RABIN

Tag

O M N I B U S   I

Rabindranath Tagore Omnibus Contents

RABINDRANATH Tagore

OMNIBUS I

RUPA

Published by
Rupa Publications India Pvt. Ltd 2003
7/16, Ansari Road, Daryaganj
New Delhi 110002

Sales centres:
Allahabad Bengaluru Chennai
Hyderabad Jaipur Kathmandu
Kolkata Mumbai

Edition copyright © Rupa Publications India Pvt. Ltd 2003

ISBN: 978-81-291-0175-4

Twentieth impression 2022

25 24 23 22 21 20

The moral right of the author has been asserted.

Typeset by Mindways Design, New Delhi

Printed in India

Contents

GITANJALI

Gitanjali

I

Thou hast made me endless, such is thy pleasure. This frail vessel thou emptiest again and again, and fillest it ever with fresh life.

This little flute of a reed thou hast carried over hills and dales, and hast breathed through it melodies eternally new.

At the immortal touch of thy hands my little heart loses its limits in joy and gives birth to utterance ineffable.

Thy infinite gifts come to me only on these very small hands of mine. Ages pass, and still thou pourest, and still there is room to fill.

II

When thou commandest me to sing, it seems that my heart would break with pride; and I look to thy face, and tears come to my eyes.

All that is harsh and dissonant in my life melts into one sweet harmony—and my adoration spreads wings like a glad bird on its flight across the sea.

I know thou takest pleasure in my singing. I know that only as a singer I come before thy presence.

I touch by the edge of the far-spreading wing of my song thy feet which I could never aspire to reach.

Drunk with the joy of singing I forget myself and call thee friend who art my lord.

III

I know not how thou singest, my master! I ever listen in silent amazement.

The light of thy music illumines the world. The life breath of thy music runs from sky to sky. The holy stream of thy music breaks through all stony obstacles and rushes on.

My heart longs to join in thy song, but vainly struggles for a voice. I would speak, but speech breaks not into song, and I cry out baffled. Ah, thou hast: made my heart captive in the endless meshes of thy music, my master!

IV

Life of my life, I shall ever try to keep my body pure, knowing that thy living touch is upon all my limbs.

I shall ever try to keep all untruths out from my thoughts, knowing that thou art that truth which has kindled the light of reason in my mind.

I shall ever try to drive all evils away from my heart and keep my love in flower, knowing that thou hast thy seat in the inmost shrine of my heart.

And it shall be my endeavour to reveal thee in my actions, knowing it is thy power gives me strength to act.

V

I ask for a moment's indulgence to sit by thy side. The works that I have in hand I will finish afterwards.

Away from the sight of thy face my heart knows no rest nor respite, and my work becomes an endless toil in a shoreless sea of toil.

To-day the summer has come at my window with its sighs and murmurs; and the bees are plying their minstrelsy at the court of the flowering grove.

Now it is time to sit quiet, face to face with thee, and to sing dedication of life in this silent and overflowing leisure.

VI

Pluck this little flower and take it. Delay not! I fear lest it droop and drop into the dust.

It may not find a place in thy garland, but honour it with a touch of pain from thy hand and pluck it. I fear lest the day end before I am aware, and the time of offering go by.

Though its colour be not deep and its smell be faint, use this flower in thy service and pluck it while there is time.

VII

My song has put off her adornments. She has no pride of dress and decoration. Ornaments would mar our union; they would come between thee and me; their jingling would drown thy whispers.

My poet's vanity dies in shame before thy sight. O master poet, I have sat down at thy feet. Only let me make my life simple and straight, like a flute of reed for thee to fill with music.

VIII

The child, who is decked with prince's robes and who has jewelled chains round his neck loses all pleasure in his play; his dress hampers him at every step.

In fear that it may be frayed, or stained with dust he keeps himself from the world, and is afraid even to move.

Mother, it is no gain, thy bondage of finery, if it keep one shut off from the healthful dust of the earth, if it rob one of the right of entrance to the great fair of common human life.

IX

O fool, to try to carry thyself upon thy own shoulders! O beggar, to come to beg at thy own door!

Leave all thy burdens on his hands who can bear all, and never look behind in regret.

Thy desire at once puts out the light from the lamp it touches with its breath. It is unholy—take not thy gifts through its unclean hands. Accept only what is offered by sacred love.

X

Here is thy footstool and there rest thy feet where live the poorest, and lowliest, and lost.

When I try to bow to thee, my obeisance cannot reach down to the depth where thy feet rest among the poorest, and lowliest, and lost.

Pride can never approach to where thou walkest in the clothes of the humble among the poorest, and lowliest, and lost.

My heart can never find its way to where thou keepest company with the companionless among the poorest, the lowliest, and the lost.

XI

Leave this chanting and singing and telling of beads! Whom dost thou worship in this lonely dark corner of a temple with doors all shut? Open thine eyes and see thy God is not before thee!

He is there where the tiller is tilling the hard ground and where the pathmaker is breaking stones. He is with them in sun and in shower, and his garment is covered with dust. Put off thy holy mantle and even like him come down on the dusty soil!

Deliverance? Where is this deliverance to be found? Our master himself has joyfully taken upon him the bonds of creation; he is bound with us all for ever.

Come out of thy meditations and leave aside thy flowers and incense! What harm is there if thy clothes become tattered and stained? Meet him and stand by him in toil and in sweat of thy brow.

XII

The time that my journey takes is long and the way of it long.

I came out on the chariot of the first gleam of light, and pursued my voyage through the wildernesses of worlds leaving my track on many a star and planet.

It is the most distant course that comes nearest to thyself, and that training is the most intricate which leads to the utter simplicity of a tune.

The traveller has to knock at every alien door to come to his own, and one has to wander through all the outer worlds to reach the innermost shrine at the end.

My eyes strayed far and wide before I shut them and said, "Here art thou!"

The question and the cry, "Oh, where?" melt into tears of a thousand streams and deluge the world with the flood of the assurance, "I am!"

XIII

The song that I came to sing remains unsung to this day.

I have spent my days in stringing and in unstringing my instrument.

The time has not come true, the words have not been rightly set; only there is the agony of wishing in my heart.

The blossom has not opened; only the wind is sighing by.

I have not seen his face, nor have I listened to his voice; only I have heard his gentle footsteps from the road before my house.

The livelong day has passed in spreading his seat on the floor; but the lamp has not been lit and I cannot ask him into my house.

I live in the hope of meeting with him; but this meeting is not yet.

XIV

My desires are many and my cry is pitiful, but ever didst thou save me by hard refusals; and this strong mercy has been wrought into my life through and through.

Day by day thou art making me worthy of the simple, great gifts that thou gavest to me unasked—this sky and the light, this body and the life and the mind—saving me from perils of overmuch desire.

There are times when I languidly linger and times when I awaken and hurry in search of my goal; but cruelly thou hidest thyself from before me.

Day by day thou art making me worthy of thy full acceptance by refusing me ever and anon, saving me from perils of weak, uncertain desire.

XV

I am here to sing thee songs. In this hall of thine I have a corner seat.

In thy world I have no work to do; my useless life can only break out in tunes without a purpose.

When the hour strikes for thy silent worship at the dark temple of midnight, command me, my master, to stand before thee to sing.

When in the morning air the golden harp is tuned, honour me, commanding my presence.

XVI

I have had my invitation to this world's festival, and thus my life has been blessed. My eyes have seen and my ears have heard.

It was my part at this feast to play upon my instrument, and I have done all I could.

Now, I ask, has the time come at last when I may go in and see thy face and offer thee my silent salutation?

XVII

I am only waiting for love to give myself up at last into his hands. That is why it is so late and why I have been guilty of such omissions.

They come with their laws and their codes to bind me fast; but I evade them ever, for I am only waiting for love to give myself up at last into his hands.

People blame me and call me heedless; I doubt not they are right in their blame.

The market day is over and work is all done for the busy. Those who came to call me in vain have gone back in anger. I am only waiting for love to give myself up at last into his hands.

XVIII

Clouds heap upon clouds and it darkens. Ah, love, why dost thou let me wait outside at the door all alone?

In the busy moments of the noontide work I am with the crowd, but on this dark lonely day it is only for thee that I hope.

If thou showest me not thy face, if thou leavest me wholly aside, I know not how I am to pass these long, rainy hours.

I keep gazing on the far-away gloom of the sky, and my heart wanders wailing with the restless wind.

XIX

If thou speakest not I will fill my heart with thy silence and endure it. I will keep still and wait like the night with starry vigil and its head bent low with patience.

The morning will surely come, the darkness will vanish, and thy voice pour down in golden streams breaking through the sky.

Then thy words will take wing in songs from every one of my birds' nests, and thy melodies will break forth in flowers in all my forest groves.

XX

On the day when the lotus bloomed, alas, my mind was straying, and I knew it not. My basket was empty and the flower remained unheeded.

Only now and again a sadness fell upon me, and I started up from my dream and felt a sweet trace of a strange fragrance in the south wind.

That vague sweetness made my heart ache with longing and it seemed to me that it was the eager breath of the summer seeking for its completion.

I knew not then that it was so near, that it was mine, and that this perfect sweetness had blossomed in the depth of my own heart.

XXI

I must launch out my boat. The languid hours pass by on the shore—Alas for me!

The spring has done its flowering and taken leave. And now with the burden of faded futile flowers I wait and linger.

The waves have become clamorous, and upon the bank in the shady lane the yellow leaves flutter and fall.

What emptiness do you gaze upon! Do you not feel a thrill passing through the air with the notes of the faraway song floating from the other shore?

XXII

In the deep shadows of the rainy July, with secret steps, thou walkest, silent as night, eluding all watchers.

To-day the morning has closed its eyes, heedless of the insistent calls of the loud east wind, and a thick veil has been drawn over the ever-wakeful blue sky.

The woodlands have hushed their songs, and doors are all shut at every house. Thou art the solitary wayfarer in this deserted street. Oh, my only friend, my best beloved, the gates are open in my house—do not pass by like a dream.

XXIII

Art thou abroad on this stormy night on thy journey of love, my friend? The sky groans like one in despair.

I have no sleep to-night. Ever and again I open my door and look out on the darkness, my friend!

I can see nothing before me. I wonder where lies thy path!

By what dim shore of the ink-black river, by what far edge of the frowning forest, through what mazy depth of gloom art thou threading thy course to come to me, my friend?

XXIV

If the day is done, if birds sing no more, if the wind has flagged tired, then draw the veil of darkness thick upon me, even as thou hast wrapt the earth with the coverlet of sleep and tenderly closed the petals of the drooping lotus at dusk.

From the traveller, whose sack of provisions is empty before the voyage is ended, whose garment is torn and dust-laden, whose strength is exhausted, remove shame and poverty, and renew his life like a flower under the cover of thy kindly night.

XXV

In the night of weariness let me give myself up to sleep without struggle, resting my trust upon thee.

Let me not force my flagging spirit into a poor preparation for thy worship.

It is thou who drawest the veil of night upon the tired eyes of the day to renew its sight in a fresher gladness of awakening.

XXVI

He came and sat by my side but I woke not. What a cursed sleep it was, O miserable me!

He came when the night was still; he had his harp in his hands, and my dreams became resonant with its melodies.

Alas, why are my nights all thus lost? Ah, why do I ever miss his sight whose breath touches my sleep?

XXVII

Light, oh, where is the light? Kindle it with the burning fire of desire!

There is the lamp but never a flicker of a flame,—is such thy fate, my heart? Ah, death were better by far for thee!

Misery knocks at thy door, and her message is that thy lord is wakeful, and he calls thee to the love-tryst through the darkness of night.

The sky is overcast with clouds and the rain is ceaseless. I know not what this is that stirs in me,—I know not its meaning.

A moment's flash of lightning drags down a deeper gloom on my sight, and my heart gropes for the path to where the music of the night calls me.

Light, oh, where is the light? Kindle it with the burning fire of desire! It thunders and the wind rushes screaming through the void. The night is black as a black stone. Let not the hours pass by in the dark. Kindle the lamp of love with thy life.

XXVIII

Obstinate are the trammels, but my heart aches when I try to break them.

Freedom is all I want, but to hope for it I feel ashamed.

I am certain that priceless wealth is in thee, and that thou art my best friend, but I have not the heart to sweep away the tinsel that fills my room.

The shroud that covers me is a shroud of dust and death; I hate it, yet hug it in love.

My debts are large, my failures great, my shame secret and heavy; yet when I come to ask for my good, I quake in fear lest my prayer be granted.

XXIX

He whom I enclose with my name is weeping in this dungeon. I am ever busy building this wall all around; and as this wall goes up into the sky day by day I lose sight of my true being in its dark shadow.

I take pride in this great wall, and I plaster it with dust and sand lest a least hole should be left in this name; and for all the care I take I lose sight of my true being.

XXX

I came out alone on my way to my tryst. But who is this that follows me in the silent dark?

I move aside to avoid his presence but I escape him not.

He makes the dust rise from the earth with his swagger; he adds his loud voice to every word that I utter.

He is my own little self, my lord, he knows no shame; but I am ashamed to come to thy door in his company.

XXXI

"Prisoner, tell me, who was it that bound you?"

"It was my master," said the prisoner. "I thought I could outdo everybody in the world in wealth and power, and I amassed in my own treasure-house the money due to my king. When sleep overcame me I lay upon the bed that was for my lord, and on waking up I found I was a prisoner in my own treasure-house."

"Prisoner, tell me, who was it that wrought this unbreakable chain?"

"It was I," said the prisoner, "who forged this chain very carefully. I thought my invincible power would hold the world captive leaving me in a freedom undisturbed. Thus night and day I worked at the chain with huge fires and cruel hard strokes. When at last the work was done and the links were complete and unbreakable, I found that it held me in its grip."

XXXII

By all means they try to hold me secure who love me in this world. But it is otherwise with thy love which is greater than theirs, and thou keepest me free.

Lest I forget them they never venture to leave me alone. But day passes by after day and thou art not seen.

If I call not thee in my prayers, if I keep not thee in my heart, thy love for me still waits for my love.

XXXIII

When it was day they came into my house and said, "We shall only take the smallest room here."

They said, "We shall help you in the worship of your God and humbly accept only our own share of his grace;" and then they took their seat in a corner and they sat quiet and meek.

But in the darkness of night I find they break into my sacred shrine, strong and turbulent, and snatch with unholy greed the offerings from God's altar.

XXXIV

Let only that little be left of me whereby I may name thee my all.

Let only that little be left of my will whereby I may feel thee on every side, and come to thee in everything, and offer to thee my love every moment.

Let only that little be left of me whereby I may never hide thee.

Let only that little of my fetters be left whereby I am bound with thy will, and thy purpose is carried out in my life—and that is the fetter of thy love.

XXXV

Where the mind is without fear and the head is held high;

Where knowledge is free;

Where the world has not been broken up into fragments by narrow domestic walls;

Where words come out from the depth of truth;

Where tireless striving stretches its arms towards perfection;

Where the clear stream of reason has not lost its way into the dreary desert sand of dead habit;

Where the mind is led forward by thee into ever-widening thought and action—

Into that heaven of freedom, my Father, let my country awake.

XXXVI

This is my prayer to thee, my lord—strike, strike at the root of penury in my heart.

Give me the strength lightly to bear my joys and sorrows.

Give me the strength to make my love fruitful in service.

Give me the strength never to disown the poor or bend my knees before insolent might.

Give me the strength to raise my mind high above daily trifles.

And give me the strength to surrender my strength to thy will with love.

XXXVII

I thought that my voyage had come to its end at the last limit of my power,—that the path before me was closed, that provisions were exhausted and the time come to take shelter in a silent obscurity.

But I find that thy will knows no end in me. And when old words die out on the tongue, new melodies break forth from the heart; and where the old tracks are lost, new country is revealed with its wonders.

XXXVIII

That I want thee, only thee—let my heart repeat without end. All desires that distract me, day and night, are false and empty to the core.

As the night keeps hidden in its gloom the petition for light, even thus in the depth of my unconsciousness rings the cry—"I want thee, only thee".

As the storm still seeks its end in peace when it strikes against peace with all its might, even thus my rebellion strikes against thy love and still its cry is—"I want thee, only thee".

XXXIX

When the heart is hard and parched up, come upon me with a shower of mercy.

When grace is lost from life, come with a burst of song.

When tumultuous work raises its din on all sides shutting me out from beyond, come to me, my lord of silence, with thy peace and rest.

When my beggarly heart sits crouched, shut up in a corner, break open the door, my king, and come with the ceremony of a king.

When desire blinds the mind with delusion and dust, O thou holy one, thou wakeful, come with thy light and thy thunder.

XL

The rain has held back for days and days, my God, in my arid heart. The horizon is fiercely naked—not the thinnest cover of a soft cloud, not the vaguest hint of a distant cool shower.

Send thy angry storm, dark with death, if it is thy wish, and with lashes of lightning startle the sky from end to end.

But call back, my lord, call back this pervading silent heat, still and keen and cruel, burning the heart with dire despair.

Let the cloud of grace bend low from above like the tearful look of the mother on the day of the father's wrath.

XLI

Where dost thou stand behind them all, my lover, hiding thyself in the shadows? They push thee and pass thee by on the dusty road, taking thee for naught. I wait here weary hours spreading my offerings for thee, while passers-by come and take my flowers, one by one, and my basket is nearly empty.

The morning time is past, and the noon. In the shade of evening my eyes are drowsy with sleep. Men going home glance at me and smile and fill me with shame. I sit like a beggar maid, drawing my skirt over my face, and when they ask me what it is I want, I drop my eyes and answer them not.

Oh, how, indeed, could I tell them that for thee I wait, and that thou hast promised to come? How could I utter for shame that I keep for my dowry this poverty? Ah, I hug this pride in the secret of my heart.

I sit on the grass and gaze upon the sky and dream of the sudden splendour of thy coming—all the lights ablaze, golden pennons flying over thy car, and they at the roadside standing agape, when they see thee come down from thy seat to raise me from the dust, and set at thy side this ragged beggar girl a-tremble with shame and pride, like a creeper in a summer breeze.

But time glides on and still no sound of the wheels of thy chariot. Many a procession passes by with noise and shouts and glamour of glory. Is it only thou who wouldst stand in the shadow silent and behind them all? And only I who would wait and weep and wear out my heart in vain longing?

XLII

Early in the day it was whispered that we should sail in a boat, only thou and I, and never a soul in the world would know of this our pilgrimage to no country and to no end.

In that shoreless ocean, at thy silently listening smile my songs would swell in melodies, free as waves, free from all bondage of words.

Is the time not come yet? Are there works still to do? Lo, the evening has come down upon the shore and in the fading light the seabirds come flying to their nests.

Who knows when the chains will be off, and the boat, like the last glimmer of sunset, vanish into the night?

XLIII

The day was when I did not keep myself in readiness for thee; and entering my heart unbidden even as one of the common crowd, unknown to me, my king, thou didst press the signet of eternity upon many a fleeting moment of my life.

And to-day when by chance I light upon them and see thy signature, I find they have lain scattered in the dust mixed with the memory of joys and sorrows of my trivial days forgotten.

Thou didst not turn in contempt from my childish play among dust, and the steps that I heard in my playroom are the same that are echoing from star to star.

XLIV

This is my delight, thus to wait and watch at the wayside where shadow chases light and the rain comes in the wake of the summer.

Messengers, with tidings from unknown skies, greet me and speed along the road. My heart is glad within, and the breath of the passing breeze is sweet.

From dawn till dusk I sit here before my door, and I know that of a sudden the happy moment will arrive when I shall see.

In the meanwhile I smile and I sing all alone. In the meanwhile the air is filling with the perfume of promise.

XLV

Have you not heard his silent steps? He comes, comes, ever comes.

Every moment and every age, every day and every night he comes, comes, ever comes. Many a song have I sung in many a mood of mind, but all their notes have always proclaimed, "He comes, comes, ever comes"

In the fragrant days of sunny April through the forest path he comes, comes, ever comes.

In the rainy gloom of July nights on the thundering chariot of clouds he comes, comes, ever comes.

In sorrow after sorrow it is his steps that press upon my heart, and it is the golden touch of his feet that makes my joy to shine.

XLVI

I know not from what distant time thou art ever coming nearer to meet me. Thy sun and stars can never keep thee hidden from me for aye.

In many a morning and eve thy footsteps have been heard and thy messenger has come within my heart and called me in secret.

I know not why to-day my life is all astir, and a feeling of tremulous joy is passing through my heart.

It is as if the time were come to wind up my work, and I feel in the air a faint smell of thy sweet presence.

XLVII

The night is nearly spent waiting for him in vain. I fear lest in the morning he suddenly come to my door when I have fallen asleep wearied out. Oh, friends, leave the way open to him—forbid him not.

If the sound of his steps does not wake me, do not try to rouse me, I pray. I wish not to be called from my sleep by the clamorous choir, of birds, by the riot of wind at the festival of morning light. Let me sleep undisturbed even if my lord comes of a sudden to my door.

Ah, my sleep, precious sleep, which only waits for his touch to vanish. Ah, my closed eyes that would open their lids only to the light of his smile when he stands before me like a dream emerging from darkness of sleep.

Let him appear before my sight as the first of all lights and all forms. The first thrill of joy to my awakened soul, let it come from his glance. And let my return to myself be immediate return to him.

XLVIII

The morning sea of silence broke into ripples of bird songs; and the flowers were all merry by the roadside; and the wealth of gold was scattered through the rift of the clouds while we busily went on our way and paid no heed. We sang no glad songs nor played; we went not to the village for barter; we spoke not a word nor smiled; we lingered not on the way. We quickened our pace more and more as the time sped by.

The sun rose to the mid sky and doves cooed in the shade. Withered leaves danced and whirled in the hot air of noon. The shepherd boy drowsed and dreamed in the shadow of the banyan tree, and I laid myself down by the water and stretched my tired limbs on the grass.

My companions laughed at me in scorn; they held their heads high and hurried on; they never looked back nor rested; they vanished in the distant blue haze. They crossed many meadows and hills, and passed chrough strange, far-away countries. All honour to you, heroic host of the interminable path! Mockery and reproach pricked me ro rise, but found no response in me. I gave myself up' for lost in the depth of a glad humiliation—in the shadow of a dim delight.

The repose of the sun-embroidered green gloom slowly spread over my heart. I forgot for what I had travelled, and I surrendered my mind without struggle to the maze of shadows and songs.

At last, when I woke from my slumber and opened my eyes, I saw thee standing by me, flooding my sleep with thy smile. How I had feared that the path was long and wearisome, and the struggle to reach thee was hard!

XLIX

You came down from your throne and stood at my cottage door.

I was singing all alone in a corner, and the melody caught your ear. You came down and stood at my cottage door.

Masters are many in your hall, and songs are sung there at all hours. But the simple carol of this novice struck at your love. One plaintive little strain mingled with the great music of the world, and with a flower for a prize you came down and stopped at my cottage door.

L

I had gone a-begging from door to door in the village path, when thy golden chariot appeared in the distance like a gorgeous dream and I wondered who was this King of all kings!

My hopes rose high and methought my evil days were at an end, and I stood waiting for alms to be given unasked and for wealth scattered on all sides in the dust.

The chariot stopped where I stood. Thy glance fell on me and thou camest down with a smile. I felt that the luck of my life had come at last. Then of a sudden thou didst hold out thy right hand and say, "What hast thou to give to me?"

Ah, what a kingly jest was it to open thy palm to a beggar to beg! I was confused and stood undecided, and then from my wallet I slowly cook out the least little grain of corn and gave it to thee.

But how great my surprise when at the day's end I emptied my bag on the floor to find a least little grain of gold among the poor heap! I bitterly wept and wished that I had had the heart to give thee my all.

LI

The night darkened. Our day's works had been done. We thought that the last guest had arrived for the night and the doors in the village were all shut. Only some said the King was to come. We laughed and said, "No, it cannot be!"

It seemed there were knocks at the door and we said it was nothing but the wind. We put out the lamps and lay down to sleep. Only some said, "It is the messenger!" We laughed and said, "No, it must be the wind!"

There came a sound in the dead of the night. We sleepily thought it was the distant thunder. The earth shook, the walls rocked, and it troubled us in our sleep. Only some said it was the sound of wheels. We said in a drowsy murmur, "No, it must be the rumbling of clouds!"

The night was still dark when the drum sounded. The voice came, "Wake up! delay not!" We pressed our hands on our hearts and shuddered with fear. Some said, "Lo, there is the King's flag!" We stood up on our feet and cried "There is no time for delay!"

The King has come—but where are lights, where are wreaths? Where is the throne to seat him? Oh, shame! Oh utter shame! Where is the hall, the decorations? Someone has said, "Vain is this cry! Greet him with empty hands, lead him into thy rooms all bare!"

Open the doors, let the conch-shells be sounded! In the depth of the night has come the King of our dark, dreary house. The thunder roars in the sky. The darkness shudders with lightning. Bring out thy tattered piece of mat and spread it in the courtyard. With the storm has came of a sudden our King of the fearful night.

LII

I thought I should ask of thee—but I dared not—the rose wreath thou hadst on thy neck. Thus I waited for the morning,

when thou didst depart, to find a few fragments on the bed.
And like a beggar I searched in the dawn only for a stray petal
or two.

Ah me, what is it I find? What token left of thy love?
It is no flower, no spices, no vase of perfumed water. It is
thy mighty sword, flashing as a flame, heavy as a bolt of
thunder. The young light of morning comes through the
window and spreads itself upon thy bed. The morning bird
twitters and asks, "Woman, what hast thou got?" No, it is
no flower, nor spices, nor vase of perfumed water—it is thy
dreadful sword.

I sit and muse in wonder, what gift is this of thine. I can
find no place where to hide it. I am ashamed to wear it, frail
as I am, and it hurts me when I press it to my bosom. Yet
shall I bear in my heart this honour of the burden of pain,
this gift of thine.

From now there shall be no fear left for me in this world,
and thou shalt be victorious in all my strife. Thou hast left
death for my companion and I shall crown him with my life.
Thy sword is with me to cut asunder my bonds, and there
shall be no fear left for me in the world.

From now I leave off all petty decorations. Lord of my
heart, no more shall there be for me waiting and weeping in
corners, no more coyness and sweetness of demeanour. Thou
hast given me thy sword for adornment. No more doll's
decorations for me!

LIII

Beautiful is thy wristlet, decked with stars and cunningly
wrought in myriad-coloured jewels. But more beautiful to me
thy sword with its curve of lightning like the outspread wings
of the divine bird of Vishnu, perfectly poised in the angry red
light of the sunset.

It quivers like the one last response of life in ecstasy of pain at the final stroke of death; it shines like the pure flame of being burning up earthly sense with one fierce flash.

Beautiful is thy wristlet, decked with starry gems; but thy sword, O lord of thunder, is wrought with uttermost beauty, terrible to behold or to think of.

LIV

I asked nothing from thee; I uttered not my name to thine ear. When thou took'st thy leave I stood silent. I was alone by the well where the shadow of the tree fell aslant, and the women had gone home with their brown earthen pitchers full to the brim. They called me and shouted, "Come with us, the morning is wear-ing on to noon." But I languidly lingered awhile lost in the midst of vague musings.

I heard nor thy steps as thou eamest. Thine eyes were sad when they fell on me; thy voice was tired as thou spokest low— "Ah, I am a thirsty traveller." I started up from my day-dreams and poured water from my jar on thy joined palms. The leaves rustled overhead; the cuckoo sang from the unseen dark, and perfume of *babla* flowers came from the bend of the road.

I stood speechless with shame when my name thou didst ask. Indeed, what had I done for thee to keep me in remembrance? But the memory that I could give water to thee to allay thy thirst will cling to my heart and enfold it in sweetness. The morning hour is late, the bird sings in weary notes, *neem* leaves rustle overhead and I sit and think and think.

LV

Languors upon your heart and the slumber is still on your eyes.

Has not the word come to you that the flower is reigning in splendour among thorns? Wake, oh, awaken! Let not the time pass in vain!

At the end of the stony path, in the country of virgin solitude, my friend is sitting all alone. Deceive him not. Wake, oh, awaken!

What if the sky pants and trembles with the heat of the midday sun—what if the burning sand spreads its mantle of thirst—

Is there no joy in the deep of your heart? At every footfall of yours, will not the harp of the road break out in sweet music of pain?

LVI

Thus it is that thy joy in me is so full. Thus it is that thou hast come down to me. O thou lord of all heavens, where would be thy love if I were not?

Thou hast taken me as thy partner of all this wealth. In my heart is the endless play of thy delight. In my life thy will is ever taking shape.

And for this, thou who art the King of kings hast decked thyself in beauty to captivate my heart. And for this thy love loses itself in the love of thy lover, and there art thou seen in the perfect union of two.

LVII

Light, my light, the world-filling light, the eye-kissing light, heart-sweetening light!

Ah, the light dances, my darling, at the centre of my life; the light strikes, my darling, the chords of my love; the sky opens, the wind runs wild, laughter passes over the earth.

The butterflies spread their sails on the sea of light. Lilies and jasmines surge up on the crest of the waves of light.

The light is shattered into gold on every cloud, my darling, and it scatters gems in profusion.

Mirth spreads from leaf to leaf, my darling, and gladness without measure. The heaven's river has drowned its banks and the flood of joy is abroad.

LVIII

Let all the strains of joy mingle in my last song—the joy that makes the earth flow over in the riotous excess of the grass, the joy that sets the twin brothers, life and death, dancing over the wide world, the joy that sweeps in with the tempest, shaking and waking all life with laughter, the joy that sits still with its tears on the open red lotus of pain, and the joy that throws everything it has upon the dust, and knows not a word.

LIX

Yes, I know, this is nothing but thy love, O beloved of my heart—this golden light that dances upon the leaves, these idle clouds sailing across the sky, this passing breeze leaving its coolness upon my forehead. The morning light has flooded my. eyes—this is thy message to my heart. Thy face is bent from above, thy eyes look down on my eyes, and my heart has touched thy feet.

LX

On the seashore of endless worlds children meet. The infinite sky is motionless overhead and the restless water is boisterous. On the seashore of endless worlds the children meet with shouts and dances.

They build their houses with sand and they play with empty shells. With withered leaves they weave their boats and smilingly float them on the vast deep. Children have their play on the seashore of worlds.

They know not how to swim, they know not how to cast nets. Pearl fishers dive for pearls, merchants sail in their ships, while children gather pebbles and scatter them again. They seek not for hidden treasures, they know not how to cast nets.

The sea surges up with laughter and pale gleams the smile of the sea beach. Death-dealing waves sing meaningless ballads to the children, even like a mother while rocking her baby's cradle. The sea plays with children, and pale gleams the smile of the sea beach.

On the seashore of endless worlds children meet. Tempest roams in the pathless sky, ships get wrecked in the trackless water, death is abroad and children play. On the seashore of endless worlds is the great meeting of children.

LXI

The sleep that flits on baby's eyes—does anybody know from where it comes? Yes, there is a rumour that it has its dwelling where, in the fairy village among shadows of the forest dimly lit with glow-worms, there hang two timid buds of enchantment. From there it comes to kiss baby's eyes.

The smile that flickers on baby's lips when he sleeps— does anybody know where it was born? Yes there is a rumour that a young pale beam of a crescent moon touched the edge of a vanishing autumn cloud, and there the smile was first born in the dream of a dew-washed morning—the smile that flickers on baby's lips when he sleeps.

The sweet, soft freshness that blooms on baby's limbs— does anybody know where it was hidden so long? Yes, when the mother was a young girl it lay pervading her heart in tender and silent mystery of love,— the sweet, soft freshness that has bloomed on baby's limbs.

LXII

When I Bring to you coloured toys, my child, I understand why there is such a play of colours on clouds, on water, and why flowers are painted in tints—when I give coloured toys to you, my child.

When I sing to make you dance I truly know why there is music in leaves, and why waves send their chorus of voices

to the heart of the listening earth—when I sing to make
you dance.

When I bring sweet things to your greedy hands I know
why there is honey in the cup of the flower and why fruits
are secretly filled with sweet juice—when I bring sweet things
to your greedy hands.

When I kiss your face to make you smile, my darling, I
surely understand what the pleasure is that streams from the
sky in morning light, and what delight that is which the
summer breeze brings to my body—when I kiss you to make
you smile.

LXIII

Thou hast made me known to friends whom I knew not. Thou
hast given me seats in homes not my own. Thou hast brought
the distant near and made a brother of the stranger.

I am uneasy at heart when I have to leave my accustomed
shelter; I forget that there abides the old in the new, and that
there also thou abidest.

Through birth and death, in this world or in others,
wherever thou leadest me it is thou, the same, the one
companion of my endless life who ever linkest my heart with
bonds of joy to the unfamiliar.

When one knows thee, then alien there is none, then no
door is shut. Oh, grant me my prayer that I may never lose
the bliss of the touch of the one in the play of the many.

LXIV

On the slope of the desolate river among tall grasses I asked
her, "Maiden, where do you go, shading your lamp with
your mantle? My house is all dark and lonesome,—lend me
your light!" She raised her dark eyes for a moment and
looked at my face through the dusk. "I have come to the
river," she said, "to float my lamp on the stream when the

daylight wanes in the west." I stood alone among tall grasses and watched the timid flame of her lamp uselessly drifting in the tide.

In the silence of gathering night I asked her, "Maiden, your lights are all lit—then where do you go with your lamp? My house is all dark and lonesome,—lend me your light." She raised her dark eyes on my face and stood for a moment doubtful. "I have come," she said at last, "to dedicate my lamp to the sky." I stood and watched her light uselessly burning in the void.

In the moonless gloom of midnight I asked her, "Maiden, what is your quest, holding the lamp near your heart? My house is all dark and lonesome,—lend me your light." She stopped for a minute and thought and gazed at my face in the dark. "I have brought my light," she said, "to join the carnival of lamps." I stood and watched her little lamp uselessly lost among lights.

LXV

What divine drink wouldst thou have, my God, from this overflowing cup of my life?

My poet, is it thy delight to see thy creation through my eyes and to stand at the portals of my ears silently to listen to thine own eternal harmony?

Thy world is weaving words in my mind and thy joy is adding music to them. Thou givest thyself to me in love and then feelest thine own entire sweetness in me.

LXVI

She who ever had remained in the depth of my being, in the twilight of gleams and of glimpses; she who never opened her veils in the morning light, will be my last gift to thee, my God, folded in my final song.

Words have wooed yet failed to win her; persuasion has stretched to her its eager arms in vain.

I have roamed from country to country keeping her in the core of my heart, and around her have risen and fallen the growth and decay of my life.

Over my thoughts and actions, my slumbers and dreams, she reigned yet dwelled alone and apart.

Many a man knocked at my door and asked for her and turned away in despair.

There was none in the world who ever saw her face to face, and she remained in her loneliness waiting for thy recognition.

LXVII

Thou art the sky and thou art the nest as well.

O thou beautiful, there in the nest it is thy love that encloses the soul with colours and sounds and odours.

There comes the morning with the golden basket in her right hand bearing the wreath of beauty, silently to crown the earth.

And there comes the evening over the lonely meadows deserted by herds, through trackless paths, carrying cool draughts of peace in her golden pitcher from the western ocean of rest.

But there, where spreads the infinite sky for the soul to take her flight in, reigns the stainless white radiance. There is no day nor night, nor form nor colour, and never, never a word.

LXVIII

Thy sunbeam comes upon this earth of mine with arms outstretched and stands at my door the livelong day to carry back to thy feet clouds made of my tears and sighs and songs.

With fond delight thou wrappest about thy starry breast that mantle of misty cloud, turning it into numberless shapes and folds and colouring it with hues everchanging.

It is so light and so fleeting, tender and tearful and dark, that is why thou lovest it, O thou spotless and serene. And that is why it may cover thy awful white light with its pathetic shadows.

LXIX

The same stream of life that runs through my veins night and day runs through the world and dances in rhythmic measures.

It is the same life that shoots in joy through the dust of the earth in numberless blades of grass and breaks into tumultuous waves of leaves and flowers.

It is the same life that is rocked in the ocean-cradle of birth and of death, in ebb and in flow.

I feel my limbs are made glorious by the touch of this world of life. And my pride is from the life-throb of ages dancing in my blood this moment.

LXX

Is it beyond thee to be glad with the gladness of this rhythm? to be tossed and lost and broken in the whirl of this fearful joy?

All things rush on, they stop not, they look not behind, no power can hold them back, they rush on.

Keeping steps with that restless, rapid music, seasons come dancing and pass away—colours, tunes, and perfumes pour in endless cascades in the abounding joy that scatters and gives up and dies every moment.

LXXI

That I should make much of myself and turn it on all sides, thus casting coloured shadows on thy radiance—such is thy *maya*. Thou settest a barrier in thine own being and then callest thy severed self in myriad notes. This thy self-separation has taken body in me.

The poignant song is echoed through all the sky in many-coloured tears and smiles, alarms and hopes; waves rise up and sink again, dreams break and form. In me is thy own defeat of self.

This screen that thou hast raised is painted with innumerable figures with the brush of the night and the day. Behind it thy seat is woven in wondrous mysteries of curves, casting away all barren lines of straightness.

The great pageant of thee and me has overspread the sky. With the tune of thee and me all the air is vibrant, and all ages pass with the hiding and seeking of thee and me.

LXXII

He it is, the innermost one, who awakens my being with his deep hidden touches.

He it is who puts his enchantment upon these eyes and joyfully plays on the chords of my heart in varied cadence of pleasure and pain.

He it is who weaves the web of this *maya* in evanescent hues of gold and silver, blue and green, and lets peep out through the folds his feet, at whose touch I forget myself.

Days come and ages pass, and it is ever he who moves my heart in many a name, in many a guise, in many a rapture of joy and of sorrow.

LXXIII

Deliverance is not for me in renunciation. I feel the embrace of freedom in a thousand bonds of delight.

Thou ever pourest for me the fresh draught of thy wine of various colours ancl fragrance, filling this earthen vessel to the brim.

My world will light its hundred different lamps with thy flame and place them before the altar of thy temple.

No, I will never shut the doors of my senses. The delights of sight and hearing and touch will bear thy delight.

Yes, all my illusions will burn into illumination of joy, and all my desires ripen into fruits of love.

LXXIV

The day is no more, the shadow is upon the earth. It is time that I go to the scream to fill my pitcher.

The evening air is eager with the sad music of the water. Ah, it calls me out into the dusk. In the lonely lane there is no passer-by, the wind is up, the ripples are rampant in the river.

I know not if I shall come back home. I know not whom I shall chance to meet. There at the fording in the little boat the unknown man plays upon his lute.

LXXV

Thy gifts to us mortals fulfil all our needs and yet run back to thee undiminished.

The river has its everyday work to do and hastens through fields and hamlets; yet its incessant stream winds towards the washing of thy feet.

The flower sweetens the air with its perfume; yet its last service is to offer itself to thee.

Thy worship does not impoverish the world.

From the words of the poet men take what meanings please them; yet their last meaning points to thee.

LXXVI

Day after day, O lord of my life, shall I stand before thee face to face. With folded hands, O lord of all worlds, shall I stand before thee face to face.

Under thy great sky in solitude and silence, with humble heart shall I stand before thee face to face.

In this laborious world of thine, tumultuous with toil and with struggle, among hurrying crowds shall I stand before thee face to face.

And when my work shall be done in this world, O King of kings, alone and speechless shall I stand before thee face to face.

LXXVII

I know thee as my God and stand apart—I do not know thee as my own and come closer. I know thee as my father and bow before thy feet—I do not grasp thy hand as my friend's.

I stand not where thou comest down and ownest thyself as mine, there to clasp thee to my heart and take thee as my comrade.

Thou art the Brother amongst my brothers, but I heed them not, I divide not my earnings with them, thus sharing my all with thee.

In pleasure and in pain I stand not by the side of men, and thus stand by thee. I shrink to give up my life, and thus do not plunge into the great waters of life.

LXXVIII

When the creation was new and all the stars shone in their first splendour, the gods held their assembly in the sky and sang, "Oh, the picture of perfection! the joy unalloyed!"

But one cried of a sudden—"It seems that somewhere there is a break in the chain of light and one of the stars has been lost."

The golden string of their harp snapped, their song stopped, and they cried in dismay—"Yes, that lost star was the best, she was the glory of all heavens!"

From that day the search is unceasing for her, and the cry goes on from one to the other that in her the world has lost its one joy!

Only in the deepest silence of night the stars smile and whisper among themselves—"Vain is this seeking! Unbroken perfection is over all!"

LXXIX

If it is not my portion to meet thee in this my life then let me ever feel that I have missed thy sight—let me not forget for a moment, let me carry the pangs of this sorrow in my dreams and in my wakeful hours.

As my days pass in the crowded market of this world and my hands grow full with the daily profits, let me ever feel that I have gained nothing—let me not forget for a moment, let me carry the pangs of this sorrow in my dreams and in my wakeful hours.

When I sit by the roadside, tired and panting, when I spread my bed low in the dust, let me ever feel that the long journey is still before me—let me not forget for a moment, let me carry the pangs of this sorrow in my dreams and in my wakeful hours.

When my rooms have been decked out and the flutes sound and the laughter there is loud, let me ever feel that I have not invited thee to my house—let me not forget for a moment, let me carry the pangs of this sorrow in my dreams and in my wakeful hours.

LXXX

I am like a remnant of a cloud of autumn uselessly roaming in the sky, O my sun ever-glorious! Thy touch has not yet melted my vapour, making me one with thy light, and thus I count months and years separated from thee.

If this be thy wish and if this be thy play, then take this fleeting emptiness of mine, paint it with colours, gild it with gold, float it on the wanton wind and spread it in varied wonders.

And again when it shall be thy wish to end this play at night, I shall melt and vanish away in the dark, or it may be in a smile of the white morning, in a coolness of purity transparent.

LXXXI

On many an idle day have I grieved over lost time. But it is never lost, my lord. Thou hast taken every moment of my life in thine own hands.

Hidden in the heart of things thou art nourishing seeds into sprouts, buds into blossoms, and ripening flowers into fruitfulness.

I was tired and sleeping on my idle bed and imagined all work had ceased. In the morning I woke up and found my garden full with wonders of flowers.

LXXXII

Time is endless in thy hands, my lord. There is none to count thy minutes.

Days and nights pass and ages bloom and fade like flowers. Thou knowest how to wait.

Thy centuries follow each other perfecting a small wild flower.

We have no time to lose, and having no time we must scramble for our chances. We are too poor to be late.

And thus it is that time goes by while I give it to every querulous man who claims it, and thine altar is empty of all offerings to the last.

At the end of the day I hasten in fear lest thy gate be shut; but I find that yet there is time.

LXXXIII

Mother, I shall weave a chain of pearls for thy neck with my tears of sorrow.

The stars have wrought their anklets of light to deck thy feet, but mine will hang upon thy breast.

Wealth and fame come from thee and it is for thee to give or to withhold them. But this my sorrow is absolutely mine own, and when I bring it to thee as my offering thou rewardest me with thy grace.

LXXXIV

It is the pang of separation that spreads throughout the world and gives birth to shapes innumerable in the infinite sky.

It is this sorrow of separation that gazes in silence all night from star to star and becomes lyric among rustling leaves in rainy darkness of July.

It is this overspreading pain that deepens into loves and desires, into sufferings and joys in human homes; and this it is that ever melts and flows in songs through my poet's heart.

LXXXV

When the warriors came out first from their master's hall, where had they hid their power? Where were their armour and their arms?

They looked poor and helpless, and the arrows were showered upon them on the day they came out from their master's hall.

When the warriors marched back again to their master's hall, where did they hide their power?

They had dropped the sword and dropped the bow and the arrow; peace was on their foreheads, and they had left the fruits of their life behind them on the day they marched back again to their master's hall.

LXXXVI

Death, thy servant, is at my door. He has crossed the unknown sea and brought thy call to my home.

The night is dark and my heart is fearful—yet I will take up the lamp, open my gates and bow to him my welcome. It is thy messenger who stands at my door.

I will worship him with folded hands, and with tears. I will worship him placing at his feet the treasure of my heart.

He will go back with his errand done, leaving a dark shadow on my morning; and in my desolate home only my forlorn self will remain as my last offering to thee.

LXXXVII

In desperate hope I go and search for her in all the corners of my room; I find her not.

My house is small and what once has gone from it can never be regained.

But infinite is thy mansion, my lord, and seeking her I have come to thy door.

I stand under the golden canopy of thine evening sky and I lift my eager eyes to thy face.

I have come to the brink of eternity from which nothing can vanish—no hope, no happiness, no vision of a face seen through tears.

Oh, dip my emptied life into that ocean, plunge it into the deepest fullness. Let me for once feel that lost sweet touch in the allness of the universe.

LXXXVIII

Deity of the ruined temple! The broken strings of *Vina* sing no more your praise. The bells in the evening proclaim not your time of worship. The air is still and silent about you.

In your desolate dwelling comes the vagrant spring breeze. It brings the tidings of flowers—the flowers that for your worship are offered no more.

Your worshipper of old wanders ever longing for favour still refused. In the eventide, when fires and shadows mingle with the gloom of dust, he wearily comes back to the ruined temple with hunger in his heart.

Many a festival day comes to you in silence, deity of the ruined temple. Many a night of worship goes away with lamp unlit.

Many new images are built by masters of cunning art and carried to the holy stream of oblivion when their time is come.

Only the deity of the ruined temple remains un-worshipped in deathless neglect.

LXXXIX

No more noisy, loud words from me—such is my master's will. Henceforth I deal in whispers. The speech of my heart will be carried on in murmurings of a song.

Men hasten to the King's market. All the buyers and sellers are there. But I have my untimely leave in the middle of the day, in the thick of work.

Let then the flowers come out in my garden, though it is not their time; and let the midday bees strike up their lazy hum.

Full many an hour have I spent in the strife of the good and the evil, but now it is the pleasure of my playmate of the empty days to draw my heart on to him; and I know not why is this sudden call to what useless inconsequence!

XC

On the day when death will knock at thy door what wilt thou offer to him?

Oh, I will set before my guest the full vessel of my life— I will never let him go with empty hands.

All the sweet vintage of all my autumn days and summer nights, all the earnings and gleanings of my busy life will I place before him at the close of my days when death will knock at my door.

XCI

O thou the last fulfilment of life, Death, my death, come and whisper to me!

Day after day have I kept watch for thee; for thee have I borne the joys and pangs of life.

All that I am, that I have, that I hope, and all my love have ever flowed towards thee in depth of secrecy. One final glance from thine eyes and my life will be ever thine own.

The flowers have been woven and the garland is ready for the bridegroom. After the wedding the bride shall leave her home and meet her lord alone in the solitude of night.

XCII

I know that the day will come when my sight of this earth shall be lost, and life will take its leave in silence, drawing the last curtain over my eyes.

Yet stars will watch at night, and morning rise as before, and hours heave like sea waves casting up pleasures and pains.

When I think of this end of my moments, the barrier of the moments breaks and I see by the light of death thy world with its careless treasures. Rare is its lowliest seat, rare is its meanest of lives.

Things that I longed for in vain and things that I got— let them pass. Let me but truly possess the things that I ever spurned and overlooked.

XCIII

I have got my leave. Bid me farewell, my brothers! I bow to you all and take my departure.

Here I give back the keys of my door—and I give up all claims to my house. I only ask for last kind words from you.

We were neighbours for long, but I received more than I could give. Now the day has dawned and the lamp that lit my dark corner is out. A summons has come and I am ready for my journey.

XCIV

At this time of my parting, wish me good luck, my friends! The sky is flushed with the dawn and my path lies beautiful.

Ask not what I have with me to take there. I start on my journey with empty hands and expectant heart. I shall put on my wedding garland. Mine is not the red-brown dress of the traveller, and though there are dangers on the way I have no fear in my mind.

The evening star will come out when my voyage is done and the plaintive notes of the twilight melodies be struck up from the King's gateway.

XCV

I was not aware of the moment when I first crossed the threshold of this life.

What was the power that made me open out into this vast mystery like a bud in the forest at—midnight?

When in the morning I looked upon the light I felt in a moment that I was no stranger in this world, that the inscrutable without name and form had taken me in her arms in the form of my own mother.

Even so, in death the same unknown will appear as ever known to me. And because I love this life, I know I shall love death as well.

The child cries out when from the right breast the mother takes it away, in the very next moment to find in the left one its consolation.

XCVI

When I go from hence let this be my parting word, that what I have seen is unsurpassable.

I have tasted of the hidden honey of this lotus that expands on the ocean of light, and thus am I blessed—let this be my parting word.

In this playhouse of infinite forms I have had my play and here have I caught sight of him that is formless.

My whole body and my limbs have thrilled with his touch who is beyond touch; and if the end comes here, let it come—let this be my parting word.

XCVII

When my play was with thee I never questioned who thou were. I knew nor shyness nor fear, my life was boisterous.

In the early morning thou wouldst call me from my sleep like my own comrade and lead me running from glade to glade.

On those days I never cared to know the meaning of songs thou sangest to me. Only my voice took up the tunes, and my heart danced in their cadence.

Now, when the playtime is over, what is this sudden sight that is come upon me? The world with eyes bent upon thy feet stands in awe with all its silent stars.

XCVIII

I will deck thee with trophies, garlands of my defeat. It is never in my power to escape unconquered.

I surely know my pride will go to the wall, my life will burst its bonds in exceeding pain, and my empty heart will sob out in music like a hollow reed, and the stone will melt in tears.

I surely know the hundred petals of a lotus will not remain closed for ever and the secret recess of its honey will be bared.

From the blue sky an eye shall gaze upon me and summon me in silence. Nothing will be left for me, nothing whatever, and utter death shall I receive at thy feet.

XCIX

When I give up the helm I know that the time has come for thee to take it. What there is to do will be instantly done. Vain is this struggle.

Then take away your hands and silently put up with your defeat, my heart, and think it your good fortune to sit perfectly still where you are placed.

These my lamps are blown out at every little puff of wind, and trying to light them I forget all else again and again.

But I shall be wise this time and wait in the dark, spreading my mat on the floor; and whenever it is thy pleasure, my lord, come silently and take thy seat here.

C

I dive down into the depth of the ocean of forms, hoping to gain the perfect pearl of the formless.

No more sailing from harbour to harbour with this my weather-beaten boat. The days are long past when my sport was to be tossed on waves.

And now I am eager to die into the deathless.

Into the audience hall by the fathomless abyss where swells up the music of toneless strings I shall take this harp of my life.

I shall tune it to the notes of for ever, and, when it has sobbed out its last utterance, lay down my silent harp at the feet of the silent.

CI

Ever in my life have I sought thee with my songs. It was they who led me from door to door, and with them have I felt about me, searching and touching my world.

It was my songs that taught me all the lessons I ever learnt; they showed me secret paths, they brought before my sight many a star on the horizon of my heart.

They guided me all the day long to the mysteries of the country of pleasure and pain, and, at last, to what palace gate have they brought me in the evening at the end of my journey?

CII

I boasted among men that I had known you. They see your pictures in all works of mine. They come and ask me, "Who is he?" I know not how to answer them. I say, "Indeed, I cannot tell." They blame me and they go away in scorn. And you sit there smiling.

I put my tales of you into lasting songs. The secret gushes out from my heart. They come and ask me "Tell me all your meanings." I know not how to answer them. I say, "Ah, who knows what they mean!" They smile and go away in utter scorn. And you sit there smiling.

CIII

In one salutation to thee, my God, let all my sense spread out and touch this world at thy feet.

Like a rain-cloud of July hung low with its burden of unshed showers let all my mind bend down at thy door in one salutation to thee.

Let all my songs gather together their diverse strains into a single current and flow to a sea of silence in one salutation to thee.

Like a flock of homesick cranes flying night and day back to their mountain nests let all my life take its voyage to its eternal home in one salutation to thee.

The Nobel Prize
Acceptance Speech

I am glad that I have been able to come at last to your country and that I may use this opportunity for expressing my gratitude to you for the honour you have done to me by acknowledging my work and rewarding me by giving me the Nobel Prize.

I remember the afternoon when I received the cablegram from my publisher in England that the prize had been awarded to me. I was staying then at the school Shantiniketan, about which I suppose you know. At that moment we were taking a party over to a forest near by the school, and when I was passing by the telegram office and the post office, a man came running to us and held up the telegraphic message. I had also an English visitor with me in the same carriage. I did not think that the message was of any importance, and I just put it into my pocket, thinking that I would read it, when I reached my destination. But my visitor supposed he knew the contents, and he urged me to read it, saying that it contained an important message. And I opened and read the message, which I could hardly believe. I first thought that possibly the telegraphic language was not quite correct and that I might misread the meaning of it, but at last I felt certain about it. And you can well understand how rejoicing it was for my boys at the school and for the teachers. What touched me more deeply than anything else was that these boys who loved me and for whom I had the deepest love felt proud of the honour that had been awarded to him for whom they had feeling of reverence, and I realized that my countrymen would share with me the honour which had been awarded to myself.

The rest of the afternoon passed away in this manner, and when the night came I sat upon the terrace alone, and I asked myself the question what the reason could be of my poems being accepted and honoured by the West—in spite of my belonging to a different race, parted and separated by seas and mountains from the children of the West. And I can assure you that it was not with a feeling of exaltation but with a searching of the heart that I questioned myself, and I felt humble at that moment.

I remember how my life's work developed from the time when I was very young. When I was about 25 years I used to live in utmost seclusion in the solitude of an obscure Bengal village by the river Ganges in a boat-house. The wild ducks which came during the time of autumn from the Himalayan lakes were my only living companions, and in that solitude I seem to have drunk in the open space like wine overflowing with sunshine, and the murmur of the river used to speak to me and tell me the secrets of nature. And I passed my days in the solitude dreaming and giving shape to my dream in poems and studies and sending out my thoughts to the Calcutta public through the magazines and other papers. You can well understand that it was a life quite different from the life of the West. I do not know if any of your Western poets or writers do pass the greatest part of their young days in such absolute seclusion. I am almost certain that it cannot be possible and that seclusion itself has no place in the Western world.

And my life went on like this. I was an obscure individual—to most of my countrymen in those days. I mean that my name was hardly known outside my own province, but I was quite content with that obscurity, which protected me from the curiosity of the crowds.

And then came a time when my heart felt a longing to come out of that solitude and to do some work for my human fellow-beings, and not merely give shapes to my dreams and meditate deeply on the problems of life, but try to give expression to my ideas through some definite work, some definitive service for my fellow-beings.

And the one thing, the one work which came to my mind was to teach children. It was not because I was specially fitted for this work of teaching, for I have not had myself the full benefit of a regular education. For some time I hesitated to take upon myself this task, but I felt that as I had a deep love for nature I had naturally love for children also. My object in starting this institution was to give the children of men full freedom of joy, of life and of communion with nature. I myself had suffered when I was young through the impediments which were inflicted upon most boys while they attended school and I have had to go through the machine of education which crushes the joy and freedom of life for which children have such insatiable thirst. And my object was to give freedom and joy to children of men.

And so I had a few boys around me, and I taught them, and I tried to make them happy. I was their playmate. I was their companion. I shared their life, and I felt that I was the biggest child of the party. And we all grew up together in this atmosphere of freedom. The vigour and the joy of the children, their chats and songs filled the air with a spirit of delight, which I drank every day I was there. And in the evening during the sun-set hour I often used to sit alone watching the trees of the shadowing avenue, and in the silence of the afternoon I could hear distinctly the voices of the children coming up in the air, and it seemed to me that these shouts

and songs and glad voices were like those trees, whi   ıe
out from the heart of the earth like fountains of life towaıds
the bosom of the infinite sky. And it symbolized, it brought
before my mind the whole cry of human life all expressions
of joy and aspirations of men rising from the heart of Humanity
up to this sky. I could see that, and I knew that we also, the
grown-up children, send up our cries of aspiration to the
Infinite. I felt it in my heart of hearts.

In this atmosphere and in this environment I used to write
my poems Gitanjali, and I sang them to myself in the midnight
under the glorious stars of the Indian sky. And in the early
morning and in the afternoon glow of sun-set I used to write
these songs till a day came when I felt impelled to come out
once again and meet the heart of the large world.

I could see that my coming out from the seclusion of my
life among these joyful children and doing my service to my
fellow creatures was only a prelude to my pilgrimage to a
larger world. And I felt a great desire to come out and come
into touch with the Humanity of the West, for I was conscious
that the present age belongs to the Western man with his
superabundance of energy.

He has got the power of the whole world, and his life
is overflowing all boundaries and is sending out its message
to the great future. And I felt that I must before I die come
to the West and meet the man of the secret shrine where the
Divine presence has his dwelling, his temple. And I thought
that the Divine man with all his powers and aspirations of
life is dwelling in the West.

And so I came out. After my Gitanjali poems had been
written in Bengali I translated those poems into English,
without having any desire to have them published, being
diffident of my mastery of that language, but I had—the
manuscript with me when I came out to the West. And you
know that the British public, when these poems were put

before them, and those who had the opportunity of reading them in manuscript before, approved of them. I was accepted, and the heart of the West opened without delay.

And it was a miracle to me who had lived for fifty years far away from activity, far away from the West, that I should be almost in a moment accepted by the West as one of its own poets. It was surprising to me, but I felt that possibly this had its deeper significance and that those years which I had spent in seclusion, separated from the life and the spirit of the West, had brought with them a deeper feeling of rest, serenity and feeling of the eternal, and that these were exactly the sentiments that were needed by the Western people with their overactive life, who still in their heart of hearts have a thirst for the peace, for the infinite peace. My fitness was that training which my muse had from my young days in the absolute solitude of the beaches of the Ganges. The peace of those years had been stored in my nature so that I could bring it out and hold it up to the man of the West, and what I offered to him was accepted gratefully.

I know that I must not accept that praise as my individual share. It is the East in me which gave to the West. For is not the East the mother of spiritual Humanity and does not the West, do not the children of the West amidst their games and plays when they get hurt, when they get famished and hungry, turn their face to that serene mother, the East? Do they not expect their food to come from her, and their rest for the night when they are tired? And are they to be disappointed.

Fortunately for me I came in that very moment when the West had turned her face again to the East and was seeking for some nourishment. Because I represented the East I got my reward from my Eastern friends.

And I can assure you that the prize which you have awarded to me was not wasted upon myself. I as an individual had no right to accept it, and therefore I have made use of it for others. I have dedicated it to our Eastern children and students. But then it is like a seed which is put into the earth and comes up again to those who have sown it, and for their benefit it is producing fruits. I have used this money which I got from you for establishing and maintaining the university which I started lately, and it seemed to me, that this university should be a place where Western students might come and meet their Eastern brethren and when they might work together in the pursuit of truth and try to find the treasures that have lain hidden in the East for centuries and work out the spiritual resources of the East, which are necessary for all Humanity.

I can remind you of a day when India had her great university in the glorious days of her civilization. When a light is lighted it can not be held within a short range. It is for the whole world. And India had her civilization with all its splendours and wisdom and wealth. It could not use it for its own children only. It had to open its gates in hospitality to all races of men. Chinese and Japanese and Persians and all different races of men, came, and they had their opportunity of gaining what was best in India, her best offering of all times and to all Humanity. And she offered it generously. You know the traditions of our country are never to accept any material fees from the students in return to the teaching, because we consider in India that he who has the knowledge has the responsibility to impart it to the students. It is not merely for the students to come and ask it from the master, but it is the master who must fulfil his mission of life by offering the best gift which he has to all who may need it. And thus it was that need of self-expression, of giving what had been stored in India and offering the best thing that she has in herself that made it possible and was the cause and the origin of these universities that were started in the different provinces of India.

And I feel that what we suffer from in the present day is no other calamity but this calamity of obscurity, of seclusion, that we have missed our opportunity of offering hospitality to Humanity and asking the world to share the best things we have got. We lost our confidence in our own civilization for over a century, when we came into contact with the Western races with their material superiority over the Eastern Humanity and Eastern culture, and in the educational establishments no provision was made for our own culture. And for over a century our students have been brought up in utter ignorance of the worth of their own civilization of the past. Thus we did not only lose touch of the great which lay hidden in our own inheritance, but also the great honour of being able to contribute to the civilization of Humanity, to have opportunity of giving what we have and not merely begging from others, not merely borrowing culture and living like eternal schoolboys.

But the time has come when we must not waste such our opportunities. We must try to do our best to bring out what we have, and not go from century to century, from land to land and display our poverty before others. We know what we have to be proud of, what we have inherited from our ancestors, and such opportunity of giving should not be lost—not only for the sake of our people, but for the sake of Humanity.

That is the reason, and that led me to the determination to establish an international institution where the Western and Eastern students could meet and share the common feast of spiritual food.

And thus I am proud to say that your awarding me the prize has made some contribution to this great object which I had in my mind. This has made me come out once again to the West, and I have come to ask you, to invite you to the feast which is waiting for you in the far East. I hope that my invitation will not be rejected. I have visited different countries of Europe, and I have accepted from them an enthusiastic welcome. That welcome has its own meaning, that the West has need of the East, as the East has need of the West, and so the time has come when they should meet.

I am glad that I belong to this great time, this great age, and I am glad that I have done some work to give expression to this great age, when the East and the West are coming together. They are proceeding towards each other. They are coming to meet each other. They have got their invitation to meet each other and join hands in building up a new civilization and the great culture of the future.

I feel certain that through my writing some such idea has reached you, even if obscurely through the translation, some idea which belongs both to the East and the West, some idea which proceeding from the East has been able to come to the West and claim its rest here, its dwelling, and to be able to receive its welcome, and has been accepted by the West. And if in my writings I have been fortunate enough to be able to interpret the voice of the need of the time I am deeply thankful to you for giving me this glorious opportunity. The acknowledgment I got from Sweden has brought me and my work before the Western public, though I can assure you that it has also given me some trouble. It has broken through the seclusion which I have been accustomed to. It has brought me out before the great public to which I have never been accustomed. And the adjustment has not been yet made. I shrink in my heart when I stand before the great concourse of Humanity in the West. I have not yet been accustomed to accept the great gift of your praise and your admiration in the manner in which you have given it to me. And I feel ashamed and shy when standing before you—I do so now. But I will only say that I am thankful to God that he has given me this great opportunity, that I have been an instrument to bring together, to unite the hearts of the East and the West.

And I must to the end of my life carry on that mission. I must do all that I can. The feeling of resentment between the East and the West must be pacified. I must do something, and with that one object I have started this institution.

I do not think that it is the spirit of India to reject anything, reject any race, reject any culture. The spirit of India has always proclaimed the ideal of unity. This ideal of unity never rejects anything, any race, or any culture. It comprehends all, and it has been the highest aim of our spiritual exertion to be able to penetrate all things with one soul, to comprehend all things as they are, and not to keep out anything in the whole universe—to comprehend all things with sympathy and love. This is the spirit of India. Now, when in the present time of political unrest the children of the same great India cry for rejection of the West I feel hurt. I feel that it is a lesson which they have received from the west. Such is not our mission. India is there to unite all human races.

Because of that reason in India we have not been given the unity of races. Our problem is the race problem which is the problem of all Humanity. We have Dravidians, we have Mohammedans, we have Hindoos and all different sects and communities of men in India. Therefore, no superficial bond of political unity can appeal to us, can satisfy us, can ever be real to us. We must go deeper down. We must discover the most profound unity, the spiritual unity between the different races. We must go deeper down to the spirit of man and find out the great bond of unity, which is to be found in all human races. And for that we are well equipped. We have inherited the immortal works of our ancestors, those great writers who proclaimed the religion of unity and sympathy, in say: He who sees all beings as himself, who realizes all beings as himself, knows Truth. That has once again to be realized, not only by the children of the East but also by the children of the West. They also have to be reminded of these great immortal truths.

Man is not to fight with other human races, other human individuals, but his work is to bring about reconciliation and Peace and to restore the bonds of friendship and love. We are not like fighting beasts. It is the life of self which is predominating in our life, the self which is creating the seclusion, giving rise to sufferings, to jealousy and hatred, to political and commercial competition. All these illusions will vanish, if we go down to the heart of the shrine, to the love and unity of all races.

For that great mission of India I have started this university. I ask you now, when I have this opportunity, I invite you to come to us and join hands with us and not to leave this institution merely to us, but let your own students and learned men come to us and help us to make this university to a common institution for the East and the West may they give the contributions of their lives and may we all together make it living and representative of the undivided Humanity of the world.

For this I have come to you. I ask you this and I claim it of you in the name of the unity of men, and in the name of love, and in the name of God. I ask you to come. I invite you.

26 May 1921, Stockholm

THE POST OFFICE

THE·CHARACTERS

MADHAV
AMAL, his adopted child
SUDHA, a little flower-girl
DOCTOR
DAIRYMAN
WATCHMAN
GAFFER
VILLAGE HEADMAN, a bully
KING'S HERALD
ROYAL PHYSICIAN

ACT I

(Madhav's House)

Madhav. What a state I am in! Before he came, nothing mattered; I felt so free. But now that he has come, goodness knows from where, my heart is filled with his dear self, and my home will be no home to me when he leaves. Doctor, do you think he——

Physician. If there's life in his fate, then he will live long. But what the medical scriptures say, it seems—

Madhav. Great heavens, what?

Physician. The scriptures have it: "Bile or palsy, cold or gout spring all alike."

Madhav. Oh, get along, don't fling your scriptures at me; you only make me more anxious; tell me what I can do.

Physician (taking snuff). The patient needs the most scrupulous care.

Madhav. That's true; but tell me how.

Physician. I have already mentioned, on no account must he be let out of doors.

Madhav. Poor child, it is very hard to keep him indoors all day long.

Physician. What else can you do? The autumn sun and the damp are both very bad for the little fellow— for the scriptures have it:

"In wheezing, swooning, or in nervous fret,
In jaundice or leaden eyes—"
Madhav. Never mind the scriptures, please. Eh, then we must
    shut the poor thing up. Is there no other method?
Physician. None at all: for "In the wind and in the sun—"
Madhav. What will your "in this and in that" do for me now?
    Why don't you let them alone and come straight to the
    point? What's to be done, then? Your system is very,
    very hard for the poor boy; and he is so quiet too with
    all his pain and sickness. It tears my heart to see him
    wince, as he takes your medicine.
Physician. The more he winces, the surer is the effect. That's
    why the sage Chyabana observes: "In medicine as in
    good advice, the least palatable is the truest." Ah, well!
    I must be trotting now.
[*Exit*

(Gaffer enters)

Madhav. Well, I'm jiggered, there's Gaffer now.
Gaffer. Why, why, I won't bite you.
Madhav. No, but you are a devil to send children off their
    heads.
Gaffer. But you aren't a child, and you've no child in the
    house; why worry, then?
Madhav. Oh, but I have brought a child into the house.
Gaffer. Indeed, how so?
Madhav. You remember how my wife was dying to adopt a
    child?
Gaffer. Yes, but that's an old story; you didn't like the idea.
Madhav. You know, brother, how hard all this getting money
    in has been. That somebody else's child would sail in
    and waste all this money earned with so much trouble—
    Oh, I hated the idea. But this boy clings to my heart
    in such a queer sort of way——

Gaffer. So that's the trouble! and your money goes all for him and feels jolly lucky it does go at all.

Madhav. Formerly, earning was a sort of passion with me; I simply couldn't help working for money. Now, I make money, and as I know it is all for this dear boy, earning becomes a joy to me.

Gaffer. Ah, well, and where did you pick him up?

Madhav. He is the son of a man who was a brother to my wife by village ties. He has had no mother since infancy; and now the other day he lost his father as well.

Gaffer. Poor thing: and so he needs me all the more.

Madhav. The doctor says all the organs of his little body are at loggerheads with each other, and there isn't much hope for his life. There is only one way to save him and that is to keep him out of this autumn wind and sun. But you are such a terror! What with this game of yours at your age, too, to get children out of doors!

Gaffer. God bless my soul! So I'm already as bad as autumn wind and sun, eh! But, friend, I know something, too, of the game of keeping them indoors. When my day's work is over I am coming in to make friends with this child of yours.

[*Exit*

(Amal enters)

Amal. Uncle, I say, Uncle!

Madhav. Hullo! Is that you, Amal?

Amal. Mayn't I be out of the courtyard at all?

Madhav. No, my dear, no.

Amal. See there, where Auntie grinds lentils in the quern, the squirrel is sitting with his tail up and with his wee hands he's picking up the broken grains of lentils and crunching them. Can't I run up there?

Madhav. No, my darling, no.

Amal. Wish I were a squirrel!—it would be lovely. Uncle, why
won't you let me go about?

Madhav. Doctor says it's bad for you to be out.

Amal. How can the doctor know?

Madhav. What a thing to say! The doctor can't know and he
reads such huge books!

Amal. Does his book-learning tell him everything?

Madhav. Of course, don't you know!

Amal (with a sigh). Ah, I am so stupid! I don't read books.

Madhav. Now, think of it; very, very learned people are all
like you; they are never out of doors.

Amal. Aren't they really?

Madhav. No, how can they? Early and late they toil and moil
at their books, and they've eyes for nothing else. Now, my
little man, you are going to be learned when you grow
up; and then you will stay at home and read such big
books, and people will notice you and say, "He's a wonder."

Amal. No, no, Uncle; I beg of you, by your dear feet—I don't
want to be learned; I won't.

Madhav. Dear, dear; it would have been my saving if I could
have been learned.

Amal. No, I would rather go about and see everything that
there is.

Madhav. Listen to that! See! What will you see, what is there
so much to see?

Amal. See that far-away hill from our window—I often long
to go beyond those hills and right away.

Madhav. Oh, you silly! As if there's nothing more to be done
but just get up to the top of that hill and away! Eh! You
don't talk sense, my boy. Now listen, since that hill
stands there upright as a barrier, it means you can't get
beyond it. Else, what was the use in heaping up so many
large stones to make such a big affair of it, eh!

Amal. Uncle, do you think it is meant to prevent us crossing
over? It seems to me because the earth can't speak it
raises its hands into the sky and beckons. And those who
live far off and sit alone by their windows can see the
signal. But I suppose the learned people—

Madhav. No, they don't have time for that sort of nonsense.
They are not crazy like you.

Amal. Do you know, yesterday I met some one quite as crazy
as I am.

Madhav. Gracious me, really, how so?

Amal. He had a bamboo staff on his shoulder with a small
bundle at the top, and a brass pot in his left hand, and
an old pair of shoes on; he was making for those hills
straight across that meadow there. I called out to him and
asked, "Where are you going?" He answered, "I don't
know; anywhere!" I asked again, "Why are you going?"
He said, "I'm going out to seek work." Say, Uncle, have
you to seek work?

Madhav. Of course I have to. There's many about looking for
jobs.

Amal. How lovely! I'll go about like them too, finding things
to do.

Madhav. Suppose you seek and don't find. Then——

Amal. Wouldn't that be jolly? Then I should go farther! I
watched that man slowly walking on with his pair of
worn-out shoes. And when he got to where the water
flows under the fig tree, he stopped and washed his feet
in the stream. Then he took out from his bundle some
gram-flour, moistened it with water and began to eat.
Then he tied up his bundle and shouldered it again;
tucked up his cloth above his knees and crossed the
stream. I've asked Auntie to let me go up to the stream,
and eat my gram-flour just like him.

Madhav. And what did your Auntie say to that?

Amal. Auntie said, "Get well and then I'll take you over there." Please, Uncle, when shall I get well?

Madhav. It won't be long, dear.

Amal. Really, but then I shall go right away the moment I'm well again.

Madhav. And where will you go?

Amal. Oh, I will walk on, crossing so many streams, wading through water. Everybody will be asleep with their doors shut in the heat of the day and I will tramp on and on seeking work far, very far.

Madhav. I see! I think you had better be getting well first; then——

Amal. But then you won't want me to be learned, will you, Uncle?

Madhav. What would you rather be, then?

Amal. I can't think of anything just now; but I'll tell you later on.

Madhav. Very well. But mind you, you aren't to call out and talk to strangers again.

Amal. But I love to talk to strangers!

Madhav. Suppose they had kidnapped you?

Amal. That would have been splendid! But no one ever takes me away. They all want me to stay in here.

Madhav. I am off to my work—but, darling, you won't go out, will you?

Amal. No, I won't. But, Uncle, you'll let me be in this room by the roadside.

[*Exit Madhav*

'Dairyman. Curds, curds, good nice curds.

Amal. Curdseller, I say, Curdseller.

Dairyman. Why do you call me? Will you buy some curds?

Amal. How can I buy? I have no money.

Dairyman. What a boy! Why call out then? Ugh! What a waste of time!

Amal. I would go with you if I could.

Dairyman. With me?

Amal. Yes, I seem to feel homesick when I hear you call from far down the road.

Dairyman (lowering his yoke-pole). Whatever are you doing here, my child?

Amal. The doctor says I'm not to be out, so I sit here all day long.

Dairyman. My poor child, whatever has happened to you?

Amal. I can't tell. You see, I am not learned, so I don't know what's the matter with me. Say, Dairyman, where do you come from?

Dairyman. From our village.

Amal. Your village? Is it very far?

Dairyman. Our village lies on the river Shamli at the foot of the Panch-mura hills.

Amal. Panch-mura hills! Shamli river! I wonder. I may have seen your village. I can't think when, though!

Dairyman. Have you seen it? Been to the foot of those hills?

Amal. Never. But I seem to remember having seen it. Your village is under some very old big trees, just by the side of the red road—isn't that so?

Dairyman. That's right, child.

Amal. And on the slope of the hill cattle grazing.

Dairyman. How wonderful! Cattle grazing in our village! Indeed there are!

Amal. And your women with red sarees fill their pitchers from the river and carry them on their heads.

Dairyman. Good, that's right! Women from our dairy village do come and draw their water from the river; but then it isn't every one who has a red saree to put on. But, my dear child, surely you must have been there for a walk some time.

Amal. Really, Dairyman, never been there at all. But the first day doctor lets me go out, you are going to take me to your village.

Dairyman. I will, my child, with pleasure.

Amal. And you'll teach me to cry curds and shoulder the yoke like you and walk the long, long road?

Dairyman. Dear, dear, did you ever? Why should you sell curds? No, you will read big books and be learned.

Amal. No, I never want to be learned—I'll be like you and take my curds from the village by the red road near the old banyan tree, and I will hawk it from cottage to cottage. Oh, how do you cry—"Curds, curds, fine curds"? Teach me the tune, will you?

Dairyman. Dear, dear, teach you the tune; what a notion!

Amal. Please do. I love to hear it. I can't tell you how queer I feel when I hear you cry out from the bend of that road through the line of those trees! Do you know I feel like that when I hear the shrill cry of kites from almost the end of the sky?

Dairyman. Dear child, will you have some curds? Yes, do.

Amal. But I have no money.

Dairyman. No, no, no, don't talk of money! You'll make me so happy if you take some curds from me.

Amal. Say, have I kept you too long?

Dairyman. Not a bit; it has been no loss to me at all; you have taught me how to be happy selling curds.

[*Exit*

Amal (*intoning*). Curds, curds, fine curds—from the dairy village—from the country of the Panch-mura hills by the Shamli bank. Curds, good curds; in the early morning the women make the cows stand in a row under the trees and milk them, and in the evening they turn the milk into curds. Curds, good curds. Hello, there's the watchman on his rounds. Watchman, I say, come and have a word with me.

Watchman. What's all this row about? Aren't you afraid of the likes of me?

Amal. No, why should I be?

Watchman. Suppose I march you off, then?

Amal. Where will you take me to? Is it very far, right beyond the hills?

Watchman. Suppose I march you straight to the King?

Amal. To the King! Do, will you? But the doctor won't let me go out. No one can ever take me away. I've got to stay here all day long.

Watchman. Doctor won't let you, poor fellow! So I see! Your face is pale and there are dark rings round your eyes. Your veins stick out from your poor thin hands.

Amal. Won't you sound the gong, Watchman?

Watchman. Time has not yet come.

Amal. How curious! Some say time has not yet come, and some say time has gone by! But surely your time will come the moment you strike the gong!

Watchman. That's not possible; I strike up the gong only when it is time.

Amal. Yes, I love to hear your gong. When it is mid-day and our meal is over, Uncle goes off to his work and Auntie falls asleep reading her *Ramayana,* and in the courtyard under the shadow of the wall our doggie sleeps with his nose in his curled-up tail; then your gong strikes out, "Dong, dong, dong!" Tell me, why does your gong sound?

Watchman. My gong sounds to tell the people, Time waits for none, but goes on for ever.

Amal. Where, to what land?

Watchman. That none knows.

Amal. Then I suppose no one has ever been there! Oh, I do wish to fly with the time to that land of which no one knows anything.

Watchman. All of us have to get there one day, my child.

Amal. Have I too?

Watchman. Yes, you too!

Amal. But doctor won't let me out.

Watchman. One day the doctor himself may take you there by the hand.

Amal. He won't; you don't know him. He only keeps me in.

Watchman. One greater than he comes and lets us free.

Amal. When will this great doctor come for me? I can't stick in here any more.

Watchman. Shouldn't talk like that, my child.

Amal. No. I am here where they have left me—I never move a bit. But, when your gong goes off, dong, dong, dong, it goes to my heart. Say, Watchman?

Watchman. Yes, my dear.

Amal. Say, what's going on there in that big house on the other side, where there is a flag flying high up and the people are always going in and out?

Watchman. Oh, there? That's our new Post Office.

Amal. Post Office? Whose?

Watchman. Whose? Why, the King's, surely!

Amal. Do letters come from the King to his office here?

Watchman. Of course. One fine day there may be a letter for you in there.

Amal. A letter for me? But I am only a little boy.

Watchman. The King sends tiny notes to little boys.

Amal. Oh, how splendid! When shall I have my letter? How do you know he'll write to me?

Watchman. Otherwise why should he set his Post Office here right in front of your open window, with the golden flag flying?

Amal. But who will fetch me my King's letter when it comes?

Watchman. The King has many postmen. Don't you see them run about with round gilt badges on their chests?

Amal. Well, where do they go?

Watchman. Oh, from door to door, all through the country.

Amal. I'll be the King's postman when I grow up.

Watchman. Ha! ha! Postman, indeed! Rain or shine, rich or poor, from house to house delivering letters— that's very great work!

Amal. That's what I'd like best. What makes you smile so? Oh, yes, your work is great too. When it is silent everywhere in the heat of the noonday, your gong sounds, Dong, dong, dong,—and sometimes when I wake up at night all of a sudden and find our lamp blown out, I can hear through the darkness your gong slowly sounding, Dong, dong, dong!

Watchman. There's the village headman! I must be off. If he catches me gossiping there'll be a great to-do.

Amal. The headman? Whereabouts is he?

Watchman. Right down the road there; see that huge palm-leaf umbrella hopping along? That's him!

Amal. I suppose the King's made him our headman here?

Watchman. Made him? Oh, no! A fussy busybody! He knows so many ways of making himself unpleasant that everybody is afraid of him. It's just a game for the likes of him, making trouble for everybody. I must be off now! Mustn't keep work waiting, you know! I'll drop in again tomorrow morning and tell you all the news of the town.

[*Exit*

Amal. It would be splendid to have a letter from the King every day. I'll read them at the window. But, oh! I can't

read writing. Who'll read them out to me, I wonder!
Auntie reads her *Ramayana;* she may know the King's
writing. If no one will, then I must keep them carefully
and read them when I'm grown up. But if the postman
can't find me? Headman, Mr. Headman, may I have a
word with you?

Headman. Who is yelling after me on the highway? Oh, it's
you, is it, you wretched monkey?

Amal. You're the headman. Everybody minds you.

Headman (looking pleased). Yes, oh yes, they do! They must!

Amal. Do the King's postmen listen to you?

Headman. They've got to. By Jove, I'd like to see——

Amal. Will you tell the postman it's Amal who sits by the
window here?

Headman. What's the good of that?

Amal. In case there's a letter for me.

Headman. A letter for you! Whoever's going to write to you?

Amal. If the King does.

Headman. Ha! ha! What an uncommon little fellow you are!
Ha! ha! the King, indeed; aren't you his bosom friend,
eh! You haven't met for a long while and the King is
pining for you, I am sure. Wait till tomorrow and you'll
have your letter.

Amal. Say, Headman, why do you speak to me in that tone
of voice? Are you cross?

Headman. Upon my word! Cross, indeed! You write to the
King! Madhav is a devilish swell nowadays. He's made
a little pile; and so kings and padishahs are every-day
talk with his people. Let me find him once and I'll make
him dance. Oh, you,—you snipper-snapper! I'll get the
King's letter sent to your house—indeed I will!

Amal. No, no, please don't trouble yourself about it.

Headman. And why not, pray! I'll tell the King about
you and he won't be long. One of his footmen will
come presently for news of you. Madhav's impudence

staggers me. If the King hears of this, that'll take some
of his nonsense out of him.

[*Exit*

Amal. Who are you walking there? How your anklets tinkle!
Do stop a while, won't you? (*A Girl enters*)

Girl. I haven't a moment to spare; it is already late!

Amal. I see, you don't wish to stop; I don't care to stay on
here either.

Girl. You make me think of some late star of the morning!
Whatever's the matter with you?

Amal. I don't know; the doctor won't let me out.

Girl. Ah me! Don't go, then! Should listen to the doctor.
People will be cross with you if you're naughty. I know,
always looking out and watching must make you feel
tired. Let me close the window a bit for you.

Amal. No, don't, only this one's open! All the others are shut.
But will you tell me who you are? Don't seem to know
you.

Girl. I am Sudha.

Amal. What Sudha?

Sudha. Don't you know? Daughter of the flower-seller here.

Amal. What do you do?

Sudha. I gather flowers in my basket.

Amal. Oh, flower-gathering! That is why your feet seem so
glad and your anklets jingle so merrily as you walk.
Wish I could be out too. Then I would pick some
flowers for you from the very topmost branches right
out of sight.

Sudha. Would you really? Do you know as much about flowers
as I?

Amal. Yes, I do, quite as much. I know all about Champa of
the fairy tale and his six brothers. If only they let me,

I'll go right into the dense forest where you can't find your way. And where the honey-sipping humming-bird rocks himself on the end of the thinnest branch, I will blossom into a *champa*. Would you be my sister Parul?

Sudha. You are silly! How can I be sister Parul when I am Sudha and my mother is Sasi, the flower-seller? I have to weave so many garlands a day. It would be jolly if I could lounge here like you!

Amal. What would you do then, all the day long?

Sudha. I could have great times with my doll Benay the bride, and Meni the pussy-cat, and—but I say, it is getting late and I mustn't stop, or I won't find a single flower.

Amal. Oh, wait a little longer; I do like it so!

Sudha. Ah, well—now don't you be naughty. Be good and sit still, and on my way back home with the flowers I'll come and talk with you.

Amal. And you'll let me have a flower, then?

Sudha. No, how can I? It has to be paid for.

Amal. I'll pay when I grow up—before I leave to look for work out on the other side of that stream there.

Sudha. Very well, then.

Amal. And you'll come back when you have your flowers?

Sudha. I will.

Amal. You will, really?

Sudha. Yes, I will.

Amal. You won't forget me? I am Amal, remember that.

Sudha. I won't forget you, you'll see.

[*Exit*

(*A Troop of Boys enter*)

Amal. Say, brothers, where are you all off to? Stop here a little.

A Boy. We're off to play.

Amal. What will you play at, brothers?

A Boy. We'll play at being ploughmen.

Another Boy (showing a stick). This is our ploughshare.

Another Boy. We two are the pair of oxen.

Amal. And you're going to play the whole day?

A Boy. Yes, all day long.

Amal. And you will come home in the evening by the road along the river bank?

A Boy. Yes.

Amal. Do you pass our house on your way home?

A Boy. Come out and play with us; yes, do.

Amal. Doctor won't let me out.

A Boy. Doctor! Do you mean to say you mind what the doctor says? Let's be off; it is getting late.

Amal. Don't go. Play on the road near this window. I could watch you, then.

A Boy. What can we play at here?

Amal. With all these toys of mine that are lying about. Here you are; have them. I can't play alone. They are getting dirty and are of no use to me.

Boys. How jolly! What fine toys! Look, here's a ship. There's old mother Jatai. Isn't this a gorgeous sepoy? And you'll let us have them all? You don't really mind?

Amal. No, not a bit; have them by all means.

A Boy. You don't want them back?

Amal. Oh, no, I shan't want them.

A Boy. Say, won't you get a scolding for this?

Amal. No one will scold me. But will you play with them in front of our door for a while every morning? I'll get you new ones when these are old.

A Boy. Oh, yes, we will. I say, put these sepoys into a line. We'll play at war; where can we get a musket? Oh, look here, this bit of reed will do nicely. Say, but you're off to sleep already.

Amal. I'm afraid I'm sleepy. I don't know, I feel like it at times. I have been sitting a long while and I'm tired; my back aches.

A Boy. It's hardly midday now. How is it you're sleepy? Listen! The gong's sounding the first watch.

Amal. Yes, Dong, dong, dong; it tolls me to sleep.

A Boy. We had better go, then. We'll come in again to-morrow morning.

Amal. I want to ask you something before you go. You are always out—do you know of the King's postmen?

Boys. Yes, quite well.

Amal. Who are they? Tell me their names.

A Boy. One's Badal.

Another Boy. Another's Sarat.

Another Boy. There's so many of them.

Amal. Do you think they will know me if there's a letter for me?

A Boy. Surely, if your name's on the letter they will find you out.

Amal. When you call in to-morrow morning, will you bring one of them along so that he'll know me?

A Boy. Yes, if you like.

Curtain

ACT II

(Amal in Bed)

Amal. Can't I go near the window to-day, Uncle? Would the doctor mind that too?

Madhav. Yes, darling; you see you've made yourself worse squatting there day after day.

Amal. Oh, no, I don't know if it's made me more ill, but I always feel well when I'm there.

Madhav. No, you don't; you squat there and make friends with the whole lot of people round here, old and young, as if they are holding a fair right under my eaves—flesh and blood won't stand that strain. Just see —your face is quite pale.

Amal. Uncle, I fear my fakir 'll pass and not see me by the window.

Madhav. Your fakir; whoever's that?

Amal. He comes and chats to me of the many lands where he's been. I love to hear him.

Madhav. How's that? I don't know of any fakirs.

Amal. This is about the time he comes in. I beg of you, by your dear feet, ask him in for a moment to talk to me here.

(Gaffer enters in a Fakir's guise)

Amal. There you are. Come here, Fakir, by my bed-side.

Madhav. Upon my word, but this is——

Gaffer (winking hard). I am the Fakir.

Madhav. It beats my reckoning what you're not.

Amal. Where have you been this time, Fakir?

Gaffer. To the Isle of Parrots. I am just back.

Madhav. The Parrots' Isle!

Gaffer. Is it so very astonishing? I am not like you. A journey doesn't cost a thing. I tramp just where I like.

Amal (clapping). How jolly for you! Remember your promise to take me with you as your follower when I'm well.

Gaffer. Of course, and I'll teach you so many travellers' secrets that nothing in sea or forest or mountain can bar your way.

Madhav. What's all this rigmarole?

Gaffer. Amal, my dear, I bow to nothing in sea or mountain; but if the doctor joins in with this uncle of yours, then I with all my magic must own myself beaten.

Amal. No. Uncle won't tell the doctor. And I promise to lie quiet; but the day I am well, off I go with the Fakir, and nothing in sea or mountain or torrent shall stand in my way.

Madhav. Fie, dear child, don't keep on harping upon going! It makes me so sad to hear you talk so.

Amal. Tell me, Fakir, what the Parrots' Isle is like.

Gaffer. It's a land of wonders; it's a haunt of birds. No men are there; and they neither speak nor walk, they simply sing and they fly.

Amal. How glorious! And it's by some sea?

Gaffer. Of course. It's on the sea.

Amal. And green hills are there?

Gaffer. Indeed, they live among the green hills; and in the time of the sunset when there is a red glow on the hillside, all the birds with their green wings go flocking to their nests.

Amal. And there are waterfalls!

Gaffer. Dear me, of course; you don't have a hill without its waterfalls. Oh, it's like molten diamonds; and, my dear, what dances they have! Don't they make the pebbles sing as they rush over them to the sea! No devil of a doctor can stop them for a moment. The birds looked upon me as nothing but a man, merely a trifling creature without wings—and they would have nothing to do with me. Were it not so I would build a small cabin for myself among their crowd of nests and pass my days counting the sea-waves.

Amal. How I wish I were a bird! Then——

Gaffer. But that would have been a bit of a job; I hear you've fixed up with the dairyman to be a hawker of curds when you grow up; I'm afraid such business won't flourish among birds; you might land yourself into serious loss.

Madhav. Really this is too much. Between you two I shall turn crazy. Now, I'm off.

Amal. Has the dairyman been, Uncle?

Madhav. And why shouldn't he? He won't bother his head running errands for your pet fakir, in and out among the nests in his Parrots' Isle. But he has left a jar of curds for you saying that he is busy with his niece's wedding in the village, and has to order a band at Kamlipara.

Amal. But he is going to marry me to his little niece.

Gaffer. Dear me, we are in a fix now.

Amal. He said she would be my lovely little bride with a pair of pearl drops in her ears and dressed in a lovely red saree; and in the morning she would milk with her own hands the black cow and feed me with warm milk with foam on it from a brand-new earthen cruse; and in the evenings she would carry the lamp round the cow-house, and then come and sit by me to tell me tales of Champa and his six brothers.

Gaffer. How charming! It would even tempt me, a hermit! But never mind, dear, about this wedding. Let it be. I tell you that when you marry there'll be no lack of nieces in his household.

Madhav. Shut up! This is more than I can stand.

[Exit

Amal. Fakir, now that Uncle's off, just tell me, has the King sent me a letter to the Post Office?

Gaffer. I gather that his letter has already started; it is on the way here.

Amal. On the way? Where is it? Is it on that road winding through the trees which you can follow to the end of the forest when the sky is quite clear after rain?

Gaffer. That is where it is. You know all about it already.

Amal. I do, everything.

Gaffer. So I see, but how?

Amal. I can't say; but it's quite clear to me. I fancy I've seen it often in days long gone by. How long ago I can't tell. Do you know when? I can see it all: there, the King's postman coming down the hillside alone, a lantern in his left hand and on his back a bag of letters; climbing down for ever so long, for days and nights, and where at the foot of the mountain the waterfall becomes a stream he takes to the footpath on the bank and walks on through the rye; then comes the sugar-cane field and he disappears into the narrow lane cutting through the tall stems of sugar-canes; then he reaches the open meadow where the cricket chirps and where there is not a single man to be seen, only the snipe wagging their tails and poking at the mud with their bills. I can feel him coming nearer and nearer and my heart becomes glad.

Gaffer. My eyes are not young; but you make me see all the same.

Amal. Say, Fakir, do you know the King who has this Post Office?

Gaffer. I do; I go to him for my alms every day.

Amal. Good! When I get well I must have my alms too from him, mayn't I?

Gaffer. You won't need to ask, my dear; he'll give it to you of his own accord.

Amal. No, I will go to his gate and cry, "Victory to thee, O King!" and dancing to the tabor's sound, ask for alms. Won't it be nice?

Gaffer. It will be splendid, and if you're with me I shall have my full share. But what will you ask?

Amal. I shall say, "Make me your postman, that I may go about, lantern in hand, delivering your letters from door to door. Don't let me stay at home all day!"

Gaffer. What is there to be sad for, my child, even were you to stay at home?

Amal. It isn't sad. When they shut me in here first I felt the day was so long. Since the King's Post Office was put there I like more and more being indoors, and as I think I shall get a letter one day, I feel quite happy and then I don't mind being quiet and alone. I wonder if I shall make out what'll be in the King's letter?

Gaffer. Even if you didn't wouldn't it be enough if it just bore your name?

(Madhav enters)

Madhav. Have you any idea of the trouble you've got me into, between you two?

Gaffer. What's the matter?

Madhav. I hear you've let it get rumoured about that the King has planted his office here to send messages to both of you,

Gaffer. Well, what about it?

Madhav. Our headman Panchanan has had it told to the King anonymously.

Gaffer. Aren't we aware that everything reaches the King's ears?

Madhav. Then why don't you look out? Why take the King's name in vain? You'll bring me to ruin if you do.

Amal. Say, Fakir, will the King be cross?

Gaffer. Cross, nonsense! And with a child like you and a fakir such as I am? Let's see if the King be angry, and then won't I give him a piece of my mind!

Amal. Say, Fakir, I've been feeling a sort of darkness coming over my eyes since the morning. Everything seems like a dream. I long to be quiet. I don't feel like talking at all. Won't the King's letter come? Suppose this room melts away all on a sudden, suppose—

Gaffer (fanning Amal). The letter's sure to come today, my boy.

(Doctor enters)

Doctor. And how do you feel to-day?

Amal. Feel awfully well to-day, Doctor. All pain seems to have left me.

Doctor (aside to Madhav). Don't quite like the look of that smile. Bad sign that, his feeling well! Chakradhan has observed—

Madhav. For goodness' sake, Doctor, leave Chakradhan alone. Tell me what's going to happen?

Doctor. Can't hold him in much longer, I fear! I warned you before—this looks like a fresh exposure.

Madhav. No, I've used the utmost care, never let him out of doors; and the windows have been shut almost all the time.

Doctor. There's a peculiar quality in the air to-day. As I came in I found a fearful draught through your front door. That's most hurtful. Better lock it at once. Would it matter if this kept your visitors off for two or three days? If some one happens to call unexpectedly— there's the back door. You had better shut this window as well, it's letting in the sunset rays only to keep the patient awake.

Madhav. Amal has shut his eyes. I expect he is sleeping. His face tells me——Oh, Doctor, I bring in a child who is a stranger and love him as my own, and now I suppose I must lose him!

Doctor. What's that? There's your headman sailing in!—What a bother! I must be going, brother. You had better stir about and see to the doors being properly fastened. I will send on a strong dose directly I get home. Try it on him—it may save him at last, if he can be saved at all.

[Exeunt Madhav and Doctor

(The Headman enters)

Headman. Hello, urchin!—

Gaffer (rising hastily). 'Sh, be quiet.

Amal. No, Fakir, did you think I was asleep? I wasn't. I can hear everything; yes, and voices far away. I feel that mother and father are sitting by my pillow and speaking to me.

(Madhav enters)

Headman. I say, Madhav, I hear you hobnob with bigwigs nowadays.

Madhav. Spare me your jokes, Headman; we are but common people.

Headman. But your child here is expecting a letter from the King.

Madhav. Don't you take any notice of him, a mere foolish boy!

Headman. Indeed, why not! It'll beat the King hard to find a better family! Don't you see why the King plants his new Post Office right before your window? Why, there's a letter for you from the King, urchin.

Amal (starting up). Indeed, really!

Headman. How can it be false? You're the King's chum. Here's your letter *(showing a blank slip of paper).* Ha, ha, ha! This is the letter.

Amal. Please don't mock me. Say, Fakir, is it so?

Gaffer. Yes, my dear. I as Fakir tell you it *is* his letter.

Amal. How is it I can't see? It all looks so blank to me. What is there in the letter, Mr. Headman?

Headman. The King says, "I am calling on you shortly; you had better have puffed rice for me.—Palace fare is quite tasteless to me now." Ha! ha! ha!

Madhav (with folded palms). I beseech you, Headman, don't you joke about these things——

Gaffer. Joking indeed! He would not dare.

Madhav. Are you out of your mind too, Gaffer?

Gaffer. Out of my mind; well then, I am; I can read plainly that the King writes he will come himself to see Amal, with the State Physician.

Amal. Fakir, Fakir, 'sh, his trumpet! Can't you hear?

Headman. Ha! ha! ha! I fear he won't until he's a bit more off his head.

Amal. Mr. Headman, I thought you were cross with me and didn't love me. I never could have believed you would fetch me the King's letter. Let me wipe the dust off your feet.

Headman. This little child does have an instinct of reverence. Though a little silly, he has a good heart.

Amal. It's hard on the fourth watch now, I suppose. Hark, the gong, "Dong, dong, ding—Dong, dong, ding." Is the evening star up? How is it I can't see——

Gaffer. Oh, the windows are all shut; I'll open them.

(A knocking outside)

Madhav. What's that?—Who is it?—What a bother!

Voice (from outside). Open the door.

Madhav. Headman—I hope they're not robbers.

Headman. Who's there?—It is Panchanan, the headman, who calls.—Aren't you afraid to make that noise? Fancy! The noise has ceased! Panchanan's voice carries far.—Yes, show me the biggest robbers!——

Madhav (peering out of the window). No wonder the noise has ceased. They've smashed the outer door. *(The Kings Herald enters)*

Herald. Our Sovereign King comes to-night!

Headman. My God!

Amal. At what hour of the night, Herald?

Herald. On the second watch.

Amal. When my friend the watchman will strike his gong from the city gates, "Ding dong ding, ding dong ding"—then?

Herald. Yes, then. The King sends his greatest physician to attend on his young friend. *(State Physician enters)*

State Physician. What's this? How close it is here! Open wide all the doors and windows. *(Feeling Amal's body.)* How do you feel, my child?

Amal. I feel very well, Doctor, very well. All pain is gone. How fresh and open! I can see all the stars now twinkling from the other side of the dark.

Physician. Will you feel well enough to leave your bed when the King comes in the middle watches of the night?

Amal. Of course, I'm dying to be about for ever so long. I'll
ask the King to find me the polar star—I must have seen
it often, but I don't know exactly which it is.

Physician. He will tell you everything. *(To Madhav.)* Arrange
flowers through the room for the King's visit. *(Indicating
the Headman.)* We can't have that person in here.

Amal. No, let him be, Doctor. He is a friend. It was he who
brought me the King's letter.

Physician. Very well, my child. He may remain if he is a friend
of yours.

Madhav (whispering into Amal's ear). My child, the King loves
you. He is coming himself. Beg for a gift from him. You
know our humble circumstances.

Amal. Don't you worry, Uncle.—I've made up my mind
about it.

Madhav. What is it, my child?

Amal. I shall ask him to make me one of his postmen that
I may wander far and wide, delivering his message from
door to door.

Madhav. (slapping his forehead). Alas, is that all?

Amal. What'll be our offerings to the King, Uncle, when he
comes?

Herald. He has commanded puffed rice.

Amal. Puffed rice. Say, Headman, you're right. You said so.
You knew all we didn't.

Headman. If you would send word to my house I could
manage for the King's advent really nice—

Physician. No need at all. Now be quiet, all of you. Sleep is
coming over him. I'll sit by his pillow; he's dropping
asleep. Blow out the oil-lamp. Only let the star-light
stream in. Hush, he sleeps.

Madhav (addressing Gaffer). What are you standing there for
like a statue, folding your palms?—I am nervous.—Say,
are there good omens? Why are they darkening the
room? How will star-light help?

Gaffer. Silence, unbeliever!

(*Sudha enters*)

Sudha. Amal!
Physician. He's asleep.
Sudha. I have some flowers for him. Mayn't I give them into his own hand?
Physician. Yes, you may.
Sudha. When will he be awake?
Physician. Directly the King comes and calls him.
Sudha. Will you whisper a word for me in his ear?
Physician. What shall I say?
Sudha. Tell him Sudha has not forgotten him.

Curtain

CREATIVE UNITY

Introduction

It costs me nothing to feel that I am; it is no burden to me. And yet if the mental, physical, chemical, and other innumerable facts concerning all branches of knowledge which have united in myself could be broken up, they would prove endless. It is some untold mystery of unity in me, that has the simplicity of the infinite and reduces the immense mass of multitude to a single point.

This One in me knows the universe of the many. But, in whatever it knows, it knows the One in different aspects. It knows this room only because this room is One to it, in spite of the seeming contradiction of the endless facts contained in the single fact of the room. Its knowledge of a tree is the knowledge of a unity, which appears in the aspect of a tree.

This One in me is creative. Its creations are a pastime, through which it gives expression to an ideal of unity in its endless show of variety. Such are its pictures, poems, music, in which it finds joy only because they reveal the perfect forms of an inherent unity.

This One in me not only seeks unity in knowledge for its understanding and creates images of unity for its delight; it also seeks union in love for its fulfillment. It seeks itself in others. This is a fact, which would be absurd had there been no great medium of truth to give it reality. In love we find a joy which is ultimate because it is the ultimate truth.

Therefore it is said in the Upanishads that the *advaitam* is *anantam*,—'the One is Infinite'; that the *advaitam* is *anandam*,—'the One is Love.'

To give perfect expression to the One, the Infinite, through the harmony of the many; to the One, the Love, through the sacrifice of self, is the object alike of our individual life and our society.

The Poet's Religion

I

Civility is beauty of behaviour. It requires for its perfection patience, self control, and an environment of leisure. For genuine courtesy is a creation, like pictures, like music. It is a harmonious blending of voice, gesture and movement, words and action, in which generosity of conduct is expressed. It reveals the man himself and has no ulterior purpose.

Our needs are always in a hurry. They rush and hustle, they are rude and unceremonious; they have no surplus of leisure, no patience for anything else but fulfillment of purpose. We frequently see in our country at the present day men utilising empty kerosene cans for carrying water. These cans are emblems of discourtesy; they are curt and abrupt, they have not the least shame for their unmannerliness, they do not care to be ever so slightly more than useful.

The instruments of our necessity assert that we must have food, shelter, clothes, comforts and convenience. And yet men spend an immense amount of their time and resources in contradicting this assertion, to prove that they are not a mere living catalogue of endless wants; that there is in them an ideal of perfection, a sense of unity, which is a harmony between parts and a harmony with surroundings.

The quality of the infinite is not the magnitude of extension, it is in the *advaitam,* the mystery of Unity. Fact occupy endless time and space; but the truth comprehending them all has no dimension; it is One. Wherever our heart touches the One, in the small or the big, it finds the touch of the infinite.

I was speaking to some one of the joy we have in our personality. I said it was because we were made conscious by it of a spirit of unity within ourselves. He answered that he had no such feeling of joy about himself, but I was sure he exaggerated. In all probability he had been suffering from some break of harmony between his surroundings and the spirit of unity within him, proving all the more strongly its truth. The meaning of health comes home to us with painful force when disease disturbs it; since health expresses the unity of the vital functions and is accordingly joyful. Life's tragedies occur, not to demonstrate their own reality, but to reveal that eternal principle of joy in life, to which they gave a rude shaking. It is the object of this Oneness in us to realize its infinity by perfect union of love with others. All obstacles to this union create misery, giving rise to the baser passions that are expressions of finitude, of that separateness which is negative and *maya.*

The joy of unity within ourselves, seeking expression, becomes creative; whereas our desire for the fulfilment of our needs is constructive. The water vessel, taken as a vessel only raises the question, 'Why does it exist at all?' Through its fitness of construction, it offers the apology for its existence. But where it is a work of beauty it has no question to answer; it has nothing to do, but to be. It reveals in its form a unity to which all that seems various in it is so related that, in a mysterious manner, it strikes sympathetic chords to the music of unity in our own being.

What is the truth of this world? It is not in the masses of substance, not in the number of things, but in their relatedness, which neither can be counted, nor measured, nor abstracted. It is not in the materials which are many, but in the expression which is one. All our knowledge of things is knowing them in their relation to the Universe, in that relation which is truth. A drop of water is not a particular assortment of elements; it is the miracle of a harmonious mutuality, in which the two reveal the One. No amount of analysis can reveal to us this mystery of unity. Matter is an abstraction; we shall never be able to realize what it is, for our world of reality does not acknowledge it. Even the giant forces of the world, centripetal and centrifugal, are kept out of our recognition. They are the day-labourers not admitted into the audience-hall of creation. But light and sound come to us in their gay dresses as troubadours singing serenades before the windows of the senses. What is constantly before us, claiming our attention, is not the kitchen, but the feast; not the anatomy of the world, but its countenance. There is the dancing ring of seasons; the elusive play of lights and shadows, of wind and water; the many coloured wings of erratic life flitting between birth and death. The importance of these does not lie in their existence as mere facts, but in their language of harmony, the mother-tongue of our own soul, through which they are communicated to us.

We grow out of touch with this great truth, we forget to accept its invitation and its hospitality, when in quest of external success our works become unspiritual and unexpressive. This is what Wordsworth complained of when he said:

The world is to much with us; late and soon,
Getting and spending, we lay waste our powers.
Little we see in Nature that is ours.

But it is not because the world has grown too familiar to us; on the contrary, it is because we do not see it in its aspect of unity, because we are driven to distraction by our pursuit of the fragmentary.

Materials as materials are savage; they are solitary; they are ready to hurt one another. They are like our individual impulses seeking the unlimited freedom of willfulness. Left to themselves they are destructive. But directly an ideal of unity raises its banner in their center, it brings these rebellious forces under its away and creation is revealed—the creation which is peace, which is the unity of perfect relationship. Our greed for eating is in itself ugly and selfish, it has no sense of decorum; but when brought under the ideal of social fellowship, it is regulated and made ornamental; it is changed into a daily festivity of life. In human nature sexual passion is fiercely individual and destructive, but dominated by the ideal of love, it has been made to flower into a perfection of beauty, becoming in its best expression symbolical of the spiritual truth in man which is his kinship of love with the Infinite. Thus we find it is the One which expresses itself in creation; and the Many, by giving up opposition, make the revelation of unity perfect.

II

I remember, when I was a child, that a row of coconut trees by our garden wall, with their branches beckoning the rising sun on the horizon, gave me a companionship as living as I was myself. I know it was my imagination which transmuted the world around me into my own world—the imagination which seeks unity, which deals with it. But we have to consider that this companionship was true; that the universe in which I was born had in it an element profoundly akin to my own imaginative mind, one which wakens in all children's natures the Creator, whose pleasure is in interweaving the web of creation with His own patterns of many-coloured stands. It is something akin to us, and therefore harmonious to our imagination. When we find some strings vibrating in unison with others, we know that this sympathy carries in it an eternal reality. The fact that the world stirs our imagination in sympathy tells us that this creative imagination is a common truth both in us and in the heart of existence. Wordsworth says:

> I'd rather be
>
> A pagan suckled in a creed outworn;
> So might I, standing on this pleasant lea,
> Have glimpses that would make me less forlorn;
> Have sight of Proteus rising from the sea,
> Or hear old Triton blow his wreathed horn.

In this passage the poet says we are less forlorn in a world which we meet with our imagination. That can only be possible if through our imagination is revealed, behind all appearances, the reality which gives the touch of companionship, that is to say, something which has an affinity to us. An immense amount of our activity is engaged in making images, not for serving any useful purpose or formulating rational propositions, but for giving varied responses to the varied touches of this reality. In this image-making the child creates his own world in answer to the world in which he finds himself. The child in us finds glimpses of his eternal playmate from behind the veil of things, as Proteus rising from the sea, or Triton blowing his wreathed horn. And the playmate is the Reality, that makes it possible for the child to find delight in activities which do not inform or bring assistance but merely express. There is an image-making joy in the infinite, which inspires in us our joy in imagining. The rhythm of cosmic notion produces in our mind the emotion which is creative.

A poet has said about his destiny as a dreamer, about the worthlessness of his dreams and yet their permanence:

> I hang 'mid men my heedless head,
> And my fruit is dreams, as theirs is bread:

The godly men and the sun-hazed sleeper,
Time shall reap; but after the reaper
The world shall glean to me, me the sleeper.

The dreams persists; it is more real than even bread which
has substance and use. The painted canvas is durable and
substantial; it has for its production and transport to market
a whole array of machines and factories. But the picture
which no factory can produce is a dream, *maya,* and yet it,
not the canvas, has the meaning of ultimate reality.

A poet describes Autumn:

I saw old Autumn in the misty morn
Stand shadowless like Silence, listening
To silence, for no lonely bird would sing
Into his hollow ear from woods forlorn.

Of April another poet sings:

April, April,
Laugh thy girlish laughter;
Then the moment after
Weep thy girlish tears!
April, that mine ears
Like a lover greetest,
If I tell thee, sweetest,
All my hopes and fears.

April, April,
Laugh thy golden laughter.
But the moment after
Weep thy golden tears!

This Autumn, this April,—are they nothing but phantasy?
Let us suppose that the Man from the Moon comes to

the earth and listens to some music in a gramophone. He seeks for the origin of the delight produced in his mind. The facts before him are a cabinet made of wood and a revolving disc producing sound; but the one thing which is neither seen nor can be explained is the truth of the music, which his personality must immediately acknowledge as a personal message. It is neither in the wood, nor in the disc, nor in the sound of the notes. If the Man from the Moon be a poet, as can reasonably be supposed, he will write about a fairy imprisoned in that box, who sits spinning fabrics of songs expressing her cry for a far-away magic casement opening on the foam of some perilous sea, in a fairyland. It will not be literally, but essentially true. The facts of the gramophone make us aware of the laws of sound, but the music gives us personal companionship. The bare facts about April are alternate sunshine and showers; but the subtle blending of shadows and lights, of murmurs and movements, in April, gives us not mere shocks of sensation, but unity of joy as does music. Therefore when a poet sees the vision of a girl in April, even a downright materialist is in sympathy with him. But we know that the same individual would be menacingly angry if the law of heredity or a geometrical problem were described as a girl or a rose—or even as a cat or a camel. For these intellectual abstractions have no magical touch for our lute-strings of imagination. They are no dreams, as are the harmony of bird-songs, rain-washed leaving glistening in the sun, and pale clouds floating in the blue.

The ultimate truth of our personality is that we are no mere biologists or geometricians; 'we are the dreamers of dreams, we are the music-makers.' This dreaming or music-making is not a function of the lotus-eaters, it is the creative impulse which makes songs not only with words and tunes, lines and colours, but with stones and metals, with ideas and men:

With wonderful deathless ditties
We build up the world's great cities,
And out of a fabulous story
We fashion an empire's glory.

I have been told by a scholar friend of mine that by
constant practice in logic he has weakened his natural
instinct of faith. The reason is, faith is the spectator in us
which finds the meaning of the drama from the unity of
the performance; but logic lures us into the greenroom
where there is stage craft but no drama at all; and then
this logic nods its head and wearily talks about
disillusionment. But the greenroom, dealing with its
fragments, looks foolish when questioned, or wears the
sneering smile of Mephistopheles; for its does not have the
secret of unity, which is somewhere else. It is for faith to
answer, 'Unity comes to us from the One, and the One in
ourselves opens the door and receives it with joy.' The
function of poetry and the arts is to remind us that the
greenroom is the grayest of illusions, and the reality is the
drama presented before us, all its paint and tinsel, masks
and pageantry, made one in art. The ropes and wheels
perish, the stage is changed; but the dream which is drama
remains true, for there remains the eternal Dreamer.

III

Poetry and the arts cherish in them the profound faith of man
in the unity of his being with all existence, the final truth of
which is the truth of personality. It is a religion directly
apprehended, and not a system of metaphysics to be analysed
and argued. We know in our personal experience what our
creations are and we instinctively know through it what
creation around us means.

When Keats said in his "Ode to a Grecian Urn":

Thou, silent form dost tease us out of thought,
As doth eternity,...

he felt the ineffable which is in all forms of perfection, the mystery of the One, which takes us beyond all thought into the immediate touch of Infinite. This is the mystery which is for a poet to realise and to reveal. It comes out in Keats' poems with struggling gleams through consciousness of suffering and despair:

Spite off despondence, of the inhuman dearth
Of noble natures, of the gloomy days,
Of all the unhealthy and o'er-darken'd ways
Made for our searching: yes, in spite of all,
Some shape of beauty moves away the pall
From our dark spirits.

In this there is a suggestion that truth reveals itself in beauty. For if beauty were mere accident, a rent in the eternal fabric of things, then it would hurt, would be defeated by the antagonism of facts. Beauty is no phantasy, it has the everlasting meaning of reality. The facts that cause despondence and gloom are mere mist, and when through the mist beauty breaks out in momentary gleams, we realize that Peace is true and not conflict, Love is true and not hatred; and Truth is the One, not the disjointed multitude. We realize that Creation is the perpetual harmony between the infinite ideal of perfection and the eternal continuity of its realization; that so long as there is no absolute separation between the positive ideal and the material obstacle to its attainment, we need not be afraid of suffering and loss. This is the poet's religion.

Those who are habituated to the rigid framework of sectarian creeds will find such a religion as this too indefinite and elastic. No doubt it is so, but only because its ambition is not to shackle the Infinite and tame it for domestic use;

but rather to help our consciousness to emancipate itself from materialism. It is as indefinite as the morning, and yet as luminous; it calls our thoughts, feelings, and actions into freedom, and feeds them with light. In the poet's religion we find no doctrine or injunction, but rather the attitude of our entire being towards a truth which is ever to be revealed in its own endless creation.

In dogmatic religion all questions are definitely answered, all doubts are finally laid to rest. But the poet's religion is fluid, like the atmosphere round the earth where lights and shadows play hide-and-seek, and the wind like a shepherd boy plays upon its reeds among flocks of clouds. It never undertakes to lead anybody anywhere to any solid conclusion; yet it reveals endless spheres of light, because it has no walls round itself. It acknowledges the facts of evil; it openly admits 'the weariness, the fever and the fret' in the world 'where men sit and hear each other groan'; yet it remembers that in spite of all there is the song of the nightingale, and 'haply the Queen Moon is on her throne,' and there is:

> White hawthorn, and the pastoral eglantine,
> Fast-fading violets covered up in leaves;
>   And mid-day's eldest child,
> The coming musk-rose, full of dewy wine,
> The murmurous haunt of flies on summer eves.

But all this has not the definiteness of an answer; it has only the music that teases us out of thought as it fills our being.

Let me read a translation from an Eastern poet to show how this idea comes out in a poem in Bengali:

> In the morning I awoke at the flutter of thy boat-sails,
> Lady of my Voyage, and I left the shore to follow the beckoning waves.

> I asked thee, 'Does the dream-harvest ripen in the island beyond the blue?'

The silence of thy smile fell on my question like the silence of sunlight on waves.

The day passed on through storm and through calm,

The perplexed winds changed their course, time after time, and the sea moaned.

I asked thee, 'Does thy sleep-tower stand somewhere beyond the dying embers of the day's funeral pyre?'

No answer came from thee, only thine eyes smiled like the edge of a sunset cloud.

It is night. They figure grows dim in the dark.

Thy wind-blown hair flits on my cheek and thrills my sadness with its scent.

My hands grope to touch the hem of thy robe, and I ask thee—'Is there thy garden of death beyond the stars, Lady of my Voyage, where thy silence blossoms into songs?'

Thy smile shines in the heart of the hush like the star-mist of midnight.

IV

In Shelley we clearly see the growth of his religion through periods of vagueness and doubt, struggle and searching. But he did at length come to a positive utterance of his faith, though he died young. Its final expression is in his 'Hymn to Intellectual Beauty'. By the title of the poem the poet evidently means a beauty that is not merely a passive quality of particular things, but a spirit that manifests itself through the apparent antagonism of the unintellectual life. This hymn rang out of his heart when he came to the end of his pilgrimage and stood face to face with the Divinity, glimpses of which had already filled his soul with restlessness. All his experiences of beauty had ever teased him with the question as to what was its truth. Some-where he sings of a nosegay which he makes of violets, daisies, tender bluebells and—

That tall flower that wets
Like a child, half in tenderness and mirth,
Its mother's face with heaven-collected tears.

He ends by saying:

And then, elate and gay,
I hastened to the spot whence I had come,
That I might there present it!—Oh! To whom?

This question, even though not answered, carries a
significance. A creation of beauty suggests a fulfillment,
which is the fulfillment of love. We have heard some poets
scoff at it in bitterness and despair; but it is like a sick child
beating its own mother—it is a sickness of faith, which hurts
truth, but proves it by its very pain and anger. And the faith
itself is this, that beauty is the self-offering of the One of
the other One.

In the first part of his 'Hymn to Intellectual Beauty'
Shelley dwells on the inconstancy and evanescence of the
manifestation of beauty, which imparts to it an appearance
of frailty and unreality:

Like hues and harmonies of evening,
Like clouds in starling widely spread,
Like memory of music fled.

This he says, rouses in our mind the question:

Why aught should fail and fade that once is
    shown,
Why fear and dream and death and birth
Cast on the daylight of this earth
Such gloom,—why man has such a scope
For love and hate, despondency and hope?

The poet's own answer to this question is:

Man were immortal, and omnipotent,
Didst thou, unknown and awful as thou art,
Keep with thy glorious train firm state within his
    heart.

This very elusiveness of beauty suggests the vision of immortality and of omnipotence, and stimulates the effort in man to realize it in some idea of permanence. The highest reality has actively to be achieved. The gain of truth is not in the end; it reveals itself through the endless length of achievement. But what is there to guide us in our voyage of realization? Men have ever been struggling for direction:

Therefore the names of Demon, Ghost and
    Heaven
Remain the records of their vain endeavour,
Frail spells,—whose uttered charm might not avail
    to sever,
From all we hear and all we see,
Doubt, chance and mutability.

The prevalent rites and practices of piety, according to this poet, are like magic spells—they only prove men's desperate endeavour and not their success. He knows that the end we seek has its own direct calls to us, its own light to guide us to itself. And truth's call is the call of beauty. Of this he says:

The light alone,—like mist o'er mountain driven,
    Or music by the night wind sent,
Thro' strings of some still instrument,
    Or moonlight on a midnight stream
Gives grace and truth to life's unquiet dream.

About this revelation of truth which calls us on, and yet which is everywhere, a village singer of Bengal sings:

My master's flute sounds in everything,

drawing me out of my house of everywhere.
While I listen to it I know that every step I take
is in my master's house.
For he is the sea, he is the river that leads to the
sea,
and he is the landing place.

Religion, in Shelley, grew with his life; it was not given to him in fixed and ready-made doctrines; he rebelled against them. He had the creative mind which could only approach Truth through its joy in creative effort. For true creation is realization of truth through the translation of it into our own symbols.

V

For man, the best opportunity for such a realization has been in men's Society. It is a collective creation of his, through which his social being tries to find itself in its truth and beauty. Had that Society merely manifested its usefulness, it would be inarticulate like a dark star. But, unless it degenerates, it ever suggests in its concerted movements a living truth as its soul, which has personality. In this large life of social communion man feels the mystery of Unity, as he does in music. From the sense of that Unity, men came to the sense of their God. And therefore every religion began with its tribal God.

The one question before all others that has to be answered by our civilizations is not what they have and in what quantity, but what they express and how. In a society, the production and circulation of materials, the amassing and spending of money, may go on, as in the interminable prolonging of a straight line, if its people forget to follow some spiritual design of life which curbs them and transforms them into an organic whole. For growth is not that enlargement which is merely adding to the dimensions of incompleteness. Growth is the movement of a whole towards a yet fuller wholeness. Living things start with this wholeness from the beginning of their career. A child has its own perfection as a child; it woud be ugly if it appeared as an unfinished man. Life is a continual process of synthesis, and not of additions. Our activities of production and enjoyment of wealth attain that spirit of wholeness when they are blended with a creative ideal. Otherwise they have the insane aspect of the eternally unfinished; they become like locomotive engines which have railway lines but no stations; which rush on towards a collision of uncontrolled forces or to a sudden breakdown of the overstrained machinery.

Through creation man expresses his truth; through that expression he gains back his truth in its fullness. Human society is for the best expression of man, and that expression, according to its perfection, leads him to the full realization of the divine in humanity. When that expression is obscure, then his faith in the Infinite that is within him becomes weak; then his aspiration cannot go beyond the idea of success. His faith in the Infinite is creative; his desire for success is constructive; one is his home, and the other is his office. With the overwhelming growth of necessity, civilization becomes a gigantic office to which the home is a mere appendix. The predominance of the pursuit of success gives to society the character of what we call *Shudra* in India. In fighting a battle, the *Kshatriya*, the noble knight,, followed his honour for his ideal, which was greater than victory itself; but the mercenary *Shudra* has success for his object. The name *Shudra* symbolizes a man who has no margin round him beyond his bare utility. The word denotes a classification which includes all naked machines that have lost their completeness of humanity, be their work manual or intellectual. They are like walking stomachs of brains, and we feel, in pity, urged to call on God and cry, 'Cover them up for mercys' sake with some veil of beauty and life!'

When Shelley in his view of the world realized the Spirit of Beauty, which is the vision of the Infinite, he thus uttered his faith:

> Never joy illumed my brow
> Unlinked with hope that thou wouldst free
> This world from its dark slavery;
> That thou,—O awful Loveliness,—
> Wouldst give whate'er these words cannot express.

This was his faith in the Infinite. It led his aspiration towards the region of freedom and perfection which was beyond the immediate and above the successful. This faith in God, this faith in the reality of the ideal of perfection, has built up all that is great in the human world. To keep indefinitely walking on, along a zigzag course of change, is negative and barren. A mere procession of notes does not make music; it is only when we have in the heart of the march of sounds some musical idea that it creates song. Our faith in the infinite reality of Perfection is that musical idea, and there is that one great creative force in our civilization. When it wakens not, then our faith in money, in material power, takes its place; it fights and destroys, and in brilliant fireworks of star-mimicry suddenly exhausts itself and dies in ashes and smoke.

VI

Men of great faith have always called us to wake up to great expectations, and the prudent have always laughed at them and said that these did not belong to reality. But the poet in man knows that reality is a creation, and human reality has to be called forth from its obscure depth by man's faith which is creative. There was a day when the human reality was the brutal reality. That was the only capital we had with which to begin our career. But age after age there has come to us the call of faith, which said against all the evidence of fact: 'You are more than you appear to be, more than your circumstances seem to warrant. You are to attain the impossible, you are immortal.' The unbelievers had laughed and tried to kill the faith. But faith grew stronger with the strength of martyrdom and at her bidding higher realities have been created over the strata of the lower. Has not a new age come to-day, borne by thunder-clouds, ushered in by a universal agony of suffering? Are we not waiting to-day for a great call of faith, which will say to us: 'Come out of your present limitations. You are to attain the impossible, you are immortal'? The nations who are not prepared to accept it, who have all their trust in their present machines of system, and have no thought or space to spare to welcome the sudden guest who comes as the messenger of emancipation, are bound to court defeat whatever may be their present wealth and power.

This great world, where it is a creation, an expression of the infinite—where its morning sings of joy to the newly awakened life, and its evening stars sing to the traveler, weary and worn, of the triumph of life in a new birth across death,— has its call for us. The call has ever roused the creator in man, and urged him to reveal the truth, to reveal the Infinite in himself. It is ever claiming from us, in our own creations, co- operation with God, reminding us of our divine nature, which finds itself in freedom of spirit. Our society exists to remind us, through its various voices, that the ultimate truth in man is not in his intellect or his possessions; it is in his illumination of mind, in his extension of sympathy across all barriers of caste and colour; in his recognition of the world, not merely as a storehouse of power, but as a habitation of man's spirit, with its eternal music of beauty and its inner light of the divine presence.

The Creative Ideal

In an old Sanskrit book there is a verse which describes the essential elements of a picture. The first in order is *Riúpa-bhédáh*—'separateness of forms.' Forms are many, forms are different, each of them having its limits. But if this were absolute, if all forms remained obstinately separate, then there would be a fearful loneliness of multitude. But the varied forms, in their very separateness, must carry something which indicates the paradox of their ultimate unity, otherwise there would be no creation.

So in the same verse, after the enumeration of separateness comes that of *pramanani*—proportions. Proportions indicate relationship, the principle of mutual accommodation. A leg dismembered from the body has the fullest licence to make a caricature of itself. But, as a member of the body, it has its responsibility to the living unity which rules the body; it must behave properly, it must keep its proportion. If, by some monstrous chance of physiological profiteering, it could outgrow by yards its fellow-stalker, then we know what a picture it would offer to the spectator and what embarrassment to the body itself. Any attempt to overcome the law of proportion altogether and to assert absolute separateness is rebellion; it means either running the gauntlet of the rest, or remaining segregated.

The same Sanskrit word *Pramanani,* which in a book of aesthetics means proportions, in a book of logic means the proofs by which the truth of a proposition is ascertained. All proofs of truth are credentials of relationship. Individual facts have to produce such passports to show that they are not expatriated, that they are not a break in the unity of the whole. The logical relationship present in an intellectual proposition, and the aesthetic relationship indicated in the proportions of a work of art, both agree in one thing. They affirm that truth consists, not in facts, but in harmony of facts. Of this fundamental note of reality it is that the poet has said, 'beauty is truth, truth beauty.'

Proportions, which prove relativity, form the outward language of creative ideals. A crowd of men is desultory, but in a march of soldiers every man keeps his proportion of time and space and relative movement, which makes him one with the whole vast army. But this is not all. The creation of an army has, for its inner principle, one single ideas of the General. According to the nature of that ruling idea, a production is either a work of art or a mere construction. All the materials and regulations of a joint-stock company have the unity of an inner motive. But the expression of this unity itself is not the end; it ever indicates an ulterior purpose. On the other hands, the revelation of a work of art is a fulfillment in itself.

The consciousness of personality, which is the consciousness of unity in ourselves, becomes prominently distinct when coloured by joy or sorrow, or some other emotion. It is like the sky, which is visible because it is blue, and which takes different aspect with the change of colours. In the creation of art, therefore, the energy of an emotional ideal is necessary; as its unity is not like that of a crystal, passive and inert, but actively expressive. Take, for example, the following verse:

Oh, fly not Pleasure, pleasant-hearted Pleasure,
Fold me thy wings, I prithee, yet and stay.
　For my heart no measure
　Knows, nor other treasure
To buy a garland for my love to-day.

And thou too, Sorrow, tender-hearted Sorrow,
Thou grey-eyed mourner, fly not yet away.
　For I fain would borrow
　Thy sad weeds to-morrow,
To make a mourning for love's yesterday.

The words in this quotation, merely showing the metre, would have no appeal to us; with all its perfection and its proportion, rhyme and cadence, it would only be a construction. But when it is the outer body of an inner idea it assumes a personality. The idea flows through the rhythm, permeates the words and throbs in their rise and fall. On the other hand, the mere idea of the above-quoted poem, stated in unrhythmic prose, would represent only a fact, inertly static, which would not bear repetition. But the emotional idea, incarnated in a rhythmic form, acquires the dynamic quality needed for those things which take part in the world's eternal pageantry.

Take the following doggerel:

Thirty days hath September,
April, June, and November.

The metre is there, and it simulates the movement of life. But it finds no synchronous response in the metre of our heart-beats; it has not in its centre the living idea which creates for itself an indivisible unity. It is like a bag which is convenient, and not like a body which is inevitable.

This truth, implicit in our own works of art, gives us the clue to the mystey of creation. We find that the endless rhythms of the world are not merely constructive; they strike our own heart-strings and produce music.

Therefore it is we feel that this world is a creation; that in its centre there is a living idea which reveals itself in an eternal symphony, played on innumerable instruments, all keeping perfect time. We know that this great world-verse, that runs from sky to sky, is not made for the mere enumeration of facts—it is not "Thirty days hath September"—it has its direct revelation in our delight. That delight gives us the key to the truth of existence; it is personality acting upon personalities through incessant manifestations. The solicitor does not sing to his client, but the bridegroom sings to his bride. And when our soul is stirred by the song, we know it claims no fees from us; but it brings the tribute of love and a call from the bridegroom.

It may be said that in pictorial and other arts there are some designs that are purely decorative and apparently have no living and inner ideal to express. But this cannot be true. These decorations carry the emotional motive of the artist, which says: 'I find joy in my creation; it is good.' All the language of joy is beauty. It is necessary to note, however, that joy is not pleasure, and beauty not mere prettiness. Joy is the outcome of detachment from self and lives in freedom of spirit. Beauty is that profound expression of reality which satisfies our hearts without any other allurements but its own ultimate value. When in some pure moments of ecstasy we realize this in the world around us, we see the world, not as merely existing, but as decorated in its form, sounds, colours and lines; we feel in our hearts that thee is One who through all things proclaims: 'I have joy in my creation.'

That is why the Sanskrit verse has given us for the essential elements of a picture, not only the manifoldness of forms and the unity of their proportions, but also *bhāvah,* the emotional idea.

It is needless to say that upon a mere expression of emotion—even the best expression of it—no criterion of art can rest. The following poem is described by the poet as 'An earnest Suit to his unkind Mistress':

And wilt thou leave me thus?
Say nay, say nay, for shame!
To save thee from the blame
Of all my grief and grame.
And wilt thou leave me thus?
   Say nay! Say nay!

I am sure the poet would not be offended if I expressed my doubts about the earnestness of his appeal, or the truth of his avowed necessity. He is responsible for the lyric and not for the sentiment, which is mere material. The fire assumes different colours according to the fuel used; but we do not discuss the fuel, only the flames. A lyric is indefinably more than the sentiment expressed in it, as a rose is more than its substance. Let us take a poem in which the earnestness of sentiment is truer and deeper than the one I have quoted above:

The sun,
Closing his benediction,
Sinks, and the darkening air
Thrills with the sense of the triumphing night,—
Night with her train of stars
And her great gift of sleep.
So be my passing!
My task accomplished and the long day done,
My wages taken, and in my heart
Some late lark singing,
Let me be gathered to the quiet West,
The sundown splendid and serene,
Death.

The sentiment expressed in this poem is a subject for a psychologist. But for a poem the subject is completely merged in its poetry, like carbon in a living plant which the lover of plants ignores, leaving it for a charcoal-burner to seek.

This is why, when some storm of feeling sweeps across the country, art is under a disadvantage. In such an atmosphere the boisterous passion breaks through the cordon of harmony and thrusts itself forward as the subject, which with its bulk and pressure dethrones the unity of creation. For a similar reason most of the hymns used in churches suffer from lack of poetry. For in them the deliberate subject, assuming the first importance, benumbs or kills the poem. Most patriotic poems have the same deficiency. They are like hill streams born of sudden showers, which are more proud of their rocky beds than of their water currents; in them the athletic and arrogant subject takes it for granted that the poem is there to give it occasion to display its powers. The subject is the material wealth for the sake of which poetry should never be tempted to barter her soul, even though the temptation should come in the name and shape of public good or some usefulness. Between the artist and his art must be that perfect detachment which is the pure medium of love. He must never make use of this love except for its own perfect expression.

In everyday life our personality moves in a narrow circle of immediate self-interest. And therefore our feelings and events, within that short range, become prominent subjects for ourselves. In their vehement self-assertion they ignore their unity with the All. They rise up like obstructions and obscure their own background. But art gives our personality the disinterested freedom of the eternal, there to find it in its true perspective. To see our own home in flames is not to see fire in its verity. But the fire in the stars is the fire in the heart of the Infinite; there, it is the script of creation.

Matthew Arnold, in his poem addressed to a nightingale, sings:

> Hark! Ah, the nightingale—
> The tawny-throated!
> Hark, from that moonlit cedar what a burst!
> What triumph! hark!—what pain!

But pain, when met within the boundaries of limited reality, repels and hurts; it is discordant with the narrow scope of life. But the pain of some great martyrdom has the detachment of eternity. It appears in all its majesty, harmonious in the context of everlasting life; like the thunder-flash in the stormy sky, not on the laboratory wire. Pain on that scale has its harmony in great love; for by hurting love it reveals the infinity of love in all its truth and beauty. On the other hands, the pain involved in business insolvency is discordant; it kills and consumes till nothing remains but ashes.

The poet sings again:

> How thick the bursts come crowding through the
>   leaves!
> Eternal Passion!
> Eternal Pain!

And the truth of pain in eternity has been sung by those Vedic poets who had said, 'From joy has come forth all creation.' They say:

Sa tapas tapatvá sarvam asrajata yadidam kincha.
(God from the heat of his pain created all that there is.)

The sacrifice, which is in the heart of creation, is both joy and pain at the same moment. Of this sings a village mystic in Bengal:

My eyes drown in the darkness of joy,
My heart, like a lotus, closes its petals in the
rapture of the dark night.

That song speaks of a joy which is deep like the blue sea,
endless like the blue sky; which has the magnificence of the
night, and in its limitless darkness enfolds the radiant worlds
in the awfulness of peace; it is the unfathomed joy in which
all sufferings are made one.

A poet of mediaeval India tells us about his source of
inspiration in a poem containing a question and an answer:

Where were your songs, my bird, when you spent
   your nights in the nest?
Was not all your pleasure stored therein?
What makes you lose your heart to the sky, the
   sky that is limitless?

The bird answers:

I have my pleasure while I rested within bounds.
When I soared into the limitless, I found my
   songs!

To detach the individual idea from its confinement of
everyday facts and to give its soaring wings the freedom of
the universal: this is the function of poetry. The ambition of
Macbeth, the jealousy of Othello, would be at best sensational
in police court proceedings; but in Shakespeare's dramas they
are carried among the flaming constellations where creation
throbs with Eternal passion, Eternal Pain.

The Religion of the Forest

I

We stand before this great world. The truth of our life depends upon our attitude of mind towards it—an attitude which is formed by our habit of dealing with it according to the special circumstance of our surroundings and our temperaments. It guides our attempts to establish relations with the universe either by conquest or by union, either through the cultivation of power or through that of sympathy. And thus, in our realization of the truth of existence, we put our emphasis either upon the principle of dualism or upon the principle of unity.

The Indian sages have held in the Upanishads that the emancipation of our soul lies in its realizing the ultimate truth of unity. They said:

Ishāvāsyam idam sarvam yat kinch jagatyām jagat.
Yéna tyakténa bhunjithā mā gradha kasyasvit
dhanam.

(Know all that moves in this moving world as enveloped by God; and find enjoyment through renunciation, not through greed of possession.)

The meaning of this is, that, when we know the multiplicity of things as the final truth, we try to augment ourselves by the external possession of them; but, when we know the Infinite Soul as the final truth, then through our union with it we realize the joy of our soul. Therefore it has been said of those who have attained their fulfillment,—'*sarvam evá vishanti*' (they enter into all things). Their perfect relation with this world is the relation of union.

This ideal of perfection preached by the forest-dwellers of ancient India runs through the heart of our classical literature and still dominates our mind. The legends related in our epics cluster under the forest shade bearing all through their narrative the message of the forest-dwellers. Our two greatest classical drama find their background in scenes of the forest hermitage, which are permeated by the association of these sages.

The history of the Northmen of Europe is resonant with the music of the sea. That sea is not merely topographical in its significance, but represents certain ideals of life which still guide the history and inspire the creations of that race. In the sea, nature presented herself to those men in her aspect of a danger, a barrier which seemed to be at constant war with the land and its children. The sea was the challenge of untamed nature to the indomitable human soul. And man did not flinch; he fought and won, and the spirit of fight continued in him. This fight he still maintains; it is the fight against disease and poverty, tyranny of matter and of man.

This refers to a people who live by the sea, and ride on it as on a wild, champing horse, catching it by its mane and making it render service from shore to shore. They find delight in turning by force the antagonism of circumstances into obedience. Truth appears to them in her aspect of dualism, the perpetual conflict of good and evil, which has no reconciliation, which can only end in victory or defeat.

But in the level tracts of Northern India men found no barrier between their lives and the grand life that permeates the universe. The forest entered into a close living relationship with their work and leisure, with their daily necessities and contemplations. They could not think of other surroundings as separate or inimical. So the view of the truth, which these men found, did not make manifest the difference, but rather the unity of all things. They uttered their in these words: *Yadidam kincha sarvam prâna éjati nihsratam* (All that is vibrates with life, having come out from life). When we know this world as alien to us, then its mechanical aspect takes prominence in our mind; and then we set up our machines and our methods to deal with it and make as much profit as our knowledge of its mechanism allows us to do. This view of things does not play us false, for the machine has its place in this world. And not only this material universe, but human beings also, may be used as machines and made to yield powerful results. This aspect of truth cannot be ignored; it has to be known and mastered. Europe has done so and has reaped a rich harvest.

The view of this world which India has taken is summed up in one compound Sanskrit word, *Sacchidānanda*. The meaning is that Reality, which is essentially one, has three phases. The first is *sat;* it is the simple fact that things are, the fact which relates us to all things through the relationship of common existence. The second is *chit;* it is the fact that we know, which relates us to all things through the relationship of knowledge. The third is *ānanda:* it is the fact that we enjoy, which unites us with all things through the relationship of love.

According to the true Indian view, our consciousness of the world, merely as the sum total of things that exist, and as governed by laws, is imperfect. But it is perfect when our consciousness realises all things as spiritually one with it, and therefore capable of giving us joy. For us the highest purpose of this world is not merely living in it, knowing it and making use of it, but realising our own selves in it through expansion of sympathy; not alienating ourselves from it and dominating it, but comprehending and uniting it with ourselves in perfect union.

II

When Vikramaditya became king, Ujjayini a great capital, and Kâlidâsa its poet, the age of India's forest retreats had passed. Then we had taken our stand in the midst of the great concourse of humanity. The Chinese and the Hun, the Scythian and the Persian, the Greek and the Roman, had crowded round us. But, even in that age of pomp and prosperity, the love and reverence with which its poet sang about the hermitage shows what was the dominant ideal that occupied the mind of India; what was the one current of memory that continually flowed through her life.

In Kâlidâsa's drama, *Shakuntalā,* the hermitage, which dominates the play, overshadowing the king's palace, has the same idea running through it—the recognition of the kinship of man with conscious and unconscious creation alike.

A poet of a later age, while describing a hermitage in his *Kādambari,* tells us of the posture of salutation in the flowering lianas as they bow to the wind; of the sacrifice offered by the trees scattering their blossoms; of the grove resounding with the lessons chanted by the neophytes, and the verses repeated by the parrots, learnt by constantly hearing them; of the wild-fowl enjoying *vaishva-deva-bali-pinda* (the food offered to the divinity which is in all creatures); of the ducks coming up from the lake for their portion of the grass seed spread in the cottage yards to dry; and of the deer caressing with their tongues the young hermit boys. It is again the same story. The hermitage shines out, in all our ancient literature, as the place where the chasm between man and the rest of creation has been bridged.

In the Western dramas, human characters drown our attention in the vortex of their passions. Nature occasionally peeps out, but she is almost always a trespasser, who has to offer excuses, or bow apologetically and depart. But in all our dramas which still retain their fame, such as *Mrit-Shakatikâ, Shakuntalā, Uttara-Rāmacharita,* Nature stands on her own right, proving that she has her great function, to impart the peace of the eternal to human emotions.

The fury of passion in two of Shakespeare's youthful poems is exhibited in conspicuous isolation. It is snatched away, naked, from the context of the All; it has not the green earth or the blue sky around it; it is there ready to bring to our view the raging fever which is in man's desires, and not the balm of health and repose which encircles it in the universe.

Ritusamhāra is clearly a work of Kâlidâsa's immaturity. The youthful love-song in it does not reach the sublime reticence which is in *Shakuntalā* and *Kumāra-Sambhava.* But the tune of the these voluptuous outbreaks is set to the varied harmony of Nature's symphony. The moonbeams of the summer evening, resonant with the flow of fountains, acknowledge it as a part of its own melody. In its rhythm sways the Kadamaba forest, glistening in the first cool rain of the season; and the south breezes, carrying the scent of the mango blossoms, temper it with their murmur.

In the third canto of *Kumāra-Sambhava,* Madana, the God Eros, enters the forest sanctuary to set free a sudden flood of desire amid the serenity of the ascetics' meditation. But the boisterous outbreak of passion so caused was shown against a background of universal life. The divine love-thrills of Sati and Shiva found their response in the world-wide immensity of youth, in which animals and trees have their life-throbs.

Not only its third canto but the whole of the *Kumāra-Sambhava* poem is painted upon a limitless canvas. It tells of the eternal wedding of love, its wooing and sacrifice, and its fulfilment, for which the gods wait in suspense. Its inner idea is deep and of all time. It answers the one question that humanity asks through all its endeavours: 'How is the birth of the hero to be brought about, the brave one who can defy and vanquish the evil demon laying waste heaven's own kingdom?'

It becomes evident that such a problem had become acute in Kâlidâsa's time, when the old simplicity of Hindu life had broken up. The Hindu kings, forgetful of their duties, had become self-seeking epicureans, and India was being repeatedly devastated by the Scythians. What answer, then, does the poem give to the question it raises? Its message is that the cause of weakness lies in the inner life of the soul. It is in some break of harmony with the Good, some dissociation from the True. In the commencement of the poem we find that the God Shiva, the Good, had remained for long lost in the self-centred solitude of his asceticism, detached from the world of reality. And then Paradise was lost. But *Kumāra-Sambhava* is the poem of Paradise Regained. How was it regained? When Sati, the Spirit, through humiliation, suffering, and penance, won the Heart of Shiva, the Spirit of Goodness. And thus, from the union of the freedom of the real with the restraint of the Good, was born the heroism that released Paradise from the demon of Lawlessness.

Viewed from without, India, in the time of Kâlidâsa, appeared to have reached the zenith of civilization excelling as she did in luxury, literature and the arts. But from the poems of Kâlidâsa it is evident that this very magnificence of wealth and enjoyment worked against the ideal that sprang and flowed forth from the sacred solitude of the forest. These poems contain the voice of warnings against the gorgeous unreality of that age, which, like a Himalayan avalanche, was slowly gliding down to an abyss of catastrophe. And from his seat beside all the glories of Vikramaditya's throne the poet's heart yearns for the purity and simplicity of India's past age of spiritual striving. And it was this yearning which impelled him to go back to the annals of the ancient Kings of Raghu's line for the narrative poem, in which he traced the history of the rise and fall of the ideal that should guide the rulers of men.

King Dilipa, with Queen Sudakshinâ, has entered upon the life of the forest. The great monarch is busy tending the cattle of the hermitage. Thus the poem opens, amid scenes of simplicity and self-denial. But it ends in the palace of magnificence, in the extravagance of self-enjoyment. With a calm restraint of language the poet tells us of the kingly glory crowned with purity. He begins his poem as the day begins, in the serenity of sunrise. But lavish are the colours in which he describes the end, as of the evening, eloquent for a time with the sumptuous splendour of sunset, but overtaken at last by the devouring darkness which sweeps away all its brilliance into night.

In this beginning and this ending of his poem there lies hidden that message of the forest which found its voice in the poet's words. There runs through the narrative the idea that the future glowed gloriously ahead only when there was in the atmosphere the calm of self-control, of purity and renunciation. When downfall had become imminent, the hungry fires of desire, aflame at a hundred different points, dazzled the eyes of all beholders.

Kâlidâsa in almost all his works represented the unbounded impetuousness of kingly splendour on the one side and the serene strength of regulated desires on the other. Even in the minor drama of *Mālavikāgnimitra* we find the same thing in a different manner. It must never be thought that, in this play, the poet's deliberate object was to pander to his royal patron by inviting him to a literary orgy of lust and passion. The very introductory verse indicates the object towards which this play is directed. The poet begins the drama with the prayer,

Sanmārgâlókayan vyapanayatu sa nastāmasi vritimishah (Let God, to illumine for us the path of truth, sweep away our passions, bred of darkness). This is the God Shiva, in whose nature Parvati, the eternal Woman, is ever commingled in an ascetic purity of love. The unified being of Shiva and Parvati is the perfect symbol of the eternal in the wedded love of man and woman. When the poet opens his drama with an invocation of this Spirit of the Divine Union it is evident that it contains in it the message with which he greets his kingly audience. The whole drama goes to show the ugliness of the treachery and cruelty inherent in unchecked self-indulgence. In the play the conflict of ideals is between the King and the Queen, between Agnimitra and Dhârini, and the significance of the contrast lies hidden in the very names of the hero and the heroine. Though the name Agnimitra is historical, yet it symbolizes in the poet's mind the destructive force of uncontrolled desire—just as did the name Agnivarna in *Raghuvamsha*. Agnimitra, 'the friend of the fire,' the reckless person who in his love-making is playing with fire, not knowing that all the time it is scorching him black. And what a great name is Dhârini, signifying the fortitude and forbearance that comes from majesty of soul! What an association it carries of the infinite dignity of love, purified by a self-abnegation that rises far above all insult and baseness of betrayal!

In *Shakuntalā* this conflict of ideals has been shown, all through the drama, by the contrast of the pompous heartlessness of the king's court and the natural purity of the forest hermitage. The drama opens with a hunting scene, where the king is in pursuit of an antelope. The cruelty of the chase appears like a menace symbolising the spirit of the king's life clashing against the spirit of the forest retreat, which is *sharanyam sarva-bhūtānām* (where all creatures find their protection of love). And the pleading of the forest-dwellers with the king to spare the life of the deer, helplessly innocent and beautiful, is the pleading that rises from the heart of the whole drama. 'Never, oh, never is the arrow meant to pierce the tender body of a deer, even as the fire is not for the burning of flowers.'

In the *Râmâyana*, Râma and his companions, in their banishment, had to traverse forest after forest; they had to live in leaf-thatched huts, to sleep on the bare ground. But as their hearts felt their kinship with woodland, hill, and stream, they were not in exile amidst these. Poets, brought up in an atmosphere of different ideals, would have taken this opportunity of depicting in dismal colours the hardship of the forest-life in order to bring out the martyrdom of Râmachandra with all the emphasis of a strong contrast. But, in the *Râmâyana*, we are led to realize the greatness of the hero, not in a fierce struggle with Nature, but in sympathy with it. Sitâ, the daughter-in-law of a great kingly house, goes along the forest paths. We read:

"She asks Râma about the flowering trees, and shrubs and creepers which she has not seen before. At her request Lakshmana gathers and brings her plants of all kinds, exuberant with flowers, and it delights her heart to see the forest rivers, variegated with their streams and sandy banks, resounding with the call of heron and duck.

'When Râma first took his abode in the Chitrakuta peak, that delightful Chitrakuta, by the Mâlyavati river, with its easy slopes for landing, he forgot all the pain of leaving his home in the capital at the sight of those woodlands, alive with beast and bird.'

Having lived on that hill for long, Râma, who was *giri-vana-priya* (lover of the mountain and the forest), said one day to Sitâ:

'When I look upon the beauties of this hill, the loss of my kingdom troubles me no longer, nor does the separation from friends cause me any pang.'

Thus passed Râmachandra's exile, now in woodland, now in hermitage. The love which Râma and Sitâ bore to each other united them, not only to each other, but to the universe of life. That is why, when Sitâ was taken away, the loss seemed to be so great to the forest itself.

III

Strangely enough, in Shakespeare's dramas, like those of Kâlidâsa, we find a secret vein of complaint against the artificial life of the king's court—the life of ungrateful treachery and falsehood. And almost everywhere, in his dramas, foreign scenes have been introduced in connection with some working of the life of unscrupulous ambition. It is perfectly obvious in *Timon of Athens*—but there Nature offers no message or balm to the injured soul of man. In *Cymbeline* the mountainous forest and the cave appear in their aspect of obstruction to life's opportunities. These only seem tolerable in comparison with the vicissitudes of fortune in the artificial court life. In *As you Like It* the forest of Arden is didactic in its lessons. It does not bring peace, but preaches, when it says:

Hath not old custom made this life more sweet
Than that of painted pomp? Are not these woods
More free from peril than the envious court?

In the *Tempest,* through Prospero's treatment of Ariel and Caliban we realize man's struggle with Nature and his longing to sever connection with her. In *Macbeth,* as a prelude to a bloody crime of treachery and treason, we are introduced to a scene of barren heath where the three witches appear as personifications of Nature's malignant forces; and in *King Lear* it is the fury of a father's love turned into curses by the ingratitude born of the unnatural life of the court that finds its symbol in the storm on the heath. The tragic intensity of *Hamlet* and *Othello* is unrelieved by any touch of Nature's eternity. Except in a passing glimpse of a moonlight night in the love scene in the *Merchant of Venice,* Nature has not been allowed in other dramas of this series, including *Romeo and Juliet* and *Antony and Cleopatra,* to contribute her own music to the music of man's love. In *The Winter's Tale* the cruelty of a king's suspicion stands bare in its relentlessness, and Nature cowers before it, offering no consolation.

I hope it is needless for me to say that these observations are not intended to minimize Shakespeare's great power as a dramatic poet, but to show in his works the gulf between Nature and human nature owing to the tradition of his race and time. It cannot be said that beauty of nature is ignored in his writings; only he fails to recognize in them the truth of the interpenetration of human life with the cosmic life of the world. We observe a completely different attitude of mind in the later English poets like Wordsworth and Shelley, which can be attributed in the main to the great mental change in Europe, at that particular period, through the influence of the newly discovered philosophy of India which stirred the soul of Germany and aroused the attention of other Western countries.

In Milton's *Paradise Lost,* the very subject—Man dwelling in the garden of Paradise—seems to afford a special opportunity for bringing out the true greatness of man's relationship with Nature. But though the poet has described to us the beauties of the garden, though he has shown to us the animals living there in amity and peace among themselves, there is no reality of kinship between them and man. They were created for man's enjoyment; man was their lord and master. We find no trace of the love between the first man and woman gradually surpassing themselves and overflowing the rest of creation, such as we find in the love scene in *Kumâra-Sambhava* and *Shakuntalā.* In the seclusion of the bower, where the first man and woman rested in the garden of Paradise—

Bird, beast, insect or worm
Dust enter none, such was their awe of man.

Not that India denied the superiority of man, but the test of that superiority lay, according to her, in the comprehensiveness of sympathy, not in the aloofness of absolute distinction.

IV

India holds sacred, and counts as places of pilgrimage, all spots which display a special beauty or splendour of nature. These had no original attraction on account of any special fitness for cultivation or settlement. Here man is free, not to look upon Nature as a source of supply of his necessities, but to realise his soul beyond himself. The Himalayas of India are sacred and the Vindhya Hills. Her majestic rivers are sacred. Lake Mânasa and the confluence of the Ganges and the Jamuna are sacred. India has saturated with her love and worship the great Nature with which her children are surrounded, whose light fills their eyes with gladness, and whose water cleanses them, whose food gives them life, and from whose majestic mystery comes forth the constant revelation of the infinite in music, scent, and colour, which brings its awakening to the soul of man. India gains the world through worship, through spiritual communion; and the idea of freedom to which she aspired was based upon the realisation of her spiritual unity.

When, in my recent voyage to Europe, our ship left Aden and sailed along the sea which lay between the two continents, we passed by the red and barren rocks of Arabia on our right side and the gleaming sands of Egypt on our left. They seemed to me like two giant brothers exchanging with each other burning glances of hatred, kept apart by the tearful entreaty of the sea from whose womb they had their birth.

There was an immense stretch of silence on the left shore as well as on the right, but the two shores spoke to me of the two different historical dramas enacted. The civilization which found its growth in Egypt was continued across long centuries, elaborately rich with sentiments and expressions of life, with pictures, sculptures, temples, and ceremonials. This was a country whose guardian-spirit was a noble river, which spread the festivities of life on its banks across the heart of the land. There man never raised the barrier of alienation between himself and the rest of the world.

On the opposite shore of the Red Sea the civilization which grew up in the inhospitable soil of Arabia had a contrary character to that of Egypt. There man felt himself isolated in his hostile and bare surroundings. His idea of God became that of a jealous God. His mind naturally dwelt upon the principle of separateness. It roused in him the spirit of fight, and this spirit was a force that drove him far and wide. These two civilizations represented two fundamental divisions of human nature. The one contained in it the spirit of conquest and the other the spirit of harmony. And both of these have their truth and purpose in human existence.

The characters of two eminent sages have been described in our mythology. One was Vashishtha and another Vishvâmitra. Both of them were great, but they represented two different types of wisdom; and there was conflict between them. Vishvâmitra sought to achieve power and was proud of it; Vashishtha was rudely smitten by that power. But his hurt and his loss could not touch the illumination of his soul; for he rose above them and could forgive. Râmachandra, the great hero of our epic, had his initiation to the spiritual life from Vashishtha, the life of inner peace and perfection. But he had his initiation to war from Vishvâmitra, who called him to kill the demons and gave him weapons that were irresistible.

Those two sages symbolize in themselves the two guiding spirits of civilization. Can it be true that they shall never be reconciled? If so, can ever the age of peace and co-operation dawn upon the human world? Creation is the harmony of contrary forces—the forces of attraction and repulsion. When they join hands, all the fire and fight are changed into the smile of flowers and the songs of birds. When there is only one of them triumphant and the other defeated, then either there is the death of cold rigidity or that of suicidal explosion.

Humanity, for ages, has been busy with the one great creation of spiritual life. Its best wisdom, its discipline, its literature and art, all the teaching and self-sacrifice of its noblest teachers, have been for this. But the harmony of contrary forces, which give their rhythm to all creation, has not yet been perfected by man in his civilization, and the Creator in him is baffled over and over again. He comes back to his work, however, and makes himself busy, building his world in the midst of desolation and ruins. His history is the history of his aspiration interrupted and renewed. And one truth of which he must be reminded, therefore, is that the power which accomplishes the miracle of creation, by bringing conflicting forces into the harmony of the One, is no passion, but a love which accepts the bonds of self-control from the joy of its own immensity—a love whose sacrifice is the manifestation of its endless wealth within itself.

An Indian Folk Religion

I

In historical time the Buddha comes first of those who
declared salvation to all men, without distinction, as by
right man's own. What was the special force which startled
men's minds and, almost within the master's lifetime, spread
his teachings over India? It was the unique significance of the
event, when a man came to men and said to them, 'I am here
to emancipate you from the miseries of the thraldom of self.'
This wisdom came, neither in texts of Scripture, nor in symbols
of deities, nor in religious practices sanctified by ages, but
through the voice of a living man and the love that flowed
from a human heart.

And I believe this was the first occasion in the history of
the world when the idea of the Avatâr found its place in
religion. Western scholars are never tired of insisting that
Buddhism is of the nature of a moral code, coldly leading to
the path of extinction. They forget that it was held to be a
religion that roused in its devotees an inextinguishable fire
of enthusiasm and carried them to lifelong exile across the
mountain and desert barriers. To say that a philosophy of
suicide can keep kindled in human hearts for centuries such
fervour of self-sacrifice is to go against all the laws of sane
psychology. The religious enthusiasm which cannot be bound

within any daily ritual, but overflows into adventures of love and beneficence, must have in its center that element of personality which rouses the whole soul. In answer, it may possibly be said that this was due to the personality of Buddha himself. But that also is not quite true. The personality which stirs the human heart to its immense depths, leading it to impossible deeds of heroism, must in the process itself reveal to men the infinite which is in all humanity. And that is what happened in Buddhism, making it a religion in the complete sense of the word.

Like the religion of the Upanishads, Buddhism also generated two divergent currents; the one impersonal, preaching the abnegation of self through discipline, and the other personal, preaching the cultivation of sympathy for all creatures, and devotion to the infinite truth of love; the other, which is called the Mahâyâna, had its origin in the positive element contained in Buddha's teachings, which is immeasurable love. It could never, by any logic, find its reality in the emptiness of the truthless abyss. And the object of Buddha's meditation and his teachings was to free humanity from sufferings. But what was the path that he revealed to us? Was it some negative way of evading pain and seeking security against it? On the contrary, his path was the path of sacrifice—the utmost sacrifice of love. The meaning of such sacrifice is to reach some ultimate truth, some positive ideal, which in its greatness can accept suffering and transmute it into the profound peace of self-renunciation. True emancipation from suffering, which is the inalienable condition of the limited life of the self, can never be attained by fleeing from it, but rather by changing its value in the realm of truth—the truth of the higher life of love.

We have learnt that, by calculations made in accordance with the law of gravitation, some planets were discovered exactly in the place where they should be. Such a law of gravitation there is also in the moral world. And when we find men's minds disturbed, as they were by the preaching of the Buddha, we can be sure, even without any corroborative evidence, that there must have been some great luminous body of attraction, positive and powerful, and not a mere unfathomable vacancy. It is exactly this which we discover in the heart of the Mahâyâna system; and we have no hesitation in saying that the truth of Buddhism is there. The oil has to be burnt, not for the purpose of diminishing it, but for the purpose of giving light to the lamp. And when the Buddha said that the self must go, he said at the same moment that love must be realised. Thus originated the doctrine of the Dharma-kâya, the Infinite Wisdom and Love manifested in the Buddha. It was the first instance, as I have said, when men felt that the Universal and the Eternal Spirit was revealed in a human individual whom they had known and touched. The joy was too great for them, since the very idea itself came to them as a freedom—a freedom from the sense of their measureless insignificance. It was the first time I repeat, when the individual, as a man, felt in himself the Infinite made concrete.

What was more, those men who felt the love welling forth from the heart of Buddhism, as one with the current of the Eternal Love itself, were struck with the idea that such an effluence could never have been due to a single cataclysm of history—unnatural and therefore untrue. They felt instead that it was in the eternal nature of truth, that the event must belong to a series of manifestations; there must have been numberless other revelations in the past and endless others to follow.

The idea grew and widened until men began to feel that this Infinite Being was already in every one of them, and that it rested with themselves to remove the sensual obstructions and reveal him in their own lives. In every individual there was, they realised, the potentiality of Buddha—that is to say, the Infinite made manifest.

We have to keep in mind the great fact that the preaching of the Buddha in India was not followed by stagnation of life—as would surely have happened if humanity was without any positive goal and his teaching was without any permanent value in itself. On the contrary, we find the arts and sciences springing up in its wake, institutions started for alleviating the misery of all creatures, human and non-human, and great centers of education founded. Some mighty power was suddenly roused from its obscurity, which worked for long centuries and changed the history of man in a large part of the world. And that power came into its full activity only by the individual being made conscious of his infinite worth. It was like the sudden discovery of a great mine of living wealth.

During the period of Buddhism the doctrine of deliverance flourished, which reached all mankind and released man's inner resources from neglect and self-insult. Even to-day we see in our own country human nature, from its despised corner of indignity, slowly and painfully finding its way to assert the inborn majesty of man. It is like the imprisoned tree finding a rift in the wall, and sending out its eager branches into freedom, to prove that darkness is not its birthright, that its love is for the sunshine. In the time of the Buddha the individual discovered his own immensity of worth, first by witnessing a man who united his heart in sympathy with all creatures, in all world, through the power of a love that knew no bounds; and then by learning that the same light of perfection lay confined within himself behind the clouds of selfish desire, and that the *Bothi-hridaya*—'the heart of the Eternal Enlightenment'—every moment claimed its unveiling in his own heart. Nâgârjuna speaks of this *Bodhi-hridaya* (another of whose names is *Bodhi-Citta*) as follows:

One who understands the nature of the *Bodhi-hridaya*, sees everything with a loving heart; for love is the essence of *Bodhi-hridaya*.[1]

My object in writing this paper is to show, by the further help of illustration from a popular religious sect of Bengal, that the religious instinct of man urges him towards a truth, by which he can transcend the finite nature of the individual self. Man would never feel the indignity of his limitations if these were inevitable. Within him he has glimpses of the Infinite, which give him assurance that this truth is not in his limitations, but that this truth can be attained by love. For love is the positive quality of the Infinite, and love's sacrifice accordingly does not lead to emptiness, but to fulfilment, to *Bodhi-hridaya*, 'the heart of enlightenment.'

The members of the religious sect I have mentioned call themselves 'Baül.' They live outside social recognition, and their very obscurity helps them in their seeking, from a direct source, the enlightenment which the soul longs for, the eternal light of love.

It would be absurd to say that there is little difference between Buddhism and the religion of these simple people, who have no system of metaphysics to support their faith. But my object in bringing close together these two religions, which seem to belong to opposite poles, is to point out the fundamental unity in them. Both of them believe in a fulfilment which is reached by love's emancipating us from the dominance of self. In both these religions we find man's yearning to attain the infinite worth of his individuality, not through any conventional valuation of society, but through his perfect relationship with Truth. They agree in holding that the realization of our ultimate object is waiting for us in ourselves. The Baül likens this fulfilment to the blossoming of a bud, and sings:

---

1. *Outlines of Mahâyâna Buddhism* by D.T. Suzaki.

Make way, O bud, make way,
Burst open thy heart and make way.
The opening spirit has overtaken thee,
Canst thou remain a bud any longer?

II

One day in a small village in Bengal, an ascetic woman from the neighbourhood came to see me. She had the name 'Sarva-khepi' given to her by the village people, the meaning of which is 'the woman who is mad about all things.' She fixed her star-like eyes upon my face and startled me with the question, 'When are you coming to meet me underneath the trees?' Evidently she pitied me who lived (according to her) perisoned behind walls, banished away from the great meeting-place of the All, where she had her dwelling. Just at that moment my gardener came with his basket, and when the woman understood that the flowers in the vase on my table were going to be thrown away, to make place for the fresh ones, she looked pained and said to me, 'You are always engaged reading and writing; you do not see.' Then she took the discarded flowers in her palms, kissed them and touched them with her forehead, and reverently murmured to herself, 'Beloved of my heart.' I felt that this woman, in her direct vision of the infinite personality in the heart of all things, truly represented the spirit of India.

In the same village I came into touch with some Baül singers. I had known them by their names, occasionally seen them singing and begging in the street, and so passed them by, vaguely classifying them in my mind under the general name of *Vairâgis*, or ascetics.

The time came when I had occasion to meet with some members of the same body and talk to them about spiritual matters. The first Baül song, which I chanced to hear with any attention, profoundly stirred my mind. Its words are so simple that it makes me hesitate to render them in a foreign tongue, and set them forward for critical observation. Besides, the best part of a song is missed when the tune is absent; for thereby its movement and its colour are lost, and it becomes like a butterfly whose wings have been plucked.

The first line may be translated thus: 'Where shall I meet him, the Man of my Heart?' This phrase, 'the Man of my Heart,' is not peculiar to this song, but is usual with the Baül sect. It means that, for me, the supreme truth of all existence is in the revelation of the Infinite in my own humanity.

'The Man of my Heart,' to the Baül, is like a divine instrument perfectly tuned. He gives expression to infinite truth in the music of life. And the longing for the truth which is in us, which we have not yet realised, breaks out in the following Baül song:

Where shall I meet him, the Man of my Heart?
He is lost to me and I seek him wandering from
    land to land.
I am listless for that moonrise of beauty,
    which is to light my life,
    which I long to see in the fullness of vision, in
    gladness of heart.

The name of the poet who wrote this song was Gagan. He was almost illiterate; and the ideas he received from his Baül teacher found no distraction from the self-consciousness of the modern age. He was a village postman, earning about ten shillings a month, and he died before he had completed his teens. The sentiment, to which he gave such intensity of expression, is common to most of the songs of his sect. And it is a sect, almost exclusively confined to that lower floor of society, where the light of modern education hardly finds an entrance, while wealth and respectability shun its utter indigence.

In the song I have translated above, the longing of the singer to realise the infinite in his own personality is expressed. This has to be done daily by its perfect expression in life, in love. For the personal expression of life, in its perfection, is love; just as the personal expression of truth in its perfection is beauty.

In the political life of the modern age the idea of democracy has given mankind faith in the individual. It gives each man trust in his own possibilities, and pride in his humanity. Something of the same idea, we find, has been working in the popular mind of India, with regard to its religious consciousness. Over and over again it tries to assert, not only that God is *for* each of us, but also that God is *in* each of us. These people have no special incarnations in their simple theology, because they know that God is special to each individual. They say that to be born a man is the greatest privilege that can fall to a creature in all the world. They assert that gods in Paradise envy human beings. Why? Because God's will, in giving his love, finds its completeness in man's will returning that love. Therefore Humanity is a necessary factor in the perfecting of the divine truth. The Infinite, for its self-expression, comes down into the manifoldness of the Finite; and the Finite, for its self-realization, must rise into the unity of the Infinite. Then is the Cycle of Truth complete.

The dignity of man, in his eternal right to Truth, finds expression in the following song, composed, not by a theologian or a man of letters, but by one who belongs to that ninety per cent of the population of British India whose education has been far less than elementary, in fact almost below zero:

My longing is to meet you in play of love, my
Lover;
But this longing is not only mine, but also yours.

For your lips can have their smile, and your flute
    its music, only in your delight in my love;
and therefore you are importunate, even as I am.

If the world were a mere expression of formative forces, then this song would be pathetic in its presumption. But why is there beauty at all in creation—the beauty whose only meaning is in a call that claims disinterestedness as a response? The poet proudly says: 'Your flute could not have its music of beauty if your delight were not in my love. Your power is great—and there I am not equal to you—but it lies even in me to make you smile, and if you and I never meet, then this play of love remains incomplete.'

If this were not true, then it would be an utter humiliation to exist at all in this world. If it were solely *our* business to seek the Lover; and *his* to keep himself passively aloof in the infinity of his glory, or actively masterful only in imposing his commands upon us, then we should dare to defy him, and refuse to accept the everlasting insult latent in the one-sided importunity of a slave. And this is what the Baül says—he who, in the world of men, goes about singing for alms from door to door, with his one-stringed instrument and long robe of patched-up rags on his back:

I stop and sit here on the road. Do not ask me to
    walk farther.
If your love can be complete without mine, let me
    turn back from seeing you.
I have been traveling to seek you, my friend, for
    long;
Yet I refuse to beg a sight of you, if you do not
    feel my need.
I am blind with market dust and midday glare,
    and so wait, my heart's lover, in hopes that your
    own love will send you to find me out.

The poet is fully conscious that his value in the world's market is pitifully small; that he is neither wealthy nor learned. Yet he has his great compensation, for he has come close to his Lover's heart. In Bengal the women bathing in the river often use their overturned water jars to keep themselves floating when they swim, and the poet uses this incident for his simile:

It is lucky that I am an empty vessel,
For when you swim, I keep floating by your side.
Your full vessels are left on the empty shore, they
     are for use;
But I am carried to the river in your arms, and I
     dance to the rhythm of your heart-throbs and
     heaving of the waves.

The great distinguished people of the world do not know that these beggars—deprived of education, honour, and wealth—can, in the pride of their souls, look down upon them as the unfortunate ones, who are left on the shore for their worldly uses, but whose life ever misses the touch of the Lover's arms.

The feeling that man is not a mere casual visitor at the palace-gate of the world, but the invited guest whose presence is needed to give the royal banquet its sole meaning, is not confined to any particular sect in India. Let me quote here some poems from a mediaeval poet of Western India—Jnândâs—whose works are nearly forgotten, and have become scarce from the very exquisiteness of their excellence. In the following poem he is addressing God's messenger, who comes to us in the morning light of our childhood, in the dusk of our day's end, and in the night's darkness:

Messenger, morning brought you, habited in gold.
After sunset, your song wore a tune of ascetic
     grey, and then came night.

> Your message was written in bright letters across
>   the black.
> Why is such splendour about you, to lure the
>   heart of one who is nothing?

This is the answer of the messenger:

> Great is the festival hall where you are to be the
>   only guest.
> Therefore the letter to you is written from sky to
>   sky,
> And I, the proud servant, bring the invitation with
>   all ceremony.

And thus the poet knows that the silent rows of stars carry
God's own invitation to the individual soul.

The same poet sings:

> What hast thou come to beg from the beggar,
>   O King of Kings?
> My Kingdom is poor for want of him, my dear
>   one,
> and I wait for him in sorrow.
> How long will you keep him waiting, O wretch,
> who has waited for your for ages in silence
>   and stillness?
> Open your gate, and make this very moment fit
>   for the union.

It is the song of man's pride in the value given to him
by Supreme Love and realized by his own love.

The Vaishnava religion, which has become the popular
religion of India, carries the same message: God's love finding
its finality in man's love. According to it, the lover, man, is
the complement of the Lover, God, in the internal love drama

of existence; and God's call is ever wafted in man's heart in the world-music, drawing him towards the union. This idea has been expressed in rich elaboration of symbols verging upon realism. But for these Baüls this idea is direct and simple, full of the dignified beauty of truth, which shuns all tinsels of ornament.

The Baül poet, when asked why he had no sect mark on his forehead, answered in his song that the true colour decoration appears on the skin of the fruit when its inner core is filled with ripe, sweet juice; but by artificially smearing it with colour from outside you do not make it ripe. And he says of his Guru, his teacher, that he is puzzled to find in which direction he must make salutation. For his teacher is not one, but many, who, moving on, form a procession of wayfarers.

Baüls have no temple or image for their worship, and this utter simplicity is needful for men whose one subject is to realise the inner-most nearness of God. The Baül poet expressly says that if we try to approach God through the senses we miss him:

> Bring him not into your house as the guest of
> your eyes; but let him come at your heart's
> invitation.
> Opening your doors to that which is seen only, is
> to lose it.

Yet, being a poet, he also knows that the objects of sense can reveal their spiritual meaning only when they are not seen through mere physical eyes:

> Eyes can see only dust and earth,
> But feel it with your heart, it is pure joy.
> The flowers of delight blossom on all sides, in
> every form, but where is your heart's thread to
> weave them in a garland?

These Baüls have a philosophy, which they call the philosophy of the body; but they keep its secret; it is only for the initiated. Evidently the underlying idea is that the individual's body is itself the temple, in whose inner mystic shrine the Divine appears before the soul, and the key to it has to be found from those who know. But as the key is not for us outsiders, I leave it with the observation that this mystic philosophy of the body is the outcome of the attempt to get rid of all the outward shelters which are too costly for people like themselves. But this human body of ours is made by God's own hand, from his own love, and even if some men, in the pride of their superiority, may despise it, God finds his joy in dwelling in others of yet lower birth. It is a truth easier of discovery by these people of humble origin than by men of proud estate.

The pride of the Baül beggar is not in his worldly distinction, but in the distinction that God himself has given to him. He feels himself like a flute through which God's own breath of love has been breathed:

My heart is like a flute he has played on.
If ever it fall into other hands,—
    let him fling it away.
My lover's flute is dear to him.
Therefore, if to-day alien breath have entered it
    and sounded stranger notes.
Let him break it to pieces and strew the dust with
    them.

So we find that this man also has his disgust of defilement. While the ambitious world of wealth and power despises him, he in his turn thinks that the world's touch desecrates him who has been made sacred by the touch of his Lover. He does not envy us our life of ambition and achievements, but he knows how precious his own life has been:

I am poured forth in living notes of joy and
　　sorrow by your breath.
Morning and evening, in summer and in rains, I
　　am fashioned to music.
Yet should I be wholly spent in some flight of
　　song,
I shall not grieve, the tune is so precious to me.

Our joys and sorrows are contradictory when self separates
them in oppositions. But for the heart in which self merges
in God's love, they lose their absoluteness. So the Baül's
prayer is to feel in all situations—in danger, or pain, or
sorrow—that he is in God's hands. He solves the problem of
emancipation from sufferings by accepting and setting them
in a higher context:

I am the boat, you are the sea, and also the
　　boatman.
Though you never make the shore, though you let
　　me sink, why should I be foolish and afraid?
Is the reaching the shore a greater prize than
　　losing myself with you?
If you are only the haven, as they say, then what
　　is the sea?
Let it surge and toss me on its waves, I shall be
　　content.
I live in you, whatever and however you appear.
Save me or kill me as you wish, only never leave
　　me in others' hands.

III

It is needless to say, before I conclude, that I had neither
the training nor the opportunity to study this mendicant
religious sect in Bengal from an ethnological standpoint. I

was attracted to find out how the living currents of religious movements work in the heart of the people, saving them from degradation imposed by the society of the learned, of the rich, or of the highborn; how the spirit of man, by making use even of its obstacles, reaches fulfilment, led thither, not by the learned authorities in the scriptures, or by the mechanical impulse of the dogma-driven crowd, but by the unsophisticated aspiration of the loving soul. On the inaccessible mountain peaks of theology the snows of creed remain eternally rigid, cold, and pure. But God's manifest shower falls direct on the plain of humble hearts, flowing there in various channels, even getting mixed with some mud in its course, as it is soaked into the underground currents, invisible, but ever-moving.

I can think of nothing better than to conclude my paper with a poem of Jnândâs, in which the aspiration of all simple spirits has found a devout expression:

> I had traveled all day and was tired; then I bowed
>   my head towards thy kingly court still far away.
> The night deepened, a longing burned in my
>   heart.
> Whatever the words I sang, pain cried through
>   them—for even my songs thirsted—
> O my Lover, my Beloved, my Best in all the
>   world.
> When time seemed lost in darkness,
>   thy hand dropped its scepter to take up the lute
>   and strike the uttermost chords;
> And my heart sang out,
>   O my Lover, my Beloved, my Best in all the
>   world.
>
> Ah, who is this whose arms enfold me?

Whatever I have to leave, let me leave; let me
leave; and whatever I have to bear, let me bear.
Only let me walk with thee,
  O my Lover, my Beloved, my Best in all the
world.

Descend at whiles from thy high audience hall,
  come down amid joys and sorrows.
Hide in all forms and delights, in love,
And in my heart sing thy songs,—
  O my Lover, my Beloved, my Best in all the
  world.

East and West

I

It is not always a profound interest in man that carries travelers nowadays to distant lands. More often it is the facility for rapid movement. For lack of time and for the sake of convenience we generalise and crush our human facts into the packages within the steel trucks that hold our travellers' reports.

Our knowledge of our own countrymen and our feelings about them have slowly and unconsciously grown out of innumerable facts which are full of contradictions and subject to incessant change. They have the elusive mystery and fluidity of life. We cannot define to ourselves what we are as a whole, because we know too much; because our knowledge is more than knowledge. It is an immediate consciousness of personality, and evaluation of which carries some emotion, joy or sorrow, shame or exaltation. But in a foreign land we try to find our compensation for the meagerness of our data by the compactness of the generalisation which our imperfect sympathy itself helps us to form. When a stranger from the West travels in the Eastern world he takes the facts that displease him and readily makes use of them for his rigid conclusions, fixed upon the unchallengeable authority of his personal experience. It is like a man who has his own boat for crossing his village steam, but, on being compelled to wade across some strange watercourse, draws angry comparisons as he goes from every patch of mud and every pebble which his feet encounter.

Our mind has faculties which are universal, but its habits are insular. There are men who become impatient and angry at the least discomfort when their habits are incommoded. In their idea of the next world they probably conjure up the ghosts of their slippers and dressing-gowns, and expect the latchkey that opens their lodging-house door on earth to fit their front door in the other world. As travelers they are a failure; for they have grown too accustomed to their mental easy-chairs, and in their intellectual nature love home comforts, which are of local make, more than the realities of life, which, like earth itself, are full of ups and downs, yet are one in their rounded completeness.

The modern age has brought the geography of the earth near to us, but made it difficult for us to come into touch with man. We go to strange lands and observe; we do not live there. We hardly meet men: but only specimens of knowledge. We are in haste to seek for general types and overlook individuals.

When we fall into the habit of neglecting to use the understanding that comes of sympathy in our travels, our knowledge of foreign people grows insensitive, and therefore easily becomes both unjust and cruel in its character, and also selfish and contemptuous in its application. Such has, too, often, been the case with regard to the meeting of Western people in our days with others for whom they do not recognise any obligation of kinship.

It has been admitted that the dealings between different races of men are not merely between individuals; that our mutual understanding is either aided, or else obstructed, by the general emanations forming the social atmosphere. These emanations are our collective ideas and collective feelings, generated according to special historical circumstances.

For instance, the caste-idea is a collective idea in India. When we approach an Indian who is under the influence of this collective idea, he is no longer a pure individual with his conscience fully awake to the judging of the value of a human being. He is more or less a passive medium for giving expression to the sentiment of a whole community.

It is evident that the caste-idea is not creative; it is merely institutional. It adjusts human beings according to some mechanical arrangement. It emphasizes the negative side of the individual—his separateness. It hurts the complete truth in man.

In the West, also, the people have a certain collective idea that obscures their humanity. Let me try to explain what I feel about it.

II

Lately I went to visit some battlefields of France which had been devastated by war. The awful calm of desolation, which still bore wrinkles of pain—death-struggles stiffened into ugly ridges—brought before my mind the vision of a huge demon, which had no shape, no meaning, yet had two arms that could strike and break and tear, a gaping mouth that could devour, and bulging brains that could conspire and plan. It was a purpose, which had a living body, but no complete humanity to temper it. Because it was passion—belonging to life, and yet not having the wholeness of life—it was the most terrible of life's enemies.

Something of the same sense of oppression in a different degree, the same desolation in a different aspect, is produced in my mind when I realise the effect of the West upon Eastern life—the West which, in its relation to us, is all plan and purpose incarnate, without any superfluous humanity.

I feel the contrast very strongly in Japan. In that country the old world presents itself with some ideal of perfection, in which man has his varied opportunities of self-revelation in art, in ceremonial, in religious faith, and in customs expressing the poetry of social relationship. There one feels that deep delight of hospitality which life offers to life. And side by side, in the same soil, stands the modern world, which is stupendously big and powerful, but inhospitable. It has no simple-hearted welcome for man. It is living; yet the incompleteness of life's ideal within it cannot but hurt humanity.

The wriggling tentacles of a cold-blooded utilitarianism, with which the West has grasped all the easily yielding succulent portions of the East, are causing pain and indignation throughout the Eastern countries. The West comes to us, not with the imagination and sympathy that create and unite, but with a shock of passion—passion for power and wealth. This passion is a mere force, which has in it the principle of separation, of conflict.

I have been fortunate in coming into close touch with individual men and women of the Western countries, and have felt with them their sorrows and shared their aspirations. I have known that they seek the same God, who is my God— even those who deny Him. I feel certain that, if the great light of culture be extinct in Europe, our horizon in the East will mourn in darkness. It does not hurt my pride to acknowledge that, in the present age, Western humanity has received its mission to be the teacher of the world; that her science, through the mastery of laws of nature, is to liberate human souls from the dark dungeon of matter. For this very reason I have realised all the more strongly, on the other hand, that the dominant collective idea in the Western countries is not creative. It is ready to enslave or kill individuals, to drug a great people with soul-killing poison, darkening their whole future with the black mist of stupefaction, and emasculating entire races of men to the utmost degree of helplessness. It is wholly wanting in spiritual power to blend and harmonize; it lacks the sense of the great personality of man.

The most significant fact of modern days is this, that the West has met the East. Such a momentous meeting of humanity, in order to be fruitful, must have in its heart some great emotional idea, generous and creative. There can be no doubt that God's choice has fallen upon the knights-errant of the West for the service of the present age; arms and armour have been given to them; but have they yet realized in their hearts the single-minded loyalty to their cause which can resist all temptations of bribery from the devil? The world to-day is offered to the West. She will destroy it, if she does not use it for a great creation of man. The materials for such a creation are in the hands of science; but the creative genius is in Man's spiritual ideal.

III

When I was young a stranger from Europe came to Bengal. He chose his lodging among the people of the country, shared with them their frugal diet, and freely offered them his service. He found employment in the houses of the rich, teaching them French and German, and the money thus earned he spent to help poor students in buying books. This meant for him hours of walking in the mid-day heat of a tropical summer; for intent upon exercising the utmost economy, he refused to hire conveyances. He was pitiless in his exaction from himself of his resources, in money, time, and strength, to the point of privation; and all this for the sake of a people who were obscure, to whom he was not born, yet whom he dearly loved. He did not come to us with a professional mission of teaching sectarian creeds; he had not in his nature the least trace of that self-sufficiency of goodness, which humiliates by gifts the victims of its insolent benevolence. Though he did not know our language, he took every occasion to frequent our meetings and ceremonies; yet he was always afraid of intrusion, and tenderly anxious lest he might offend us by his ignorance of our customs. At last, under the continual strain of work in an alien climate and surroundings, his health broke down. He died, and was cremated at our burning-ground, according to his express desire.

The attitude of his mind, the manner of his living, the object of his life, his modesty, his unstinted self-sacrifice for a people who had not even the power to give publicity to any benefaction bestowed upon them, were so utterly unlike anything we were accustomed to associate with the Europeans in India, that it gave rise in our mind to a feeling of love bordering upon awe.

We all have a realm, a private paradise, in our mind, where dwell deathless memories of persons who brought some divine light to our life's experience, who may not be known to others, and whose names have no place in the pages of history. Let me confess to you that this man lives as one of those immortals in the paradise of my individual life.

He came from Sweden, his name was Hammargren. What was most remarkable in the event of his coming to us in Bengal was the fact that in his own country he had chanced to read some works of my great countryman, Ram Mohan Roy, and felt an immense veneration for his genius and his character. Ram Mohan Roy lived in the beginning of the last century, and it is no exaggeration when I describe him as one of the immortal personalities of modern time. This young Swede had the unusual gift of a farsighted intellect and sympathy, which enabled him even from his distance of space and time, and in spite of racial differences, to realize the greatness of Ram Mohan Roy. It moved him so deeply that he resolved to go to the country which produced this great man, and offer her his service. He was poor, and he had to wait some time in England before he could earn his passage money to India. There he came at last, and in reckless generosity of love utterly spent himself to the last breath of his life, away from home and kindred and all the inheritances of his motherland. His stay among us was too short to produce any outward result. He failed even to achieve during his life what he had in his mind, which was to found by the help of his scanty earnings a library as a memorial to Ram Mohan Roy, and thus to leave behind him a visible symbol of his devotion. But what I prize most in this European youth, who left no record of his life behind him, is not the memory of any service of goodwill, but the precious gift of respect which he offered to a people who are fallen upon evil times, and whom it is so easy to ignore or to humiliate. For the first time in the modern days this obscure individual from Sweden brought to our country the chivalrous courtesy of the West, a greeting of human fellowship.

The coincidence came to me with a great and delightful surprise when the Nobel Prize was offered to me from Sweden. As a recognition of individual merit it was of great value to me, no doubt; but it was the acknowledgement of the East as a collaborator with the Western continents, in contributing its riches to the common stock of civilization, which had the chief significance for the present age. It meant joining hands in comradeship by the two great hemispheres of the human world across the sea.

IV

To-day the real East remains unexplored. The blindness of contempt is more hopeless than the blindness of ignorance; for contempt kills the light which ignorance merely leaves unignited. The East is waiting to be understood by the Western races, in order not only to be able to give what is true in her, but also to be confident of her own mission.

In Indian history, the meeting of the Mussulman and the Hindu produced Akbar, the object of whose dream was the unification of hearts and ideals. It had all the glowing enthusiasm of a religion, and it produced an immediate and a vast result even in his own lifetime.

But the fact still remains that the Western mind, after centuries of contact with the East, has not evolved the enthusiasm of a chivalrous ideal which can bring this age to its fulfilment. It is everywhere raising thorny hedges of exclusion and offering human sacrifices to national self-seeking. It has intensified the mutual feelings of envy among Western races themselves, as they fight over their spoils and display a carnivorous pride in their snarling rows of teeth.

We must again guard our minds from any encroaching distrust of the individuals of a nation. The active love of humanity and the spirit of martyrdom for the cause of justice and truth which I have met with in the Western countries have been a great lesson and inspiration to me. I have no doubt in my mind that the West owes its true greatness, not so much to its marvellous training of intellect, as to its spirit of service devoted to the welfare of man. Therefore I speak with a personal feeling of pain and sadness about the collective power which is guiding the helm of Western civilization. It is a passion, not an ideal. The more success it has brought to Europe, the more costly it will prove to her at last, when the accounts have to be rendered. And the signs are unmistakable, that the accounts have been called for. The time has come when Europe must know that the forcible parasitism which she has been practising upon the two large Continents of the world—the two most unwieldy whales of humanity— must be causing to her moral nature a gradual atrophy and degeneration.

As an example, let me quote the following extract from the concluding chapter of *From the Cape to Cairo*, by Messrs.

Grogan and Sharp, two writers who have the power to inculcate their doctrines by precept and example. In their reference to the African they are candid, as when they say, 'We have stolen his land. Now we must steal his limbs.' These two sentences, carefully articulated, with a smack of enjoyment, have been more clearly explained in the following statement, where some sense of that decency which is the attenuated ghost of a buried conscience, prompts the writers to use the phrase 'compulsory labour' in place of the honest word 'slavery'; just as the modern politician adroitly avoids the word 'injunction' and uses the word 'mandate.' 'Compulsory labour in some form,' they say, 'is the corollary of our occupation of the country.' And they add: 'It is pathetic, but it is history,' implying thereby that moral sentiments have no serious effect in the history of human beings.

Elsewhere they write: 'Either we must give up the country commercially, or we must make the African work. And mere abuse of those who point out the impasse cannot change the facts. We must decide, and soon. Or rather the white man of South Africa will decide.' The authors also confess that they have seen too much of the world 'to have any lingering belief that Western civilization benefits native races.'

The logic is simple—the logic of egoism. But the argument is simplified by lopping off the greater part of the premise. For these writers seem to hold that the only important question for the white men of South Africa is, how indefinitely to grow fat on ostrich feathers and diamond mines, and dance jazz dances over the misery and degradation of a whole race of fellow-beings of a different colour from their own. Possibly they believe that moral laws have a special domesticated breed of comfortable concessions for the service of the people in power. Possibly they ignore the fact that commercial and political cannibalism, profitably practised upon foreign races, creeps back nearer home; that the cultivation of unwholesome appetites has its final reckoning with the stomach which has been made to serve it. For, after all, man is a spiritual being, and not a mere living money-bag jumping from profit to profit, and breaking the backbone of human races in its financial leapfrog.

Such, however, has been the condition of things for more than a century; and to-day, trying to read the future by the light of the European conflagration, we are asking ourselves everywhere in the East: 'Is this frightfully overgrown power really great? It can bruise us from without, but can it add to our wealth of spirit? It can sign peace treaties, but can it give peace?'

It was about two thousand years ago that all-powerful Rome in one of its eastern provinces executed on a cross a simple teacher of an obscure tribe of fishermen. On that day the Roman governor felt no falling off of his appetite or sleep. On that day there was, on the one hand, the agony, the humiliation, the death; on the other, the pomp of pride and festivity in the Governor's palace.

And to-day? To whom, then, shall we bow the head?

Kasmai devaya havisha vidhema?
(To which God shall we offer oblation?)

We know of an instance in our own history of India, when a great personality, both in his life and voice, struck the keynote of the solemn music of the soul—love for all creatures. And that music crossed seas, mountains, and deserts. Races belonging to different climates, habits, and languages were drawn together, not in the clash of arms, not in the conflict of exploitation, but in harmony of life, in amity and peace. That was creation.

When we think of it, we see at once what the confusion of thought was to which the Western poet, dwelling upon the difference between East and West, referred when he said,

'Never the twain shall meet.' It is true that they are not yet showing any real sign of meeting. But the reason is because the West has not sent out its humanity to meet the man in the East, but only its machine. Therefore the poet's line has to be changed into something like this:

Man is man, machine is machine,
And never the twain shall wed.

You must know that red tape can never be a common human bond; that official sealing-wax can never provide means of mutual attachment; that it is a painful ordeal for human beings to have to receive favours from animated pigeon-holes, and condescensions from printed circulars that give notice but never speak. The presence of the Western people in the East is a human fact. If we are to gain anything from them, it must not be a mere sum-total of legal codes and systems of civil and military service. Man is a great deal more to man than that. We have our human birthright to claim direct help from the man of the West, if he has anything great to give us. It must come to us, not through mere facts in a juxtaposition, but through the spontaneous sacrifice made by those who have the gift, and therefore the responsibility.

Earnestly I ask the poet of the Western world to realise and sing to you with all the great power of music which he has, that the East and the West are ever in search of each other, and that they must meet not merely in the fullness of physical strength, but in fullness of truth; that the right hand, which wields the sword, has the need of the left, which holds the shield of safety.

The East has its seat in the vast plains watched over by the snow-peaked mountains and fertilised by rivers carrying mighty volumes of water to the sea. There, under the blaze of a tropical sun, the physical life has bedimmed the light of its vigour and lessened its claims. There man has had the repose of mind which has ever tried to set itself in harmony with the inner notes of existence. In the silence of sunrise and sunset, and on star-crowded nights, he has sat face to face with the Infinite, waiting for the revelation that opens up the heart of all that there is. He has said, in a rapture of realization:

'Hearken to me, ye children of the Immortal, who dwell in the Kingdom of Heaven. I have known, from beyond darkness, the Supreme Person, shining with the radiance of the sun.'

The man from the East, with his faith in the eternal, who in his soul had met the touch of the Supreme Person—did he never come to you in the West and speak to you of the Kingdom of Heaven? Did he not unite the East and the West in truth, in the unity of one spiritual bond between all children of the Immortal, in the realization of one great Personality in all human persons?

Yes, the East did once meet the West profoundly in the growth of her life. Such union became possible, because the East came to the West with the ideal that is creative, and not with the passion that destroys moral bonds. The mystic consciousness of the infinite, which she brought with her, was greatly needed by the man of the West to give him his balance.

On the other hand, the East must find her own balance in Science—the magnificent gift that the West can bring to her. Truth has its nest as well as its sky. That nest is definite in structure, accurate in law of construction; and though it has to be changed and rebuilt over and over again, the need of it is never-ending and its laws are eternal. For some centuries the East has neglected the nest-building of truth. She has not been attentive to learn its secret. Trying to cross the trackless infinite, the East has relied solely upon her wings. She has spurned the earth, till, buffeted by storms, her wings are hurt and she is tired, sorely needing help. But has she then to be told that the messenger of the sky and the builder of the nest shall never meet?

The Modern Age

I

Wherever man meets man in a living relationship, the meeting finds its natural expression in works of art, the signatures of beauty, in which the mingling of the personal touch leaves its memorial.

On the other hand, a relationship of pure utility humiliates man—it ignores the rights and needs of his deeper nature; it feels no compunction in maltreating and killing things of beauty that can never be restored.

Some years ago, when I set out from Calcutta on my voyage to Japan, the first thing that shocked me, with a sense of personal injury, was the ruthless intrusion of the factories for making gunny-bags on both banks of the Ganges. The blow it gave to me was owing to the precious memory of the days of my boyhood, when the scenery of this river was the only great thing near my birthplace reminding me of the existence of a world which had its direct communication with our innermost spirit.

Calcutta is an upstart town with no depth of sentiment in her face and in her manners. It may truly be said about her genesis:—In the beginning there was the spirit of the Shop, which uttered through its megaphone, 'Let there be the Office!' and there was Calcutta. She brought with her no dower of distinction, no majesty of noble or romantic origin; she never gathered around her any great historical associations, any annals of brave sufferings, or memory of mighty deeds. The only thing which gave her the sacred baptism of beauty was the river. I was fortunate enough to be born before the smoke-belching iron dragon had devoured the greater part of the life of its banks; when the landing-stairs descending into its waters, caressed by its tides, appeared to me like the loving arms of the villages clinging to it; when Calcutta, with her up-tilted nose and stony stare, had not completely disowned her foster-mother, rural Bengal, and had not surrendered body and soul to her wealthy paramour, the spirit of the ledger, bound in dead leather.

But as an instance of the contrast of the different ideal of a different age, incarnated in the form of a town, the memory of my last visit to Benares comes to my mind. What impressed me most deeply, while I was there, was the mother-call of the river Ganges, ever filling the atmosphere with an 'unheard melody,' attracting the whole population to its bosom every hour of the day. I am proud of the fact that India has felt a most profound love for this river, which nourishes civilization on its banks, guiding its course from the silence of the hills to the sea with its myriad voices of solitude. The love of this river, which has become one with the love of the best in man, has given rise to this town as an expression of reverence. This is to show that there are sentiments in us which are creative, which do not clamour for gain, but overflow in gifts, in spontaneous generosity of self-sacrifice.

But our minds will nevermore cease to be haunted by the perturbed spirit of the question, 'What about gunny-bags?' I admit they are indispensable, and am willing to allow them a place in society, if my opponent will only admit that even gunny-bags should have their limits, and will acknowledge the importance of leisure to man, with space for joy and worship, and a home of wholesale privacy, with associations of chaste love and mutual service. If this concession to humanity be denied or curtailed, and if profit and production are allowed to run amuck, they will play havoc with our love of beauty, of truth of justice, and also with our love for our fellow-beings. So it comes about that the peasant cultivators of jute, who live on the brink of everlasting famine, are combined against, and driven to lower the price of their labours to the point of blank despair, by those who earn more than cent per cent profit and wallow in the infamy of their wealth. The facts that man is brave and kind, that he is social and generous and self-sacrificing, have some aspect of the complete in them; but the fact that he is a manufacturer of gunny-bags is too ridiculously small to claim the right of reducing his higher nature to insignificance. The fragmentariness of utility should never forget its subordinate position in human affairs. It must not be permitted to occupy more than its legitimate place and power in society, nor to have the liberty to desecrate the poetry of life, to deaden our sensitiveness to ideals, bragging of its own coarseness as a sign of virility. The pity is that when in the centre of our activities we acknowledge, by some proud name, the supremacy of wanton destructiveness, or production not less wanton, we shut out all the lights of our souls, and in that darkness our conscience and our consciousness of shame are hidden, and our love of freedom is killed.

I do not for a moment mean to imply that in any particular period of history men were free from the disturbance of their lower passions. Selfishness ever had its share in government and trade. Yet there was a struggle to maintain a balance of forces in society; and our passions cherished no delusions about their own rank and value. They contrived no clever devices to hoodwink our moral nature. For in those days our intellect was not tempted to put its weight into the balance on the side of over-greed.

But in recent centuries a devastating change has come over our mentality with regard to the acquisition of money. Whereas in former ages men treated it with condescension, even with disrespect, now they bend their knees to it. That it should be allowed a sufficiently large place in society, there can be no question; but it becomes an outrage when it occupies those seats which are specially reserved for the immortals, by bribing us, tampering with our moral pride, recruiting the best strength of society in a traitor's campaign against human ideals, thus disguising, with the help of pomp and pageantry, its true insignificance. Such a state of things has come to pass because, with the help of science, the possibilities of profit have suddenly become immoderate. The whole of the human world, throughout its length and breadth, has felt the gravitational pull of a giant planet of greed, with concentric rings of innumerable satellites, causing in our society a marked deviation from the moral orbit. In former times the intellectual and spiritual powers of this earth upheld their dignity of independence and were not giddily rocked on the tides of the money market. But, as in the last fatal stages of disease, this fatal influence of money has got into our brain and affected our heart. Like a usurper, it has occupied the throne of high social ideals, using every means, by menace and threat, to seize upon the right, and, tempted by opportunity, presuming to judge it. It has not only science for its ally, but other forces also that have some semblance of religion, such as nation-worship and the idealising of organised selfishness. Its methods are far-reaching and sure. Like the claws of a tiger's paw, they are softly sheathed. Its massacres are invisible, because they are fundamental, attacking the very roots of life. Its plunder is ruthless behind a scientific system of screens, which have the formal appearance of being open and responsible to inquiries. By whitewashing its stains it keeps its respectability unblemished. It makes a liberal use of falsehood in diplomacy, only feeling embarrassed when its evidence is disclosed by others of the trade. An unscrupulous system of propaganda paves the way for widespread misrepresentation. It works up the crowd psychology through regulated hypnotic doses at repeated intervals, administered in bottles with moral labels upon them of soothing colours. In fact, man has been able to make his pursuit of power easier to-day by his art of mitigating the obstructive forces that come from the higher region of his humanity. Within his cult of powers and his idolatry of money he has, in a great measure, reverted to his primitive barbarism, a barbarism whose path is lit up by the lurid light of intellect. For barbarism is the simplicity of a superficial life. It may be bewildering in its surface adornments and complexities, but it lacks the ideal to impart to it the depth of moral responsibility.

II

Society suffers from a profound feeling of unhappiness, not so much when it is in material poverty as when its members are deprived of a large part of their humanity. This unhappiness goes on smouldering in the subconscious mind of the community till its life is reduced to ashes or a sudden combustion is produced. The repressed personality of man generates an inflammable moral gas deadly in its explosive force.

We have seen in the late war, and also in some of the still more recent events of history, how human individuals freed from moral and spiritual bonds find a boisterous joy in a debauchery of destruction. There is generated a disinterested passion of ravage. Through such catastrophe we can realize what formidable forces of annihilation are kept in check in our communities by bonds of social ideas; nay, made into multitudinous manifestations of beauty and fruitfulness. Thus we know that evils are, like meteors, stray fragments of life, which need the attraction of some great ideal in order to be assimilated with the wholesomeness of creation. The evil forces are literally outlaws; they only need the control and cadence of spiritual laws to change them into good. The true goodness is not the negation of badness, it is in the mastery of it. Goodness is the miracle which turns the tumult of chaos into a dance of beauty.

In modern society the ideal of wholeness has lost its force. Therefore its different sections have become detached and resolved into their elemental character of forces. Labour is a force; so also is Capital; so are the Government and the People; so are Man and Woman. It is said that when the forces lying latent in even a handful of dust are liberated from their bond of unity, they can lift the buildings of a whole neighbourhood to the height of a mountain. Such disfranchised forces, irresponsible free-booters, may be useful to us for certain purposes, but human habitations standing secure on their foundations are better for us. To own the secret of utilising these forces is a proud fact for us, but the power of self-control and the self-dedication of love are truer subjects for the exultation of mankind. The genii of the Arabian Nights may have in their magic their lure and fascination for us. But the consciousness, of God is of another order, infinitely more precious in imparting to our minds ideas of the spiritual power of creation. Yet these genii are abroad everywhere; and even now, after the late war, their devotees are getting ready to play further tricks upon humanity by suddenly spiriting it away to some hill-top of desolation.

III

We know that when, at first, any large body of people in their history became aware of their unity, they expressed it in some popular symbol of divinity. For they felt that their combination was not an arithmetical ones; its truth was deeper than the truth of number. They felt that their community was not a mere agglutination but a creation, having upon it the living touch of the infinite Person. The realization of this truth having been an end in itself, a fulfilment, it gave meaning to self-sacrifice, to the acceptance even of death.

But our modern education is producing a habit of mind which is ever weakening in us the spiritual apprehension of truth—the truth of a person as the ultimate reality of existence. Science has its proper sphere in a analysing this world as a construction, just as grammar has its legitimate office in analysing the syntax of a poem. But the world, as a creation, is not a mere construction; it too is more than a syntax. It is a poem, which we are apt to forget when grammar takes exclusive hold of our minds.

Upon the loss of this sense of a universal personality, which is religion, the reign of the machine and of method has been firmly established, and man, humanly speaking, has been made a homeless tramp. As nomads, ravenous and restless, the men from the West have come to us. They have exploited our Eastern humanity for sheer gain of power. This modern meeting of men has not yet received the blessing of God. For it has kept us apart, though railway lines are laid far and wide, and ships are plying from shore to shore to bring us together.

It has been said in the Upanishads:

Yastu sarvāni bhutāni ātmānyevānupashyati
Sarva bhuteshu chātmānam na tato vijugupsate

(He who sees all things in *ātmā,* in the infinite spirit, and the infinite spirit in all beings, remains no longer unrevealed.)

In the modern civilization, for which an enormous number of men are used as materials, and human relationships have in a large measure become utilitarian, man is imperfectly revealed. For man's revelation does not lie in the fact that he is a power, but that he is a spirit. The prevalence of the theory which realizes the power of the machine in the universe, and organises men into machines, is like the eruption of Etna, tremendous in its force, in its outburst of fire and fume; but its creeping lava covers up human shelters made by the ages, and its ashes smother life.

IV

The terribly efficient method of repressing personality in the individuals and the races who have failed to resist it has, in the present scientific age, spread all over the world; and in consequence there have appeared signs of a universal disruption which seems not far off. Faced with the possibility of such a disaster, which is sure to affect the successful peoples of the world in their intemperate prosperity, the great Powers of the West are seeking peace, not by curbing their greed, or by giving up the exclusive advantages which they have unjustly acquired, but by concentrating their forces for mutual security.

But can powers find their equilibrium in themselves? Power has to be made secure not only against power, but also against weakness; for there lies the peril of its losing balance. The weak are as great a danger for the strong as quicksands for an elephant. They do not assist progress because they do not resist; they only drag down. The people who grow accustomed to wield absolute power over others are apt to forget that by so doing they generate an unseen force which some day rends that power into pieces. The dumb fury of the downtrodden finds its awful support from the universal law of moral balance. The air which is so thin and unsubstantial gives birth to storms that nothing can resist. This has been proved in history over and over again, and stormy forces arising from the revolt of insulted humanity are openly gathering in the air at the present time.

Yet in the psychology of the strong the lesson is despised and no count taken of the terribleness of the weak. This is the latent ignorance that, like an unsuspected worm, burrows under the bulk of the prosperous. Have we never read of the castle of power, securely buttressed on all sides, in a moment dissolving in air at the explosion caused by the weak and outraged besiegers? Politicians calculate upon the number of mailed hands that are kept on the sword-hilts: they do not possess the third eye to see the great invisible hand that clasps in silence the hand of the helpless and waits its time. The strong form their league by a combination of powers, driving the weak to form their own league alone with their God. I know I am crying in the wilderness when I raise the voice of warning; and while the West is busy with its organization of a machine-made peace, it will still continue to nourish by its iniquities the underground forces of earthquake in the Eastern Continent. The West seems unconscious that Science, by providing it with more and more power, is tempting it to suicide and encouraging it to accept the challenge of the disarmed; it does not know that the challenge comes from a higher source.

Two prophecies about the world's salvation are cherished in the hearts of the two great religions of the world. They represent the highest expectation of man, thereby indicating his faith in a truth which he instinctively considers as ultimate— the truth of love. These prophecies have not for their vision the fettering of the world and reducing it to tameness by means of a close-linked power forged in the factory of a political steel trust. One of the religions has for its meditation the image of the Buddha who is to come, Maitreya, the Buddha of love; and he is to bring peace. The other religion waits for the coming of Christ. For Christ preached peace when he preached love, when he preached the oneness of the Father with the brothers who are many. And this was the truth of peace. Christ never held that peace was the best policy. For policy is not truth. The calculation of self-interest can never successfully fight the irrational force of passion—the passion which is perversion of love, and which can only be set right by the truth of love. So long as the powers build a league on the foundation of their desire for safety, secure enjoyment of gains, consolidation of past injustice, and putting off the reparation of wrongs, while their fingers still wriggle for greed and reek of blood, rifts will appear in their union; and in future their conflicts will take greater force and magnitude. It is political and commercial egoism which is the evil harbinger of war. By different combinations it changes its shape and dimensions, but not its nature. This egoism is still held sacred, and made a religion; and such a religion, by a mere change of temple, and by new committees of priests, will never save mankind. We must know that, as, through science and commerce, the realization of the unity of the material world gives us power, so the realization of the great spiritual Unity of Man alone can give us peace.

The Spirit of Freedom

When Freedom is not an inner idea which imparts strength to our activities and breadth to our creations, when it is merely a thing of external circumstance, it is like an open space to one who is blindfolded.

In my recent travels in the West I have felt that out there freedom as an idea has become feeble and ineffectual. Consequently a spirit of repression and coercion is fast spreading in the politics and social relationships of the people.

In the age of Monarchy the king lived surrounded by a miasma of intrigue. At court there was an endless whispering of lies and calumny, and much plotting and planning among the conspiring courtiers to manipulate the king as the instrument of their own purposes.

In the present age intrigue plays a wider part, and affects the whole country. The people are drugged with the hashish of false hopes and urged to deeds of frightfulness by the goadings of manufactured panics; their higher feelings are exploited by devious channels of unctuous hypocrisy, their pockets picked under anaesthetics of flattery, their very psychology affected by a conspiracy of money and unscrupulous diplomacy.

In the old order the king was given to understand that he was the freest individual in the world. A greater semblance of external freedom, no doubt, he had than other individuals. But they built for him a gorgeous prison of unreality.

The same thing is happening now with the people of the West. They are flattered into believing that they are free, and they have the sovereign power in their hands. But this power is robbed by hosts of self-seekers, and the horse is captured and stabled because of this gift of freedom over space. The mob-mind is allowed the enjoyment of an apparent liberty, while its true freedom is curtailed on every side. Its thoughts are fashioned according to the plans of organised interests; in its choosing of ideas and forming of opinions it is hindered either by some punitive force or by the constant insinuation of untruths; it is made in an artificial world of hypnotic phrases. In fact, the people have become the storehouse of a power that attracts round it a swarm of adventurers who are secretly investing its walls to exploit it for their own devices.

Thus it has become more and more evident to me that the ideal of freedom has grown tenuous in the atmosphere of the West. The mentality is that of a slave-owning community, with a mutilated multitude of men tied to its commercial and political treadmill. It is the mentality of mutual distrust and fear. The appalling scenes of inhumanity and injustice, which are growing familiar to us, are the outcome of a psychology that deals with terror. No cruelty can be uglier in its ferocity than the cruelty of the coward. The people who have sacrificed their souls to the passion of profit-making and the drunkenness of power are constantly pursued by phantoms of panic and suspicion, and therefore they are ruthless even where they are least afraid of mischances. They become morally incapable of allowing freedom to others, and in their eagerness to curry favour with the powerful they not only connive at the injustice done by their own partners in political gambling, but participate in it. A perpetual anxiety for the protection of their gains at any cost strikes at the love of freedom and justice, until at length they are ready to forgo liberty for themselves and for others.

My experience in the West, where I have realized the immense power of money and of organized propaganda,— working everywhere behind screens of camouflage, creating an atmosphere of distrust, timidity, and antipathy,—has impressed me deeply with the truth that real freedom is of the mind and spirit; it can never come to us from outside. He only has freedom who ideally loves freedom himself and is glad to extend it to others. He who cares to have slaves must chain himself to them; he who builds walls to create exclusion for others builds walls across his own freedom; he who distrusts freedom in others loses his moral right to it. Sooner or later he is lured into the meshes of physical and moral servility.

Therefore I would urge my own countrymen to ask themselves if the freedom to which they aspire is one of external conditions. Is it merely a transferable commodity? Have they acquired a true love of freedom? Have they faith in it? Are they ready to make space in their society for the minds of their children to grow up in the ideal of human dignity, unhindered by restrictions that are unjust and irrational?

Have we not made elaborately permanent the walls of our social compartments? We are tenaciously proud of their exclusiveness. We boast that, in this world, no other society but our own has come to finality in the classifying of its living members. Yet in our political agitations we conveniently forget that any unnaturalness in the relationship of governors and governed which humiliates us, becomes an outrage when it is artificially fixed under the threat of military persecution.

When India gave voice to immortal thoughts, in the time of fullest vigour of vitality, her children had the fearless spirit of the seekers of truth. The great epic of the soul of our people—the Mahabharata—gives us a wonderful vision of an overflowing life, full of the freedom of inquiry and experiment. When the age of the Buddha came, humanity was stirred in our country to its uttermost depth. The freedom of mind which it produced expressed itself in a wealth of creation, spreading everywhere in its richness over the continent of Asia. But with the ebb of life in India the spirit of creation died away. It hardened into an age of inert construction. The organic unity of a varied and elastic society gave way to a conventional order which proved its artificial character by its inexorable law of exclusion.

Life has its inequalities, I admit, but they are natural and are in harmony with our vital functions. The head keeps its place apart from the feet, not through some external arrangement or any conspiracy of coercion. If the body is compelled to turn somersaults for an indefinite period, the head never exchanges its relative function for that of the feet. But have our social divisions the same inevitableness of organic law? If we have the hardihood to say 'yes' to that question, then how can we blame an alien people for subjecting us to a political order which they are tempted to believe eternal?

By squeezing human beings in the grip of an inelastic system and forcibly holding them fixed, we have ignored the laws of life and growth. We have forced living souls into a permanent passivity, making them incapable of moulding circumstance to their own intrinsic design, and of mastering their own destiny. Borrowing our ideal of life from a dark period of our degeneracy, we have covered up our sensitiveness of soul under the immovable weight of a remote past. We have set up an elaborate ceremonial of cage-worship, and plucked all the feathers from the wings of the living spirit of our people. And for us,—with our centuries of degradation and insult, with the amorphousness of our national unit, with our helplessness before the attack of disasters from without and our unreasoning self-obstructions from within,—the punishment has been terrible. Our stupefaction has become so absolute that we do not even realize that this persistent misfortune, dogging our steps for ages, cannot be a mere accident of history, removable only by another accident from outside.

Unless we have true faith in freedom, knowing it to be creative, manfully taking all its risks, not only do we lose the right to claim freedom in politics, but we also lack the power to maintain it with all our strength. For that would be like assigning the service of God to a confirmed atheist. And men, who contemptuously treat their own brothers and sisters as eternal babies, never to be trusted in the most trivial details of their personal life,—coercing them at every step by the cruel threat of persecution into following a blind lane leading to nowhere, driving a number of them into hypocrisy and into moral inertia,—will fail over and over again to rise to the height of their true and severe responsibility. They will be incapable of holding a just freedom in politics, and of fighting in freedom's cause.

The civilization of the West has in it the spirit of the machine which must move; and to that blind movement human lives are offered as fuel, keeping up the steam-power. It represents the active aspect of inertia which has the appearance of freedom, but not its truth, and therefore gives rise to slavery both within its boundaries and outside. The present civilization of India has the constraining power of the mould. It squeezes living man in the grip of rigid regulations, and its repression of individual freedom makes it only too easy for men to be forced into submission of all kinds and degrees. In both of these traditions life is offered up to something which is not life; it is a sacrifice, which has no God for its worship, and is therefore utterly in vain. The West is continually producing mechanical power in excess of its spiritual control, and India has produced a system of mechanical control in excess of its vitality.

The Nation

The people are living beings. They have their distinct personalities. But nations are organizations of power, and therefore their inner aspects and outward expressions are everywhere monotonously the same. Their differences are merely differences in degree of efficiency.

In the modern world the fight is going on between the living spirit of the people and the methods of nation-organizing. It is like the struggle that began in Central Asia between cultivated areas of man's habitation and the continually encroaching desert sands, till the human region of life and beauty was choked out of existence. When the spread of higher ideals of humanity is not held to be important, the hardening method of national efficiency gains a certain strength; and for some limited period of time, at least, it proudly asserts itself as the fittest to survive. But it is the survival of that part of man which is the least living. And this is the reason why dead monotony is the sign of the spread of the Nation. The modern towns, which present the physiognomy due to this dominance of the Nation, are everywhere the same, from San Francisco to London, from London to Tokyo. They show no faces, but merely masks.

The peoples, being personalities, must have their self-expression, and this leads to their distinctive creations. These creations are literature, art, social symbols and ceremonials.

They are like different dishes at one common feast. They add richness to our enjoyment and understanding of truth. They are making the world of man fertile of life and variedly beautiful.

But the nations do not create, they merely produce and destroy. Organisations for production are necessary. Even organisations for destruction may be so. But when, actuated by greed and hatred, they crowd away into a corner the living man who creates, then the harmony is lost, and the people's history runs at a break-neck speed towards some fatal catastrophe.

Humanity, where it is living, is guided by inner ideals; but where it is a dead organisation it be comes impervious to them. Its building process is only an external process, and in its response to the moral guidance it has to pass through obstacles that are gross and non-plastic.

Man as a person has his individuality, which is the field where his spirit has its freedom to express itself and to grow. The professional man carries a rigid crust around him which has very little variation and hardly any elasticity. This professionalism is the region where men specialise their knowledge and organise their power, mercilessly elbowing each other in their struggle to come to the front. Professionalism is necessary, without doubt; but it must not be allowed to exceed its healthy limits, to assume complete mastery over the personal man, making him narrow and hard, exclusively intent upon pursuit of success at the cost of his faith in ideals.

In ancient India professions were kept within limits by social regulation. They were considered primarily as social necessities, and in the second place as the means of livelihood for individuals. Thus man, being free from the constant urging unbounded competition, could have leisure to cultivate his nature in its completeness.

The Cult of the National is the professionalism of the people. This cult is becoming their greatest danger, because it is bringing them enormous success, making them impatient of the claims of higher ideals. The grater the amount of success, the stronger are the conflicts of interest and jealousy and hatred which are aroused in men's minds, thereby making it more and more necessary for other peoples, who are still living, to stiffen into nations. With the growth of nationalism, man has become the greatest menace to man. Therefore the continual presence of panic goads that very nationalism into ever-increasing menace.

Crowd psychology is a blind force. Like steam and other physical forces, it can be utilized for creating a tremendous amount of power. And therefore rulers of men, who, out of greed and fear, are bent upon turning their peoples into machines of power, try to train this crowd psychology for their special purposes. They hold it to be their duty to foster in the popular mind universal panic, unreasoning pride in their own race, and hatred of others. Newspapers, school-books, and even religious services are made use of for this object; and those who have the courage to express their disapprobation of this blind and impious cult are either punished in the law-courts, or are socially ostracized. The individual thinks, even when he feels; but the same individual, where he feels with the crowd, does not reason at all. His moral sense becomes blurred. This suppression of higher humanity in crowd minds is productive of enormous strength. For the crowd mind is essentially primitive; its forces are elemental. Therefore the Nation is for ever watching to take advantage of this enormous power of darkness.

The people's instinct of self-preservation has been made dominant at particular times of crisis. Then, for the time being, the consciousness of its solidarity becomes aggressively wide-awake. But in the Nation this hyper-consciousness is kept alive for all time by artificial means. A man has to act the part of a policeman when he finds his house invaded by burglars. But if that remains his normal condition, then his consciousness of his household becomes acute and over-wrought, making him fly at every stranger passing near his house. This intensity of self-consciousness is nothing of which a man should feel proud; certainly it is not healthful. In like manner, incessant self-consciousness in a nation is highly injurious for the people. It serves its immediate purpose, but at the cost of the eternal in man.

When a whole body of men train themselves for a particular narrow purpose, it becomes a common interest with them to keep up that purpose and preach absolute loyalty to it. Nationalism is the training of a whole people for a narrow ideal; and when it gets hold of their minds it is sure to lead them to moral degeneracy and intellectual blindness. We cannot but hold firm the faith that this Age of Nationalism, of gigantic vanity and selfishness, is only a passing phase in civilization, and those who are making permanent arrangements for accommodating this temporary mood of history will be unable to fit themselves for the coming age, when the true spirit of freedom will have sway.

With the unchecked growth of Nationalism the moral foundation of man's civilisation is unconsciously undergoing a change. The ideal of the social man is unselfishness, but the ideal of the Nation, like that of the professional man, is, selfishness. This is why selfishness in the individual is condemned while in the nation it is extolled, which leads to hopeless moral blindness, confusing the religion of the people with the religion of the nation. Therefore, to take an example, we find men more and more convinced of the superior claims of Christianity, merely because Christian nations are in possession of the greater part of the world. It is like supporting a robber's religion by quoting the amount of his stolen property.

Nations celebrate their successful massacre of men in their churches. They forget that *Thugs* also ascribed their success in manslaughter to the favour of their goddess. But in the case of the latter their goddess frankly represented the principle of destruction. It was the criminal tribe's own murderous instinct deified—the instinct, not of one individual, but of the whole community, and therefore held sacred. In the same manner, in modern churches, selfishness, hatred and vanity in their collective aspect of national instincts do not scruple to share the homage paid to God.

Of course, pursuit of self-interest need not be wholly selfish; it can even be in harmony with the interest of all. Therefore, ideally speaking, the nationalism, which stands for the expression of the collective self-interest of a people, need not be ashamed of itself it is maintains its true limitations. But what we see in practice is, that every nation which has prospered has done so through its career of aggressive selfishness either in commercial adventures or in foreign possessions, or in both. And this material prosperity not only feeds continually the selfish instincts of the people, but impresses men's minds with the lesson that, for a nation, selfishness is a necessity and therefore a virtue. It is the emphasis laid in Europe upon the idea of the Nation's constant increase of power, which is becoming the greatest danger to man, both in its direct activity and its power of infection.

We must admit that evils there are in human nature, in spite of our faith in moral laws and our training in self-control. But they carry on their foreheads their own brand of infamy, their very success adding to their monstrosity. All through man's history there will be some who suffer, and others who cause suffering. The conquest of evil will never be a fully accomplished fact, but a continuous process like the process of burning in a flame.

In former ages, when some particular people became turbulent and tried to rob others of their human rights, they sometimes, achieved success and sometimes failed. And it amounted to nothing more than that. But when this idea of the Nation, which has met with universal acceptance in the present day, tries to pass off the cult of collective selfishness as a moral duty, simply because that selfishness is gigantic in stature, it not only commits depredation, but attacks the very vitals of humanity. It unconsciously generates in people's minds an attitude of defiance against moral law. For men are taught by repeated devices the lesson that the Nation is greater than the people, while yet it scatters to the wind the moral law that the people have held sacred.

It has been said that a disease becomes most acutely critical when the brain is affected. For it is the brain that is constantly directing the siege against all disease forces. The spirit of national selfishness is that brain disease of a people which shows itself in red eyes and clenched fists, in violence of talk and movements, all the while shattering its natural restorative powers. But the power of self-sacrifice, together with the moral faculty of sympathy and cooperation, is the guiding spirit of social vitality. Its function is to maintain a beneficent relation of harmony with its surroundings. But when it begins to ignore the moral law which is universal and uses it only within the bounds of its own narrow sphere, then its strength becomes like the strength of madness which ends in self-destruction.

What is worse, this aberration of a people, decked with the showy title of 'patriotism', proudly walks abroad, passing itself off as a highly moral influence. Thus it has spread its inflammatory contagion all over the world, proclaiming its fever flush to be the best sign of health. It is causing in the hearts of peoples, naturally inoffensive, a feeling of envy at not having their temperature as high as that of their delirious neighbours and not being able to cause as much mischief, but merely having to suffer from it.

I have often been asked by my Western friends how to cope with this evil, which has attained such sinister strength and vast dimensions. In fact, I have often been blamed for merely giving warning, and offering no alternative. When we suffer as a result of a particular system, we believe that some other system would bring us better luck. We are apt to forget that all systems produce evil sooner or later, when the psychology which is at the root of them is wrong. The system which is national to-day may assume the shape of the international tomorrow; but so long as men have not forsaken their idolatry of primitive instincts and collective passions, the new system will only become a new instrument of suffering. And because we are training to confound efficient system with moral goodness itself, every ruined system makes us more and more distrustful of moral law.

Therefore I do not put my faith in any new institution, but in the individuals all over the world who think clearly, feel nobly, and act rightly, thus becoming the channels of moral truth. Our moral ideals do not work with chisels and hammers. Like trees, they spread their roots in the soil and their branches in the sky, without consulting any architect for their plans.

Woman and Home

Creative expressions attain their perfect form through emotions modulated. Woman has that expression natural to her—a cadence of restraint in her behaviour, producing poetry of life. She has been an inspiration to man, guiding, most often unconsciously, his restless energy into an immense variety of creations in literature, art, music and religion. This is why, in India, woman has been described as the symbol of *Shakti*, the creative power.

But if woman begins to believe that, though biologically her function is different from that of man, psychologically she is identical with him; if the human world in its mentality becomes exclusively male, then before long it will be reduced to utter inanity. For life finds its truth and beauty, not in any exaggeration of sameness, but in harmony.

If woman's nature were identical with man's, if Eve were a mere tautology of Adam, it would only give rise to a monotonous superfluity. But that she was not so was proved by the banishment she secured from a ready-made Paradise. She had the instinctive wisdom to realize that it was her mission to help her mate in creating Paradise of their own on earth, whose ideal she was to supply with her life, whose materials were to be produced and gathered by her comrade.

However, it is evident than an increasing number of women in the West are ready to assert that their difference from men is unimportant. The reason for the vehement utterance of such a paradox cannot be ignored. It is rebellion against a necessity, which is not equal for both the partners

Love in all forms has its obligations, and the love that binds women to their children binds them to their homes. But necessity is a tyrant, making us submit to injury and indignity, allowing advantage over us to those who are wholly or comparatively free from its burden. Such has been the case in the social relationship between man and woman. Along with the difference inherent in their respective natures, there have grown up between them inequalities fostered by circumstances. Man is not handicapped by the same biological and psychological responsibilities as woman, and therefore he has the liberty to give her the security of home. This liberty exacts payment when it offers its boon, because to give or to withhold the gift is within its power. It is the unequal freedom in their mutual relationships which has made the weight of life's tragedies so painfully heavy for woman to bear.

Some mitigation of her disadvantage has been effected by her rendering herself and her home a luxury to man. She has accentuated those qualities in herself which insidiously impose their bondage over her mate, some by pandering to his weakness, and some by satisfying his higher nature, till the sex-consciousness in our society has grown abnormal and overpowering. There is no actual objection to this in itself, for it offers a stimulus, acting in the depth of life, which leads to creative exuberance. But a great deal of it is a forced growth of compulsion bearing seeds of degradation. In those ages when men acknowledged spiritual perfection to be their object, women were denounced as the chief obstacle in their way. The constant and conscious exercise of allurements, which gave women their power, attacked the weak spots in man's nature, and doing so added to its weakness. For all relationships tainted with repression of freedom must become sources of degeneracy to the strong who impose such repression.

Balance of power, however, between man and woman was in a measure established when home wielded a strong enough attraction to make men accept its obligations. But at last the time has come when the material ambition of man has assumed such colossal proportions that home is in danger of losing its center of gravity for him, and he is receding farther and farther from its orbit.

The arid zone in the social life is spreading fast. The simple comforts of home, made precious by the touch of love, are giving way to luxuries that can only have their full extension in the isolation of self-centred life. Hotels are being erected on the ruins of homes; productions are growing more stupendous than creations; and most men have, for the materials of their happiness and recreation, their dogs and horses, their pipes, guns, and gambling clubs.

Reactions and rebellions, not being normal in their character, go on hurting truth until peace is restored. Therefore, when woman refuses to acknowledge the distinction between her life and that of man, she does not convince us of its truth, but only proves to us that she is suffering. All great suffering indicate some wrong somewhere. In the present case, the wrong is in woman's lack of freedom in her relationship with man, which compels her to turn her disabilities into attractions, and to use untruths as her allies in the battle of life, while she is suffering from the precariousness of her position.

From the beginning of our society, women have naturally accepted the training which imparts to their life and to their home a spirit of harmony. It is their instinct to perform their services in such a manner that these, through beauty, might be raised from the domain of slavery to the realm of grace.

Women have tried to prove that in the building up of social life they are artists and not artisans. But all expressions of beauty lose their truth when compelled to accept the patronage of the gross and the indifferent. Therefore when necessity drives women to fashion their lives to the taste of the insensitive or the sensual, then the whole thing becomes a tragedy of desecration. Society is full of such tragedies. Many of the laws and social regulations guiding the relationships of man and woman are relics of a barbaric age, when the brutal pride of an exclusive possession had its dominance in human relations, such as those of parents and children, husbands and wives, masters and servants, teachers and disciples. The vulgarity of it still persists in the social bond between the sexes because of the economic helplessness of woman. Nothing makes us so stupidly mean as the sense of superiority which the power of the purse confers upon us.

The powers of muscle and of money have opportunities of immediate satisfaction, but the power of the ideal must have infinite patience. The man who sells his goods, or fulfils his contract, is cheated if he fails to realise payment, but he who gives form to some ideal may never get his due and be fully paid. What I have felt in the women of India is the consciousness of this ideal—their simple faith in the sanctity of devotion lighted by love which is held to be divine. True womanliness is regarded in our country as the saintliness of love. It is not merely praised there, but literally worshipped; and she who is gifted with it is called *Devi,* as one revealing in herself Woman, the Divine. That this has not been a mere metaphor to us is because, in India, our mind is familiar with the idea of God in an eternal feminine aspect. Thus the Eastern woman, who is deeply aware in her heart of the sacredness of her mission, is a constant education to man. It has to be admitted that there are chances of such an influence failing to penetrate the callousness of the coarse-minded; but that is the destiny of all manifestations whose value is not in success or reward in honour.

Woman has to be ready to suffer. She cannot allow her emotions to be dulled or polluted, for these are to create her life's atmosphere, apart from which her world would be dark and dead. This leaves her heart without any protection of insensibility, at the mercy of the hurts and insults of life. Women of India, like women everywhere, have their share of suffering, but it radiates through the ideal, and becomes, like sunlight, a creative force in their world. Our women know by heart the legends of the great women of the epic age—Savitri who by the power of love conquered death, and Sita who had no other reward for her life of sacrifice but the sacred majesty of sorrow. They know that it is their duty to make this life an image of the life eternal, and that love's mission truly performed has a spiritual meaning. It is a religious responsibility for them to live the life which is their own. For their activity is not for money-making, or organising power, or intellectually probing the mystery of existence, but for establishing and maintaining human relationships requiring the highest moral qualities. It is the consciousness of the spiritual character of their life's work, which lifts them above the utilitarian standard of the immediate and the passing, surrounds them with the dignity of the eternal, and transmutes their suffering and sorrow into a crown of light.

I must guard myself from the risk of a possible misunderstanding. The permanent significance of home is not in the narrowness of its enclosure, but in an eternal moral idea. It represents the truth of human relationship; it reveals loyalty and love for the personality of man. Let us take a wider view, in a perspective truer than can be found in its present conventional associations. With the discovery and development of agriculture there came a period of settled life in our history. The nomad ever moved on with his tents and cattle; he explored space and exploited its contents. The cultivator of land explored time in its immensity, for he had leisure. Comparatively secured from the uncertainty of his outer resources, he had the opportunity to deal with his moral resources in the realm of human truth. This is why agricultural civilisation, like that of India and China, is essentially a civilisation of human relationship, of the adjustment of mutual obligations. It is deep-rooted in the inner life of man. Its basis is co-operation and not competition. In other words, its principle is the principle of home, to which all its outer adventures are subordinated.

In the meanwhile, the nomadic life with its predatory instinct of exploitation has developed into a great civilisation. It is immensely proud and strong, killing leisure and pursuing opportunities. It minimises the claims of personal relationship and is jealously careful of its unhampered freedom for acquiring wealth and asserting its will upon others. Its burden is the burden of things, which grows heavier and more complex every day, disregarding the human and the spiritual. Its powerful pressure from all sides narrows the limits of home, the personal region of the human world. Thus, in this region of life, women are every day hustled out of their shelter for want of accommodation.

But such as state of things can never have the effect of changing woman into man. On the contrary, it will lead her to find her place in the unlimited range of society, and the Guardian Spirit of the personal in human nature will extend the ministry of woman over all developments of life. Habituated to deal with the world as machine, man is multiplying his materials, banishing away his happiness and sacrificing love to comfort, which is an illusion. At last the present age has sent its cry to women, asking her to come out from her segregation in order to restore the spiritual supremacy of all that is human in the world of humanity.

She has been aroused to remember that womanliness is not chiefly decorative. It is like that vital health, which not only imparts the bloom of beauty to the body, but joy to the mind and perfection to life.

An Eastern University

In the midst of much that is discouraging in the present state of the world, there is one symptom of vital promise. Asia is awakening. This great event, if it be but directed along the right lines, is full of hope, not only for Asia herself, but for the whole world.

On the other hand, it has to be admitted that the relationship of the West with the East, growing more and more complex and widespread for over two centuries, far from attaining its true fulfillment, has given rise to a universal spirit of conflict. The consequent strain and unrest have profoundly disturbed Asia, and antipathetic forces have been accumulating for years in the depth of the Eastern mind.

The meeting of the East and the West has remained incomplete, because the occasions of it have not been disinterested. The political and commercial adventures carried on by Western races—very often by force and against the interest and wishes of the countries they have dealt with—have created a moral alienation, which is deeply injurious to both parties. The perils threatened by this unnatural relationship have long been contemptuously ignored by the West. But the blind confidence of the strong in their apparent invincibility has often led them, from their dream of security, into terrible surprises of history.

It is not the fear of danger or loss to one people or another, however, which is most important. The demoralising influence of the constant estrangement between the two hemispheres, which affects the baser passions of man,—pride, greed and hypocrisy on the one hand; fear, suspiciousness and flattery on the other,—has been developing, and threatens us with a world-wide spiritual disaster.

The time has come when we must use all our wisdom to understand the situation, and to control it, with a stronger trust in moral guidance than in any array of physical forces.

In the beginning of man's history his first social object was to form a community, to grow into a people. At that early period, individuals were gathered together within geographical enclosures. But in the present age, with its facility of communication, geographical barriers have almost lost their reality, and the great federation of men, which is waiting either to find its true scope or to break asunder in a final catastrophe, is not a meeting of individuals, but of various human races. Now the problem before us is of one single country, which is this earth, where the races as individuals must find both their freedom of self-expression and their bond of federation. Mankind must realise a unity, wider in range, deeper in sentiment, stronger in power than ever before. Now that the problem is large, we have to solve it on a bigger scale, to realise the God in man by a larger faith and to build the temple of our faith on a sure and world-wide basis.

The first step towards realisation is to create opportunities for revealing the different peoples to one another. This can never be done in those fields where the exploiting utilitarian spirit is supreme. We must find some meeting-ground, where there can be no question of conflicting interests. One of such places is the University, where we can work together in a common pursuit of truth, share together our common heritage, and realise that artists in all parts of the world have created forms of beauty, scientists discovered secrets of the universe, philosophers solved the problems of existence, saints made the truth of the spiritual world organic in their own lives, not merely for some particular race to which they belonged, but for all mankind. When the science of meteorology knows the earth's atmosphere as continuously one, affecting the different parts of the world differently, but in a harmony of adjustments, it knows and attains truth. And so, too, we must know that the great mind of man is one, working through the many differences which are needed to ensure the full result of its fundamental unity. When we understand this truth in a disinterested spirit, it teaches us to respect all the differences in man that are real, yet remain conscious of our oneness; and to know that perfection of unity is not in uniformity, but in harmony.

This is the problem of the present age. The East, for its own sake and for the sake of the world, must not remain unrevealed. The deepest source of all calamities in history is misunderstanding. For where we do not understand, we can never be just.

Being strongly impressed with the need and the responsibility, which every individual to-day must realise according to his power, I have formed the nucleus of an International University in India, as one of the best means of promoting mutual understanding between the East and the West. This Institution, according to the plan I have in mind, will invite students from the West to study the different systems of Indian philosophy, literature, art and music in their proper environment, encouraging them to carry on research work in collaboration with the scholars already engaged in this task.

India has her renaissance. She is preparing to make her contribution to the world of the future. In the past she produced her great culture, and in the present age she has an equally important contribution to make to the culture of the New World which is emerging from the wreckage of the Old. This is a momentous period of her history pregnant with precious possibilities, when any disinterested offer of co-operation from any part of the West will have an immense moral value, the memory of which will become brighter as the regeneration of the East grows in vigour and creative power.

The Western Universities give their students an opportunity to learn what all the European peoples have contributed to their Western culture. Thus the intellectual mind of the West has been luminously revealed to the world. What is needed to complete this illumination is for the East to collect its own scattered lamps and offer them to the enlightenment of the world.

There was a time when the great countries of Asia had, each of them, to nurture its own civilisation apart in comparative seclusion. Now has come the age of co-ordination and co-operation. The seedlings that were reared within narrow plots must now be transplanted into the open fields. They must pass the test of the world-market, if their maximum value is to be obtained.

But before Asia is in a position to co-operate with the culture of Europe, she must base her own structure on a synthesis of all the different cultures which she has. When, taking her stand on such a culture, she turns toward the West, she will take, with a confident sense of mental freedom, her own view of truth, from her own vantage-ground, and open a new vista of thought to the world. Otherwise, she will allow her priceless inheritance to crumble into dust, and, trying to replace it clumsily with feeble imitations of the West, make herself superfluous, cheap and ludicrous. If she thus loses her individuality and her specific power to exist, will it in the least help the rest of the world? Will not her terrible bankruptcy involve also the Western mind? If the whole world grows at last into an exaggerated West, then such an illimitable parody of the modern age will die, crushed beneath its own absurdity.

In this belief, it is my desire to extend by degrees the scope of this University on simple lines, until it comprehends the whole range of Eastern cultures—the Aryan, Semitic, Mongolian and others. Its object will be to reveal the Eastern mind to the world.

Of one thing I felt certain during my travels in Europe, that a genuine interest has been roused there in the philosophy and the arts of the East, from which the Western mind seeks fresh inspiration of truth and beauty. Once the East had her reputation of fabulous wealth, and the seekers were attracted from across the sea. Since then, the shrine of wealth has changed its site. But the East is famed also for her storage of wisdom, harvested by her patriarchs from long successive ages of spiritual endeavour. And when, as now, in the midst of the pursuit of power and wealth, there rises the cry of privation from the famished spirit of man, an opportunity is offered to the East, to offer her store to those who need it.

Once upon a time we were in possession of such a thing as our own mind in India. It was living. It thought, it felt, it expressed itself. It was receptive as well as productive. That this mind could be of any use in the process, or in the end, of our education was overlooked by our modern educational dispensation. We are provided with buildings and books and other magnificent burdens calculated to suppress our mind. The latter was treated like a library-shelf solidly made of wood, to be loaded with leather-bound volumes of second-hand information. In consequence, it has lost its own colour and characters, and has borrowed polish from the carpenter's shop. All this has cost us money, and also our finer ideas, while our intellectual vacancy has been crammed with what is described in official reports as Education. In fact, we have bought our spectacles at the expense of our eyesight.

In India our goddess of learning is *Saraswati*. My audience in the West, I am sure, will be glad to know that her complexion is white. But the signal fact is that she is living and she is a woman, and her seat is on a lotus-flower. The symbolic meaning of this is, that she dwells in the centre of life and the heart of all existence, which opens itself in beauty to the light of heaven.

The Western education which we have chanced to know is impersonal. Its complexion is also white, but it is the whiteness of the white-washed classroom walls. It dwells in the cold-storage compartments of lessons and the ice-packed minds of the schoolmasters. The effect which it had on my mind when, as a boy, I was compelled to go to school, I have described elsewhere. My feeling was very much the same as a tree might have, which was not allowed to live its full life, but was cut down to be made into packing-cases.

The introduction of this education was not a part of the solemn marriage ceremony which was to unite the minds of the East and West in mutual understanding. It represented an artificial method of training specially calculated to produce the carriers of the white man's burden. This want of ideals still clings to our education system, though our Universities have latterly burdened their syllabus with a greater number of subjects than before. But it is only like adding to the bags of wheat the bullock carries to market; it does not make the bullock any better off.

Mind, when long deprived of it natural food of truth and freedom of growth, develops an unnatural craving for success; and our students have fallen victims to the mania for success in examinations. Success consists in obtaining the largest number of marks with the strictest economy of knowledge. It is a deliberate cultivation of disloyalty to truth, of intellectual dishonesty, of a foolish imposition by which the mind is encouraged to rob itself. But as we are by means of it made to forget the existence of mind, we are supremely happy at the result. We pass examinations, and shrivel up into clerks, lawyers and police inspectors, and we die young.

Universities should never be made into mechanical organisations for collecting and distributing knowledge. Through them the people should offer their intellectual hospitality, their wealth of mind to others, and earn their proud right in return to receive gifts from the rest of the world. But in the whole length and breadth of India there is not a single University established in the modern time where a foreign or an Indian student can properly be acquainted with the best products of the Indian mind. For that we have to cross the sea, and knock at the doors of France and Germany. Educational institutions in our country are India's alms-bowl of knowledge; they lower our intellectual self-respect; they encourage us to make a foolish display of decorations composed of borrowed feathers.

This it was that led me to found a school in Bengal, in face of many difficulties and discouragements, and in spite of my own vocation as a poet, who finds this true inspiration only when he forgets that he is a schoolmaster. It is my hope that in this school a nucleus has been formed, round which an indigenous University of our own land will find its natural growth—a University which will help India's mind to concentrate and to be fully conscious of itself; free to seek the truth and make this truth its own wherever found, to judge by its own standard, give expression to its own creative genius, and offer its wisdom to the guests who come from other parts of the world.

Man's intellect has a natural pride in is own aristocracy, which is the pride of its culture. Culture only acknowledges the excellence whose criticism is in its inner perfection, not in any external success. When this pride succumbs to some compulsion of necessity or lure of material advantage, it brings humiliation to the intellectual man. Modern India, through her very education, has been made to suffer this humiliation. Once she herself provided her children with a culture which was the product of her own ages of thought and creation. But it has been thrust aside, and we are made to tread the mill of passing examinations, not for learning anything, but for notifying that we are qualified for employments under organisations conducted in English. Our educated community is not a cultured community, but a community of qualified candidates. Meanwhile the proportion of possible employments to the number of claimants has gradually been growing narrower, and the consequent disaffection has been widespread. At last the very authorities who are responsible for this are blaming their victims. Such is the perversity of human nature. It bears its worst grudge against those it has injured.

It is as if some tribe which had the primitive habit of decorating its tribal members with birds' plumages were some day to hold these very birds guilty of the crime of being extinct. There are belated attempts on the part of our governors to read us pious homilies about disinterested love of learning, while the old machinery goes on working, whose product is not education but certificates. It is good to remind the fettered bird that its wings are for soaring; but it is better to cut the chain which is holding it to its perch. The most pathetic feature of the tragedy is that the bird itself has learnt to use its chain for its ornament, simply because the chain jingles in fairly respectable English.

In the Bengali language there is a modern maxim which can be translated, 'He who learns to read and write rides in a carriage and pair.' In English there is a similar proverb, 'Knowledge is power.' It is an offer of a prospective bribe to the student, a promise of an ulterior reward which is more important than knowledge itself. Temptations, held before us as inducements to be good or to pursue uncongenial paths, are most often flimsy lies or half-truths, such as the oft-quoted maxim of respectable piety, 'Honesty is the best policy,' at which politicians all over the world seem to laugh in their sleeves. But unfortunately, education conducted under a special providence of purposefulness, of eating the fruit of knowledge from the wrong end, *does* lead one to that special paradise on earth, the daily rides in one's own carriage and pair. And the West, I have heard from authentic sources, is aspiring in its education after that special cultivation of worldliness.

Where society is comparatively simple and obstructions are not too numerous, we can clearly see how the life-process guides education in its vital purpose. The system of folk-education, which is indigenous to India, but is dying out, was one with the people's life. It flowed naturally through the social channels and made its way everywhere. It is a system of widespread irrigation of culture. Its teachers, specially trained men, are in constant requisition, and find crowded meetings in our villages, where they repeat the best thoughts and express the ideals of the land in the most effective form. The mode of instruction includes the recitation of epics, expounding of the scriptures, reading from the Puranas, which are the classical records of old history, performance of plays founded upon the early myths and legends, dramatic narration of the lives of ancient heroes, and the singing in chorus of songs from the old religious literature. Evidently, according to this system, the best function of education is to enable us to realise that to live as a man is great, requiring profound philosophy for its ideal, poetry for its expression, and heroism in its conduct. Owing to this vital method of culture the common people of India, though technically illiterate, have been made conscious of the sanctity of social relationships, entailing constant sacrifice and self-control, urged and supported by ideals collectively expressed in one word, *Dharma*.

Such a system of education my sound too simple for the complexities of modern life. But the fundamental principle of social life in its different stages of development remains the same; and in no circumstance can the truth be ignored that all human complexities must harmonise in organic unity with life, failing which there will be endless conflict. Most things in the civilised world occupy more than their legitimate space. Much of their burden is needless. By bearing this burden civilised man may be showing great strength, but he displays little skill. To the gods, viewing this from on high, it must seem like the flounderings of a giant who has got out of his depth and knows not how to swim.

The main source of all forms of voluntary slavery is the desire of gain. It is difficult to fight against this when modern civilisation is tainted with such a universal contamination of avarice. I have realised it myself in the little boys of my own school. For the first few years there is no trouble. But as soon as the upper class is reached, their worldly wisdom—the malady of the aged—begins to assert itself. They rebelliously insist that they must no longer learn, but rather pass examinations. Professions in the modern age are more numerous and lucrative than ever before. They need specialisation of training and knowledge, tempting education to yield its spiritual freedom to the claims of utilitarian ambitions. But man's deeper nature is hurt; his smothered life seeks to be liberated from the suffocating folds and sensual ties of prosperity. And this is why we find almost everywhere in the world a growing dissatisfaction with the prevalent system of teaching, which betrays the encroachment of senility and worldly prudence over pure intellect.

In India, also, a vague feeling of discontent has given rise to numerous attempts at establishing national schools and colleges, but, unfortunately, our very education has been successful in depriving us of our real initiative and our courage of thought. The training we get in our schools has the constant implication in it that it is not for us to produce but to borrow. And we are casting about to borrow our educational plans from European institutions. The trampled plants of Indian corn are dreaming of recouping their harvest from the neighbouring wheat fields. To change the figure, we forget that, for proficiency in walking, it is better to train the muscles of our own legs than to strut upon wooden ones of foreign make, although they clatter and cause more surprise at our skill in using them than if they were living and real.

But when we go to borrow help from a foreign neighbourhood we are apt to overlook the real source of help behind all that is external and apparent. Had the deep-water fishes happened to produce a scientist who chose the jumping of a monkey for his research work, I am sure he would give most of the credit to the branches of the trees and very little to the monkey itself. In a foreign University we see the branching wildernesses of its buildings, furniture, regulations, and syllabus, but the monkey, which is a difficult creature to catch and more difficult to manufacture, we are likely to treat as a mere accident of minor importance. It is convenient for us to overlook the fact that among the Europeans the living spirit of the University is widely spread in their society, their parliament, their literature, and the numerous activities of their corporate life. In all these functions they are in perpetual touch with the great personality of the land which is creative and heroic in its constant acts of self-expression and self-sacrifice. They have their thoughts published in their books as well as through the medium of living men who think those thoughts, and who criticise, compare and disseminate them. Some at least of the drawbacks of their academic education are redeemed by the living energy of the intellectual personality pervading their social organism. It is like the stagnant reservoir of water which finds its purification in the showers of rain to which it keeps itself open. But, to our misfortune, we have in India all the furniture of the European University except the human teacher. We have, instead, mere purveyors of book-lore in whom the paper god of the bookshop has been made vocal.

A most important truth, which we are apt to forget, is that a teacher can never truly teach unless he is still learning himself. A lamp can never light another lamp unless it continues to burn its own flame. The teacher who has come to the end of his subject, who has no living traffic with his knowledge, but merely repeats his lessons to his students, can only load their minds; he cannot quicken them. Truth not only must inform but inspire. If the inspiration dies out, and the information only accumulates, then truth loses its infinity. The greater part of our learning in the schools has been wasted because, for most of our teachers, their subjects are like dead specimens of once living things, with which they have a learned acquaintance, but no communication of life and love.

The educational institution, therefore, which I have in mind has primarily for its object the constant pursuit of truth, from which the imparting of truth naturally follows. It must not be a dead cage in which living minds are fed with food artificially prepared. It should be an open house, in which students and teachers are at one. They must live their complete life together, dominated by a common aspiration for truth and a need of sharing all the delights of culture. In former days the great master-craftsmen had students in their workshops where they co-operated in shaping things to perfection. That was the place where knowledge could become living—that knowledge which not only has its substance and law, but its atmosphere subtly informed by a creative art, in which the man who explores truth expresses something which is human in him—his enthusiasm, his courage, his sacrifice, his honesty, and his skill. In merely academical teaching we find subjects, but not the man who pursues the subjects; therefore the vital part of education remains incomplete.

For our Universities we must claim, not labelled packages of truth and authorised agents to distribute them, but truth in its living association with her lovers and seekers and discoverers. Also we must know that the concentration of the mind-forces scattered throughout the country is the most important mission of a University, which, like the nucleus of a living cell, should be the centre of the intellectual life of the people.

The bringing about of an intellectual unity in India is, I am told, difficult to the verge of impossibility owing to the fact that India has so many different languages. Such a statement is as unreasonable as to say that man, because he has a diversity of limbs, should find it impossible to realise life's unity in himself, and that only an earthworm composed of a tail and nothing else could truly know that it had a body.

Let us admit that India is not like any one of the great countries of Europe, which has its own separate language; but is rather like Europe herself, branching out into different peoples with many different languages. And yet Europe has a common civilisation, with an intellectual unity which is not based upon uniformity of language. It is true that in the earlier stages of her culture the whole of Europe had Latin for her learned tongue. That was in her intellectual budding time, when all her petals of self-expression were closed in one point. But the perfection of her mental unfolding was not represented by the singularity of her literary vehicle. When the grate European countries found their individual languages, then only the true federation of cultures became possible in the West, and the very differences of the channels made the commerce of ideas in Europe so richly copious and so variedly active. We can well imagine what the loss to European civilisation would be if France, Italy and Germany, and England herself, had not through their separate agencies contributed to the common coffer their individual earnings.

There was a time with us when India had her common language of culture in Sanskrit. But, for the complete commerce of her thought, she required that all her vernaculars should attain their perfect powers, through which her different peoples might manifest their idiosyncrasies; and this could never be done through a foreign tongue.

In the United States, in Canada and other British Colonies, the language of the people is English. It has a great literature which had its birth and growth in the history of the British Islands. But when this language, with all its products and acquisitions, matured by ages on its own mother soil, is carried into foreign lands, which have their own separate history and their own life-growth, it must constantly hamper the indigenous growth of culture and destroy individuality of judgement and the perfect freedom of self-expression. The inherited wealth of the English language, with all its splendour, becomes an impediment when taken into different surroundings, just as when lungs are given to the whale in the sea. If such is the case even with races whose grandmother-tongue naturally continues to be their own mother-tongue, one can imagine what sterility it means for a people which accepts, for its vehicle of culture, an altogether foreign language. A language is not like an umbrella or an overcoat, that can be borrowed by unconscious or deliberate mistake; it is like the living skin itself. If the body of a draught-horse enters into the skin of a race-horse, it will be safe to wager that such an anomaly will never win a race, and will fail even to drag a cart. Have we not watched some modern Japanese artists imitating European art? The imitation may sometimes produce clever results; but such cleverness has only the perfection of artificial flowers which never bear fruit.

All great countries have their vital centres for intellectual life, where a high standard of learning is maintained, where the minds of the people are naturally attracted, where they find their genial atmosphere, in which to prove their worth and to contribute their share to the country's culture. Thus they kindle, on the common altar of the land, that great sacrificial fire which can radiate the sacred light of wisdom abroad.

Athens was such a centre in Greece, Rome in Italy; and Paris is such today in France. Benares has been and still continues to be the centre of our Sanskrit culture. But Sanskrit learning does not exhaust all the elements of culture that exist in modern India.

If we were to take for granted, what some people maintain, that Western culture is the only source of light for our mind, then it would be like depending for daybreak upon some star, which is the sun of a far distant sphere. The star may give us light, but not the day; it may give us direction in our voyage of exploration, but it can never open the full view of truth before our eyes. In fact, we can never use this cold starlight for stirring the sap in our branches, and giving colour and bloom to our life. This is the reason why European education has become for India mere school lessons and no culture; a box of matches, good for the small uses of illumination, but not the light of morning, in which the use and beauty, and all the subtle mysteries of life are blended in one.

Let me say clearly that I have no distrust of any culture because of its foreign character. On the contrary, I believe that the shock of such extraneous forces is necessary for the vitality of our intellectual nature. It is admitted that much of the spirit of Christianity runs counter, not only to the classical culture of Europe, but to the European temperament altogether.

And yet this alien movement of ideas, constantly running against the natural mental current of Europe, has been a most important factor in strengthening and enriching her civilisation, on account of the sharp antagonism of its intellectual direction. In fact, the European vernaculars first woke up to life and fruitful vigour when they felt the impact of this foreign thought-power with all its oriental forms and affinities. The same thing is happening in India. The European culture has come to us, not only with its knowledge, but with its velocity.

Then, again, let us admit that modern Science is Europe's great gift to humanity for all time to come. We, in India, must claim it from her hands, and gratefully accept it in order to be saved from the curse of futility by lagging behind. We shall fail to reap the harvest of the present age if we delay.

What I object to is the artificial arrangement by which foreign education tends to occupy all the space of out national mind, and thus kills, or hampers, the great opportunity for the creation of a new thought-power by a new combination of truths. It is this which makes me urge that all the elements in our own culture have to be strengthened, not to resist the Western culture, but truly to accept and assimilate it; to use it for our sustenance, not as our burden; to get mastery over this culture, and not to live on its outskirts as the hewers of texts and drawers of book-learning.

The main river in Indian culture has flowed in four streams,—the Vedic, the Puranic, the Buddhist, and the Jain. It has its source in the heights of the Indian consciousness. But a river, belonging to a country, is not fed by its own waters alone. The Tibetan Brahmaputra is a tributary to the Indian Ganges. Contributions have similarly found their way to India's original culture. The Muhammadan, for example, has repeatedly come into India's original culture. The Muhammadan, for example, has repeatedly come into India from outside, laden with his own stores of knowledge and feeling and his wonderful religious democracy, bringing freshet after freshet to swell the current. To our music, our architecture, our pictorial art, our literature, the Muhammadans have made their permanent and precious contribution. Those who have studied the lives and writings of our medieval saints, and all the great religious movements that sprang up in the time of the Muhammadan rule, know how deep is our debt to this foreign current that has so intimately mingled with our life.

So, in our centre of Indian learning, we must provide for the co-ordinate study of all these different cultures,—the Vedic, the Puranic, the Buddhist, the Jain, the Islamic, the Sikh and the Zoroastrian. The Chinese, Japanese, and Tibetan will also have to be added; for, in the past, India did not remain isolated within her own boundaries. Therefore, in order to learn what she was, in her relation to the whole continent of Asia, these cultures too must be studied. Side by side with them must finally be placed the Western culture. For only then shall we be able to assimilate this last contribution to our common stock. A river flowing within banks is truly our own, and it can contain its due tributaries; but our relations with a flood can only prove disastrous.

There are some who are exclusively modern, who believe that the past is the bankrupt time, leaving no assets for us, but only a legacy of debts. They refuse to believe that the army which is marching forward can be fed from the rear. It is well to remind such persons that the great ages of renaissance in history were those when man suddenly discovered the seeds of thought in the granary of the past.

The unfortunate people who have lost the harvest of their past have lost their present age. They have missed their seed for cultivation, and go begging for their bare livelihood. We must not imagine that we are one of these disinherited peoples of the world. The time has come for us to break open the treasure-trove of our ancestors, and use it for our commerce of life. Let us, with its help, make our future our own, and not continue our existence as the eternal rag-pickers in other people's dustbins.

So far I have dwelt only upon the intellectual aspect of Education. For, even in the West, it is the intellectual training which receives almost exclusive emphasis. The Western universities have not yet truly recognized that fulness of life. And a large part of man can never find its expression in the mere language of words. It must therefore seek for its other languages,—lines and colours, sounds and movements. Through our mastery of these we not only make our whole nature articulate, but also understand man in all his attempts to reveal his innermost being in every age and clime. The great use of Education is not merely to collect facts, but to know man and to make oneself known to man. It is the duty of every human being to master, at least to some extent, not only the language of intellect, but also that personality which is the language of Art. It is a great world of reality for man,—vast and profound,—this growing world of his own creative nature. This is the world of Art. To be brought up in ignorance of it is to be deprived of the knowledge and use of that great inheritance of humanity, which has been growing and waiting for every one of us from the beginning of our history. It is to remain deaf to the eternal voice of Man, that speaks to all men the messages that are beyond speech. From the educational point of view we know Europe where it is scientific, or at best literary. So our notion of its modern culture is limited within the boundary lines of grammar and the laboratory. We almost completely ignore the aesthetic life of man, leaving it uncultivated, allowing weeds to grow there. Our newspapers are prolific, our meeting-places are vociferous; and in them we wear to shreds the things we have borrowed from our English teachers. We make the air dismal and damp with the tears of our grievances. But where are our arts, which, like the outbreak of spring flowers, are the spontaneous overflow of our deeper nature and spiritual magnificence?

Through this great deficiency of our modern education, we are condemned to carry to the end a dead load of dumb wisdom. Like miserable outcasts, we are deprived of our place in the festival of culture, and wait at the outer court, where the colours are not for us, nor the forms of delight, nor the songs. Ours is the education of a prison-house, with hard labour and with a drab dress cut to the limits of minimum decency and necessity. We are made to forget that the perfection of colour and form and expression belongs to the perfection of vitality,—that the joy of life is only the other side of the strength of life. The timber merchant may think that the flowers and foliage are mere frivolous decorations of a tree; but if these are suppressed, he will know to his cost that the timber too will fail.

During the Moghal period, music and art in India found a great impetus from the rulers, because their whole life— not merely their official life—was lived in this land; and it is the wholeness of life from which originates Art. But our English teachers are birds of passage; they cackle to us, but do not sing,—their true heart is not in the land of their exile.

Construction of life, owing to this narrowness of culture, must no longer be encouraged. In the centre of Indian culture which I am proposing, music and art must have their prominent seats of honour, and not be given merely a tolerant nod of recognition. The different systems of music and different schools of art which lie scattered in the different ages and provinces of India, and in the different strata of society, and also those belonging to the other great countries of Asia, which had communication with India, have to be brought there together and studied.

I have already hinted that Education should not be dragged out of its native element, the life-current of the people.

Economic life covers the whole width of the fundamental basis of society, because its necessities are the simplest and the most universal. Educational institutions, in order to obtain their fulness of truth, must have close association with this economic life. The highest mission of education is to help us to realise the inner principle of the unity of all knowledge and all the activities of our social and spiritual being. Society in its early stage was held together by its economic co-operation, when all its members felt in unison a natural interest in their right to live. Civilisation could never been started at all if such was not the case. And civilisation will fall to pieces if it never again realises the spirit of mutual help and the common sharing of benefits in the elemental necessaries of life. The idea of such economic co-operation should be made the basis of our University. It must not only instruct, but live; not only think, but produce.

Our ancient *tapovanas*, or forest schools, which were our natural universities, were not shut off from the daily life of the people. Masters and students gathered fruit and fuel, and took their cattle out to graze, supporting themselves by the work of their own hands. Spiritual education was a part of the spiritual life itself, which comprehended all life. Out centre of culture should not only be the centre of the intellectual life of India, but the centre of her economic life also. I must co-operate with the villages round it, cultivate land, breed cattle, spin cloths, press oil from oil from oil-seeds; it must produce all the necessaries, devising the best means, using the best materials, and calling science to its aid. Its very existence should depend upon the success of its industrial activities carried out on the co-operative principle, which will unite the teachers and students and villagers of the neighbourhood in a living and active bond of necessity. This will give us also a practical industrial training, whose motive force is not the greed of profit.

Before I conclude my paper, a delicate question remains to be considered. What must be the religious ideal that is to rule our centre of Indian culture? The one abiding ideal in the religious life of India has been *mukti*, the deliverance of man's soul from the grip of self, its communion with the Infinite Soul through its union in *ânanda* with the universe. This religion of spiritual harmony is not a theological doctrine to be taught, as a subject in the class, for half an hour each day. It is the spiritual truth and beauty of our attitude towards our surroundings, our conscious relationship with the Infinite, and the lasting power of the Eternal in the passing moments of our life. Such a religious ideal can only be made possible by making provision for students to live in intimate touch with nature, daily to grow in an atmosphere of service offered to all creatures, tending trees, feeding birds and animals, learning to feel the immense mystery of the soil and mater and air.

Along with this, there should be some common sharing of life with the tillers of the soil and the humble workers in the neighbouring villages; studying their crafts, inviting them to the feasts, joining them in works of co-operation for communal welfare; and in our intercourse we should be guided, not by moral maxims or the condescension of social superiority, but by natural sympathy of life for life, and by the sheer necessity of love's sacrifice for its own sake. In such an atmosphere students would learn to understand that humanity is a divine harp of many strings, waiting for its one grand music. Those who realise this unity are made ready for the pilgrimage through the night of suffering, and along the path of sacrifice, to the great meeting of Man in the future, for which the call comes to us across the darkness.

Life, in such a centre, should be simple and clean. We should never believe that simplicity of life might make us unsuited to the requirements of the society of our time. It is the simplicity of the tuning-fork, which is needed all the more because of the intricacy of strings in the instrument. In the morning of our career our nature needs the pure and the perfect note of a spiritual ideal in order to fit us for the complications of our later years.

In other words, this institution should be a perpetual creation by the co-operative enthusiasm of teachers and students, growing with the growth of their soul; a world in itself, self-sustaining, independent, rich with ever-renewing life radiating life across space and time, attracting and maintaining round it a planetary system of dependent bodies. Its aim should lie in imparting life-breath to the complete man, who is intellectual as well as economic, bound by social bonds, but aspiring towards spiritual freedom and final perfection.

GORA

My thanks are due to Mr. Surendanath Tagore, who very kindly made the final corrections and revisions for this translation. Any merits it possesses are due to his painstaking efforts to rectify my mistakes.—TRANSLATOR.

ONE

It was the rainy season in Calcutta; the morning clouds had scattered, and the sky overflowed with clear sunlight.

Binoy-bhusan was standing alone on the upper verandah of his house, watching in leisurely idleness the constant ebb and flow of the passers-by. He had finished his college course some time before, but had not yet started any regular work. He had written a little for the papers, it is true, and had organised meetings,—but this had not satisfied his mind. And now, this morning, for want of anything in particular to do, he was beginning to feel restless.

In front of the shop opposite, a Bāul mendicant was standing, dressed in the motley robe of those wandering minstrels, and singing:

> Into the cage flies the unknown bird,
>   It comes I know not whence.
> Powerless my mind to chain its feet,
>   It goes I know not where.

Binoy felt that he would like to call the Bāul upstairs and take down this song about the unknown bird. But, just as in the middle of the night, when it turns suddenly cold, it is too much exertion to reach for an extra blanket, so the Bāul remained uncalled, the song of the unknown bird remained unwritten, and only its strains kept echoing through Binoy's mind.

Just then an accident occurred in front of his house. A hackney-cab was run into by a grand carriage and pair, which went off at full speed taking no notice of the half-overturned gharry which it had left in its trail.

Running out into the street, Binoy saw a young girl getting out from the cab, and an oldish gentleman trying to descend. He rushed to their assistance, and seeing how pale the old man looked, he asked him: "You are not hurt, sir, I hope?"

"No, it's nothing," he answered with an attempt to laugh it off, but his smile died away and it was easy to see that he was on the point of fainting.

Binoy seized hold of his arm, and turning to the anxious girl, said: "This is my house, just here, do come in "

When they had placed the old gentleman on a bed, the girl looked round for some water, and taking a pitcher sprinkled some on his face and began to fan him, saying meanwhile to Binoy: "Can you send for a doctor?"

As a doctor lived nearby, Binoy sent off his servant at once to call him.

There was a mirror in the room, and standing behind the girl Binoy gazed at her reflection. From childhood he had been busy with his studies in his Calcutta home, and what little knowledge he had of the world he had gained from books. He had never known any womenfolk outside his own family circle, and the picture he now saw in the mirror fascinated him. He was not skilled in scrutinising the details of feminine features, but in that youthful face, bowed in affectionate anxiety, it seemed to Binoy as if a new world of tender brightness had been unfolded before him.

When, after a while, the old man opened his eyes and sighed, the girl bent down towards him and asked in a tremulous whisper: "Father, are you hurt?"

"Where am I?" asked the man, attempting to sit up. But Binoy hastened to his side saying: "Don't move, please, till the doctor comes."

As he was speaking the doctor's footsteps were heard, and presently he entered. But as, on examining the patient, he found nothing seriously wrong, he left after prescribing some brandy to be given with warm milk.

On his departure the girl's father showed signs of agitation and concern, but his daughter, guessing the cause, quieted him with the assurance that she would send on the doctor's fee and the cost of the medicine when they got home. She then turned to Binoy.

What wonderful eyes! It never occurred to him to ask whether they were large or small, black or brown. At the very first glance they gave an impression of sincerity. They had no trace of either shyness or hesitation, but were full of a serene strength.

Binoy ventured haltingly: "Oh! the doctor's fee is nothing—you need not trouble—I—I will—"

But the girl's eyes, which were on him, not only prevented him from finishing his sentence, but made it certain that he would have to accept the cost of the doctor's visit.

When the old man protested against sending for the brandy, his daughter insisted, saying: "But, father, the doctor ordered it?"

To this he replied: "Doctors have a bad habit of ordering brandy on the slightest pretext. A glass of milk will be quite enough for my little weakness." And after drinking some milk he turned to Binoy and said: "Now we must be going. We have put you to a lot of trouble, I'm afraid."

The girl now asked for a cab, but her father exclaimed diffidently: "Why put him to more inconvenience? Our house is so close that I can easily walk."

But she refused to allow this, and as her father did not persist, Binoy himself went to call a cab.

Before leaving, the old gentleman asked the name of his host, and on being told "Binoy-bhusan Chatterji," he gave his own in return as "Paresh-chandra Bhattacharya," saying that he lived close by, at No. 78 in the same street. He added: "Whenever you have time to spare, we shall be delighted if you will call." And the eyes of the girl gave a silent consent to this invitation.

Binoy felt that he wanted to accompany them home then and there, but as he was not quite sure whether that would be good manners, he stood hesitating, and just as their carriage was about to start, the girl gave a slight bow, which took Binoy so unawares that in his confusion he omitted to return the salutation.

Back in his room, Binoy reproached himself again and again for this trifling omission. He mentally reviewed every detail of his behaviour from the time he had met them to the moment of parting, and he felt that from start to finish his manners had been atrocious. What he ought to have done and what he ought not to have done, what he ought to have said and what he ought not to have said, in the different situations, he was trying in vain to settle in his mind, when his eyes suddenly fell on a handkerchief which the girl had been using and had left lying on the bed. As he hurriedly snatched it up the refrain of that Bāul's song haunted him:

Into the cage flies the unknown bird,
It comes I know not whence.

The hours passed and the sun's heat became intense. The stream of gharries began to flow swiftly officewards, but Binoy could not give his mind to any work that day. His tiny home and the ugly city that surrounded it suddenly seemed to him an abode of illusion. The flaming radiance of the July sun burnt into his brain and coursed through his veins,— screening from his inner mind all the pettiness of his everyday life with a curtain of blazing light.

Just then he noticed a seven-or eight-year-old boy standing outside peering at the numbers on the doors. Somehow he had not the least doubt that it was his house the boy was looking for, so he called out to him: "This is the house all right," and, quickly running down into the street, almost dragged the little fellow indoors. He eagerly scanned the boy's face as he handed him a letter, on which he saw his name written in English in a woman's clear hand. The boy said: "My sister sent me with this." The envelope contained no letter, only some money.

The boy then turned to go, but Binoy insisted on taking him upstairs to his room. He was darker than his sister, but still there was a strong resemblance, and Binoy, with a sense of gladness at heart, felt greatly attracted to him.

The youngster was clearly quite self-possessed, for on entering the room he pointed to a portrait hanging on the wall and asked: "Whose picture is that?"

"It is the picture of a friend of mine," replied Binoy.

"A friend's picture!" exclaimed the boy. "Who is he?"

"Oh, you won't know him," said Binoy, laughing. "His name is Gourmohan. But I call him Gora. We've been to school together ever since we were children."

"Do you still go to school?"

"No, I've finished with my studies."

"Have you really? Finished your—?"

Binoy could not resist the temptation of winning the admiration of this little messenger, and said: "Yes, I've finished everything!"

The boy looked at him in wide-eyed wonder and gave a sigh. He doubtless thought that some day he too would attain to such heights of learning.

On being asked his name the boy replied: "My name is Master Satish-chandra Mukerji."

"Mukerji?" repeated Binoy blankly.

They were fast friends in no time, and Binoy soon found out that Paresh Babu was not their own father, but had brought them up from childhood. The sister's name had formerly been Radharani, but Paresh Babu's wife had changed it to the less aggressively orthodox name of Sucharita.

When Satish was about to go, Binoy asked him: "Can you go all alone?" to which the little fellow answered with injured pride: "I always do!" When Binoy said: "Let me see you home," he became quite distressed at such a slight on his manliness, and said: "Why should you? I can easily get along by myself," and he began to give all kinds of precedents to show how usual it was for him to go about alone.

Why Binoy should nevertheless, insist on going with him to the door of his house was more than the boy could fathom.

Further, when Satish asked him to come in with him Binoy resolutely refused, saying: "No, not now. I will come another day."

On returning home Binoy took out the envelope and read and re-read the address written on it so minutely that he soon knew every stroke and flourish of it by heart. Then he placed it, together with the contents, in his box with such care,— one could feel sure that there was no chance of this money ever being used, even in the direst emergency.

TWO

O n a dark evening, during the rains, the sky lowered heavy with its load of moisture. Beneath the silent sway of the dull, drab stretch of cloud, the city of Calcutta lay motionless like a huge disconsolate dog curled up with its head resting on its tail. Since the previous night it had been drizzling steadily, persistently enough to make the streets muddy, yet not with sufficient determination to wash the mud away. The rain had ceased at four o'clock that afternoon, but still the clouds looked threatening. It was in this gloomy state of the weather, when it was as unpleasant to stay indoors as it was unsafe to venture out, that two young men were seated on wicker stools on the damp roof-terrace of a three-storied building.

On this terrace, when they had been small, these two friends had played together on return from school; before their examinations it was here that they had loudly committed their lessons to memory, pacing up and down as though in a frenzy; and in the hot weather it was here that they used to take their evening meals on returning from college, often arguing till two o'clock in the morning, waking up startled when the sun arose to find that they had fallen asleep together on the mat. When they had no more college examinations to pass then it was on this roof that the meetings of the Hindu Patriots' Society were held once a month with one of the friends as Chairman and the other as Secretary.

The name of the Chairman was Gourmohan, called by his friends and his relations Gora. He seemed to have utterly outgrown all around him. One of his college Professors used to call him the Snow Mountain, for he was outrageously white, his complexion unmellowed by even the slightest tinge of pigment. He was nearly six feet tall, with big bones, and fists like the paws of a tiger. The sound of his voice was so deep and rough that you would be startled if you suddenly heard him call out, "Who is there?" His face seemed needlessly large and excessively strong, the bones of his jaws and chin being like the massive bolts of a fortress. He had practically no eyebrows, his forehead sloping broadly to the ears. His lips were thin and compressed, his nose projecting over them like a sword. His eyes, small but keen, seemed to be aimed at some unseen distant object like the point of an arrow, yet able to turn in a flash to strike something near at hand. Gourmohan was not exactly good-looking, but it was impossible to overlook him, for he would have been conspicuous in any company.

His friend Binoy was modest and yet bright, like the ordinary run of educated Bengali gentlemen. The delicacy of his nature and the keenness of his intellect combined to give a special quality to the expression of his face. At college he always got high marks and won scholarships, while Gora had been quite unable to keep pace with him, not having the same taste for reading. He could not understand things so quickly as Binoy, nor had he such a good memory. So Binoy, as his faithful steed, had to bear Gora along with himself through all their college examinations.

This was the conversation which engrossed the two friends that wet August evening.

"Let me tell you," Gora was saying. "When Abinash abused the Brahmos the other day, it only showed what a healthy moral vigour he enjoys. What made you flare up at him like that?"

"What nonsense!" replied Binoy. "Surely there can be no two opinions about his taste!"

"If you think so, the evil must be in your own thoughts. You cannot expect of society that while some of its renegade members are trying to overturn it, by insisting on doing just as they please, it should calmly look on, making sweetly reasonable allowances. Society is naturally bound to misunderstand such people and regard as crooked that which they might be doing quite sincerely. If society cannot help looking upon their 'good' as evil, that is but one of the many penalties which must fall on those who wilfully flout it."

"It may be natural," said Binoy, "but I cannot agree that all that is natural is good."

"Oh, bother the good!" broke out Gora. "The world is welcome to the few really good people it may contain. For me, let the rest be but natural! Otherwise work would not get on, nor would life be worth living. If people want to pose sanctimoniously as Brahmos, they must be ready to put up with the little inconvenience of being misunderstood and abused by non-Brahmos. To have your opponents' applause while you strut about like a peacock, is too much to ask of this world,— if that did happen, the world would be a mighty poor place."

"I have no objection to any sect or party being reviled," explained Binoy. "But when the abuse becomes personal—"

"What is the point in reviling the sect? That only amounts to criticising their opinions. I want to show up individuals. As for you, O saint, have you never indulged in personalities yourself?"

"Indeed I have," avowed Binoy. "Very often, I am afraid. And I am heartily ashamed of it too."

"No, Binoy!" exclaimed Gora with a sudden excitement. "This will not do. Never!"

Binoy was silent for a moment. "Why, what is the matter?" he asked at length. "What alarms you?"

"I see clearly enough that you are treading the path of weakness."

"Weakness indeed!" Binoy exclaimed irritably. "You know well enough that I could go to their house this very moment if I wanted to—they have even invited me—and yet you see I do not go."

"Yes, I know. But you never seem able to forget that you are keeping away. Day and night you are harping on it to yourself. 'I do not go. I do not go!' Better far to go and be done with it!"

"Do you seriously mean to advise me to go, then?" asked Binoy.

Gora thumped his knee as he replied: "No, I do *not* advise you to go. I can put it down in black and white that the day you do go to their house, you will go over there completely. The very next day you will begin to take your meals with them; and then down goes your name as a militant preacher of the Brahmo Samaj!"

"Indeed! and what next, pray?" smiled Binoy.

"What next?" rejoined Gora bitterly. "There is no 'next' after you are dead and gone from your own world. You, the son of a Brahmin, will throw away all sense of restraint and purity and will end by being thrown on the refuse heap like some dead animal. Like a pilot with a broken compass you will lose your bearings, and it will gradually seem mere superstition and narrowness to guide the ship into port,— your idea of the best method of navigation will be reduced to drifting anyhow. But I have not the patience to go on bandying words with you. So I simply say: go and be done with it, if you must. But do not keep racking our nerves by this continual hesitation on the brink of inferno."

Binoy burst out laughing. "The patient who has been given up by the doctor does not necessarily die," said he. "I cannot detect any sign of my approaching end."

"You cannot?" sneered Gora.

"No."

"You don't find your pulse failing?"

"By no means. There's plenty of strength left in it yet."

"It doesn't seem to you that if a certain fair hand were to serve you the food of an outcaste, that might make it a feast fit for the gods?"

"That will do, Gora!" said Binoy, blushing deeply. "Shut up!"

"Why?" protested Gora. "I intended no insult. The fair lady in question does not pride herself on being 'invisible even to the sun.'[1] If the least allusion to her tender petal of a hand, which any male person is at liberty to shake, strikes you as a desecration, then indeed you're as good as lost!"

"Look here, Gora, I reverence Woman, and in our scriptures also—"

"Don't quote scripture in support of the kind of sentiment you feel. That's not called reverence, but goes by another name which it would make you still angrier to hear me mention."

"It pleases you to be dogmatic," said Binoy with a shrug.

"The scriptures tell us," persisted Gora, "that Woman is deserving of worship because she gives light to the home,— the honour which is given her by English custom, because she sets fire to the hearts of men, had better not be termed worship."

"Would you contemptuously dismiss a great idea because it occasionally gets clouded over?" asked Binoy.

"Binu," answered Gora impatiently. "Now that you have clearly lost your own power of judgment you ought to be guided by me. I affirm that all the exaggerated language about women that you find in English books has at bottom merely

---

1 A Sanskrit phrase for those women who observe very strict *purdah*.

desire. The altar at which Woman may be truly worshipped is her place as Mother, the seat of the pure, right-minded Lady of the House. There is some insult hidden in the praise of those who remove her from there. The cause of your mind hovering about Paresh Babu's house, like a moth round a candle, is in plain language what the English call 'Love'; but for God's sake don't ape the English cult by placing this love above all other considerations, as the one object of man's worship."

Binoy jumped up like a fresh horse under a whip "Enough, enough!" he cried. "You go too far, Gora!"

"Too far?" retorted Gora. "I haven't even come to the point yet. Simply because our sense of reality about the true relations of man and woman is bemisted by passion, we need must make it a subject for poetising."

"If it is our passion which besmirches our idea of the right relationship of man and woman, is the foreigner alone to blame? Is it not the same passion which leads our moralists to exaggerated vehemence when they preach that woman is an evil to be shunned? These are merely two opposite aspects of the same attitude of mind in two different types. If you abuse the one, it will not do to excuse the other."

"I misunderstood you, I see!" smiled Gora. "Your condition is not so hopeless as I feared. So long as philosophy finds scope in your brain, you may make love without fear. But take care that you save yourself before it is too late,—that is the prayer of your well-wishers."

"You have gone quite crazy, my dear fellow!" Binoy expostulated. "What have I to do with love? To ease your mind I will confess that, from what I have heard and seen of Paresh Babu and his family, I have come to entertain a great respect for them. Maybe, for that reason, I have a certain attraction for seeing what their home life is like."

"'Attraction' let it be, if you prefer it; but of that attraction you must beware. What harm if your zoological researches remain uncompleted? This much is certain, that they belong to the genus predatory; and if your studies lead you too near them, you will go so far in that not even the tip of your tail will be visible."

"You have one great fault, Gora," objected Binoy. "You seem to believe that all the strength God had to give was bestowed on you alone, and that the rest of us are mere weaklings."

This remark seemed to strike Gora with the force of a new idea. "Right!" he shouted, giving Binoy an enthusiastic thump on the back. "Quite right! That is a great fault of mine."

"Love!" groaned Binoy. "You have a still greater fault, Gora, and that is your utter inability to estimate the force of concussion which the ordinary spinal cord is able to bear."

At this moment Gora's elder stepbrother, Mohim, came upstairs, stout and panting, and called out, "Gora!"

Gora at once left his seat and stood up respectfully as he answered "Sir?"

"I just came," said Mohim "to see if the thunder-clouds had burst on our roof. What's the excitement to-day? I suppose by now you have driven the English half-way across the Indian Ocean! I haven't noticed much loss to the Englishmen, but your sister-in-law below is lying in bed with a headache, and your leonine roaring is somewhat of a trial to her."

With this Mohim left them and went back downstairs.

THREE

Just as Gora and Binoy were about to go down from the roof, Gora's mother arrived there, and Binoy respectfully saluted her, taking the dust of her feet.

To see Anandamoyi no one would think she was Gora's mother. She had a slender but well-knit figure; and though her hair was grey in places, it did not show. At first sight you would take her for under forty. The curves of her face were very tender, seemingly chiselled by a master hand with the utmost care. Her spare contour was devoid of all exaggeration, and her face had the impress of a pure and keen intelligence. Her complexion was dark, without the least resemblance to that of Gora. One thing about her struck all her acquaintances, namely, that with her *sari* she wore a bodice. At the time of which we are speaking, though certain modern young women had begun to adopt it as part of their dress, ladies of the old school looked askance at the wearing of a bodice as savouring of Christianity. Anandamoyi's husband, Krishnadayal Babu, had held a post in the Commissariat Department, and Anandamoyi had spent most of her days with him, from childhood, away from Bengal. So she had not the idea that to cover the body properly was a matter to be ashamed of, or to laugh at. In spite of her devotion to household work, from scrubbing the floors and doing the washing to sewing, mending, and keeping the accounts, and her practical interest in all the members of her own family as well as those of her neighbours, she never seemed too fully occupied.

Anandamoyi acknowledged Binoy's salutation, saying: "When Gora's voice reaches down to us below, then we are certain that Binu has come. The house has been so quiet all these days that I was wondering what was the matter with you, child. Why haven't you been for so long? Have you been ill?"

"No," replied Binoy rather hesitatingly. "No, mother, I've not been ill, but just think of the heavy rain!"

"Rain indeed!" broke in Gora. "And when the rainy season is over Binoy will make the sun his excuse! If you put the blame on the outside elements they cannot defend themselves, but the real reason is known to his inner conscience."

"What nonsense you talk, Gora!" protested Binoy.

"That's true, child," agreed Anandamoyi. "Gora shouldn't have put it like that. The mind has its moods, sometimes sociable, sometimes downcast, it cannot always be the same. It is wrong to tax people about it. Come, Binoy, come to my room and have something to eat. I have kept your favourite sweetmeats ready for you."

Gora shook his head vehemently as he said: "No, no, mother, none of that, please! I cannot allow Binoy to eat in your room."

"Don't be absurd, Gora," said Anandamoyi. "I never ask you to do so. And as for your father, he has become so orthodox that he will eat nothing not cooked by his own hands. But Binu is my good boy; he's not a bigot like you, and you surely do not want to prevent him by force from doing what he thinks right?"

"Yes, I do!" answered Gora. "I must insist on it. It is impossible to take food in your room so long as you keep on that Christian maidservant Lachmi."

"Oh, Gora dear, how can you bring yourself to utter such words!" exclaimed Anandamoyi, greatly distressed. "Have you not all along eaten food from her hand, for it was she who nursed you and brought you up? Only till quite lately, you could not relish your food without the chutney prepared by her. Besides, can I ever forget how she saved your life, when you had smallpox, by her devoted nursing?"

"Then pension her off," said Gora impatiently. "Buy her some land and build a cottage for her; but you must not keep her in the house, mother!"

"Gora, do you think that every debt can be paid off with money?" said Anandamoyi. "She wants neither land nor cash; she only wants to see you, or she will die."

"Then keep her if you like," said Gora resignedly. "But Binoy must not eat in your room. Scriptural rules must be accepted as final. Mother, I wonder that you, the daughter of such a great Pandit, should have no care for our orthodox customs. This is too—"

"Oh, Gora, you silly boy!" smiled Anandamoyi. There was a time when this mother of yours was very careful about observing all these customs; and at the cost of many a tear too!—Where were you then? Daily I used to worship the emblem of Shiva, made by my own hands, and your father used to come and throw it away in a fury. In those days I even felt uncomfortable if I ate rice cooked by any and every Brahmin. We had but little of railways then, and through many a long day I have had to fast when travelling by bullock-cart, or on a camel, or in a palanquin. Your father won the approbation of his English masters because of his unorthodox habit of taking his wife wherever he travelled; for that he gained promotion, and was allowed to stay at headquarters instead of being kept constantly on the move. But for all that, do you think he found it an easy matter to break my orthodox habits? Now that he has retired in his old age with a heap of savings, he has suddenly turned orthodox and intolerant,— but I cannot follow him in his somersaults. The traditions of seven generations of my ancestors were uprooted, one by one,—do you think they can now be replanted at a word?"

"Well, well," answered Gora, "leave aside your ancestors— they are not making objections. But surely out of regard for us you must agree to certain things. Even if you do not regard the scriptures, you ought to respect the claims of love."

"Need you explain these claims with so much insistence?" asked Anandamoyi wearily. "Do I not know only too well what they mean? What happiness can it be for me, at every step I take, to come into collision with husband and child? But do you know that it was when I first took you in my arms that I said good-bye to convention? When you hold a little child to your breast then you feel certain that no one is born into this world with caste. From that very day the understanding came to me that if I looked down upon anyone for being of low caste, or a Christian, then God would snatch you away from me. Only stay in my arms as the light of my home, I prayed, and I will accept water from the hands of anyone in the world!"

At these words of Anandamoyi, for the first time, a vague disquiet flitted across Binoy's mind, and he glanced quickly from Anandamoyi to Gora's face. But he immediately banished all shadow of doubt from his thoughts.

Gora also seemed perplexed. "Mother," he said, "I don't follow your reasoning. Children find no difficulty in living and thriving in the homes of those who obey the scriptures— who put the idea in your head that God has given some special dispensation in your case?"

"He who gave you to me also inspired me with this idea," answered Anandamoyi. "What could I do? I had no hand in the matter. Oh, my dear crazy boy, I don't know whether to laugh or to cry at your foolishness. But never mind, let it be. So Binoy is not to be allowed to eat in my room—is that the latest?"

"If he gets an opportunity he will dart off like an arrow," laughed Gora, "and he's got the appetite too! But mother, I am not going to let him. He is the son of a Brahmin. It won't do to make him forget his responsibilities for the sake of a few sweetmeats. He will have to make many sacrifices, to exercise severe self-control, before becoming worthy of his glorious birthright. But, mother, don't be angry with me, I beg by the dust of your dear feet."

"What an idea!" exclaimed Anandamoyi. "Why should I be angry? You know not what you do, let me tell you that much. It is my sorrow that I should have brought you up, and yet—anyhow, however that may be, it is impossible for me to accept what you call your religion. What if you will not eat in my room, it is enough for me that I should have you with me mornings and evenings.—Binoy dear, don't look so sad. You are too sensitive; you think that I am hurt, but I am not really. Don't worry, child! I shall invite you some other day and have your food prepared by a regular Brahmin! But as for myself, I give you all notice I intend to go on taking water from Lachmi's hand!" And with that she went downstairs.

Binoy stood silent for a time, and then he turned and said slowly: "Isn't this going a little too far, Gora?"

"Who is going too far?"

"You!"

"Not by a hair's breadth!" said Gora emphatically. "I am for each one of us keeping to our limits; once you yield a pin's point of ground, there is no knowing where you will end."

"But she is your mother!" protested Binoy.

"I know what a mother is," answered Gora; "you needn't remind me of that! How many possess a mother like mine! But if I once begin to show disrespect for tradition, then one day perhaps I shall cease to respect my mother also. Look here, Binoy, I have one word to say to you: the heart is a good thing, but it is not the best of all."

After a pause Binoy said hesitatingly: "Listen, Gora. To-day, as I heard your mother's words, I felt somehow strangely disturbed. It seemed to me as if there is something on your mother's mind which she cannot explain to us, and that hurts her."

"Ah, Binoy!" said Gora impatiently, "don't give so much rein to your imagination—it does no good and only wastes your time."

"You never give heed to what is going on around you," replied Binoy, "and so you dismiss as imaginary what you fail to see. But I assure you that I have often noticed that your mother seems to have some secret on her mind—something that she feels is out of tune with her surroundings and which makes her home life sad. Gora, you ought to give more careful ear to her words."

"I am careful enough about what the ear can tell," replied Gora. "If I do not try to go deeper, that is because I fear to deceive myself."

FOUR

Abstract ideas are all very well as opinions, but when applied to persons they cease to have the same force of certainty,—at any rate that was so in the case of Binoy, for he was largely guided by the heart. Therefore, however loud he might be in support of a principle in argument, when it was a question of dealing with men, human considerations would prevail. So much so that it was difficult to say how far he accepted the principles Gora preached for their own sake and how far because of his great friendship for him.

On his return from Gora's house, as he walked slowly along the muddy streets on that rainy evening, a struggle was going on in his mind between the claims of principle and his personal feelings.

When Gora had contended that, to save society at the present time from various kinds of open and hidden attack, it was necessary to be constantly on the alert on matters relating to eating and caste, Binoy had easily assented. He had even argued the point hotly with those who disagreed. He had said that when the enemy attacks a fortress from all sides it shows no lack of a liberal mind to guard with your very life every road, lane, door, window, and even crack leading into the fortress.

But Gora's refusal to let him take food in his mother's room was a blow which hurt him intensely.

Binoy had no father, and he had lost his mother also at an early age. He had an uncle in the country, but from boyhood he had lived a lonely student-life in Calcutta, and from the very day he had been introduced to Anandamoyi, by his friend Gora, he had called her "Mother."

Often had he gone to her room, and teased her till she would make for him his favourite confections. Many a time had he pretended to be jealous of Gora, accusing his mother of showing partiality to him when serving the food. Binoy knew it quite well if he omitted to visit her for two or three days how anxious she would get in the hope of watching him do justice to her delicacies,—how impatiently she would wait for their meetings to break up. And to-day in the name of society he had been forbidden to eat with her! Could she bear such a thing, and could he himself tolerate it?

She had said with a smile: "After this I will not touch your food when I invite you, but will get hold of a good Brahmin to prepare your meals!" But how wounded she must have felt!—thought Binoy as he reached his lodgings.

His empty room was dark and untidy with books and papers scattered everywhere. Striking a match, Binoy lighted the lamp which was smeared with the servant's finger-prints. On the white table-cloth which covered his writing-table there were spots of grease and ink-stains. In this room he felt choked. The want of human companionship and love made him feel terribly depressed. All such duties as the rescue of his country and the protection of his society seemed vague and false. Far more true seemed that "unknown bird" which one bright, beautiful morning of July had flown to the door of his cage and then flown away again. But Binoy had determined not to allow his thoughts to dwell on that "unknown bird"; so to quieten his mind he tried to picture to himself Anandamoyi's room from which Gora had banished him.

The polished cement floor kept scrupulously clean—on one side the soft bed with its white counterpane spread over it like a swan's wing, and on a little stool beside it, the lighted lamp. Bending over her work, Anandamoyi must be stitching away with different-coloured threads at the patchwork quilt, with the maidservant Lachmi sitting at her feet and chattering away in her queer Bengali. It was this quilt that Anandamoyi always worked at when her mind was troubled with anything and Binoy fixed his thoughts on the picture of her calm face absorbed in her work. He said to himself: "May the lovelight of her face guard my mind from all distractions. May it be as the reflection of my motherland and keep me firm in the path of duty." In his thoughts he called her "Mother," and said: "No scripture shall prove to me that food from your hand is not nectar for me."

In the silence of the room the steady ticking of the big clock could be heard, and Binoy felt it unbearable to stay there. Near the lamp a lizard on the wall was catching insects. Binoy watched it for a little and then got up, seized his umbrella, and went out.

He was undecided where to go. Probably his original purpose had been to go back to Anandamoyi, but he suddenly remembered that the day was Sunday, and he decided to go to hear Keshub Babu preach at the Brahmo Samaj service. He knew that the sermon must be nearly over by this time, but that made no difference to his resolve.

As he reached the place, the congregation was dispersing, and as he stood with his umbrella up at a corner of the street, he saw Paresh Babu coming out with a peaceful benevolence written on his countenance. Four or five members of his family were with him, but Binoy's eyes were on the youthful face of only one of them, lighted up for a moment by the street lamp as they passed by—then there was a rattle of carriage-wheels and it vanished like a bubble in a vast sea of darkness.

Binoy did not manage to reach Gora's house that evening, but returned to his lodgings lost in thought. When, after making a fresh start the next afternoon, he did actually find himself at Gora's house after a long detour, the darkness of a clouded evening had already set in.

Gora had just lit his lamp and had sat down to write as Binoy came in. He looked up from his paper and said, "Well, Binoy, which way is the wind blowing to-day?"

Without taking any notice of the question Binoy said: "I want to ask you one thing, Gora. Tell me, is India very real, absolutely clear, to you? India is your thoughts day and night, but in what way do you think of her?"

Gora left off his writing and looked keenly at Binoy for a short time. Then he put down his pen and, leaning back in his chair, said: "As the captain of a ship when he is out on the ocean keeps in mind the port across the sea, both while at work and during his leisure, so is India in my mind at all times."

"And where is this India of yours?" pursued Binoy.

"Where the point of this compass of mine turns by day and by night," exclaimed Gora, placing his hand on his heart. "There,—not in your Marshman's *History of India.*"

"And is there any particular port to which your compass points?" continued Binoy.

"Isn't there!" replied Gora with intense conviction. "I may miss my task, I may sink and drown, but that Port of a great Destiny is always there. That is my India in its fullness—full of wealth, full of knowledge, full of righteousness. Do you mean to say that such India is nowhere? Is there nothing but this falsehood on every side! This Calcutta of yours, with its offices, its High Court, and its few bubbles of brick and mortar! Poof!"

He stopped and looked steadily at Binoy, who remained silent lost in thought.

Gora went on: "Here, where we read and study, where we go about seeking employment, slaving away from ten to five without rhyme or reason,—because we call this falsehood of some evil genie India, is that any reason why 350 millions of people should honour what is false and go about intoxicated with the idea that this world of falsity is a real world? How can we gain any life, for all our efforts, out of this mirage? That is why we are gradually dying of inanition. But there is a true India, rich and full, and unless we take our stand there, we shall not be able to draw upon the sap of life either by our intellect or by our heart. Therefore, I say, forget everything—book-learning, the illusion of titles, the temptations of servile livelihood; renounce the attractions of all these and let us launch the ship towards its port. If we must sink, if we must die, let us. It is because it is so vital for us that I at least can never forget the true and complete image of India!"

"Is this merely the ferment of excitement, or the truth?" asked Binoy.

"The truth of course!" thundered Gora.

"And what about those who cannot see as you do?" inquired Binoy gently.

"We must make them see!" replied Gora, clenching his fist. "That is our work. If people are unable to see a clear picture of truth, they will surrender themselves to any phantom. Hold up before all the unbroken image of India, and men will become possessed by it. Then you won't have to go begging for paltry subscriptions from door to door—people will jostle one another in their efforts to offer up their lives."

"Well, then, show me this image, or else send me to join the unseeing multitudes!"

"Try and realise it for yourself," replied Gora. "If only you have faith, you will find joy in the austerity of your devotion. Our fashionable patriots have no faith in truth, that is why they cannot make any strong claim, either on themselves or on others. If the God of Wealth himself offered them a boon, I verily believe they would not have the courage to ask for more than the gilt badge of the Viceroy's orderlies. They have no faith, therefore they have no hope."

"Gora," protested Binoy, "every one has not the same nature. You have faith yourself, and you can take shelter in your own strength, that is why you cannot fully understand the mental condition of other people. I tell you plainly, give me some task, it doesn't matter what. Make me work day and night. Otherwise I feel as if I had got hold of something tangible only while I am with you; but as soon as I am away from you, I find nothing at hand to cling to."

"You speak of work?" replied Gora. "At present our only task is to infuse in the unbelievers our own unhesitating and unflinching confidence in all that belongs to our country. Through our constant habit of being ashamed of our country, the poison of servility has overpowered our minds. If each one of us will, by his own example, counteract that poison, then we shall soon find our field of service. So far, in whatever we try to do, we simply copy what our school-book history teaches us that others have done. Can we ever give our heart and mind truly to such second-hand service? In this way we can only follow the path of degradation."

At this juncture Mohim entered the room, hookah in hand, with slow and leisurely steps. This was his time, after returning from office and taking some refreshment, for sitting at the door of his house with his betel chew and his smoke. One by one his friends from the neighbourhood would join him, and then they would retire to the sitting-room for a game of cards.

At his entry Gora stood up, and Mohim, puffing at his hookah, said: "You, who are so busy trying to save India, I wish you'd save your brother!"

Gora looked inquiringly at Mohim, who went on: "The new Burra Sahib at our office is a regular rogue. He has a face like a bulldog, and calls us Babus 'baboons.' If anyone loses his mother he won't give him leave, saying that it is a lie. Not a single Bengali clerk gets his full pay at the end of the month, their salaries being completely riddled with fines. An anonymous letter about him has appeared in the papers recently, and the fellow will have it that it is my work. Not that he's altogether wrong either! He threatens to dismiss me unless I write a strong contradiction over my own name. You two bright jewels of our University must help me to concoct a good letter, scattering broadcast such phrases as 'even-handed justice,' 'never-failing generosity', 'kindly courteousness,' etc., etc."

Gora remained silent, but Binoy laughed and said: "Dada,[1] how can one manage to express so many falsehoods in one breath?"

"One must give a tooth for a tooth and an eye for an eye," replied Mohim. "I've had long experience of these sahibs, and there is nothing unfamiliar about them to me. The way they can collect falsehoods is beyond all praise. Nothing stands in their way if necessity arises. If one of them tells a lie, the whole crowd of them howl in chorus like jackals,—not as we do, who are not above taking credit for turning approver. Be assured that it is no sin to deceive them, so long as you are not found out!"

With his last words Mohim laughed loud and long, and Binoy also could not help smiling.

"You hope to shame them by confronting them with the truth!" went on Mohim. "If the Almighty had not endowed you with this kind of intelligence, the country would not have come to such a plight! You really must begin to understand

---

1 Dada—elder brother.

that the strong fellow from across the sea does not bow his head in shame when you catch him in the act of housebreaking. On the contrary, he raises his crowbar on you with all the assurance of innocence itself. Isn't that so?"

"True enough," answered Binoy.

"Well then," continued Mohim, "if we use a little oil from the mill of falsehood to flatter them, saying: 'O righteous one, O holy saint, kindly throw us something from your satchel, even if it be only its dust,' then some small part of our own may be restored to us. At the same time we shall avoid all chance of a breach of the peace. If only you think of it, this is real patriotism. But Gora is angry with me. He has taken to showing great respect to me, his elder brother, ever since he turned orthodox. But to-day my words don't strike him as coming from an elder. What am I to do, brother mine? I must speak the truth even about falsehood. However that may be, Binoy you must write that letter. Wait a moment and I will bring you my rough notes of the points." And Mohim went off, pulling hard at his hookah.

Gora turned to Binoy and said: "Binu, do go to Dada's room, there's a good fellow, and keep him quiet while I finish my writing."

FIVE

Anandamoyi knocked at the door of her husband's prayer-room. "Are you listening?" she called to him. "I'm not trying to enter, you needn't be afraid, but when you've finished I want a word with you. Now that you have got hold of a new *sannyasi,* I won't get a sight of you for a good long time, I know, so I've come here. Don't forget to come to me, for a minute, when you've done." And with these words she returned to her household duties.

Krishnadayal Babu was a dark man, not very tall and inclined to be stout. The most prominent of his features were his large eyes, the rest of his face being almost hidden under a bushy grey beard and moustache. He always affected ochre silk robes and wooden sandals, and carried a brass pot, in the manner of ascetics. The front part of his head was bald, but he wore his hair long and coiled up on the top.

There had been a time, while his work kept him upcountry, when in the company of the soldiers of the regiment he had indulged in forbidden meat and wine to his heart's content. In those days he used to consider it a sign of moral courage to go out of his way to revile and insult priests and *sannyasis* and men of any kind of religious profession. But nowadays anything savouring of orthodoxy had his allegiance. He no sooner caught sight of a *sannyasi* than he would sit at his feet in the hope of learning some novel form of religious exercise.

His greed for finding some hidden short cut to salvation, some esoteric method of gaining mystical powers, was boundless. While he had recently been busy taking lessons in Tantric practices, his latest discovery had been a Buddhist monk, and this had unsettled his mind all over again.

His age was only twenty-three when his first wife had died in childbirth. Unable to bear the sight of the son who had been the cause of this mother's death, Krishnadayal handed over the infant to his father-in-law and went off west in a fit of despairing renunciation. Within six months he had married Anandamoyi, the fatherless granddaughter of a great Benaras pandit.

Upcountry he procured an appointment in the Commissariat Department, and by various shifts managed to win the favour of his employers. On the death of his wife's grandfather, he was compelled, for lack of any other guardian, to take her to live with himself.

Meanwhile the Sepoy Mutiny had broken out, and he did not miss certain opportunities of contriving to save the lives of some highly placed English people, for which he was rewarded both by honour and a grant of land. Shortly after the mutiny had been quelled, he gave up his appointment and returned to live in Benaras with the newly born Gora. When the child was five years old, Krishnadayal went on to Calcutta and taking his elder boy, Mohim, away from his uncle, began to educate him. Now Mohim, by favour of his father's patrons, had been taken into the Government Treasury, where, as we have seen, he was working enthusiastically.

Gora from his childhood had been a leader amongst the boys of his neighbourhood and his school. His chief work and amusement was to make the lives of his teachers unbearable. When he was a little older he led the Students' Club in their national songs, gave lectures in English, and was the acknowledged leader of a band of little revolutionaries. At last, when he had been hatched from the egg of the Students' Club and started cackling in public at meetings of adults, that seemed to afford Krishnadayal Babu considerable amusement.

Gora began to gain quite a reputation outside his home but none of his own family took him very seriously. Mohim felt it due to his Government service to try his best to restrain Gora, at whom he jeered, calling him "Patriotic Prig," "Harish Mookerjee the Second," etc., over which, sometimes, the two nearly came to blows. Anandamoyi was very much upset at heart over Gora's militant antagonism to everything English, and tried every expedient to calm him down, but without effect. Gora would in fact be only too delighted if he got a chance in the street of quarrelling with an Englishman. At the same time, he was greatly attracted towards the Brahmo Samaj, being under the spell of Keshub Chandra Sen's eloquence.

It was just at this time that Krishnadayal all of a sudden turned strictly orthodox, so much so that he felt exceedingly put out even if Gora stepped into his room. He actually had a part of the house reserved specially for his own use, calling it the "Hermitage," and going to the length of displaying the name on a signboard. Gora's mind revolted against these ways of his father. "I can't put up with all this folly," he said; "I simply won't stand it." Gora, in fact, was on the point of cutting off all connection with his father, when Anandamoyi intervened and managed somehow to reconcile them.

Gora, whenever he got the opportunity, argued hotly with the Brahmin pandits who gathered round his father. It could scarcely be called argument, however, his words being more like slaps on the face. Most of these pandits had little scholarship, but an immense avidity for their perquisites. They could not manage Gora at all, and were mortally afraid of his tigerish onslaughts.

But there was one of them for whom Gora began to entertain a great respect. His name was Vidyavagish, and he

had been engaged by Krishnadayal for expounding the Vedanta
philosophy. At first Gora tried to dispose of him with the same
insolence, but he was soon disarmed. The man, he found, had
not only great learning, but his liberality of mind was something
wonderful. Gora had never imagined that any one, read only
in Sanskrit lore, could have such a keen and open intelligence.
There was such power and peace, such unwavering patience
and depth, in the character of Vidyavagish that Gora could
not but feel himself restrained in the pandit's presence. Gora
began to study the Vedanta philosophy with him, and, as he
could never do anything half-heartedly, he plunged headlong
into all its speculations.

As it happened, this coincided with a controversy started
in the papers by some English missionary, in which he attacked
Hindu religion and Hindu society and invited discussion.
Gora fired up at once, for although he was only too ready
himself, when he got the chance, to worry his opponents by
crying down scriptural injunctions and popular customs alike,
he was goaded to the quick at this disrespect shown to Hindu
society by a foreigner. So he rushed into the fray, and took
up the defence. He would not acknowledge a single one, not
even the smallest fraction, of the faults imputed to the Hindus
by the opposite party. After many letters had been exchanged,
the editor finally closed the correspondence.

But Gora had been thoroughly roused, and he set to work
on a book in English on "Hinduism," in which he exerted
himself to the utmost to get together arguments from reason
and scripture to prove the blameless excellence of Hindu
religion and society. He ended by succumbing to his own
advocacy. He said: "We must refuse to allow our country to
stand at the bar of a foreign court and be judged according
to a foreign law. Our ideas of shame or glory must not depend
on minute comparisons at every step with a foreign standard.
We must not feel apologetic about the country of our birth—

whether it be about its traditions, faith, or its scriptures—neither to others nor even to ourselves. We must save our country and ourselves from insult by manfully bearing the burdens of our motherland with all our strength and all our pride."

Full of these ideas, Gora began religiously to bathe in the Ganges, regularly to perform ceremonial worship morning and evening, to take particular care of what he touched and what he ate, and even to grow a *tiki*.[1] Every morning he went to take the dust of his parents' feet, and as for Mohim, whom he had had no compunction in calling "cad" and "snob"—now, whenever he came into the room, Gora stood up and made to him the obeisance due to an elder. Mohim did not spare his sneers at Gora for this sudden change, but Gora never answered him back.

By his preaching and example Gora created a regular party of young enthusiasts round himself. They seemed to have gained from his teaching freedom from the strain of opposing pulls on their conscience. "We need no longer offer explanations," they seemed to say to themselves with a sigh of relief. "It matters not whether we are good or bad, civilised or barbarian, so long as we are but ourselves."

But, curiously enough, it did not appear that Krishnadayal was pleased at this sudden change in Gora. On the contrary he one day called Gora and said to him: "Look here, my son, Hinduism is a very profound subject. It is not easy for any and every person to sound the depths of the religion established by the Rishis. It is just as well not to meddle with it without a full understanding. Your mind is not yet mature, moreover you have all along been educated in English. Your first impulse towards the Brahmo Samaj was more suited for your type of

---

1 A tuft of heir at the back of the head, grown by Brahmins in Bengal as a mark of orthodoxy.

mind. So I was not at all annoyed about it, rather it pleased me. But the path you are now following is not your path at all. I am afraid it will not do."

"What are you saying father?" protested Gora. "Am I not a Hindu? If I cannot understand the deeper meaning of Hinduism to-day I shall do so to-morrow. Even if I can never grasp its full significance, its path is the only one for me to pursue. The merit of some previous Hindu birth has brought me this time into a Brahmin family, and in this way, after repeated re-births through Hindu religion and society, I shall reach my final goal. If by mistake I swerve from my appointed path, that will only mean redoubled travail in returning to it."

But Krishnadayal kept on shaking his head as he said: "But, my boy, simply to call oneself a Hindu is not to become one. It is easy to become a Mohammedan, easier still to become a Christian—but a Hindu! Good Lord, that's a different matter!"

"That's true enough," replied Gora; "but since I have been born a Hindu I have at least crossed the threshold. If only I keep on the true path I shall gradually make good progress."

"I am afraid, my son," answered Krishnadayal, "I shall hardly be able to convince you by argument. What you say is quite right in its way. Whatever religion is really yours according to your own *karma,* to it you will have to return sooner or later,—no one can stand in your way. God's will be done! What are we but His instruments."

Krishnadayal had a way of accepting, with equally open arms, the doctrine of Karma and trust in God's will, identity with the Divine and worship of the Divinity,—he never even felt the need for reconciling these opposites.

SIX

Remembering his wife's request, Krishnadayal, after finishing his bath and taking his food, went to her room. It was the first time he had been there for many days, and he spread his own mat on the floor and sat bolt upright, as if carefully dissociating himself from his surroundings.

Anandamoyi opened the conversation: "You are making a bid for sainthood and do not trouble yourself about domestic matters, but I am getting worried to death about Gora."

"Why, what is there to be afraid of?" asked Krishnadayal.

"I can't exactly tell," replied Anandamoyi. "But I'm thinking that if Gora goes on with this Hinduism of his at this rate, it cannot last—some catastrophe is sure to happen. I warned you not to invest him with the sacred thread, but in those days you were not so particular and said: 'What does a piece of string matter one way or the other?' But it has come to mean much more than the thread now. And where are you going to draw the line?"

"Oh yes!" grumbled Krishnadayal. "Put all the blame, on me, of course! But was not the original mistake yours? You *would* insist on not giving him up. In those days I too was hot-headed, with no thought of the claims of religion. I could not dream of doing such a thing to-day!"

"Say what you like," replied Anandamoyi, "I will never admit having done anything wrong. You remember that I left nothing untried in order to have a child of my own. I did whatever was suggested,—how many *mantras* I uttered! how many charms I wore! Well, one day in a dream I saw myself offering to God a basket of white flowers.—After a time the flowers disappeared, and in their place I saw a little child, as white as they were. I cannot tell you what I felt when I saw it,—my eyes filled with tears. I was just about to snatch it to my bosom when I awake. It was just ten days after that I got Gora—God's gift to me. How could I give him up to anyone else? I must have held him in my womb in some previous life, at the cost of great pain, and that is why he has come now to call me 'Mother.' Just think how strangely he came to us! That midnight, when all around us there was bloodshed, and we ourselves went in fear of our lives, the English lady took shelter in our home. You were afraid to keep her in the house, but I put her in the cowshed unknown to you. That very night she died on giving birth to a son. If I had not cared for that orphan child it would not have lived. What did you care? You wanted to hand him over to a padre. Why? Why should I give him to the padre? What was the padre to him? Had he saved the child's life? Was such a way of getting the child less wonderful than giving birth to it myself? Whatever you may say, unless he who gave to me my child takes him away from me, I will never give him up."

"Don't I know that?" said Krishnadayal. "Anyhow, do as you will with your Gora, I have never tried to interfere. I had to go through the thread investiture because, having given him out to be our son, society would not have it otherwise. There are only two questions remaining to be settled. Legally Mohim is entitled to all that I have—so—"

"Who wants to share in your property?" interrupted Anandamoyi. "You may leave all your earnings to Mohim,—Gora will not claim a piece of them. He's a man and well educated. He can earn his own living; why should he hanker after another's wealth? As for me, it is enough that he lives,—I have no need for any other possessions."

"No, I don't want to leave him altogether penniless," objected Krishnadayal. "There is the land which was granted to me,—that ought to bring in a thousand rupees a year. The more knotty question is that of his marriage. What's already been done is done—but I can't now go further and actually marry him into a Brahmin family, according to Hindu rites—whether it pleases you to get angry or not."

"So you think I have no conscience merely because I am not like you, sprinkling holy Ganges water all over the place? Why should I want to marry him into a Brahmin family, or get angry about it, either?"

"What! Aren't you yourself a Brahmin's daughter?"

"And what if I am?" replied Anandamoyi. "I have long ceased to take pride in my caste. Why, when our relatives made a fuss at Mohim's wedding because of my unorthodox habits, I simply kept at a distance without a word of protest. Nearly everybody calls me a Christian, and whatever else comes to their lips. I accept all that they say in good part, contenting myself with the reply: Aren't Christians human beings? If you alone are the elect of God, why has He made you grovel in the dust first before the Pathans, then before the Moghuls, and now before the Christians?"

"Oh, that's a long story," answered Krishnadayal somewhat impatiently. "You're a woman and wouldn't be able to understand. But there is such a thing as society and you can't ignore it—that at least you can understand."

"I'd rather not bother my head about all that," said Anandamoyi. "But this much I do understand, that, if, after having brought up Gora as my child, I now start playing at orthodoxy, then, apart from its offending society, it would offend my own conscience. It is only because of my fear of *dharma* that I have never hidden anything and let every one know that I do not conform to orthodox customs, bearing patiently all the hard words this has earned for me. There is one thing, however, which I have concealed, and for this I go in constant dread of God's retribution.—Look here, I think we ought to make a clean breast of it to Gora, let come what may."

"No, no!" exclaimed Krishnadayal, greatly perturbed at this suggestion. "Not while I live. You know Gora. If once he hears the truth, there's no telling what he will do, and then the whole of society will be about our ears. Not only that, but the Government may also give trouble, for, although Gora's father was killed in the Mutiny and we knew that his mother died, yet when the trouble was over we ought to have informed the magistrate. If once we raise this mare's nest, all my religious exercises will be done for, and there's no knowing what further calamity may descend upon me."

Anandamoyi remained silent, and after a pause Krishnadayal went on: "With regard to Gora's marriage I have an idea. Paresh Bhattacharya was a fellow-student of mine. He has just retired from a school-inspectorship with a pension and is staying in Calcutta. He's a full-fledged Brahmo, and I have heard that there are many marriageable girls in his house. If only we could steer Gora to that establishment, then, after a few visits he might easily take a fancy to one of them. After that we may safely leave matters to the God of Love."

"What! Gora go visiting in a Brahmo household? Those days for him are long past!" exclaimed Anandamoyi.

As she spoke Gora himself came into the room calling out in his thundering voice, "Mother!" but, seeing his father sitting there, he paused for a moment in astonishment. Anandamoyi went quickly up to him as she asked, with affection radiating from her countenance: "What is it, my child? what do you want of me?"

"Nothing very urgent, it can wait." With which Gora turned to go, but Krishnadayal stopped him, saying: "Wait a moment, Gora, I have something to say to you. I have a Brahmo friend who has recently come to Calcutta, and is living near Beadon Street."

"Is it Paresh Babu?" asked Gora.

"How do you come to know him?" asked Krishnadayal in surprise.

"I've heard of him from Binoy, who lodges near his house," explained Gora.

"Well," pursued Krishnadayal, "I want you to call and inquire after him."

Gora hesitated a moment, apparently revolving something in his mind and then came out with: "All right, I'll go over to-morrow first thing."

Anandamoyi was rather surprised at Gora's ready compliance, but the very next moment he said: "No, I forgot, I can't go to-morrow."

"Why not?" asked Krishnadayal.

"To-morrow I have to go to Tribeni."

"Tribeni of all places!" exclaimed Krishnadayal.

"There is the bathing festival for to-morrow's eclipse of the sun," explained Gora.

"You make me wonder, Gora," said Anandamoyi. "Haven't you the Ganges here in Calcutta, that you can't bathe without going all the way to Tribeni?—You are out-doing orthodoxy itself!"

But Gora left the room without answering.

The reason why Gora had decided to bathe at Tribeni was because there would be crowds of pilgrims there. Gora snatched at every opportunity for casting away all his diffidence, all his former prejudices, and, standing on a level with the common people of his country, to say with all his heart: "I am yours and you are mine."

SEVEN

In the morning Binoy awoke and saw the early light blos soming as pure as the smile of a newborn child. A few white clouds were floating aimlessly in the sky.

As he stood in the verandah recalling the happy memory of another such morning, he saw Paresh Babu coming slowly along the street, a stick in one hand and Satish holding the other.

As soon as Satish caught sight of Binoy he clapped his hands and shouted, "Binoy Babu!" Paresh Babu also looked up and saw him, and Binoy hurrying downstairs met them both as they entered the house.

Satish seized Binoy's hand, saying: "Binoy Babu, why haven't you been to see us? You promised to come in that day."

Binoy, putting his hand affectionately on the boy's shoulder, smiled at him, while Paresh Babu, carefully placing his stick upright against the table, sat down and said: "I don't know what we should have done without you the other day. You were so very good to us."

"Oh, that was nothing; pray don't speak of it," said Binoy deprecatingly.

"I say, Binoy Babu, haven't you got a dog?" asked Satish suddenly.

"A dog?" replied Binoy with a smile. "No, I am afraid I haven't."

"Why don't you keep a dog?" inquired Satish.

"Well,—the idea of keeping one never occurred to me."

"I am told," said Paresh Babu, coming to his rescue, "that Satish came here the same day. I'm afraid he must have pestered you a lot. He talks so much that his sister has nicknamed him Mr. Chatterbox."

Binoy said: "I too can chatter when I like, so we got on very well together,—didn't we, Satish Babu?"

Satish went on with his questions and Binoy with his answers, but Paresh Babu spoke very little. He only threw in a word now and then with a happy and tranquil smile. When about to go, he said: "The number of our house is 78; from here it is straight along the road to the right."

"He knows our house quite well," interrupted Satish. "He came right up to the door with me that very day."

There was no earthly reason for feeling ashamed of this fact; nevertheless, Binoy was overcome with a sense of bashfulness, as though he had been suddenly found out.

"Then you know our house," said the old gentleman. "So if you are ever—"

"That goes without saying—whenever I—" faltered Binoy.

"We are such near neighbours," said Paresh Babu as he rose. "It is only because we live in Calcutta that we have remained so long unacquainted."

Binoy saw his guests to the street and stood at the door for a little, watching them, as Paresh Babu walked slowly along leaning on his stick, while Satish carried on a ceaseless chatter by his side.

Binoy thought to himself—"I have never seen an old man like Paresh Babu. I feel I want to take the dust of his feet. And what a delightful boy Satish is! When he grows up he will be a real man. He is as frank as he is clever."

However good the old man and the boy might be, that was hardly enough to account for this sudden outburst of respect and affection. But Binoy's state of mind did not need a longer acquaintanceship.

"After this," added Binoy in his mind, "I shall *have* to go to Paresh Babu's house unless I want to be rude."

But the India of Gora's party admonished him: "Beware! Thou shalt not enter there!"

At every step Binoy had been obeying the prohibitions of this partisan India. He was sometimes beset with doubts, and yet he had obeyed. A spirit of rebelliousness now showed itself within him, for this India to-day seemed merely Negation incarnate.

The servant came to announce his midday meal, but Binoy had not yet even taken his bath. It was past noon, and with a determined shake of the head he sent the servant away, saying: "I shall not be eating at home to-day; you need not stay on for me." And without even putting on his scarf he took up an umbrella and went out into the street.

He made straight for Gora's house, for he knew that everyday at twelve o'clock Gora went to the office of his Hindu Patriots' Society in Amherst Street, where he spent the afternoon writing rousing letters to members of his party all over Bengal. Here his admirers used to gather, waiting on his words, and here his devoted assistants felt themselves honoured by being allowed to serve him.

As he had anticipated, Gora had gone as usual to the office, and Binoy, almost running into the inner apartments, burst into Anandmoyi's room. She was just beginning her meal, and Lachmi was in attendance, fanning her.

"Why, Binoy, what is the matter?" cried Anandamoyi in astonishment.

"Mother, I'm hungry," said Binoy, seating himself before her. "Give me something to eat."

"How awkward!" said Anandamoyi, much disturbed. "The Brahmin cook has just gone and you—"

"Do you think I have come to eat a Brahmin's cooking!" exclaimed Binoy. "What was the matter with my own Brahmin cook? I'll share your meal, mother. Lachmi, bring me a glass of water, will you?"

Binoy gulped down the water, and then Anandamoyi, fetching another plate for him, helped him from her dish with the greatest solicitude and affection. Binoy ate like a man who has been starving for days.

Anandamoyi, to-day, was relieved of one great source of pain, and, seeing her happy, a weight seemed to be lifted from Binoy's mind also.

Anandamoyi sat down to her sewing. The scent of some Keya flowers filled the room. Binoy reclined at her feet, with his head resting on his arm, and, forgetting all the rest of the world, went on chattering to her as in the old days.

EIGHT

With the breaking down of this last barrier a fresh flood of rebelliousness surged through Binoy's heart, and when he left the house he seemed to be flying through the air,—his feet touched ground so lightly. He wanted to proclaim to all whom he met that at last he was free from the bonds which had held him so long.

Just as he was passing No. 78, he met Paresh Babu coming from the opposite direction.

"Come in, come in," said Paresh Babu. "I'm delighted to see you, Binoy Babu." And he took him into his sitting-room which looked on the street. It was furnished with a small table, with a wooden-backed bench on one side, and two cane chairs on the other. On one wall was hanging a coloured picture of Christ, and on the other a photograph of Keshub Chandra Sen. On the table were some newspapers neatly folded and kept in place by a lead paper-weight. A small bookcase stood in the corner, on the upper shelf of which stood a complete set of Theodore Parker's works arranged in a row. On the top of the bookcase was a globe covered with a cloth.

Binoy took a seat, and his heart began to beat with agitation at the thought of one who might enter by the door behind him.

However, Paresh Babu said: "Sucharita goes every Monday to teach the daughter of a friend of mine, and, as they have a boy of the same age as Satish, he has gone with his sister.

I have just returned from escorting them there. If I had been a little later, I might have missed you."

At this piece of news Binoy felt both a sense of relief and a pang of disappointment.

It was easy enough, however, to talk with Paresh Babu, and in the course of conversation Binoy had soon told him all about himself,—how he was an orphan and how his uncle lived with his aunt in the country, looking after some landed property,—how he had studied together with his two cousins until the elder had taken up practice as a pleader in the district court, and the younger had died of cholera. His uncle's desire had been to make Binoy a deputy magistrate, but Binoy, having no ambition for such a life, was spending his time in all kinds of profitless tasks.

In this way nearly an hour passed, and to stay on without any apparent reason would have appeared impolite, so Binoy rose to go and said, "I'm sorry to have missed seeing my friend Satish. Tell him that I called."

"If you wait a little you will see them," replied Paresh Babu. "They will be back very soon."

Binoy felt ashamed to take advantage of such a casual suggestion. If he had been·pressed ever so little more, he would have stayed on, but Paresh Babu was a man of few words and not given to urging people against their will, so he had to bid farewell,—Paresh Babu merely saying: "I shall be happy to see you now and then, if you will come."

Binoy had nothing urgent to take him home. It is true he wrote for the papers, and every one praised his English style, but for some days he had not been able to give his mind to writing, and whenever he sat at his table his mind would begin to wander. So, without any particular reason, he sauntered along in the opposite direction.

He had hardly gone a few steps before he heard a shrill boyish voice calling out, "Binoy Babu! Binoy Babu!" and, looking up, he saw Satish peeping out of a hackney-cab and beckoning to him. From the glimpse of a *sari* and the white sleeve of a bodice it was not difficult to guess who the other occupant of the cab was.

According to Bengali etiquette it was not possible for Binoy to look into the cab, but before another moment had passed Satish had jumped out and, seizing him by the hand, was saying: "Come into the house, Binoy Babu."

"I have just this moment come from there," explained Binoy.

"But I wasn't at home, so you must come in again," Satish persisted.

Binoy was unable to resist Satish's pleading, and entering the house with his captive, Satish called out: "Father, I have brought Binoy Babu back again!"

The old gentleman came out of his room smiling and saying: "You've fallen into firm hands, Binoy Babu, and won't easily escape this time. Satish, go and call your sister."

Binoy stepped into the room, his heart beating fast and furiously. Paresh Babu remarked, "You're out of breath, I see. That Satish is a *caution!*"

When Satish brought his sister into the room, Binoy first became aware of a delicate perfume. Then he heard Paresh Babu saying: "Radha, Binoy Babu has come. You remember him, of course."

As Binoy looked up timidly he saw Sucharita bow and take a chair opposite him, and this time he did not omit to return the salutation.

"Yes," said Sucharita, "Binoy Babu was passing along, and the moment Satish saw him he jumped out of the gharry and captured him. Perhaps, Binoy Babu, you were going on some business—I hope he has not inconvenienced you?"

Binoy had not dared to hope that Sucharita would address any words to him personally, and he was so taken aback that he could but reply hurriedly: "No, no, I had nothing to do and am not at all inconvenienced."

Satish, pulling at his sister's dress, said: "Didi, give me the key, please. I want to show Binoy Babu our musical box."

Sucharita laughed as she said: "What! Already begun? Mr. Chatterbox's friends never know any peace. The musical box they must hear to begin with, to say nothing of their other trials and tribulations. Binoy Babu, I must warn you, the exactions of this little friend of yours are endless. I doubt whether you'll manage to bear them."

Binoy for the life of him could not see how to reply to Sucharita with equal naturalness. He vowed not to show the least bashfulness, but all that he succeeded in uttering were a few broken phrases: "No, no,—not at all,—please don't be—I'd really enjoy it."

Satish took away the keys from his sister and brought in the musical box. It consisted of a glass case with a model ship reposing on silken waves inside. On its being wound up a tune was played and the ship rocked to the rhythm. Satish's glances beamed from the ship to Binoy's face and back again to the ship—he could hardly contain his excitement.

Thus was Satish the means of helping Binoy to breakthrough his awkwardness, and it gradually became possible for him to look straight up at Sucharita's face while talking to her.

A little later Lila, one of Paresh Babu's own daughters, came in and said: "Mother wants all of you to come upstairs into the verandah."

NINE

Upstairs, on the terrace over the portico, a table was spread with a white cloth, and round it chairs were arranged. On the cornice outside the railings there stood a row of plants in tubs, and looking down, one could see by the side of the street the glossy rain-washed foliage of Sirish and Krishnachura trees.

The sun had not yet set, and its slanting rays shone wanly on one corner of the terrace.

There was no one there when Paresh Babu took Binoy upstairs, but in a moment Satish arrived bringing with him a black-and-white hairy terrier. Its name was Khudè (Tiny), and Satish showed off all its tricks. It could *salaam* with one of its paws, bow its head down to the ground, and beg for biscuits. For the glory that Khudè thus earned Satish took all the credit. Khudè himself was not an enthusiast for credit,— to him the biscuit was the more real thing.

Now and then, from a room nearby, the prattle of girls' voices, mingled with little bursts of laughter, could be heard, together with the occasional sound of a man's voice. Along with this stream of gaiety, there was borne into Binoy's mind a new sense of sweetness, touched with a pang of envy. Never before in his life had he come across the rippling merriment of girls at home. Now this music sounded so close, and yet for him it was so far away. Poor distracted Binoy was quite unable to give any attention to what Satish was chattering about beside him.

Paresh Babu's wife now arrived on the scene with her three daughters and a young man who was a distant relative. Her name was Baroda. She was no longer young, though it was easy to see that she had dressed with special care. She had lived quite a simple life in her early days, and then had all of a sudden developed an anxiety to keep pace with advanced society. Therefore it was that her silk *sari* rustled so vigorously and her high-heeled shoes made such a clatter. She was always careful about keeping clear the distinction between things that were Brahmo and things that were not. It was on this account she had changed the orthodox name of Radharani to Sucharita.

Her eldest daughter's name was Labonya. She was stout, of a cheery and sociable disposition, and loved gossip. Her face was chubby, her eyes large, and her complexion dark and glossy. She herself was inclined to be rather careless about her dress, but in this matter she was kept strictly under her mother's control. She hated high-heeled shoes but had to wear them, and whenever she went out in the afternoon her mother insisted on putting powder and rouge on her cheeks. Because of her stoutness her bodices were made so tight that when Labonya was released by her mother from the dressing-room she looked like a bale just out of the press.

The middle daughter's name was Lolita. She was almost exactly the opposite of her elder sister. She was taller and darker, quite thin, followed her own rules, and though sparing of words, she could on occasion make very cutting remarks. Her mother, in her heart of hearts, was afraid of her, and took care not to rouse her temper.

The youngest, Lila, was only ten years old. She was a regular tomboy, always struggling and fighting with Satish. Especially it was a disputed point as to who could claim the rightful ownership of Khudè. If the dog itself had been consulted it is doubtful whether it would have chosen either of them as its master, though, if anything, it probably had a slight preference for Satish, whose discipline it found easier to bear than the onslaught of Lila's caresses.

As soon as Mistress Baroda came out on to the terrace, Binoy stood up and made her a low bow. Paresh Babu introduced him with: "This is the friend in whose house the other day—"

"Oh!" exclaimed Baroda effusively. "How kind you were! We are most grateful to you." But Binoy became so bashful at this display of gratitude that he was at a loss for a suitable answer.

He was also introduced to the young man who had accompanied the girls. His name was Sudhir, and he was still at college reading for his B.A. He was pleasant-looking, fair in complexion, wore spectacles, and had a small moustache. He seemed a fidgety kind of person as he could not sit still for a moment, but was always on the move, keeping the girls lively with his teasing and joking. The girls kept on scolding him, but nevertheless could not get on without their Sudhir. He was always ready to do their shopping for them, and accompany them to the Circus or the Zoological Gardens. Sudhir's unrestrained familiarity with these girls was quite new to Binoy, in fact it gave him something of a shock. His first impulse was one of condemnation, but this soon became tempered with a tinge of jealousy.

"It seems to me I've seen you once or twice at the Brahmo Samaj services," observed Baroda by way of introduction.

Binoy suddenly felt as if he had been found out in some crime as he admitted, with unnecessary apology in his tone, that he had once or twice been to hear Keshub Babu preach.

"I suppose you are reading at college?" Baroda next asked him.

"No, I've finished with college."

"How far did you read?"

"I have taken my M.A."

This seemed to inspire Baroda with a due sense of respect for this boyish-looking youth. Heaving a sigh, she looked towards Paresh Babu as she remarked: "If our Manu had lived he would by now have taken his M.A."

Her first child, Manoranjan, had died at the age of nine and whenever she heard of any young man who had done well in his examination, or had obtained a good post, or had written a good book, Mistress Baroda immediately thought that if only her son had lived he would have done the same.

However that may be, after his loss she had taken it on herself, as a special duty, to make known to society the virtues of her three daughters. She did not neglect this opportunity of informing Binoy how studious her daughters were, nor did she conceal from him what their English governess had said about their intelligence and high qualities. When on the Prize Day of the Girls' School, the Lieutenant-Governor and his wife had been present, Labonya had been specially selected from amongst the girls of the whole school for garlanding them, and Binoy was even privileged to hear the exact words of the complimentary remark which the Governor's wife had addressed to her.

At length Baroda wound up by saying to Labonya: "Bring that piece of embroidery, dear, for which you got a prize."

This figure of a parrot worked in wool had long been known to all their relatives and visitors. It had been manufactured, with infinite pains and after many months, with the constant help of her governess, so that there was not much of Labonya's own handiwork in it; but there was no escaping the ceremony of exhibiting it to each new visitor.

At first Paresh Babu used to object, but had ceased to do so on finding that his protests were fruitless.

While Binoy was engaged in showing the proper amount of wonder and appreciation for this work of art, the servant came in with a letter for Paresh Babu. When he read it, Paresh Babu's face lighted up with pleasure as he said to the servant: "Bring the gentleman upstairs."

"Who is it?" asked Mistress Baroda.

"The son of my old friend Krishnadayal has come to call on me," replied Paresh Babu.

Binoy's heart suddenly stood still and he turned pale. He sat with his hands clenched as though preparing to stand firm under some attack. He felt sure that Gora would be struck unfavourably with the ways of these people, and that he would judge them accordingly, and he made ready to champion them in anticipation.

TEN

Sucharita was arranging the eatables on a tray in the pas sage—this she now made over to a servant to be handed round, and came and sat out on the terrace. And as the servant came in, he was followed by Gora. Everyone was struck with his size and the whiteness of his complexion. He had a caste-mark of Ganges-clay on his forehead, and was wearing a coarse *dhuti* and an old-fashioned short jacket tied with ribbon. His shoes were country-made, with turned-up toes. He came in like an incarnate image of revolt against Modernity. Even Binoy had never before seen him in such martial guise.

It was true that Gora to-day was full of fiery protest against things as they happened to be, and there was a special reason for it.

He had started the day before, on a steamer, for the bathing festival at Tribeni. At the wayside stations crowds of women pilgrims, accompanied by one or two men, had been getting on as passengers. In their anxiety to get a place there had been some elbowing and jostling, and what with the mud on their feet and the single slippery plank which served as gangway, some slipped and fell, while others were actually pushed over into the water by the sailors. Many of those who had managed to get a place for themselves missed their companions in the crush. On the top of all this was the rain, occasional showers of which kept on drenching them, and the deck, where they had to sit, was coated with a slimy mud. Their faces betokened hopeless harassment, their eyes a pitiful anxiety. Only too well did they know that such weak and insignificant creatures could expect no help from captain or crew, so that every movement of theirs was full of a timid apprehension. Gora was the only one who was doing his best to help these pilgrims in their distressful plight.

Leaning over the railings of the upper first-class deck stood an Englishman and a modernised Bengali babu, smoking cigars and laughing and talking together as they watched the fun. Every now and then, when one of the unfortunate pilgrims got into a specially awkward predicament, the Englishman laughed, and the Bengali joined in.

After they had passed two or three stations in this manner, Gora could bear it no longer. Going on to the upper deck he said in a voice of thunder: "Enough of this! Aren't you ashamed of yourselves?"

The Englishman merely stared fiercely at Gora from head to foot, but the Bengali vouchsafed a reply: "Ashamed?" he sneered. "Of course I am, to see the utter stupidity of these animals!"

"There are worse beasts than ignorant people," flung out Gora with a flaming face,—"men without hearts."

"Get out of here!" retorted the Bengali, getting excited. "You have no business to come up to the First Class."

"No, indeed," replied Gora, "my place is not with such as you; it is with those poor pilgrims there. But I warn you not to compel me to come again to this class of yours!"— with which he rushed back to the lower deck.

After this incident the Englishman leaned back in his deck-chair, with his feet upon the railing, and was immersed in a novel. His Bengali fellow-passenger made one or two attempts to pick up the thread of their conversation, but without success. Then, to prove that he was not on the side of the common herd of his countrymen, he called the *khansama* and asked him whether he could give him some roast chicken. The *khansama* replied that he had nothing but tea and bread and butter, whereupon he exclaimed in English, so that the *sahib* could hear: "The arrangements for our creature comforts on this steamer are scandalous!" His companion, however, ignored the overture; and even when, shortly after, the Englishman's newspaper blew off the table, and the Bengali jumped out of his chair to pick it up and put it back, he was not rewarded with a word of thanks.

When getting off at Chandernagore, the *sahib* suddenly went up to Gora and, lifting his hat slightly, said, "I beg your pardon for my conduct. I *am* ashamed of myself,"—and then hurried off.

What was burning within Gora, however, was the sense of outrage that his educated countryman could go to the length of joining a foreigner in exulting over the sorry plight of his own people, and laugh at them with an assumption of superiority. That the people of his country had laid themselves open to all kinds of insult and insolent behaviour, that they had come to the pass of accepting it as inevitable to be treated like animals by their more fortunate compatriots, and of regarding such treatment as but natural and proper,— the root-cause of all this Gora knew to be the deep-seated ignorance which pervaded the country, and this thought nearly broke his heart. But what hurt him most was the fact that the educated people did not take on their own shoulders the burden of this eternal shame and insult, but rather could glory in their own comparative immunity. It was for this reason that Gora, to show his contempt for all the book-learning and slavish conventions of such educated people, had come to the Brahmo's house with the mark of the Ganges-clay on his forehead, and these peculiar rustic shoes on his feet.

"O Lord!" said Binoy to himself, "Gora is out in full war-paint." His heart sank within him at the bare thought of what Gora might say and do next, and he in turn felt called upon to gird himself for the defence.

While Mistress Baroda had been talking with Binoy, Satish had perforce to be content with amusing himself with a top in one corner of the terrace; but at the sight of Gora he lost all interest in this occupation and, edging slowly up to Binoy's chair, stared at the new visitor as he asked in a whisper: "Is that your friend?"

"Yes," replied Binoy.

Gora had given just one glance at Binoy and thereafter ignored his presence. He saluted Paresh Babu in due form, and then, without any appearance of constraint, he drew one of the chairs a little away from the table and sat down. As for the ladies, orthodox etiquette demanded that he should not give any sign that he was even aware of their presence.

Mistress Baroda had just decided to remove her daughters from the neighbourhood of this unmannerly boor, when Paresh Babu introduced him to her as the son of an old friend, whereupon Gora turned towards her and bowed.

Sucharita had heard Binoy refer to Gora, but she did not understand that this visitor was he, and at first sight she felt a certain resentment towards him, for she had neither the training nor the patience to put up with educated people who could still hold on to strict orthodoxy.

Paresh Babu began to make inquiries after his boyhood's friend Krishnadayal, and to recount incidents of their student days. "Amongst the college students of those days," said he, "we were the worst pair of iconoclasts you could imagine—we had no vestige of respect for traditions—we regarded the taking of unorthodox food as our actual duty. How many evenings have we spent eating forbidden food in a Mussulman's shop near College Square, and then sitting up till midnight discussing how we would reform Hindu society!"

Baroda here interposed the question: "And what are your friend's views nowadays?"

"Now he strictly observes all orthodox customs," replied Gora.

"Is he not ashamed of himself?" asked Baroda, ablaze with indignation.

"Shame is a sign of a weak character," laughed Gora. "Some people are even ashamed to acknowledge their own fathers."

"Wasn't he formerly a Brahmo?" inquired Baroda.

"I also was once a Brahmo," replied Gora.

"And you now have faith in a deity that has finite form?" asked Baroda.

"I'm not so superstitious as to show contempt for finite forms without justification," answered Gora. "Can form be belittled merely by reviling it? Has anyone been able to penetrate its mystery?"

"But form is limited," interrupted Paresh Babu in his gentle voice.

"Nothing can become manifest unless it has limits," persisted Gora. "The Infinite has taken the help of form in order to manifest Himself, otherwise how could He be revealed? That which is unrevealed cannot attain perfection. The formless is fulfilled in forms just as thought is perfected in words."

"You mean, to say that is more perfect than the formless?" exclaimed Baroda, shaking her head unconvinced.

"It matters little what I mean," replied Gora. "The world does not depend for its form on what I say. If the formless had been the real perfection, then form would have found no place in the universe at all."

Sucharita heartily wished someone would humiliate this arrogant youth by vanquishing him in argument, and she was angry to see Binoy sitting quietly by without opening his mouth. Gora's very violence of tone seemed to be bringing her strength for a crushing reply. At this moment, however, the servant brought in a kettle of hot water and Sucharita had to busy herself making the tea, while Binoy occasionally darted an inquiring glance in her direction.

Although there was not much difference between Gora and Binoy on matters relating to worship, yet that Gora should have come uninvited into this Brahmo home and shown such uncompromising hostility, pained Binoy deeply. He was filled with admiration for Paresh Babu's calm self-control,—his benign serenity, raised into the heights of aloofness above, both sides of the argument,—when he contrasted it with Gora's aggressive demeanour. Opinions are nothing, thought he to himself,—better than all is the self-contained calm of true realisation. What does it matter which argument is true and which is false—what has been gained within is the real thing.

Paresh Babu in the course of the discussion every now and then closed his eyes and took a plunge into the depths of his being—this was a habit of his—and Binoy watched, fascinated, the peace that shone on his countenance while his mind was thus turned inwards. It was a great disappointment to him to find that Gora's reverence did not flow out towards this venerable man and help him to keep a restraint on his tongue.

When Sucharita had finished pouring out several cups of tea, she looked inquiringly towards Paresh Babu. She was in perplexity as to which of the guests she should offer tea to.

Mistress Baroda looked at Gora and burst out with: "You, I suppose, do not take any of these things!"

"No," replied Gora with decision.

"Why?" persisted Baroda. "Are you afraid of losing caste?"

"Yes," answered Gora.

"Then you believe in caste?"

"Is caste a thing of my own creation that I should not believe in it? Since I own allegiance to society, I must respect caste also."

"Are you then bound to obey society in all matters?" asked Baroda.

"Not to obey society is to destroy it," replied Gora.

"What if it is destroyed?"

"You might as well ask what harm there is in cutting off the branch on which one is seated!"

"Mother, what's the good of all this useless argument?" called out Sucharita in vexation. "He will not eat with us and there's an end of it!"

Gora fixed his gaze on Sucharita for a moment, while she, looking towards Binoy, asked with some hesitation: "Do you—?"

Binoy had never in his life taken tea. He had given up eating bread or biscuits made by Mussulmans long ago, but to-day he felt that he was in duty bound to eat and drink whatever was offered, so with an effort he looked up straight as he said: "Yes, of course I will!" and then he glanced at Gora, on whose face there played a faint sarcastic smile.

Binoy manfully drank up his tea, though it was bitter and unpalatable to his taste.

"What a nice boy, this Binoy!" was Baroda's unspoken comment, and, turning her back on Gora, she gave all her attention to him. When he observed this, Paresh Babu quietly drew his chair up to Gora and began to talk with him apart, in an undertone.

Another visitor was now announced. They all welcomed him as Panu Babu, though his real name was Haran-chandra Nag. He had a reputation in his own circle for extraordinary learning and intelligence, and though nothing had been actually said on either side, it was in the air that he would marry Sucharita. There was certainly no room for doubt that he had an inclination in that direction, and all her girl friends persistently chaffed Sucharita on the subject.

Haran taught in a school, for which reason Mistress Baroda did not think much of this mere schoolmaster. She indeed made it quite plain that it was as well he had not dared to make up to any of her own daughters. The sons-in-law of her dreams were enterprising knights-errant whose one object of pursuit should be a deputy-magistrateship.

As Sucharita offered Haran a cup of tea, Labonya from a safe distance gave her a meaning glance and puckered up her mouth in a smile.

This did not escape Binoy, for within this brief space of time his vision had become unusually alert and penetrating in certain matters, though he had not formerly been famous for his powers of observation. It struck Binoy as an unfair disposition of Providence that these two, Haran and Sudhir, should be so intimately bound up with the family history as to have become objects of secret signs between the girls of the house.

Into Sucharita's mind, on the other hand, the arrival of Haran on the scene brought a glimmer of hope. If but this new champion of hers should succeed in bringing the haughty conqueror to the dust, she would feel avenged. At any other time Haran's argumentativeness only irritated her, but to-day she welcomed this knight of wordiness with joy, and she was lavish in her supply of armour in the shape of tea and cakes.

"Panu Babu, here is our friend—" began Paresh Babu.

But Haran cut him short with: "Oh, I know him very well! At one time he was an enthusiastic member of our Brahmo Samaj." And with this he turned away from Gora and gave all his attention to his cup of tea.

At that time only one or two Bengalis had passed the Civil Service examination, and Sudhir was describing the reception given to one of them on his return home from England.

"What does it matter," snapped out Haran, "how well Bengalis may do in their examinations, they will never be any good as administrators." And in order to demonstrate that no Bengali could carry on the work of a district, he waxed eloquent on the various defects and weaknesses of the Bengali character.

Gora's face reddened visibly as this tirade proceeded, but, subduing his lion's roar as far as he could, he broken in at length with: "If that is your honest opinion, aren't you ashamed to be sitting comfortably at this table munching bread and butter?"

"What would you have me do?" asked Haran, raising his eyebrows in astonishment.

"Either try to remove these stains from the Bengali character, or go and hang yourself!" replied Gora. "Is it such an easy thing to say that our nation will never accomplish anything? I wonder your bread doesn't choke you!"

"Mustn't I speak out the truth?" asked Haran.

"I beg your pardon," continued Gora with heat, "but if you really believed what you say, you could not have held forth about it so glibly. It is because you know it to be false that it comes so easily from your lips. Let me tell you, Haran Babu, falsehood is a sin, false censure is a still greater sin, but there are few sins to compare with the false revilement of one's own people!"

Haran was quivering with rising anger, and when Gora added: "Do you imagine that you are the one superior person amongst all your countrymen? that you alone are entitled to give vent to your fulminations against them, and the rest of us, on behalf of our forefathers, are quietly to submit to your indictment?"—it became impossible for Haran to give up his position, and his abuse of the Bengalis was continued in a still higher pitch. He referred to many kinds of evil customs prevalent in Bengali society: so long as these remained, said he, there was absolutely no hope for the race.

"What you say about evil customs," said Gora scornfully, "you have merely learnt off by heart from English books— you know nothing at all about the matter at first hand. When you are able to condemn all the evil customs of the English with as much honest indignation, you will have a right to talk."

Paresh tried his best to change the subject, but it was impossible to check the infuriated Haran. Meanwhile the sun went down, and the sky became glorious with the radiance which shone through the fringe of clouds, and in spite of all the turmoil of the wordy warfare, the strains of some music seemed to fill Binoy's heart.

As this was the time for his evening meditation, Paresh left the terrace and, going down into the garden, seated himself beneath a champak tree.

Baroda had conceived a thorough dislike for Gora, nor was Haran a favourite of hers; so when she could stand their discussion no longer she turned to Binoy and said: "Come, Binoy Babu, let's go inside." And Binoy could do no less to mark his appreciation of the special favour thus shown to him by Mistress Baroda than meekly to follow her into the room.

Baroda called to her daughters to follow them, while Satish, seeing the hopelessness of the discussion coming to an end, made his exit with his dog.

Baroda turned the opportunity to account by discoursing to Binoy on the accomplishments of her daughters, and turning to Labonya said, "Bring your album, dear, and show it to Binoy Babu, will you?"

Labonya was so accustomed to showing this album to the latest visitor that she was always on the look-out for this request, and in fact had been feeling disappointed that the discussion should be proving so unending.

On opening the album Binoy saw some English poems of Moore and Longfellow written in it. The capital letters and titles of the poems were done in ornamental characters, and the handwriting showed the greatest neatness and care. His admiration was unaffected, for in those days it reflected no small credit on a girl to be able to copy English poetry so well.

When she found Binoy duly overwhelmed, Mistress Baroda turned to her second daughter with the request, "Lolita, darling, that recitation of yours—"

But Lolita replied very firmly, "No, mother, I really cannot. I don't remember it very well," and turned to look out of the window.

Baroda explained to Binoy that she really remembered it perfectly well, but was so modest that she did not care to show off. She said that she had been like this from childhood, and in proof of her assertion she recounted one or two instances of her remarkable attainments. She added that she was so brave that even if she was hurt she would not cry, and stated that in these respects she much resembled her father.

Now it was Lila's turn. At first when she was told to recite she began to giggle, but as soon as she started she was like a machine wound up, and in one breath she reeled off "Twinkle, twinkle, little star" without the least sign of understanding its meaning.

Knowing that the next item on the programme was a display of singing, Lolita went out of the room.

The discussion outside had now reached its height. Haran had given up all attempts at argument and was indulging freely in the hottest of words, while Sucharita, ashamed and vexed at Haran's lack of self-control, was taking Gora's part: and this fact did not add to Haran's peace of mind, or tend to console him.

The evening sky became dark with heavy rain-clouds. Hawkers began to sell garlands of jasmine in the street with their peculiar cries. Fire-flies twinkled out on the foliage of the trees by the roadside, and a deep shadow darkened the water of the neighbouring tank.

Binoy now reappeared on the verandah to say good-bye, and Paresh Babu said to Gora: "Come and see us whenever you like. Krishnadayal was like my own brother, and though our opinions differ nowadays, and we never see or write to each other, yet the friendships of boyhood's days always remain part of our flesh and blood. I feel very close to you because of my old relations with your father."

The tranquil and affectionate voice of Paresh Babu acted like a charm in calming down the argumentative heat of Gora's mind. There had not been much of reverence in Gora's first salutation to the old man, but now at parting he bowed to him with real respect. Of Sucharita he took not the slightest notice, for to have shown by the least gesture that he was noticing her presence would to him have been the height of rudeness. Binoy, making a low obeisance to Paresh Babu, bowed slightly to Sucharita in turn, and then, as if somewhat ashamed of what he had done, he hurried after Gora.

To avoid the ceremony of leave-taking Haran had gone inside and was turning over the leaves of a Brahmo hymn-book which lay on the table; but the moment the two guests had gone he hastened back to the verandah, and said to Paresh Babu: "My dear sir, it's hardly right to introduce the girls to any and every one."

Sucharita felt so annoyed that she could no longer conceal her feelings, and exclaimed: "If father had followed that advice, then we should have never become acquainted with you!"

"It's all right if you confine yourself to people belonging to your own society," explained Haran.

Paresh Babu laughed. "You want us to go back to the zenana system over again by restricting our expansion within our own community. But I myself think that girls ought to mix with people of all shades of opinion, otherwise they will simply remain narrow-minded. Why need we be so squeamish about it?"

"I never said they should not mix with people of a variety of opinions," replied Haran. "But these fellows don't even know how to behave towards ladies."

"No, no!" expostulated Paresh. "What you take for lack of manners is merely shyness—and unless they come into ladies' society that will never be cured."

ELEVEN.

Haran had been specially anxious the other day to put Gora in his proper place and to raise the standard of victory before Sucharita's very eyes. At the beginning this had been Sucharita's hope also. But, as it turned out, exactly the opposite happened. On social and religious matters Sucharita could not agree with Gora, but regard for her own race and sympathy for her countrymen came naturally to her, and although she had never before discussed the condition of her country, yet, when she heard Gora thunder forth his protest on hearing his own people abused, her whole mind echoed a sympathetic assent. Never before had she heard anyone speak with such force and firm faith about the motherland.

Then, when Haran had spitefully returned to the charge behind their backs, calling Binoy and Gora ill-mannered boors, Sucharita in protest against such meanness was again drawn to take their side.

Not that her feeling of revolt against Gora was altogether quelled. Even now his aggressively countrified dress hurt her somewhat. She understood somehow that in this protesting orthodoxy there was a spirit of defiance,—that it had not the naturalness of real conviction,—that it did not find its full satisfaction in his own faith,—that in fact it was assumed in anger and arrogance in order to hurt others.

That evening, in whatever she did when at her meal or while telling Lila stories, Sucharita was conscious of some gnawing pain, deep down in her being, which kept on hurting her. A thorn can only be extracted if you know where it is, and Sucharita sat alone on the verandah trying to locate the thorn which so galled her. She tried, in the cool of the darkness, to allay the uncalled-for fever of her heart, but all in vain. The undefined burden which she carried made her want to weep, but tears would not come.

Nothing could be more absurd than to suppose that Sucharita should be so grievously exercised merely because some unknown young man had come with a defiantly prominent caste-mark on his brow, or because it had not been possible to defeat him in argument and humble his pride to the dust. She dismissed this explanation from her mind as altogether impossible. Then she blushed with shame as the real reason at length dawned on her. For two or three hours she had been sitting face to face with this young man, and had even now and again taken his part in the argument, and yet he had not taken any notice of her, nor, when he said good-bye, did not he seem even aware of her presence. It became clear beyond doubt that it was this complete indifference to her that hurt her so deeply. Binoy had also shown the awkwardness which is natural to those not accustomed to ladies' society, but this awkwardness of his had merely been a modest, shrinking diffidence, of which Gora had not a trace.

Why was it so impossible for Sucharita to bear this hard indifference of Gora's, or to dismiss it from her mind with contempt? She felt ready to die at the remembrance that, even in face of such neglect, she had not had the self-control to refrain from thrusting herself into the discussion. Once, indeed, when she had shown heat at the unfairness of one of Haran's arguments, Gora had looked up at her. In his glance there was clearly no sign of shyness, but what there *was* in it did not seem so clear. Did he think her to be forward, or wanting to show off,—thus to be joining uninvited in an argument between men? What did it matter what he thought? Nothing at all, and yet Sucharita could not help feeling pained. She strove hard to forget all about it, to wipe it from her memory, but she could not. Then she felt angry with Gora, and tried to feel a withering contempt for him as an arrogant, superstitious youth; but still she felt humbled as she recalled the unflinching gaze of that immense man with a voice like thunder, and she was quite unable to maintain the dignity of her own attitude.

Thus torn between her own conflicting feelings, Sucharita sat alone till far into the night. The lights were out and everyone had retired. She heard the front door being shut, and by this she knew that the servants had finished their work and were preparing for bed.

At this moment Lolita came out in her night-dress and, without saying anything, went and stood by the balustrade. Sucharita smiled to herself, for she realised that Lolita was vexed with her, as she had promised to sleep with her that night and had entirely forgotten about it. But merely to acknowledge the forgetfulness would not have been any good for appeasing Lolita,—being able to forget her was the real fault. And Lolita was not the sort of girl to remind anyone of a promise. She had determined to keep still in bed, without a sign of being hurt, but as time passed the keenness of her disappointment increased until, able to bear it no longer, she had left her bed, just to show quietly that she was still awake.

Sucharita left her chair and, going slowly up to Lolita, embraced her, saying: "Lolita, dear, don't be angry with me."

But Lolita moved away, murmuring: "Angry? Why should I be angry? Pray keep your seat."

"Come, dear, let's go to bed," pleaded Sucharita, taking hold of her hand.

But Lolita remained where she was without answering, till at last Sucharita dragged her along to their bedroom.

Then, at last, Lolita asked in a choked voice: "Why are you so late? Don't you know it is eleven o'clock? I have heard all the hours strike, and now you'll be too sleepy for a chat."

"I am so sorry, dear," said Sucharita, drawing her closer to her.

The fault having been acknowledged, Lolita's anger evaporated, and she was mollified at once.

"Of whom were you thinking sitting alone all this time, Didi? Was it of Panu Babu?" she asked.

"Oh, get away!" cried Sucharita with a gesture of reproof. Lolita could not bear Panu Babu. In fact she would not even chaff Sucharita about him as her other sisters did. The very idea that Haran wished to marry Sucharita infuriated her.

After a few moments of silence Lolita started again: "What a nice man Binoy Babu is, isn't he, Didi?" And it could not be said that in this question there was no attempt to test what was in Sucharita's mind.

"Yes, dear, Binoy Babu seems quite a nice sort of person," was the reply.

This, however, was not at all in tune with what Lolita had been expecting, so she went on: "But whatever you say, Didi, that Gourmohan Babu is altogether insufferable. What a nasty complexion, and what hard features! And such an awful prig! How did he strike you?"

"He is far too orthodox for my taste," replied Sucharita.

"No! No! It's not that," exclaimed Lolita. "Why, uncle is very orthodox too—but that is so different—I—I can't quite explain what I mean."

"Yes, quite different indeed!" laughed Sucharita, and as she recalled Gora's high white brow with the caste-mark on

it, her anger against him flamed up over again, for was it not
thus that Gora had announced to them all in big letters:
"From you am I different"? Nothing less than levelling this
immense pride of aloofness to the dust could have soothed
her sense of outrage.

Gradually they stopped talking and fell asleep. When it
was two o'clock, Sucharita woke up and heard the rain pouring
down in torrents. The lamp in the corner of the room had
gone out, and every now and then the lightning flashed
through their mosquito-net. In the stillness and gloom of
night, with the sound of the ceaseless rain in her ears, Sucharita
felt heavy of heart. She tossed from side to side in her effort
to sleep, and looked with envy at the face of Lolita, who was
in deep slumber—but sleep refused to come.

In her vexation she left the bed and went to the door.
Opening it, she stood looking out on the roof with the rain
spraying in on her with every gust of wind. All the incidents
of that evening came across her mind one by one. The picture
of Gora's face, all aglow with excitement and lighted by the
rays of the setting sun, flashed out, and all the arguments
which she had heard, but forgotten, now came back to her
together with the sound of his deep, strong voice.

His words rang again in her ears: "Those whom *you* call
illiterate are those to whose party *I* belong. What *you* call
superstition, that is *my* faith! So long as you do not love your
country and take your stand beside your own people, I will
not allow one word of abuse of the motherland from you."—
To which Haran had replied: "How can such an attitude make
for the country's reform?" Whereupon Gora had roared out:
"Reform? That can wait a while yet. More important than
reforms are love and respect. Reform will come of itself from
within, after we are a united people. You would break up the
country into a hundred bits by your policy of separateness.
Because, forsooth, our country is full of superstitions, you,

the non-superstitious, must keep superior and aloof! What I say is,—may it be my greatest desire never to keep apart from the rest, even by becoming superior! When at last we are really one, then which of our orthodox practices shall remain and which be abolished, the country, and He who is the God of our country, shall decide."

Haran had retorted: "The country is full of just such practices and customs as do not allow it to become united." To which Gora answered: "If you believe that you must first root up all evil practices and customs before our country can become one, then, every time you have to cross the ocean, you would have to begin by scooping out the water. Put away all your pride and contempt, and in true humility become inwardly one with all, and then shall your love overcome a thousand defects and evils. In every society there are faults and weaknesses, but so long as the people are united to one another by the bonds of love, they are able to neutralise all the poison. The cause of rottenness is always present in the air, but so long as you are alive it cannot work,—only dead things decay. Let me tell you that we are not going to submit to outside attempts to reform us, whether it be from you or from foreign missionaries."

"Why not?" Haran had asked, and Gora had replied: "There is a good reason. We can take correction from our parents, but when the police come to do it there is more of insult than of improvement in the process, and we only lower our manhood if we suffer it. First acknowledge kinship with us, then come to reform us, else even good advice from you will but harm us."

In this way Sucharita recalled Gora's words in every detail, and, as she did so, her heart ached more and more. Tired out at last, she went back to bed and, pressing her eyes with her hands, tried to thrust away these thoughts from her mind and go off to sleep; but her face and ears burned, and her brain seethed with the rival ideas which struggled within it.

TWELVE

W hen Binoy had left Paresh Babu's house and was in the
street, he said: "You might walk a little more slowly,
Gora, old chap,—your legs are longer than mine, and if you
don't moderate your pace a little I shall get out of breath
trying to keep up with you."

"I want to walk by myself to-night," answered Gora
gruffly; "I have got a lot of things to think over." And he went
off rapidly at his usual rate.

Binoy felt deeply hurt. By revolting against Gora he had
to-day broken his usual rule, and he would have felt relieved
if Gora had scolded him. A storm would have cleared the
sultry air which hung over the sky of their lifelong friendship,
and he could have breathed freely again.

Binoy could not feel that Gora was to blame for leaving
him in a temper; but this was the first time in all their long
friendship, that there had been any real disagreement between
them, and Binoy had a heavy heart as he walked through the
dismal rainy night with the dark thunder-clouds rumbling at
intervals. It seemed as if his life had suddenly left its beaten
track and started off in a new direction. In the darkness Gora
had gone one way and he another.

Next morning, on getting up, his mind was easier. He felt
that in the night he had worked himself up into uncalled-for
torment of mind, and now, in the morning, he did not feel

that his friendship for Gora and his acquaintanceship with Paresh Babu were so very incompatible. He even smiled at the idea of having made so much of the affair, and at the misery he had felt the night before.

So, throwing his shawl[1] over his shoulders, he went off at a good round pace to Gora's house. Gora was seated downstairs, reading. He had caught sight of Binoy in the street, but to-day Binoy's arrival did not make him take his eyes off the paper. Binoy, without saying a word, took away the newspaper from Gora's hands.

"I think you've made some mistake," observed Gora coldly. "I am Gourmohan—a superstitious Hindu."

"The mistake is perhaps yours," replied Binoy. "I am Binoy-bhusan, that same Gourmohan's superstitious friend."

"But Gourmohan is such an incorrigible fellow that he never apologises for his superstitions to any one at all."

"Binoy too is like that. But he does not try to force his superstitions down others' throats."

In less than no time the two friends were in the middle of a hot discussion, and the neighbours speedily became aware that Gora and Binoy had met.

"What need was there for you that day to deny that you visited at Paresh Babu's?" Gora asked at length.

"There's no question of need at all," smiled Binoy. "I denied it simply because I had not visited there. Yesterday was the first time that I entered their house."

"It strikes me you know the way to enter all right, but I doubt if you will find the way out so easily!" sneered Gora.

"That may be so," said Binoy. "Perhaps I was born that way. I don't find it easy to leave anyone for whom I have

---

1 A *dhuti* for the lower part and a tunic for the upper, is the usual Bengali costume at home; over this is added a scarf or a shawl when going out.

love or respect. You yourself have had proof of this nature of mine."

"So then your goings there will continue indefinitely from now onwards?"

"Why should I be the only one to come and go? You also have the power of movement: you are not a nailed-down fixture, are you?"

"I may go, but I return," said Gora; "but in the signs I observed in you, there was no suggestion of returning. How did you like your tea?"

"It tasted rather bitter."

"Why then—"

"To have refused it would have been still more bitter."

"Is good manners, then, all that is needed to preserve society?" asked Gora.

"Not always. But look here, Gora, when social conventions conflict with the dictates of the heart—"

Gora in his impatience would not let Binoy finish. "Heart indeed!" he roared out. "It is because society is so insignificant for you that at every turn you can find your heart in conflict with it. If only you could have realised how deep the pain of a blow against society goes, you would be ashamed to be sentimentalising over that heart of yours. It rends your heart to give the least bit of offence to Paresh Babu's daughters: it breaks mine to see how easily you can hurt the whole of society on such a slight pretext!"

"But really, Gora," expostulated Binoy, "if it is a blow to society for someone to drink a cup of tea, then all I can say is that such blows are good for the country. If we try to protect the country from this kind of thing, we shall only make it weak and effeminate."

"My dear sir," replied Gora, "I know every one of these stock arguments—don't take me for an absolute fool. But all this does not arise in the present circumstances. When a sick child does not want to take its medicine, the mother, though quite well, drinks some herself to console the child with the idea that both are in the same plight. That is not a question of medical treatment, but of personal love, and if that love is lacking, however reasonable the mother's actions may be, the relation of mother and child is hurt, and with it is lost the desired effect. I do not quarrel with the tea-cup—it is the breaking of the relations with our country which hurts me. Far easier is it to refuse the tea,—even to give offence to Paresh Babu's daughters! In the present state of our country, to become one in spirit with all is our chief task. When once we have accomplished that, the question of whether we should drink tea or not will be settled in two words."

"Then I see it will be long enough before I drink my second cup of tea!" observed Binoy.

"No, there's no reason why it should be so very long," replied Gora. "But, Binoy, why do you insist on holding on to me? The time has come for you to give me up along with the other things in Hindu society which are displeasing to you. Otherwise Paresh Babu's daughters will feel hurt!"

At this moment Abinash entered the room. He was a disciple of Gora's, and whatever he heard from Gora's lips his mind made petty and his language made vulgar, as he went on publishing it broadcast. As it happened, however, those who were unable to understand Gora felt that they understood Abinash perfectly, and praised his words accordingly. Abinash was especially jealous of Binoy, and whenever he got the chance he would try conclusions with him with the most foolish arguments. Binoy had no patience with his stupidity and would cut him short; whereupon Gora, taking up the argument, would himself enter the arena; while Abinash would plume himself that it was *his* ideas which Gora was expounding.

Feeling that the arrival of Abinash on the scene effectually spoilt for the time all chance of his becoming reconciled to

Gora, Binoy went upstairs to where Anandamoyi was seated outside her store-room, cutting up vegetables for the kitchen.

"I have been hearing your voice for some time," said Anandamoyi. "Why so early? Did you take your breakfast before coming out?"

If it had been any other day, Binoy would have said: "No, I did not"—and would there and then have sat down and had a good time, doing justice to Anandamoyi's hospitality. But to-day he replied: "Thanks, mother, I had my breakfast before starting."

To-day he did not want to give Gora further occasion for offence,—he knew he had not yet been fully forgiven, and the feeling that he was still being kept somewhat at a distance was inwardly oppressing him.

Taking a knife out of his pocket he sat down and began to help Anandamoyi to peel potatoes. After a quarter of an hour he went downstairs again, and finding that Gora and Abinash had gone out together, he remained sitting silently in Gora's room for a time; then he took up the paper and absently glanced over the advertisement columns. At length he heaved a deep sigh and left the house.

After his midday meal he again began to feel restless to see Gora. He had never had any hesitation in humbling himself to his friend, but even if he had no pride of his own to stand in the way, the dignity of his friendship had its claims. It is true he felt that his single-hearted loyalty to Gora had suffered because of his allowing room for intimacy with Paresh Babu, and for that he was prepared for Gora's sneers and upbraidings, but to be cast off in this way was more than he could have imagined possible. After going a short distance from his house, Binoy retraced his steps;—he dared not venture up Gora's house again, lest his friendship should again be subject to insult.

THIRTEEN

After several days had passed in this way, one afternoon Binoy sat down after his midday meal, pen in hand, to write a letter to Gora. Putting his utter lack of progress down to the bluntness of his pen, he spent a long time mending it with a knife, with the utmost care. While he was thus engaged, Binoy heard his name called out down below. Throwing the pen on the table, he ran quickly downstairs crying, "Come up, Mohim Dada."

Mohim came upstairs and made himself a comfortable seat on Binoy's bed. After he had finished scrutinising the furniture of the room at some length, he said: "Look here, Binoy, it's not that I don't know your address—nor that I have no desire to inquire after your welfare, but the fact is, with you model young men of the present generation there's no chance of getting *pan* or a smoke in your rooms, so unless there is anything very special, I never—" Here he stopped, seeing that Binoy was looking flurried, but went on: "If you are thinking of going out to buy a hookah, I beg you to have pity on me. I can forgive you for not offering me tobacco, but I would never survive a new hookah filled by the hand of a clumsy novice." Mohim took up a fan which was lying nearby, and, after he had fanned himself awhile, he managed to come to his point: "That fact is, I have a reason for coming to see you at the sacrifice of my Sunday afternoon's nap. I want you to do me a favour."

"What favour may that be?" asked Binoy.

"Promise first, and then I'll tell you," replied Mohim.

"Of course, if it is anything I can do—"

"It is a thing you alone can do. You have only to say, yes."

"Why are you so diffident to-day?" asked Binoy. "You know quite well that I am like one of the family—if I can help you in any way, of course I will."

Mohim produced a wrap of *pan* leaves from his pocket and, offering some to Binoy, stuffed the rest into his own mouth, and, as he chewed them, he said: "You know my daughter Sasi. She's not so bad-looking; for she does not take after her father in that respect. She is getting on in years, and I must be arranging for her marriage. I can't sleep of nights for thinking that she might fall into the hands of some good-for-nothing fellow."

"What makes you so anxious?" said Binoy comfortingly. "There's plenty of time for her marriage yet."

"If you had a daughter of your own you would understand my anxiety," replied Mohim, sighing. "As the years pass, up goes her age of itself, but a bridegroom, does not come of himself. So as the time flies I am getting into an awful state of mind. If, however, you can give me some hope, then of course I don't mind waiting for a time."

Binoy was in a quandary. "I am afraid I don't know many likely people," he muttered. "In fact, you may say I practically don't know anybody at all in Calcutta, outside your family— still, I will look around."

"You know Sasi, at all events,—what kind of a girl she is and all that?" said Mohim.

"Of course I do!" laughed Binoy. "Why, I've known her since she was a tiny-tot—she's fine girl."

"Then you need not look very far, my boy. I offer her to you!" With which Mohim beamed triumphantly.

"What!" cried Binoy, now thoroughly alarmed.

"I beg your pardon if I have put my foot in it," said Mohim. "Of course your family is better than ours, but surely, with one of your modern education, that need not stand in the way?"

"No, no!" exclaimed Binoy. "It is not a question of family,—but just think of her tender age—"

"What do you mean?" protested Mohim. "Sasi is quite old enough! The girls of Hindu homes are not *mem-sahibs*—it would never do to fly in the face of our own customs."

Mohim was not a man to let his victim off so easily, and in his clutches Binoy felt he hardly knew what to do. At last he said: "Well, let's have a little time to think it over."

"Take your time by all means. You need not think I came to fix the happy day straight off."

"I have my people to consult—" began Binoy again.

"Of course, of course," broke in Mohim. "They certainly must be consulted. So long as your uncle is alive, we could not think of doing anything against his wishes." And taking some more *pan* from his pocket he went away, appearing to regard the matter as settled.

Some time ago Anandamoyi had thrown out a suggestion as to the possibility of Binoy marrying Sasi, but Binoy had not paid any heed to it. To-day also the match did not appear to him any the more suitable, but nevertheless he allowed the idea a place in his mind. If the marriage took place, thought he to himself, then he would really become one of Gora's family, not to be so easily cast off. He had always considered as laughable the English custom of regarding marriage as an affair of the heart, and so to him there was nothing impossible in the idea of his union with Sasi. In fact, he felt a special pleasure for the moment, because this proposal of Mohim's would give him an excuse for seeking Gora's advice. He half hoped that his friend would even press him to accept it, for he was sure that, if he didn't agree too readily, Mohim would ask Gora to intercede.

These thoughts gradually drove away Binoy's depression, and, in his eagerness to see Gora at once, he started out towards his house. He had not gone far when he heard Satish calling to him from behind.

He returned to his lodgings with the boy, who produced from his pocket something tied up in his handkerchief. "Guess what' in here!" said Satish.

Binoy named all kinds of impossible things such as "A skull," "A puppy," but only succeeded in winning Satish's disapproval.

At last, opening the bundle, Satish displayed some black-looking fruits and asked: "Can you tell me what these are?"

Binoy ventured a few random guesses, and when he had given it up, Satish explained that an aunt who lived in Rangoon had sent a parcel of these fruits for the family, and his mother had sent a few to Binoy Babu as a present.

Burmese mangosteens were not often seen in Calcutta in those days, so Binoy shook them and pinched them and then asked: "How on earth is one to eat this fruit, Satish Babu?"

Satish, laughing at Binoy's ignorance, said: "See here, you must not try and bite them—you must cut them with a knife and then eat the inside."

Satish, only a short while before, had caused great amusement to his relatives with his fruitless attempts to bite into one of them; he was now able to forget his own discomfiture by laughing at Binoy.

After these two friends of unequal age had joked together for a little, Satish said: "Binoy Babu, mother says that if you have time you must come with me. To-day is Lila's birthday."

"I'm sorry I shan't have time to-day," said Binoy. "I am going somewhere else."

"Where are you going?" asked Satish.

"To my friend's house."

"What, that friend of yours?"

"Yes."

Satish could not understand the logic which prevented Binoy from going to their house, but compelled him to go to another friend—and that too a friend whom he, for his part, could not bear. Satish disliked the very idea of Binoy's wanting to see such a friend, who looked even more severe than his head master, and from whom any appreciation of his wonderful musical box seemed quite out of the question. So he insisted: "No, Binoy Babu, you must come home with me."

It did not take long before Binoy had to capitulate. For all the conflict of his inclinations, for all the objections which occurred to his mind, he at last took his captor's hand and started towards No. 78. It was impossible for Binoy not to feel pleased at being specially chosen to share the rare fruits from Burma, or to ignore the overture of intimacy which this implied.

When Binoy was approaching Paresh Babu's house he saw Haran coming out with several other unknown people who had been invited to Lila's birthday feast. Haran Babu, however, went off without appearing to notice him.

As he entered the house Binoy heard the sound of laughter and scampering. Sudhir had stolen the key of the drawer where Labonya kept her album hidden. Amongst the poems selected by this youthful aspirant for literary fame were some which would have been fit subject for jest, and Sudhir was threatening to read these out before the assembled company. It was when the struggle between the two sides was at its height that Binoy appeared on the battle-field. On his arrival Labonya's party vanished in the twinkling of an eye, and Satish ran after them to share in the fun. Presently Sucharita came into the room and said: "Mother asks you to wait a little, she will be here directly. Father has gone to call on Anath Babu, and will not be late coming back either."

With the idea of putting Binoy more at ease Sucharita began to talk to him about Gora. She said with a laugh: "I imagine he'll never enter our house again!"

"What makes you think so?" asked Binoy.

"He certainly was shocked to see us girls appear in the presence of men," explained Sucharita. "I don't suppose he has any respect for women who don't give themselves entirely to domestic duties."

Binoy found it difficult to answer this remark. He would have been only too pleased to be able to contradict it, but how could he say what he knew was untrue? So he merely said: "Gora's opinion is, I think, that unless girls give their whole mind to housework they are wanting in their loyalty to their duty."

To this Sucharita replied: "Then would not it be better for men and women to have a complete division of duties? If you allow men into the house, their duty to the world outside may likewise suffer! Are you also of the same opinion as your friend?"

About the social code for women Binoy had up till this time agreed with Gora, and had even written articles about it in the papers. But he could hardly bring himself to admit such opinions now. "Don't you think," he said, "that in all such matters we are really the slaves of convention? We are first of all shocked to see women outside their homes because we are not accustomed to it, and then we try to justify our feelings by making it out to be unseemly or improper. Tradition is really at the bottom, the arguments are only an excuse."

Sucharita, with little questions and suggestions, kept the conversation to the subject of Gora, and Binoy said whatever he had to say about his friend with a sincere eloquence. He had never before arranged his illustrations and arguments so well. It is doubtful, indeed, whether even Gora himself could have expounded his own principles so clearly and so brilliantly. Stimulated by his own unexpected cleverness and power of expression, Binoy felt a joyous exhilaration which made his face radiant. He said: "Our scriptures say: *Know thyself*—for knowledge is liberation. I can tell you that my friend Gora is India's self-knowledge incarnate. I can never think of him as an ordinary man. While the minds of all the rest of us are scattered in different directions by every trifling attraction, or by the temptation of novelty, he is the one man who stands firm amidst all distractions, uttering in a voice of thunder the *mantram: Know thyself.*"

The talk would have gone on indefinitely, for Sucharita was listening eagerly, but suddenly there came from the adjoining room the sound of Satish's shrill voice reciting—

Tell me not, in mournful numbers,
"Life is but an empty dream!"

Poor Satish never got the chance of displaying his attainments before visitors. Guests were often made hot and uncomfortable by being made to listen to Lila's recitations of English poetry, but Baroda never called upon Satish, although in everything there was a keen rivalry between the two. Satish's greatest joy in life was to humble Lila's pride, if he could find any way to do so. The day before Lila had been put to the test before Binoy, but then Satish had no opportunity of proving his superiority without being invited. He would only have been snubbed if he had tried. So to-day he began to recite in the adjoining room as if doing it for himself, at which Sucharita could not restrain her laughter.

At that moment Lila rushed into the room, her hair swinging in braids, and, running up to Sucharita, whispered something in her ear.

Meanwhile the clock struck four. Binoy had determined, on his way to Paresh Babu's house, that he would leave it early and to see Gora. And the more he had talked about his friend, the more eager he had become to meet him. Thus reminded of the hour, he got up hurriedly from his chair.

"Must you be going so soon?" exclaimed Sucharita. "Mother is preparing tea for you. Won't it do if you go a little later?"

To Binoy this was not a question, but a command, so he sat down again at once. Labonya in a fine silk dress now came in and announced that tea was ready, and her mother wanted them to come up on to the terrace.

While Binoy took his tea Mistress Baroda entertained him with the complete biography of each of her children. Lolita took Sucharita away with her out of the room, and there was only Labonya left, sitting with her head bent over her knitting. Somebody had once complimented her on the play of her delicate fingers when she knitted, and ever since she had made a habit of starting this work without any special reason, whenever there were visitors present.

Paresh Babu came in just as evening fell, and as it was Sunday he proposed that they should go to the Brahmo Samaj service. Mistress Baroda turned to Binoy and said that, if he had no objection, they would be glad of his company. After this Binoy could not see his way to make any objection.

They divided themselves between two gharries and set off for the Samaj. When the service was over and they were just preparing to get into the cabs, Sucharita with a little start exclaimed: "Why, there goes Gourmohan Babu!"

There was not a doubt that Gora had seen the party, but he had hurried away as if he had not noticed them. Binoy was ashamed at his friend's rudeness, but he understood at once the reason of this precipitate retreat. Gora had caught sight of him in that company. The happiness which had lit up his mind all this time was suddenly extinguished. Sucharita immediately read Binoy's thoughts and divined the cause of them, and because Gora could judge a friend like Binoy so unfairly, all the more because of his unjust prejudice against Brahmos, her indignation against him once more gained the mastery. She longed more than ever for Gora's discomfiture, no matter by what means.

FOURTEEN

When Gora sat down to his midday meal, Anandamoyi tried to introduce the subject that was uppermost in her thoughts. "Binoy came here this morning," she said by way of an opening. "Did you not see him?"

Without looking up from his food, Gora answered shortly: "Yes, I did."

"I asked him to stay," returned Anandamoyi after a long silence, "but he went off in an absent-minded sort of way."

Gora made no reply, and Anandamoyi went on: "Gora, there's something on his mind, I'm sure. I've never seen him like this before. I don't like it at all."

Gora went on eating without a word. Anandamoyi was a little afraid of Gora just because she loved him so dearly, so she was generally reluctant to press him on any matter when he himself did not open his mind to her. On any other occasion she would have let the subject drop, but to-day she was so anxious about Binoy that she went on: "Look here, Gora, don't be annoyed if I speak plainly. God has created many kinds of men, but He does not intend them all to tread the same path. Binoy loves you as his own life, that is why he will put up with anything from you—but nothing good can come of your trying to force him to your way of thinking."

"Mother, bring me some more milk, will you?" was Gora's only reply.

Here the conversation ended. After her own meal was over, Anandamoyi sat thoughtfully sewing on her bed, while Lachmi, having vainly tried to draw her into a discussion about the special wickedness of one of the servants, lay down to have her nap on the floor.

Gora spent a long time over finishing his correspondence. Binoy had seen quite plainly in the morning how angry he was, and it was unthinkable to Gora that he would not come to make it up. So in all that he was doing he kept listening for Binoy's footsteps. But the day wore on and yet Binoy did not come.

Gora had just made up his mind to stop writing when Mohim entered the room. He dropped into a chair, and plunged right into the subject by asking: "What have you been thinking about Sasi's marriage?"

As Gora had never given a single thought to the question he could not but maintain a guilty silence.

Mohim then tried to bring Gora to a due sense of his duties as uncle by expatiating on the high price of bridegrooms in the marriage market, and the difficulty of furnishing the requisite dowry in the present circumstances of the family. And, having duly cornered Gora into the confession that he could see no way out of the difficulty, Mohim relieved him of the problem by suggesting Binoy as a solution. There was no need for Mohim to take such a roundabout way, but, whatever he might say to Gora's face, in his heart of hearts Mohim was a little afraid of him.

Gora had never even dreamt that Binoy's name could come up in such a connection, especially as they had both decided to remain unmarried in order to devote their love to the service of their country. So he simply said: "But will Binoy agree to marry at all?"

"Is this the kind of Hindu you are?" broke out Mohim. "For all your caste-marks and *tikis,* your English education has got right into your bones. Surely you know that the scriptures enjoin marriage as the duty of every son of a Brahmin!"

Mohim neither ignored the traditional customs like modern young men, nor did he particularly affect the scriptures. He thought it absurd to make a show of eating at hotels; nor did he think it necessary for plain, sober folk to be always quoting sacred texts, as Gora loved to do. But his policy was "In Rome do as the Romans do," and so to Gora he did not neglect an appeal to the scriptures.

Had this proposal been made two days earlier, Gora would simply not have listened to it. To-day, however, it did not seem to him to be so entirely unworthy of regard. At all events it gave him an immediate excuse for going to see Binoy. So eventually he said: "All right, I'll find out what Binoy thinks about it."

"You needn't worry about finding that out," replied Mohim. "He will think just as you tell him to think. If you put in a word in favour, it will be all right, so we may take it as settled."

Gora went off to Binoy's lodgings the same evening and burst like a storm into his room, only to find it empty. He called the servant-boy and heard that Binoy had gone to No. 78.

A poisonous flood of antipathy against Paresh Babu, his family, and the whole Brahmo Samaj filled Gora's heart, and, bearing this overflowing revolt within him, he rushed off to Paresh Babu's house. His intention was to speak out quite straight, so as to make it too hot for that Brahmo household, and not too comfortable for Binoy either. But on reaching the house he found that all of them had gone out to the evening service.

For a moment he was in doubt as to whether Binoy had accompanied them—perhaps he might this very moment be at Gora's house. Gora could hardly contain himself, and with his usual impetuosity he at once made for the Brahmo Samaj. As he reached the door he saw Binoy following Mistress Baroda into a cab. There was this shameless fellow, in full view of the open street, seated in the company of a lot of strange girls! The fool! To have got so completely caught in the coils—so quickly too, and so easily! Friendship, then, no longer had any charms. Gora went off like the wind, while Binoy in the darkness of the carriage sat silently looking out into the street.

Mistress Baroda, thinking that the sermon had moved him, did not care to interrupt his meditations.

FIFTEEN

Gora, on returning home that night, went straight up to the roof-terrace and there began to pace up and down.

After a while Mohim came up panting. "Since man has not been provided with wings," he grumbled, "why on earth does he build three-storied houses? The heaven-dwelling gods will never tolerate these land animals trying to creep right up to the skies! Did you go to see Binoy?"

Without giving a direct answer Gora said: "Sasi's marriage with Binoy is impossible."

"Why, doesn't Binoy agree?"

"I don't agree!"

"What!" cried Mohim, raising his hands in dismay. "What new caprice have you on the brain now?—may I know why you won't?"

"I have realised," explained Gora, "that it will be next to impossible to keep Binoy orthodox for long, so it won't do to bring him into our family."

"Well, I never!" ejaculated Mohim. "Many a bigot have I seen in my day, but this beats them all. You are going one better than even the Benaras or Nadia pandits. They are satisfied when they see orthodoxy. You want orthodoxy warranted to last. You'll be wanting to purify someone next, because you dreamt he became a Christian!"

After some more words had been exchanged, Mohim said: "But I can't hand the child over to the first uneducated boor

I come across. Educated people are bound to miss some rule of scripture or other now and then—for that, you may wrangle with them, or even mock at them, but why punish my poor girl by forbidding them to marry? What a fellow you are for getting things wrong side up!"

When Mohim came back downstairs he went straight to Anandamoyi and said: "Mother, do put the brake on your Gora!"

"Why, what's he been doing?" asked Anandamoyi.

Mohim explained: "I had practically settled that Binoy should marry my Sasi, and got Gora to agree to it too; but now he has suddenly found out that Binoy is not enough of a Hindu for him—it appears that his views do not square with the ancient law-givers in every particular! So Gora has turned nasty—and you know what it means when he does that. Next to the law-givers, you are the only one in the world for whose opinion Gora cares. If only you say the word, my daughter's future is assured. It won't be possible to find another such husband for her."

Mohim then gave a detailed account of the talk he had had with Gora. Anandamoyi was much upset, feeling more than ever that some difference was widening into a real gulf between Gora and Binoy.

Going upstairs she found that Gora had stopped pacing the terrace, and was reading, seated on a chair in his room with his feet upon another. She drew up another chair and sat down beside him, whereupon Gora put his feet down and, sitting upright, looked her in the face.

"Gora, my darling," began Anandamoyi. "Listen to me, and don't get into a quarrel with Binoy. To me you are like two brothers, and I can't bear the thought of any difference between you."

"If my friend wants to cut himself adrift," said Gora, "I'm not going to waste my time running after him."

"My dear, I don't know what the trouble between you is, but if you can bring yourself to believe that Binoy wants to cut the ties that bind him to you, where is the strength of your friendship?"

"Mother," replied Gora, "you know I like to follow a straight path. If anyone wants to keep astride the fence, I'll ask him to take away his leg from my side, and I don't care whether he or I get hurt in the process."

"What after all has happened?" expostulated Anandamoyi. "He has been visiting at a Brahmo house—isn't that the whole of his fault?"

"That's a long story, mother."

"Let it be as long as it may, but I have one little word to put in. You plume yourself on your steadfastness—that you never give up what you once take hold of. Why then is your hold on Binoy so loose? Had your Abinash wanted to secede from the party, would you have let him go so easily? Does the keeping of Binoy mean so little to you, just because he is such a true friend?"

Gora remained silent and thoughtful, for Anandamoyi's words had made his own mind clear to him. All this while he had been thinking he was sacrificing friendship to duty. He now saw that the exact opposite was the truth. He had been ready to inflict on Binoy love's extreme penalty merely because the exactions of his friendship had not been submitted to. The strength of their friendship claimed to keep Binoy tied fast to his will, and Gora felt sore simply because that had not happened.

As soon as Anandamoyi saw that her words had made an impression, she rose to go without saying any more. Go oo, jumped off his chair and snatched his shawl from the rack.

"Where are you off to?" asked Anandamoyi.

"To Binoy's."

"Won't you have your dinner first? It's ready."

"I'll bring Binoy back with me and we'll dine together."

Anandamoyi turned to go downstairs, but stopped as she heard footsteps coming up, saying: "Here's Binoy himself!" and a moment later Binoy appeared.

Anandamoyi's eyes filled with tears as she saw him. "I hope you haven't dined yet, Binoy, my child?" she asked him affectionately.

"No, mother," he replied.

"Then you are to dine here."

Binoy looked towards Gora, and Gora said: "Binoy, you will live long. I was just going to see you!"

Anandamoyi felt a load lifted from her mind as she hurried away, leaving the friends to themselves.

When the two were seated, neither of them could muster up the courage to begin on the subject uppermost in their minds. Gora led off with small talk. "Do you know that new gymnastic instructor we have got for the boys of the club?" he began. "He is a splendid teacher!" And thus they went on till they were summoned downstairs for dinner.

When they sat down to their meal Anandamoyi could see from their conversation that the veil between them had not yet been lifted. So when they had finished, she said: "Binoy, it's now so late that you must stay the night here. I'll send a message to your lodgings."

Binoy cast an inquiring glance at Gora's face and then he said: "The Sanskrit adage tells us that he who has dined should bear himself right royally—therefore will I not walk the streets this night, but rest here."

The two then went up on to the roof, and rested on a mat spread on the open terrace. The sky was flooded with the autumn moonlight. Thin white clouds, like short spells of drowsiness, passed over the moon and then floated away. On every side, up to the horizon, stretched rows of roofs of all heights and sizes, mingling here and there with the tops of trees, like an unmeaning, unsubstantial phantasy of light and shade.

The clock of a neighbouring church struck eleven. The hawkers of ices had given their last call. The sound of the traffic grew faint. There was not a sign of wakefulness in the lane nearby, expect for the occasional bark of a dog, or the sound of the neighbours' horses kicking against the wooden floor of their stables.

For a long time neither of them spoke, till at last Binoy, hesitatingly at first, but gradually giving full vent to his emotion, spoke out his mind. "My heart is too full to contain itself, Gora," he said. "I know that you yourself are not interested in the subject of my thoughts, but I cannot rest until I have told you all. I cannot judge whether the thing is good or evil, but this much I know for certain,—it is not to be trifled with. I have read a great deal about it, and up till now I imagined I knew all there was to be known,—just as one may dream of the delights of swimming when looking on the picture of a lake; but now that I am in the water, I don't find it such an easy matter!"

With this introduction Binoy began to unfold to Gora, as best as he could, the wonderful experience which had come into his life. Nowadays, he averred, it seemed as if all his days and nights enveloped him completely—as if the sky had no gap in it, but was filled with sweetness, like the beehive with honey in the springtime. Everything nowadays came close to him, touched him, had for him a new meaning. He had never known before that he loved the world so deeply, that the sky was so wonderful, the light so marvellous, that even the stream of unknown wayfarers along the streets could be so profoundly real! He longed to do something for everyone he came across,—to dedicated his powers to the eternal service of the world, as did the sun.

From the way Binoy spoke, one would hardly infer that he had any particular person in mind. He seemed to have a delicacy about mentioning any name—or even giving a hint that there was a name to mention. He almost felt guilty to be talking thus at all. It was a liberty, an insult,—but it was too tempting to be resisted on such a night, seated by the side of his friend, under the silent sky.

What a wonderful face! How the glow of life delicately revealed itself in the tenderness of her forehead! What a glorious intelligence, what inexpressible depths in her features! How radiantly did her innermost thoughts blossom out in her eyes when she smiled!—how unutterably did they lurk beneath the shade of her eyelashes! And those two hands of hers! They seemed to speak, so eager were they to express in beauty of service the tender devotion of her mind. Binoy felt this life and youth to be fulfilled with this vision—great waves of joy dashed against his breast as it repeatedly flooded his heart.

What could be more wonderful than to be privileged to experience what so many other people in this world have to go through life without even seeing? Could this be some madness? Was it in any way wrong? What if it were—it was too late to check it now. If the current should carry him to some shore, well and good; but if it should float him off, or drown him, that could not be helped. The trouble was he did not even wish to be rescued—it seemed as if the true goal of all his life was thus to be swept away from all bonds of tradition and habit.

Gora listened on in silence. On many such moonlit nights, seated alone together amidst the stillness all around, the two friends had discussed all manner of things—literature, people, the welfare of society, how they two would spend their future lives—but never anything so intimate. Gora had never come face to face with such a true revelation, such a vivid expression of the inner truth of the human heart. He had always looked

down upon this kind of thing as rubbishy poetic outpourings—
but to-day it touched him so closely, he could ignore it no
longer. Not only so, the violence of its outburst knocked at
the door of his mind too,—its rapture thrilled through his
being like flashes of lightning. For an instant the veil was lifted
off an unsuspected region of his heart, and the magic of the
autumn moonlight found entrance and irradiated that erstwhile
obscure chamber.

They were not aware, as they talked on, when the moon
descended behind the roofs, and its place was taken by a faint
hint of light in the east, like the smile on the face of a sleeping
child. When at length the burden that lay on Binoy's mind
was lightened, he began to feel a little ashamed. After a pause
he went on: "This thing that has happened to me must seem
very trivial in your eyes. Perhaps it makes you feel a contempt
for me,—but what am I to do? I have never kept anything
back from you, and I've unburdened myself to you now,
whether you understand me, or not."

Gora replied: "Binoy, I can't honestly say that I exactly
understand this kind of thing, nor would you have understood
it any better a few days ago. I can't even deny that, amidst
all the immensity of life, this side of it, for all its effusiveness
and passion, has struck me as utterly trivial. But perhaps it
may not be really so—that much I am free to admit. It has
seemed to me thin and unsubstantial because I have never
experienced its power or its depths. But now I cannot dismiss
as false what you have realised so tremendously. The fact of
the matter is, that if the truths outside the field of one's own
work did not appear of less moment, no man could have
carried on with his duty. Therefore God has not confused man
by making all objects equally clear to his vision. We must
select for ourselves the field on which we would focus our
attention, and forgo our greed for all the rest outside it, else
we shall never find the truth at all. I cannot worship at the

shrine where you have seen truth's image for if I did I should have to lose the inner truth of my own life. We must choose one course or the other."

"I see!" exclaimed Binoy. "Either Binoy's course, or Gora's. I am out to fulfil myself—you to give yourself up."

Gora interrupted impatiently: "Binoy, don't try to be epigrammatic! I can quite see that to-day you stand face to face with a great truth, with which there can be no trifling. You have to give yourself entirely up to it if you want to realise any truth—there's no other way of getting at it. It is the one desire of my life that my truth may come before me as vividly some day. So long, you have been content with what you knew of love from books. I also have only a book knowledge of the love of country. Now that you have experienced the real thing, you realise how much more true it is than the thing you read about. It claims nothing less than the whole of your universe; there is no place where you can get away from it. When once my love of country becomes so overwhelmingly self-evident, then also there will be no escape for me,—it will draw out all my wealth and life, my blood, the very marrow of my bones; my sky light, in fact my all. How wonderful, how beautiful, how clear, how obvious that true image of my country will be,—how fierce and overpowering will be its joy, over passing in a moment both life and death by its turbulent flood,—of this I caught glimpses as I listened to you speaking. This experience that has come into your life has brought new life to me also. Whether I shall ever be able to understand what you have felt I know not, but I seem to have been able to experience through you some taste of what I have been yearning for myself."

As he spoke Gora had left the mat and was walking up and down. The tinge of dawn in the east seemed like a spoken message to him; his very soul was moved, as if he had heard the chanting of Vedic mantras in some ancient forest retreat of India. For a moment he stood motionless, thrilling through and through, while it seemed to him that through the top of his brain a lotus-stem had pierced its way and unfolded into a radiant blossom, filling the skies above him with its expanding petals. His whole life, its consciousness, its power, seemed to lose itself in the bliss of its supreme beauty.

When Gora came to himself again, he said suddenly: "Binoy, even this love of yours you will have to transcend—I tell you it will not do to stop there. One day I will show you how great and true is He who has called me with His mighty power. To-day I am filled with a great joy—I know I will never give you up into any lesser hands."

Binoy rose from the mat and came and stood beside Gora, who with an unwonted enthusiasm pressed Binoy to his bosom as he said: "Brother, for us 'tis death—the same death. We two are one; none shall separate us, none shall ever hinder us."

Gora's tumultuous emotion sent its waves pulsing through Binoy's heart, and without a word he surrendered himself completely to his friend's influence. They paced the terrace together in silence, while the eastern sky flushed crimson.

Gora spoke again: "Brother, the goddess of my worship does not come to me enshrined in beauty. I see her where there is poverty and famine, pain and insult. Not where worship is offered with song and flower, but where life's blood is sacrificed. To me, however, it is the greatest joy that no element of mere pleasantness is there to seduce one; there one must rouse himself with his full strength and be prepared to give up his all. No sweetness cloys such manifestation; it is an irresistible, unbearable awakening, cruel and terrible, in which the strings of being are struck so harshly that all the tones of the gamut cry out as they are snapped asunder. When I think of it, my heart leaps—such joy I feel is fit joy for a man—it is Siva's dance of life. The whole quest of man is the vision of the New as it appears in all its beauty on the flaming crest of the Old as it is destroyed. On the background of this blood-red sky I can see a radiant Future, freed from its bonds,—I can see it in to-day's approaching dawn—listen, you can hear its drum-beats in my breast!" And Gora, taking Binoy's hand, placed it over his heart.

"Gora, my brother," said Binoy, deeply moved, "I will be your comrade through and through. But I warn you never to let me hesitate. Like cruel fate itself, you must drag me along without mercy. We are both on the same road, but our strength is not the same."

"Our natures are different, its is true," replied Gora, "but a supreme joy will make our different natures one. A greater love than that which binds us to each other will unite us. So long as such greater love does not become true for both of us, there will be friction, and falling out at every step. Then will come a day when, forgetting all our differences, forgetting even our friendship, we shall be able to stand together, immovable, in an immense passion of self-abandonment. In that austere joy we shall find the ultimate fulfilment of our friendship."

"So may it be!" responded Binoy, pressing Gora's hand.

"But meanwhile I shall give you much pain," Gora went on. "You will have to bear with all my tyranny—for it will not do to look upon our friendship as an end in itself—we must not dishonour it by trying to preserve it at any cost. If our friendship must perish for the sake of the greater love, that can't be helped; but if it can survive, then it will be fulfilled indeed."

They both started on hearing footsteps behind them, and, looking round, they saw that Anandamoyi had come up. She took a hand of each of them and drew them towards the bedroom, saying: "Come, get along to bed!"

"No, mother, we can't sleep now," exclaimed both together.

"Oh yes, you can!" said Anandamoyi, as she made the two friends lie down. Then, shutting the door, she sat by their pillow fanning them.

"All your fanning will not do, mother," said Binoy. "Sleep won't come to us now."

"Won't it? We'll see about that!" replied Anandamoyi. "At any rate, if I stay here you won't be able to begin talking again."

When the two of them had fallen asleep, Anandamoyi crept quietly out of the room, and on her way downstairs met Mohim coming up. "Not now," she cautioned him. "They've been awake all night. I've only just sent them off to sleep."

"My goodness—this is friendship with a vengeance," said Mohim. "Do you know if they discussed the marriage question at all?"

"No, I don't," replied Anandamoyi.

"They must have come to some decision," Mohim mused aloud. "When on earth will they wake up? Unless the marriage takes place soon, there may be all kinds of complications."

"There will be no complications," laughed Anandamoyi, "if they are allowed a little more sleep. They are sure to wake sometime to-day."

SIXTEEN

"Aren't you going to get Sucharita married at all?" cried Mistress Baroda.

Paresh Babu stroked his beard in his customary quiet manner, as he asked in his gentle voice: "Where is the bridegroom?"

To which his wife replied: "Why, it's practically settled that she is to marry Panu Babu—at least we all think so—Sucharita herself knows it too."

"I'm not sure that Sucharita looks with favour on Panu Babu," ventured Paresh Babu.

"Now look here," cried his spouse, "that's just the sort of thing I can't stand. What if we have always treated the girl like one of our own daughters—why need she put on such airs? If such an educated and religious man as Panu Babu is taken with her, is that a thing to be treated lightly? Whatever you may say, although my Labonya is much better-looking, I can assure you she will never say 'No' to anyone we are pleased to marry her to. If you go on encouraging Sucharita's conceit, it will be a hard task to find a bridegroom for her."

Paresh Babu never argued with his wife, especially about Sucharita, so he kept silent.

When, on the birth of Satish, Sucharita's mother died, the girl had been only seven years old. Her father, Ram-sharan Haldar, had, on losing his wife, joined the Brahmo Samaj, and to avoid the persecution of his neighbours had taken refuge at Dacca. It was while he was working in the Post Office there that Paresh Babu had become his intimate friend, so much so that Sucharita from that time loved him like her own father. Ram-sharan Babu died suddenly, leaving whatever money he had to his two children, and making Paresh Babu trustee. It was from then that the two orphans had come to live in Paresh Babu's family.

The reader already knows what an enthusiastic Brahmo Haran was. He had a hand in all the activities of the Samaj,— he was a teacher in the Night School, editor of their Journal, secretary of the Girls' School,—in fact he was indefatigable. Everyone expected that this young man would eventually take a very high position in the Brahmo Samaj. Even outside the Samaj he had become famous, through the pupils of his school, for his mastery of the English language and his knowledge of philosophy.

For these various reasons Sucharita had shown a special respect towards Haran, just as she did to all other good Brahmos. When she had come to Calcutta from Dacca, she had even been eager to make his acquaintance.

Eventually not only had Sucharita become acquainted with this renowned person, but he had not hesitated to show his preference for her. Not that Haran openly declared his love for Sucharita, but he devoted himself so single-mindedly to the task of removing her imperfections, correcting her faults, increasing her enthusiasm, and generally improving her, that it became clear to all that he wished to make this particular girl worthy of being a helpmate unto himself. As for Sucharita, when she realised that she had won the heart of this famous man, she could not help a feeling of pride in herself mingling with her respect for him.

Although no definite proposal had been made to the authorities concerned, since everybody had settled that Haran was to marry her, Sucharita also accepted it as a settled fact, and it became her special concern to see how, by study and practice, she could become worthy of the man who had sacrificed his life to the welfare of the Brahmo Samaj. The thought of this marriage appeared to her like a stone fortress of fear, awe, and responsibility—not a place for merely living in happily, but for strenuous striving—not a family event, but a matter of history.

Had the marriage taken place at this juncture, the bride's people, at any rate, would have regarded it as a piece of good fortune. Unfortunately, however, Haran had come to regard the responsibilities of his own important life as so immense that he thought it unworthy of himself to marry merely because of mutual attraction. He felt unable to take the step without first considering in all aspects how far the Brahmo Samaj would be benefited by the marriage. It was with this in view that he first began to test Sucharita.

But when you venture thus to test others you get yourself tested likewise. So when Haran came to be known in this home by his more familiar title "Panu Babu," it was no longer possible to see in him only that storehouse of English learning and receptacle of metaphysical wisdom who stood like an incarnation of all that benefited the Brahmo Samaj,—the fact that he was a man had also to be taken into account; and in such capacity he ceased to be a mere object of reverence, but became also a subject of likes and dislikes.

The strange thing was, that the very aspect which from a distance had aroused Sucharita's reverence, on closer acquaintance struck her unfavourably. The way in which Haran constituted himself the guardian and protector of whatever was true, good or beautiful in the Brahmo Samaj, made him appear ridiculously small. The real relationship of man with truth is the relationship of a devotee—for in that spirit a man's nature becomes humble. When a man is proud and overbearing, he shows only too clearly his own comparative smallness. In this respect Sucharita could not help noticing the difference between Paresh Babu and Haran. To look at Paresh Babu's calm face, the nobility of the truth he bore within him became apparent. With Haran it was quite the reverse, for his Brahmoism, with its aggressive self-conceit, obscured everything else, and came out, in all its ungainliness, in whatever he said or did.

When, obsessed with his own idea of the welfare of the Brahmo Samaj, Haran would not hesitate to impugn even Paresh Babu's judgment, Sucharita would writhe like a wounded snake. At that time in Bengal, English educated people did not study the *Bhagavadgita,* but Paresh Babu used to read it occasionally to Sucharita, and had even read nearly the whole of the *Mahabharata* to her. Haran disapproved of this, for he wanted to banish all such books from Brahmo households. He himself never read them, wishing to keep aloof from all such literature favoured by the orthodox. Amongst the scriptures of the world-religions his only support was the Bible. The fact that Paresh Babu drew no line between Brahmo and non-Brahmo in such things as the study of scriptures, and other matters which he regarded as unessential, was a thorn in the side of Haran. But Sucharita could not bear that anyone should have the arrogance to find fault with Paresh Babu's conduct, even secretly. And it was this open display of arrogance on his part which lowered Haran in her eyes.

But although Sucharita felt herself becoming estranged every day by the violence of Haran's sectarianism and by his dry narrow-mindedness, the probability of her marriage with him had never yet been questioned by either side. In a religious community, a man who labels himself with a high-priced ticket gradually comes to be taken at his own valuation. So much so that even Paresh Babu did not dispute Haran's claims, and because everyone regarded him as one of the future pillars of the Samaj, he also gave his tacit consent to the idea. Nay, further, the only questioning that ever exercised him was as to whether Sucharita was good enough for such a husband; it had never so much as occurred to him to inquire how far Haran was pleasing to Sucharita.

As no one thought it necessary to consult Sucharita's point of view in this matter she also got into the way of ignoring her own personal inclination. Like the rest of the Brahmo Samaj, she also took it for granted that when it suited Haran to say he was ready to marry her, it would be her part to accept such marriage as her life's chief duty.

Matters had been going on thus when Paresh Babu, on hearing the few hot words Sucharita had exchanged with Haran in defence of Gora, began to have misgivings as to whether she had a sufficient respect for him. Perhaps, he thought, there might be some deeper reason for their differences of opinion, thus come to light. So when Baroda returned to the question of Sucharita's marriage he had not shown his former complaisance.

That very day Mistress Baroda drew Sucharita aside and said to her: "You've been making father anxious."

Sucharita started in dismay,—even unconsciously she could be a cause of anxiety to Paresh Babu caused her the greatest concern. She turned pale as she asked: "Why, what have I done?"

"How can I know, dear?" replied Baroda. "He imagines that you do not like Panu Babu. Practically everyone in the Brahmo Samaj believes that your marriage with him is a settled thing—and if you now—"

"Why, mother," interrupted Sucharita in surprise, "I've never said a word about it to anybody."

She had reason to be astonished. She had often been irritated by Haran's behaviour, but she had never for a moment, even in thought, protested against the idea of marrying him, for, as we have seen, it had been impressed on her that the question of her personal happiness had nothing to do with the case.

Then she remembered that she had the other day unguardedly allowed her displeasure with Haran to be visible to Paresh Babu, and thinking that this was what had upset him, she felt immensely penitent. She had never permitted herself to break out like this before, and vowed she would never let it happen again.

Haran himself happening to come that afternoon, Mistress Baroda called him to her room and said: "By the way, Panu Babu, everyone is saying that you are going to marry our Sucharita, but I've never heard anything about it from your own lips. If such be really your intention, why don't you speak out?"

Haran was unable to keep his avowal back any longer. He felt he must play for safety by definitely making Sucharita captive. The question of her fitness for helping him in his work for the Samaj, and of her devotion to himself personally, could be put to the test later. So he replied: "That goes without saying. I was only waiting for her to reach her eighteenth year."

"You are over-scrupulous," said Baroda. "It is enough that she has passed her fourteenth."[1]

Paresh Babu was astonished to see Sucharita's behaviour at the tea-table that afternoon, for she had given Haran such a cordial reception for a long time past. In fact, when he was about to go, she actually pressed him to sit down again, so that she might show him a new piece of embroidery of Labonya's.

Paresh Babu was relieved. He thought he must have been mistaken, and smiled to himself, thinking that some secret

---

1 The legal age.

lovers' quarrel had occurred between the two and had now been made up.

Before leaving that evening Haran made a formal proposal for Sucharita's hand to Paresh Babu, adding that he did not wish the wedding to be delayed for long.

Paresh Babu was somewhat mystified. "But you used to say," he objected, "that it is wrong to marry a girl under eighteen. You've even written to that effect in the papers."

"That does not apply to the case of Sucharita," explained Haran, "for her mind is unusually developed for her age."

"That may be so," protested Paresh Babu, firm in spite of his mildness. "But, Panu Babu, unless there be any very special reason, you should act according to your own convictions by waiting till she comes of age."

Haran, ashamed at having been betrayed into this weakness, hastened to make amends by saying: "Of course, that is my duty. My only idea was that we should have a formal betrothal at an early date in the presence of friends and of God."

"Certainly, an excellent suggestion," agreed Paresh Babu.

SEVENTEEN

When, after two or three hours' sleep, Gora awoke and saw Binoy sleeping beside him, his heart was filled with joy. He felt as relieved as one who has dreamt that he has lost something very precious, and wakes up to find that it was only a dream. He realised, with Binoy beside him, how crippled his life would have been if he had given up his friend. Gora felt so elated that he shook Binoy out of his slumber, shouting: "Come along, there's work to do."

Gora had a regular social duty to perform every morning: to visit the poor people of his neighbourhood. It was not with the idea of preaching to them, or of doing them good, but simply with the desire for their companionship. In fact, he was hardly so intimate with his circle of educated friends as he was with these people. They used to call him "Uncle" and offer him a hookah specially set apart for higher folk, and Gora had actually forced himself to smoke simply in order to come closer to them.

The chief admirer of Gora was one Nanda, the son of a carpenter. He was twenty-two years of age, and worked in his father's shop at making wooden boxes. He was a first-rate sportsman and the best bowler in the local cricket team. Gora had formed a Sports and Cricket Club into which he had introduced these sons of carpenters and blacksmiths on a footing of equality with the well-to-do members. In this mixed company Nanda stood easily first in every kind of manly exercise. In consequence, some of the better-class students were jealous of him, but under Gora's strict discipline they had to acquiesce in his election as their Captain.

A few days previously Nanda had wounded his foot with a chisel and had not been attending at the cricket-field for some days, and Gora, being so preoccupied about Binoy all this time, had not been able to make any inquiries, so to-day they started together for the carpenters' quarter to call on Nanda.

As they reached the door of Nanda's house they heard the sound of women weeping within. Neither Nanda's father nor any other men-folk of the household were at home, and from a neighbouring shopkeeper Gora learnt that Nanda had died that very morning and his body had just been taken to the burning-ghat.

Nanda dead! So healthy and strong, so vigorous and good-hearted, and so young too!—dead, that very morning! Gora stood petrified in every limb. Nanda was a common carpenter's son: the gap caused in his circle would be felt by few, and that perhaps only for a short time; but to Gora, Nanda's death seemed cruelly incongruous and impossible. He had seen what immense vitality he had—so many people were alive, but where could one find such abundance of life?

On inquiring into the cause of his death they learnt that it was tetanus. Nanda's father had wanted to call in a doctor, but his mother had insisted that her son was possessed of devil, so she had sent for an exorcist, who had spent the whole night uttering spells and tormenting the sufferer, searing his body with red-hot wires. At the beginning of the illness Nanda had asked for Gora to be informed, but, fearing lest he should insist on their having medical aid, Nanda's mother had not sent him the message.

"What stupidity, and what a terrible penalty!" groaned Binoy, as they turned away from the house.

"Don't comfort yourself, Binoy," said Gora bitterly, "by simply calling it stupidity and trying to remain out of it. If you had really a clear vision of how great this stupidity is, and how far-reaching its penalty, you could not have dismissed the matter with just an expression of regret!"

Gora quickened his pace more and more as his excitement grew on him, while Binoy without answering tried to keep up with him.

Gora after a short silence suddenly continued: "Binoy, I can't let the matter end here so easily. The torments inflicted by that charlatan on my Nanda are torturing me, they are torturing the whole of my country. I can't look upon this as a trivial or isolated event."

Finding Binoy still silent, Gora roared out: "Binoy, I know quite well what's in your mind! You are thinking that there's no remedy, or if there is, it's a long way off. But I can't bear to think in that strain. If I could, I should not have remained alive. Whatever wounds my country, no matter how serious it may be, has its remedy—and that remedy is in my own hands. Because I believe this, I am able to bear all the sorrow and distress and insult that I see around me."

"I have not the courage," said Binoy, "to keep my faith erect in face of such widespread and terrible misery."

"I shall never bring myself to believe that misery is eternal," answered Gora. "The whole will-power and thought-power of the universe is attacking it, within and without. Binoy, I urge you again and again, never even in your dreams think it impossible for our country to become free. With the conviction of its freedom firm in our hearts, we must keep ourselves in readiness. You want to rest content with the vague idea that at some propitious moment the battle for India's freedom will commence. I say the fight has already begun, and is being carried on every moment. Nothing could be more cowardly than for us to remain unanxious and unwatchful."

"Look here, Gora," answered Binoy. "Between you and the rest of us I see this difference: our everyday happenings seem to strike you with new force every time, even things that have gone on happening for a long time. But, as for us, we are as unconscious of them as of the breath we take,— they move us neither to hope nor to despair, neither to rejoicing nor to despondency. Our days slip emptily by, and we realise neither ourselves nor our country in the midst of surrounding events."

Gora suddenly turned scarlet and the veins started out on his forehead, as he clenched his fists and began to run furiously after a man driving a pair of horses, while in a voice that startled the whole street he called out—"Stop! Stop!" The stout, dressy Bengali babu who was driving the turn-out gave one look round and then, with a flourish of his whip on the flanks of his spirited horses, disappeared.

An old Mohammedan cook had been crossing the road with a basket of provisions for some European master on his head. The pompous babu had called out to him to get out of the way, but the deaf old man was nearly run over. He managed to save himself, but tripped and the contents of the basket—fruits, vegetables, butter and eggs—were scattered all over the road. The angry driver turning on his seat had shouted, "You damned pig!" and given the old man such a stinging stroke with his whip that he drew blood.

"Allah! Allah!" sighed the old man as he meekly proceeded to gather up what things were not spoilt into his basket, while Gora, returning to the spot, began to help him at his task. The poor cook was greatly distressed at seeing this well-dressed gentleman taking so much trouble, and said: "Why are you troubling yourself, Babu? These things are no longer any good."

Gora knew quite well that he was doing was really no help at all, and that it would only embarrass the man he was seeming to help—but he felt that it was impossible not to do something to show passers-by that one gentleman at least was anxious to atone for the brutality of another by taking the insult upon himself, and thus to uphold outraged right.

When the basket was refilled Gora said: "This loss will be too heavy for you to bear. Come along to our house and I will make it up to you. But let me tell you one thing, Allah will not forgive you for submitting to such insult without a word of protest."

"Allah will punish the wrongdoer," replied the Mohammedan. "Why should he punish me?"

"He who submits to wrong," said Gora, "is also a wrongdoer, for it is he who is the cause of all evil in the world. You may not understand me, but remember that religion is not merely being pious, for that simply encourages the evildoer. Your Mohammed understood that all right, and that's why he did not go about preaching meek submission."

As Gora's house was rather far away, he took the old man to Binoy's lodgings, and standing in front of the writing-table, said: "Get out your money."

"Wait a moment," replied Binoy. "Let me get the key."

But the tug of the impatient Gora was too much for the lock, and the drawer flew open. The first thing that came into view inside was a large photograph of Paresh Babu's whole family, which Binoy had managed to procure from his youthful friend Satish. Gora sent the old man away with the necessary sum of money, but he said not a word about the photograph; and seeing Gora silent, Binoy did not care to refer to it either, though his mind would have been relieved by the exchange of a few words on the subject.

"Well, I'm off!" said Gora suddenly.

"That's nice of you!" exclaimed Binoy. "To go off alone! Don't you know that mother invited me to breakfast with you? I'm off with you too!"

They left the house together. On the way back Gora did not speak a word. The photograph had reminded him that the main current in Binoy's heart was carrying him along a path with which his life had no connection.

Binoy understood well enough the cause of Gora's silence, but he shrank from trying to break through the barrier of his reserve, for he felt that Gora's mind had touched upon a point where there was a real obstacle to their intercourse.

When they reached home they found Mohim standing at the door, looking down the street. "What's been happening?" he cried, on catching sight of the two friends. "As you have been awake all last night, I was picturing you both comfortably asleep on the footpath somewhere. But it's getting late. Go and have your bath, Binoy."

Having thus driven off, Mohim turned to Gora and said: "Look here, Gora, you must think seriously of the matter I spoke about. Even if Binoy is not orthodox enough for you, where in the world shall we find a better? It's not sufficient to secure mere orthodoxy—we must have education too. I concede that the usual compound of education-cum-orthodoxy is not strictly in accord with our scriptures, but for all that, they do not make such a bad combination either. If you had a daughter of your own, I am sure you would have come to my opinion."

"That's all right, Dada," answered Gora. "I don't think Binoy will have any objection."

"Just listen to him!" exclaimed Mohim. "Who is worrying as to whether Binoy will object? It is your objecting that I am afraid of. If only you will request Binoy with your own lips, I shall be perfectly satisfied. If that will not serve, let it drop."

"I'll do that," said Gora.

Whereupon Mohim felt that nothing remained but to order the wedding feast.

At the first opportunity Gora said to Binoy: "Dada has begun to press hard for your marriage with Sasi. What say you to it?"

"First tell me what you wish."

"I say that it wouldn't be such a bad thing."

"But you used to think differently. Didn't we agree that neither of us should marry? I thought that was settled."

"Well, now let it be settled that you will marry and I won't."

"Why? Why different goals for the same pilgrimage?"

"It is because I am afraid of different goals that I suggest this arrangement. God sends some men into the world with heavy burdens ready made, while others are let off delightfully light—if you yoke these two kinds of creatures together, one has to be loaded up to pull evenly with the other. We shall be able to keep pace together properly, only after you have been duly weighted down by a spell of married life."

"All right!" smiled Binoy. "Pile the weight on this side, by all means!"

"But, as to the particular load itself, have you any objection?"

"Since weighing down is the object, anything will serve equally well—brick or stone—what does it matter?"

Binoy could divine the exact reason for Gora's eagerness about this marriage, and was only amused by his evident anxiety to rescue his friend from entanglement with one of Paresh Babu's girls.

The rest of the afternoon, after their midday meal, was spent in making up for the loss of their night's rest by a long nap. There was no further talk between the two friends till the shades of evening had fallen and they had gone on to the roof-terrace.

Binoy looked up into the sky and said: "See here, Gora, I want to say one thing to you. It appears to me that in our love for our country there is one great imperfection. We only think of the half of India."

"How? What do you mean?" asked Gora.

"We look on India only as a country of men; we entirely ignore the women," explained Binoy.

"Like the Englishman," said Gora, "you want to see women everywhere,—in the home and in the world outside; on the land, the water, and in the sky; at our meals, our amusements and our work,—with the result that for you the women will eclipse the men, and your outlook will remain just as one-sided."

"No, no!" replied Binoy. "It won't do for you to dismiss my argument like that. Why raise the question whether I look at things like the English or not? What I say is, that we do not give the women of our country their rightful place in our consideration. Take yourself, for instance. I can say, for certain, that you never give a moment's thought to the women,—for you the idea of our country is womanless, and such idea can never be the true one."

"Since I have seen and known my mother," observed Gora, "I have seen, in her, all the women of our country, and known as well the place they should occupy."

"You are simply making phrases in order to delude yourself," said Binoy. "The familiarity which one gets in the home with women at their household work, does not make for true knowledge. I know that you will only get furious if I venture to make any comparison between English society and ours,—and I don't want to do it either, nor do I pretend to know exactly to what extent and in what ways our womenfolk may show themselves in public without overstepping the limits of propriety,—but my point is, that so long as our women remain hidden behind the *purdah,* our country will be a half-truth to us, and will not be able to win our full love and devotion."

"As time has its two aspects—day and night, so society has its two sections—man and woman," argued Gora. "In a natural condition of society, woman remains unseen, like night—all her work is done unobtrusively, behind the scenes. Where society has become unnatural, there night usurps the province of day, and both work and frivolity are carried on by artificial light. And what is the result? Night's secret functioning ceases, fatigue increases progressively, recuperation becomes impossible, and man carries on only by recourse to intoxication. Similarly, if we try to drag our women out onto the field of outside duty, then their characteristic quiet work will be interfered with, the peace and happiness of society will be destroyed, and frenzy will prevail in their stead. At first sight such frenzy may be mistaken for power, but it is a power which makes for ruin. Of the two aspects of society, man is patent, but not, therefore, necessarily more patent. If you try to bring the latent force of woman to the surface, then society will be made to live on its capital and soon descend towards bankruptcy. I say that, if we men attend the place of feasting and women keep guard over the stores, then only will the festivity be a success, even though the women remain invisible. Only intoxication can want all powers to be spent in one direction, in the same place, and in an identical manner."

"Gora," said Binoy, "I don't want to dispute what you say—but neither have you disproved what I argued. The real question is—"

"Look here, Binoy," interrupted Gora, "if we go on disputing further about this matter it will only lead to a regular wrangle. I confess that women have not thrust themselves on my consciousness in the way they have recently done on yours. So you can never make me feel about them as you do. Let us for the present agree to differ."

Gora thrust aside the subject. But a seed cast aside may nevertheless fall to the ground, and there it only waits for an opportunity to sprout. Up till now Gora had completely shut out women from his field of vision, and had never even dreamt that his life lacked anything, or suffered any loss, thereby. To-day Binoy's exaltation of feeling had made real to him the fact of their existence and the extent of their power in society. But as he could not decide what their proper place was, or what special need they served, he felt averse to this discussion with Binoy. He could neither master the subject nor dismiss it as worthless, so he felt he would rather not talk about it at all.

As Binoy was leaving that night, Anandamoyi called him to her and asked: "Has your marriage with Sasi been settled?"

Binoy answered with a slightly embarrassed laugh: "Yes, mother,—Gora has played the rôle of matchmaker!"

"Sasi is quite a good girl," said Anandamoyi; "but don't do anything childish, Binoy. I know you well enough, my child. You have hurried yourself into a decision because you found you could not really make up your mind. There is plenty of time to think it over. You're old enough to judge for yourself: don't decide such a serious question without consulting your real feelings."

As she spoke she patted Binoy gently on the shoulder, while he, without answering, went slowly away.

EIGHTEEN

Binoy kept thinking over Anandamoyi's words on the way home. He had never yet disregarded her advice in the least particular, and he felt a burden weighing him down the whole of that night.

Next morning he woke up with a sense of being relieved of all obligation by having paid at last an adequate price for Gora's friendship. He felt that the lifelong bond which he had accepted, by agreeing to this marriage with Sasi, had earned him the right to loosen his bonds in other directions. This marriage-bond was a surety which would secure him for ever from Gora's unfounded suspicions as to his being drawn away from orthodoxy by the temptation of marrying into a Brahmo family. So Binoy began to visit Paresh Babu's house constantly and without any scruples, and for him it had never been difficult to make himself completely at home in the house of people whom he liked. Having once disposed of the hesitation he had felt on Gora's account, it was not long before he was treated like one of Paresh Babu's own family.

At first Lolita was up in arms against Binoy, but this lasted only so long as she suspected Sucharita to have a liking for him. As soon as she saw clearly that Sucharita had no special partiality for him, she was no longer in revolt, and allowed herself to admit without a struggle that Binoy Babu was an exceptionally nice man.

Even Haran was not antagonistic; on the contrary, he seemed to desire to emphasise the fact that Binoy had really some notion of good manners, the implication being that Gora had none. And because Binoy never started an argument with Haran, in which tactics he was abetted by Sucharita, he had never been the occasion of any breach of the peace at the tea-table.

But when Haran was not there, Sucharita would encourage Binoy to explain his opinions on social matters. She could not get over her curiosity as to how educated men like Gora and Binoy could justify the ancient superstitions of their country. If she had not known these two personally, she would have dismissed such attempts with contempt as not worth a thought. But from her very first encounter with Gora she had been unable to dismiss him from her mind with contempt. So whenever she got an opportunity she always led the conversation round to a discussion of Gora's mode of life and his opinions, and tried to get further and further into the matter by her questions and objections. Paresh Babu always believed that it was a liberal education for Sucharita to hear the opinions of all sects, so he never put a stop to these discussions out of any fear of their leading her astray.

One day Sucharita asked: "Now tell me, does Gourmohan Babu really believe in caste, or are his professions merely an exaggerated form of his devotion to his country?"

"You acknowledge the steps of a staircase, don't you?" replied Binoy. "You don't object to some having to be higher than the others?"

"I don't object to that, only because I have to go up them. I wouldn't have acknowledged any such necessity on level ground."

"Just so," said Binoy. "The object of the staircase, which is our society, is to enable people to mount up from below— right up to the goal of man's life. If we had regarded society, or the world itself, as our goal, then there would have been no necessity for acknowledging these differences, then the European social condition of a continual scramble to occupy the maximum space would also have been good enough for us."

"I am afraid I don't understand you very clearly," objected Sucharita. "My question is this. Do you mean to tell me you find the purpose, for which you say caste distinctions were created in our society, to have been successful?"

"It is not so easy to see the face of success in this world," answered Binoy. "India offered one great solution to the social problem, namely the caste system—that solution is still being worked out before the eyes of all the world. Europe has not yet been able to give anything more satisfactory, for there society is one long struggle and wrangle. Human Society is still waiting for the final success of the solution offered by India."

"Please don't be angry with me," said Sucharita timidly. "But do tell me, are you merely echoing Gourmohan Babu's opinions, or do you really believe all this yourself?"

"To tell you the truth," said Binoy, smiling, "I have not the same force of conviction as Gora has. When I see the defects of our society, the abuses of our caste system, I cannot but express my doubts; but Gora tells me that doubt is only the result of trying to see great things in too much detail,— to regard the broken branches and withered leaves as the ultimate nature of a tree is simply the result of intellectual impatience. Gora says he does not ask for any praise of the decaying boughs, but asks us to look at the whole tree and then try to understand its purpose."

"Let us leave aside the withered boughs by all means," said Sucharita. "But surely we have a right to consider the fruit. What kind of fruit has caste produced for our country?"

"What you call the fruit of caste is not merely that, but the result of the totality of the conditions of our country. If you try to bite with a loose tooth you suffer pain,—for that you don't blame the teeth, but only the looseness of that particular tooth. Because, owing to various causes, disease and weakness have attacked us, we have only been able to distort the idea which India stands for, and not lead it to success. That is why Gora continually exhorts us: Become healthy, become strong!"

"Very well then, do you regard the Brahmin as a kind of divine man?" pursued Sucharita. "Do you really believe that the dust of a Brahmin's feet purifies a man?"

"Is not much of the homage we pay in this world of our own creation? Would it have been a small thing for our society if we could have created real Brahmins? We want divine men—supermen, and we shall get them too if only we can desire them with all our hearts and all our minds. But if we want them in a foolish manner, then we need must be content to burden the earth with demons to whom no evil doing is foreign, and whom we allow to earn their livelihood by shaking the dust of their feet on our heads."

"Have these supermen of yours come into being anywhere at all?" asked Sucharita.

"They are there, in India's inner need and purpose, just as the tree is hidden in the seed. Other countries want generals like Wellington, scientists like Newton, and millionaires like Rothschild, but our country wants the Brahmin, the Brahmin who knows not what fear is, who hates greed, who can vanquish sorrow, who takes no account of loss—whose being is united with the Supreme Being. India wants the Brahmin of firm, tranquil and liberated mind—when once she gets him then only will she be free! It is not to kings that we bow our heads, nor do we submit our necks to the yoke of oppressors. No, it is through our own fear that our heads are bowed low; we are caught in the web of our own greed, we are slaves to our own folly. May the true Brahmin by his austere discipline deliver us from that fear, that greed, that folly,—we don't want them to fight for us, or to trade for us, or to secure for us any other worldly advantage."

Up to this point Paresh Babu had been merely a listener, but now he interposed, saying softly: "I cannot say that I know India; and I certainly do not know what India wanted for herself, or whether she ever succeeded in getting it,—but can you ever go back to the days that are gone? Our striving should be concerned with what is possible in the present,— what good can we do by stretching out our arms in vain appeals to the past?"

"I have often thought and spoken as your are doing," said Binoy; "but as Gora says, can we kill the past by merely speaking of it as dead and gone? The past is always with us, for nothing that once was true can ever depart."

"The way your friend puts these things," objected Sucharita. "is not the way they are put by the ordinary man. How then can we be sure that you speak for the whole country?"

"Please don't think," protested Binoy, "that my friend Gora is one of those ordinary people who pride themselves on being very strict Hindus. He looks at the inner significance of Hinduism, and so seriously that he has never regarded the life of a true Hindu as a matter of luxury which would wither at the least touch, and die if handled roughly."

"But it seems to me that he is rather particular about avoiding the least touch," said Sucharita, smiling.

"That watchfulness of his has its own peculiarity," explained Binoy. "If you question him about it he will reply at once: 'Yes, I believe every bit of it—that caste can be lost by contact, that purity can be lost through improper food—all that is unmistakably true.' But I know quite well that is merely his dogmatism,—the more absurd his opinions sound to his hearers, the more positively will he express them. He insists on rigid, indiscriminate observance, lest, by his yielding on minor points, foolish people may be led to feel a disrespect for more vital matters, or lest the opposite party should claim a victory. So he dare not display any laxity, even to me."

"There are plenty of such people amongst Brahmos also," said Paresh Babu. "They want to sever all connections with Hinduism without discrimination, lest outsiders should mistakenly think they condone also its evil customs. Such people find it difficult to lead a natural life, for they either pretend or exaggerate, and think that truth is so weak that it is part of their duty to protect it by force or by guile. The bigots are those whose idea is, 'Truth depends upon me. I do not depend upon truth.' As for myself, I pray to god that I may always be a simple, humble worshipper of truth, whether in a Brahmo temple or at a Hindu shrine,—that no external barrier may obstruct or hinder my worship."

After these words Paresh Babu remained silent for a while, allowing his mind to rest as it were in the very depths of his being. These few words of his seemed to have lifted the whole tone of the discussion—not that this was due to anything in the words themselves, but to the peace which welled up from the experiences of Paresh Babu's own life. The faces of Lolita and Sucharita lighted up with a glow of devotion. Binoy also did not feel like saying any more. He could see that Gora was too high-handed—the simple and assured peace which clothes the thought and word and deed of those who are the bearers of truth, was not one of Gora's possessions—and on hearing Paresh Babu speak, this struck Binoy all the more painfully.

When Sucharita had gone to bed that night, Lolita came and sat on the edge of her bed. Sucharita saw clearly enough that Lolita was turning something over in her mind, and, as she also knew, that something was about Binoy. So she herself gave her an opening by saying: "Really, I like Binoy Babu immensely."

"That's because he is all the time talking about Gourmohan Babu," observed Lolita.

Although Sucharita saw the insinuation, she pretended she did not, and said innocently: "That's true; I hugely enjoy hearing Gour Babu's opinions from his mouth. It almost makes me see the man himself before my eyes."

"I don't enjoy it at all!" snapped Lolita. "It makes me angry."

"Why?" asked Sucharita in surprise.

"It's nothing but Gora, Gora, Gora day in and day out," replied Lolita. "His friend Gora may be a great man, but isn't he himself a man also?"

"That's true, but how does his devotion prevent him from being one?" asked Sucharita laughing.

"His friend has overshadowed him so completely that Binoy Babu has no chance of showing himself. It is as though a cockroach had swallowed a midge. I have no patience with the midge for allowing itself to be caught, and it doesn't heighten my respect for the cockroach."

Sucharita, amused at the heat in Lolita's tone, merely laughed and said nothing, while Lolita continued: "You may laugh if you like, Didi, but I can tell you that if anyone tried to put me in the shade like that, I would not stand it for a single day. Take yourself,—whatever people may think, you never keep me in the background; that's not your nature and that's why I love you so. The fact is, you have learnt that lesson from father—he keeps a place for everybody."

In that household these two girls were the most devoted of all to Paresh Babu. At the very mention of "father" their hearts seemed to expand.

"Just fancy, comparing anybody with father!" protested Sucharita. "But whatever you may say, dear, Binoy Babu can talk wonderfully well."

"But, my dear girl, don't you see that his ideas sound so wonderful just because they are not his own. If he had talked of what he himself really thought, then his words would have been just simple and sensible,—not sounding like manufactured phrases, and that's the way I'd have much preferred them."

"Why be angry about it, dear?" said, Sucharita. "It only means that Gourmohan Babu's opinions have become his own."

"If that is so then I think it's horrid," said Lolita. "Has God given us intelligence to expound other people's ideas, and a mouth simply to repeat other people's phrases, however wonderfully well? Bother such wonderfulness, I say!"

"But, why can't you see that, because Binoy Babu loves Gourmohan Babu so much, they have really come to think in the same way?"

"No, no, no!" broke out Lolita, "no much thing has happened at all. Binoy Babu has simply acquired the habit of accepting everything Gourmohan Babu says—that's not love, it's slavery. He wants to deceive-himself into thinking that he holds the same opinions as his friend, but why? Where one loves, one can follow without agreeing—one can surrender oneself with eyes open. Why cannot he plainly admit that he accepts Gourmohan Babu's opinions because of his love for him? Isn't it clear enough that he does so? Tell me truly, Didi, don't you think that's the truth?"

Sucharita had not thought of it in this light,—all her curiosity had been about Gora and she had not felt any eagerness to study Binoy as a separate problem. So without giving a direct answer to Lolita's question, she said: "Well, suppose you are right, what's to be done about it?"

"I should love to untie his bonds for him and free him from his friend," replied Lolita.

"Why not try it, dear?"

"My trying will not do much, but if you put your mind to it, something is sure to happen."

Sucharita was not unaware, in her heart of hearts, of having acquired an influence over Binoy, but she tried to laugh the matter off, and Lolita went on: "The one thing I like him for, is the way he is struggling to free himself from Gourmohan Babu's control after coming under your influence. Anyone else in his place would have started writing a play in abuse of Brahmo girls—but he still keeps an open mind, as is proved by his regard for you and his respect for father. We must try and help Binoy Babu to stand on his own feet. It is unbearable that he should exist merely to preach Gourmohan Babu's opinions."

At this moment Satish came running into the room calling out, "Didi! Didi!" Binoy had taken him to the circus, and although it was so late, Satish could not check his enthusiasm for the performance which he had seen for the first time. After describing his experiences, he said: "I tried to bring Binoy Babu in to stay the night with me, but after coming into the house he went away again, saying he would come again to-morrow. Didi, I told him that he would have to take all of you to see the circus one day."

"And what did he say to that?" asked Lolita.

"He said that girls would be frightened if they saw a tiger. But *I* wasn't at all afraid!" With which Satish swelled out his chest with manly pride.

"Oh, indeed!" said Lolita. "I know well enough the kind of brave man your friend Binoy Babu is—I say, Didi, we must really compel him to take us to the circus."

"There will be an afternoon performance to-morrow," said Satish.

"That's good. We'll go to-morrow," settled Lolita; and next day, when Binoy arrived, Lolita exclaimed: "I see you've come in good time, Binoy Babu. Let's make a start."

"Where to?" asked Binoy, in surprise.

"To the circus, of course," declared Lolita.

To the circus! To sit with a party of girls before everybody in the tent, in broad daylight! Binoy was dumbfounded.

"Is suppose Gourmohan Babu will be angry, will he?" pursued Lolita.

Binoy pricked up his ears at the question, and when Lolita repeated: "Gourmohan Babu has views about taking girls to the circus, hasn't he?" he replied firmly: "Certainly he has."

"Please give us an exposition of them," begged Lolita. "I'll go and call my sister so that she may hear it too."

Binoy felt the sting but laughed, whereupon Lolita continued: "What makes you laugh, Binoy Babu? Yesterday you told Satish that girls are afraid of tigers—aren't you ever afraid of anyone?"

After this Binoy simply had to accompany the girls to the circus. Not only that, but on his way there he had plenty of time to ponder agitatedly on the figure he seemed to be cutting, not only to Lolita but also to the other girls of the house, so far as his relations to his friend went.

The next time Lolita saw Binoy she asked him with an air of innocent inquiry: "Have you told Gourmohan Babu about our visit to the circus the other day?"

The point of the question penetrated deeply this time, and made Binoy wince and blush as he replied: "No, not yet."

NINETEEN

Gora was at his work one morning when Binoy arrived unexpectedly and said abruptly: "The other day I took Paresh Babu's daughters to the circus."

Gora went on with his writing, saying: "So I hear."

"From whom did you hear?" asked Binoy in astonishment.

"From Abinash, who happened to be at the circus the same day," replied Gora, and continued writing without further remark.

That Gora should have already heard of it, and of all people from Abinash, who could not have spared any embellishments in his account of the matter, made all Binoy's old instincts rise up to shame him. At the same time it flashed across his memory that he had not slept till late last night because he was mentally occupied in quarrelling with Lolita. "Lolita thinks that I am afraid of Gora, as a schoolboy of his master. How unfairly people can judge one another! It's true that I respect Gora for his unusual qualities, but not in the way Lolita thinks, which is as unjust to me as to him. Just imagine taking me for a child, with Gora as my guardian!" This had been the burden of his thoughts overnight.

Gora went on with his writing, and Binoy recalled again those two or three pointed questions which Lolita had fired off at him. He found it hard to dismiss them from his mind. Suddenly a feeling of revolt rose in his heart. "What if I did go to the circus?"—he flared up within. "Who is Abinash to come and discuss my affairs with Gora?—and why on earth does Gora allow that idiot to launch into such a discussion? Is Gora my keeper that I am to be answerable to him as to where I go and with whom? This is an outrage on our friendship!"

Binoy would hardly have been so indignant with Gora and Abinash had he not suddenly realised his own cowardice. He was merely trying to shift on to his friend the guilt of the secrecy which he had felt impelled to preserve so long. If only Gora had spoken a few angry words to him on the subject, the friends could have come on to the same level, and Binoy would have been consoled. But Gora's solemn silence made him appear to be sitting in judgment on him. This made the memory of Lolita's cutting remarks gall him all the more.

Mohim now entered the room, hookah in hand, and, after offering *pan* from his box, said: "Everything is settled on our side, Binoy, my son. Now, if only your uncle gives his approval we shall all feel relieved. Have you written to him yet?"

This pressure on the subject of his marriage was specially irritating to Binoy to-day. Of course he knew that it was no fault of Mohim's—Gora having given him to understand that Binoy had consented—but he himself felt very small over this consent of his. Anandamoyi had practically tried to dissuade him: neither had he ever felt drawn to his prospective bride. How then had a clear decision at all come out of the confusion? It could not exactly be said that Gora had hurried him in any way, for he would never have pressed him if Binoy had seriously made the least objection, and yet why—? In that "yet" he felt again the sting of Lolita's remarks. For it was nothing that had actually happened on this occasion, but the complete ascendancy which Gora had acquired over him during all these years of their friendship, which was behind it. Binoy had habitually put up with this ascendancy only because of his exceeding love and his soft complaisant nature. And so the masterful relationship had come to prevail over the friendship itself. Hitherto Binoy had not realised this, but now there was no denying it. And so he was in duty bound to marry Sasi!

"No, I've not yet written to my uncle," was his reply to Mohim's question.

"My mistake entirely!" said Mohim. "Why should *you* write any letter; that's my duty. What's his full name, my son?"

"Why are you in such a hurry about it?" replied Binoy "Weddings can't take place in the months of *Aswin* and *Kartik*. In *Aghran*—but I forget, there's a difficulty about that month too. It's an unlucky month in our family history, and we never have auspicious ceremonies in *Aghran*."

Mohim put down his hookah in a corner against the wall and said: "Look here, Binoy, if you are going to stick to all that sort of superstition, then is all this modern education of yours only so many phrases learnt by rote? In this wretched country it is difficult enough to find auspicious days in the calendar, and if, on top of that, every household is going to consult its own private family records, how is business going to be carried on at all?"

"Then why do you accept even *Aswin* and *Kartik* as inauspicious?" asked Binoy.

"Do I?" cried Mohim. "Not a bit of it. But what can I do—in this country of ours you need not honour God, but if you don't honour all the rules about the months of *Bhadra, Aswin* and *Kartik,* and about Thursdays and Saturdays, and all the special phases of the moon, you'll not be allowed in the house! And I must confess that, though I say I don't accept all this, in practice if I don't go by the calendar I feel uncomfortable,—our atmosphere breeds fear just as it breeds malaria, so I can't shake off that kind of feeling."

"Similarly, in my family," said Binoy, "they can't throw off their fear of the month of *Aghran*! At least my aunt would never consent."

Thus did he manage, somehow, to put off the matter for the time, while Mohim, at a loss what move to try next, made his retreat.

Gora could divine from the tone of Binoy's remarks that his friend was beginning to hesitate. Binoy had not been coming for some days, and he suspected that he must be visiting at Paresh Babu's more frequently than ever. And, now that he had tried to put off the question of his marriage, Gora began to have serious misgivings, so, leaving his writing, he turned and said: "Binoy, when once you have given your word to my brother, why plunge him into all these needless uncertainties?"

Binoy, with a sudden impatience, blurted out: "Did I give my word, or was it snatched from me?"

Gora was taken by surprise at this sign of sudden revolt, and, with hardening mind, he asked incisively: "Who was it snatched this from you?"

"You!"

"I? Why, I hardly spoke half-a-dozen words to you on the subject—and you call that extorting a promise!"

As a matter of fact Binoy had no very convincing proof of his accusation—what Gora said was true—very few words had been exchanged—and in what he had said there had not been sufficient insistence to deserve being called pressure. And yet it was also true in a sense that Gora had robbed Binoy of his consent. The less the outward proof the more importunate becomes the accuser, so Binoy, with a note of unreasonable excitement in his voice, said: "Many words are not required to extort a promise!"

"Take back your word!" shouted Gora, getting up from the table "Your promise is not of such immense value that

I should want to beg or rob it of you!"—"Dada," he then roared out to Mohim, who was in the next room, and who came in at once in a great flurry. "Dada," cried Gora, "didn't I tell you at the very beginning that Binoy's marriage with Sasi was impossible?—that I didn't approve of it?"

"Of course you did. No one else could have said such a thing. Any other uncle would have shown some keenness about his niece's marriage!"

"What made you use me as a cat's-paw to obtain Binoy's consent?" flung out Gora.

"No other reason except that I thought it the best way of gaining his consent," answered Mohim ruefully.

Gora turned red in the face. "Please leave me out of all this!" he cried. "I'm not a professional matchmaker; I've other work to do." And with these words he left the room.

Before the unfortunate Mohim could pursue the matter any further, Binoy also had reached the street, and Mohim's only resource was his hookah, which he now took up from the corner where he had placed it.

Binoy had had many quarrels with Gora, but such a volcanic upheaval as the present one had never occurred before, and at first he was aghast at the result of his own work. When he got back home, darts seemed to be piercing his conscience. He had no appetite for eating, or for sleep, as he thought of what a blow he had dealt Gora in that one brief moment. He felt specially repentant to think of the extraordinary and unreasonable way in which he had put all the blame on Gora. "I've done wrong, wrong, wrong," he kept on saying to himself.

Later in the day, just as Anandamoyi was sitting down to her sewing after her midday meal, Binoy turned up and came and sat beside her. She had heard something of what had happened from Mohim, but when she had seen Gora's face at meal-time she knew that a storm had raged.

"Mother," said Binoy, "I've done wrong. What I said to Gora this morning about my marriage with Sasi was nonsense!"

"What of that, Binoy? That kind of thing is bound to happen whenever you try to suppress some pain in the mind. And it's just as well that it should have happened. In a short time both of you will have forgotten all about this quarrel."

"But, mother, I want you to know that I have no objection to marrying Sasi."

"Don't make matters worse, my child, by trying to patch up your quarrel in a hurry. Marriage is for life, while a quarrel is only for the time."

Binoy, however, was not able to accept this advice. He felt he could not go straight to Gora with his proposal, so he went to Mohim and let him know that there was now no obstacle in the way of the marriage, that it could take place in four months' time, and that he himself would see to it that his uncle made no objection.

"Shall we have the betrothal ceremony at once?" urged Mohim.

"All right, that you can settle after consulting Gora," replied Binoy.

"What! consult with Gora again!" complained Mohim irritably.

"Yes, yes, that is absolutely essential!"

"Well, if it must be done, I suppose it must, but—" With which Mohim stopped his mouth with the *pan* which he stuffed into it.

Mohim said nothing that day, but next morning he went to Gora's room, fearing that he would have a hard fight to obtain his consent over again. But the moment he mentioned how Binoy had come the previous afternoon and had spoken of his willingness to marry Sasi, and had even told him to ask Gora's advice about the betrothal, Gora at once expressed his approval and said: "Good! Let's have the betrothal by all means!"

"You're quite complaisant now, I see, but for the Lord's sake don't raise some new objection next time."

"It was not my objection, but my request, which raised the trouble," said Gora.

"Well, then," said Mohim, "my humble petition is, that you neither object nor make any request. I'll be quite satisfied with what I can do myself. How could I know that your request was going to have such a contrary effect? All that I want to know is, do you really wish the marriage to take place?"

"Yes, I do."

"Then let the wish be enough, and don't meddle any further in the matter."

TWENTY

G ora now came to the conclusion that it would be difficult to keep a hold on Binoy from a distance, so that a watch must be kept where the field of danger was. The best way to keep Binoy within bounds, he felt, would be to keep up a frequent intercourse with Paresh Babu himself. So, the very day after the quarrel, he went in the afternoon to Binoy's lodgings.

That Gora would come so soon was more than Binoy had expected, and he was as astonished as he was happy. He was still more surprised when Gora introduced the topic of Paresh Babu's daughters without any sign of hostility towards them. It was not necessary to try very hard to arouse Binoy's interest in this subject, and the two friends went on discussing the topic from every point of view till far into the night.

Even when walking home that night Gora could not keep the subject out of his head, nor was he able to dismiss it from his thoughts so long as he was awake. Never before in his life had such a disturbance invaded his mind—in fact, the subject of women had never been included in his cogitations. Binoy had now proved to him that they were a part of the world problem, which must be dealt with by solution or compromise, but which could not be ignored.

So next day, when Binoy said to Gora, "Come along with me to Paresh Babu's, he has often inquired after you," Gora agreed without the least demur. Not only did he consent, but there was no longer the same indifference in his mind. At first he had been utterly incurious about Sucharita and Paresh Babu's daughters, then a contemptuous hostility towards them had arisen in his mind, but now he actually felt an eagerness to know them better. He was anxious to discover what the attraction was that exercised such an influence over Binoy's heart.

It was evening when they reached the house, and in the parlour upstairs Haran was reading one of his English articles to Paresh Babu by the light of a table-lamp. Paresh Babu was, however, only a means to an end, for Haran's real object was to impress Sucharita. She was listening in silence at the foot of the table, shading her eyes from the glare of the lamp with a palm-leaf fan. With her naturally obedient nature she was trying her best to attend, but every now and then her mind would wander.

When the servant announced the arrival of Gora and Binoy, she started, and was preparing to leave the room when Paresh Babu stopped her, saying: "Where are you going, Radha? It is only our Binoy and Gour who have come."

Sucharita sat down in some confusion, though relieved that the reading of Haran's tedious article had been interrupted. She was certainly excited at the prospect of seeing Gora again, but she felt both shy and uneasy at the idea of his coming while Haran was there. It is difficult to say whether it was fear lest they should quarrel again, or something else.

The very name of Gora had set Haran on edge. He barely returned Gora's salutation and then sat silent, looking glum. As for Gora, the moment he saw Haran all his fighting instincts were aroused.

Mistress Baroda had gone visiting with her three daughters, and it had been arranged that Paresh Babu should call for them in the evening to bring them home. It was already time for Paresh Babu to go when Gora and Binoy's arrival delayed him; and when he could no longer put off going, he whispered to Haran and Sucharita that he would be back as soon as possible, and left them to entertain the guests.

The entertainment began soon enough, for in less than no time a regular pitched battle had begun. The subject under discussion was this. There was a certain District Magistrate named Brownlow, stationed near Calcutta, with whom Paresh Babu had been friendly when at Dacca. He and his wife had shown great regard for Paresh Babu because he did not keep his wife and daughters secluded in the *zenana*. Every year the *sahib* used to celebrate his birthday by holding an agricultural fair. Mistress Baroda had been lately calling on Mrs. Brownlow, and had as usual been expatiating on her daughters' cleverness in English literature and poetry, whereupon the *mem-sahib* had enthusiastically suggested that as the Lieutenant-Governor was bringing his wife to the fair this year, it would be nice if Paresh Babu's girls could act a short English play before them. This suggestion had met with Baroda's delighted approval, and to-day she had taken her daughters to a friend's house for a rehearsal. When asked whether it would be possible for him to attend the fair, Gora replied with unnecessary violence—"No!" Whereupon a heated controversy ensued about the English and the Bengalis, and the difficulties in the way of social intercourse between them in India.

Haran said: "It is the fault of our own people. We have so many bad customs and superstitions that we are not worthy."

To which Gora replied: "If that is really true, then, however unworthy we may be, we ought to be ashamed of going about slavering for the society of English people."

"But," returned Haran, "those who are really worthy are received with the highest regard by the English—as for instance our friends here."

"This kind of regard for some persons which only accentuates the humiliation of the rest of their countrymen, is nothing but an insult in my eyes," said Gora.

Haran's anger soon got the better of him, and Gora, by egging him on, quickly had him at his mercy.

While the discussion was going on in this way, Sucharita was gazing at Gora from behind the shelter of her fan,—the words which she heard making no impression on her mind. If she had been conscious that she was staring at Gora she would doubtless have felt ashamed, but she was utterly oblivious of herself. Gora sat opposite to her, leaning over the table with his powerful arms stretched out before him. The light of the lamp fell on his broad white brow, while he now laughed contemptuously and then frowned angrily. Put in all the play of his features there was a dignity which showed that he was not indulging in any play of words, but that his opinions had long years of thought and practice behind them. It was not merely his voice that spoke, but the expression of his face and every movement of his body seemed to show deep conviction. Sucharita wondered as she watched him. It seemed as if for the first time in her life she was looking at a real man, who could not be confounded with the ordinary run of men. Beside him Haran Babu appeared so ineffective that his features, his gestures, and even his dress began to look ludicrous. She had so often discussed Gora with Binoy that she had come to think of him merely as the leader of a special party with a decided opinions of his own, and at best, it seemed to her, he might be of some kind of service to the country. Now, as she looked on his face, she could see, beyond all party opinion or ulterior benefit, the man Gora. For the first time in her life she now saw what a man was, and what his soul was, and in the joy of this rare experience she completely forgot her own existence.

Sucharita's absorbed expression had not escaped Haran, who had, in consequence, been unable to put all his force into his arguments. At length he got up from his seat impatiently and calling her as if she were a close relative, said: "Sucharita, will you come into the other room? I want to speak to you."

Sucharita shrank as though she had been struck, or although Haran was on terms familiar enough to call her like that, and at any other time she would have thought nothing of it, yet to-day, in the presence of Gora and Binoy, it seemed like an insult, especially as Gora cast a swift glance at her in such a way as seemed to make Haran's offence the more unpardonable. At first she pretended not to have heard him, but when Haran, with some show of irritation, repeated: "Don't you hear me, Sucharita? I have something to say to you. I must ask you to come into the next room," she replied, without looking at him: "Wait till father comes back, and then you can tell me."

At this juncture Binoy got up, saying: "I am afraid we are in the way; it's time for us to be going," to which Sucharita hurriedly replied: "No, Binoy Babu, you mustn't go away so soon. Father asked you to wait for him. He will be here immediately," and there was a note of anxious pleading in her voice, as though there had been a proposal to hand over a deer to its hunter.

Haran now strode out of the room saying: "I can't wait now, I must be going." Once outside, he began to repent of his rashness, but he could think of no excuse for returning.

After his departure Sucharita felt hot with shame and sat with bent head, not knowing what to do or say.

It was then that Gora got an opportunity for studying her features. Where was the least trace of the immodest forwardness which he had always associated with educated girls? No doubt her expression was one of bright intelligence, but how beautifully softened it was by her modest shyness. Her brow was pure and stainless like a glimpse of autumn sky: her lips were silent, but how like a tender bud with the soft curves of the unspoken word. Gora had never before looked closely at a modern woman's dress, having contemned it without seeing it, but to-day the new-fashioned *sari* which enfolded Sucharita's figure seemed to him admirable.

One of her hands rested on the table, and, as it peeped out of the puckered sleeve of her bodice, it seemed to Gora's eyes like the gracious message of a responsive heart. In the quiet evening lamp-light which surrounded Sucharita, the whole room with its shadows, the pictures on its walls and all the neatness of its furniture, seemed to form one complete image in which stood out, not its material appurtenances, but the home into which it had been transformed by the deft touches of a woman's care, which all in a moment had been revealed to Gora.

Gradually, as he watched her, she became intensely real and concrete to him, from the stray locks of hair over her temples to the border of her *sari*. At one and the same time he could see Sucharita in her completeness and Sucharita in her every detail.

For a short time they all felt the awkward silence, then Binoy looked towards Sucharita and reverted to some subject he had been discussing with her a few days before. He said: "As I was telling you the other day, I once believed there was no hope either for our country or for our society—that we should always be regarded as minors, and the English would ever remain our guardians. And this is still the opinion of the majority of our countrymen. In such frame of mind, people either remain immersed in their selfish interests or grow indifferent to their fate. I, at one time, seriously thought of securing a Government post through the influence of Gora's father. But Gora brought me to my senses by his protests."

Gora, seeing a slight trace of surprise on Sucharita's face at this remark, said: "Don't think that anger against the Government had anything to do with what I said. Those who are in Government service generally come to acquire a pride in the Government's power, as if it were their own, and thus tend to form a class apart from their other countrymen. I see this more clearly every day. A relative of mine was once a Deputy Magistrate. He has retired now, but when he was in service the District Magistrate used to censure him, saying: "Babu, why are so many people acquitted in your court?" and he would answer: "There is a good reason for that, *sahib*. Those whom you send to gaol are merely like cats and dogs to you, but those whom I have to send are my brothers." In those days there were plenty of our countrymen able to say such noble words, and Englishmen who would listen to them were not lacking either. But nowadays the shackles of service are becoming an ornament and the Deputy Magistrates of the present time are gradually coming to look upon their fellow-countrymen as little better than dogs. And experience shows us that the higher they rise in the service the more they deteriorate. If you are raised up on another man's shoulders you need must look down on your own people, and the moment you regard them as inferior you are bound to do them injustice. That cannot lead to any good." And as he spoke Gora thumped the table so that the lamp shook.

"Gora," said Binoy, smiling, "that table is not Government property, and the lamp belongs to Paresh Babu."

Gora roared with laughter at this remark, filling the whole house with his merriment, and Sucharita was surprised and also delighted to find that Gora could laugh with the heartiness of a boy at a joke against himself. She had not apparently realised that those who have great ideas can also laugh heartily.

Gora talked on many topics that evening, and although Sucharita remained silent, her face showed such obvious approval that his heart was filled with enthusiasm. At length he said, specially addressing Sucharita: "I want you to remember one thing. If we have the mistaken notion that because the English are strong we can never become strong unless we become exactly like them, then that impossibility will never be achieved, for by mere imitation we shall eventually be neither one thing nor the other. To you I make only this request: come inside India, accept all her good and her evil: if there be deformity then try and cure it from within, but see it with your own eyes, understand it, think over it, turn your face towards it, become one with it. You will never understand if you stand opposed and, imbued to the bone with Christian ideas, view it from outside. Then you will only try to wound and never be of any service."

Gora called this his request, but it was rather a command. There was such tremendous force in his words that there was no waiting for the other's consent.

Sucharita listened with bowed head, her heart palpitating to find Gora addressing her specially, with such great eagerness. She put aside all her shyness and said with simple modesty: "I have never before thought about my country so greatly and so truly. But one question I would ask you: what is the relation between country and religion? Does not religion transcend country?"

This question in her soft voice sounded very sweet to Gora's ears, and the expression in Sucharita's eyes as she addressed him made it even sweeter. He replied: "That which transcends country, which is greater than country, can only reveal itself through one's country. God has manifested His one, eternal nature in just such a variety of forms. But those who say that Truth is one, and therefore that only one form of religion is true, accept only this truth, namely, that Truth is one, but omit to acknowledge the truth that Truth is limitless. The limitless One manifests itself in the limitless Many. I can assure you that through the open sky of India you will be able to see the sun—therefore there is no need to cross the ocean and sit at the window of a Christian church."

"You mean to say that for India there is a special path leading to God. What is this speciality?" asked Sucharita.

"The speciality is this," replied Gora. "It is recognised that the Supreme Being who is without definition is manifest within limits,—the endless current of minute and protracted, subtle and gross, is of Him. He is at one and the same time with endless attributes and without attribute; of infinite forms and formless. In other countries they have tried to confine God within some one definition. In India no doubt there have also been attempts to realise God in one or other of His special aspects, but these have never been looked upon as final, nor any of them conceived to be the only one. No Indian devotee has ever failed to acknowledge that God in His infinity transcends the particular aspect which may be true for the worshipper personally."

"That may be true of the wise devotee, but what of the others?" asked Sucharita.

"I always admit that in every country the ignorant will distort the truth," replied Gora.

"But has not such distortion gone further in our country than elsewhere?" persisted Sucharita.

"That may be so," answered Gora. "It is just because India has desired to acknowledge, fully, both the opposite aspects of subtle and gross,—inner and outer, spirit and body,—that those who cannot grasp the subtle aspect have the opportunity to seize upon the gross, and their ignorance working on it, results in these extraordinary distortions. All the same, it would never do for us to cut ourselves off from the great, the varied, the wonderful way in which India has tried to realise in body, mind and action, and from every point of view, the One who is true, both in forms and in formlessness, in material as well as in spiritual manifestation, alike to outer sense and inner perception;—or to commit the folly of accepting instead, as the only religion, the combination of

Theism and Atheism, dry, and unsubstantial, evolved by eighteenth-century Europe."

Sucharita remained lost in thought awhile, and finding her silent, Gora went on: "Please don't think me to be a bigoted person, least of all one of those who have suddenly turned orthodox,—my words are not meant in *their* sense. My mind is in an ecstasy with the deep and grand unity which I have discovered running through all of India's various manifestations and her manifold strivings, and this prevents me from shrinking to stand in the dust with the poorest and most ignorant of my countrymen. This message of India some may understand, some may not,—that makes no difference in my feeling that I am one with all India, that all her people are mine; and I have no doubt that through all of them the spirit of India is secretly but constantly working."

Gora's words, spoken out in his powerful voice, seemed to vibrate through the walls and furniture of the room. These were not words which Sucharita could be expected fully to understand, but the first tide of impending realisation sets in strongly, and the realisation that life is not confined within the bonds of family or sect overwhelmed her with a painful force.

No more was said, for from the staircase came the sound of running feet and of girlish laughter. Paresh Babu had returned with his daughters, and Sudhir was playing one of his usual pranks on the girls.

On entering the room and seeing Gora, Lolita and Satish recovered their gravity and remained there, but Labonya went out precipitately, while Satish sidled up to Binoy's chair and began whispering to him, and Lolita drew a chair up behind Sucharita and sat down half-hidden.

Paresh Babu then entered, saying: "I am rather late in getting back. Panu Babu has gone, I suppose?"

Sucharita making no answer, Binoy said: "Yes, he wasn't able to wait." And Gora got up and, making a respectful bow to Paresh Babu, said: "We too must be going."

"I've not had much chance of a talk with you this evening," said Paresh Babu. "I hope you'll call now and then, when you find the time."

Just as Gora and Binoy were going out of the room, Mistress Baroda came in. They both bowed to her, and she cried: "What! going already?"

"Yes," replied Gora abruptly whereupon Baroda turned to Binoy, saying: "But, Binoy Babu, I cannot let you go; you must stay to dinner with us. Besides, I have something to speak to you about."

Satish jumped with delight at this invitation and, seizing Binoy's hand, said: "Yes, yes, don't let Binoy Babu go, mother; he must sleep with me here to-night."

Finding that Binoy hesitated to give his answer, Baroda turned to Gora with: "Must you take Binoy Babu away? Do you need him specially?"

"No, no, not at all," replied Gora hastily. "Binoy, you stay; I'm off." And he went quickly out.

When Mistress Baroda asked Gora's consent to his staying, Binoy could not help casting a furtive glance at Lolita, who turned her face away with a smile. Binoy could hardly resent these little railleries in which Lolita indulged, and yet they pricked him like thorns. When he had sat down again Lolita said: "Binoy Babu, you would have been wiser to have made your escape to-day."

"Why?" asked Binoy.

"Mother has a scheme for putting you into an awkward position," explained Lolita. "We are one actor short for the play at the Magistrate's fair, and mother has fixed on you to fill up the gap."

"Good heavens!" exclaimed Binoy. "I'd never be able to do that."

"I told mother that at the start," said Lolita, laughing. "I said that your friend would never allow you to take a part in this play."

Binoy winced at the thrust as he said: "We needn't discuss my friend's opinion. But I've never done any acting in my life—why pitch on me?"

"What about us?" complained Lolita. "Do you suppose we have been acting all our lives?"

At this point Mistress Baroda returned and Lolita said: "Mother, it is useless to invite Binoy Babu to join in our play, unless you can induce his friend to agree—"

"Its not a matter for my friend's consent at all," interrupted Binoy in distress. "I simply have not the ability to act."

"Don't you worry about that," cried Baroda. "We'll soon be able to put you in the way. Do you mean to say these girls can do it and you can't? What nonsense!" And there was no further way of escape left to Binoy.

TWENTY ONE

Gora, on leaving the house, did not walk at his usual pace, and instead of going straight home he absently sauntered down to the river. In those days the Ganges and its banks had not been invaded by the ugliness which commercial greed has since brought in its train. There was no railway beside it, and no bridge across it, and the sky on a winter evening was not obscured by the soot-laden breath of the crowded city. The river used then to bring its message of peace from the stainless peaks of the distant Himalayas into the midst of Calcutta's dusty bustle.

Nature had never found an opportunity for attracting Gora's attention, for his mind had always been busily engaged in its own efforts. He had never so much as noticed any part of his surroundings which was not directly the object of those efforts.

This evening, however, the message of the sky, with its star-lit darkness, moved his heart with all kinds of little touches. The river was without a ripple. The lights of the boats tied to the landing-places twinkled out, and all the gloom seemed massed in the dense foliage of the trees on the opposite bank. Over the whole scene the planet Jupiter kept watch like the wakeful conscience of the night.

All this time Gora had been living aloof in his own world of thought and action—what was it that had now happened?

He had been brought up against some point of contact with Nature; and, thereupon, the deep dark water of the river, the dense dark banks, and the illimitable dark sky overhead had offered him welcome. Gora felt that to-night he had surrendered himself to Nature's overtures.

From the garden of a merchant's office by the roadside the unfamiliar fragrance of some exotic flowering creeper laid its soothing touch over Gora's restless heart, and the river beckoned him away from the field of man's untiring labour towards some dim unexplored region, where the trees bore wondrous flowers and cast mysterious shadows, on the banks of unknown waters; where, beneath the pure open skies, the days seemed like the frank gaze of a wide-open eye, the nights like the bashful shadows trembling beneath downcast eyelashes.

A very vortex of sweetness surrounded Gora and seemed to draw him into unknown primal depths never experienced by him before. His whole being was assailed, at one and the same time, with shocks of pain and of joy. He seemed to be standing in utter self-forgetfulness on this autumn night by the river-bank,—the vague starlight in his eyes, the undefined city sounds in his ears,—in the presence of the veiled elusive mystery which pervades the universe. Because, so long, he had not acknowledged her sway, Nature had now taken her revenge by enmeshing him in her magic net, binding him close to earth, water and sky, and cutting him off from his everyday life.

Gora lost in wonder at his own condition, sank down on the steps of the deserted ghat. Again and again he asked himself, as he sat there, what was this sudden experience, what its meaning for him, what place had it in the scheme of life which he had planned for himself? Was it a thing to be fought against and overcome?

But as Gora clenched his fists fiercely, there came to him the memory of the questioning glances of two entrancing eyes, soft with modesty, bright with understanding—and in imagination he felt the touch of the perfect fingers of two gentle hands. He thrilled through and through with ineffable joy as all his questions and misgivings were completely set at rest by the depth of this experience in the darkness, and he felt loath to lose it by leaving the place.

When he returned home that night, Anandamoyi asked him: "Why so late, child? Your dinner is quite cold."

"Oh, I don't know, mother; I was sitting for a long time by the river."

"Wasn't Binoy with you?"

"No, I was alone."

Anandamoyi felt considerably astonished, for she had never known Gora do such a thing before—meditating alone by the Ganges till so late an hour! It has never been his habit to sit still in silent thought. Anandamoyi watched him as he sat eating absently, and noticed a new kind of restless excitement in his features. After a pause she asked quietly: "I suppose you have been to Binoy's to-day?"

"No, we were both at Paresh Babu's house this afternoon."

This gave Anandamoyi fresh food for thought, and after awhile she ventured another question: "Did you make the acquaintance of all the family?"

"Yes, without any reserve," replied Gora.

"I suppose their girls have no objection to come out before everybody?"

"None at all," said Gora.

At any other time there would have been a note of emphasis in Gora's reply, and its absence mystified Anandamoyi more than ever.

Next morning Gora did not get through his preparations for the day's work with his accustomed rapidity. He stood for quite a long time looking absent-mindedly out of his bedroom window, which faced the east. At the end of the lane, on the opposite side of the main thoroughfare into which it led, was a school. In the school grounds stood an old *jambolan* tree, over the foliage of which floated a thin veil of morning mist letting the red beams of the rising sun dimly through. Gradually, as Gora stood looking at it, the mist melted away and bright shafts of sunlight pierced the network of leaves like so many glittering bayonets, while the city street became busy with passers-by and the sound of traffic.

Suddenly Gora's glance fell upon Abinash and some of his fellow-students, who were coming up the lane towards his house, and with a strong effort he threw off the web of absorption that had cast its spell around him. "No, this will never do!" he said to himself with a force which smote his mind like a blow, and he rushed out of his room.

He reproached himself bitterly for not being ready in time to receive his colleagues—a thing that he had never before allowed to happen. He made up his mind not to go to Paresh Babu's house again, and to contrive some means to banish all thoughts of the family, even by avoiding Binoy for a time.

In the course of the talk with his friends they decided on a plan for going on a tramp along the Grand Trunk Road. They would take no money with them, subsisting on whatever hospitality was offered them on the way.

This determination arrived at, Gora displayed unbounded enthusiasm. An intense joy took possession of him at the idea of thus escaping from all fetters and taking to the open road. It seemed to him that the very notion of this adventure had freed his heart from the net in which it had become entangled. Like a boy released from school, Gora almost ran out of the house to make his preparations for this outing, as he tossed to and fro in his mind the argument that work alone was true and all these sentiments, which had so overpowered him, only illusions.

Just as Krishnadayal was entering the house, carrying a vessel of sacred Ganges water in his hand, wearing a scarf inscribed with the names of the gods, and repeating sacred *mantras,* Gora in his haste ran into him. Dismayed at what he had done, Gora hastily bent to touch his feet in apology; but Krishnadayal shrank away from him, and saying hurriedly, "Never mind now, never mind," sidled past, feeling that Gora's touch had destroyed all the efficacy of his morning bath in the Ganges.

Gora had never realised that all Krishnadayal's carefulness was specially directed towards avoiding him in particular; he merely put down his squeamishness as being part of his insane desire to avoid contamination by guarding against the touch of all and sundry, for did he not keep even his wife Anandamoyi at a distance, as though she were an outcaste, and hardly came into contact all with Mohim, who was always too busy. The only member of the family he had anything to do with was his granddaughter Sasi, and he used to get her to memorise Sanskrit texts and teach her the correct ritual of worship.

So when Krishnadayal shrank away, Gora merely smiled to himself at his father's ways, which in fact had gradually and so completely estranged him that, in spite of his disapproval of Anandamoyi's unorthodox habits, all his devotion had been centred in this unconventional mother of his.

After finishing his breakfast, Gora put a change of clothes into a bundle and, strapping it on his back in the manner of English travellers, he went to Anandamoyi and said: "Mother, I'm thinking of going away for a few days. Give me your leave."

"Where are you going, my son?" she asked.

"I don't know myself, exactly," he replied.

"Is it on any business?"

"Not business as it is usually understood. The journey itself is the business."

Seeing that Anandamoyi remained silent, Gora implored her anxiously: "Mother, you really must not say no. You know me well enough. You need have no fear of my turning ascetic and taking to the road for good! I cannot stay away from you for many days, you know that, don't you?"

Gora had never before expressed his affection for his mother in such clear terms, and no sooner had he done so than he felt a little awkward.

Anandamoyi, though inwardly delighted, detected, this, and in order to put him at his ease she said: "Binoy's going with you, of course, isn't he?"

"Just like you, mother! Without Binoy to guard him, you think someone will kidnap your Gora. Binoy is not going, and I am going to cure this superstitious faith of yours in him by coming back safe and sound, even without his protection!"

"But you'll let me have news now and then?" said Anandamoyi.

"Better make up your mind that you'll not get any news, then if you do you'll be all the happier. No one is going to steal your Gora,—never fear. He isn't the kind of priceless treasure you imagine him to be! If anyone takes a fancy to this little luggage of mine I'll make him a present of it and come home,—I'm not to stick to it at the risk of my life, I can assure you!"

Gora bent low to take the dust of Anandamoyi's feet, and she blessed him by kissing her own fingers which had touched his head, but made no attempt to dissuade him from his project. She never stood in the way of anything being done because it gave herself pain, or for fear of some imaginary evil. In her own life she had been through many obstacles and dangers, and she was not ignorant of the outside world. She had never known fear, and her anxiety to-day was not because of anything that might happen to Gora, but because, from the night before, she had guessed that he was going through some mental distress, which she now felt sure was the reason of his suddenly going off on this tramp.

Just as Gora set foot in the street with his bundle on his back, Binoy appeared carrying with the greatest care two deep-red roses. "Binoy," said Gora, "whether you are a bird of good or evil omen will soon be put to the test."

"Are you going on a journey, then?" asked Binoy.

"Yes."

"Where?"

"Echo answers where!" laughed Gora.

"Have you no better answer?"

"No. Go to mother and she will tell you all about it. I must be off." And with these words Gora marched off at a quick pace.

On entering her room Binoy made his obeisance to Anandamoyi and placed the two roses at her feet. Picking them up she asked: "Where did you get these, Binoy?"

Binoy, without giving her a definite answer, said: "When I get something good I want first of all to offer it in worship at your feet. But you are thoughtful, mother?"

"What makes you think so?" asked Anandamoyi.

"Because you have forgotten to offer me the usual betel leaf," said Binoy.

When Anandamoyi had supplied this deficiency, the two of them went on talking till midday. Binoy was unable to throw any light on the object of Gora's purposeless journey; but when, in the course of conversation, Anandamoyi asked him whether he had not taken Gora to Paresh Babu's house the day before, he gave her a full account of all that had happened there, and she listened closely to every word.

When departing Binoy said: "Mother is my worship accepted, and may I take the flowers away now that they have received your blessing?"

Anandamoyi laughed as she handed the roses to Binoy. She could see that these blossoms were not receiving such care merely for their beauty—that there was assuredly a deeper object in them than their botanical interest.

When Binoy had gone she pondered long on what she had heard, and prayed fervently to God that Gora might not be unhappy, and that nothing might happen to injure his friendship with Binoy.

TWENTY TWO

There was a history attached to these two roses.

The night before, when Gora had departed alone from Paresh Babu's house, he had left poor Binoy in a great fix at the proposal that he should take part in the play at the Magistrate's fair.

Lolita had no great enthusiasm for this play, rather she was bored by the whole affair, but she felt an obstinate wish to entangle Binoy in it somehow. She was provoked with Gora, and wanted to use Binoy for doing whatever she could contrary to Gora's wishes. She did not herself understand why it was so unbearable for her to think of Binoy as subservient to his friend, but whatever the reason might be, she felt that she could breathe freely if only she could make Binoy independent of all such bondage.

So, shaking her head roguishly, she had said to him: "Why, sir, what's wrong with the play?"

"There may be nothing wrong in the play itself," answered Binoy, "but it is acting in the Magistrate's house that I object to.

"Is that your own opinion or someone else's?"

"I'm not responsible for expressing other people's ideas," said Binoy; "and, further, they are not easy to explain. Perhaps you may find it hard to believe, but I'm giving you my own opinions, sometimes in my own words, sometimes perhaps in another's."

Lolita merely smiled without replying, but a short time afterwards she said: "Your friend Gour Babu imagines, I suppose, that there is great heroism in setting no value on a magistrate's invitation,—that it is a way of fighting the English?"

"My friend may or may not think so, but I myself certainly do," replied Binoy with some heat. "Isn't it a method of fighting? How can we preserve our self-respect unless we give up our subserviency to those who think they honour us by beckoning us with their little finger?"

Lolita was naturally of a proud disposition, and she liked to hear Binoy speaking of this need for self-respect; but, feeling the weakness of her argument, she went on hurting Binoy by her needless mockery.

"Look here," said Binoy at length. "Why do you go on arguing? Why don't you say 'It is my wish that you take part in this play,' then I could get some pleasure from the sacrifice of my own opinions out of regard for your request."

"Bah!" exclaimed Lolita. "Why should I say that? If you have an honest opinion, why should you act against it at my request? But it must be honestly yours!"

"Have it that way if you like," said Binoy. "Let it be granted that I have no real opinion,—if I am not allowed to sacrifice it at your request, let me at least own defeat at the hands of your arguments and consent to take part in the play."

As Mistress Baroda entered the room at this moment, Binoy got up and at once said: "Will you please tell me what I have to do to get up my part?"

"There's no need for you to worry about that," answered Baroda triumphantly. "We'll see that you are coached properly. All you have to do is to come regularly to the rehearsals."

"Very well, then I'll be going now."

"No, no, you must stay to dinner," urged Mistress Baroda.

"Will you not excuse me to-night?"

"No, Binoy Babu, you really must stay," insisted Baroda.

So Binoy stayed, but he did not feel as much at ease as usual. Even Sucharita sat silent to-night, absorbed in her own thoughts. She had not taken any part in the conversation either, while Lolita had been arguing with Binoy, but had got up and been pacing up and down the verandah. Anyhow the thread of their intercourse somehow seemed to have snapped.

When parting from Lolita, Binoy looked at her serious face and said: "Just my luck! I own defeat, but fail to please you all the same."

Lolita made no answer and turned away.

She was not a girl to cry readily, but to-night she felt the tears irresistibly coming to her eyes. What was the matter? What made her keep on trying to wound Binoy and only getting wounded herself?

As long as Binoy was unwilling to take part in the play, Lolita's pertistence had only increased, but, as soon as he consented, all her enthusiasm had vanished. In fact all the arguments against his taking part waxed turbulent in her mind, and she was tormented with the thought that he ought not to have agreed merely at her request. What mattered her request to him? Was this merely his politeness?—As if she had been pining for his politeness!

But why should she be so contrary now? Had she not done her best to drag poor Binoy into the play? What right had she to be angry with him because he had yielded to her persistence, even though it was out of politeness? Lolita was clearly more exercised over this affair, with her self-reproaches, than was merely natural.

On other occasions when she was disturbed, she used to go for comfort to Sucharita, but to-night she did not. For she could not fully understand why her heart beat at her breast and the tears struggled to come.

Next morning Sudhir brought a bouquet for Labonya, and in it there were two red roses which Lolita immediately took out of the bunch. On being asked why, she replied: "I can't bear to see beautiful blossoms squashed in the middle of a nosegay. It's barbarous to herd a number of flowers together like that," and she untied the bouquet and distributed the flowers in different parts of the room.

Satish now came running up to her crying: "Didi, where did you get these flowers?"

Without answering his question Lolita asked: "Aren't you going to call on your friend to-day?"

Up to that moment Satish had not been thinking of Binoy, but at the mere mention of him he began to dance, saying: "Yes, of course I will", and he wanted to start there and then.

"What do you do when you're there?" asked Lolita, detaining him, to which Satish replied concisely: "We talk."

"He gives you so many pictures, why don't you give him something?" continued Lolita.

Binoy had cut out all kinds of pictures from English magazines and Satish had started a scrap-book with them. He had become so keen about filling its pages that the moment he saw a picture, even in a valuable book, his fingers itched to cut it out, and this avidity of his had brought upon his guilty head heaps of scoldings from his sisters.

That in this world reciprocity of gifts is expected, now came as a sudden and uncomfortable revelation to Satish. It was not easy for him to contemplate the idea of giving up any of the cherished possessions which he guarded with such care in an old tin box, and his face showed alarm. Lolita pinched his cheek and said with a laugh: "Never mind, don't you worry about that. Just give him these two roses."

Delighted at such an easy solution of the problem, Satish set off with the flowers to settle his debt with his friend. On the road he met Binoy and called out: "Binoy Babu, Binoy

Babu!" and, concealing the roses under his coat, he said: "Can you guess what I've got for you here?"

When Binoy had acknowledged defeat as usual, Satish produced the two red blossoms and Binoy exclaimed: "Oh, how lovely! But, Satish Babu, these are not your own, are they? I hope I shan't be falling into the hands of the police as a receiver of stolen goods!"

Satish felt a sudden doubt as to whether he could call these flowers his own or not, so he said after a moment's thought: "Of course not! Why, my sister Lolita gave them to me to give to you!"

So now the question was settled, and Binoy said good-bye to Satish with a promise to call in the afternoon.

Binoy had not been able to forget the pain he had experienced the previous night at Lolita's hands. He seldom quarrelled with people, so he had never expected such sharp words from anybody. At first he had regarded Lolita as merely following in Sucharita's wake, but recently his condition with regard to her had been like that of a goaded elephant which gets no time to forget its driver. His chief concern had been to please Lolita anyhow and get for himself a little peace. But on returning home at night her pungent, mocking words recurred to his mind, one after another, till he found sleep difficult.

"I am merely like Gora's shadow. I have no opinions of my own.—Lolita despises me because she thinks this, but it is absolutely false." Thus ran his thoughts, and he marshalled in his mind all kinds of arguments against the idea. But these were of no avail, for Lolita had never brought against him any definite accusation, and had avoided giving him any opportunity for arguing the point. Binoy had so many answers to the charge, and yet he never got a chance of stating them,— this was what vexed him so. And then to crown it all, even when he had admitted defeat, Lolita had shown no sign of pleasure. This upset him entirely. "Am I then such a contemptible object?" he bitterly asked himself.

So when he heard from Satish that Lolita had sent these roses to him by proxy, he was exultant. He took them as a peace-offering, in token of his surrender. At first he thought he would carry them home, but at length he decided to get them sanctified by offering them at Mother Anandamoyi's feet.

That same evening, when Binoy arrived at Paresh Babu's house, Lolita was hearing Satish repeat his school lessons.

Binoy's first words were: "Red is the colour of warfare; flowers of reconciliation ought to have been white."

Lolita looked at him blankly, at a loss to understand his meaning, until he brought out from under his shawl a bunch of white oleanders and held them towards her, saying: "No matter how beautiful your roses are, they have still the tinge of anger about them. These flowers of mine can't compare with them for beauty, but they are nevertheless, not unworthy of your acceptance in their white garb of humility."

"What flowers do you call mine?" asked Lolita, blushing deeply.

"Have I then made a mistake?" stammered Binoy in confusion. "Satish Babu, whose flowers did you give me?"

"Why, didn't Lolita Didi tell me to give them?" replied Satish with an injured air.

"To whom did she tell you to give them?" questioned Binoy.

"To you, of course."

Lolita, turning redder than ever, gave Satish a push as she said: "I never saw such a little stupid! Didn't you want the flowers to give to Binoy Babu in exchange for his pictures?"

"Yes, I did but didn't you tell me to give them?" cried Satish, altogether puzzled.

Lolita realised that bandying words with Satish only got her more entangled than ever, for Binoy now clearly saw that Lolita had given him the roses but did not want him to know it.

Binoy said: "Never mind. I relinquish my claim to your flowers: but let me tell you, there is no mistake about these flowers of mine. These are my peace-offering, on the making up of our quarrel."

Lolita interrupted him with a toss of her head: "When did we ever quarrel, and what is this making up you speak of?"

"Has everything, then been an illusion from start to finish?" exclaimed Binoy. "No quarrel, no flowers, no reconciliation either! It seems not only a case of mistaking the glitter for gold, but there never was any glitter even! That proposal about the play, was that—?"

"There's no mistake about that, anyway," interrupted Lolita. "But who ever quarrelled about it? What makes you imagine that I've been in a conspiracy to win your consent? You agreed, and I was duly gratified, that was all. But if you have any real objection to taking part in the play, why should you have agreed, no matter who asked you?" With which she went out of the room.

Everything had turned out contrary. That very morning Lolita had decided that she would confess her defeat at Binoy's hands, and would request him to give up the idea of the play. But things had developed in just the opposite way.

Binoy was led to think that Lolita had not got over her annoyance at his previous opposition, and was still angry because she thought that although Binoy had outwardly capitulated he yet was, at heart, against the performance. He felt greatly pained that Lolita should have taken the matter so seriously, and he made up his mind that he would never raise any objection again, even in joke; that he would take up his part in the play with such devotion and ability that no one would be able to accuse him of indifference.

Sucharita had been sitting alone in her bedroom since early morning, trying to read the *Imitation of Christ.* This morning she had not given any attention to her other regular work. Every now and again her mind would wander and the pages of the book become blurred, and then, with redoubled energy, she would force herself to apply her mind to the book, unwilling to acknowledge her weakness.

Once she thought she heard the sound of Binoy's voice, and on the impulse of the moment she put her book on the table and started up to go into the sitting-room. But, annoyed with herself for this lack of interest in the subject, she took up the book again and sat down, with her hands over her ears lest any distracting sounds should again disturb her.

It often happened that when Binoy called, Gora came also, and she could not help wondering whether he had come to-day. She was afraid lest Gora had come, and then again she was racked by the doubt that he had not.

While she was in this distracted state, Lolita entered the room. "Why, what's the matter, my dear?" exclaimed Sucharita at the sight of her face.

"Nothing!" replied Lolita, shaking her head.

"Where were you all this time?" asked Sucharita.

"Binoy Babu has come," said Lolita. "I think he wants to talk to you."

Sucharita was afraid to ask whether anyone else had come with Binoy. If anybody had come Lolita would certainly have mentioned it; but still her mind was in suspense, and at length she went out, deciding to perform the duties of hospitality and give up her attempts at self-restraint, first asking Lolita: "Won't you come too?"

"You go first, I'll come along later," replied Lolita a little impatiently.

When Sucharita entered the sitting-room she found only Binoy and Satish talking together, and she said: "Father is out, but he will be back soon. Mother has taken Labonya and Lila to our teacher's house to learn their parts. She left word that if you came we were to ask you to wait."

"Aren't you going to be in this play too?" inquired Binoy.

"If everyone were to act where would the audience be?" replied Sucharita.

Generally, when Binoy and Sucharita were together, there was no lack of conversation between them, but to-day there seemed to be some obstacle on both sides which prevented them from talking freely. Sucharita had come determined not to raise the usual topic of Gora; nor did Binoy find it any easier to mention his name, imagining that Lolita, and perhaps the rest of that household, regarded him as his friend's satellite.

After a few random remarks to Binoy, Sucharita, seeing no other way of escape, began to discuss with Satish the merits and demerits of his scrap-book. She managed to rouse Satish's anger by finding fault with his method of arranging his pictures, and Satish, getting excited, disputed with her in his shrill voice.

Binoy meanwhile was looking disconsolately at his rejected bunch of white oleander blossoms which lay on the table, and was thinking to himself with wounded pride: "Lolita ought to have accepted these flowers of mine, if only for the sake of politeness."

Suddenly footsteps were heard, and Sucharita started violently on seeing Haran enter the room. Her startled expression persisted so glaringly that she blushed at Haran's glance.

Haran said to Binoy as he sat down: "Well, hasn't your Gora Babu come to-day?"

"Why?" asked Binoy, irritated at this unnecessary question. "Have you any need of him?"

"It is rare to see you and not to see him," replied Haran. "That is why I asked."

Binoy felt so annoyed that, afraid lest he should show it, he said abruptly: "He is not in Calcutta."

"Gone preaching, I suppose," sneered Haran.

Binoy's anger increased, and he remained silent.

Sucharita left the room without speaking. Haran rose and followed her at once, but she passed out too quickly for him to overtake her, so he called after her: "Sucharita, I want a word with you."

"I'm not well to-day," replied Sucharita, and she went and shut herself in her bedroom.

Mistress Baroda now arrived on the scene and called Binoy to another room to give him his instructions about the play. When, a short time afterwards, he returned, he found that his flowers had disappeared from the table.

Lolita did not turn up that evening for the rehearsal.

As for Sucharita, she sat alone in her room till far into the night with the *Imitation of Christ* lying closed on her lap, and gazed from her corner into the darkness outside.

It seemed as if some unknown and wonderful country had appeared before her eyes like a mirage, from which all the experiences of her past life were in some way completely different, so that the lights which shone there, like chaplets of stars in the darkness of night, struck her mind with awe, as at the mystery of the ineffably remote.

"How insignificant my life has been," she felt. "What I thought of as certain up to now has become full of doubt; what I have been doing everyday seems meaningless. In that mystic realm, perhaps, all knowledge will become perfect, all work noble, and the true significance of life will at length be revealed. Who has brought me before the secret portal of this wonderful, unknown, terrible region? Why does my heart tremble so?—why do my limbs seem to fail me when I try to advance?"

TWENTY THREE

For several days Sucharita spent much time at her prayers, and seemed more and more to be in need of Paresh Babu's support. One day when Paresh Babu was reading alone in his room, Sucharita came in and sat quietly beside him, whereupon he laid down his book and asked: "What is it, Radha dear?"

"Nothing, father," answered Sucharita as she began to arrange the books and papers on his writing-table, although everything was quite tidy. Then after a few moments she said: "Father, why don't you read with me as you used to do?"

"My pupil has passed out of my school," said Paresh Babu, smiling affectionately. "Now you can understand things for yourself."

"No, I can't understand anything at all!" protested Sucharita. "I want to read with you as before."

"So be it," agreed Paresh Babu. "We'll begin from to-morrow."

"Father," said Sucharita suddenly, after a short silence, "why did you not explain to me what Binoy Babu was saying the other day about caste?"

"You know, my dear child," replied Paresh Babu, "I have always wanted you girls to think for yourselves, and not simply to take my opinions, or anyone else's, at second hand. To offer instruction on any question before it has really arisen in the mind is like giving food before one is hungry,—it spoils the appetite and leads to indigestion. But whenever you ask me any question, I am always ready to tell you what I know about it."

"Well, then," said Sucharita, "I *am* asking you a question. Why do we condemn caste distinctions?"

"There's no harm in a cat sitting by and eating right beside you," explained Paresh Babu, "but if certain men so much as enter the room, the food has to be thrown away! How can one not condemn the caste system which has resulted in this contempt and insult of man by man? If that is not unrighteous, I do not know what is. Those who can despise their fellow-men so terribly can never rise to greatness; for them, in turn, shall be reserved the contempt of others."

"The present degenerate condition of our society has bred many faults," said Sucharita, repeating something she had heard from Gora's lips, "and these faults have found their way into every aspect of our life, but are we therefore entitled to blame the real thing itself?"

"I could have answered you," replied Paresh Babu with his usual gentleness, "had I known where the real thing is to be found. But what I actually see before me is the intolerable aversion of man for man in our country,—and how this is dividing and subdividing our people. Can we gain any consolation in such circumstances by trying to dwell on some imaginary 'real' thing?"

"But," asked Sucharita, again echoing Gora's words, "was it not one of the ultimate truths of our country to look on all men with impartial vision?"

"That impartial vision," said Paresh Babu, "was an intellectual achievement,—it had nothing to do with the heart. In it there was room for neither love nor hate, it transcended likes and dislikes. But man's heart can never find its rest in an abstraction so empty of the heart's requirements. So in spite of the existence of this philosophical equality in our

country, we see that the low caste is not allowed entry even
into God's temple. If equality be not observed even on God's
own ground, what matters it whether its conception is to be
found in our philosophy or not?"

Sucharita silently revolved Paresh Babu's words in her
own mind, trying to understand them, and at length she
asked: "Why then, father, didn't you explain all this to Binoy
Babu and his friend?"

Paresh Babu smiled a little as he answered: "They do not
understand, not because they lack the intelligence,—they are,
rather, too clever to want to understand; they prefer explaining
to others! When once the desire comes to them really to
understand from the point of view of the highest truth,—that
is, of righteousness,—they won't have to depend on your
father's intelligence for the explanation. At present they view
it from quite a different standpoint, and nothing that I can
say will be of any use to them."

Although Sucharita had listened to Gora's talk with
respect, the divergence of his standard from her own had
nevertheless pained her, and prevented her finding
consolation in his conclusions. As Paresh Babu was speaking,
she felt for the time relieved of her internal conflict. She
would never admit for a moment the idea that Gora, or
Binoy, or for that matter anybody at all, could understand
any subject better than Paresh Babu. On the contrary, she
had never been able to help feeling angry with anyone whose
opinions did not conform to his. Lately, however, she had
not been able to dismiss Gora's opinions with such ready
contempt as of old. It was for the same reason that she now
felt this restless desire in her heart to be constantly
taking shelter under Paresh Babu's wing, as she had done
when a child.

She rose from her seat and went as far as the door; then
she came back and, resting her hand on the back of Paresh

Babu's chair, said: "Father, will you let me sit with you at your evening meditation to-day?"

"Certainly, my dear," said Paresh Babu.

After this Sucharita finally retired into her bedroom and, closing the door, sat down and tried hard to reject all that Gora had said.

But at once Gora's face, radiant with confident assurance, rose before her, and she thought to herself: "Gora's words are not mere words, they are Gora himself. His speech has form and movements, it has life; it is full of the power of faith and the pain of love for his country. His are not opinions that can be settled by contradicting them. They are the whole man himself—and that, too, no ordinary man."

How could she have the heart to raise her hand against him in rejection? Sucharita felt a tremendous struggle going on within her, and she burst into tears. That he could throw her into such a plight, and yet have no compunction in deserting her like this, made her heart ache, and because it ached she was woefully ashamed.

TWENTY FOUR

It had been decided that Binoy should recite in a dramatic style Dryden's poem on "The Power of Music," and that the girls in suitable costumes should present tableaux illustrative of the subject of the poem. In addition to this, songs and English recitations were to be given by the girls as well.

Mistress Baroda had repeatedly assured Binoy that they would prepare him well for the day, for although she herself knew very little English, she depended for help on one or two of her circle who were well versed in the language. But when the rehearsal took place Binoy astonished these expert friends of hers by his recitation, and Baroda was completely cheated of the pleasure of training up this newcomer. Even those who formerly had not regarded Binoy as anyone in particular, were compelled to respect him when they found how proficient he was in English. Haran himself requested Binoy to contribute occasional articles to his paper, and Sudhir began to press him to deliver English lectures at his Students' Society.

As for Lolita, she was in a strange state of mind. She was pleased, in a way, that Binoy should be independent of anyone else's help, and yet she also felt piqued. It upset her to think that Binoy, now conscious of his own powers, might give up expecting to learn anything from them.

What exactly Lolita wanted of Binoy, and in what event she would regain her former peace of mind, she was herself at a loss to understand. As a result, her discontent began to show itself in every little thing, and every time it had Binoy for its target. Lolita could see well enough that this was neither fair nor polite to Binoy; this hurt her, and she tried hard to restrain herself, but on the slightest pretext some inward resentment would suddenly get the better of her and burst out unreasonably in a way she could not account for.

Just as she had at first pestered Binoy till he had consented to take part in this affair, so now she worried him to withdraw. But how could Binoy escape at this stage without upsetting all their plans? Besides, probably with the discovery of his new powers, he himself seemed to have become quite keen about it.

Finally, one day Lolita said to her mother: "I really can't go on with this performance any longer!"

Mistress Baroda knew this second daughter of hers only too well, so she asked in dismay: "Why, what's the trouble?"

"I simply can't do it," repeated Lolita.

As a matter of fact, from the time it was no longer possible to regard Binoy as a novice, Lolita had been quite unwilling to recite her piece, or rehearse her part, in his presence. She practised alone by herself, to the great inconvenience of everyone else; but it was impossible to do anything with her, and at length they had to yield and carry on the rehearsals without her.

But when, at the last moment, Lolita declared her intention of withdrawing altogether, Baroda was nonplussed. She knew well enough that nothing she could say or do would be any good at all, so she was driven to ask Paresh Babu's help.

Though he never meddled in the matter of his daughters' likes or dislikes in unimportant matters, yet as they had given a promise to the Magistrate, and there was very little time left for making other arrangements, Paresh Babu called Lolita to him and, putting his hand on her head, said: "Lolita, would it not be wrong if you withdrew now?"

"I can't do it, father," said Lolita with suppressed tears in her voice. "It's quite beyond me."

"It won't be your fault if you can't do it well," said Paresh Babu. "But if you don't do it at all, that will really be wrong of you."

Lolita hung her head as her father went on: "My dear, when you have once taken up a responsibility, you must see it through. This is not the time to try and escape, merely because your pride is hurt. What if your pride does suffer, can you not bear that in order to do your duty? Won't you try dear?"

"I will," said Lolita as she lifted her face to her father's.

That very evening she made a special effort, and throwing off all hesitation due to Binoy's presence, she entered into her part with zest, almost with defiance. It was the first time that Binoy had heard her recite, and he was really astonished at the vigour and clearness of her enunciation, the unhesitating force with which she interpreted the meaning of the poem. He was delighted beyond his expectations, and her voice sounded in his ears for long after the recitation was over. A good reciter exercises a peculiar fasination over the hearer,— the poem lends its own charm to the reciter's mind, as do flowers to the branches on which they bloom. And from that moment Lolita, for Binoy, became enveloped in poetry.

Hitherto Lolita had all the time kept Binoy goaded by her sharp tongue; and just as one's hand constantly seeks only the painful spot, had Binoy been unable to discern anything of Lolita save her stinging words and her ironical smiles. All his thoughts about her had been confined to trying to discover what made her say this or do that, and the more mysterious had seemed her displeasure the busier had he been kept worrying about it. It had often been his first waking thought, and, every time he started for Paresh Babu's house, he had anxiously wondered what Lolita's mood would be. Whenever he had found her gracious, an immense load seemed to be lifted from Binoy's mind, and then his problem had been how to contrive to make this mood permanent,—a problem, however, of which the solution was clearly beyond his powers.

That is why, after the mental disquiet of all these days, Lolita's recitation of this poem stirred him in a strangely forcible way, so much so that he was at a loss to find any words to express the pleasure he felt. But he did not dare to make any remark to Lolita, for there was no knowing whether his praise would please her, whether such usual sequence of cause and effect would apply to her at all,—the chances were it wouldn't, just because it was usual! So Binoy went over to Mistress Baroda, and to her unburdened himself of his admiration for Lolita's performance, whereupon Baroda's opinion of Binoy's wisdom and intelligence became higher than ever.

The effect on the other side was no less curious. As soon as Lolita felt that her elocution had been a success, that she had ridden the waves of her difficulties like a good seaworthy boat, all her irritation against Binoy vanished, and no vestige of her desire to annoy him remained. Thenceforth she became quite keen about the rehearsals, and in the process was drawn closer to Binoy. She even had no compunction in asking Binoy's advice.

At this change in Lolita's attitude towards him, Binoy felt as if a stone had been rolled off his breast. He felt so light-hearted that he wanted to go to Anandamoyi and play his old childish pranks with her. Many ideas crowded into his mind which he felt he would like to talk over with Sucharita, but he hardly ever saw her nowadays.

Whenever Binoy got the chance of a chat with Lolita he took it, but yet he felt he still would have to be very careful.

He knew how critically he and his friend would be judged by her, so that his conversation did not flow with its natural speed.

Sometimes Lolita would say to him: "Why do you talk as though you were speaking out of a book?" to which Binoy would answer: "I've spent all my time reading, so I suppose my mind must have become like a printed page."

Then again Lolita would say: "Please don't try to talk so well,—just say whatever you really think. You talk so beautifully that one suspects you are merely expounding somebody else's ideas."

For this reason, whenever any idea occurred to Binoy's orderly mind, in an appropriate, well-finished phrase he would, before expressing it to Lolita, try to condense and simplify it, and if a chance metaphor happened to escape him he felt abashed.

Lolita herself shone out as if after the passing of some inexplicable cloud. Even Mistress Baroda was astonished to see the change in her. She no longer turned contrary, as of old, making objections to anything and everything, but joined heartily in what they were doing, rather overwhelming them with the abundance of her ideas and suggestions for the coming play. In this matter Baroda's own exuberance was somewhat tempered by her love for economy, so she was now as embarrassed at her daughter's keenness as she had formerly been at her lack of it.

Lolita, full of her newborn zeal, would often seek out Sucharita with an eager expectation, but although Sucharita laughed and talked with her, Lolita somehow felt herself checked in her presence, and had to come away every time with a sense of disappointment.

One day she went to Paresh Babu and said: "Father, it's not fair that Didi should be sitting alone with her books while we are slaving away at the performance. Why should't she join us?"

Paresh Babu himself had noticed that Sucharita seemed to be holding aloof from her companions, and had been fearing that such moodiness was not healthy for her. Now, at Lolita's words, he came to the conclusion that unless she was induced to join in the amusements of the others, this might become a habit. So he said to Lolita: "Why don't you speak to your mother about it?"

"I will speak to mother," said Lolita, "but you will have to do the persuading, or else Didi will never agree."

When finally Paresh Babu did speak to Sucharita, he was agreeably surprised to find that she had no excuse to make, but at once came forward to do her allotted duty.

As soon as Sucharita came out of her seclusion Binoy tried to get on the same intimate terms with her as before, but something seemed to have happened meanwhile which prevented his reaching up to her. There was such a far-away look in her eyes, such detachment in her expression that he shrank from thrusting himself on her. There had always been a kind of distance in her manner which now became more pronounced, in spite of her joining the rehearsals. She would get through just her own part, and then leave the room. And in this way she receded farther and farther away from Binoy.

Now that Gora was away, Binoy was free to become more intimate than ever with Paresh Babu's household, and the more he relapsed into his own true nature the more were they all drawn to him, and the better pleased was he with himself at experiencing this expansive freedom, hitherto unknown. It was at this juncture that he found Sucharita drifting away from him. At any other time he would have found the pain of such loss hard to bear, but now he easily rose above it.

The strange thing was that Lolita, though noticing this change in Sucharita, made no grievance of it, as she would have done before. Was it because enthusiasm for the play and her recitations had taken such complete possession of her?

Haran, for his part, finding Sucharita taking part in the entertainment, also waxed enthusiastic over it. He himself offered to recite a passage from *Paradise Lost,* and deliver a short lecture on the Charms of Music as a kind of prelude to the recitation of Dryden's poem. This suggestion annoyed Mistress Baroda, and Lolita too was far from pleased; but Haran had already written to the Magistrate about it and settled the matter. So when Lolita hinted that the Magistrate might object to the proceedings being too long, Haran silenced her by triumphantly producing the Magistrate's letter of thanks from his pocket.

No one knew when Gora would be coming back from his expedition. Although Sucharita had determined that she would dismiss the matter from her thoughts, everyday the hope was born afresh in her mind that perhaps this would be the day of his return. Just when she was feeling keenly both this indifference of Gora's and the unruliness of her own mind, and was anxiously seeking for some way of extricating herself from such a predicament, Haran came and once more requested Paresh Babu to celebrate, in God's name his betrothal ceremony with Sucharita.

"There is still a long time before the marriage can take place," objected Paresh Babu. "Do you think it wise to bind yourselves so soon?"

"I think it very essential for both of us," answered Haran, "that we should go through a period of being thus bound to each other before marriage. It will be good for our souls to have this kind of spiritual relationship as a bridge between our first acquaintance and the married state,—a tie without the bondage of duties."

"You had better see what Sucharita has to say," suggested Paresh Babu.

"But she has already given her consent," urged Haran.

Paresh Babu, however, was still in doubt as to Sucharita's

real feelings for Haran, so he called her himself and told her about Haran's proposal.

Sucharita had come to the point of clutching at any support for setting at rest her distracted condition, so she agreed so readily and unhesitatingly that all Paresh Babu's doubts were dispelled. He again asked Sucharita to consider well all the responsibilities attaching to a long engagement, and when, even then, she had no objection to raise, it was settled that, as soon as Mr. Brownlow's entertainment was over, a day should be fixed for the betrothal ceremony.

After this Sucharita felt for a time as though her thoughts had been rescued from some devouring dragon, and she made up her mind that she would prepare herself sternly for serving the Brahmo Samaj on marrying Haran. She decided to have daily readings with Haran, from English books on religious subjects, so as to be able to shape her life according to his ideas; and she felt a sense of uplift in having thus accepted a difficult, even unpleasant, burden.

Of late she had not been reading the paper of which Haran was editor. The day after her decision she received a copy fresh from the press, sent probably by the editor's own hand. Sucharita took the paper to her room and sat down to read it from start to finish, as a kind of religious duty, prepared like a devoted pupil to take to heart all the instruction it offered.

But instead, like a ship in full sail, she ran against a rock. There was an article entitled "The Mania for Looking Back," which consisted of a bitter attack on those people who, although living in modern times, persistently turn their faces towards the past. The reasoning was not unsound—in fact, Sucharita had been searching for just such arguments,—but as soon as she read the article she could see that the object of the attack was Gora. There was, indeed, no mention of this name nor any reference to his writings, but it was evident that just as a soldier takes pleasure in seeing every bullet fired from his gun kill a man, so a spiteful joy expressed itself in this article because every word wounded a living person.

The whole spirit of the paper was intolerable to Sucharita, and she wanted to tear every one of its arguments into shreds. She said to herself: "Gourmohan Babu could have powdered this article into dust!" And as she did so his radiant face shone out before her eyes, and his powerful voice rang in her ears. In the presence of this image and in contrast with the uncommon quality of his speech, this article and its writer appeared so contemptibly trivial that she threw the paper on the floor.

For the first time after many days Sucharita then came and sat by Binoy, and in the course of her talk she said: "What has happened to the copies of the paper in which your writings, and your friend's, appear? Didn't you promise to give me them to read?"

Binoy did not tell her that he had not had the courage to keep his promise because of the change he had noticed in her, so he merely said: "I've kept them all ready for you, and will bring them to-morrow."

Next day Binoy brought with him an armful of magazines and newspapers and left them with Sucharita. But, when she thus got them, she would not read them, and put them away in a box. She did not read them simply because she was so eager to do so. Once more she sought peace for her rebellious heart by refusing to allow it to be distracted and forcing it to accept Haran's undisputed sway.

TWENTY FIVE

On a Sunday morning Anandamoyi was preparing *pan,*
and Sasi, seated beside her, was slicing piles of betel-
nut, when Binoy entered the room. Sasi bashfully made her
escape, scattering the nuts on her lap all over the floor.
Anandamoyi smiled.

Binoy had the habits of making friends with everybody
all round, and had always been on specially good terms with
Sasi. They were always teasing each other. Sasi had hit upon
the device of hiding away Binoy's shoes and returning them
only on his promising to tell her a story, while Binoy in
revenge would invent stories based on highly coloured versions
of actual events from Sasi's own life. This proved to be
condign punishment for her; for she would first try to escape
by accusing the story-teller of falsehood, then by contradicting
him in a voice louder than his own, and finally by flying from
the room in utter rout. Sometimes she would try to retaliate
by manufacturing similar stories about Binoy, but she was no
match for her opponent in the power of invention.

However that may be, whenever Binoy used to come to
the house she would leave everything else and come running
to have her fun with him. Sometimes she would pester Binoy
so badly that Anandamoyi had to rebuke her, but the fault
was not hers alone, for Binoy used to ask for trouble so
successfully that it was impossible for her to control herself.

So now, when that same Sasi self-consciously fled from the room at Binoy's entry, Anandamoyi smiled, it is true, but it was not a smile of happiness.

Binoy himself was so much upset by this trifling incident that he sat for some time without uttering a word. It suddenly made him realise how unnatural these new relations with Sasi really were.

When he had consented to the proposal of marriage he had been thinking only of his friendship with Gora, but he had never visualised clearly what it would mean in other connections. Besides, as Binoy had so often written in their paper, in our country marriage is mainly a social matter, not a personal one, nor had he indulged in any personal likes or dislikes in his own case. Now that he had seen Sasi retire at the sight of her future husband, overwhelmed with bashfulness, he got a glimpse of what their future relationship would be like.

As he realised how far Gora had dragged him along, against his own nature, he became angry with his friend and also reproached himself. And when he remembered how, from the very first, Anandamoyi had discouraged the proposal, he was filled with an admiration for her, not unmixed with astonishment at her keenness of perception.

Anandamoyi understood what was passing in Binoy's mind, and in order to turn his thoughts into other channels she said: "Binoy, I had a letter from Gora yesterday."

"What does he say?" asked Binoy somewhat absently.

"Nothing much about himself," replied Anandamoyi. "But he writes sorrowfully about the plight of the poorer people in the country. He has a long description of all the wrongs perpetrated by the magistrate in some village called Ghosepara."

Feeling in a state of excited antagonism towards Gora, Binoy said somewhat impatiently: "Gora's eyes are always for other's faults: he would excuse all the social outrages, which we ourselves are every day heaping upon our own fellows, and call them virtuous acts!"

Anandamoyi smiled to see Binoy making a stand as champion of the opposite party, in the process of having his fling at Gora, but she said nothing.

Binoy went on: "Mother, you smile and wonder why I have suddenly become indignant. I will tell you what makes me angry. The other day Sudhir took me to a friend's house in the country. When we started from Calcutta it began to rain, and when the train stopped at the junction I saw a Bengali in European dress holding an umbrella well over himself and watching his wife getting out of the carriage. The woman had a child in her arms and she barely managed to protect her baby with her shawl, as she stood exposed on the open platform, shrinking with cold and diffidence. When I saw that the husband stood there, unabashed, under his umbrella, and the drenched wife also took it uncomplainingly, as a matter of course,—nor did anybody else on the station seem to regard it as in anyway wrong,—it seemed to me as if there was not a single woman in the whole of Bengal, whether poor or rich, who had any protection against rain or sun. From that moment I vowed never again to utter the lie that we treat our womenfolk with great reverence, as our good angels, our goddesses, and so forth!"

Binoy stopped short as he realised how his feelings had led him to raise his voice. He concluded in his natural tone: "Mother, you perhaps think I am delivering a lecture to you, as I sometimes do elsewhere. It may be I have got into the habit of talking as if I were lecturing, but that is not what I am doing now. I have never realised before how much our women mean to our country. I never even gave a thought to them.—But I won't chatter much more now, mother. Because I talk so much no one believes that my words express my own ideas. I shall be more careful in future!" and, as abruptly as he had come, Binoy departed, full of his newfound emotion.

Anandamoyi, calling Mohim, said: "Binoy's marriage with Sasi will never take place."

"Why?" asked Mohim. "Are you opposed to it?"

"Yes, I'm against the proposal because I know it will never come off in the end, otherwise why should I object?"

"Gora has consented, and so has Binoy, so why shouldn't it come off? Though, of course, if you disapprove I know that Binoy will never marry her."

"I know Binoy better than you do."

"Better even than Gora does?"

"Yes, I know him more thoroughly than Gora does, and therefore, after considering it from every point of view, I feel I ought not to give my consent."

"Well, let Gora come back first."

"Mohim, listen to me. If you try and press this matter too far it will lead to trouble, I can assure you. I do not wish Gora to talk to Binoy on the subject again."

"All right, we'll see about that," said Mohim as he stuffed some *pan* into his mouth and went out of the room.

TWENTY SIX

When Gora started on his expedition he had with him four companions. Abinash, Motilal, Basanta and Ramapati. But they all found difficult to keep pace with Gora's pitiless enthusiasm. Abinash and Basanta returned to Calcutta after the first few days on the plea of ill health. As for the other two, it was only because of their devotion for Gora that they did not do likewise, leaving their leader alone. And indeed Motilal and Ramapti suffered in no small degree for their loyalty, because no amount of tramping seemed to tire Gora, nor was he ever bored, however long they might be held up on the way. He would stay on day after day in the home of those who were eager to offer hospitality to these Brahmin wayfarers, would crowd round to listen to Gora and were loath to part with him.

This was the first time Gora had seen what the condition of his country was like, outside the well-to-do and cultured society of Calcutta. How divided, how narrow, how weak was this vast expanse of rural India,—how supinely unconscious of its own power, how ignorant and indifferent as to its own welfare! What gulfs of social separation yawned between villages only a few miles apart. What a host of self-imposed imaginary obstacles prevented them from taking their place in the grand commerce of the world. The most trivial things looked so big to them; the least of their traditions seemed so unbreakable.

Without such an opportunity to see it for himself, Gora would never have been able even to imagine how inert were their minds, how petty their lives, how feeble their efforts.

One day a fire occurred in one of the villages in which Gora was staying, and he was astounded to see how utterly they failed to combine their resources even when faced by so grave a calamity. All was confusion, everyone running hither and thither, weeping and wailing, without the least sign of method anywhere. There was no source of drinking-water nearby, the women of the neighbourhood having to bring water from a great distance for their household work, even those who were comparatively well off never dreaming of digging a tank to mitigate this daily inconvenience in their own households. There had been fires before, but as everyone had accepted them merely as visitations of Fate, it never occurred to them to try to make some arrangement for a nearer supply of water.

It began to appear ridiculous to Gora for him to be lecturing these people about the condition of their country, when their power of understanding even the most urgent needs of their own neighbourhood was so overcast by blind habit. What, however, astonished him most was to find that neither Motilal nor Ramapati seemed to be the least disturbed by all that they were seeing—rather they appeared to regard Gora's perturbation as uncalled for. "This is how the poor are accustomed to live," they said to themselves; "what to us would be hardship they do not feel at all." They even thought it mere sentimentality to be so concerned about a better life for them. But to Gora it was a constant agony to be brought face to face with this terrible load of ignorance, apathy and suffering, which had overwhelmed rich and poor, learned and ignorant alike, and clogged their advance at every step.

Then Motilal received news of the illness of a relative and left for home, so that Ramapati alone remained with Gora.

As these two proceeded they came to a Mohammedan village on the bank of a river. After a long search for some place where they could accept hospitality, they discovered at last a solitary Hindu house,—that of a barber. When this man had duly offered welcome to the Brahmin visitors, they saw on entering his house that one of the inmates was a Mohammedan boy who, they learnt, the barber and his wife had adopted. The orthodox Ramapati was thoroughly disgusted, and when Gora taxed the barber with his un-Hindu conduct, he said: "What's the difference, sir? We call on Him as Hari, they as Allah, that's all."

Meanwhile the sun had risen high and had begun to shine fiercely. The river was far off, across a wide stretch of burning sand. Ramapati, tortured with thirst, wondered where he could get any drinking-water, fit for a Hindu. There was a small well near the barber's house, but the water polluted by this renegade's touch could not serve for his need.

"Has this boy no parents of his own?" asked Gora.

"He has both mother and father living, but he is as good as an orphan all the same," answered the barber.

"How do you mean?"

The barber then related the boy's history.

The estate on which they were living had been farmed out to Indigo Planters, who were always disputing with the agriculturist tenants the rights to till the fertile alluvial land on the river-banks. All the tenants had given in to the *sahibs* except those living in this village of Ghosepara, who refused to be ousted by the Planters. They were Mohammedans, and their leader Faru Sardar was afraid of no one. During these disputes with the Planters he had twice been put in gaol for fighting the police, and he had at length been reduced to such straits that he was practically starving, yet he would not be tamed.

This year the cultivators had managed to reap an early crop off the fresh alluvial deposits by the river-side, but the

Planter himself had come later on, only about a month ago, with a band of club-men and forcibly taken away the harvested grain. It was on this occasion that Faru Sardar, in defending his fellow-villagers, had hit the *sahib* such a blow on his right hand that it had to be amputated. Such daring had never been known in these parts before.

From then onwards the police had been engaged in devastating the whole neighbourhood, like a raging fire. No household was safe from their inquisitorial depredations, nor the honour of the women. Others besides Faru had been put away in gaol, and of those who were left, many had fled from the village. In the house of Faru there was no food, and his wife had only one piece of cloth to wear as a *sari*, the condition of which was such that she could not come out in public. Their only son, this boy Tamiz, used to call the barber's wife "Auntie," and when she saw that he was practically starving, the kind-hearted woman took him away to her own home.

At a distance of about two or three miles were the offices of the Indigo Factory and there the Inspector of Police and his force were quartered. When they would next descend upon the village, and what they would do in the name of investigation, no one could say. Only the previous day they had suddenly appeared in the house of the barber's old neighbour, Nazim. This Nazim had a young brother-in-law who had come from a different district to see his sister. At sight of him the Police Inspector, without rhyme or reason, had remarked: "Ha, we have a fighting cock here, I see! Throws out his chest, does he?" With which he struck him over the face with his staff, knocking out his teeth and making his mouth bleed. When the man's sister, at sight of this brutality, came running up to tend her brother, she was sent reeling to the ground with a savage blow. Formerly the police had not the courage to commit such atrocities in this quarter, but now that all the able-bodied men had either been arrested or had fled, they could wreak their wrath on the villagers with impunity, and there was no knowing how long their shadow would continue to darken the locality.

Gora could not tear himself away from the barber's recital, but Ramapati had become desperate with thirst, so before the barber had finished his story he repeated his question: "How far is the nearest Hindu quarter?"

"The rent collector of the Indigo Factory is a Brahmin, by name Madhav Chatterjee," said the barber. "He is the nearest Hindu. He lives in the office buildings, 2 or 3 miles away."

"What kind of a man is he?" asked Gora.

"A regular limb of Satan," replied the barber. "You couldn't get another scoundrel so cruel, and yet so soft-spoken. He has been entertaining the Police Inspector all these days, but will collect the expenses from us, with a little profit for himself, too!"

"Come, Gora Babu, let's be going," interposed Ramapati impatiently. "I can't stand this any longer." His patience had been brought to breaking point by the sight of the barber's wife drawing water from the well in the courtyard and pouring pitchers full over that wretch of a Mohammedan boy for his bath! His nerves were so set on edge that he felt he could not remain in that house for another moment.

Gora, as he was going, asked the barber: "How is it that you are lingering on here in spite of these outrages? Have you no relatives to go to, elsewhere?"

"I've been living here all my life," explained the barber, "and have got attached to all the neighbours. I am the only Hindu barber near about, and, as I have nothing to do with land, the Factory people don't molest me. Besides, there's hardly another man left in the whole village, and if I went away the women would die of fright."

"Well, we're off," said Gora, "but I'll come and see you again after we've had some food."

The effect of this long story of oppression on the famished and thirsty Ramapati was to turn all his indignation against the recalcitrant villagers, who had brought all this trouble on their own head. This upraising of the head in the presence of the strong seemed to him the very height of folly and pig-headedness on the part of these Mohammedan roughs. He felt they were served right thus to be taught a lesson, and to have their insolence broken. It is just this class of people, thought he, who always fall foul of the police, and for that they themselves are mainly responsible. Why could not they give in to their lords and masters? What was the use of this parade of independence—where was their foolhardy boasting now? In fine, Ramapati's sympathies were inwardly ranged on the side of the *sahibs*.

As they walked across the burning sand, in the full heat of the mid-day sun, Gora never spoke a single word. When at length the roof of the Indigo Factory's office showed through the trees, he stopped suddenly and said: "Ramapati, you go and get something to eat, I'm going back to that barber's."

"Whatever do you mean?" exclaimed Ramapati. "Aren't you going to eat anything yourself? Why not go after we've had something at this Brahmin's house?"

"I'll take care of myself, don't you worry!" replied Gora. "You get some food and then go back to Calcutta. I expect I shall have to stay on at that Ghosepara village for a few days,—you'll not be able to do that."

Ramapati broke out into a cold sweat. He could not believe his ears. How could Gora, good Hindu as he was, even talk of staying in the home of those unclean people? Was he mad, or determined to starve himself to death? But this was not the time to do much thinking; every moment seemed to him an age; and it did not need much persuasion to make him take this opportunity of escape to Calcutta. Before he went into the office, however, he turned to cast one glance at Gora's tall figure as he strode across the burning, deserted sands.

How lonely he looked!

Gora was almost overcome with hunger and thirst, but the very idea of having to preserve his caste by eating in the house of that unscrupulous scoundrel, Madhav Chatterjee, became more and more unbearable the longer he thought of it. His face was flushed, his eyes bloodshot, his brain on fire with the revolt in his mind. "What terrible wrong have we been doing," he said to himself, "by making purity an external thing! Shall my caste remain pure by eating from the hands of this oppressor of the poor Mahomedans, and be lost in the home of the man who has not only shared their miseries but given shelter to one of them at the risk of being outcasted himself? Let the final solution be what it may, I cannot accept such conclusion now."

The barber was surprised to see Gora, return alone. The first thing Gora did was to take the barber's drinking-vessel and after carefully cleaning it, fill it with water from the well. After drinking he said: "If you have any rice and *dal* in the house please let me have some to cook." His host busied himself in getting everything ready for the cooking, and when Gora had prepared and eaten his meal he said: "I will stay on with you for a time."

The barber was beside himself at the idea, and putting his hands together in entreaty, he said: "I am indeed fortunate that you should think of condescending so far, but this house is being watched by the police, and if they find you here it may lead to trouble."

"The Police won't dare to harm you while I am here,— if they do, I'll take care of you."

402 ❖ RABINDRANATH TAGORE OMNIBUS

"No, no," implored the barber. "Pray don't think of such a thing. If you try to protect me I shall indeed be a lost man. These fellows will think I am trying to get them into trouble by calling in an outsider as witness of their misdeeds. So far, I've managed to steer clear of them, but once I am a marked man, I'll have to leave, and after that the village will go to rack and ruin."

It was hard for Gora, who had spent all his days in the city, to comprehend the reason of the man's apprehensions. He had always imagined that you only had to stand firmly enough on the side of right, for evil to be overcome. His sense of duty would not allow him to think of leaving these afflicted villagers to their fate. But the barber fell on his knees and clasped his feet saying: "You a Brahmin, sir, have deigned to come as my guest,—to ask you to depart is nothing less than a crime for me. But because I see you really pity us, I make bold to tell you that if you try to prevent any of this police oppression while staying in my house, you will only get me into trouble."

Gora, annoyed at what he considered the unreasonable cowardice of the barber, left him that very afternoon. He even had a revulsion of feeling for having taken food under the roof of this good-for-nothing renegade! Tired and disgusted he arrived towards evening at the Factory office. Ramapati had lost no time in starting for Calcutta after his meal, and was no longer there.

Madhav Chatterjee showed the greatest respect for Gora, and invited him to be his guest, but Gora, full of his angry reflections, broke out with: "I won't even touch your water!"

On the astonished Madhav inquiring the reason, Gora began to tax him bitterly for his outrageous acts of oppression and refused to take a seat.

The Police Inspector was reclining on a *tukta* fitted with a huge bolster, puffing away at his *hookah,* and at Gora's outburst he sat up and asked rudely: "Who the deuce are you, and where do you come from?"

"Ah! the Inspector, I suppose?" remarked Gora, without giving any answer to his question. "Let me tell you that I've taken note of all your doings at Ghosepara. If you don't mend your ways, even yet, then—"

"You'll have us all hanged, will you?" sneered the Inspector, turning towards his friend. "We seem to have got hold of a bumptious sort of a bounder, I see. I thought it was a beggar, but just look at his eyes!—Sergeant, come forward!" he shouted to one of his men.

Madhav, with a perturbed air, took the Inspector by the hand as he pleaded: "Oh, I say, Inspector, go slow.—Don't be insulting a gentleman!"

"Nice sort of gentleman, indeed!" flung out the Inspector. "Who is he to abuse you like that—wasn't that an insult?"

"What he said wasn't exactly untrue, was it, so why let's get angry about it?" replied Madhav unctuously. "I am the agent of the Indigo Planters for my sins,—what worse can be said of me? And don't take it amiss, old fellow, but does it really amount to any further abuse to call a Police Inspector an emissary of Satan? It's the business of tigers to kill and eat their prey, so what's the sense in calling them types of meekness?—Well, well, there we are, we've got to make a living somehow!"

No one had ever seen Madhav get into a fit of temper unless he had anything to gain by it. Who could tell beforehand what kind of person could be of help and which could do an injury? So he always went into the *pros* and *cons* before he decided to injure or insult any one. He did not believe in unnecessary waste of energy.

"Look here, Babu," then said the Inspector to Gora. "We have come here to carry out Government orders. If you try to meddle in this business you'll get into hot water, I promise you!"

Gora went off without answering, but Mahdav followed after him and said: "What you say is quite true, sir, ours is butcher's work; and as for that rogue of an Inspector over there, it is a sin to sit on the same seat with him! I can't speak of all the wrong I have had to get done through that fellow. But it won't be for much longer. After a few years I shall have earned enough to pay the expenses of my daughter's marriage and then I and my wife can retire to a religious life in Benaras. I'm getting tired of this sort of thing—sometimes I feel inclined to hang myself and end it all! Anyhow, where are you proposing to stay the night? Why not dine with me and sleep here. I'll make separate arrangements for you, so that you need not even cross that blackguard's shadow."

Gora was blessed with an appetite of more than the usual dimensions,—he had moreover eaten very little through all that dismal day, but his whole body was afire with indignation, and he simply could not stay on there for anything, so he excused himself, saying that he had business elsewhere.

"Let me at least send a lantern with you," said Madhav.

But Gora went off quickly, without waiting to reply, while Madhav, returning to the house, said to the Inspector: "That fellow's sure to go and report us, old fellow. If I were you I would send someone on to the Magistrate, beforehand."

"What for?" asked the Inspector.

"Just to warn him," suggested Madhav, "that there's a young Babu from somewhere, going about trying to get at the witnesses in your case."

TWENTY SEVEN

The Magistrate, Mr. Brownlow, was taking an evening walk by the river and with him was Haran. Some way off, his wife was having her drive with Paresh Babu's daughters.

Mr. Brownlow was in the habit of inviting to an occasional garden-party at his house a few of his respectable Bengali acquaintances, and would preside at the prize distribution of the local High School. If he was requested to honour a wedding celebration in some wealthy home he would graciously yield to the importunate invitation. He would even, when asked to grace a *Jatra* party, sit for some time in a big armchair and try patiently to stay through some of the songs. The year before, at a *Jatra* performance given in a pleader's house, he was so pleased with the acting of two of the boy performers that, at his special request, they repeated their dialogue before him.

His wife was a missionary's daughter, and she often had the missionary ladies of the station to tea-parties at her home. She had founded a Girls' School for the District and tried hard to keep up the number of its pupils. Seeing how studious Paresh Babu's daughters were at their lessons, she was always encouraging them, and even now, when they lived at a distance, she used to write letters to them, and every Christmas she sent them presents of religious books.

The Fair had started, and Mistress Baroda had arrived on the scene with all the girls, as well as Haran, Sudhir and

Binoy. Accommodation had been provided for them in the Government Bungalow. Paresh Babu, being unable to stand all this excitement and bustle, had been left behind in Calcutta all alone. Sucharita had tried her best to remain with him for company, but Paresh Babu, regarding the acceptance of the Magistrate's invitation as a duty, insisted on sending her along too.

It had been settled that the play and recitations should be given at an evening party to be held two days later at the Magistrate's house. The Commissioner of the District, as well as the Lieutenant-Governor and his wife, were to be present, and the Magistrate had invited many English friends, not only from the neighbouring districts, but also from Calcutta. Arrangements had also been made for a few select Bengalis, for whom, it was rumoured, a separate tent would be provided in the garden, with orthodox refreshments.

Haran had managed to please the Magistrate in a very short time by the high standard of his conversation, and had astonished the *sahib* by his unusual knowledge of the Christian scriptures, so much so that Mr. Brownlow had asked him why, when he got so far, he stopped short of becoming a Christian himself!

This evening they were engaged, as they walked along the river-bank, in a grave discussion about the methods of the Brahmo Samaj and the best means for the reform of the Hindu Social System. In the middle of their talk Gora suddenly came up and accosted the *sahib* with a "Good evening, sir."

He had tried to obtain an interview with the Magistrate the day before, but he had soon made the discovery that in order to obtain an audience of the *sahib* he would have to pay toll to his servants. Being unwilling to countenance such a disgraceful practice, he had taken this opportunity of waylaying the *sahib* during his evening walk. At his interview neither Haran nor Gora showed any sign of their previous acquaintance.

The Magistrate was rather surprised at this sudden apparition. This kind of six-foot tall, big-boned, stalwart figure he could not remember to have come across before in this province. Neither was his complexion like that of the ordinary Bengali. He was wearing a khaki shirt and a coarse and somewhat soiled *dhuti*. He had a bamboo stick in his hand, and his shawl was twisted into a kind of turban on his head.

"I have just come from Ghosepara," began Gora.

Whereupon the Magistrate gave a half-subdued whistle. Only the day before he had received intimation that a stranger was trying to interfere in the Ghosepara investigations. So this was the fellow! He looked Gora up and down with a keen inquiring stare and asked: "To what part of the country do you belong?"

"I am a Bengali Brahmin," said Gora.

"Oh! Connected with some newspaper, I suppose?"

"No."

"Then what were you doing at Ghosepara?"

"I happened to be staying there in the course of a walking tour, and seeing signs of police oppression, with apprehension of more to come, I have come to you in the hope of remedy."

"Are you aware that the Ghosepara people are a set of rogues?" said the Magistrate.

"They're not rogues, but they are fearless and independent, and cannot endure injustice without protest," answered Gora.

This enraged the Magistrate. Here was one of those modern youths whose brains had been turned by education. "Insufferable," he muttered under his breath, adding aloud: "You know nothing about local conditions round here," in a stern voice which was expected to clinch the matter.

But Gora answered in his big voice: "You know much less of those conditions than I do!"

"Look here," said the Magistrate. "Let me warn you that if you meddle with this Ghosepara affair you will not get off cheaply."

"Since you have a prejudice against the villagers, and have made up your mind not to remedy their wrongs," said Gora, "I've no other course but to go back to Ghosepara, and encourage the people, so far as I can, to stand up for themselves against this police oppression."

The Magistrate stopped short in his walk to turn on Gora like a flash of lightning with the shout: "What confounded insolence."

Gora left slowly, without answering back further.

"What is all this a symptom of in your countrymen, nowadays?" scornfully asked the Magistrate of Haran.

"It simply shows that their education is not going deep enough," replied Haran in a superior tone. "There is no spiritual and moral teaching at all. These fellows have not been able to assimilate the best in English culture. It is because they have only learnt their lessons by rote, and not had any moral training, that these ingrates will not acknowledge British rule in India to be a dispensation of Providence."

"Such moral culture they will never get until they accept Christ," remarked the Magistrate sententiously.

"In a way that is true," admitted Haran, and proceeded to plunge into a subtle analysis of where he agreed and where he disagreed with the Christian point of view.

The Magistrate was held so engrossed by this discourse that it was not till his wife had returned in the carriage, after leaving Paresh Basu's daughters at the Bungalow, and called out: "Aren't you coming home, Harry?" that he suddenly realised how late it was.

"By Jove," he exclaimed as he looked at his watch, "it's twenty past eight!" and as he got into the carriage he warmly pressed Haran's hand saying: "The evening has passed most pleasantly in this interesting talk with you."

Haran, on his return to their Bungalow, retailed at length the conversation he had been having with the Magistrate, but he failed to touch upon the incident of Gora's sudden appearance.

TWENTY EIGHT

Forty-seven of the unfortunate villagers had been put into the lock-up, without a regular trial, simply as an example to the rest.

After leaving the Magistrate, Gora went in search of a lawyer, and was told that Satkori Haldar was one of the best in the locality. On calling at his house it turned out that this lawyer was an old fellow-student of Gora's.

"Well I declare, it's Gora!" he exclaimed. "Whatever are you doing here?"

Gora explained that he wanted an application to be made to the Court for bailing out the Ghosepara prisoners.

"Who will stand surety?" asked Satkori.

"I will, of course."

"Are you able to go bail for 47 people?"

"If the *mukhtears* will stand surety I am ready to pay the usual fees."

"It will cost quite a lot."

In the Magistrate's Court, the next day, the application for bail was duly made. No sooner did the Magistrate catch sight of yesterday's tall figure, with dusty clothes and turban, than he curtly refused the application. So amongst the others, boys of fourteen and old men of eighty were left to wear out their hearts in confinement.

Gora requested Satkori to fight the case, but said the latter: "Where are you going to get witnesses? All those who were on the spot are now in gaol! Besides that the whole neighbourhood has been terrorised by the investigations, which followed upon the injury to the *sahib*. The Magistrate has begun to suspect a conspiracy of educated seditionists. If I push myself forward too much he may even suspect me! The Anglo-Indian newspapers are continually complaining that Englishmen's lives in the moffusil will become unsafe if the natives are allowed to become too uppish. Meanwhile it is becoming well-nigh impossible for the natives to live in their own country! I know that the oppression is terrible, but there's no means of resisting it."

"No means!" cried out Gora. "Why can't we—?"

"I see you've not changed one bit since your school days!" laughed Satkori. "We can't do anything simply because we have wife and children to support—they'll starve unless we can make something for them everyday. How many people are there ready to risk death for their families by taking other people's perils on their own shoulders, especially in our country, where the families are by no means small? Those who are responsible for the welfare of more than a dozen people already cannot afford to look after another dozen or so, in addition!"

"Then will you do nothing for these poor people?" pressed Gora. "Could you not make an application to the High Court, or—"

"You don't seem to realise the situation!" interrupted Satkori impatiently. "It is an Englishman who has been hurt! Every Englishman is of the King's race,—an injury to the least of White-men amounts to a petty rebellion against the British Raj! I'm not going to fall foul of the Magistrate by tilting against this system, without the least chance of any result."

Next day Gora decided to start for Calcutta by the 10.30 train to see whether he could get any help from some Calcutta lawyer. He was on his way to the station when he met with a check.

A cricket match had been arranged between a Calcutta team of students and the local team for the last day of the Fair, and the visiting team was practising, when one of the players got badly hit by the ball on his leg. There was a large tank by the side of the field and two students had just taken the injured player to the bank, and were binding the boy's leg with a piece of cloth dipped in the water, when suddenly a police constable turned up from somewhere and began hitting the students right and left, using unspeakably abusive language.

The Calcutta students did not know that this was a reserved tank and that it was forbidden to use it, and even if they had known, they were not used to being insulted without cause by the police. They were muscular youths, so they set about avenging the insult as it deserved. Hearing the row, more constables came running up and at the same moment Gora also appeared on the scene.

Gora knew the students well, for he had often taken them to play cricket matches, and when he saw the boys being bullied, he could not help coming to their rescue. "Have a care," he shouted to the police. "Keep your hands off the boys!" Whereupon the constables turned upon him with their filthy abuse, and soon there was a regular fight on. A crowd began to gather, and in less than no time scores of students had flocked to the place. Encouraged by Gora's support and leadership they soon made a successful attack on the police and scattered their forces. To the spectators the affair was great fun, but it is needless to say that for Gora it proved to be no joke.

At about three or four o'clock Binoy, Haran and the girls were rehearsing the play in the Bungalow when two students, who were known to Binoy, came and informed him that Gora and some of the boys had been arrested and were now in the police cell awaiting their trial, which was to take place before the Magistrate next day.

Gora in the lock-up! The news startled them all, except Haran. Binoy rushed off immediately to his old school-fellow, Satkori Haldar, and took him along to the Police Station.

Satkori suggested trying for bail, but Gora resolutely refused either to employ a pleader or to accept any surety.

"What!" cried Satkori as he looked at Binoy. "Who would think Gora had come out of school! He doesn't seem to have acquired any more commonsense than he used to have then."

"I don't want to get free merely because I happen to have friends or money," said Gora. "According to our scriptures the urgency of doing justice appertains to the King. On him recoils the crime of injustice. But if, under this Government, people have to buy their way out of gaol, spending their all to get their bare rights, then I for one will not spend a single pice for the sake of such justice."

"Under Mohammedan rule you had to pawn your head to pay the bribes," said Satkori.

"That was a defect of the dispensers of justice, not of the King. Even now, bad judges may take bribes. But, under the present system, it is sheer ruination for the unfortunate man, whether plaintiff or defendant, innocent or guilty, who has to present himself at the King's door for judgment. Over and above that, when the Crown is plaintiff, and people like myself defendants, then all the attorneys and advocates are ranged on the King's side and none left for me, except my fate. If a just cause be sufficient, why have a Government pleader for the Crown? If, on the other hand, the pleading of advocates be a necessary part of the system, why should not the opposite side be provided with one also? Is this a policy of Government, or of waging war against the subject?"

"Why get so warm, old fellow?" laughed Satkori. "Civilisation is not a cheap commodity. If you are called upon for subtle judgments, you have to make subtle laws, and if there are subtle laws then you must make a trade of law, in which buying and selling is bound to come in. Therefore civilised courts naturally become markets for the buying and selling of justice, and those who have no money stand every chance of getting swindled. What would you have done if you had been King, let me ask you?"

"If I had made such extra subtle laws," replied Gora, "that even the intelligence of highly paid judges could not fathom their mystery, then at all events I would have provided expert advocates for both sides at Government expense. And, in any case, I would not have plumed myself on being superior to Moghul or Pathan rulers, while I kept saddling my poor subjects with all the cost of obtaining fair judgments."

"Ah, I see!" said Satkori. "However, since that blessed day has not come, and you are not the King, but only a prisoner at the bar of a civilised Emperor, you must either spend money or get the help of some lawyer friend gratis. The only alternative will not result in a happy ending."

"Let that ending be mine which will happen without any effort on my part," said Gora emphatically. "I want my fate to be the same as the fate of those who are without means in this empire."

Binoy begged him to be more reasonable, but Gora would not listen, and asked Binoy: "How do you happen to be here?"

Binoy flushed slightly. If Gora had not been in prison he would probably have told the reason of his visit with a certain amount of defiance in his tone, but in the circumstances he was unable to come out with a direct answer, so he merely said: "I'll talk about myself later—now it is your—"

"To-day I am a guest of the King," interrupted Gora. "The King himself is looking after me; none of you need worry about it."

Binoy knew that it would not be possible to shake Gora's resolve, so he gave up the idea of engaging a pleader for the defence. He said, however: "I know you won't be able to eat prison diet, so I'll arrange to have your meals sent from outside."

"Binoy," said Gora impatiently, "why do you waste your energy? I don't want anything from outside. I don't want anything better than what is the common lot of everyone in gaol."

Binoy returned in great agitation to the Bungalow, where Sucharita was on the look out for him at the open window of her bedroom. She had shut herself in, being unable to bear company or conversation.

When she saw Binoy coming towards the Bungalow with an anxious and harassed look on his face, her heart beat fast in apprehension, but she controlled her feelings with a great effort and, taking up a book, came out of her room. Lolita was in a corner of the sitting-room, occupied with her sewing, which she usually loathed, while Labonya was playing word-making and word-taking with Sudhir, with Lila as onlooker. Haran was discussing with Mistress Baroda the arrangements for the coming entertainment.

Sucharita listened spell-bound to Binoy's account of Gora's encounter with the police that morning, while the blood mounted to Lolita's face and her sewing slipped off her lap on to the floor.

"Don't you be anxious, Binoy Babu," said Mistress Baroda. "I will myself speak to the Magistrate's wife about Gourmohan Babu this evening."

"Please don't do any such thing," begged Binoy. "If Gora should hear of it he would never forgive me to the end of his life."

"Some steps must be taken for defending him, surely," remarked Sudhir.

Binoy then went on to tell them everything about their attempts to get Gora released on bail, and how Gora had objected to having the services of a pleader.

"What silly affectation!" sneered Haran, unable to restrain his impatience at the story.

Up to this time, whatever her real feelings towards Haran may have been, Lolita had shown him outward respect, and had never argued with him, but now she shook her head vehemently as she cried: "It is not affectation at all—what Gour Babu has done is quite right. Is the Magistrate here to bully us, that we should have to be defending ourselves? Have we to pay them fat salaries and then pay pleaders as well to rescue us from their clutches? Rather than have this kind of justice, it is truly much better to be in gaol."

Haran stared at Lolita in surprise. He had seen her as a child, and never suspected that she had developed opinions of her own. He gravely rebuked her for her unseemly outburst, saying: "What do you understand about such matters? Your head seems to have been turned by the irresponsible ravings of raw college youths, who have learnt a few books by rote, but have no ideas or culture of their own!"

He then proceeded to give a description of Gora's meeting with the Magistrate the previous evening, and also gave out what the Magistrate had said about it to him afterwards. The affair of Ghosepara was news to Binoy, and it only alarmed him still more, for he now realised that the Magistrate would not let Gora off easily.

Haran Babu's motive in telling the story missed its object altogether. Sucharita was deeply wounded at the meanness which had allowed Haran to keep silent about the interview all this time, and every one of them began to despise Haran for his petty spite against Gora, which was now disclosed.

Sucharita kept silent throughout; for a moment it had seemed as if she also would break out with some protest, but she controlled herself and picking up her book turned its pages with trembling hands.

Lolita said defiantly: "I don't care if Haran Babu sides with the Magistrate. To me the whole affair only shows Gour Babu's true nobility of mind!"

TWENTY NINE

As the Lieutenant-Governor was to arrive that day, the Magistrate came to Court punctually at half-past ten, hoping to finish the work of dispensing justice early.

Satkori Babu, who was defending the students, tried to use that opportunity to assist his friend. From the look of things, taken all round, he had come to the conclusion that much the best course was to plead guilty, which he did, putting in a plea for leniency on the ground of the youth and inexperience of his clients.

The Magistrate sentenced the boys to whippings of 5 to 25 stripes according to their age and the extent of their offence. Gora had no pleader acting for him, and in his own defence he tried to show how unwarrantable the violence of the police had been, but the Magistrate cut him short with a sharp rebuke, and sentenced, him to a month's rigorous imprisonment for interfering with the police in the discharge of their duties, telling him that he ought to be grateful for being let off so lightly.

Sudhir and Binoy were present in Court, but the latter could not bear to look at Gora's face. He felt a sense of suffocation as he hurriedly left the Court-room. Sudhir urged him to return with him to the Government Bungalow, and take his bath and have something to eat. But Binoy paid no attention to his words, and crossing over the Court grounds he sat down beneath a tree, saying to Sudhir: "You go back to the Bungalow, I will follow shortly."

How long Binoy sat thus after Sudhir had left, he knew not. But after the sun had passed the meridian, a carriage came and stopped immediately in front of him, and on looking up Binoy saw Sudhir and Sucharita descending from the carriage and coming towards him. He stood up hurriedly as they approached, and heard Sucharita saying to him in a voice charged with emotion: "Binoy Babu, won't you come?"

Binoy suddenly became conscious that they were becoming an object of curiosity to passers-by, so he immediately accompanied them back to the carriage, but on the way back none of them could speak a word.

When they returned to the Bungalow, Binoy saw at once that a serious quarrel had been in progress. Lolita had declared her determination not to go that evening to the Magistrate's house, and Mistress Baroda was in a terrible dilemma, while Haran was furious at this unreasonable revolt on the part of a chit like Lolita. Again and again he deplored the malady which had attacked these modern boys and girls, making them refuse all discipline. It was the result of being allowed to meet all sorts of people, and talk all kinds of nonsense with them!

When Binoy arrived Lolita said: "Binoy Babu, I ask your forgiveness. I've done you a great wrong by not being able to understand the justice of the objections you used to make. It's because we know nothing of things outside our own narrow circle that we misunderstand things so completely! Panu Babu, here, says that this Magistrate's administration is a dispensation of Providence for India. If that be so, all I can say is that our hearty desire to curse such administration is also a dispensation of Providence."

Haran interjected angrily: "Lolita, you—"

But Lolita, turning her back on him, exclaimed: "Be quiet please! I'm not speaking to you!—Binoy Babu, don't you allow yourself to be persuaded by anybody. There must not be any play to-night, not for anything!"

"Lolita!" cried Mistress Baroda, trying to cut short her remarks. "You're a nice girl to be sure! Aren't you going to let Binoy Babu take his bath or have anything to eat? Don't you know it's already half-past one? See how pale and tired he looks!"

"I can't eat in this house," said Binoy. "We are the Magistrate's guests here."

Mistress Baroda first tried to smooth matters, humbly entreating Binoy to stay on, and then, seeing that her daughters were all silent, she broke out angrily: "What's come over you all? Suchi, will you please explain to Binoy Babu that we have given our word, and people have been invited, so that we must get through the day somehow, otherwise what will they all think of us? I shall never be able to show my face before them again."

But Sucharita remained silent with eyes downcast.

Binoy went off to the River Steamer Station nearby, and found that a boat would start in about two hours' time for Calcutta, arriving there next day at about eight o'clock in the morning.

Haran poured the vials of his wrath on both Binoy and Gora in his most abusive manner, whereupon Sucharita hastily departed and shut herself up in the next room. She was followed shortly after by Lolita, who found her lying on the bed, covering her face with her hands.

Lolita, bolting the door from inside, went gently up to Sucharita and, sitting beside her, began to pass her fingers through her hair. After some time, when Sucharita had recovered her composure, Lolita quietly lifted her hands away from her face, and when she could thus see her freely she whispered in her ears: "Didi, let us leave this place and return to Calcutta. We can't possibly go to the Magistrate's place to-night."

For a long time Sucharita made no reply, but when Lolita had repeated her suggestion several times, she sat up on the bed and said: "How can we do that, dear? I never wanted to come at all, but since father has sent me, how can I leave till I have fulfilled his objects?"

"But father knows nothing of all that has happened now," argued Lolita. "If he knew he would never have asked us to stay."

"How can we be so sure, dear?" said Sucharita wearily.

"But tell me, Didi," said Lolita, "will you really be able to go through your part? How can you ever go to that Magistrate's house? And then to stand on the stage, all dressed up, and recite poetry! I couldn't utter a single word even if I bit my tongue till the blood flowed!"

"I know, dear," said Sucharita. "But one has to endure even the torments of hell. There's no escape for us now. Do you think I shall ever in my life forget this day?"

Lolita became angry at Sucharita's submissiveness, and returning to her mother, said: "Aren't you going, mother?"

"What's the matter with the girl?" exclaimed the mystified Baroda. "We'll have to be there at nine o'clock at night!"

"I was talking about going to Calcutta," said Lolita.

"Just listen to her!" cried Baroda.

"And Sudhir-dada," said Lolita, turning to him, "are you also going to stay on her?"

Sudhir had been upset at Gora's sentence of imprisonment, but he was not strong-minded enough to resist the temptation to show off his talent before such a distinguished company of *sahibs*. He mumbled out something to the effect that he had his hesitations, but he would nevertheless have to go to the entertainment.

"We are wasting time in all this to-do," said Mistress Baroda. "Let us go and take a rest, or else we shall look so worn out to-night that we shan't be fit to be seen. No one must leave their beds till half-past five." With which she packed them all off to their bedrooms.

They all fell asleep except Sucharita, to whom sleep would not come, and Lolita, who remained sitting bolt upright on her bed.

The steamer's siren was sounding repeatedly for the passengers to come aboard, till at length it was time for her to cast off, when, just as the sailors were on the point of raising the gangway planks, Binoy, who was standing on the upper deck, saw a Bengali lady hastening towards the boat. Her dress and figure resembled Lolita's, but at first Binoy could hardly believe his eyes. When, however, she came nearer there could no longer be any doubt. For a moment he thought that she had come to fetch him, but then he remembered that Lolita also had been against going to the Magistrate's house that night.

Lolita just managed to catch the steamer, and as the sailors were engaged in casting off, Binoy came hurrying down in great alarm to meet her.

"Let us go up on to the upper deck," she said.

"But the steamer is starting," exclaimed Binoy in dismay.

"I know that," replied Lolita, and without waiting for Binoy she went up the stairs.

The steamer started with its siren hooting, and Binoy, having found a chair for Lolita on the upper deck, looked at her with silent question in his eyes.

"I am going to Calcutta," explained Lolita, "I found I couldn't possibly stay on."

"And what do the others say?" asked Binoy.

"Up to now no one knows," said Lolita. "I left a note and they will know when they read it."

Binoy was taken aback at this exhibition of self-will on Lolita's part, and he began hesitatingly: "But—"

Lolita stopped him with: "Now that the steamer has started what is the use of saying 'But'? I don't see why, because

I happen to have been born a girl, I should have to put up with everything without protest. For us, also, there are such words as possible and impossible, right and wrong. It would have been easier for me to commit suicide than to have taken any part in that play of theirs."

Binoy saw that what was done was done, and no good would now come of worrying as to whether it was good or bad.

After some moments of silence Lolita went on: "I have been very unfair to your friend, Gourmohan Babu. I don't know why, but somehow, from the time I first saw him and heard him talk, my mind has been set against him. He always spoke with such vehemence, and you all seemed to say 'Yes' to whatever he said, it used to make me angry. I never could bear to be forced into anything, whether by speech or action. But now I see Gourmohan Babu forces things on himself as well as on other people—that's real power—I've not seen another man like him."

Thus Lolita talked on, not only because of her contrition for the way she had misjudged Gora, but because misgiving about what she had done just now would persist in raising its head in her inner consciousness; nor had she been able to realise how awkward it would be to have Binoy as her sole companion on board the steamer; but knowing full well that the more shame you show the more shameful it all gets to be, she began to chatter away for all she was worth.

Binoy, however, was at a loss for words. He was thinking on the one hand of the trouble and insult which had befallen Gora at the hands of the Magistrate, and on the other of his own disgrace in having come here to perform at the house of that same Magistrate. Over and above this there was this awkward situation with Lolita. These had combined to render him speechless.

In the old days such foolhardiness on Lolita's part would have earned her his censure, but now he could not entertain any such feeling. In fact, mixed with his surprise at her escapade was a certain amount of admiration for her pluck, and there was further the joy at the thought that, out of the whole party, he and Lolita were the only ones who had shown any real feeling about the insult to which Gora had been subjected.

For this defiance of theirs Binoy alone of the two would not have to suffer any untoward consequences, but Lolita would have to taste its bitter fruit for many a long day to come. How strange that Binoy should always have considered this very Lolita to be against Gora. The more he pondered over it, the higher grew his admiration for her intolerance of wrongdoing, her courage of conviction, regardless of the dictates of mere prudence,—so much so that he knew not how to contain his feelings.

He felt that Lolita had rightly looked down upon him as lacking in strength and courage of conviction. He would never have been able to thrust aside so boldly all considerations of praise and blame from his own people, in order to pursue what he himself considered the right course. How often had he failed to be his own true self for fear of displeasing Gora, or lest Gora should think him weak, and then had deceived himself by subtle argument into the belief that Gora's view was his own!

He realized how superior Lolita had proved herself to him in the independence of her intellect, and honoured her accordingly. He badly wanted to ask Lolita's pardon for the way he had so often misjudged and inwardly blamed her in the past,—but could think of no way of putting his feelings into words. The vision of womanhood which he had gained to-day in the light of the glory which Lolita's beautifully courageous act had cast round her, made him feel that his very life was indeed fulfilled.

THIRTY

As soon as they arrived in Calcutta, Binoy took Lolita to Paresh Babu's house.

Before they had thus been together on the steamer, Binoy did not know what his exact feelings towards Lolita were. His mind had been fully occupied with his disputes with her, and his chief object had been, almost every day he met her how to patch up a peace with this untameable girl. Sucharita had risen on the horizon of Binoy's life like the evening star, radiant with the pure sweetness of womanhood, and he had realised how his nature had expanded into completeness with the joy of this wonderful manifestation. But other stars had also arisen, and he could not clearly recollect when it had come to pass, that the first star, which had heralded for him the world's festival of light, had again vanished below the horizon.

From the moment the rebel Lolita had stepped on to the steamer, Binoy had said to himself: "Lolita and I now stand alone, side by side, against the rest of Society," and he could not put out of his mind the fact that in her trouble Lolita had left everyone else to come and join him. No matter what her reason or purpose might be, it was plain that Binoy was no longer merely one amongst others to Lolita, he was alone beside her, in fact the only one. All her own people were far away while he was near, and this sense of nearness thrilled in his heart like a tremor of an impending flash in clouds laden with lightning.

When Lolita had retired to her cabin for the night, Binoy felt unable to sleep. So taking off his shoes he began to pace noiselessly up and down the deck. There was no special reason for guarding Lolita during the journey, but Binoy could not bring himself to forgo any of the delights of the novel and unexpected responsibility which had been thrown on him and so took on himself this needless vigil.

There was ineffable depth in the darkness of the night. The cloudless sky was filled with stars. The trees lining the bank were massed together like a solid black plinth supporting the sky overhead. Below flowed the swift silent current of the broad river. And in the midst of it all lay the sleeping Lolita. Just this much had happened,—that Lolita had trustfully placed in his hands this slumber of hers in all its peaceful beauty,—and nothing more; which charge Binoy had accepted as the most precious of all gifts, and was keeping watch accordingly.

Neither father, nor mother, nor any relative was near, and yet Lolita was able to entrust her beautiful body to this strange bed, allowing herself to sleep without care or fear; the regular heaving of her breast keeping time to the rhythm of the poem of her slumber; not a stray lock of her skilfully bound tresses out of place; both her hands, so soft in their expression of womanly tenderness, resting on the counterpane with all the languor of complete confidence; her restless tripping feet in repose at last, like the ended cadence of the music of a festival just over,—this was the picture that filled Binoy's imagination.

Like a pearl in its shell, Lolita lay wrapped in the silent darkness, enveloped by the starry heavens, and to Binoy this repose, in its rounded-off perfection, seemed the only thing that mattered in all the world that night. "I am awake! I am awake!" were the words which rose, like a triumphant trumpet-blast, from the depths of Binoy's awakening manhood, and mingled with the silent message of the ever-awake Bridegroom, who watches over the universe.

But there was also another thought which kept recurring to him through the darkness of this moonless night: "To-night Gora is in gaol!" Up to now Binoy had shared all his friend's joys and sorrows,—this was the first time it had happened otherwise. He knew quite well that; to a man like Gora, gaol meant no real hardship, but from first to last, throughout this important episode in Gora's life, Binoy had been away from his friend, and had had no hand in the affair. When the separated currents of their two lives would be coming together once more, would the void created by this separation ever be filled again? Did it not mean the end of their rare and unbroken friendship?

So, as the night wore on, Binoy felt, at one and the same time, both fulfilment and emptiness, and stood overcome, at the meeting-place of creation and destruction, gazing out into the darkness.

When the cab had drawn up at Paresh Babu's door, and Lolita descended, Binoy saw that she was trembling and that it was costing her a great effort to pull herself together. The fact was, she had up to now been wholly unable to estimate the enormity of her offence against society in having ventured on this risky proceeding. She knew quite well that her father would never reproach her in words, but for that very reason she feared his silence more than anything else.

Binoy was puzzled to decide what was the right thing to do under the circumstances. In order to test whether she would feel still worse if he remained with her, he said haltingly: "I suppose I had better be going."

"No, no, come along and see father," replied Lolita hurriedly.

Binoy was inwardly delighted at the eagerness in her words. His duty, then, was not finished with merely bringing her home. Owing to this accident his life had become bound to Lolita's by a special tie. He felt he must now stand by her with even greater firmness. The thought that Lolita imagined she could depend upon him touched him deeply, and he felt as if she had grasped his hand for support. If Paresh Babu became angry with Lolita for her rash and unconventional conduct, then he felt, he must take the responsibility on himself, accepting all the blame, and like protecting armour save her from censure.

But Binoy did not quite understand what was passing in Lolita's mind. It was not that she wanted Binoy to act as a protecting barrier, the real reason was that she never liked concealment and now wanted Paresh Babu to know exactly what she had done in the fullest detail. She wanted to bear the full brunt of her father's judgment, whatever it might be.

From early morning she had been feeling angry with Binoy. That this was unreasonable she knew, but curiously, this knowledge increased rather than diminished her annoyance.

Her state of mind, on board the steamer, had been different. From her childhood she had been subject to fits of temper, which led her into doing silly things. But the present escapade was a really serious one. That Binoy should have got mixed up in the affair made it all the more awkward, but then again, she also felt a certain secret exultation, as at some forbidden indulgence.

This taking shelter with a comparative stranger, this coming so close to him without any screen of family or society between them, was no doubt a critical situation to be gravely exercised about, but Binoy's natural delicacy of behaviour had cast such a protecting veil of purity over it, that she felt free to delight in his innate modesty which was thus revealed to her. This hardly seemed to be the same Binoy who had joined in all their fun and amusements, who had talked and joked so freely with them, and even been so familiar with the very servants. He could so easily have thrust himself on her now, on the pretext of taking care of her,—he came all the nearer to her heart because he had so carefully kept at a distance.

In her cabin, that night, all these thoughts kept her wakeful, and after tossing restlessly about in her bed through the long hours, at length it seemed to her that the night had passed and dawn was breaking. She softly opened her cabin door and peeped out. The night was near its end, but its dew-laden darkness still clung to the river-bank and to the rows of trees which lined it. A cool breeze had sprung up and was rippling the surface of the water, and from the engine-room below came sounds of the resumption of the next day's work.

Lolita, coming out of her cabin, became aware, as she stepped towards the front deck, that Binoy was lying asleep on a deck-chair, wrapped in his shawl. Her heart beat quickly as she realised that he must have been keeping watch over her all night,—so near, and yet so far! Immediately she slipped back to her cabin with tremulous footsteps and, standing at the door, gazed on Binoy sleeping amidst the darkness of those unfamiliar river scenes,—his figure, for her, becoming the centre of the galaxy of stars which watched over the world.

As she looked on, her heart filled with an indescribable sweetness and her eyes brimmed over with tears. It seemed as though the God, whom her father had taught her to worship, had come to-day and blessed her with outstretched hand; and, at the sacred moment when, on the slumbering bank of the river, cosy under the foliage of its dense woods, the first secret union of the coming light with the departing darkness took place, the poignant music of some divine *vina* seemed to ring through this vast star-spangled chamber of the universe.

At a sudden sleepy movement of Binoy's hand Lolita slipped back into her cabin, and shutting the door lay down on her bed again. Her hands and feet were cold, and for a long time she was unable to control the beating of her heart.

The darkness gradually melted away, and the steamer began to move. Lolita, after performing her toilet, came out and stood by the railing of the deck. Binoy also had wakened on hearing the warning whistle of the steamer, and with his eyes towards the east was awaiting the first blush of the coming dawn.

When he saw Lolita come out on deck he rose, and was preparing to retire into his cabin, when Lolita greeted him, and said: "I'm afraid you did not get much sleep last night."

"Oh, I didn't have a bad night," replied Binoy.

After this they had nothing more to say to each other.

The dew on the bamboo clumps on the river-bank began to glisten golden in the first rays of sunrise. Never before had these two witnessed such a dawn. Never before had the light touched them in such a way. For the first time they realised that the sky is not empty, but gazes, filled with a silent joy of wonder, at each fresh unfolding of creation. The consciousness of each of them was so stimulated that it also became alive to its own close touch with the grand consciousness underlying the universe. And so it was that neither of them could utter a word.

The steamer reached Calcutta. Binoy hired a cab and, placing Lolita inside, took his seat beside the driver. Who can say why it was that, while driving through the streets of Calcutta, the wind for Lolita had veered round and become contrary? That in this difficult situation Binoy should have been with her on the steamer, and had become entangled with her affairs so intimately; that he should now be taking her along home, as if he were her guardian; this was what weighed heavily on her mind. It seemed unbearable to her that, by force of circumstances, Binoy should seem to have acquired the rights of authority over her. Why had it turned out so?

Why did the music of the previous night stop on such a harsh note as soon as she was confronted with her work-a-day life? Therefore, when Binoy had said, as they arrived at the door of her home: "Now I must be going," she felt her irritation increasing. Did he believe she was afraid to go into her father's presence with him? She wanted to show in the clearest manner that she was not in the least ashamed of herself, and was quite ready to tell her father everything. So she could not have Binoy slinking away from the door, as if she were indeed a culprit. She wished to make her relationship with Binoy as clear as it had been before; she did not want to belittle herself in his eyes by allowing any of last night's illusions and hesitations to persist in the broad light of day.

THIRTY ONE

The moment Satish caught sight of Binoy and Lolita, he rushed up between them and, holding a hand of each, said: "Where's Sucharita? Hasn't she come?"

Binoy felt in his pocket, and looked all about him. "Sucharita!" he cried. "Yes, that's so, where can she be? By Jove, she's lost!"

"Don't be silly," cried Satish, giving Binoy a push. "Do tell me, Lolita Didi, where is she?"

"Sucharita will come to-morrow," answered Lolita, and with that she proceeded towards Paresh Babu's room.

Satish tried to pull them along, saying: "Come and see who has come."

But Lolita snatched her hand away and said: "Don't worry us now. I want to see father."

"Father has gone out," Satish informed her, "and won't be back for a long time."

At this both Binoy and Lolita felt that they had gained some breathing space.

"Who has come, did you say?" asked Lolita.

"I won't tell you!" said Satish.—"You try, Binoy Babu, see if you can guess who has come. You'll never be able to, I'm sure! Never!"

Binoy suggested all sorts of impossible names, such as Nawab Surajuddaula, King Nabakrishna and even

Nandakumar. Satish said "No" to each name in a shrill voice, giving conclusive proof of the impossibility of such guests coming to their house. Binoy acknowledged his defeat humbly, saying: "That is so, I had forgotten that Nawab Surajuddaula would find a good many inconveniences in this house. However, first let your sister go and investigate the mystery, and then if necessary you can call me."

"No, you must both come together!" persisted Satish.

"Which room must we go to?" asked Lolita.

"Top floor," said Satish.

Right at the top of the house was a little room in one corner of the terrace, with a tiled verandah on the south as a protection against sun and rain. Obediently following Satish they went upstairs and saw, seated on a small mat under the tiled verandah, a middle-aged woman with spectacles, reading the *Ramayana*. One side-spring of her glasses was broken and the string which took its place was hanging over her ear. Her age seemed about forty-five. Her hair was getting rather thin in front, but her complexion was fresh, and her face still plump like a ripe fruit. Between her eyebrows was a permanent caste mark, but she wore no ornaments and her dress was that of a widow.

As her glance fell on Lolita, she quickly took off her spectacles, put down her book, and gazed at her with a certain amount of eagerness. Then when she saw Binoy behind, she rose hastily and, drawing her *sari* over the back of her head, made as if she would retire into the room. But Satish seized hold of her and said: "Auntie, why are you running away? This is my sister Lolita, and that is Binoy Babu. My elder sister will come to-morrow." This brief introduction seemed sufficient, and there was no doubt that Satish had given a full and particular account of his friends beforehand, for whenever Satish got the opportunity to speak on such subjects as were of interest to him, he never kept anything back.

Lolita stood speechless, at a loss to make out who this "Auntie" of Satish's might be. But finding that Binoy promptly made his salutation by bending to take the dust off her feet, she followed suit.

Auntie now brought a large mat from the room and, spreading it out, said: "Sit down, my son; sit down, little mother." And when Binoy and Lolita were seated she took her own seat; whereupon Satish snuggled up to her. With her arm round Satish, she said to the newcomers: "You probably do not know me. I am Satish's aunt—Satish's mother was my sister."

It was not so much the few words of this introduction, but something in her face and tone of voice, which seemed to hint of a tear-purified life of sorrow.

When she said " I am Satish's aunt," pressing little Satish to her bosom, Binoy, without knowing anything further of her history, felt a deep sense of compassion. He said: "It won't do for you to be only Satish's auntie. I shall have my quarrel with him if he monopolises you like that! It's bad enough that he should insist on calling me Binoy Babu, and not Dada,— on top of that I will not stand his doing me out of an aunt!"

It never took long for Binoy to win over people, and this pleasant-spoken, bright-looking young man was in less than no time joint proprietor of Auntie's heart. "And where is my sister, your mother, my son?" she inquired.

"I lost my own mother long years ago," said Binoy, "but I can't bring myself to say that I have no mother," and his eyes became moist at the thought of what Anandamoyi meant to him.

They were soon talking away together so briskly that no one could have guessed they had only just met. Satish now and then joined in with his irrelevant chatter, but Lolita remained silent.

Lolita had always been reserved, and it took her long to overcome the barrier of unfamiliarity with a new acquaintance. Moreover, her mind was not at ease. So she did not quite like the readiness with which Binoy had taken to this unknown person. She blamed him in her mind for being too light-hearted and not taking seriously enough the extremely difficult position into which she had been plunged. Not that Binoy would have fared any better in her good graces, by sitting silent with a glum face. Had he dared do so, Lolita would certainly have resented such assumption of responsibility on his part for a burden which rested between her and her father alone.

The real fact was that what had seemed music overnight now only jangled on her nerves, and in consequence nothing that Binoy could do seemed to her right, or to mend matters. God alone knew what could have served to get rid of the root of the trouble! Why blame as unreasonable these women, whose very life is emotion, for the curious courses into which their hearts lead them? If the foundation of love be right, the leadership of the heart becomes so simple and sweet that reason has to hide its head in shame, but if there be any defect in this foundation, then the intellect is powerless to correct it, and it becomes futile to ask for any explanation, whether it be of attraction or repulsion, laughter or tears.

It was getting later and later, and yet Paresh Babu had not returned. The impulse to get up and go home became stronger and stronger, and Binoy tried to control it by not allowing the conversation with Satish's aunt to flag for a moment. At last Lolita could restrain her vexation no longer, and she suddenly interrupted Binoy by saying: "For whom are you waiting? There's no saying how long father will be. Shouldn't you rather be going to Gourmohan Babu's mother?"

Binoy winced,—this vexed tone of Lolita's was only too well known to him! He cast one glance at her face and then leapt to his feet with the suddenness of a bow when its string has snapped. For whom had he been waiting indeed? He had never plumed himself on his presence being indispensable here at this juncture,—in fact at the door he had been about to take his departure, and had only stayed on at Lolita's express desire; and now to be asked this question by her!

Lolita was startled at the suddenness with which Binoy rose from his seat. She could see that the usual smile on his face had vanished as completely as the light of a lamp which has been blown out. She had never before seen him so crestfallen, so wounded, and as she looked on him her remorse stung her like a whip-lash.

Satish jumped up and, hanging on to Binoy's arm, begged and pleaded: "Binoy Babu, do sit down, don't go yet.— Auntie, please ask Binoy Babu to stay to breakfast.—Lolita, why did you tell Binoy Babu to go?"

"No, Satish my boy, not to-day!" said Binoy. "If Auntie will be kind enough to remember me, I'll come and have something with you another day. It's too late to-day."

Even Satish's aunt noticed the pain in his voice, and her heart went out to him. She glanced timidly from Binoy to Lolita, and could divine that some drama of fate was being played behind the scenes.

Lolita made some excuse and retired to her room, to weep, as she had made herself weep so many times before.

THIRTY TWO

Binoy went off at once to Anandamoyi's house, tortured with mixed feelings of humiliation and self-reproach. Why had he not come straight to mother? What a fool he had been to imagine that Lolita had any special need of him! God had punished him rightly for not having left every other duty to run to Anandamoyi, the moment he arrived in Calcutta,—so that the question had to come from Lolita's lips: "Shouldn't you go to see Gora's mother?" Was it possible for a single moment that the thought of Gora's mother should be more important to Lolita than to Binoy? Lolita knew her only as Gour Babu's mother but to Binoy she was the image of all mothers in the world!

Anandamoyi had just finished her bath and was sitting alone in her room, seemingly wrapt in meditation, when Binoy came in and prostrated himself at her feet with the cry: "Mother!"

"Binoy!" she said, caressing his bowed head with her hands.

Whose voice is like that of a mother's? The very sound of his name uttered by Anandamoyi seemed to soothe his whole being. Controlling his emotion with an effort, he said softly: "Mother, I've been too long in coming!"

"I've heard everything, Binoy," said Anandamoyi gently.

"You've already heard the news!" exclaimed the startled Binoy.

It appeared that Gora had written a letter from the police station and had sent it through the lawyer, in which he had told her of the probability of his having to go to gaol. At the end of this letter he wrote:

"Prison can do no harm to your Gora, but he won't be able to bear it if it gives you the least pain. Your sorrow can be his only punishment,—the Magistrate can give no other. But, mother, don't be thinking only of your child. There are many other mother's sons lying in gaol,—through no fault of theirs,—I would stand on the same ground with them and share their hardships. If this wish of mine is fated to be fulfilled this time, pray do not let that distress you.

"You may not remember it, mother, but in the year of the famine I once left my purse on the table, in the room looking out on to the street. When I came back after a few minutes I saw that the purse had been stolen. In it were the fifty rupees of my scholarship, which I was saving up for a silver basin for bathing your feet. While I was burning with useless anger against the thief, God suddenly brought me to my senses, and I said to myself: 'But that money is my gift to the famine-stricken man who took it.' No sooner had I said this than that fruitless regret vanished, leaving my mind in peace. So to-day I say to myself: 'I am going to gaol voluntarily, of my own accord, without regrets, or anger, simply to take its shelter.' There is a certain amount of inconvenience in its food and other arrangements, but during my recent tramp I accepted hospitality of all sorts and conditions of people and did not always get my accustomed comforts, or even necessities, in their houses. What we accept of our own free will ceases to be a hardship, so you may rest assured that it is not a question of anyone forcibly keeping me in gaol,—I go there, willing and content.

"While in the enjoyment of our comforts at home, we are quite unable to appreciate what an immense privilege it is to have the freedom of the outside air and light—we are all the time forgetful of the multitudes who, with or without fault of their own, are subjected to confinement and insult and deprived of this God-given privilege. We give no thought to these multitudes, nor feel any kinship with them. I now want to be branded with the same stigma as they, not to keep myself clear by hanging on to the goody-goody majority who are dressed up to look respectable.

"I have learnt much of life, mother, after this experience of the world. Those who are content to pose as judges are, most of them, to be pitied. Those who are in prison are bearing the punishment for the sins of those who judge others, but not themselves. The faults of many go to the making of a crime, but only these unfortunates have to bear the brunt of it. When, or how, or where, the sin of those who are living comfortable and respectable lives outside the prison walls will be expiated, we do not know. But for myself, I cry shame on that smug respectability of theirs, and prefer to carry on my breast the brand of man's infamy. Give me your blessing, mother, and do not weep for me. Sree Krishna all his days bore on his breast the mark of Bhrigu's kick, and so do the assaults of arrogance make deeper and deeper their impress on the breast of God. If He has accepted this mark as His ornament, then why be anxious for me, what cause have you for sorrow on my account?"

On receiving this letter Anandamoyi had tried to send Mohim to Gora, but Mohim said: "There's my office. The *sahib* will never give me leave"; and he proceeded to fly out against Gora for his rashness and folly. "I'll be losing my job one of these days simply because of our relationship," he concluded.

Anandamoyi did not think it necessary to approach Krishnadayal at all, for on the subject of Gora she was abnormally sensitive so far as her husband was concerned. She knew quite well that he had never given to Gora the place of a son in his heart, rather he felt a sort of hostility against him. Gora had always stood between them as the Vindhya mountain range, dividing their married life. On the one side was Krishnadayal with all his paraphernalia of strict orthodoxy, and on the other Anandamoyi alone with her untouchable Gora. It seemed as though all intercourse was closed between these two who alone in the whole world knew Gora's history.

Thus Anandamoyi's affection for Gora had become wholly her own treasure. She tried in every way to make his life in that family, where he was merely on sufferance, as easy as possible. Her incessant anxiety was to prevent anyone from being able to say: this has happened because of your Gora, or we have had to submit to this calumny owing to your Gora, or we have suffered this loss through your Gora! The whole burden of Gora, she felt, rested on herself alone. And as luck would have it, the refractoriness of this Gora of hers was far from ordinary! It was no easy task to keep his presence anywhere from violently obtruding itself.

She had so far succeeded in bringing up this crazy Gora of hers, in midst of these antagonistic surroundings, with the exercise of constant vigilance by day and by night. In the midst of this hostile family she had submitted in much revilement and had endured much sorrow, without being able to ask anyone else to share it.

Deserted by Mohim, Anandamoyi remained sitting in silence before the window, and watched Krishnadayal return from his morning bath with the sacred Ganges clay smeared on his brow, his breast and his arms, muttering sacred *mantras*. While so purified, no one, not even Anandamoyi, was allowed to come near him. Prohibition, prohibition, nothing but prohibition!

With a sigh she left the window and went into Mohim's room, where she found him sitting on the floor, reading the newspaper and having his chest rubbed with oil by his servant, preparatory to his morning bath. Anandamoyi said to him: "Mohim, you must find someone to go with me, I want to see Gora. He seems to have made up his mind to go to gaol, but I suppose they'll allow me to see him before he's sentenced?"

For all Mohim's outward brusqueness, he had a real affection for Gora. "Confound the fellow!" he shouted. "Let the scamp go to gaol—it's a wonder he didn't get there long ago!" But all the same he lost no time in calling his confidential man, Ghosal, and sending him off at once with some money for legal expenses; also making up his mind that if his office master gave him leave, and the mistress of his house her consent, he himself would follow.

Anandamoyi knew that Mohim would never be able to see Gora in trouble without bestirring himself about it, and when she found he was ready to do the little that could be done, she had no more to say to him. For she also knew that it would be impossible to get any member of this orthodox household to take her, the lady of the house, to the lock-up where Gora was, to face the curious glances and inquisitive remarks of the crowd. So she forbore to press her request, and returned to her own room with compressed lips and the shadow of suppressed pain in her eyes. When Lachmiya broke out into loud wailing she rebuked her and sent her out of the room. It had always been her habit to adjust all her anxieties silently within herself. Joy and sorrow alike found her tranquil. The travail of her heart was known only to her God.

What consolation he could offer to Anandamoyi was more than Binoy could make out and after the first few words he had remained silent. In fact her nature did not depend on any words of comfort from others; rather she shrank from any discussion of troubles for which there was no remedy. So Anandamoyi also did not refer further to the matter but simply said: "Binu, I see you haven't had your bath yet. Go and make yourself ready soon, it's getting late for your breakfast."

When he had taken his bath and sat down to his breakfast, the empty place beside Binoy made her heart ache for Gora; and when she thought of the other being served with coarse gaol food, unsweetened by a mother's care, even made doubly bitter by insulting gaol regulations, Anandamoyi could no longer bear it, and, making some excuse, she had to leave the room.

THIRTY THREE

On arriving home and finding Lolita there so unexpectedly, Paresh Babu guessed that this self-willed girl of his had got involved in more than ordinary trouble. In answer to his look of inquiry she said: "Father, I've come away from there. I found it impossible to stay on." In answer to his question as to what had happened, Lolita added: "The Magistrate has put Gour Babu into gaol."

How Gora came to be mixed up in the matter, Paresh Babu was at first puzzled to make out, but after he had heard from Lolita a full account of all that had occurred, he for a while was lost in silent thought. His first anxiety was for Gora's mother. It was just as easy, he pondered, for the Magistrate to sentence Gora as to sentence a common thief, because such callousness was the outcome of the easy disregard for justice to which he had become habituated. How much more terrible was man's tyranny over man than all the other cruelties in the world, and how vast and intolerable it had become with the combined power of Society and the Government behind it! The whole thing came vividly before his mind as he listened to the story of Gora's imprisonment.

Seeing Paresh Babu silent and thoughtful, Lolita asked him eagerly: "Isn't this injustice terrible, father?"

He replied in his usual unruffled, manner: "We don't know exactly how far Gora went, but this much at least we can say, that even if Gora was carried away, by his convictions, beyond his legal rights, there can be no doubt that he is quite incapable of committing what in English is called a crime. But what is to be done, my child? The sense of justice of our times has not attained to fullness of wisdom. The same penalty awaits the trivial fault as the crime, both have to tread the same mill in the same gaol. No one man can be blamed for this—the combined sin of all men is responsible."

Suddenly changing the subject, Paresh Babu asked: "With whom did you come?"

Lolita drew herself up as she replied with rather more than usual emphasis: "With Binoy Babu." But, for all her emphasis, there was behind it a sense of weakness. She was unable to make the statement with unabashed simplicity, the flush of shame insisted on rising to her face, to add to her confusion.

Paresh Babu had for this capricious and unruly daughter of his even more affection than for the rest of his children, and his regard for her fearless truthfulness was all the greater because it so often got her into trouble with the rest of the family. Lolita's faults were obvious enough, and he could see how they prevented this special quality of hers from being appreciated—he was therefore all the more careful to keep it under his fostering care, lest in the process of bringing her waywardness under control her inner nobility should also be crushed.

The beauty of his other daughters was readily acknowledged by all who saw them, for their features were regular and their complexion fair. But Lolita was darker and her more complex face admitted of differences of opinion. For this reason Mistress Baroda had always expressed to her husband her anxiety about finding a suitable husband for her. But the beauty which Paresh Babu saw in her face was not that of complexion or features, but of the soul which there found its expression,—not just the pleasantness of a faultless shape but the firmness of strength, the brightness of independence,—characteristics which attract a chosen few, but repel most others.

Feeling that Lolita would never be popular, but always be genuine, Paresh Babu had drawn her near to him almost with painful solicitude, and was the more lenient towards her errors because he knew that none else would forgive them. He had realised in a moment all that she would have to bear for days to come, as soon as Lolita had told him that she had come away alone with Binoy—that Society would award for this slight transgression of hers a punishment suited to much worse misconduct.

As he was revolving the situation in his mind, Lolita continued: "Father, I know I've done wrong, but I've now come to understand one thing clearly—the relationship between the magistrate and the people of our country is such that his patronising hospitality does us no honour. Ought I to have stayed on there, and put up with such patronage, after I had realised this?"

To Paresh Babu the question was not an easy one to answer, so without attempting any reply he gave his little madcap of a daughter a playing pat on the head.

That afternoon Paresh Babu was walking up and down outside the house, thinking it all over, when Binoy came up and made his obeisance. Paresh Babu discussed with him Gora's imprisonment and all that it meant, at considerable length, but he never so much as referred to Binoy's coming away with Lolita on the steamer. And as it got dark he said: "Come Binoy, let's go indoors."

But Binoy would not, saying: "I must be going home now."

Paresh Babu did not repeat his invitation, and Binoy, casting a rapid glance in the direction of the second floor verandah, walked slowly away.

Lolita had seen Binoy from the verandah, and when her father came inside alone, she came down to his room thinking that Binoy would be following later. But as Binoy did not come, Lolita, after fidgeting a while with the books and papers on the table, was about to leave the room, when Paresh Babu called her back, and with an affectionate look at her downcast countenance said: "Lolita, sing a hymn to me, will you?" and with that he shifted the lamp, so as to throw the light off her face.

THIRTY FOUR

The next day Mistress Baroda returned with the rest of her party.

Haran felt so outraged at Lolita's conduct that, unable to contain himself, he came in at once to see Paresh Babu, without going to his own house first.

Baroda swept past Lolita without a word, too indignant even to look at her, and went straight to her own room.

Labonya and Lila were also greatly incensed with Lolita, because, on having to leave both her and Binoy out of the programme, it became so curtailed that they had experienced endless humiliation.

As for Sucharita, she had shared neither Haran's angry fulminations, nor Baroda's tearful regrets, nor the sense of humiliation of Labonya and Lila, but had maintained an icy silence and gone about her appointed tasks like a machine. Today, also, she entered the room last of all, moving like an automation.

Sudhir was so ashamed of the part he had played, that he shrank from coming in with them at all; whereupon Labonya, vexed at his unresponsiveness to her entreaties, vowed she would have nothing more to do with him!

"This is too bad!" exclaimed Haran as he strode into Paresh Babu's room.

Lolita, who overheard him from the next room, came in at once and, standing behind her father with both hands on the back of his chair, looked Haran straight in the face.

"I have heard all about what happened from Lolita herself," said Paresh Babu, "and do not think there's any good in discussing it further."

Haran regarded the habitual calm of Paresh Babu only as a sign of his weakness of character, so he replied with a touch of superciliousness: "What has happened is over certainly, but the fault of character which caused it still persists, and so its discussion remains necessary. It would never have been possible for Lolita to do as she has done, but for the over-indulgence which you have always shown her. What harm you have thus done you will realise when you hear all the details of the shameful story!"

Paresh Babu, feeling all the signs of a gathering storm at the back of his chair, drew Lolita round to his side and, taking her hand in his, said to Haran with a gentle smile: "Panu Babu, when your turn comes you will learn that to bring up a child there is need also of affection!"

Lolita bending over her father and putting one arm round his neck, whispered in his ear: "Father, the water is getting cold, go and take your bath."

"I'll be going in a minute," replied Paresh Babu meaningly, referring to Haran's presence, "it's not so late yet."

"Don't you worry, father," Lolita gently insisted. "We'll look after Panu Babu while you are bathing."

When Paresh Babu had left the room, Lolita took possession of his chair and ensconced firmly therein, fixed her gaze on Haran's face as she said to him: "You seem to think that you have the right to say what you please to everybody here!"

Sucharita knew Lolita well, and in former days she would have taken alarm at the look on her face. But now she quietly took a seat near the window and calmly rested her eyes on

the open pages of a book. It had always been Sucharita's
nature and habit to keep herself under control, and the repeated
wounds she had suffered during the past few days had only
made her more silent than ever. But the strain of this silence
had at length come near breaking-point, making her welcome
Lolita's challenge to Haran as a much-needed outlet for her
own pent-up feelings.

"I suppose you think," went on Lolita, "that you understand
father's duty to us better than he does himself! You would
be Headmaster to the whole Brahmo Samaj!"

Haran was thunderstruck at Lolita's daring to talk thus
to him, and he was on the point of giving her a severe
snubbing, but before he could speak Lolita continued: "We
have put up with your superior airs long enough, but let me
tell you that if you want to lord it over father, not a soul in
this house will stand it,—not even the servants!"

"Lolita," gasped Haran, "really—"

But Lolita would not let him proceed. "Listen to me,
please," she interrupted. "We've heard you talk often enough,
hear me out for once. If you won't take it from me, ask sister
Suchi: our father is much greater even than what you can
imagine yourself to be,—that's what we want to tell you
plainly. Now if you have any advice to offer, let's have it."

Haran's face was black with rage. "Sucharita!" he called
out as he rose from his chair. Sucharita looked up from her
book. "Will you let Lolita insult me before your face?"

"She has not tried to insult you," said Sucharita slowly.
"What Lolita wants is, that you should show a proper
respect for father. I assure you, we cannot even think anyone
to be more worthy of respect."

For a moment it looked as if Haran would leave the room,
but he did not. He fell back into his chair with an intensely
solemn air. The more he felt that he was gradually losing the
respect of everyone in this house, the more desperately he

struggled to maintain his position in it, forgetting that to clutch tighter a weakening support only makes it give way the sooner.

Finding Haran reduced to a gloomy and sullen silence Lolita went and sat next to Sucharita and began to converse with her as though nothing special had happened.

Then Satish came running into the room and, seizing Sucharita by the hand, dragged her up saying: "Come along, Didi, do come!"

"Where am I to go?" asked Sucharita.

"Oh do come along," insisted Satish. "I have something to show you.—Lolita, you have not told her yet, have you?

"No," said Lolita. She had promised not to divulge the secret of this new Auntie to Sucharita, and had kept her word.

But, not being able to leave their guest, Sucharita said: "All right, Mr. Chatterbox, I'll come a little later. Let father first finish his bath."

Satish became restless. He never left a stone unturned when it was a question of getting away from Haran. But as he stood in great awe of him he dared not press the matter further in his presence. Haran, for his part, had never shown much interest in Satish, except when occasionally he tried to correct him. Satish lay in wait, however, and the moment Paresh Babu came from his bath he dragged both the sisters away after him.

Haran said: "About that proposal of my formal betrothal with Sucharita, I am anxious not to delay it any longer. Let it be fixed for next Sunday."

"For myself," replied Paresh Babu, "I have no objection, but it is for Sucharita to decide."

"But you have already obtained her consent," pressed Haran.

"Let it be as you wish, then," said Paresh Babu.

THIRTY FIVE

Binoy did not feel up to going again to Paresh Babu's house, and as for his own lodgings their loneliness felt so oppressive that the very next morning he went quite early to Anandamoyi and said: "Mother, I want to stay with you here for a few days."

Binoy had it also in mind that he could comfort Anandamoyi in her sorrow at Gora's enforced absence, and her heart was touched when she saw this. She put her hand affectionately on his shoulder, but said nothing.

As soon as he was settled, Binoy began to make all kinds of petulant demands and even playfully to quarrel with Anandamoyi over his not being properly looked after, with the idea of distracting her, as well as himself, from their sorrowful reflections. And when, in the gloom of evening, it became difficult to keep his feelings under control, Binoy pestered Anandamoyi till she left all her housework, and came with him to the verandah in front of his room, and there he made her sit down on the mat and tell him stories about her childhood's days and about her father's home,—stories of the days before her marriage when, as the grandchild of the preceptor, she had been the pet of all the students in her grandfather's school; and because everyone joined in lavishing on this fatherless girl every kind of indulgence, she had been a cause of anxious solicitude to her widowed mother.

"Mother!" cried Binoy at the end, "I can't even think that there was ever a time when you were not our mother! I believe that the students of your grandfather's school used to look on you as their tiny little mother, and that it was really you who had to bring up your grandfather!"

The next evening Binoy was lying on a mat with his head resting on Anandamoyi's lap and was saying: "Mother, I sometimes wish that I could give back to God all my book learning and take refuge in this lap of yours as a child once more—with only you in the whole world, you and no one else but you."

Binoy's tone was so full of weariness and seemed to reveal such an overburdened heart that Anandamoyi was surprised as well as greatly troubled. She moved up closer and began gently to stroke his head, and after a long silence asked him: "Binu, is everything all right at Paresh Babu's?"

At this question the abashed Binoy gave a start. "Nothing can be hidden from mother," thought he. "She sees right into one!" Aloud he said somewhat haltingly: "Yes, they are all very well."

"I should very much like to know Paresh Babu's girls," continued Anandamoyi. "Gora did not have a good opinion of them, to begin with, but from the way they have been able to win him over since, they seem to be different from ordinary people."

"I also have often wished," said Binoy eagerly, "that I could introduce them to you. But I was afraid Gora might object, so I never suggested it."

"What is the name of the eldest?" pursued Anandamoyi. And in this way several questions were asked and answered, but when the name of Lolita came up Binoy tried to turn the subject with an evasive reply. Anandamoyi, however, with a smile at his tactics, refused to be put off.

"I've heard that Lolita is a very clever girl," she went on.

"Who told you?" asked Binoy.

"Why, *you* of course!" answered Anandamoyi.

There had been a time when Binoy had no special awkwardness in speaking of Lolita. He had now clean forgotten how, during that free-minded stage, he had given Anandamoyi glowing accounts of the keenness of Lolita's intellect.

Anandamoyi, rounding all obstacles like an expert captain, had soon steered the subject so skilfully ahead, that no important detail of Lolita's friendship with Binoy remained hidden from her. Binoy even came out with how Lolita's acute distress at Gora's sudden arrest, and imprisonment had led to her escape alone with him on the steamer. And in his excitement as he talked on all trace of his former weariness vanished. It seemed to him such a piece of good fortune to be able thus to talk freely about so wonderful a character!

When at length dinner was announced and the conversation was interrupted, Binoy seemed to awake, as if from a dream, to realise that he had been telling Anandamoyi absolutely everything that was in his mind. She had listened to and appreciated everything so simply, that nowhere did the recital call for any feeling of awkwardness or shame.

Up to this point in his life Binoy had never come across anything which had needed to be kept from this mother of his, and he had got into the habit of coming to her even with his most trivial concerns. But since his acquaintance with Paresh Babu's people, a sense of hesitation had crept in, which had not been healthy for Binoy's mind. Now that he had once again poured all his troubles into her sympathetic and understanding ears, he felt great elation. The purity of his last experience would have suffered, he was sure, if he had been unable to offer it at mother Anandamoyi's feet,—in that case some stain of unworthiness would have remained to tarnish his love.

In the night Anandamoyi turned the matter over and over in her mind. She felt that the puzzle of Gora's life was getting more and more tangled, but that possibly its solution might be found in Paresh Babu's house. She decided, in the end, that no matter what was fated to happen, she would have to get to know these girls.

THIRTY SIX

Mohim and all his part of the family had begun to take
Sasi's marriage with Binoy as a settled thing. Sasi, with
her newly developed bashfulness, had given up coming near
him. As for Sasi's mother, Lakshmi, Binoy hardly ever came
across her.

Not that Mistress Lakshmi was shy, but her disposition
was inordinately secretive, and the door of her room was
almost always closed. Every one of her possessions was kept
under lock and key, except only her husband; and even he
was not as free as he would have liked under his wife's strict
regime,—the circle of his acquaintance and the orbit of his
movements being alike restricted. Lakshmi kept her little
world well under her own control, and it was as difficult for
the outsider to get in as for the insider to get out! So much
so that even Gora was not a welcome visitor in Lakshmi's part
of the house.

This realm of Mistress Lakshmi's was never torn with any
internal conflict between legislature, judiciary or executive,
for she herself would execute the laws of her own making
and combined in herself both the court of first instance and
that of final appeal. In his outside relations Mohim passed
for a man of strong will, but that will of his found no scope
within the jurisdiction of Lakshmi, not even in the most
insignificant matters.

Lakshmi had made her own estimate of Binoy from behind her purdah and had bestowed on him the seal of her approval. Mohim, having known Binoy from boyhood, had got into the way of regarding him as merely Gora's friend. It was his wife who had first drawn his attention to the possibilities of Binoy as bridegroom, not the least of his merits, which she had pressed on her husband, being that he would never insist on a dowry!

Now, although Binoy had come to stay in the house, Mohim was tantalised to find himself unable to get in a word with him about the marriage, because of his depression at Gora's misadventure.

When Sunday came round, however, the exasperated mistress of his home took the matter in her own hands, broke into Mohim's Sabbath siesta, and drove him forth, *pan*-box and all, to where Binoy was reading out to Anadamoyi something from the last number of the *Bangadarshan*, then recently started by Bankim-chandra.

Mohim, after offering a *pan* to Binoy, started off with a homily on Gora's irrepressible folly; then as he proceeded to count up the days remaining for Gora's sentence to expire, he was quite naturally—and causally—reminded that nearly half the month of *Aghran* was already over; whereupon he felt he could come to the point.

"Look here, Binoy," he then said. "Your idea about not having wedding in *Aghran* is all nonsense. As I was saying, if you add a family almanac to all our other rules and prohibitions there'll never be any marriages at all in this country!"

Seeing how awkward Binoy felt, Anandamoyi came to his rescue and interposed with: "Binoy has known Sasi since she was a tiny little thing, he can't quite see himself marrying her. That was why he made the excuse about the month of *Aghran*."

"He should have said so plainly, then, at the very start," said Mohim.

"It takes some time to understand even one's own mind," replied Anandamoyi. "But, Mohim, what makes you so anxious? There's no dearth of bridegrooms, surely. Let Gora come back—he knows plenty of marriageable young men— he will be able to fix up a suitable match with one of them."

"Humph!" grunted Mohim, pulling a long face. Then after a short silence he broke out with: "If you had not put in a spoke, mother, Binoy would never have raised any objections."

Binoy, all in a flurry, was about to protest, but Anandamoyi would not let him. "You are not far out, Mohim," she said, "I have not been able to give Binoy any encouragement in this matter. Binoy is still young, and might perhaps have agreed on the impulse of the moment, but it would never have turned out well."

Thus did Anandamoyi shelter Binoy from Mohim's attack by drawing all his anger on herself, making Binoy feel quite ashamed of his own weakness. But Mohim, did not wait to give Binoy an opportunity of mending matters by expressing his unwillingness for himself. "A stepmother can never feel as one's own mother," was his unspoken comment as he left the room in a huff.

Anandamoyi knew perfectly well that Mohim would not hesitate to bring this charge. She knew that all family unpleasantness was bound to be put down to the stepmother in Society's code of justice, but she was never in the habit of regulating her conduct by what people might think of her. From the day she had taken Gora in her arms she had entirely cut herself away from tradition and custom, and in fact had taken to a course which consistently brought social censure upon her.

But her constant self-reproach, due to the suppression of truth which she had been led to connive at, rendered her impervious to the caustic comments of others. When people accused her of being a Christian she used to clasp Gora to her bosom and say: "God knows it is no accusation to call me a Christian!" Thus had she gradually become accustomed to ignore the dictates of her social circle and to follow simply her own nature. So it was not possible for any charge made by Mohim, silent or spoken, to move her from what she considered right.

"Binu," said Anandamoyi suddenly, "you haven't been to Paresh Babu's house for many days now, have you?"

"Hardly *many*, mother," answered Binoy.

"Well, you have certainly not been since the day after you returned on the steamer," said Anandamoyi.

That was indeed not very many days, but Binoy knew that his visits to Paresh Babu's house had, just before that, become so frequent that Anandamoyi scarcely ever got a glimpse of him. From that point of view he was open to the comment that his recent absence had been fairly long—for him!

He began to pick out a thread from the border of his *dhuti*, but remained silent.

Just then the servant came in and announced that some ladies had called, whereupon Binoy got up hurriedly, so as not to be in the way, but while they stood debating who it could be, Sucharita and Lolita entered the room, and then it was no longer possible for him to retire. So he stayed on, awkwardly silent.

The girls took the dust off Anandamoyi's feet. Lolita did not take any special notice of Binoy, but Sucharita bowed and greeted him with a "How are you?" and then turning to Anandamoyi introduced themselves saying: "We have come from Paresh Babu's."

Anandamoyi welcomed them affectionately, protesting: "You need no introduction, my dears. I have never seen you, it is true, but I feel as if you belonged to our own family," and in a very short time she had made them quite at home.

Sucharita tried to draw Binoy, who was sitting apart in silence, into the conversation by remarking: "You have not been to see us for some time."

Binoy glanced towards Lolita as he replied: "That's because I was afraid of exhausting my welcome by presuming on it too much."

"I suppose you don't know that affection expects presumption," said Sucharita with a smile.

"Doesn't he?" laughed Anandamoyi. "Why, if I could only tell you how he orders me about all day long—I don't get a moment's peace with his whims!" and she looked lovingly at Binoy.

"God is only using me to test the patience with which he has endowed you," retorted Binoy.

At this remark Sucharita nudged Lolita slyly and said: "Do you hear this, Lolita? Have we been tested too, and found wanting, I wonder!"

Seeing that Lolita paid no attention to this remark, Anandamoyi laughed and said: "This time Binu is engaged in putting his own patience to the test. You people little know what you mean for him. Why, in the evenings he can talk about nothing else, and Paresh Babu's very name is enough to send him into ecstasies," and as she spoke Anandamoyi gazed at Lolita, who, although she was making strenuous efforts to look up naturally, was unable to do so without blushing all over.

"You can't imagine with what a number of people he has quarrelled by standing up for Paresh Babu!" continued Anandamoyi. "All his orthodox friends twit him with being a Brahmo, and some of them have even tried to outcaste him.— You need not look so uncomfortable about it, Binu dear, it's nothing to be ashamed of.—What do you say, my little mother?"

This time Lolita had been looking up, but lowered her eyes when Anandamoyi turned towards her, and it was

Sucharita who replied for her: "Binoy Babu has been good enough to give us his friendship—that's not due to our merit alone, but to his largeness of heart."

"There I cannot agree!" smiled Anandamoyi. "I've known Binoy ever since he was a youngster and all these days he has never made friends with anyone except my Gora. He does not get on even with the other men of his own set. But since he has come to know you, he has got quite beyond our reach! I was ready to pick a quarrel with you over this, but now, I see, I've got into the same plight—you are too irresistible, my dears!" With this Anandamoyi caressed each of the girls in turn by touching them under the chin and then kissing her own fingers.

Binoy had begun to look so uncomfortable that Sucharita took pity on him and said: "Binoy Babu, father came with us, and is now downstairs talking with Krishnadayal Babu."

This gave Binoy the opportunity to make his escape, leaving the ladies to themselves. Anandamoyi then talked to the girls of the extraordinary friendship which existed between Gora and Binoy, and she was not long in discovering how interested both her hearers were.

To Anandamoyi herself there was no one in the whole world so dear as these two, to whom she had offered the full adoration of a mother's love, from their early childhood. She had, indeed, shaped them with her own hands, like the images of Shiva which girls make for their own worship, and they had appropriated to themselves the whole of her devotion.

The story of these two idols of hers sounded so sweet from her own lips, and so vivid, that Sucharita and Lolita both felt they could not have enough of it. They had no lack of regard for Gora and Binoy, but they seemed to see them in a new light through the magic radiance of a mother's love.

Now that she had come to know Anandamoyi, Lolita's anger against the Magistrate flamed up afresh. But Anandamoyi smiled at her pungent remarks and said: "My dear, God alone knows what Gora's being in gaol has meant to me, but I can't bring myself to be angry with the *sahib*. I know Gora. He cannot allow any man-made laws to stand in the way of what he feels to be right. Gora has done his duty. The authorities are doing theirs. Those whom the result hurts must submit. If only you will read my Gora's letter, little mother, you will realise that he has not shirked pain, nor is he venting childish anger against anyone. He weighed all the consequences of what he has done." And she brought Gora's letter out of a box in which she had carefully put it away and handed it to Sucharita, saying: "Will you read it aloud, my dear. I would like to heart it again."

After the reading of Gora's wonderful letter all three of them kept silent a while. Anandamoyi wiped away some tears which came, not merely from a mother's grief, but also from a mother's joy and pride. What a Gora was this Gora of hers! Not the poltroon to cringe to the Magistrate for pity or pardon. Had he not accepted the whole responsibility for his deed, knowing full well all the hardship of gaol life! For that he had no quarrel with anyone, and if he could bear it without wincing, his mother, too could endure it!

Lolita gazed at Anandamoyi's face in admiration. All the prejudices of a Brahmo household were strongly ingrained in her. She had never felt much respect for women whom she considered to be steeped in the superstitions of orthodoxy. From her childhood she had heard Mistress Baroda, whenever she wanted to be particularly scathing about any fault of Lolita's, denounce it as fit only for girls of Hindu homes, and thereupon had always felt duly humiliated.

Anandamoyi's words, to-day, repeatedly filled her with wonder. Such calm strength, such sound sense, such keen discernment! Lolita felt very small besides this woman when she realised how uncontrolled were her own emotions. How effectually had her agitation prevented her from speaking to Binoy or even looking in his direction! But now the calm compassion in Anandamoyi's face brought peace to her own turbulent mind, and her relations with her surroundings became simple and natural. "Now that I have seen you," she exclaimed, "I understand clearly where Gour Babu got his strength from."

"I am afraid," smiled Anandamoyi, "your understanding of this matter is not quite clear. If Gora had been like an ordinary child to me, from where could I have got the strength myself? Could I then have borne this trouble of his so easily?"

THIRTY SEVEN

In order to understand the cause of Lolita's special agitation on the occasion of her visit to Anandamoyi's, it is necessary to go back a little.

For some days past the first thought in Lolita's mind, every morning, had been: "Binoy Babu will not come to-day." And yet she had not been able for the rest of the day to get rid of the hope that he would come after all. Every now and then she would imagine that perhaps he had already come, but instead of coming up to the parlour, was with Paresh Babu downstairs. And when this idea took hold of her, she would be wandering from room to room, over and over again. Then when the day wore to its close, and at last she was in her bed, Lolita did not know what to do with the thoughts which crowded on her. At one moment she could hardly restrain her tears, and the next she would be feeling angry with she knew not whom,—probably with herself! She could only exclaim to herself: "What is this? What is to happen to me? I see no way out, in any direction. How much longer can I go on like this?"

Lolita knew that Binoy was in orthodox society, and marriage with him was out of the question,— and yet thus to be wholly unable to control her own heart! What a shame,— what an awful plight to be in! She could see that Binoy was not averse to her, and it was because of this that she found it so difficult to keep her heart in check. It was because of this that while she waited so ardently for Binoy's coming, she was also consumed with the fear lest he should really come.

After struggling in this way all these days, she had felt on that morning that it had become too much for her. She decided that if it was Binoy's absence which was causing all this torment, perhaps the sight of him might serve to allay it. So she had drawn Satish into her room and said: "You have been having a quarrel with Binoy Babu, I see!"

Satish indignantly denied the accusation, although, now that he had got his Auntie, he had for some days forgotten his friendship with Binoy.

"Then he's a fine kind of a friend, I must say!" went on Lolita. "You are so full of Binoy Babu, Binoy Babu, all the time and he doesn't even turn to look at you!"

"Doesn't he?" cried Satish. "What do you know about it! Of course he does!"

Satish usually relied on emphatic assertion alone for keeping up the glory which he claimed as the due of this smallest member of the family. In this case he felt that some tangible proof was necessary, so he promptly made off to Binoy's lodgings. He was soon back with the news: "He's not at home at all, that's why he hasn't come!"

"But why couldn't he have come before!" persisted Lolita.

"Because he's not been there for a long time," said Satish.

It was then that Lolita went to Sucharita and said: "Didi, dear, don't you think we ought to go and call on Gour Babu's mother?"

"But we don't know her," objected Sucharita.

"Bah!" exclaimed Lolita. "Isn't Gour babu's father an old friend of father's?"

Sucharita remembered that this was so. "Yes, that is true," she agreed, and then, becoming even enthusiastic, added: "Go and ask father about it, dear."

But this Lolita refused to do and Sucharita had to go herself. "Certainly!" said Paresh Babu at once. "We ought to have thought of it long ago."

It was settled that they should go after breakfast, but no sooner was the decision come to than Lolita changed her mind. Some hesitation, some wounded pride, came up to the surface and pulled her back. "You accompany father," she said to Sucharita. "I'm not going!"

"That will never do!" cried Sucharita. "How can I go alone, with father? Do come, there's a dear, there's a darling! Don't be obstinate and upset things."

Lolita was at last persuaded. But was not this admitting defeat at Binoy hands? He had found it so easy to keep away, and was she to go running after him like this? The ignominy of her surrender made her furious with Binoy. She tried hard to deny to herself that she had any idea of calling on Anandamoyi because of the chance of getting a glimpse of Binoy, and it was to keep up this attitude that she had refused to greet or even to look at him.

Binoy, for his part, had concluded that her behaviour was due to her discovery of his secret sentiments, which she thus wished to show him that she repulsed. That Lolita could possibly be in love with him was a supposition which he had not sufficient self-conceit to entertain.

Binoy now came timidly up to the door and stood there, saying that Paresh Babu had sent word that he was ready to go home. He took shelter behind the door, so that Lolita could not see him.

"What!" cried Anandamoyi. "Does he think I'll allow them to go without some refreshments? I won't be long, Binoy. You come in and sit down, while I go and see about it. What makes you keep standing at the door like that?"

Binoy came in and took his seat as far away from Lolita as he could. But Lolita had recovered her composure and without a trace of her former awkwardness she said quite naturally: "Do you know, Binoy Babu, your friend Satish went off to your lodgings this morning to find out whether you had forsaken him completely?'

Binoy started with amazement as if he had heard a voice from heaven, and then was abashed because his astonishment was so ill-concealed. His gift of ready repartee forsook him completely. "Satish went to my place, did he?" he repeated, colouring to the ears. "I've not been at home these days."

These few words of Lolita, however, gave Binoy immense joy, and in a single moment the doubts which had overwhelmed his whole world like a choking nightmare were lifted. He felt there was nothing left to desire in the universe. "I am saved, saved!" cried his heart. "Lolita does not doubt me. Lolita is not angry with me!"

Very quickly all barriers slipped away from between them, and Sucharita was saying with a laugh: "Binoy Babu seems at first to have mistaken us for some kind of clawed, tusked or horned creature, or perhaps he thought we had come in arms to the assault!"

"The silent are always found guilty," said Binoy. "In this world those who lodge their plaints first win their suits. But I did not expect this kind of judgment from you, Didi! You yourself drift away, and then accuse others of becoming distant!"

This was the first time Binoy had addressed Sucharita as "Didi," acknowledging her sisterly relationship; and it sounded sweet in her ears, for she felt that the intimacy which had been theirs, almost from their first meeting, had now taken concrete and delightful shape.

At this juncture Anandamoyi returned and took charge of the girls, sending Binoy downstairs to look after Paresh Babu's refreshment.

It was nearly dark when at length Paresh Babu went away with his daughters, and Binoy said to Anandamoyi: "Mother,

I'm not going to let you do any more work to-day. Come, let's go upstairs."

Binoy could hardly contain himself. He took Anandamoyi to the terrace and, spreading a mat with his own hands, he made her sit down.

"Well, Binu, what is it?" then asked Anandamoyi. "What do you want to say to me?"

"Nothing at all," replied Binoy, "I want *you* to talk." The fact was that Binoy was on tenterhooks to know what Anandamoyi thought of Paresh Babu's girls.

"Well, I declare," cried Anandamoyi. "And is that why you dragged me away from my work? I thought you had something important to tell me."

"If I hadn't brought you up here, you wouldn't have seen this beautiful sunset," said Binoy.

The November sun was indeed setting over the roofs of Calcutta, but in somewhat dismal mood. There was no particular beauty of colouring, all its golden splendour being absorbed by the pall of smoke lying over the horizon. But this evening even the dullness of this murky sunset was to Binoy aflame with colour. It seemed to him as if all the world stood round and enfolded him in its embrace and that the sky came near and caressed him with its touch.

"The girls are very charming," observed Anandamoyi.

But that was not enough for Binoy and he contrived to keep the subject going with little touches, bringing out many a detail of his intercourse with Paresh Babu's family. All of these were not of much moment, but Binoy's keen interest and Anandamoyi's ready sympathy, the complete seclusion of the terrace and the deepening shades of the November evening, combined to invest every little point in that domestic history with a wealth of immense meaning.

Anandamoyi suddenly said with a sigh: "How I should love to see Gora marry Sucharita!"

Binoy sat up straight as he said: "Exactly what I've often thought, mother! Sucharita would just suit Gora."

"But can it ever be?" mused Anandamoyi.

"Why not?" exclaimed Binoy. "I'm not at all sure that Gora is not attracted by Sucharita."

Anandamoyi had not failed to notice that Gora was under the influence of some attraction, and had also guessed, from occasional remarks which Binoy had let fall, that the attraction proceeded from none other than Sucharita herself. After a few moments' silence she said: "What I doubt is, whether Sucharita would consent to marry into an orthodox family."

"The question is, rather," said Binoy, "whether Gora would be allowed to marry into a Brahmo family. Have you no such objection?"

"None whatever, I assure you," replied Anandamoyi.

"Haven't you really?" cried Binoy.

"To be sure I haven't, Binu," repeated Anandamoyi. "Why should there be any? Marriage, is a matter of hearts coming together—if that happens, what matters it what *mantras* are recited? It's quite enough if the ceremony be performed in God's name."

Binoy felt a great weight lifted from his mind, and he said enthusiastically: "Mother, it really fills me with wonder to hear you talk like that. However did you come to have such a liberal mind?"

"Why, from Gora of course!" answered Anandamoyi, laughing.

"But what Gora says is exactly the opposite," protested Binoy.

"What does it matter what he says?" said Anandamoyi. "Whatever I have learnt comes from Gora all the same!—how true man is himself, and how false the things about which his quarrels divide man from man. What after all is the difference, my son, between Brahmo and orthodox Hindu? There is no case in men's hearts—there God brings men together and there He Himself comes to them. Will it ever do to keep Him at a distance and leave the duty of uniting men to creeds and forms?"

"Your words are honey to me, mother," said Binoy as he bent to take the dust of her feet. "My day with you has been fruitful indeed!"

THIRTY EIGHT

With the arrival of Sucharita's aunt, Harimohini, the atmosphere in Paresh Babu's house became considerably disturbed. Before describing how this happened it may be well, first, to give a brief account of Harimohini in the words with which she told Sucharita all about herself.

"I was two years older than your mother, and there was no end to the loving care which we both enjoyed in our father's home. The reason of this was, that we were the only two children in the house, and our uncles were so fond of us that we were hardly allowed to put out feet to the ground.

"When I was eight years old I was married into the well-known Palsha family of Roy Chowdhuries, who were as wealthy as they were high-born. But my fate was not meant to be a happy one, for some misunderstanding arose between my father and my father-in-law over my dowry, and my husband's people could not for a long time forgive what they regarded as my father's parsimoniousness. They used to hurl dark threats at me, saying: 'What if our boy married again? We should like to see what their girl's condition will be then!'

"When my father saw my miserable plight he swore that he would never marry another daughter of his into a rich family, and that is how a wealthy match was not sought for your mother.

"In my husband's home the family was a large one, and when I was only nine years of age I had to help in the cooking for sixty or seventy people. I could never have my own meal until everyone had been served, and even then I had only what was left, sometimes nothing but rice, or rice and *dal*. I used to have my first meal as late as two o'clock and on some days not till almost evening, and then the moment I had finished my own food I had to start cooking again for the evening meal, and not till eleven or twelve o'clock in the night did I get a chance to have my supper. There was no specially appointed place for me to sleep in, and I simply slept with anyone who could find a place for me, sometimes without any mattress at all.

"This neglect to which I was deliberately subjected did not fail to have its effect on my husband as well, who for a long time kept me at a distance.

"When I reached my seventeenth year my daughter Monorama was born. My position became still worse because I had given birth to a mere girl. And yet my little girl was a great joy and comfort to me in the midst of all this humiliation. Deprived of all affection, whether from her father or anyone else in the house, Monorama became to me an object of care as dear as life itself.

"After three years I gave birth to a boy and then my condition changed for the better, as I attained at length my due place as mistress of the house. I had never known a mother-in-law, and my husband's father died two years after Monorama's birth. After his death my husband and his younger brothers went to law over the division of the family property, and at length, after much of it had been lost in litigation, the brothers separated.

"When Monorama became old enough to be married I was so afraid lest I should lose sight of her, that I gave her in marriage in a village called Shimula at a distance of about ten miles from Palsha. The bridegroom was an exceptionally good-looking young man, a regular *Kartik*.[1] His features were as handsome as his complexion was fair, and his people too were well-to-do.

"Before my doom finally overtook me, providence gave me a short taste of happiness which, while it lasted, seemed, to make good all the years of neglect and misery I had endured before. Towards the end, I won my husband's love and also his respect, so that he would not undertake anything important without first consulting me. But it was all too good to last. An epidemic of cholera broke out in our neighbourhood and my husband and son died within four days of each other. God must have kept me alive to teach me that sorrow, which it is unbearable even to imagine, can be borne by man.

"Gradually I got to know my son-in-law. Who could have thought that such a venomous snake could lie hidden in the heart of that charming exterior? My daughter had never told me that her husband had got into the habit of drinking through the bad company he kept; and when he used to come and wheedle money out of me on various pretexts I felt rather pleased than otherwise, for I had no one else in the world for whom I needed to save.

"Very soon, however, my daughter began to forbid me to do so, and would caution me, saying: "You are only spoiling him by letting him have money like that. There's no knowing where he wastes it when once he gets hold of it." I thought that Monorama was only afraid of the disgrace he would get into with his own people by taking money from his wife's relations. And as my folly would have it, I took to giving him in secret the money which carried him on the road to ruin. When my daughter got to know this she came to me in tears and disclosed everything. You can imagine how I then beat

---

1 Corresponding to Adonis.

my breast in despair! And to think that it was a younger brother of my husband's whose example and encouragement had been my son-in-law's undoing!

"When I stopped giving him money and he began to suspect that it was my daughter who was at the bottom of it, he gave up all attempts at concealment. He then began to ill-treat Monorama so cruelly, not hesitating even to insult her before outsiders, that once more I had to go on giving him money without her knowledge, knowing full well that I was only helping him on the road to hell. But what could I do? I simply could not bear to have Monorama thus tortured.

"Then came a day—how well I still remember that day! It was towards the end of February. The hot weather had commenced unusually early. We were remarking to each other how the mango trees in the back garden were already laden with blossom. At mid-day a palanquin stopped at our door, out of which stepped Monorama, who, with a smile on her face, came up to me and took the dust of my feet.

" 'Well, Monu,' I exclaimed. 'What's the news?'

"She replied, still smiling: 'Can't I come to see my mother without having any news to give her?'

"My daughter's mother-in-law was not a bad sort of person, and the message she had sent was: 'Monorama is expecting a child and I think it best for her to stay with her mother till her confinement is over.' I naturally thought that this was the true reason,—how was I to guess that my daughter's husband had begun beating her again although she was in this condition, and that her mother-in-law had packed her off in sheer dread of the possible consequences?

"Monorama, as well as her mother-in-law, thus conspired to keep me in the dark. When I wanted to anoint her with oil or help her when taking her bath, she always made some excuse,—she did not want me to see the marks of her husband's blows!

"Several times my son-in-law came round and made a fuss, trying to get his wife to go back with him, for he knew that so long as she stayed with me he would find it difficult to extort money. But even this ceased in time to be an obstacle for him, and he had no qualms in openly pestering me for money, even in Monorama's presence. Monorama herself was firm and forbade me to listen to him, but the fear that his rising wrath against my daughter might overstep all bounds kept me weak.

"At last Monorama said: 'Mother, let me take charge of your cash,' with which she took possession of my box and my keys. When my son-in-law found that there was no longer any chance of getting money from me, and that Monorama's determination could not be broken, he began to press for his wife's return home. I tried to persuade Monorama, saying: 'Let him have what he wants, dear, if only to get rid of him, else who knows to what lengths he may go.'

"But my Monorama was as firm in some things as she was gentle in others, and she would say: 'Never, mother, it simply can't be done.'

"One day her husband came with bloodshot eyes, and said: 'To-morrow afternoon I'll have a palanquin sent, and if you don't let my wife come, it will be the worse for you, I promise you.'

"When the palanquin arrived next day, just before evening, I said to Monorama: 'It's not safe to put it off now, my dear, but I'll send someone over to bring you back again next week.' But Monorama said: 'Let me stay just a while, mother, I can't bring myself to go to-night. Tell them to come again after a few days.' 'My dear,' I said, 'if I send the palanquin back again, shall we be able to control that turbulent husband of yours? No, Monu, you had better go now.' 'No, mother, not to-day,' she pleaded. 'My father-in-law will be returning by the middle of *Phalgun,* I will go then.

"Nevertheless I still insisted that it would not be safe, and at length Monorama went to get ready, while I got busy over preparing some food for the servants and bearers who had come with the palanquin,—so busy that I did not get the chance to put the finishing touches to Monorama's toilet, or make up some little favourite dainty for her, or even to have a few words with her before she left. Just before she stepped into the palanquin, Monorama stooped to touch my feet, and said: 'Mother—good-bye!'

"I did not realise then that it was good-bye for ever! Even to this day my heart is breaking at the thought that she would not go, and I made her. Never in this life will that wound be healed.

"That very night Monorama died of a miscarriage and, even before the news reached me, her body had been hurriedly and secretly cremated.

"What can you understand, my dear, about the agony of a sorrow for which there is nothing to be said or done, and which cannot be washed away, even with life-long weeping? Nor were my troubles at an end with the loss of my all.

"After the death of my husband and my son, my husband's younger brothers cast covetous eyes on my property. They knew that after my death it would all go to them, but they had not the patience to wait. I can hardly blame them, for was it not almost a crime for a wretched woman like myself to remain alive? How can people who have no end of wants be expected to put up with one who has none and yet bars the way to their enjoyment?

"So long as Monorama was living I stood firm for my rights, determined not to be taken in by any persuasion, for I wanted to leave my savings to her. But my brothers-in-law could not bear the idea of my saving money for my daughter, for to them it seemed like stealing it from their pockets. There was an old and trusted servant of my husband's named

Nilkanta, who was my ally. He would not hear of it if, for the sake of peace, I proposed any kind of compromise with them. 'We'll see,' he would say, 'who can deprive us of our just rights.'

"It was in the middle of this fight for my rights that Monorama died, and the very day after her death one of my brothers-in-law came to me and advised me to renounce my possessions and take to the ascetic life. 'Sister,' he said, 'God evidently does not intend you to live a worldly life. For the days that remain to you why not go to some holy place and devote yourself to religious works? We will arrange for your maintenance.'

"I sent for my religious preceptor, and asked him: 'Tell me, Master, how to save myself from this unbearable suffering which has come upon me. I am consumed by an all-encompassing fire, I can see no escape from this anguish whichever way I turn.'

"My *Guru* took me to our temple and, pointing to the image of Krishna, said: 'Here is your husband, your son, your daughter, your all. Serve and worship Him and all your longings will be satisfied and your emptiness will be filled.'

"So I began to spend all my time in the temple and tried to give my whole mind to God. But how was I to give myself unless He took me? Alas, He has not done so yet!

"I called Nilkanta and said to him: 'Nil-dada, I have decided to give away my life-interest in the property to my brothers-in-law, asking only for a small monthly allowance for myself.' But Nilkanta said: 'No, that can never be. You are a woman, don't you worry yourself with these business matters.'

"'But what further need have I of property?' I asked. 'What an idea!' exclaimed Nilkanta. 'To give up our legal rights! Don't you dream of doing such a mad thing.' For Nilkanta there was nothing greater than one's legal rights. But I was in a terrible quandary. I had come to detest worldly concerns like poison, and yet how could I distress old Nilkanta, the only trustworthy friend I had in the world?

"At length one day, without Nilkanta's knowledge, I put my signature to a document. What its meaning was I did not fully understand, but as I had no thought of keeping anything back I had no fear of being cheated. What belonged to my father-in-law, I felt, let his children have.

"When the document had been registered, I called Nilkanta and said: 'Nil-dada, don't be angry with me, please, I have signed away the property. I have no further need of it.' 'What!' cried Nilkanta, aghast. 'What have you gone and done!'

"When he read the draft of the document and saw that I really had given up all my rights, his indignation knew no bounds, for from the time of his master's death his one object in life had been to preserve this property of mine. All his thoughts and efforts had been incessantly engaged in this task. It had been his one recreation to dance attendance at lawyers' offices, and search out legal points and hunt up evidence, so much so, indeed, that he did not find time to attend to his own affairs. When he saw that by a stroke of the pen of a foolish woman the rights for which he had fought had taken flight, it was impossible for him to brook it. 'Well, well,' said he, 'I've done with the affairs of this estate. I'm off!'

"That Nil-dada should go away like this and part from me in anger was to touch the lowest depth of my misfortunes. I called him back and begged him not to go, saying: 'Dada, don't be angry with me. I have some money saved up. Take these five hundred rupees and give them to your boy when he gets married to buy ornaments for his bride, with my blessings.' 'What do I want with more money?' cried Nilkanta. 'With all my master's wealth gone, five hundred rupees will be no consolation to me. Let them be!' and saying this my husband's last real friend left me.

"I took refuge in the temple. My brothers-in-law constantly pestered me, saying: 'Go and live in some holy place,' but I replied: 'My husband's ancestral home is my only holy place. The seat of our family god shall be my place of refuge.' But it seemed to them intolerable that I should encumber any part of that house with my presence. They had already brought in their own furniture and had apportioned the different rooms between themselves. At last they said: 'You may take our family god with you if you like, we shall make no objection.' When I still hesitated, they asked: 'How do you propose to manage about your expenses?'

"To this I answered: 'The allowance which you have fixed for my maintenance will be quite sufficient for me.' But they pretended not to understand: 'What do you mean?' they said. 'There was no word of any allowance.'

"Then it was that, just thirty-four years after my marriage, I left my husband's home one day, taking my god with me. When I sought Nil-dada, I found that he had already retired to Brindaban.

"I joined a party of pilgrims going from our village to Benaras, but for my sins I could get no peace even there. Every day I called upon my god, and said: 'O God, make Thyself as real to me as were my husband and children.' But He did not listen to my prayer. My heart is not yet comforted, and my whole mind and body are flooded with tears. Oh my God, how cruel and hard is man's life!

"I had not been to my father's home for a single day since the time I had been taken to my husband's house at the age of eight. I had tried my best to be allowed to go for your mother's wedding, but in vain. Then I heard the news of your birth, and after that of my sister's death, but up to the present time God did not give me the opportunity of taking you, my children, who have lost your own mother, into my arms.

"When I found that even after wandering about to many places of pilgrimage my mind was still full of attachment, and thirsted for some object of affection, I began to make inquiries as to your whereabouts. I heard that your father had given up orthodox religion and society, but what difference could that make to me? Was not your mother my own sister?

"At last I discovered where you were living, and came along here with a friend, from Benaras. I have heard that Paresh Babu does not honour our gods, but you have only to look on his face to know that the gods honour him. It takes more than mere offerings to please God—that I know well enough—and I must find out how Paresh Babu has managed to win Him over so completely.

"However that may be, my child, the time for me to retire from the world has not yet come. I am not ready to live all alone by myself. When it is His gracious will, I shall be able to do so, but in the meantime I feel I cannot bear the idea of living away from you, my new-found children."

THIRTY NINE

Paresh Babu had taken Harimohini into his house while Mistress Baroda was away from home, and had made all arrangements for her to occupy the lonely room at the top of the house, where she could live in her own way and so have no difficulty with her caste observances.

But when Baroda returned home and found her housekeeping complicated by this unexpected arrival, she felt angry all over, and made it known to Paresh Babu, in pretty plain terms, that this was too much to expect of her.

"You can bear the burden of the whole family of us," said Paresh Babu, "surely you can also bear with this unfortunate widow as well?"

Mistress Baroda regarded Paresh Babu as being devoid of all practical commonsense and knowledge of the world. Having no idea of what would be convenient in domestic matters, she was sure that any step he took of himself would be certain to be the wrong one. But she also knew that, when he did decide upon taking any step, you might argue with him, or get angry with him, or even dissolve into tears, he would be as immovable as an image of stone. What could be done with such a man? What woman could get on with one with whom it was impossible even to quarrel when need arose! She felt she would have to admit defeat.

Sucharita was of about the same age as Monorama, and to Harimohini she seemed much the same in appearance. Even their natures were similar, tranquil yet firm. Now and then, when she saw Sucharita suddenly from behind, Harimohini's heart gave a jump.

One evening when Harimohini was sitting alone in the dark, weeping silently, and Sucharita came to her, Harimohini strained her niece to her bosom, murmuring with closed eyes: "She has come back, come back to my heart! She would not go, but I sent her away. Could I ever be punished enough for that in this life? But perhaps I have suffered enough, so now she comes back to me! Here she is, with the same smile on her face. Oh, my little mother, my treasure, my jewel!" and then she fell to stroking Sucharita's face and kissing her, deluging her with tears.

Whereupon Sucharita also began to sob, and said in a choking voice: "Auntie, neither did I enjoy a mother's love for long, but now that lost mother of mine, too, has come back. How often, when I had not the strength to call upon God in my sorrow, when my whole soul seemed to be shrivelled up, I have called upon my mother. To-day mother has heard my call and come to me!"

But Harimohini said: "Don't talk so, my child, don't talk so. When I hear you say that, I feel so happy that I am afraid! O God, don't rob me of this too. I have tried to get rid of all attachment—to make my heart like stone, but I cannot— I am so weak! Have pity on me, do not strike me again, my God! O Radharani! my dear, go away from me and leave me! Do not cling to me so. O Lord of my life, my Krishna, my Gopal, what calamity are you preparing for me again!"

"Auntie," said Sucharita, "you will never be able to send me away, say what you like; I am not going to leave you,— never,—I will stay beside you always," and she snuggled up against her aunt's breast and lay there like a child.

Within these few days so deep a feeling of kinship had sprung up between Sucharita and her aunt that time could be no measure of it. This seemed to add to Mistress Baroda's vexation. "Just look at the girl!" she exclaimed. "As if she has never received any care or affection from us! Where was her aunt all these years, I should like to know! We take all the trouble to bring her up from a child and now it's nothing but Auntie, Auntie! Haven't I always said to my husband that this Sucharita, whom they are all never tired of praising up to the skies, looks as if butter would not melt in her mouth, but there's no melting her heart, either. All that we have done has been thrown away on her."

Baroda knew well enough that she would not get Paresh Babu's sympathy in her grievance, and not only that, but if she showed her annoyance with Harimohini she would lose the place she had in his respect. This made her all the angrier and determined more than ever, whatever her husband might think, to prove that all understanding people were on her side. So she began to discuss the affair of Harimohini with every member of the Brahmo Samaj, important and unimportant, so as to win them over to her view. There was no end to her complaints as to how bad for the children it was to have the example of this superstitious, ill-fated, idol-worshipping woman always before them in the house.

Mistress Baroda's suppressed vexation not only found expression outside the house, it resulted, inside, in making Harimohini thoroughly uncomfortable. The high-caste servant, who had been told off to draw water for Harimohini's cooking, would be put on to some other work just when his services were required. If the matter was ever mentioned, Baroda would say: "Why, what's the trouble? Isn't Ramdin there?" knowing very well that Harimohini could not use the water handled by the low-caste Ramdin. If anyone pointed this out to her, she would say; "If she's so high caste as all that, what makes her come to a Brahmo home? We can't have all these silly distinctions here, and I for one am not going to allow it."

On such occasions her sense of duty became almost fierce. She would say: "The Brahmo Samaj is getting quite lax over social matters—that's why it's doing much less for social uplift than it used to do." And would go on to make it clear that she, for her part, would lend no countenance to such laxity—no, none whatever, so long as she had any strength left in her! If she was to be misunderstood, that couldn't be helped; if her own relations were against her, she was prepared to submit to it! And in conclusion, she did not neglect to remind her hearers that all the saints of the world who had done anything great, had to endure opposition and insult.

But no amount of inconvenience seemed to tell on Harimohini,—it appeared, rather, that she gloried in thus being able to rise to the full height of her penance. The hardships due to her self-imposed asceticism seemed to be more in tune with the permanent torture which raged within her. Her's seemed to be the cult of welcoming sorrow and making it one's own, so as to win the more real victory over it.

When Harimohini found that the water-supply for her cooking was causing trouble in the family, she gave up cooking altogether, and subsisted only on fruit and milk which she had first offered before her god. Sucharita was grievously exercised over this. Whereupon her aunt, in order to soothe her, said: "But this is very good for me, my dear. It is a necessary discipline, and gives me joy, not pain."

"Auntie," was Sucharita's reply, "if I stop taking water or food from the hands of lower-caste people, will you allow me to wait on you?"

"You, my dear," said Harimohini, "should do as you have been taught to believe—you must not follow a different path for my sake. I have you near me, in my very arms, that is happiness enough for me. Paresh Babu has been like a father, like a *guru* to you; you should honour his teaching; God will bless you for it."

Harimohini herself put up with all the petty annoyances inflicted on her by Mistress Baroda so simply that she did not seem to be even aware of them, and when Paresh Babu came to see her every morning with the question: "Well, and how are you to-day? You are not feeling at all inconvenienced, I hope?" she would answer: "No, thank you, I'm getting along very happily."

But these annoyances tormented Sucharita without respite. She was not the sort of girl to complain. More especially was she careful not to let anything against Baroda escape her in Paresh Babu's hearing. But though she bore it all in silence, without the least sign of resentment, it had the result of drawing her nearer and nearer to her aunt, and eventually, in spite of Harimohini's protests, she gradually took upon herself to attend to all her aunt's wants.

At last, when Harimohini saw what trouble she was giving Sucharita, she decided to take to cooking her own food again. Whereupon Sucharita said: "Auntie, I will regulate my conduct exactly as you want me to, but you positively must allow me to draw the water for you. I'll take no denial."

"My dear," said Harimohini, "you must not be offended, but that water has to be offered to my God."

"Auntie!" protested Sucharita. "Is your God in orthodox society that he should observe caste? Can pollution affect him too?"

At length Harimohini had to acknowledge herself vanquished by Sucharita's devotion, and she accepted her niece's services without reserve. Satish too, in imitation of his sister, began to be seized with the desire to share his Auntie's food, and finally it reached such a pass that these three combined to form a separate little family in one corner of

Paresh Babu's home. Lolita was the only bridge between the two divisions, for Mistress Baroda saw to it that none of her other daughters should approach Harimohini's little corner,— she would have prevented Lolita also, if she had dared.

FORTY

M istress Baroda often invited her Brahmo lady friends
to the house, and sometimes they would all congregate
on the terrace in front of Harimohini's room. On such occasions
Harimohini, in the simplicity of her nature, would try to help
in making them welcome, but they on their side hardly disguised
their contempt. They would even look pointedly at her, while
Baroda was making pungent comments on orthodox manners
and customs, in which some of them would join.

Sucharita, who was always with her aunt, had to put up
with these attacks in silence. All she could do was to show
by her actions that they touched her too, because she followed
her aunt's ways. When refreshments were served, Sucharita
would decline to have anything, saying: "I don't take these
things, thanks."

At which Mistress Baroda would burst out with: "What!
D'you mean to say you cannot eat with us?"

And when Sucharita repeated that she would rather not,
Baroda would wax sarcastic, saying to her friends: "D'you
know, our young lady is getting to be mighty high caste. Our
touch is contamination for her!"

"What! Sucharita turned orthodox! Wonders will never
cease!" the visitors would remark.

Harimohini would get worried and say: "No, Radharani,
this will never do, dear; do go and have something with

them!" That her niece should have to endure these sarcasms for her sake was too much for her aunt, but Sucharita remained firm.

One day one of the Brahmo visitors, just out of curiosity, was about to step into Harimohini's room with her shoes on, when Sucharita blocked the way, saying: "Not into this room, please!"

"Why, what's the matter?"

"My aunt's family God is kept there."

"Ah, an idol! And so she worships idols?"

"Yes, mother, of course I do," replied Harimohini.

"How can you have faith in idols?"

"Faith! Where is a miserable creature like me to get faith? Had I but faith, it would have saved me."

Lolita happened to be there on this occasion, and her face was scarlet as she turned on the questioner and asked her: "Have you then faith in Him you worship?"

"What nonsense! How could it be otherwise?" was the answer.

Lolita shook her head scornfully as she said: "You not only have no faith, but what is more, you don't even know that you haven't.

Thus was Sucharita's alienation from her people complete, in spite of all that Harimohini could do to keep her from doing things which Baroda would specially resent.

Baroda and Haran had in the past never been able to pull on well together, but now they came to a mutual understanding against the rest. Whereupon Mistress Baroda was pleased to remark that no matter what people might say, if there was one man who was trying to keep pure the ideals of the Brahmo Samaj it was Panu Babu. While Haran made out to all and sundry that Mistress Baroda was a shining example of a Brahmo housewife who, with devoted conscientiousness, was trying in every way to preserve the fair name of Brahmo

Society from all stain. In this praise of his there was, of course, a veiled insinuation against Paresh Babu.

One day Haran said to Sucharita in the presence of Paresh Babu: "I have heard that nowadays you take only sanctified food offered to idols. Is that true?"

Sucharita's face flushed, but she tried to look as though she had not heard the remark, and began to shift about the pens and inkstand on the table, while Paresh Babu, with sympathetic glance towards her, said to Haran: "Panu Babu, whatever we eat is food sanctified by God's grace."

"But Sucharita is ready to give up our God, it seems," said Haran.

"Even if that were possible, is it any remedy to worry her about it?" asked Paresh Babu.

"When we see a person being carried off by the current, are we not to try and draw him back to the bank?" replied Haran.

"Pelting him with clods is not the same as drawing him to the bank," said Paresh Babu. "But, Panu Babu, you need not be alarmed. I have known Sucharita ever since she was a tiny little thing, and if she had fallen into the water I should have known it before any of you, and would not have remained indifferent about it either."

"Sucharita is here to answer for herself," said Haran. "I am told she has taken to refusing to eat with everybody. Ask her whether that is true."

Sucharita, relaxing the unnecessarily close attention which she had been giving to the inkstand, said: "It is known to father that I have given up eating food touched by all kinds of people, and if he can tolerate it, that is enough for me. If it be displeasing to any of you, you are at liberty to call me what names you like, but why trouble father about it? Do you not know what immense forbearance he has for each one of us? Is this the way you requite him?"

Haran was taken aback at this plain speaking. "Even Sucharita has learnt to speak up for herself!" thought he, wonderingly.

Paresh Babu was a man who loved peace, and he did not like much discussion either about himself or about others. He had lived his life quietly, not seeking any position of importance in the Brahmo Samaj. Haran had put this down to Paresh Babu's lack of enthusiasm for the cause and had even taxed him with it, but in explanation Paresh Babu had only said: "God has created two classes of bodies, mobile and inert. I belong to the latter. God will make use of men like myself for accomplishing such work as we are fit for. Nothing is to be gained by becoming restless to achieve something which one is not capable of. I am getting old, and what I have the power to do, and what not, has been settled long ago. You can do no good by trying to hustle me on."

Haran plumed himself on being able to infuse enthusiasm even in an unresponsive heart. His belief was that he had an irresistible power of stimulating the inert into activity, of melting into repentance the fallen,—that no one for long could stand in the way of his forceful single-mindedness. He had come to the conclusion that all the changes for the better which had taken place in the individual members of the Samaj were mainly to be ascribed to him.

He had not a doubt that it was his influence which was at work all the time behind the scenes, and when anyone specially praised Sucharita in his presence, he beamed with a sense of self-satisfaction. He felt that he was shaping Sucharita's character by his advice, example, and companionship, and had begun to hope that her life itself would be one of the most glorious achievements standing to his credit. His pride suffered no check, even now, by this deplorable backsliding of Sucharita's, for he put all the blame for it on Paresh Babu's shoulders.

Haran had never been able to join whole-heartedly in the chorus of praise of Paresh Babu which was on everyone's lips, and he now thought he had reason to congratulate himself that they would soon find how well justified his more intelligent silence had been.

Haran could forgive almost anything, except the following of an independent path, according to their own judgment, by those whom he had tried to guide aright. It was wellnigh impossible for him to let his victims escape without making a struggle, and the more clear it became that his advice was having no effect, the more insistent did he become. Like a wound-up machine not yet run down, he could not check himself, and would go on dinning the same thing over and over again into unwilling ears, not knowing when he was defeated.

This peculiarity of his used to trouble Sucharita very much, not on her own account, but for Paresh Babu. Paresh Babu had become an object of discussion to the whole Brahmo Samaj,—what could be done to counteract that?

Then, again, there was Harimohini, who was coming to realise, as the days passed by, that the more she tried to keep herself in the background, the more did she become a cause of disturbance in the family circle; and the humiliations to which she was subjected distressed Sucharita more and more everyday. She could discover no way out of these difficulties.

On the top of this there was Mistress Baroda, who had begun to press Paresh Babu to hasten forward Sucharita's marriage. "We can't be responsible for Sucharita any longer," she insisted, "now that she has begun to follow her own sweet will. If her wedding is delayed much longer I shall have to take the other girls elsewhere, for Sucharita's preposterous example is most pernicious for them. You will have to repent for your indulgence towards her, I warn you. Look at Lolita. She was never like this before. Who d'you think is at the root of her perverse behaviour,—listening to nobody and making herself an all-round nuisance? That affair the other day, which nearly made me die of shame,—do you imagine that Sucharita had no hand in it? I have never complained before, because you love Sucharita more than your own daughters, but let me tell you plainly, now, that it can't go on much longer."

Paresh Babu was greatly worried, not at Sucharita's ways, but because of this disturbance in the family. He had not a doubt that, when once Mistress Baroda had made up her mind, she would leave no stone unturned to gain her object, and if she saw that her efforts seemed fruitless she would simply redouble them. He felt that if Sucharita's marriage could possibly be expedited, it would also make for her own peace of mind in the present circumstances, so he said to Baroda: "If Panu Babu can get Sucharita to fix the day, I have no objection at all."

"How many more times has her consent to be asked, I should like to know," cried Mistress Baroda. "You positively astound me! Why all this waiting on her pleasure? Will you tell me where she can get another such husband? You may get angry or not, as you please, but if the truth is to be told, Sucharita is not worthy of Panu Babu!"

"I have not been able to understand clearly," said Paresh Babu, "how Sucharita really feels towards Panu Babu. So until they come to some settlement between themselves, I would rather not interfere."

"Ah, so you do *not* understand!" exclaimed Baroda. "At last you admit it? That girl is not so easy to understand, I tell you. You may take it from me, she's very different inwardly from what she makes herself out to be!"

FORTY ONE

There had been an article in the newspaper on the falling off in the zeal of the Brahmo Samaj. In it there were such clear references to Paresh Babu's family that, although no names were mentioned, everyone could see plainly who were meant, nor was it hard to guess from the style who the writer was. Sucharita had managed, somehow, to read on to the end of the article, and was now engaged in tearing the paper to pieces,—it seemed from the way she had set about it that nothing short of reducing it into its original atoms would appease her!

It was at this moment that Haran entered the room, and drew his chair up beside her. But Sucharita did not even so much as lift her eyes to look at him—so absorbed was she in her task.

"Sucharita," said Haran, "I have a very important matter to discuss with you to-day, so you must give me your attention."

Sucharita went on tearing up the paper and, when it was no longer possible to tear the pieces with her fingers, she took out her scissors and began to cut them into still smaller fragments. Before she had finished, Lolita came into the room.

"Lolita," said Haran, "I have something to talk over with Sucharita."

But when Lolita turned to go, Sucharita caught hold of her dress and detained her, whereupon Lolita protested: "But

Panu Babu has something particular to say to you!" Sucharita, however, took no notice of this remark, and made Lolita come and sit down beside her.

As for Haran, he was constitutionally incapable of taking a hint. So he plunged into his subject without any further ado. He said: 'I do not think that our wedding ought to be delayed any longer. I have had a talk with Paresh Babu, and he says that as soon as you give your consent the day can be fixed. So I have decided that next Sunday week—" But Sucharita, without giving him time to finish his sentence, simply said: "No."

Haran was taken aback by this very concise and determined negative. He had always known Sucharita as a paragon of obedience, and had never even imagined that she could check his proposal before it had been half expressed with just this one word.

"No!"—he repeated irately. "What do you mean by 'no'?— do you want a later day to be fixed?"

"No," simply repeated Sucharita.

"Then what on earth *do* you mean?" gasped Haran, quite disconcerted.

"I do not consent to the marriage," replied Sucharita, with head bent low.

"You don't consent! Whatever can you mean?" repeated Haran, like one stupefied.

"It seems, Panu Babu," interposed Lolita sarcastically, "that you have forgotten your mother-tongue!"

Haran looked crushingly at Lolita as he said: "It is easier to confess that I no longer understand my mother-tongue than to have to admit that I have all along misunderstood the oft-repeated words of one for whom I never entertained anything but respect!"

"It takes time to understand people," observed Lolita, "and perhaps that applies to you also."

"From first to last,"said Haran, "there has been no discrepancy between my deeds and words. I can positively declare that I have never given any one cause to misunderstand me. Let Sucharita herself say whether I am right or wrong!"

Lolita was about to make some rejoinder when Sucharita stopped her and said: "What you say is quite true! I don't wish to blame you for a moment."

"If you don't blame me," exclaimed Haran, "then why treat me in this disgraceful manner?"

"You have the right to call it disgraceful," replied Sucharita firmly, "but this disgrace I must accept, for I cannot—"

A voice was heard outside: "Didi, may I come in?"

With an expression of immense relief Sucharita called out at once: "Oh, it's you, Binoy Babu, is it? Come in, do."

"You have made a mistake, Didi, it's not Binoy Babu, but only Binoy. You must not overwhelm me with all this formality!" said Binoy as he entered the room. Then, as he caught sight of Haran and noted the expression on his face, he added jocosely: "Ah, you are annoyed with me, I see, because I have not been coming for so many days!"

Haran made an attempt to enter into the joke. "A good reason for being angry too," he began concluding however with: "But I am afraid you have come just now at rather an inopportune moment. I was discussing an important matter with Sucharita."

"Just my luck!" said Binoy as he got up hurriedly. "One never knows what is the propitious time to come; that's why one hardly dares come at all."

He was about to leave the room, when Sucharita interposed: "Don't you go, Binoy Babu. We have finished our talk. Sit down."

Binoy could divine that his arrival had been the means of rescuing Sucharita from some awkward situation, so he sat down cheerfully, saying: "I never refuse a kindness. If I'm offered a seat, I promptly accept it. That's my nature. Therefore, Didi, beware! Never say what you don't mean, or you'll rue the consequence!"

Haran was reduced to speechlessness, but his demeanour betokened a rising determination, warning all beholders that he was not the man to leave the room till he had had his say to the last word.

As soon as Lolita had heard Binoy's voice from outside the door, her blood was sent coursing through her body, making unsuccessful all her efforts to keep natural. Consequently, when Binoy entered the room, she found it impossible to address him like an ordinary friend, all her attention being taken up in deciding which way she should look and what she should do with her hands. She would have left the room, but Sucharita still had hold of her dress.

Binoy for his part also directed his conversation ostensibly towards Sucharita, not daring, for all his ready wit, to address Lolita directly. He tried to hide his embarrassment by talking volubly, without a pause.

But all the same this new shyness between Lolita and Binoy did not pass unobserved by Haran. He was chagrined to see that Lolita, who had been recently adopting such an impudent attitude towards himself, should be so subdued before Binoy. His anger against Paresh Babu increased at this evidence of the evils which he had brought on the family by introducing his daughters to people outside the Brahmo Samaj. And the feeling that Paresh Babu should live to repent of his folly came upon him with all the force of a curse.

When it became evident that Haran had no intention of moving, Sucharita said to Binoy: "You haven't seen Auntie for a long time. She often inquires about you. Wouldn't you like to come up and see her?"

"Don't you be thinking," protested Binoy as he got up to follow Sucharita, "that I required your words to remind me of Auntie. She was in my thoughts already."

When Sucharita had left with Binoy, Lolita also rose and said: "I don't suppose, Panu Babu, that you have anything special to say to me?"

"No," replied Haran. "As I presume you are wanted elsewhere, I give you leave to go."

Lolita understood his insinuation, and drawing herself up, to show that she did not shrink from the point of his remark, she said: "It is so long since Binoy Babu has called that I really must go and have a chat with him. Meanwhile, if you want to read your own writings—but I forget, my sister has just torn your paper into little pieces. However, if you can bear to read anything written by another, you may look through these." With which she took from a table in the corner some articles of Gora's which had been carefully put away there and, placing them before Haran, went upstairs.

Harimohini was delighted at Binoy's visit. It was not simply because she had conceived an affection for this youth, but because he was so different from the other visitors, who made no secret of regarding her as belonging to some different species. These were all Calcutta people, superior to her in their English and Bengali culture, and their stand-offishness was gradually making her shrink within herself.

In Binoy, Harimohini felt a sense of support. He also was a Calcutta man, and she had heard that his learning was not to be scoffed at, and yet he had never shown the least sign of disrespect for her, but rather a loving regard. It was especially for this reason that in this short time Binoy had found a place in her heart, like a near relation.

Lolita would never have found it easy to follow so closely after Binoy into Harimohini's room, but for the blow to her pride which Haran's sneer had dealt. This not only forced her to go, but also, when she arrived there, it took away from her all hesitation in talking freely to Binoy. In fact some snatches of their laugher floated downstairs, reaching the ears and getting on the nerves of the deserted Haran, sitting there all by himself.

Haran soon got tired of his own company and thought of assuaging the pain of the wounds he had received by a talk with Mistress Baroda. When he had sought her out and she learned that Sucharita had expressed her unwillingness to marry Haran, her indignation knew no bounds.

"Panu Babu," she admonished him, "it won't do for you to be too good-natured in this matter. She has given her consent, time and again, and in fact the whole Brahmo Samaj has taken it as settled long ago. It will never do for you to allow everything to be turned topsy-turvy simply because to-day she shakes her head. You must not give up your claim so easily. Be firm, and we shall see what she can do!"

It was indeed superfluous to incite Haran to firmness. All the time he had been stiffly saying to himself: "I must see this thing through for the sake of principle. For me it may not be a great matter to give up Sucharita, but the dignity of the Brahmo Samaj is at stake!"

Binoy, in order to get rid of all formality in his relationship with Harimohini, had asked her to give him something to eat, whereupon Harimohini, fluttered at the request, bustled about, and, arranging some fruit, sweetmeats and roasted grain on a brass salver, placed it before Binoy together with a glass of milk.

Binoy laughed as he said: "I thought I would be able to put Auntie in a fix by saying I was hungry at such an unusual time, but I see I have to own defeat!"

With this he was preparing to fall to with a great show of appetite when, all of a sudden, Mistress Baroda made her appearance.

Binoy bent as low as he could over his plate at her entry, saying: "How is it I didn't see you downstairs? I've been there for some time."

But Baroda took no notice of his remark or greeting, and looking towards Sucharita, exclaimed: "So our young lady is here, is she? I guessed as much! She's having her fling, while poor Panu Babu has been waiting for her all the morning as if he were a supplicant for favour! I've brought up all these girls from childhood, and never had such a thing happened before. Who's been putting her up to all this, I wonder? To think of these doings going on in our family! How are we to show our faces in the Brahmo Samaj any more?"

Harimohini felt greatly perturbed at this and said to Sucharita: "I didn't know that any one was waiting for you downstairs. How wrong of me to detain you! Go, my dear, go at once! I should have known better."

Lolita was on the point of breaking out with a protest that it could not possibly be Harimohini's fault, but Sucharita with a firm pressure of her hand made her a sign to keep quiet, and without making any reply went away downstairs.

We have told how Binoy had at first won his way into Baroda's good graces. She felt quite sure that through the influence of their family he would before long become a member of the Brahmo Samaj, and she felt a special pride in the thought that she would thus be the making of this young man. In fact she had on several occasions boasted of her exploit to some of her Brahmo friends. It made her all the more bitter to find this same Binoy established in the camp of the enemy, with her own daughter, Lolita, as his ally in rebellion.

"Lolita, have you any special business here?" she asked cuttingly.

"Yes, Binoy Babu came up, so—"

"Leave Binoy Babu to be entertained by those he came to visit. You are wanted downstairs!"

Lolita at once jumped to the conclusion that Haran had been coupling her name with Binoy's in a way he had no right to do. This stiffened her attitude, and what she had haltingly begun, she finished with an uncalled-for effusiveness: "Binoy Babu has called after a long time. I want to have a good talk with him first, and then I'll come down."

Mistress Baroda understood from her tone that Lolita refused to be intimidated and, fearing to have to confess defeat in Harimohini's presence, she said nothing more, leaving the room without taking any notice of Binoy.

Of Lolita's eagerness for a chat with Binoy, which she had just expressed to her mother, not a trace was to be found after Baroda left. For a little time the three of them sat in awkward silence, and then Lolita rose and, going to her own room, shut herself in.

Binoy clearly realised what Harimohini's position in that household was, and directing the conversation to that end he gradually heard all her past history.

When she had finished telling him everything, Harimohini said: "My child, the world is not the proper place for an unfortunate woman like me. It would have been better for me if I had been able to go to some sacred place and had tried to serve God there. I had a small sum of money left, and could have lived on it for some time, and even if I had lived still longer I could have managed to get along somehow by cooking in some family. Plenty of people live in Benaras like that!

"But my mind is so sinful, I could not bring myself to do it. Whenever I am alone, all my sorrows seem to press on me and prevent me even from thinking about God. Sometimes I feel I shall go mad. Radharani and Satish have been to me what a raft is to a drowning man,—the very thought of having to leave them again almost chokes me. Therefore it is that, day and night, I am haunted by the fear that I shall have to give them up too—otherwise, after losing my all, why should I again have come to love them so much in such a short time?

"I don't mind speaking out my heart to you, my son, so I tell you, ever since I have got these two, I seem to be able to worship God with my whole heart—and if I lose them, my God will become nothing but hard stone."

With these words she wiped the tears from her eyes.

FORTY TWO

Sucharita went downstairs and standing in front of Haran said: "What is it you are waiting to tell me?"

"Sit down," said Haran.

But Sucharita remained as she was.

"Sucharita, you have done me a wrong," went on Haran.

"You too have done wrong to me," said Sucharita.

"The word I plighted is still as good—" Haran was about to continue when Sucharita interrupted him.

"Do people wrong each other only with words? Would you force me to act against my inclination because of a word? Is not the truth greater than any number of false words? Merely because I have repeated the same mistake many times, is the mistake to prevail? Now that I have realised where it was wrong I cannot abide by my former consent,—to do that would be truly wrong."

Haran was at a loss to understand how such a change could have come over Sucharita. He had neither the penetration nor the modesty to guess that it was due to his inconsiderate persistence that she had been compelled to break through her natural reserve and quietness. So, mentally putting all the blame on her new companions, he asked: "What is this mistake you say you have discovered?"

"Why ask me that?" said Sucharita. "Is it not enough that I tell you I have withdrawn my consent?"

"But surely we are called upon to offer some explanation to the Brahmo Samaj," urged Haran. "What will you say, and what shall I say, to our members?"

"As for myself," said Sucharita, "I will say nothing. If you must say something, then you can tell them that Sucharita is too young, or too foolish, or too changeable. Say just what you like. But as between us, there is nothing more to be said."

"It cannot end like this," cried Haran. "If Paresh Babu—'

At this moment Paresh Babu himself came in. "Well, Panu Babu," he inquired, "were you wanting to say anything to me?"

Sucharita was passing out of the room, but Haran called her back and said: "No, Sucharita, you must not go now. Let us discuss the matter in the presence of Paresh Babu."

Sucharita turned and stood where she was, while Haran said: "Paresh Babu, after all this time Sucharita now says that she does not consent to our marriage. Was it right for her to play like this with a matter of such vital importance? Won't you, too, have to take some of the responsibility for this ugly business?"

Paresh Babu stroked Sucharita's hair as he said gently: "My dear, there is no need for you to stay on, you may go."

At these simple words of sympathetic understanding, the tears came rushing into Sucharita's eyes and she hurried away from the room.

Paresh Babu then continued: "It is because I feared that Sucharita had given her consent without fully understanding her own mind that I was hesitating to grant your request about the formal betrothal."

"Does it not occur to you," replied Haran, "that perhaps she understood her own mind right enough when she gave her consent, but that it is her refusal which is due to her not understanding her own mind?"

"Both suppositions are possible," admitted Paresh Babu. "But in such a state of doubt surely no marriage can take place."

"Will you not advise Sucharita in her own interest?"

"You should know that I could not advise Sucharita otherwise than in her own interest."

"If that had really been the case," broke out Haran, "then Sucharita could never have come to this pass. All that is happening in your family nowadays, I tell you to your face, is due simply to your lack of judgment."

Paresh Babu laughed slightly as he replied: "You are quite right there,—if I do not take the responsibility for what happens in my own family, who else is to do so?"

"Well, I can assure you that you will have to repent some day," concluded Haran.

"Repentance is a gift of God's grace. I fear to do wrong, Panu Babu, but not to repent," replied Paresh Babu.

At this point Sucharita came back and taking Paresh Babu by the hand said: "Father, it is time for your worship."

"Panu Babu, will you wait a little?" asked Paresh Babu.

With an abrupt "No" Haran at length departed.

FORTY THREE

Sucharita was dismayed at the struggle which it now seemed she was in for, both with her own self as well as with her surroundings. Her feelings towards Gora had all this time, unknown to herself, been growing in strength, and when after his arrest they had become so clear—almost irresistible—she had no idea how it would end. She felt unable to take anybody into her confidence about it, she even shrank from facing it herself.

She did not get any opportunity for the solitude in which she might have tried to end the conflict within her by some kind of compromise, for Haran had contrived to bring the angry members of their Samaj buzzing all round her. There were even signs that he would sound the tocsin in the newspapers.

Over and above this there was the problem of her aunt, which had reached such a point that unless a solution could be found very quickly, disaster was inevitable. Sucharita realised that life had come to a crisis, and that the day for following her accustomed path and for thinking in the old habitual channel was past.

Her one and only support in this time of difficulty was Paresh Babu. Not that she asked advice or counsel from him, for there was much in her thoughts about which she felt a delicacy, and something also which seemed too shameful to mention before him. It was simply his life and his companionship which seemed silently to draw her into the refuge of the fostering care of a father and the loving devotion of a mother.

In these autumn evenings Paresh Babu did not go into the garden for his worship, but used to sit in prayer in a little room on the western side of the house. Through the open door the rays of the setting sun fell on his white hair and tranquil face, and at such times Sucharita would quietly step in and sit beside him. She felt as if her own restless and tortured heart could be quieted in the still depths of Paresh Babu's meditation. So when he opened his eyes Paresh Babu would generally find this daughter of his seated beside him— a still and silent disciple—and the ineffable sweetness in which she seemed steeped would make his blessing silently flow out to her from the very depths of his heart.

Because of the union with the Supreme which Paresh Babu's life consistently sought, his mind was always turned towards what was best and truest; worldly concerns had never been able to become predominant for him. The freedom which he had himself gained in this way made it impossible for him to seek to coerce others in regard to belief or conduct. He had such a natural reliance upon goodness and such patience with the ways of the world that he often drew on himself the censure of sectarian enthusiasts. But though such censure might wound him, it never disturbed his equanimity. He often repeated to himself the thought: "I will take nothing from others' hands, but will accept all from Him."

It was to get a touch of this deep tranquillity of Paresh Babu's that Sucharita nowadays used to keep going to him on various pretexts. When the conflict in her heart and the conflict all around her bid fair utterly to distract this inexperienced girl, she would feel that her mind could be filled with peace only if she could lay her head for a while at her father's feet.

She had hoped that if she could but gain the strength to bide her time in patience, the opposing forces would exhaust themselves and own defeat. But that was not fated to be, and she had been forced to venture out into unfamiliar paths.

When Mistress Baroda found that it was not possible to move Sucharita from her course by her reproaches, and that there was no hope of getting Paresh Babu on her side, all her rage was turned with redoubled force upon Harimohini. The very thought of the presence in her house of this woman made her feel beside herself.

On the day of annual celebration in memory of her father, Baroda had invited Binoy to be present. The family and friends were to meet for the service in the evening, and she was busy decorating the room for the ceremony, with the help of Sucharita and her daughters.

While thus engaged, Baroda happened to notice Binoy going upstairs to see Harimohini, and as the veriest trifle assumes importance when the mind is worried, this sight became in a moment so unbearable to her that she could not go on with what she was doing and felt impelled to follow Binoy to Harimohini's room, where she found Binoy already seated on the mat, chatting familiarly with Harimohini.

"Look here," burst out Baroda, "I don't mind your staying in this house as long as you like, and we'll look after you too, with pleasure, but let me tell you, once for all, that we can't have you keeping your idol here."

Harimohini had spent all her days in a village, and her idea of the Brahmos was that they were merely a sect of Christians. How far one could safely associate with them had been the only problem of which she was aware in their connection. That they also might not care to associate with her was a view which had now gradually been borne in on her and had lately set her thinking what ought to be done in the circumstances.

Mistress Baroda's plain speech made it clear that it would not do to go on thinking much longer, but that a decision had become immediately necessary. At first she thought of moving to some other lodgings in Calcutta, so that she could still occasionally see her Sucharita and her Satish; but then, she pondered, would her slender resources be enough to meet the cost of living in Calcutta?

When, like a sudden storm, Mistress Baroda had come and gone, Binoy sat still a while with bowed head.

Then Harimohini broke the silence saying: "I am thinking of going on a pilgrimage. Could any of you accompany me on the journey, my son?"

"I should be only too glad to take you along," replied Binoy. "But it will be some days before we can get ready to start, so in the meantime will you not come and stay with my mother?"

"You little know, child," said Harimohini, "what a burden I am. God has placed such a heavy load on my shoulders that no one can bear me. When I saw that the burden of my presence had become unbearable even in my own husband's home, I ought to have understood! But this understanding comes with such difficulty to me. I have been wandering about all this time trying to fill the emptiness in my heart and, wherever I have been, I have carried my misfortunes with me. No more of it, my son, let me be. Why invade again somebody else's house? Let me at last take shelter at the feet of Him who bears the burden of the whole world. I cannot struggle any more," and as she spoke, Harimohini wiped her eyes again and again.

"No, no, Auntie," said Binoy, "I cannot allow you to say that. You cannot possibly compare my mother with anyone else at all! One who has been able to dedicate all the burdens of life to God never feels it too much to carry another's sorrow. Such a one is my mother, and such also is Paresh Babu here. No, I won't hear of it. Let me first take you to my own place of pilgrimage, and then I will accompany you to yours."

"But," said Harimohini, 'surely we must inform them that we—"

"Our arrival will be information enough," interrupted Binoy, "in fact the best of information!"

"Then, to-morrow morning—" began Harimohini, but Binoy interrupted her again: "Why to-morrow—better to-night!"

Sucharita now came to call Binoy saying: "Mother sent me to tell you that it is time for the service."

"I am afraid I can't attend it now. I've something I want to talk over with Auntie," said Binoy. The fact was that after what had happened, Binoy did not feel like accepting Baroda's invitation any more. It all seemed such a mockery to him.

But Harimohini became agitated and urged him to go, saying: "You can talk to me afterwards. Finish with the memorial ceremony first and then come back to me."

"It *would* be better for you to come, I think," added Sucharita.

Binoy understood that if he did not attend the service he would only be assisting the revolution, which had already begun in that household, to come to a head. So he went to the room prepared for the ceremony. But his complaisance did not fully serve its purpose.

Refreshments were handed round after the service, but Binoy excused himself saying: "I am afraid I have no appetite."

"Small blame to your appetite, when you've just been having all kinds of dainties upstairs," sneered Baroda.

Binoy laughingly admitted the charge. "That's the fate of greedy people!" he said. "They lose the future by yielding to the temptation of the present."

With this he was preparing to leave, when Baroda asked him: "Going upstairs again, I suppose?"

Binoy answered with a brief "Yes," and went out of the room, saying to Sucharita in a whisper, as he passed the door: "Didi, come and see Auntie for a moment. She has special need of you."

Lolita was engaged in serving the guests, and at a moment when she was passing near Haran he remarked apropos of nothing: "Binoy Babu is not here, he has gone upstairs."

Lolita stopped in front of him and, looking him full in the face, said cuttingly: "I know that. But he won't depart without saying good-bye to me. Besides, I'll be going upstairs, too, as soon as I have finished with my duties here."

It had not escaped Haran that Binoy had said something to Sucharita and that she had almost immediately followed him out of the room. He had just before made more than one unsuccessful attempt to draw Sucharita into conversation, and her avoidance of his overtures had been so conspicuous before all the assembled Brahmos, that he had felt thoroughly insulted. His suppressed feelings became more bitter than ever when he thus failed to bring Lolita to a due sense of her delinquency.

When Sucharita came upstairs she found that Harimohini was sitting with all her belongings packed up, as if she was leaving immediately, and she asked her aunt what the matter was.

Harimohini was unable to make any reply and began to weep. "Where is Satish?" she said at length. "Ask him to come and see me for a moment, little mother, will you?"

Sucharita looked in perplexity at Binoy, who said: "If Auntie stays in this house, it will only make it awkward all round, so I am taking her away to my mother's".

"I am thinking of going on to some place of pilgrimage from there," added Harimohini. "It's not right for people like me to stop in anyone's home. Why should other people be saddled with me always?"

This was just what Sucharita had been thinking about, all these days, and she also had come to the conclusion that it could mean nothing but insult for her aunt to stay on. So she could make no reply, and simply went and sat down beside Harimohini without speaking. It was already dark, but the lamps had not been lighted. The stars shone dimly through the misty autumn sky, and in the darkness it could not be seen which of them were weeping.

Suddenly the sound of Satish's shrill voice calling "Auntie! Auntie!" could be heard from the stairs, and Harimohini got up hurriedly.

"Auntie," said Sucharita, "you can't go anywhere to-night. To-morrow morning we shall see about it. How can you run away like this without taking leave of father properly? How hurt he would feel!"

Binoy, in his excitement at the insult offered to Harimohini by Mistress Baroda, had not thought of this. He had felt it would not do for her to stay even one more night under that roof, and he wanted to show Baroda that she need not think that Harimohini would have to endure her insults helplessly, because she had nowhere else to go to. So his one anxiety had been to get her away from there as quickly as possible.

At Sucharita's words it struck him that Harimohini's relations with the Mistress were not the only ones that mattered in this home,—that it would not do to put more stress on the insult received from her than on the hospitality so generously and affectionately offered by the Master of the house, so he said: "That is quite true. You can't go without saying good-bye to Paresh Babu."

Satish here came in shouting, "Auntie, do you know that the Russians are going to invade India? Won't it be fun?"

"And which side will you be on?" asked Binoy.

"I am with the Russians!" said Satish.

"Ah, then they need have no further anxiety," smiled Binoy. As soon as she saw that the crisis had passed, and Binoy was himself again, Sucharita left them and slipped back down-stairs.

FORTY FOUR

Paresh Babu was sitting alone in his little room, before going to bed, reading a volume of Emerson near the lighted lamp, and when Sucharita came in and gently drew a chair up close to him, he laid down his book and looked in her face.

Sucharita could not mention the purpose for which she had come. She felt quite unable to bring up any worldly matter. She said merely: "Father, do read to me a little."

Paresh Babu went on reading and explaining to her until it was ten o'clock. After the reading Sucharita again did not feel like talking about any troublesome subject, which might disturb her father's rest, so she was about to retire to her own room, when Paresh Babu called her back and said: "You came to speak about your Auntie, didn't you?"

Sucharita was astonished that he had been able to guess what was on her mind and said: "Yes, father, but don't trouble about that to-night. We can talk about it to-morrow."

But Paresh Babu made her sit down and said: "It has not escaped me that your aunt is finding it inconvenient here. I did not realise before how strongly her religious beliefs and customs would clash with your mother's habits and ideas. Now that I see how it distresses her, I feel sure your aunt, too, cannot help feeling uncomfortable about it."

"Auntie has already made ready to leave," said Sucharita.

"I knew that she would want to do that," said Paresh Babu, "but I know too that, as her only relatives, you cannot possible let her go homeless. So I've been thinking over the matter for some time."

Sucharita had never guessed that Paresh Babu had discovered the awkward position in which her aunt had been placed and was actually engaged in thinking it out. She had been very circumspect all this time, fearing lest the discovery should give him pain, and when she heard him speak in this way her eyes brimmed over with thankfulness.

"I have just thought of a suitable house for her," Paresh Babu went on.

"But, I am afraid, she—she—" stammered Sucharita.

"She won't be able to afford the rent, you mean? But why should she? You're not going to charge her rent, are you?"

Sucharita looked at him in speechless wonder, and he laughed as he went on: "Let her live in your own house, and then she won't have to pay any rent."

This only served to mystify Sucharita still more, until Paresh Babu explained: "Don't you know that you have two houses in Calcutta? One is yours, and the other belongs to Satish. When your father died he left some money in my care, and I lent it out at interest, and when it increased sufficiently I invested it in buying two houses in town. All these years I have been getting rent for them, which I have also laid by. The tenant of your house left a short time ago and, as it is now vacant, there will be nothing to inconvenience your aunt."

"But will she be able to live there all by herself?" asked Sucharita.

"While she has you, her own relative, why should she be alone?" said Paresh Babu.

"This was just what I came to speak to you about tonight," exclaimed Sucharita. "Auntie has already decided on leaving this house and I was wondering how I could let her go alone. I wanted to ask you, and will do exactly as you tell me to."

"You know the lane that runs by the side of our house?" observed Paresh Babu. "Well, your house is only three doors away down that lane. You can even see it from our verandah. If you are living there you won't feel deserted, for we can see you as often as if you were in the same house."

Sucharita felt an immense weight lifted from her mind, for the thought of having to leave Paresh Babu was unbearable to her, though she had begun to feel certain that her duty would compel her to do so very soon.

With a heart too full for words, Sucharita remained sitting beside Paresh Babu, who also sat rapt in his own thoughts. Sucharita was his pupil, his daughter, his friend. She had become a part of his very life. Without her even his worship of God seemed incomplete. On the days when Sucharita came and joined him at his meditation it seemed to him that his devotions were more fruitful, and that as his tender affection sought to lift her thoughts towards the Good, his own life too was uplifted.

None of the others had ever come to him with such devotion and such single-hearted humility as did Sucharita. Just as a flower looks towards the sky, so her whole nature turned towards him and opened into blossom. Such devoted claim cannot but evoke a corresponding response, making the full heart bend to shower its gifts like a rain-laden cloud.

What could be a more wonderful opportunity than thus to be able daily to give of one's best and truest to one whose soul was open to receive. Such opportunity Sucharita had bestowed on Paresh Babu and therefore it was that his relationship with her was so deep.

Now the time had arrived for the severance of their outward connection. The parent tree had ripened the fruit with its own life-sap and now must free it to drop off. The secret pain at his heart Paresh Babu was now offering to the Dweller within.

He had been noticing for some time that the call to live her own life had come to Sucharita. He was sure that she had put by ample provision for her pilgrimage, and with it she must now fare forth on the high road of the world, to gain new experience from its joys and sorrows, from the trials she would suffer and the endeavours she would make.

Go forth, my child, he was saying in his heart. It can never be that you are to remain overshadowed forever by my guidance, or even my watchful care. God will free you from me and draw you through every kind of experience towards your final destiny,—may your life have its fulfilment in Him. And thus he dedicated to God, as a sacred offering, the Sucharita whom he had tended from childhood with all the wealth of his affection.

Paresh Babu had not allowed himself to entertain any feelings of annoyance with Mistress Baroda, nor to harbour any resentment at these differences within his own family circle. He knew quite well that when the freshet suddenly begins to course through the old narrow channel, a turbulent flood arises, and that the only remedy is to let the water find its freedom over the broad fields. He could see how the grooves of tradition and habit in the life of his family had been disturbed by the unforeseen happenings which had centred round Sucharita, and that peace could only be gained by freeing her from all trammels and allowing her to find her own true relations with the outside world. And so he had been quietly making preparations for giving her such freedom to live her own life in harmony.

They both sat without speaking till the clock struck eleven, when Paresh Babu rose, and taking Sucharita's hand in his, drew her on to the verandah. The stars were shining in a sky which was now free from cloud, and, with Sucharita standing

beside him, Paresh Babu prayed in the quietness of the night:
"Deliver us from all that is untrue and let the True shed its
pure radiance over our lives."

FORTY FIVE

Next morning when Harimohini, on taking her leave of Paresh Babu, made to him the obeisance due to an elder, he hurriedly withdrew his feet from her touch. "Don't do that to me!" he exclaimed greatly embarrassed.

Harimohini said with tears in her eyes: "I shall never, in this or any other life, be quit of my obligation to you. You have made life possible, even for an unfortunate creature like me,—no one else could have done it,—not even if they had wished to. But God is kind to you and that is why you are able to rescue even me."

Paresh Babu became quite distressed. "I have not done anything out of the ordinary," he muttered. "All this is Sucharita's—"

But Harimohini would not allow him to finish. "I know, I know," she said, "but Radharani herself is yours,—whatever she does is your doing. When her mother died, and then she also lost her father, I thought she was doomed to be unfortunate—how could I know that God would bless her in her misfortunes? When, after all my wanderings, I at length arrived here, and got to know you, then I understood that God could have pity even for me."

At this moment Binoy came in and announced: "Auntie, mother has come to fetch you."

"Where is she?" exclaimed Sucharita, rising all in a flurry.

"Down below with your mother," answered Binoy, whereupon Sucharita hurried away downstairs.

Paresh Babu said to Harimohini: "Let me go in advance and put your new home in order for you."

When he had gone, Binoy said in astonishment: "Auntie, I never heard of your having a house!"

"I too never heard of it, my child, till to-day," said Harimohini. "It was known only to Paresh Babu. It seems it belongs to Radharani."

When Binoy had heard all about it he said: "I had thought that at last Binoy was going to be of some use in the world to someone, but I see that I am to be deprived of that pleasure. Up to now I have never been able to do anything, even for mother,—it is she who has always been doing things for me. For my auntie too, I can do nothing, it seems, but must be content to receive her kindness. My fate is to accept, I see, not to give!"

After a little Anandamoyi arrived escorted by Lolita and Sucharita. Harimohini came forward to greet her, saying: "When God bestows his favours, He is not miserly about it. Didi, to-day I have got you for my own, too," and with these words she took Anandamoyi's hand and made her sit down beside her.

"Didi," continued Harimohini, "Binoy can talk about nothing but you!"

"That has been a way of his from childhood," answered Anandamoyi with a smile; "when once he is interested in a subject he can never leave it alone. It will soon be his aunt's turn, I can assure you."

"Quite true!" exclaimed Binoy. "So be warned beforehand! I have got my auntie late in life, and self-acquired, too! Since I've been cheated of her for all these years, I must make the most of her now!"

Anandamoyi, looking towards Lolita, said with a meaning smile. "Our Binoy not only knows how to get what he wants, but he also has the art of taking good care of what he gets! Don't I know how he values all of you like some undreamt of good fortune? I cannot tell you how happy I am that he should have come to know your people—it has made a different man of him, and he knows it!"

Lolita tried to make some reply to this, but she was at a loss for words, and became so confused that Sucharita had to come to her rescue with: "Binoy can see the good in every one, and so earns the right to enjoy the best side of his friends; that's due to his own merit, mostly."

"Mother," interposed Binoy, "the world does not look on your Binoy as quite the interesting creature to deserve all your harping on him! I have often wanted to make this clear to you, but my vanity has stood in the way. At last I feel I cannot keep this damaging revelation back any longer. Now, mother, let us change the subject."

At this juncture Satish came up with his new puppy, his latest acquisition, in his arms. On seeing what he carried Harimohini shrank back in dismay, entreating him: "Satish, my dear, please take that dog away. Do, there's darling."

"It will not hurt you, Auntie," expostulated Satish. "It won't even go into your room. It will be quite quiet if you will just pet it a little."

Harimohini moved farther and farther away from the untouchable animals, as she kept imploring him: "No, my dear, for goodness' sake take it away!"

Then Anandamoyi drew Satish towards her, dog and all, and taking the puppy in her lap, said: "So you are Satish, are you our Binoy's friend?"

Satish saw nothing unreasonable in being called a friend of Binoy's and said "yes" without the least diffidence. He then stood staring at Anandamoyi, who explained to him that she was Binoy's mother.

Sucharita admonished her brother saying: "Mr. Chatterbox, make your *pronam* to mother," whereupon Satish made a shamefaced attempt at an obeisance.

Meanwhile Mistress Baroda arrived on the scene and without taking the least notice of Harimohini, asked Anandamoyi whether she could offer her any refreshment.

"I have no scruples about what I eat," replied the latter, "but I won't have anything now, thank you. Let Gora come back and then we'll honour your hospitality, if we may." For Anandamoyi did not like to do anything, which might be contrary to Gora's wishes, in his absence.

Baroda then looked towards Binoy and said: "Oh! Binoy Babu, so you are here, too, I was not aware that you had come!"

"I was just going to let you know that I'm here, with a vengeance!" answered Binoy.

"Well, you gave us the slip yesterday, though an invited guest! What do you say to joining us at breakfast without an invitation?"

"That only makes it all the more inviting," said Binoy. "A tip is always more jolly than the usual wages."

Harimohini was astonished at this conversation. Evidently, then, Binoy was in the habit of taking meals in this house, and over and above that, here was Anandamoyi too, who seemed to have no scruples about her caste. She was far from pleased at all this.

When Baroda had left the room, she ventured to ask diffidently: "Didi, isn't your husband—?"

"My husband is a strict Hindu," replied Anandamoyi.

Harimohini was altogether puzzled, and showed it so plainly that Anandamoyi had to explain: "Sister, so long as society seemed to me the most important thing in the world, I used to respect its rules, but one day God revealed Himself to me in such a way that He would not allow me to regard society any more. Since He Himself took away my caste, I have ceased to fear what others may think of me."

"And what of your husband?" asked Harimohini, none the wiser for this explanation.

"My husband does not like it," said Anandamoyi.

"And your children?"

"They too are not pleased. But is my life given to me merely to please husband and children? Sister, this matter is not one which can well be explained to others. He alone understands who knows all!" with which Anandamoyi joined her hands in silent salutation.

Harimohini thought that perhaps some missionary lady had seduced her towards Christianity, and she felt at heart a great shrinking from her.

FORTY SIX

Labonya, Lolita and Lila would not leave Sucharita for a moment. And though they helped her to arrange her new home with a great show of enthusiasm, it was an enthusiasm which served only to veil their tears.

All these years Sucharita, on various pretexts, had everyday been doing some little service or other for Paresh Babu, arranging flowers in his room, keeping his books and papers in order, airing his clothes with her own hands, and when his bath was ready, coming to remind him about it. Neither of them had ever looked on these little things as anything special.

But now that the time was fast approaching when they would come to a stop, though the same little things could as well be done by others, or even left undone, the difference that this would make kept gnawing at the hearts of both.

Whenever Sucharita nowadays came into Paresh Babu's room, every little thing she did would assume immense proportions for both of them. Some oppression at his heart would bring forth a sigh, some pain in hers would make her eyes brim over.

On the day on which it was settled that Sucharita was to move into her new house after the midday meal, Paresh Babu, when he went to his room for his morning meditation, found flowers already arranged before his seat and Sucharita waiting for him. Labonya and Lila had thought of all having their prayers together that morning, but Lolita had dissuaded them, knowing how much it meant to Sucharita to be allowed to share their father's devotions, and that she must be specially feeling the need of his blessing to-day. Lolita did not want the presence of others to disturb the intimacy of the communion of these two.

When at the close of their prayers Sucharita's tears overflowed, Paresh Babu said: "Do not be looking back, my child. Have no hesitations, but face bravely whatever fate may have in store for you. Go forward rejoicing, ready with all your strength to choose the Good from whatever may come before you. Surrender yourself fully to God, accepting Him as your only help, and then, even in the midst of loss and error, you will be able to follow the path of the Best. But if you remain divided, offering part of yourself to God and part elsewhere, then everything will become difficult. May God so deal with you that you will no longer have any need of the little help we can give you."

When they came out of the prayer-room, they found Haran waiting for them, and Sucharita, unwilling to-day to harbour any feelings of resentment, greeted him with gentle cordiality.

Haran at once sat bolt upright in his chair and said in a solemn voice: "Sucharita, this day of your backsliding from the truth which you have so long professed is indeed a day of mourning for us."

Sucharita made no answer, but the discordant note jarred on the harmony which had filled her mind.

"Only one's own conscience can tell who is advancing and who is backsliding," remarked Paresh Babu. "We often needlessly exercise ourselves, misjudging things from the outside."

"Do you mean to say that you have no misgivings for the future?" asked Haran—"and no cause of repentance for the past?"

"Panu Babu," replied Paresh Babu, "I never give place to imaginary fears in my mind, and as to whether anything has happened to cause repentance, that I shall know when repentance comes."

"Is it all imaginary that your daughter, Lolita, came away alone on the steamer with Binoy Babu?" persisted Haran.

Sucharita flushed and Paresh Babu replied: "You seem to be labouring under some excitement, Panu Babu, and it would not be doing you justice to ask you to discuss these matters in this frame of mind."

Haran tossed his head. "I never discuss anything excitedly," he said. "I always have a due sense of responsibility for whatever I may say; so you need have no qualms on that score. What I said was not meant personally. I spoke on behalf of the Brahmo Samaj, and because it would have been wrong for me to remain silent. Unless you had been blind, you would have seen, from the one circumstance of Lolita travelling alone with Binoy Babu, that your family is beginning to drift away from its former safe anchorage. It is not only that it will give you cause to repent, but what is more, it will bring discredit on the Samaj."

"If censure be your object, such outside view is enough; but if you would judge, you must enter into the matter more deeply. The happening of an event is not enough to prove the guilt of a particular person."

"But what happens does not happen of itself," replied Haran. "Something has gone wrong within you people which is making these things possible. You have been bringing outsiders into the family circle, who are seeking to drag it away from its traditions. Can't you see for yourself how far they have actually made you drift away?"

"I am afraid, Panu Babu, we do not see eye to eye in these matters." There was a shade of annoyance in Paresh Babu's tone.

"You may refuse to see, but I ask Sucharita herself to bear witness. Let her tell us whether Binoy's relationship with Lolita is only an external circumstance. Has it not penetrated deeply into their lives?—No, Sucharita, it won't do for you to go away; you must answer me first. The matter is a serious one."

"No matter how serious it may be, it is none of your business!" answered Sucharita sternly.

"Had that been so," said Haran, "I would not have given the matter a thought, much less insisted on talking about it. You may not care for the Samaj, but so long as you are members, the Samaj cannot help passing its judgment on you."

Lolita suddenly rushed in from somewhere, like a veritable whirlwind, saying: "If the Brahmo Samaj has appointed you its judge, it is better for us to be out of it altogether!"

"Lolita, I am glad you are here," said Haran as he rose from his chair. "It's but right that the charge against you should be discussed in your presence."

Sucharita was really angry this time, and her eyes flashed fire she cried: "Hold court in your own house, Haran Babu, if you will. But we shall not submit to this right, which you arrogate to yourself, of insulting people in their homes.— Come, Lolita, let us go."

But Lolita would not budge. "No, Didi," she said. "I am not going to run away. I am prepared to hear everything that Panu Babu has to say. Come, sir, what is it you were saying?"

Haran being at a loss how to proceed, Paresh Babu intervened: "Lolita, my dear, Sucharita is leaving us to-day. We must not have any wrangling this morning.—Panu Babu, whatever our faults may have been, for this occasion you must excuse us."

Haran was reduced to solemn silence, but the more Sucharita showed that she would have nothing to do with him, the more obstinately did he become determined to secure her for his own. It was because he had not, even now, given up hopes of her, that Sucharita's impending departure with her orthodox aunt had made him feel desperate, knowing that he could not follow her there.

So, to-day, he had come with all his deadliest weapons ready sharpened, prepared to force a decision that very morning. He had been sure that his moral shafts would go home every time. He had never dreamt that Sucharita and Lolita would make a stand with no less sharp arrows out of their own quiver.

But even his disappointment at the actual turn of events had not made him downhearted. Truth—that is to say Haran—must win: was not that his motto? Of course he would have to fight for it; and he girded up his loins for a renewed struggle from that day onwards.

Sucharita, meanwhile, had gone over to her aunt, and was saying to her: "You must not mind, Auntie, if I take my meals with all of them to-day."

To this Harimohini said nothing. She had thought that Sucharita had come entirely over to orthodoxy, and moreover, now that she was so independent by right of her own property, and was to live in a separate house, Harimohini had hoped that at last they would be able to have everything their own way. She did not at all like this sudden lapse of Sucharita's, and so kept silent.

Sucharita understood what was passing in her mind, and said: "Let me assure you, Auntie, that your God will be pleased at this. He who is Lord of my heart has told me to eat together with them all to-day. If I don't obey His command He will be angry, and I fear His anger more than yours."

Harimohini could not understand this at all. So long as there had been the necessity of submitting to Mistress Baroda's insults, Sucharita had joined in her orthodoxy, and shared in her humiliations. Now that the day had come for their deliverance, how was it that Sucharita did not jump at the chance?

It was clear that Harimohini had not fathomed the depth of her niece's mind—perhaps it was beyond her altogether.

Though she did not actually forbid Sucharita, she felt annoyed with her. "Where did the girl get this shocking taste for impure food?" she grumbled to herself. "And she was born in a Brahmin home too!"

Then after a short silence she said aloud: "One word, though, my dear. Do as you please about eating with them, but at least don't drink water drawn by that bearer!"

"Why Auntie!" exclaimed Sucharita. "Isn't he that very Ramdin who milks his cow for you and brings you your milk every morning?"

Harimohini's eyes opened wide in astonishment as she said: "You take my breath away, my dear! To compare water with milk,—as if the same rules apply to both!"

"All right, Auntie," said Sucharita, laughing, "I won't take any water from Ramdin's hand to-day. But let me warn you that you had better not forbid Satish, because then he will be sure to do just the opposite."

"Oh, Satish is another matter," observed Harimohini. "— Were not the stronger sex privileged to break all rules and evade all discipline, imposed even by orthodoxy?"

FORTY SEVEN

Haran had been on the war path.

About two weeks had passed since the day Lolita had accompanied Binoy on the steamer to Calcutta. A few people had already heard about it, and more had been coming to hear of it in the usual course, but now within two days the news spread like a fire in dry straw.

Haran had explained to many people how important it was to check this kind of individual misconduct, in the interests of the very structure of Brahmo family life. This did not prove a difficult task, for it is always easy to obey with alacrity the call of truth and duty, when it prompts us to contemn and punish others' transgressions. And the majority of the important members of the Samaj were not deterred by any false modesty from joining Haran with the enthusiasm in the performance of this painful duty. These pillars of the sect did not even grudge the hire of the conveyances which took them from house to house in order to proclaim the danger in which the Brahmo Samaj stood if this kind of thing were to be condoned.

In addition to this, the news soon went the round—with embellishments—that Sucharita had not only turned orthodox but had taken shelter in the house of a Hindu aunt, and was spending her days in worshipping idols, making sacrifices, and indulging in all kinds of superstitious austerities.

Meanwhile, after Sucharita's departure to her own home, a great struggle had been going on in Lolita's mind. Every night when she went to bed she vowed she would never own defeat, and every morning when she got up she would repeat her resolve. For it had come to this pass, that the thought of Binoy had taken complete possession of her mind. If she heard his voice in the room below, her heart would begin to beat faster. If he did not happen to call for two or three days her mind was tortured with injured pride. She would then contrive to send Satish to his friend's lodgings on various pretexts, and when Satish returned she would try to worm out of him every detail of what Binoy had said and done when he was there.

The more uncontrollable this obsession of Lolita's grew, the more anxious did she become with the fear of impending defeat. So much so, that she sometimes even felt angry with her father because he had not put a stop to their intimacy with Binoy and Gora.

Anyhow, she was now fully determined to fight to the bitter end, feeling she would rather die than admit defeat. She began to imagine all kinds of ways in which she would pass her days. She even thought that it would be quite possible for her to emulate the glories of some of the European women of whom she had read, by devotion to a life of philanthropy.

One day she went to Paresh Babu and said: "Father, wouldn't it be possible for me to take up teaching work in some Girl's School?"

Paresh Babu looked in his daughter's face, and could see that her eyes were pleading to be saved from the hunger of her heart. He said soothingly: "Why not my dear? But is there a suitable Girl's School?"

At this time there were not many suitable schools, for although there were one or two elementary institutions for girls, women of the upper classes had not taken to teaching work. "Aren't there any then?" asked Lolita with a note of despair.

"Not that I know of," Paresh Babu had to admit.

"Then, father, couldn't we start one?" pursued Lolita.

"That would require a great deal of money, I am afraid," said Paresh Babu, "and also many people to help."

Lolita had always thought that the difficulty was in encouraging the desire to do good works,—she had never known before what obstacles there could be in the fulfilment of such a desire. After a short silence she got up and left the room, leaving Paresh Babu trying to fathom the cause of this pain at his beloved daughter's heart.

He was suddenly reminded of the insinuation about Binoy, made by Haran the other day, and heaving a sigh he asked himself: "Have I then indeed been acting injudiciously?" In the case of any of his other daughters it would not have mattered so much, but to Lolita her life was something very true. She could not do things by halves, and her joys and sorrows were never half real, half imaginary.

That same noon Lolita went over to Sucharita's house. It was but sparingly furnished. A country-made *durry* covered the floor of the principal room, on one side of which her bed was spread and on the other Harimohini's; for, as her aunt did not use a bedstead, Sucharita followed her example by making her bed on the floor in the same room. On the wall hung a portrait of Paresh Babu, and in the next room, which was a small one, was Satish's bed, with books and exercises and inkstand and pens lying scattered about in confusion on a table against the wall. Satish himself had gone to school. The house was steeped in silence.

Harimohini was preparing for her siesta after her meal, and Sucharita, her loose hair hanging over her shoulders, was seated on her own bed, with a pillow on her lap, on which rested the book that she was deeply engrossed in reading. In front of her lay several other books. When she suddenly saw Lolita come into the room, Sucharita shut her book in some confusion, but immediately her sense of shame itself got the better of her shame, and she reopened the book at the page she had been reading. These were volumes of Gora's writings.

Harimohini sat up and cried: "Come in, come in, my little mother. Don't I know how Sucharita's heart must be aching for the sight of you! She always reads those books when she is sad. I was just thinking, as I lay here, how nice it would be if one of you were to come round, and here you are! You will live long, my dear!"

Lolita at once plunged into the subject which was uppermost in her mind. The moment she had sat down she said: "Suchi Didi, how would it be if we started a school for the girls of our neighourhood?"

"Just listen to her!" exclaimed Harimohini aghast. "What will you do with a school?"

"How could we start one, dear?" asked Sucharita. "Who would help us? Have you spoken to father about it?"

"Both of us can teach, surely!" explained Lolita, "and perhaps Labonya will join us."

"It is not only a question of teaching," observed Sucharita. "There'll have to be rules and regulations for managing the school; we must have a suitable house, secure pupils and collect funds. What can girls like us do about all this?"

"Didi, you mustn't talk like that!" exclaimed Lolita. "Because we have been born girls, are we to wear our hearts out within the four walls of our home? Are we never to be of any use to the world?"

The pain that was in these words found a response in Sucharita's heart. She began to revolve the matter seriously in her mind.

"There are plenty of girls in our neighbourhood," went on Lolita. "Their parents would be only too pleased if we offered to teach them free of charge. And, as for a house, we can easily find room for the few pupils who are likely to join at first, in this very house of yours. So the money question would not be any great difficulty."

Harimohini became thoroughly alarmed at the idea of all the strange girls of the neighbourhood invading the house for their schooling. All her efforts were concentrated on regulating her conduct and performing her religious ceremonies, according to scriptural injunctions, carefully secluded from all chance of contamination. And she was roused into making a definite protest at this danger of her seclusion being violated.

Sucharita said: "You needn't be afraid, Auntie. If we get the pupils at all, we can manage quite well to carry on our class downstairs. We won't let them come up to worry you. So, Lolita, if we can but get any pupils, I am quite ready to join you."

"There's no harm in our having a good try, anyway," said Lolita.

Harimohini continued to grumble mildly saying: "What makes you always want to do as the Christians do, my little mothers? I have never heard of Hindu gentlewomen wanting to teach in a school—never in my life!"

From the roof of Paresh Babu's house a regular intercourse had been kept up with the girls on the roofs of the neighbouring houses. There was, however, one obstacle to the progress of their intimacy, and that was the surprise which the others did not hesitate to express, and the inquisitive questions which they did not refrain from asking, as to why the girls of Paresh Babu's family, who grown so big, were not yet married. Lolita, in fact, for this reason, rather avoided these roof-to-roof conversations.

Lobonya, on the other hand, was the most enthusiastic member of these meetings, for she had unbounded curiosity in regard to the family histories of her neighbours. Her afternoon *at homes,* under the open sky, while engaged in doing her hair on the roof terrace, were well attended, and all kinds of news passed between the neighbours by aerial service.

So Lolita entrusted to Labonya the task of collecting pupils for her intended school, and when the proposal was thus proclaimed from the roof-tops many of the girls showed great enthusiasm. In the meantime Lolita began to make ready the lower room of Sucharita's house, sweeping and scrubbing and decorating it with great eagerness.

But the schoolroom remained empty. The heads of the neighbouring families were furious at this attempt to inveigle their daughters into a Brahmo house on the pretext of teaching them. They even regarded it as their duty to forbid their daughters to hold any further communication with Paresh Babu's girls, and not only were they thus deprived of their evening airing on the roof terrace, but had to hear a great deal about their Brahmo friends which was not exactly complimentary. Poor Labonya, when she now went up in the evening, comb in hand, found the neighbouring roofs peopled with the elder generation of her neighbours, with not a sign of the younger, nor of the cordial greetings which she was accustomed to receive from them.

But Lolita did not stop here. "There are quite a number of poor Brahmo girls," she said, "who cannot afford to go to the Bethune school. It would be doing them a service if we take charge of their schooling;" and she not only began to look out for such pupils, but asked Sudhir to help her.

The fame of Paresh Babu's daughters' accomplishments had spread far, in fact what was rumoured far surpassed the truth. So when they heard that these girls were ready to teach without taking any fees, many parents were only too delighted.

In a very few days Lolita's school had made a fair start with about half a dozen pupils, and she was so busy discussing with Paresh Babu all the rules and arrangements for her school that she had not a single moment to give to her own thoughts. She even had a hot discussion with Labonya as to what kind of prizes should be given after the examination at the end of the year; and also as to who should be the examiner.

Although no love was lost between Labonya and Haran, yet Labonya was under the spell of Haran's great reputation for learning, and she had not the least doubt that if he were to assist in the work of the school, whether by teaching or examining, it would add greatly to its glory. But Lolita would not hear of it. She could not bear that Haran should have any hand in this work of theirs at all.

Shortly after the start, however, pupils began to dwindle, until one day the class was altogether empty. Sitting in her silent schoolroom, Lolita started at every footstep, hoping against hope that it was some pupil turning up at last, but no one came. When thus it came on to two o'clock, she felt sure that something had gone wrong, so she went off to the house of a girl who lived quite close. There she found her pupil on the brink of tears. "Mother would not let me go," she cried. "It upsets the house so," explained the mother herself, without making it at all clear what there was so upsetting about it. Lolita was a sensitive girl, and never cared to press anyone in whom she saw any sign of unwillingness, nor even to ask the reason, so she merely said: "If it is not convenient, then why worry about it?"

At the next house she went to, she heard another reason. "Sucharita has become orthodox," they blurted out. "She observes caste, she worships idols which are kept in the house."

"If that be the objection, we can hold the school in our own house," suggested Lolita.

But as even this did not seem to remove their objection. Lolita felt sure that there must be something more behind it. So without going round to any other houses, she went home, sent for Sudhir, and asked him: "Tell me, Sudhir, what is it that has really happened?"

"Panu Babu is up in arms against this school of yours," replied Sudhir.

"What?" asked Lolita. "Is it because idols are worshipped in Didi's house, or what?"

"Not only that," began Sudhir, but stopped short.

"What else is it then?" asked Lolita impatiently. "Won't you tell me?"

"Oh! It's a long story!" evaded Sudhir.

"Anything to do with my own shortcomings?"

When Sudhir still remained silent, Lolita's face flushed angrily as she exclaimed: "My punishment for the steamer incident, I see! There's no way, then, of atoning for indiscretions in our Samaj,—is that the idea? So I'm to be shut out from all good work in our own community! That's the kind of method you have adopted for my moral uplift and that of the Samaj, is it?"

Sudhir tried to soften the indictment by saying: "It's not quite that. What they are really afraid of is, least Binoy Babu and his friends might gradually get mixed up in this school work."

This made Lolita angrier still. "Afraid?" she retorted. "Why, that would be a splendid stroke of luck for us! Do they think they could furnish us with any helpers half as competent?"

"Yes, that's true enough," faltered Sudhir, confused by her excitement. "But then, Binoy Babu isn't—"

"Isn't a Brahmo, I know," interrupted Lolita. "So he is taboo to the Brahmo Samaj! I don't see much to be proud of in such a Samaj!"

Sucharita meanwhile had at once divined the real reason for the desertion of their school by its pupils. She had left the schoolroom without a word, and had gone upstairs to Satish to prepare him for his ensuing examination.

There Lolita found her, after she came back from Sudhir, and said: "Have you heard what has happened?"

"I have not heard anything, but I have understood, all the same," replied Sucharita.

"And must we quietly suffer all this?" asked Lolita.

Sucharita took Lolita by the hand as she said: "Let us quietly suffer whatever may befall, for there is no disgrace in suffering. Haven't you seen how calmly father suffers everything?"

"But Suchi Didi," expostulated Lolita. "It has often seemed to me that one puts a premium on evil by suffering it without protest. The proper remedy for evil is to fight against it."

"Well, what kind of fight would you put up, dear?" inquired Sucharita.

"I haven't thought about that yet," replied Lolita. "I don't even know what I have the power to do—but something certainly must be done. Those who can attack mere girls like us, in this underhand way, are no better than cowards, no matter how great they may think themselves to be. But I am not going to take defeat at their hands, I tell you,—never! I don't care what trouble they may put us to, for showing fight!" and she stamped her foot as she spoke.

Sucharita, without giving any answer, gently stroked Lolita's hand, and then after a little said: "Lolita, dear, let us first see what father thinks about it."

"I'm just going to him," said Lolita, getting up.

As she came near the door of their house, Lolita caught sight of Binoy coming out with downcast face. On seeing her he stopped awhile, as though he were debating with himself whether to speak to her or not, and then restraining himself, he bowed towards her slightly and went off, without raising his eyes to her face.

Lolita felt as if her heart had been pierced by burning arrows, and entering the house hurriedly, she went straight to her mother's room. There she found Mistress Baroda sitting at the table and apparently trying to give her mind to an account-book which lay open before her.

Baroda was quick to take alarm at sight of Lolita's face, and her glance at once fell back on her accounts, the study of which she pursued with such zeal that it appeared as if the family solvency entirely depended on their being properly balanced.

Lolita drew a chair up to the table and sat down, but still her mother did not look up. At last Lolita called her: "Mother!"

"Wait a moment, child," complained Baroda, " can't you see. I am—" and she bent lower over her figures.

"I'm not going to disturb you for long," said Lolita. "I just want to know one thing. Has Binoy Babu been here?"

Without lifting her eyes from the account-book, Mistress Baroda said: "Yes."

"What did you say to him!"

"Oh, that's long story."

"I only want to know whether you talked about me or not," persisted Lolita.

Seeing no means of escape, Baroda threw down her pen and looking up, said: "Yes, child, we did! Haven't I seen that things have gone too far—everyone in the Samaj is talking about it, so I had to give him a warning."

Lolita flushed all over with the shame of it, and the blood mounted to her head. "Has father forbidden Binoy Babu to come here any more?" she asked.

"Do you think he bothers his head about all these matters?" replied Baroda. "If he had done so, all this need never have happened."

"And is Panu Babu to be allowed to come here just the same?" pursued Lolita.

"Just listen to her! Why shouldn't Panu Babu come?" exclaimed Mistress Baroda.

"Then why shouldn't Binoy Babu too?"

Mistress Baroda drew the account-book towards her again, and said: "Lolita, I can't argue with you! Don't worry me now, I've got such a lot of work to get through."

Baroda had taken the opportunity of Lolita's absence at her school during the middle of the day to call Binoy to her and give him a piece of her mind. Lolita would never know anything about it, she had thought, so she was now thoroughly upset to find that her little stratagem had been discovered. She realised that the peaceful solution she had tried to bring about was no longer in sight,—rather greater trouble loomed ahead. But all her anger was directed towards that irresponsible husband of hers. What a plight for a woman to have to keep house with such a dunderhead!

Lolita went away with a devastating storm raging in her heart. Going downstairs she found Paresh Babu writing letters in his room, and without any preliminary she asked him point-blank: "Father, is Binoy Babu not worthy of mixing with us?"

Paresh Babu immediately understood the situation. He had not been unaware of the agitation against his family which was taking place in their Samaj, and he had been giving serious thought to the matter. Had he not suspected the nature of Lolita's feelings towards Binoy, he would not have taken the least notice of what outsiders were saying. But if love for Binoy had grown in Lolita's heart, then, he asked himself again and again, what was his duty towards them?

This was the first time a crisis had occurred in his family since he had openly left orthodoxy to embrace Brahmoism. So that, while on the one hand apprehensions and misgivings assailed him from all sides, on the other, his conscience, roused to alertness, was warning him that just as when leaving his original religion he had looked to God alone, now in this time of trial he should once again place the truth above all social or prudential considerations, and therewith win through.

So, in answer to Lolita's question, Paresh Babu said: "I regard Binoy as a very fine man indeed. His character is excellent, and he is as cultured as he is clever."

"Gour Babu's mother has been to see us twice within the last few days," said Lolita, after a brief silence. "So I was thinking of taking Suchi Didi along to return her call."

Paresh Babu was unable to give an answer immediately, for he knew that at such a time, when every movement of theirs was being discussed, such a visit would only add to the scandal that surrounded them. But, so long as he saw nothing wrong in it, he felt he could not forbid it, so he said: "All right, you two go along. I would have come too, if I had not been so busy."

FORTY EIGHT

Binoy had never in his dreams imagined that his coming and going so thoughtlessly like a guest and friend, to Paresh Babu's house, would be the cause of such an active volcanic eruption in their society. When he had first gone there he had felt a certain shyness, and because he was not sure to what limits he had the right to go he always walked circumspectly. But gradually as his timidity decreased, it never even occurred to him that there was the least fear of danger, and now that he heard for the first time that his conduct had given rise in the Brahmo Society to scandal about Lolita, he was thunderstruck. He was above all distressed because he was well aware that his feeling for Lolita far exceeded that of ordinary friendship, and in the present state of society he regarded it as crime to entertain such feelings where there was such a difference of social customs. He had often thought that it was difficult for him to define his exact position as a trusted guest of that family. In one particular moment he had felt that he was a fraud, and that if he made his real feelings clear to them all it would be a matter to be ashamed of.

It was while his feelings were in this state that one day he received a note from Bordashundari asking him to come specially at noon to see her. When he arrived she asked him: "Binoy Babu, you are a Hindu, aren't you?" and when he admitted the fact he was asked the further question: "You are

not ready to leave the Hindu society are you?" To this he
replied that he was not, whereupon Bordashundari said: "Then
why do you—?" To this half-finished question Binoy was
unable to give any definite answer, but he sat with his face
averted, feeling as if he had at last been found out. Something
which he had wanted to keep secret even from the sun, and
the moon, and the air was then known to everyone here! He
could only think to himself: "What does Paresh Babu think
about it, what does Lolita think about it, and what does
Sucharita think of me?" By some angel's blunder he had found
a place in this heaven for a short time—and now, so soon after
entering it, he must be banished for ever with his head bowed
in shame.

And then, when he had seen Lolita just as he was leaving
Paresh Babu's house, for a moment he thought that at this
last parting from her he would destroy completely every
vestige of their former friendship by confessing to her his
grave fault—but he could not think how he was to do it—
so instead he bowed slightly without looking in her direction
and went off.

Only a short time ago Binoy had been to Paresh Babu's
family an outsider, and now again he stood there—an outsider.
But what a difference! Why did he feel to-day such a void?
In his life before he had seemed to lack nothing—he had his
Gora and his Anandamoyi. But now he felt like a fish out of
water, and whichever way he turned he could find no support.
In the midst of that crowded highway of the busy city he saw
everywhere a pale and shadowy image of ruin menacing his
own life. He was surprised himself at this widespread and
barren emptiness, and he asked again and again from the
heartless and unanswering sky why this had happened and
when, and how it had become possible.

Suddenly he heard someone calling: "Binoy Babu! Binoy
Babu!" and looking round he saw Satish running after him.

Catching him in his arms, Binoy exclaimed: "Well, my little brother! What is it, my friend?" but there were tears in his voice as he spoke, for he had never realised, as he did to-day, what sweetness there was in his relationship with this boy of Paresh Babu's household.

"Why don't you come to our house?" asked Satish. "To-morrow Labonya and Lolita Didi are coming to dinner with us, and Auntie has sent me to invite you too.

Binoy understood from this that Auntie had not heard the news, so he said: "Satish Babu, give Auntie my *pronams,* but tell her that I shall not be able to go."

Satish caught hold of Binoy's hand and begged him, saying: "Why can't you come? You must come, for we will not let you off no matter for what."

Now Satish had a special reason for his eagerness. At his school he had been given an essay to write on "Kindness towards Animals," and he had been given forty-two marks out of fifty for it, so he was very anxious to show it to Binoy. He knew that his friend was a very wise and learned person, and he had made up his mind that a man of such good taste as Binoy would certainly be able to appreciate the true value of his writing. And if once Binoy could be got to confess the excellence of his essay, then the unappreciative Lila could be looked down upon with contempt if she ventured to express disrespect for his genius. It was he in fact who had induced his Auntie to send the invitation, for he wanted his sisters to be present when Binoy gave out his opinion about the essay.

On hearing that it would be quite impossible for Binoy to come, Satish became greatly downcast, so Binoy put his arm round his neck and said: "Come, Satish, come home with me."

As Satish had his essay in his pocket, he was not able to refuse this invitation, so this boy in search of literary fame went to Binoy's house in spite of the fact that he would be wasting precious time with the school examinations so near at hand.

Binoy seemed as if he could not let the boy go, and not only did he listen to the essay, but praised it with a lack of discrimination which was hardly in keeping with sound principles of criticism. Over and above that he sent to the bazaar for some sweetmeats and plied Satish with refreshments.

He then accompanied the boy nearly to Paresh Babu's door, and said with somewhat unnecessary confusion as he was parting from him: "Well, Satish, I must be going now."

But Satish seized hold of his hand and tried to drag him in, saying: "No, no, you must come into the house!"

To-day, however, his importunity bore no fruit.

Binoy walked as though in a dream to Anandamoyi's house, but as she was not to be seen, he entered the solitary room on the roof where Gora had been in the habit of sleeping. How many happy days and nights had they spent together in that room during the years of their boyhood's friendship! What joyous talks, what resolutions, what serious discussions! What friendly quarrels they had had there, and with what affection these quarrels had terminated! Binoy wanted to enter this realm of his early days and to forget the present—but these newly-made acquaintances stood as obstacles across the path—somehow they would not allow him to enter. Up to now Binoy had not realised clearly when the centre of his life had shifted and when its direction had changed—now that he understood all without any doubts, he was afraid.

Anandamoyi had put out her cloth to dry on the roof, and when she came up to fetch it at midday she was surprised to see Binoy in Gora's room. Going up to him quickly, she put her hand on his shoulder and asked: "What is the matter, Binoy? Whatever has happened to make you look so pale?"

Binoy sat up and said: "Mother, when first I used to go to Paresh Babu's house Gora used to get angry with me. At that time I used to think his anger was wrong—but it was not his anger that was wrong but my own stupidity."

Anandamoyi laughed slightly as she said: "I don't say that you are a specially intelligent boy, but I would like to know what was wrong with your intelligence in this particular instance?"

"Mother," replied Binoy, "I never for a moment considered the complete difference there is in our social customs. I merely thought what pleasure and profit I obtained from their example, and friendship, and was drawn to them for that reason. It never occurred to me for an instant that I had any other cause for anxiety!"

"On hearing what you have said," interposed Anandamoyi, "it would never have occurred to me either."

"Mother, you do not know," said Binoy, "that I have raised a regular storm about them in their society—people have made such a scandal about it that never again can I go to their—"

"Gora used repeatedly to say something," interrupted Anandamoyi, "which I always thought very true. He says the worst possible thing that can happen is for there to be outward peace where there is an inner wrong. If there is a storm in their Samaj, then there is no need to feel any regret about it that I can see. You will find that good will come out of it. So long as your own conduct has been sincere it will be all right."

That was just where Binoy felt there was a hitch. He was not at all sure whether his own conduct had been entirely blameless or not. Seeing that Lolita belonged to a different society from his and marriage with her was therefore impossible, Binoy felt as though his love for her were like a secret sin, and he was tortured at the thought that now the time had come for the inevitable penance.

"Mother," Binoy exclaimed impulsively, "it would have been better if that proposal for me to marry Soshimukhi had been carried out. I ought to be kept by some strong bond to the place where I really belong—I ought to be bound in such a way that I could never break away."

"In other words," laughed Anandamoyi, "instead of making Soshimukhi your bride you want to make her your chain! What a fate for Soshi!"

At this moment the servant came in with the news that Paresh Babu's daughters had called. On hearing this announcement Binoy's heart began to beat fast, for he made sure that they had come to complain to Anandamoyi about him and to ask her to warn him to be careful. He stood up hastily, and said: "Then I must be going, mother."

But Anandamoyi took his hand and said: "Don't leave the house altogether, Binoy. Wait a little downstairs."

As he went downstairs Binoy kept saying to himself: "This is quite superfluous on their part. What has taken place can't be helped, but I would sooner die than go to their house again. When the punishment for a sin once begins to burn like a fire, even when it has burned the sinner to a corpse, it does not want to be extinguished."

As he was about to enter the room downstairs in which Gora used to sit, Mohim came in on his way back from his office, with the buttons of his chapkan undone so as to give more freedom to his swelling girth. "Well, well, so here is Binoy!" exclaimed Mohim as he took Binoy by the hand. "Why, I have been wanting to see you." And he took Binoy into the room and offered him a betel leaf from the pan box which he carried.

"Bring some tobacco," he shouted, and then plunged straight into the business he had in mind, asking: "That matter was practically settled, wasn't it? So now—"

He saw at once that Binoy's attitude was not so antagonistic as before. Not that he showed very great enthusiasm, but there was no sign of his trying to waive the question in any way, and when Mohim wanted to settle the date definitely, Binoy said: "Let Gora come back and then we can decide the day."

"That will be only a few days!" exclaimed Mohim in a satisfied tone, and he added: "What do you say to having some refreshments, Binoy? You are looking quite washed out to-day. I hope you're not going to be ill!"

When Binoy had succeeded in extricating himself from the danger of refreshments, Mohim departed inside the house to satisfy the pangs of his own hunger, while Binoy began to turn over the pages of the first book he picked up from Gora's table. Then he threw the book down and began pacing up and down the room, until, a servant appeared saying that he was wanted upstairs.

"Who is wanted?" asked Binoy.

"You are," replied the servant.

"Are they all upstairs?" asked Binoy.

"Yes," answered the servant.

Binoy followed the man upstairs with a face like that of a student called to the examination room. He hesitated a little at the door, but Sucharita called out to him in her usual frank and friendly voice: "Come in, Binoy Babu!" and on hearing her speak in such a tone Binoy felt as though he had suddenly been presented with unexpected wealth.

When he entered the room both Sucharita and Lolita were astounded at his appearance, for he already bore traces of the shock that this harsh and unexpected blow had been to him, and his usually bright and happy face was quite devastated. Though Lolita felt pained and touched at the sight, yet she was unable to disguise some feeling of joy.

On any other day Lolita would not have found it easy to begin talking to Binoy—but to-day the moment he entered the room she exclaimed: "Oh, Binoy Babu, we have something we want to consult you about!"

These words were to Binoy like a sudden shower of joy, and he started with pleasure, and in an instant his pale sad face became radiant.

"We three sisters," went on Lolita, "want to start a small Girls' School."

"Why," exclaimed Binoy enthusiastically, "for a long time it has been a dream of my life to start a Girls' School!

"You will have to help us in this matter," said Lolita.

"You won't find *me* neglectful in anything that I am capable of doing," said Binoy. "But you must tell me what you want me to do."

"The Hindu guardians," explained Lolita, "do not trust us because we are Brahmos. So you will have to help us in this difficulty.

"Oh, you needn't have any anxiety on that score," exclaimed Binoy excitedly, "I shall be able to manage all right."

"That he will be able to do I know," added Anandamoyi. "Binoy hasn't his equal for winning people over by the charm of his persuasive words."

Lolita went on: "You will have to advise us how the School regulations should be worded, how the time should be divided, and what subjects should be taught, and how many classes there should be, and all that sort of thing."

Although these matters would be easy enough for Binoy, somehow he felt bewildered. Was Lolita entirely ignorant of the fact that Bordashundari had forbidden him to mix with them anymore, and that there was a regular agitation against them going on in their Samaj? He was perplexed by the question as to whether it would be wrong for him, or injurious to Lolita, if he agreed to her proposal, and yet had he the strength of mind to refuse a request of Lolita's to help her in a charitable work?

Sucharita also on the other hand was equally astonished. She had never so much as dreamt that Lolita would suddenly make such a request to Binoy. Already her relationship with Binoy was complicated enough, and now there was this unexpected affair. That Lolita, knowing everything, should make such a proposal of her own free will made Sucharita frightened. She realised that Lolita's mind was in revolt, but was it right for her to involve the unfortunate Binoy still further? So Sucharita said somewhat anxiously: "We must discuss this matter with father first, so don't be too elated, Binoy Babu, at your appointment as Inspector of Girls' Schools."

From this remark Binoy saw that Sucharita was trying tactfully to check the proposal, and began to have still further misgivings. Seeing clearly enough that Sucharita knew all about the difficulty that had arisen in the family circle it was not conceivable that Lolita was ignorant of it. Why then did Lolita—? but it was all a puzzle.

"Of course we must talk to father about it," assented Lolita. "Now that Binoy Babu has expressed his willingness to help us we can tell him. He will raise no objection I am sure. We'll make him help us in the School as well, and you too," looking towards Anandamoyi, "will not be let off."

"Certainly, I will be able to sweep your schoolroom," laughed Anandamoyi. "I can't think of anything else that I am capable of doing."

"That will be more than enough, mother!" said Binoy. "Then at least our School will be absolutely clean!"

When Sucharita and Lolita had gone Binoy started walking towards the Eden Gardens, and after his departure Mohim went to Anandamoyi and said: "I see that Binoy has become much more amenable, so it would be a good thing to get the matter settled quickly. Who knows when he will change his mind again!"

"What do you say!" exclaimed Anandamoyi in astonishment. "Since when has Binoy become willing again? He never said anything to me about it."

"Why, he spoke to me about it only to-day," answered Mohim. "He said that the day could be fixed when Gora came home."

Anandamoyi shook her head and said: "No, Mohim, you misunderstood him, I assure you."

"However dull my intellect may be," expostulated Mohim, "I'm old enough to understand the meaning of plain language. I'm sure of that."

"My child," said Anandamoyi, "I know you will be angry with me, but I see that you are only going to make trouble over this."

"If you want to make trouble," said Mohim with a serious face, "then of course trouble will come."

"Mohim, I can bear whatever you say to me no matter what it is," said Anandamoyi, "but I can't give my consent to what can only cause trouble—it is for the good of all of you that I say this."

"If only," replied Mohim rather harshly, "you would leave the question of what is good for us, for us to settle ourselves, you wouldn't have to listen to any complaints, and perhaps it would be the best for all in the long run. What do you say to leaving the matter of what is best for us till after Soshimukhi is safely married?"

To this Anandamoyi gave no reply; she only heaved a sigh while Mohim, taking his *pan* box from his pocket, went out chewing the inevitable betel leaf.

FORTY NINE

Going to Paresh Babu Lolita said: "Because we are Brahmos no Hindu girls want to come and be taught by us, so I have been thinking that it would be a good thing for the work if we could get some Hindu to help in it. What do you think, father?"

"Where can you find anyone from amongst the Hindus?" asked Paresh Babu.

Lolita had come to her father girded for the difficult task of mentioning Binoy's name, but when it came to the point she suddenly felt shy. However, making a great effort, she said: "Why should it be so difficult? There are plenty of suitable people. There is Binoy Babu—or—"

This use of the word "or" was quite superfluous—it was in fact a prodigal use of it, and her sentence remained uncompleted.

"Binoy!" exclaimed Paresh Babu. "But why should Binoy be willing?"

Lolita's pride received a blow at this remark. Binoy Babu unwilling! Did he not know that Lolita at least had the power of making him willing? She only said: "There's no reason why he should not be."

After a short silence Paresh Babu said: "When he has looked at it from every point of view he will never agree to help."

Lolita flushed deeply, and began to rattle the bunch of keys that was tied to her *sari*. Paresh Babu's heart was pained as he watched his daughter's troubled face, but he could not think of any word of consolation. After a little time Lolita looked up slowly, and said: "Then, father, is this school of ours going to be impossible after all?"

"I see at present all kinds of difficulties," said Paresh Babu. "If you try you will only raise all sorts of unpleasant criticisms."

Nothing could be more painful to Lolita than for her to have finally to accept this wrong in silence and for Haran Babu to be victorious, and she would not for a moment have taken the order for retreat from anyone else than her father. She herself was not afraid of any unpleasantness, but how was she to bear what was wrong? Quietly she got up and went away.

When she got to her own room she found a letter waiting for her, and from the handwriting she saw that it was from an old school friend named Shailabala, who was now married and living at Bankipure.

In the course of the letter she wrote: "My mind has been much disturbed by many rumours which I have heard concerning you all, and I have been thinking of writing to you for news for a long time, but have not found time. But the day before yesterday I had a letter from someone (whose name I will not mention) which contained news about you which dumbfounded me. In fact, I should find it almost impossible to believe if it were not for the trustworthy character of the one who wrote it. Is it possible that you are contemplating marriage with some Hindu young man? If this is true—" etc. etc.

Lolita became hot with indignation, and without waiting a moment she sat down to write her answer, which was to the following effect:

"It astonishes me that you should write to ask me whether the news is true or not. Have you so little faith that you have to test the truth of a statement made by a member of the Brahmo Samaj? Further than that you tell me that you are thunderstruck at being told that I am likely to marry some Hindu young man! But let me assure you that there are certain well-known pious young men of the Brahmo Samaj the very thought of marrying whom would fill me with apprehension, and I know one or two young Hindus to whom it would be a matter of pride for any Brahmo girl to be married. I have not anything more that I specially want to write to you just now."

As for Paresh Babu he gave up all his work for that day, and sat in deep thought for a long time. Then at length he went to see Sucharita, who was quite alarmed on seeing the troubled expression of his face. She knew what it was that was causing him anxiety, for she herself had for several days been thinking over the same problem.

Going with Sucharita into her lonely room and sitting down, Paresh Babu said: "Mother, the time has come to think seriously about Lolita."

"I know that, father," answered Sucharita, looking tenderly towards him.

"I'm not thinking of the scandal in our society," said Paresh Babu, "I was wondering—well, is Lolita—"

Seeing Paresh Babu hesitate, Sucharita tried to express clearly what was in her own mind, and said: "Lolita always used to speak to me quite freely about what she thought, but lately I have noticed that she has not been so open. I understand well enough that—"

"Lolita has got a burden on her mind of such a nature," interrupted Paresh Babu, "that she doesn't want to acknowledge it even to herself. I am perplexed as to what is the best course to take—what do you think, have I been injuring her by allowing Binoy to come and go freely in our home?"

"Father, you know that there is no fault in Binoy Babu," said Sucharita, "his character is spotless—in fact, I have seen very few natures like his amongst the educated people of our acquaintance."

"You are right, Radha, you are quite right!" exclaimed Paresh Babu eagerly, as if he had just discovered a new truth. "It is to the goodness of his character that we should look— that is what God also looks to. That Binoy is a good man, and that we have made no mistake in that, is a matter to thank God for."

Paresh Babu breathed freely again feeling that he was delivered from some snare. He was never unjust to his God, and he accepted the scales with which God weighed men as being the scales of eternal truth, and because he had not mixed false weights fabricated by his own society he had no feeling of self-reproach. He was only astonished at himself that he had suffered so much simply from not having for so long understood so obvious a fact. He placed his hand on Sucharita's head and said: "To-day, mother, I have learnt a lesson from you!"

Sucharita immediately touched his feet and exclaimed. "No! No! What are you saying, father?"

"Sectarianism," said Paresh Babu, "is a thing which makes people entirely forget the simple and obvious truth that man is man—it creates a kind of whirlpool in which the society-made distinction between Hindu and Brahmo assumes greater importance than universal truth—all this time I have been vainly whirled round in this eddy of falsity."

"Lolita is not able to give up her determination to start a Girls' School," went on Paresh Babu after a pause. "She wanted me to agree to her asking Binoy to help her in it."

"No, no, father," exclaimed Sucharita, "wait a little first!"

The picture of Lolita's distressed look as she had left him, after he had discouraged her proposal of seeking help from

Binoy, arose before him and gave him intense pain. He knew well that his spirited daughter was not feeling so much troubled at the wrong done her by their society as at being prevented from declaring war against that wrong, more especially when it was her father that prevented her. He was therefore eager to change his attitude on the subject, so he said: "Why, Radha, why should we wait?"

"Because otherwise mother will be vexed," answered Sucharita.

Paresh Babu saw that she was right, but before he could answer Satish came in and whispered something to Sucharita, to which she replied: "No, Mr. Chatterbox, not now! Tomorrow will do!"

"But to-morrow I have to go to school," pouted Satish, crestfallen.

"What is it, Satish, what do you want?" asked Paresh Babu with an affectionate smile.

"Oh, it's one of Satish's—"Sucharita was beginning, when Satish stopped her hastily by putting his hand over her mouth, and expostulated: "No, no, don't tell him! Don't tell him!"

"If it's a secret why should you be afraid of Sucharita telling?" asked Paresh Babu.

"No, father," said Sucharita, "he's really very anxious for you to hear this secret."

"Never, never!" shouted Satish as he ran away.

The fact was that Binoy had praised his essay so highly that he had promised to show it to Sucharita, and it is superfluous to add that the reason he had reminded her in Paresh Babu's presence was clear enough to Sucharita. Poor Satish had not realised that in this world the object of his most secret thoughts could be ascertained so easily.

FIFTY

Four days later Haran Babu called on Bordashundari with a letter in his hand. Nowadays he had given up all hope of influencing Paresh Babu.

Handing the letter to Bordashundari, Haran Babu remarked: "From the first I have been trying to warn you to be careful! You were even displeased with me for doing so. Now you will be able to see from this letter how far things have gone behind the scenes," and he handed her the letter which Lolita had written in answer to her friend Shailabala.

When she had finished reading it, Bordashundari exclaimed: "How could I have foreseen this, tell me! I could never have even dreamt of this happening. But let me tell you that you cannot lay the blame on me for this. You have all conspired together and turned Sucharita's head by your chorus of praises of her goodness—there was no girl to compare with her in the whole Brahmo Samaj—now it is for you to check the doings of this ideal Brahmo girl of yours. It was my husband who brought Binoy and Gour Babu to our home, and although I did my best to guide Binoy to our way of thinking, that business of his 'Auntie,' who was brought from somewhere into our house, began, and idol-worship was started, and now Binoy has been so completely spoilt that he runs away at the sight of me. Sucharita is at the root of all these troubles that are happening. I always knew what kind of a girl she was—

but I never spoke about it; I actually brought her up in such a way that no one would have known she was not my own child. And now this is what I get for it all! It is useless for you to have shown me this letter—you must do whatever you think best now!"

Haran Babu generously acknowledged his regret and confessed quite candidly that he had at one time totally misunderstood Bordashundari. At length Paresh Babu was called.

"Just look at this!" exclaimed Bordashundari, throwing the letter down on the table before him.

After reading the letter carefully twice, Paresh Babu looked up, and said: "Well, what of it?"

"What of it, indeed!" repeated Bordashundari angrily. "What more do you want? What further proof is lacking? You've allowed the worship of idols, observance of caste, practically everything. There's only one thing wanting now, and that is for you to marry one of your girls into a Hindu family! After that I suppose you will do penance and enter the Hindu society yourself—but let me tell you—"

"You need not tell me anything," said Paresh Babu with a slight laugh. "The time for telling me has not come yet! The real question is why you have all made up your mind that Lolita intends to marry into a Hindu family. There is nothing in this letter to make you say so, at least nothing that I can see."

"Up to now I have never been able to discover what can open your eyes," exclaimed Bordashundari impatiently. "If only you had not been so blind from the very start all this would never have happened. Tell me, what could anyone write that is plainer than this letter?"

"I think perhaps," interposed Haran Babu, "that we ought to ask Lolita herself to explain what she meant by this letter. I can inquire from her if I have your permission."

But before anything further could be said Lolita herself came rushing into the room in a regular storm saying: "Father, just look at that! It is from our Brahmo Samaj that such anonymous letters are coming!"

Paresh Babu read the epistle handed to him, and saw that it was full of abuse and advice of various kinds which the writer, taking for granted that her marriage with Binoy had been secretly settled, thought fit to inflict upon Lolita. In addition to this, the writer imputed evil motives to Binoy, and said that he would soon get tired of his Brahmo wife and, forsaking her, would marry again into a Hindu family.

Haran Babu took the letter from Paresh Babu and when he had read it he turned to Lolita with the words: "Lolita, this letter has made you angry, but are you not yourself the cause of such a letter being possible? Tell us how you yourself could write such a letter as this which is in your own handwriting!"

"So it is with you that Shaila has been corresponding about me is it?" asked Lolita after a momentary surprise.

Haran Babu evaded answering plainly, but said: "Remembering her duty to the Brahmo Samaj she was bound to send your letter to me."

"Tell me once and for all what the Brahmo Samaj wants to say," said Lolita, standing firmly before him.

"This rumour that is current throughout our Samaj," explained Haran Babu, "in regard to you and Binoy Babu, is one which I for my part do not credit, but I would like to hear a denial from your own lips."

With blazing eyes Lolita answered him, placing her trembling hands on the back of a chair. She said: "And why, tell me, do you find it impossible to credit it?"

"Lolita," said Paresh Babu, placing his hand on her shoulder, "you are too excited just now to discuss this matter, you can talk to me about it later. Let us drop the subject for the present."

"Don't try, Paresh Babu, to hush the matter up now that we have begun it!" interposed Haran Babu.

At this remark Lolita became still more angry, and she exclaimed: "Father hush it up indeed! Father is not like you people, afraid of the truth—let me tell you that he knows truth to be greater even than your Brahmo Samaj! I can assure you that I see nothing either wrong or impossible in my marrying Binoy!"

"But has he decided to be initiated in the Brahmo religion?" inquired Haran Babu.

"Nothing has been decided," said Lolita, "and as for his being initiated as a Brahmo what need is there for that?"

Up to now Bordashundari had been silent—her wish being that to-day Haran Babu should be the victor, and that Paresh Babu would be bound to confess his fault and show repentance. But she could not contain herself at this, and she joined in, saying: "Lolita, are you mad? What are you saying?"

"No, mother," answered Lolita, "I'm not mad—what I am saying I say after due consideration! I refuse to be hedged round on all sides like this—I am determined to be free from this society of Haran Babu and his set!"

"You, I suppose, call unrestraint freedom!" said Haran Babu sarcastically.

"No," replied Lolita, "liberty for me means freedom from the slavery of falsehood, and from the attacks of meanness. Where I see nothing wrong or contrary to my religion why should the Brahmo Samaj interfere, and put obstacles in my way?"

With a display of arrogance Haran Babu turned on Paresh Babu with the words: "There, you see, Paresh Babu! I always knew that in the end it would lead to something of this kind! I did my best to warn you but without any result!"

"Look here, Panu Babu," said Lolita. "I have one warning to give you—do not have the conceit to offer your advice to people who are far greater than you in every respect," and with this parting thrust she left the room.

"See what a fuss!" exclaimed Bordashundari; "now let us consider what should be done!"

"We shall have to do our duty," said Paresh Babu, "but we can't find out what our duty is in such a disturbed atmosphere. You will have to excuse me, but I can't discuss this matter now, I want to be left alone for a little."

FIFTY ONE

On hearing what had happened Sucharita began to think that Lolita had made a fine muddle of everything, and after remaining silent for a little, she said, putting her arm round Lolita's neck: "Sister, dear, but this makes me feel afraid!"

"What are you afraid of?" asked Lolita.

"Such a to-do is being made throughout the Brahmo Samaj," said Sucharita, "but supposing after all Binoy Babu is unwilling!"

"He will be willing," said Lolita with assurance, though her face was lowered.

"You know," went on Sucharita, "mother has been encouraged by Panu Babu to hope that Binoy would never consent to this marriage when it would mean his leaving his own society. Lolita, why didn't you think well of all the difficulties before you spoke like that to Panu Babu?"

"You needn't think that I am sorry I spoke!" cried Lolita. "If Panu Babu and his party think that by driving me to the edge of the ocean like a hunted animal they will be able to capture me there, they will soon find out their mistake. He doesn't know that I'm not afraid of jumping into the sea, and that I would sooner do that than fall into the jaws of his pack of yelping hounds."

"Let us consult father about it," suggested Sucharita.

"I can assure you," answered Lolita, "that father will never join forces with the hunters. He has never wanted to keep us in fetters. Has he ever shown any anger towards us when our opinions differed from his, or tried to limit our freedom by appealing to us in the name of the Brahmo Samaj? How often mother has been annoyed with him for this, but father's only fear for us was lest we should lose the power of thinking for ourselves. After he has brought us up like this do you imagine he will in the end surrender us into the hands of a gaol superintendent of the Samaj like Panu Babu?"

"Very well," observed Sucharita, "and supposing father offers no objection, what do you propose to do then?"

"If none of you will do anything, then I will myself——" began Lolita, but Sucharita interrupted her anxiously: "No, no, my dear, you will not have to take any steps! I have thought of a plan."

That evening just as Sucharita was preparing to go round to see Paresh Babu he himself called at her house. It was his habit at this time to walk up and down in the garden alone with his head bowed in thought—it was as if he were smoothing out from his mind all the creases of the day's work in the pure darkness of evening and preparing himself for the night's rest by storing up in his heart deep draughts of unsullied peace. To-night when he entered Sucharita's room with a careworn face, having sacrificed the peace of his lonely evening meditation, Sucharita felt her affectionate heart touched with a pain like that of a mother who sees her child, who ought to be playing happily, lying still and silent in pain and sickness.

"You have heard everything, I suppose, Radha?" asked Paresh Babu.

"Yes, father," replied Sucharita, "I've heard. But why are you so anxious?"

"I'm only worried about one thing," answered Paresh Babu, "and that is whether Lolita will be able to bear the brunt of this storm which she has raised. In the face of excitement a blind pride obscures our minds, but when one by one the fruits of our actions begin to ripen the strength to bear the consequences of our acts vanishes. Having thought well of the consequences of her own actions, has Lolita decided what is the best course for her to follow?"

"I can tell you for certain one thing," answered Sucharita, "and it is that Lolita will never be overcome by any penalties which society may see fit to inflict upon her."

"I only want to be sure," explained Paresh Babu, "that Lolita is not merely showing this spirit of revolt in a moment of anger."

"No, father," said Sucharita, looking down, "if that had been the case I would never have listened to her for a moment. What she had been thinking quite seriously for a long time came out fully when she received a sudden blow! For a girl like Lolita it will never do now to try and check her. Besides that, father, Binoy Babu is such a good man."

"But is Binoy ready to become a member of the Brahmo Samaj?" asked Paresh Babu.

"That I can't say for certain," replied Sucharita. "What do you say to our going to see Gour Babu's mother once?"

"I had been thinking myself that it would be a good thing if you went," assented Paresh Babu.

FIFTY TWO

From Anandamoyi's house Binoy used to go to his lodgings every morning, and one day on reaching his room he found a letter awaiting him. The letter was an anonymous one, and contained a considerable amount of advice as to the undesirability of Binoy marrying Lolita. It was pointed out that not only would Binoy himself be unhappy in the match but that it would be a disaster for Lolita also. If however Binoy still persisted, in spite of these warnings, in contemplating the marriage, it would be well for him to consider the fact that Lolita's chest was weak and the doctors had even suspected phthisis.

Binoy was dumbfounded at receiving such a letter, for he had never imagined that any one could invent such palpable falsehoods. Surely it was plain to everybody that the difference in their social customs made it impossible for his marriage with Lolita to take place! It was because of this that he had so long felt his love for Lolita to be blameworthy. But since such a letter had been sent to him it seemed as if it was regarded as a certainty in Brahmo Samaj circles, and it pained him excessively to think how the members of her society must be heaping abuse on Lolita on this score. It seemed to him not only a matter of diffidence, but even of shame, that Lolita's name should have been thus coupled with his so plainly and made a subject of common discussion. He could only suppose that now Lolita must be reproaching herself for her acquaintanceship with him and cursing the day they had met, and that she would never again be able to bear even the sight of him.

Alas for the human heart! For even in the midst of this excessive self-reproach there was mixed such a deep and keen joy that his heart was aglow with it. It refused to acknowledge either insult or shame, and in order that he should not harbour this feeling Binoy began to pace rapidly up and down the verandah. But with the morning light there mingled a kind of madness, so that even the cry of the hawkers as they passed along the street awakened in his heart a deep restlessness. Had not this flood of abuse which had overwhelmed Lolita taken her and floated her to the secure refuge of his heart? He could not banish from his mind the image of Lolita borne by this flood away from her own society towards him, and his heart could cry only these words: "Lolita is mine! Mine alone!" He had never before had the courage to utter these words with such assurance, but to-day, as he heard the wish of his heart echoed so plainly from outside, he could no longer restrain himself.

While he was pacing the verandah in this excited condition he suddenly caught sight of Haran Babu coming towards the house. At once he understood what was behind this anonymous letter.

When he had offered Haran Babu a chair, Binoy waited without displaying his usual self-confidence. At last Haran Babu began:

"Binoy Babu, you are a Hindu, aren't you?"

"Yes, of course I am!" replied Binoy.

"You must not be angry with my question," begged Haran Babu. "We are often blind when we do not consider things from all points of view—when there is a danger of our conduct causing trouble in any society; at such a time we should welcome as a friend one who asks us what our conduct will lead to, and to what limit we can safely go."

"Such a long preamble is quite unnecessary," said Binoy with an attempt at a laugh. "It's not my nature to become distracted at being asked unpleasant questions, nor shall I do any violence to the questioner! What you have to ask me you can ask me without any fear, no matter what it is."

"I don't wish to accuse you of any wilful transgression," apologised Haran Babu, "and it is unnecessary to tell you that the fruit of an indiscretion is often laden with poison."

"What it is unnecessary to tell me," exclaimed Binoy with a shade of annoyance, "you can leave out. Tell me only what you really want to say."

"Is it right," asked Haran Babu, "for you who are a Hindu, and who cannot leave the Hindu society, to come and go in Paresh Babu's home in such a manner as to give rise to talk about his daughters?"

"Look here, Panu Babu," complained Binoy. "I can't accept all responsibility for what the people of any society choose to fabricate from any particular occurrence—that depends upon the nature of the people themselves to a large extent. If it is possible for the members of your Brahmo Samaj to discuss Paresh Babu's daughters in such a way as to create scandal that is a matter of shame for your Samaj rather than for them."

"If," exclaimed Haran Babu, "any girl is allowed to leave the protection of her mother and go wandering off alone on a steamer with some outsider, is that not a matter which her society has a right to discuss? Answer me that question!"

"If you are going to place on an equality some purely external event with a fault of the inner life, then what need was there for you yourself to leave the Hindu society and become a Brahmo?" asked Binoy. "No matter what has happened, Panu Babu, I can't see the necessity for arguing about all these matters. I can very well decide for myself what my own duty is, and you won't be able to help me in that in the least degree."

"I don't want to say much to you," answered Haran Babu. "I have one last word to say, and it is that from now you must keep away from there, for if you don't it will be very wrong of you. By frequenting Paresh Babu's home you have only caused trouble, none of you know what injury you have done them all."

When Haran Babu had gone Binoy felt tortured with doubts. The noble and simple-hearted Paresh Babu had welcomed both himself and Gora into his home with such obvious affection; possibly Binoy had on several occasions overstepped the limits of his rights in the household, but never for one day had he been deprived of his regard and affection;—in this Brahmo home Binoy had found a shelter such as he had not found anywhere else, and it had been so congenial to his nature that through his acquaintance with them all his whole life seemed to have gained special strength. And in the family where he had found such a refuge, and had experienced such affection and such happiness, was the memory of him to be a cause of pain? He had been the cause of a stain of reproach falling on Paresh Babu's daughters! And it was he who had brought such a humiliation on the whole future life of Lolita! Was there any remedy for such a crime? Alas! Alas! What a tremendous hindrance in the way of truth does the thing which is called society raise! There was no true obstacle to the union of Lolita and Binoy. God, the inner Lord of both their hearts, knew how ready Binoy was to sacrifice the whole of his life for her welfare and happiness—was it not He who had drawn Binoy so close to her from the very first?—there was no obstacle in His eternal decrees. Was the God who was worshipped in the Brahmo Samaj by people like Panu Babu some different Being? Was He not the Ruler of human hearts? Some dreadful prohibition stands, with its teeth bared, trying to prevent their union. But if he only heeded the commands of society and not the precepts of the Lord of all human hearts, would not such prohibition be sinful? But alas! perhaps it was just such prohibition that would have most weight with Lolita! And besides that perhaps Lolita's feeling for Binoy was—but there was no end to the doubts with which he was beset.

FIFTY THREE

At the time that Haran Babu was visiting Binoy, Abinash had called on Anandamoyi with the news that it had been settled that Binoy was to marry Lolita.

"That can never be true," expostulated Anandamoyi.

"Why should it be untrue?" asked Abinash. "Is such a match impossible for Binoy?"

"That I don't know," answered Anandamoyi, "but I'm sure that he could not have kept such an important matter a secret from me. Never!"

But Abinash persisted, saying that he had heard it from reliable sources in the Brahmo Samaj, and that it must be true. He further said that he had foreseen this sad end for Binoy long ago, and had even argued with Gora on the subject. When he had proclaimed the news to Anandamoyi, he went downstairs and retailed the news with great gusto to Mohim.

When Binoy returned that morning, Anandamoyi saw from his face that he was greatly troubled. When she had given him his meal she called him into her own room, and asked him: "Why Binoy, what's happened?"

"Mother, just read this letter, will you?" said Binoy.

When she had finished reading it, Binoy went on: "This morning Panu Babu came to see me, and gave me a regular scolding."

"What about?" asked Anandamoyi.

"He said that my conduct had given rise to a scandal about Paresh Babu's daughters in the Brahmo Samaj," explained Binoy.

"People are saying that it has been settled that you are to marry Lolita," said Anandamoyi. "I don't see any cause for scandal in that!"

"If the marriage had been a possible one there would have been no cause for scandal," said Binoy, "but how wrong it is to spread such a rumour when such a thing is impossible! It is especially cowardly to do so where Lolita is concerned."

"If you had any manhood," said Anandamoyi, "you could easily save her from the clutches of such a rumour."

"Tell me how!" exclaimed Binoy in astonishment.

"How indeed!" cried Anandamoyi. "Why, by marrying her!"

"What are you saying mother?" said the astounded Binoy. "I can't make out what you think of your Binoy! Do you imagine that Binoy has only to say, 'I will marry," and then the world will have nothing further to say on the subject— that everything simply waits for a nod from me?"

"I don't see any reason for such a lot of discussion," said Anandamoyi. "It will be all right if only you do what it is in your power to do. You can surely say that you are ready to marry."

"Would not such an unreasonable proposal be an insult to Lolita?" asked Binoy.

"Why do you call it unreasonable?" expostulated Anandamoyi. "Since the rumour has got abroad that you are going to marry her, then certainly the marriage is regarded as reasonable. I assure you that you need not hesitate for a moment."

"But, mother, we must think of Gora, mustn't we?" argued Binoy.

"No, my child," said Anandamoyi decisively, "this is not a matter in which Gora should be consulted. I know he will be angry, and I don't want him to be angry with you. But what can we do? If you have any regard for Lolita you can never allow her to be an object of scandal to her Samaj all her days."

But this was more easily said than done! Since Gora had been sent to gaol Binoy's love for him had flowed with redoubled force, and how could he prepare such a heavy blow for him? Further than that there was social custom. To transgress against society is easy enough in mind—but, when the time comes to act, in how many places do we find that the shoe pinches! A horror of the unknown, a refusal to face the unaccustomed, these make one look back without any reason.

"The more I know of you, mother," exclaimed Binoy, "the more astonished I am at you! However do you manage to have such a clear mind? It seems to me that you don't have to walk. Has God given you wings? Nothing seems able to obstruct you!"

"God hasn't put any obstructions in my way!" laughed Anandamoyi. "He has made everything clear to me!"

"But, mother," said Binoy, "whatever I may say with my lips, my mind does not keep pace with it! After all my education, and intelligence, and arguing I suddenly see that I am an absolute fool!"

At this point Mohim came into the room and began to question Binoy so rudely about his relationship with Lolita that he was humiliated almost beyond endurance, but controlling himself as well as he could, he sat with eyes downcast without answering, until Mohim had left the room after abusing every party in a most scurrilous manner. He gave them to understand that a shameless plot had been hatched in Paresh Babu's family to snare Binoy to his destruction, and that Binoy had been fool enough to allow himself to be caught in the trap. "Just let us see whether they can deceive Gora like that!" he had exclaimed. "They'll find him a tougher problem!"

Seeing himself surrounded on all sides by reproaches, Binoy remained seated in silent dismay till Anandamoyi startled him by saying: "Do you know, Binoy, what you ought to do? You ought to go and see Paresh Babu. If once you can discuss things with him everything will become clear."

FORTY FOUR

On suddenly seeing Anandamoyi, Sucharita exclaimed in astonishment: "Why, I was just on the point of setting out to call on you!"

"I did not know that you were getting ready to come," laughed Anandamoyi, "but I know what it was that was bringing you. I have come on the same errand, for the moment I heard the news I could not contain myself, and felt I must see you."

Sucharita was rather surprised to hear that the news had reached Anandamoyi's ears, and she listened carefully as Anandamoyi said: "Mother, I have always regarded Binoy as my own child. When I came to know how he had been taken up by you all you don't know how I blessed you in my heart! So how could I remain inactive when I heard that you were in trouble? I don't know whether I can do anything to help you or not—but somehow my mind was so upset that I had to come running to you. My dear, is Binoy the cause of all this trouble?"

"Not at all!" exclaimed Sucharita. "Lolita is responsible for all the agitation that has arisen. Binoy never dreamt that Lolita would come to the steamer without saying a word to anyone, and yet people are talking as though the two of them had discussed the plan secretly beforehand. And Lolita is such a spirited girl that she would never contradict the rumour or explain what actually happened."

"But something will have to be done about it!" said Anandamoyi. "Since Binoy heard all this he has not had a moment's peace of mind—he is even taking all the blame on himself."

Sucharita flushed slightly and, lowering her face, inquired: "Well, do you think that Binoy Babu—

"Look here, my child," interrupted Anandamoyi on seeing Sucharita's painful hesitation. "I can assure you that whatever Binoy is told to do for Lolita he will do. I have known him from his childhood, and I have seen that if once he surrenders himself he can keep nothing back. For that reason I have often had to go in constant fear lest his heart should take him to such a place that there would be no hope of extricating him from it."

"You needn't have any anxiety as to whether Lolita will give her consent," said Sucharita, feeling a weight lifted from her mind. "I know her heart quite well. But will Binoy Babu be ready to leave his own society?"

"No, doubt he would be ready if necessary," said Anandamoyi, "but why do you talk about his leaving his society at this stage? Is there any need for that?"

"Why, what do you mean, mother?" cried Sucharita. "Do you mean to say that Binoy Babu can marry a Brahmo girl while remaining a Hindu?"

"If he is willing to do so," answered Anandamoyi, "then what objection have you?"

"I can't myself see how that could be possible!" observed Sucharita in confusion.

"It seems to me the easiest thing in the world, mother," explained Anandamoyi. "Look here, in my own home I cannot observe the customs which the rest of the family observe—that's why so many people call me a Christian. At the time of any special ceremonies I voluntarily keep myself apart. You may smile, my dear, but do you know that even Gora will

not take water in my room! But why should I for that reason
say that the house is not my home, and that their Hindu
society is not my society? I personally can never say that. I
remain in that society, and in that house, accepting all the
abuse they like to give me—but I don't find that such a great
hindrance. If the obstacles become insurmountable then I
shall take the path which God will point out to me, but what
I feel I shall say to the very end, and it is their lookout whether
they accept me or not."

"But," said Sucharita in some perplexity, "look here,—
you know the opinions of the Brahmo Samaj,—supposing
Binoy Babu—"

"His opinions are of the same kind," interrupted
Anandamoyi. "The opinions of the Brahmo Samaj are not
something outside the rest of creation. All those articles which
appear in your periodicals he has read to me quite often—
and I don't see anything wonderfully out of the way in your
opinions."

Here she was interrupted by Lolita entering the room in
search of Sucharita. On seeing Anandamoyi there Lolita blushed
shyly, for she saw from Sucharita's face that they had been
talking about her. She felt that she would like to have escaped,
but there was no excuse for getting away so immediately.

"Come, Lolita, come, little mother!" exclaimed
Anandamoyi, taking her by the hand, and making her sit
down close beside her as though Lolita were her special
possession.

Continuing what she had been saying Anandamoyi went
on to Sucharita: "See here, mother, it is one of the most
difficult things to make bad and good harmonise—and yet in
this world they are found together—and in that union sorrow
and happiness are found—it is not always evil that is seen but
also good. And if that is possible then I fail to understand why
it should be difficult for two people whose opinions differ

to unite happily. Is true union between two human beings merely a matter of opinion?"

Sucharita remained with her head bent low, and Anandamoyi went on: "Will this Brahmo Samaj of yours not permit two people to unite if they wish to? Will your society keep apart, by its external decrees, two beings whom God has made one in heart? Little mother, is there no society anywhere in this world which will ignore small differences of opinion, and allow union in the things that really matter! Are human beings meant only to quarrel thus with their God! Is it only for this that the thing called society has been created?"

Was this heartfelt enthusiasm which Anandamoyi was displaying in her discussion merely due to her desire to banish opposition to Binoy's marriage with Lolita? Had she not some idea that by her arguments she would be able to remove what little hesitation was still left in Sucharita's mind on this subject? For it would never do for Sucharita to keep such an impression. If it were her conclusion that Binoy could not marry Lolita unless he became a Brahmo, then the one hope which had been buoying up Anandamoyi during these days of anxiety would be shattered in the dust! That very day Binoy had asked her the question: "Mother, shall I have to enroll my name in the Brahmo Samaj? Shall I have to accept that also?" and she had replied: "No, no! I don't see any need of that!"

Binoy had asked further: "And suppose they bring pressure to bear on me?"

"No," had observed Anandamoyi after a short silence, "this is not a matter in which pressure can be brought to bear."

But Sucharita did not agree with what Anandamoyi had said, and as she made no answer, Anandamoyi realised that Sucharita's mind had not yet given its assent.

Anandamoyi began to say to herself: "It was only through my affection for Gora that I was able to break through the traditions of my society. But is not Sucharita's heart attracted to Gora? If it had been, then surely she would not have made so much of such a trivial matter."

Anandamoyi felt somewhat depressed. There wanted only two or three more days before Gora's release from gaol, and she had been thinking that there was a field lying ready for him in which he would find happiness. She felt that now was the time for binding Gora, if ever, for otherwise there was no saying what difficulties he would get into. But to win Gora and keep him bound was not the task of an ordinary girl. On the other hand it would be wrong to give him in marriage to a girl in any Hindu family—that was why she had refused so many applications from fathers of marriageable daughters. Gora used to say that he would not marry at all, and people were astonished that she, as his mother, had never protested against his decision. Then when at last she had detected signs of his weakening she had rejoiced greatly, so Sucharita's silent opposition was a great blow to her. But she was not a person easily to let go the helm, and she said to herself: "All right, let us wait and see."

FIFTY FIVE

Paresh Babu was saying: "Binoy, I don't want you to do anything foolhardy just because of your anxiety to save Lolita from her dilemma. This agitation in our society has not much value—what is exciting them so much just now they will forget entirely in a few days."

Binoy felt that he had come braced up to do his duty by Lolita. He knew that such a marriage would be inconvenient from the point of view of society—and over and above that there was Gora's anger to be considered—but at the call of duty he had tried to banish all these unpleasant thoughts from his mind. And now when Paresh Babu suddenly wanted to dismiss this appeal of duty altogether Binoy felt all the more averse to turning back. He said:

"I shall never be able to repay you for all the affection you have shown towards me, and it is unbearable to me to think that I have been the cause of the least unhappiness in your family, even for a day."

"Binoy, you don't quite follow me," expostulated Paresh Babu. "I am personally delighted that you have such regard for us, but for you to offer to marry my daughter as a means of showing your respect does not show much regard for my daughter's feelings. So I explained to you that this difficulty is by no means of such a serious nature that you have to offer to make the least sacrifice."

Now at any rate Binoy was freed from any sense of responsibility, but his mind did not run along the unobstructed path of freedom with quite the same eagerness as a bird rises in the air when released from its cage. Even now he did not show any sign of moving, although the dam of restraint which he had been building for so long from a sense of duty had been found unnecessary. Where until recently he had taken every step in fear and trembling, drawing back at every moment, he was now occupying the whole space and found it hard to retreat. In the very place to which duty had taken him, dragging him by the hand, and was now saying: "Now, brother, retreat, you have no need to go further," his heart was saying, "You can retreat if you like, but I remain here."

Now that Paresh Babu had not given him any further excuse Binoy said: "You must not think that I was wanting to do something hard at the call of duty. If only you will give your consent nothing could give me greater joy than such good fortune as—I was only afraid lest—"

"There is not the least ground for your fears," interrupted Paresh Babu without a moment's hesitation. He loved truth so greatly that he even confessed: "I have heard from Sucharita that Lolita is not averse to you."

A flash of joy shot through Binoy's heart on hearing that this secret of Lolita's inner soul had been revealed to Sucharita. He wondered when and how she had spoken of it. An intense and mysterious joy thrilled his heart at the thought that he had been an object of intimate talk between these two friends. He at once said:

"If you think me worthy of her, then nothing could be a matter of more intense happiness to me."

"Just wait a little," said Paresh Babu. "Let me go upstairs and see my wife."

On going to ask Bordashundari her opinion, she urged: "Binoy will have to be initiated in the Brahmo Samaj."

"That goes without saying," answered Paresh Babu.

"We must first settle that," said Bordashundari, "so send for Binoy."

"Then we must settle a day for the initiation ceremony," said Bordashundari without further preamble, as soon as Binoy had come.

"Is initiation absolutely essential?" asked Binoy hesitatingly.

"Absolutely essential indeed!" exclaimed Bordashundari. "What do you mean? How else can you marry into a Brahmo family?"

Binoy hung his head without answering. So it seemed that Paresh Babu, on hearing that he wanted to marry his daughter, had taken it for granted that he would naturally enter the Brahmo Samaj.

"I have the greatest respect for the Brahmo Samaj," he faltered, "and up to now there has been nothing in my conduct which is contrary to its teaching. But is it absolutely necessary for me to become a member?"

"If your opinions are in harmony with ours, then what harm is there in being initiated?" asked Bordashundari.

"It is impossible for me to say that Hindu society means nothing to me," explained Binoy.

"Then it was wrong of you ever to raise this question," complained Bordashundari. "Have you shown yourself ready to marry our daughter just out of pity for us or to do us good?"

This was a great blow to Binoy, for he saw that his proposal really did seem to be insulting to them.

Just about a year before, the new Law of Civil Marriage had been passed, and at that time both he and Gora had written very strongly against it in the papers. It was therefore difficult for Binoy now to declare that he was not a Hindu and marry according to the Civil Marriage Law.

He saw now that Paresh Babu could not be expected to approve of the idea of his marrying Lolita while still remaining a Hindu, so heaving a sigh he stood up to go, and making his obeisance to both of them, said apologetically: "Please forgive me, I will not say more to aggravate my fault," and with that he left the room. As he was going downstairs he saw Lolita seated alone at a small desk in the corner of the verandah writing letters. At the sound of his footsteps she looked up, and for a moment gazed at him with an agitated expression. Lolita's acquaintanceship with Binoy was not recent—how often had she looked in his face, but to-day there seemed to be some mysterious secret expressed in her glance. That secret of Lolita's thoughts, known only to Sucharita, was to-day revealed to Binoy in the shadow of her dark eyelashes, and the tenderness of her glance was like a cloud laden with the coming coolness of rain. In the momentary glance which Binoy gave her in return her heart felt a sudden flash of pain. Without speaking a word he bowed to Lolita and went on down the stairs.

FIFTY SIX

W hen Gora came out of gaol he found Paresh Babu and Binoy waiting for him at the gate.

A month is by no means a long time. When Gora had been on his walking tour he had been separated from his friends and relations for more than that, but when, after his one month's separation in prison, he came out and saw Binoy and Paresh Babu, he felt as if he had been born again into the familiar world of his old friends. When he saw, in the early morning light, the gentle affection on Paresh Babu's peaceful face, he bowed down and took the dust of his feet with a joy of devotion such as he had never felt before. Paresh Babu embraced the two friends, and then Gora seized Binoy's hand and exclaimed with a laugh: "Binoy, from our school days we have taken all our education together, but I have stolen a march on you by taking instruction in this school of studies!"

As Binoy did not feel in a mood to join in his mirth he was silent. He felt that his friend had come out, having passed through the mysterious hardships of gaol life, more his friend than ever! He maintained an almost reverent and solemn silence until Gora asked: "How is mother?"

"Mother is well," answered Binoy.

"Come along, my friend," called Paresh Babu, "a carriage is waiting for you."

Just as they were about to get into the carriage Abinash came running up, panting, with a group of students behind him.

On seeing him, Gora hurried to take his seat, but Abinash was too quick for him and stood in his way, requesting him to stand there for a moment.

As he was making the request the students began to sing in loud voices:

> "To-day, after the dark night of sorrow,
>   Dawn has come!
> The bonds of subjection are shattered.
>   Dawn has come!"

"Be quiet!" shouted Gora, his face becoming scarlet. The students at once stopped singing and looked at him in surprise as he went on: "Abinash, what's all this to-do about?"

Abinash, without answering, brought out from under his shawl a thick garland carefully wrapped in a plantain leaf, while a young boy began to read an address in a high-pitched voice, at a speed like that of an organ which has been wound up. It was printed in letters of gold and the subject was Gora's release from gaol.

Rejecting Abinash's proffered garland, Gora exclaimed in a voice full of anger: "What's all this pantomime about? Have you been making preparations all this month for dressing me up as a member of your troupe by the side of the road here?"

As a matter of fact Abinash had been planning this for a long time. He had thought that it would make a great impression, and had not taken Binoy into his counsels, as he was covetous of the kudos which he felt sure such an unusual performance would bring. For at the time of which we speak such forms of nuisance had not become common. Abinash had even written a description of the scene for the papers and only left one or two details to be filled in on his return to Calcutta before sending it to the Press.

"It is wrong of you to speak like that," protested Abinash. "The fact is that we have been sharing your sufferings while you have been in prison. Our ribs have been scorched by a steady fire of heartfelt pain during every moment of this past month."

"You are mistaken, Abinash," observed Gora. "If only you look closely enough you will see that the fire has not even been kindled, and that no irreparable injury has been done to your ribs."

But Abinash was not to be squashed, and persisted: "The Government has tried to disgrace you, but to-day, as representatives of the Motherland India, we place this garland of honour—"

"This is getting beyond a joke!" expostulated Gora, and pushing Abinash and his followers to one side he turned to Paresh Babu and invited him to get into the carriage.

Paresh Babu heaved a sigh of relief as he took his seat, and Gora and Binoy followed him without delay.

Gora reached home next morning, having made the journey to Calcutta by steamer, and found a crowd waiting to do him honour outside his house. Managing somehow to free himself from their clutches he went in to see Anandamoyi. She had taken her bath early that morning and was ready waiting for him, and when Gora came in and touched her feet, she could not keep back the tears which all these days she had managed to control.

When Krishnadayal returned from his bath in the Ganges Gora went to see him, but he made his *pronams* from a distance and did not touch his feet. Krishnadayal having taken his seat at a safe distance, Gora said: "Father, I want to do penance."

"I don't see any need for that," answered Krishnadayal.

"I did not feel any hardship in gaol," explained Gora, "except that I found it impossible to keep myself from contamination. I don't feel free from self-reproach even now. That's why I must do ceremonial penance."

"No, no!" cried Krishnadayal in dismay. "There's no need for you to exaggerate so much. I can't give my approval to such a course."

"All right then," said Gora, "let me take the opinion of the pandits on the subject."

"You needn't consult any pandit," objected Krishnandayal. "I can give you an assurance that no penance will be necessary in your case."

Gora had never yet been able to comprehend, why a man, who was so particular with regard to ceremonial cleanliness as Krishnadayal was, never liked any kind of rule or restraint to apply to Gora—and not only did not wish to give his assent but positively opposed any attempt of Gora's in the direction of orthodox observances.

Anandamoyi had to-day placed Binoy's seat for the meal beside Gora's, but Gora expostulated: "Mother, please move Binoy's seat a little farther off!"

"Why, what is wrong with Binoy!" exclaimed Anandamoyi in surprise.

"There's nothing wrong with Binoy," answered Gora, "the fault lies with me. I am contaminated."

"No matter," answered Anandamoyi, "Binoy is not one to care about that sort of thing."

"Binoy may not care, but I do," said Gora.

When, after their meal, the two friends went upstairs to the deserted room on the top storey, they were at a loss what to say. Binoy could not think how he could broach to Gora the subject which had been uppermost in his own mind for the past month. Questions about Paresh Babu's family also occurred to Gora's mind, but he did not mention them, waiting for Binoy to introduce the subject. It is true that he had asked after his daughters from Paresh Babu, but that was merely for the sake of politeness. His mind was eager to hear much more detailed news of them than merely that they were well.

At this juncture Mohim came into the room and sat down, panting with the exertion of climbing the stairs. As soon as he had recovered his breath he said: "Binoy, we have been waiting all this time for Gora. Now that he has come there's no need for further delay. Let us decide the day at once. What do you say, Gora? You know to what I refer of course?"

Gora answered with a laugh, and Mohim continued: "You laugh, do you? You are thinking that your Dada hasn't yet forgotten about that! But let me tell you that a daughter is no dream—I am beginning to see that she is a very real object—one that you can't easily forget! Don't laugh about it, Gora, this time we must settle it finally."

"The man is present upon whom everything depends for a settlement!" exclaimed Gora.

"Oh, Hell!" protested Mohim. "Do you expect anything to be settled by a man who is so unsettled himself? Now that you have come you must shoulder the burden."

To-day Binoy maintained a solemn silence, even on the pretext of a jest at his own expense he did not try to say anything, and Gora, realising that there was some hitch somewhere, observed: "I can take charge of issuing the invitations, and even of ordering cakes and sweetmeats, I am even ready to give my services at the time of the wedding feast, but it is beyond me to take the responsibility for Binoy marrying your daughter. I myself am not on intimate terms with the one who is responsible for all this business of love— I keep at a safe distance and make my obeisances from afar."

"Don't for a moment imagine that because you keep at a distance he will spare you," said Mohim. "There's no telling when you will receive a surprise visit from him. I have no idea what his plans are with regard to you, but I know that with regard to Binoy he is making a fine mess. Let me tell you that you will have cause to repent it if you do not yourself become active in the matter instead of leaving it all to Cupid."

"I am quite willing to repent for not accepting a responsibility which is not mine," laughed Gora, "for I should have to repent even more bitterly if I did accept it. I want to be saved from such a fate."

"Will you stand by and see a Brahmin boy squandering his honour, his caste, and his respectability without protest?" inquired Mohim. "You give up your food and sleep in your anxiety to keep people good Hindus, and now your best friend is about to sacrifice his caste and marry into a Brahmo family, and you will not be able to show your face before people again. Binoy, I suppose you will be angry with me, but there are plenty of people who are ready to say all this to Gora behind your back, in fact they are falling over one another in their eagerness. I at least say it in your presence, and that is good for all parties concerned. If the rumour is false, then say so and the matter ends there, but if it is true, then settle it once for all."

When Mohim had left them Binoy did not speak a word, but Gora turned to him, and asked: "Why, Binoy, what's all this about?"

"It is difficult," began Binoy, "to explain everything properly by referring to only a few items of news, so I had decided that I would tell you the whole story gradually, but in this world nothing happens in the way we want it to—events seem first of all to go about silently, prowling like tigers hunting for their prey, and then, suddenly, without any warning, they have pounced on one's neck. News too seems at first to remain smothered like a fire, and then suddenly it bursts out into a blaze and there is no putting it out. For this reason

I sometimes think the only way for man to be free is for him to remain absolutely stationary."

"Where is the freedom if only you yourself remain stationary?" asked Gora, laughing. "If the rest of the world sees fit to remain moving, why should it allow you to be still? In fact just the opposite effect will be produced, for when the world is at work and you alone remain idle you will only find yourself cheated. Therefore you must be on the look-out that your attention is not distracted, lest while everything else is moving you find that you yourself are not ready."

"That is true enough," assented Binoy, "I'm never ready! This time too I was unprepared. I never understand from what direction something will take place, but when once it has happened then one must surely accept responsibility for it. It won't do to dissent from something unpleasant because it would have been better if it had never happened at all."

"Without knowing what has happened I find it difficult to discuss the matter," observed Gora.

Bracing himself for the confession Binoy began: "Through unavoidable circumstances I was placed in such a position with reference to Lolita that unless I marry her she will have to endure unfounded reproaches from her society for the rest of her life."

"Let me hear more definitely what kind of a position you were placed in," interposed Gora.

"That's a long story," answered Binoy. "I'll tell you everything by degrees; in the meantime you must be content with what I have told you."

"All right," said Gora, "I'm content. I have only this to say, that if the circumstances were unavoidable then all regret for the result is also unavoidable. If Lolita has to bear insult from her society then it can't be helped."

"But," expostulated Binoy, "the means of preventing that are in my hands!"

"It that is so, then it's a good thing," remarked Gora. "But you can't make it so simple by stating the fact vociferously. When men are in need it is in their power to steal and murder, but does that fact make such acts right? You say that you want to do your duty to Lolita by marrying her, but are you sure that it is your highest duty? Have you no duty to society?"

Binoy did not answer that he had decided against marrying into a Brahmo family because he had remembered his duty to society, instead of that he began to argue hotly, saying: "In this matter I don't think that you and I will agree. I am not speaking against society because of an attraction for an individual. What I contend is that there is something above both society and the individual to which we ought to look, and that is religion. Just as it is not my chief duty to save the individual, neither is it my chief duty to save society, my highest duty being to preserve the one and only religion."

"I can't respect a religion," expostulated Gora, "which denies the rights of the individual and of society and claims everything for itself."

"But I can!" exclaimed Binoy, his mettle up. "Religion is not built up on the foundations of society and the individual, it is society and the individual which depend on religion. If you once begin to call that religion which society happens to want, then society itself will be ruined; if society puts any obstacles in the way of a right religious freedom, then by surmounting such unreasonable obstructions we are doing our duty to society. If it is not wrong for me to marry Lolita, if indeed I ought to do so, then it would be actually irreligious for me to be deterred from doing so merely because it happened to be unfavourable to society."

"Are you to be the sole judge of what is right and wrong?" asked Gora. "Will you not consider what sort of a position you will be placing your children in by such a marriage?"

"If you once begin to think like that," urged Binoy, "then you will be making all social injustices permanent. Why then do you blame the poor clerk who continually puts up with insults and kicks from his European master? He also is thinking of the position of his children, isn't he?"

Binoy had come to a point in his argument with Gora which he had never reached before. Only a few weeks before he would have shrunk with all his being from the very possibility of any severance from society. On this subject he had not ventured to argue even to himself, and if the matter had not been discussed by Gora like this things would have taken quite the opposite direction, in conformity with the long-established habits of Binoy's mind. But as the argument went on, his inclination, supported by his own sense of duty, became stronger and stronger.

The discussion with Gora raged hot and fierce. In this kind of argument Gora did not usually appeal to reason—he simply expressed his views with a violence which few people could equal. To-day too he tried his best to shatter into dust every argument brought forward by Binoy, but on this occasion he discovered that there were obstacles in his way. So long as there had been only a question of Gora's opinion as against Binoy's, Gora had invariably been victorious—but to-day two real men were opposed to each other; Gora was no longer able to ward off wordy arrows by his own stock of verbal weapons, for wherever an arrow touched him it found a human heart sensitive and full of pain.

Finally Gora exclaimed: "I don't want to bandy words with you, for there is not much in this which is worth arguing about, it is more a matter for the heart to understand. But that you should want to separate yourself from the people of your own country, by marrying a Brahmo girl, is a matter of intense pain to me personally. You may be able to do such a thing, but I never could—that's where you and I differ—it is neither in wisdom nor in intelligence. It is your affections that are turned in a different direction from mine. You can hardly be expected to feel for society when you want to deal it such a stab, just where I feel the throb of life. What I want is India, no matter how you may find fault with her or how much you may abuse her. I don't want anyone greater than her, whether myself or another! I do not wish to do the least thing which might separate me from her even by a hair's breadth!"

And before Binoy could get out his answer Gora cried: "No, Binoy, it is futile to argue with me about this! When the whole world has forsaken India and heaps insults upon her, I for my part wish to share her seat of dishonour—this caste-ridden, this superstitious, this idolatrous India of mine! If you want to separate yourself from her then you must separate yourself from me also."

Gora got up and, going out on to the verandah, began to pace up and down, while Binoy remained sitting in silence, till the servant came and announced that a crowd of people was waiting to see Gora outside, and Gora, glad of the opportunity for escape, went downstairs.

On going outside he saw that amongst a crowd of others was Abinash. Gora had made up his mind that Abinash was angry with him, but there was not the least sign of anger in him at present. In fact he began to make a speech praising, in exaggerated language, the incident of Gora's refusal to accept the garland the previous day. He declared before all: "My respect for Gourmohan Babu has increased greatly. I had known for a long time that he was an uncommon man, but yesterday I discovered that he is a great personage. We went yesterday, to show him honour, but he rejected the honour in a manner that you would find few people showing nowadays! Is that a thing to be scoffed at?"

Gora was overcome with confusion at such words and his annoyance with Abinash made him quite hot. He exclaimed impatiently: "Look here, Abinash, you insult a man by your kind of honour! Could you not expect from me modesty enough to refuse your invitation for me to join in that dance of yours by the roadside? And you call this the sign of a great personage! Have you the idea of starting a strolling *Jatra* party, and of going round collecting dole? Is no one ready to do even the least bit of real work? If you want to work with me, all right, and if you want to fight against me, all right too, but I beg you not to go about like this, shouting 'Bravo! Bravo!'"

But this only made Abinash's devotion the greater, and he turned with a beaming face to those who were present, as though to draw the attention of them all to the wonderful spirit of Gora's words! He exclaimed: "By your blessing we have been able to see such true disinterestedness on your part as it is to the everlasting glory of the Motherland. We can surrender our lives to such a one," and with these words he bent down to touch Gora's feet, but Gora moved away impatiently.

"Gourmohan Babu," said Abinash, "you refuse to accept any honour from us, but it will not do for you to refuse us the pleasure of your presence at a feast which we intend to hold one day. We have all been discussing it and you must consent to come."

"Until I have done penance," answered Gora, "I can't sit down with any of you to a meal."

Penance! Abinash's eyes became bright, as he exclaimed: "Such an idea would never have occurred to any of us, but Gourmohan Babu can never neglect any of the rules laid down by the Hindu religion."

All agreed that it would be an excellent plan for them all to meet for the feast on the occasion of the ceremony of penance. Some of the big pandits of the country would have to be invited, and they would receive ocular demonstration, on seeing Gourmohan's insistence on making penance, that even in these days the Hindu religion is a living thing.

When and where the ceremony should take place was also discussed, and when Gora declared that it would be inconvenient at his own home, one of his devoted followers, who had a garden house on the banks of the Ganges, proposed that the arrangements should be made there. It was also decided that the expenses of the occasion should be defrayed by all the members of the party combined.

Just before their departure Abinash began an eloquent and impassioned address in which, waving his hands at the audience, he said: "Gourmohan Babu may be angry with me, but when the heart is full it is impossible to restrain one's feelings. For the rescue of the Vedas, avatars[1] have been born in this holy land of India, and so to-day we have obtained an avatar who has been born for the preservation of the Hindu religion. In the whole world our country is the only one which has six seasons—and in this country of ours avatars have been born from time to time and will take birth again. We are indeed fortunate that we have had proof that this is true! Brothers, let us cry, 'Victory to Gourmohan!'"

Excited by Abinash's eloquence the whole crowd began to cheer vociferously, but Gora fled in great confusion.

To-day, his first free day after his gaol experiences, an intense weariness seemed to overcome him. In the confinement of gaol life he had for many days been dreaming of how he would work for his country with new enthusiasm, but to-day he kept asking himself only one question: "Alas, where is my country? Is it real only to myself? Here is my earliest friend, he with whom I have discussed all my life's plans and hopes, ready at a moment's notice to sever all connection after so many years with his past and future, with complete callousness,

----

1 Avatar is an incarnation.

in order to marry some girl he has taken a fancy to! And here are those who belong to what everyone called my party, after my having explained my views to them so many times, deciding that I am an avatar born only to preserve the Hindu religion! I am merely a personified form of the Scriptures! And is India to be given no place? Six seasons, indeed! In India there are six seasons! If the only product of these six seasons is the ripening of a fruit such as Abinash, where would have been the loss in having two or three seasons less?"

At this moment the servant came saying that his mother called him, and on receiving this message Gora started suddenly, and repeated to himself, "Mother has called me!" and it seemed to him that the words had a new significance to him. He said to himself, "No matter what happens, I have my mother. And she is calling for me. She will unite me with everyone. She will not permit me to remain at a distance from anyone. I shall see that those who are my own are with her sitting in her room. In the gaol, too, mother was calling me, there I was able to see her, and now outside the prison walls she calls me and I will go to see her." As he spoke thus to himself he looked out towards the cold sky of that winter noonday, and his differences with Binoy and Abinash suddenly seemed to him to become trivial. In this sunlight of midday, India seemed to be stretching out her arms towards him, and he saw spread out before him all her rivers and mountains, her cities and oceans, and from the infinite there poured a clear and stainless light in which the whole of India shone radiantly. Gora's heart was so full that tears came to his eyes and all despondency vanished from his mind. His nature was preparing joyfully for that work for India which was so endless, the fruits of which seemed so far off. Though he was not able to see with his own eyes the greatness of India which he had seen in his meditations, he did not feel the least shadow of regret. He said to himself again and again: "Mother is calling me! Let me go to where the Bestower of all food, the One who maintains the Universe, is seated so infinitely far away in time and yet present at each instant, the One who is beyond death and yet in the midst of life, the One who sheds the glorious light of the Future on the imperfect and miserable Present—let me to there—mother calls me to that infinitely far and yet infinitely close." In the midst of this joy Gora felt the presence of Binoy and Abinash—as though they too were not separated from him—all the trifling differences of that day being merged in a complete harmony.

When Gora first entered Anandamoyi's room his face was almost transfigured with the radiance of his happiness, and it seemed to him as if there was behind everything that he saw before him some wonderful presence. Coming in suddenly he did not at first recognise who it was who was sitting beside his mother!

It was Sucharita who stood up and bowed to him.

"It is you then that has come?" said Gora to her. "Sit down please!"

When he said, "It is you that has come!" he spoke as though it were no ordinary event, but some special advent.

At one time Gora had avoided Sucharita, and so long as he had been on his tour, engaged in work and undergoing various hardships, he had been able to put the thought of her more or less out of his mind. But during his days of confinement in gaol the memory of Sucharita haunted him. There had been a time when the fact that there were women in India hardly entered Gora's mind, but now he had made a new discovery of this truth through Sucharita, and the sudden and complete revelation of such a great and ancient fact made the whole of his strong nature tremble as though from a blow. When the sunlight and free air of the outer world entered into his prison cell and filled his mind with pain, he saw that world not merely as his own field of work composed only of the society of men—there appeared before him in his meditations the faces of two presiding deities of that beautiful outside world, the light of the sun, moon, and stars illumining them with a special radiance, with the cool blue sky surrounding them as a tender background—the one lighted by a mother's love known to him from his birth, and the other the beautiful and tender face of his new acquaintance.

In the midst of this narrow and joyless gaol life Gora found it impossible to feel antagonistic when the memory of this face rose in his mind. The unique joy of this meditation brought into his prison a sense of deep freedom, and the hardships of gaol seemed to him like some false and unsubstantial dream. All the waves of his throbbing heart transcended the prison walls and mingled with the sky, played on the shimmering leaves and blossoms, and broke on the shores of the work-a-day world.

Gora had thought to himself that there was no reason to be afraid of an image of his fancy, so for the whole of that month he had let his thoughts flow freely in that channel, arguing to himself that it is only of real things that we need to be afraid.

But when, on coming out of gaol, Gora had seen Paresh Babu his heart was filled with joy. That his joy was not merely because of meeting Paresh Babu, but with it there was mingled the magic of that image which had haunted his fancy for so many days—all this Gora, at first, did not realise. But gradually it dawned on him, as he was on the steamer going to Calcutta, that Paresh Babu did not have such a strong attraction for him by reason only of his own virtues.

Now Gora braced himself again for the conflict, saying to himself that he would not be defeated. As he sat on the steamer he determined that again he would go away to a distance, and would never allow his mind to be bound by even the finest of fetters.

It was while in this frame of mind that the argument with Binoy had taken place. At this first meeting with his friend after their separation, such a violent altercation would not have occurred if it had not been that Gora was really arguing with himself. It was becoming increasingly clear to him that the issues involved in this argument affected his own honour. And it was for that reason he spoke so vehemently on that day—his vehemence was a necessity for himself. When to-day his violence aroused in Binoy an opposing violence, and when in his mind Binoy was only tearing to pieces all Gora's arguments, and calling them stupid bigotry, when his whole mind arose in revolt against him, Binoy never dreamed for a moment that Gora would not have been giving him such heavy blows unless he had been dealing those blows at himself also.

After his discussion with Binoy, Gora decided that it would not do to leave the field of battle. He thought, "If out of fear for my own life I let go of Binoy, then Binoy cannot be saved."

FIFTY SEVEN

Gora was deep in thought just then—he regarded Sucharita, not as a special individual, but rather as an idea. The womanhood of India was revealed to him in the figure of Sucharita, and he regarded her as the manifestation of all that was sweet and pure, loving and virtuous in the homes of his Motherland. His heart overflowed with happiness as he saw, seated beside his mother, this incarnation of the grace which shone upon India's children, served the sick, consoled the afflicted, and consecrated with love even the most insignificant. He saw in her a manifestation of the power which never forsakes the meanest of us in our sorrows or misfortunes, which never despises us, and although entitled to worship offers its devotions to even the most unworthy amongst us. She seemed to him to be the one whose skilful and beautiful hands put the seal of sacrifice on all our works, and to be like some imperishable gift of ever-patient and all-powerful love which God's hands have bestowed upon us, and he said to himself: "We have allowed this gracious gift to pass unnoticed—we have put it in the background hidden behind all else—what clearer sign of our misery could there be!" He thought to himself that it is woman who ought to be called the motherland—she it is who is seated on the hundred-petalled lotus, in the innermost abode of India's heart—we are her servitors. The misfortunes of the country are insults to her, and it is because we are indifferent to those insults that in these days we have cause to be ashamed of our manhood.

Gora was astonished at his own thoughts. He had never realised before how imperfect his perception of India had been so long as he had failed to acknowledge the women of India. What a lack there had been in Gora's conception of his duty to his country so long as its women were so shadowy and unreal to him! It was as though his idea of duty had power but no life, muscles but no nerves. Gora realised in a single moment that the further we banish woman from us, and the smaller the place we give to her in our lives, the weaker does our manhood become.

So when Gora said to Sucharita: "So you have come!" there was more in his words than mere conventional politeness! His salutation conveyed his newly discovered joy and wonder.

Gora bore some traces of his gaol experiences. He looked less healthy than he had done before, for the gaol food was so distasteful to him that he had practically fasted the whole month he was in prison. His complexion had lost much of the clear brightness it had shown before and he looked quite pale, and because his hair had been cropped short the thinness of his face was even more apparent.

On seeing how thin Gora looked, Sucharita felt a special regard for him awaken in her mind, though with it there was much pain. She wanted to bow down and take the dust of his feet! Gora was revealed to her like the pure flame of a fire which is blazing so brightly that neither smoke nor fuel is visible, and a devotion mixed with tender compassion so trembled in her breast that she was unable to utter a single word.

Anandamoyi was the first to speak. She said: "Now I understand what happiness mine would have been if I had

had a daughter. How can I tell you what a comfort Sucharita has been to me all the time you have been away! Before I got to know her, I did not realise that one of the glories of sorrow is that at such a time we become acquainted with many great and good things. We get distressed because we do not know always in how many ways God has given us consolation for our sorrows. You may feel shy, little mother, but I feel compelled to tell in your presence what a happiness you have been to me during these sad days!"

Gora looked towards Sucharita's shy face with an expression of solemn gratitude, and then addressed Anandamoyi, saying: "Mother, she came to share your sorrow in your days of sadness, and now she has come to increase your joy on this day of happiness—those who have large hearts are such disinterested friends."

"Didi," exclaimed Binoy, on seeing how shy she was, "when a thief is caught he gets punished from all sides, and so now that you have been caught by them all you have got to enjoy the fruits. Where can you fly to? I have known you for a long time, but I have never given you away. I have kept silent, though I have known quite well that it couldn't be concealed for long."

"You have kept silent, have you?" laughed Anandamoyi. "You are such a silent boy by nature, aren't you? Why, from the very first day he got to know you he has been singing your praises, and there has been no restraining him!"

"Just listen to her, Didi!" cried Binoy. "The witness and proof that I am appreciative of merits and am not ungrateful are both present!"

"You are now only singing your own praises!" exclaimed Sucharita.

"But you will never get me to make known my virtues," protested Binoy. "If you want to hear them you must come to mother—you will be dumbfounded—even when I myself hear her I am astonished! If only mother will write my biography I am willing to die young!"

"Just hear the boy talk!" exclaimed Anandamoyi.

And in this way the first shyness was broken.

At the time of departure Sucharita said to Binoy: "Won't you come and see us one day?"

Sucharita invited Binoy to come but she could not ask Gora. He did not understand the real reason and he felt rather hurt. That Binoy found it so easy to mix with everyone and took his own place in every society, and Gora could not, had never before been a matter of regret to Gora, but to-day he acknowledged to himself that this lack in his character was a real failing.

FIFTY EIGHT

Binoy understood that Sucharita had invited him to discuss with her the proposed marriage with Lolita. It seemed then that although he had given his final decision the matter was by no means finished with! So long as he had life he would not be able to get free from either party.

Up to now Binoy's chief anxiety had been how he could break the news to Gora! By Gora he was not thinking merely of the individual, for Gora stood for certain ideas—a certain faith, and he had been a kind of support in life. Binoy's constant connection with him had become a matter of habit as well as joy to him, and any sort of quarrel with him was like a quarrel with himself.

But the blow had fallen and the first feeling of shrinking from the task had disappeared. Binoy had got a certain strength from having told Gora about his connection with Lolita. Before an operation there is no limit to a patient's fears, but when the knife begins to cut, the sick man sees that even with the pain there is relief also, and what in imagination seems so serious a matter is not so in reality.

Until then Binoy had not been able to bring himself to argue even with himself, but now the door for discussion was open, and in his mind he was constantly thinking of answers to Gora's arguments. And objections which it seemed to him likely that Gora might make he would pick to pieces from various standpoints. If only he had been able to argue the whole matter out with Gora, then, although he might have got excited, he would have come to some final conclusion, but Binoy saw that Gora would not discuss matters to the end. This made Binoy rather hot—he thought, "Gora will not understand, and will not explain either, he simply wants to use violence. Violence! How can I ever bow my head before violence? Let what will happen, I am on the side of truth!" and as he uttered the word truth it seemed to clutch hold of his heart as though it were a living thing. To make a stand against Gora it was necessary to side with the strongest possible party, and so making truth his chief support Binoy repeated the word again and again to himself. In fact, feeling that he had taken refuge in the truth, he began to feel a great respect for himself, and when he started for Sucharita's house he walked with head erect. Whether he felt so confident because he was inclined towards truth, or because his inclination was towards something else, Binoy was not in a condition to understand.

When he arrived Harimohini was busy cooking, and Binoy stood at the kitchen door, and having put forward a claim for a midday meal suitable for a Brahmin's son, he went upstairs.

Sucharita was engaged with some needlework, and without lifting her eyes from her task she at once broached the subject she had on her mind. She said: "Look here, Binoy Babu, where there is no inner obstacle ought we to respect an opposition which is purely external?"

When he had been arguing with Gora, Binoy had taken one point of view, and now that he was arguing with Sucharita he took just the opposite. How could anyone have guessed now that he had any difference of opinion with Gora?

"But aren't you making too little of external obstacles?" inquired Binoy.

"There's a reason for that, Binoy Babu!" explained Sucharita. "Our obstacles are not exactly external ones, for our society is founded upon religious principles, whereas the society you belong to is hemmed round by social bonds. Therefore if Lolita has to leave her society it will be a serious matter for her, whereas for you to leave your society would not be much of a loss to you."

Then began a discussion between them as to whether or not man's personal religion ought to be entangled in any society or not.

While this was going on Satish came into the room with a letter and a newspaper. On seeing Binoy he became very excited and wished that he could by some means change Friday to a Sunday. In less than no time Satish and his friend Binoy were talking happily together, while Sucharita began to read the newspaper and the note which accompanied it, which was from Lolita.

In this Brahmo newspaper there was an item of news which said that in a well-known Brahmo family there had been a fear that a marriage was to take place with a Hindu, but the danger had passed owing to the young man's unwillingness. With this news as the theme the article went on to compare the deplorable weakness of the Brahmo family with the firm faith of the Hindu young man, and the comparison was by no means in favour of the Brahmo family.

Sucharita thought within herself that no matter what might be said, Lolita's marriage with Binoy must be brought about somehow. But she saw it would not be by arguing with this young man, so she sent a note to Lolita asking her to come round at once, without any mention that Binoy was there.

Since there was no calendar accommodating enough to make Friday into Sunday, Satish had perforce to leave to get ready for school, and Sucharita too got up to take her bath and begged Binoy to excuse her for a little.

When the heat of the discussion had cooled down and
Binoy was left alone in the room the inner spirit of his young
manhood awoke. It was about nine o'clock, and in the lane
there were few passers-by. The ticking of the small clock on
Sucharita's writing-table was the only sound that disturbed
the silence. The spirit of the room began to exert its influence
over Binoy's mind, and it seemed as if all the little details of
its furnishing became suddenly familiar to him. The neatness
of her table, the embroidered chair covers, the deerskin spread
beneath the chair, the two or three pictures hanging on the
walls and the row of books bound in red cloth and arranged
on a little bookshelf, all exercised a deep fascination over his
mind. A beautiful mystery seemed to gather in the interior
of this room, and the memory of the discussions which had
taken place in its lonely stillness at midday, between the two
companions, seemed even now to be hidden there like some
shy and beautiful presence. Binoy began to try and imagine
how and where each one had sat as they talked, and he
fashioned in his mind many pictures of the confidences to
which Paresh Babu had referred when he said: "I have heard
from Sucharita that Lolita is not averse to you." An
indescribable current, like the tender tune of some wandering
minstrel, began to flow through Binoy's mind, and in the
secret places of his heart there arose such a speechless and
inexpressible feeling, that being neither a poet nor an artist
Binoy became inwardly restless. He felt as if he would be all
right if he could only do something, but the means of action
seemed out of his power. It was as though a veil separated
him from what was quite close so that it seemed to be at an
infinite distance, and yet he had not the power to rend the
veil.

Harimohini came into the room and asked Binoy if he
would take any refreshments, and when Binoy replied in the
negative she came into the room and sat down.

So long as Harimohini had been living in Paresh Babu's house she had been greatly attracted to Binoy, but, from the time she had come with Sucharita to a home she could call her own, all outside visitors had become very distasteful to her. She had come to the conclusion that Sucharita's recent lapses in matters of social conduct were entirely the fault of her friends. Even though she knew that Binoy was not a Brahmo she felt only too clearly that he was not very strict in observing Hindu customs, so she was not so eager nowadays to invite this son of a Brahmin to partake of the sacred food offered to her gods.

To-day in the course of her talk she asked Binoy: "Well, my child, you are the son of a Brahmin, but don't you observe the evening worship?"

"Auntie," said Binoy apologetically, "through learning so many things by heart day and night I have forgotten all the right texts for evening worship!"

"Paresh Babu has also learned a great deal," answered Anandamoyi, "but according to his own religion he always observes some form of worship both morning and evening."

"But, Auntie," expostulated Binoy, "what he does cannot be managed by merely learning off a few texts. If ever I become like him I shall do as he does."

"So long as you are not like him," said Harimohini rather harshly, "why can't you follow your ancestors? Is it good to be neither one thing nor the other? Man after all is a religious being. But neither Ram, nor the Ganges! How can that be?"

She was interrupted at this point by the entrance of Lolita, who on seeing Binoy started violently and asked Harimohini where Sucharita was.

"Radharani has gone to take her bath," said Harimohini and Lolita, as though she thought some explanation of her appearance were necessary, said: "It was Sucharita who called me here."

"Well, sit down till she comes," said Harimohini, "she will be here directly."

Harimohini had no very kindly feelings towards Lolita either, for she wanted now to get Sucharita away from her old surroundings and to keep her entirely under her own control. Paresh Babu's other daughters were not so intimate, but Harimohini was not at all pleased at the way Lolita dropped in at all times for a chat with Sucharita. She used to try and interrupt their talks by calling Sucharita away on the pretext of some housework, or she would express her regret that nowadays Sucharita's studies were not making such progress as they used to do. She would say this in spite of the fact that when Sucharita did give her time to study she would never forget to say that education was not only not necessary for girls but was positively injurious. The real truth was that, because she was not able to hedge Sucharita round as she wanted to do, she was in the habit of blaming sometimes her companions and sometimes her studies.

She was not at all pleased at having to sit with Binoy and Lolita, but because she was angry with them she remained seated. She felt that there was some mysterious relationship between the two, and she said to herself: "No matter what the rules of your society may be I will never allow this sort of shameless intimacy, all this Christian kind of behaviour, to go on in any house of mine."

In Lolita's mind also there was an uncomfortable feeling of opposition. The previous day she had decided that she would accompany Sucharita to Anandamoyi's house, but when it came to the point she could not bring herself to go. She felt great respect for Gora but at the same time her hostility towards him was very keen, for she could not get the idea out of her mind that Gora's attitude towards her was unfavourable in all kinds of ways. She felt this to such an extent that from the very day of Gora's release from prison her feelings towards Binoy also had undergone a change. Previous to that she had been actually priding herself on her influence over Binoy, and the very idea that he was not to extricate himself from his friend's clutches made her feel antagonistic towards him for his weakness.

Binoy, on the other hand, the moment he saw Lolita come into the room, began to feel greatly agitated. With regard to Lolita he could never keep his ideas clear, for from the time their names had been connected together in the gossip of the community his mind would become agitated like a magnetic needle disturbed by a storm the moment he saw her.

As for Lolita, she felt very angry with Sucharita when she found that Binoy was seated there. She saw that she had been sent for to straighten out what had become tangled, and in the hope of making the mind of the unwilling Binoy favourable towards her again. So she turned to Harimohini and said: "Tell Didi that I can't stay just now, and that I'll come another time." And without so much as looking at Binoy she went quickly out of the room.

Now that it was no longer necessary for Harimohini to stay she also got up and went to do some housework.

The look, as of suppressed fire, on Lolita's face was not unfamiliar to Binoy, but it was a long time since he had seen it. He had been feeling free from anxiety as the evil days had apparently passed for good when Lolita had been so ready to produce her fiery arrows against him, but to-day he saw that she had taken out those old weapons from her armoury, and there was not the least sign of rust on them. It is hard enough to bear anger, but for a person like Binoy it was doubly difficult to bear contempt. He remembered with what keen dislike she had regarded him when she thought him to be a mere satellite of the planet Gora, and now he felt upset at the thought that to Lolita his hesitation must seem like a sign of cowardice. It was unbearable to him that she should be regarding as timidity what was really a hesitation born of a sense of duty, and yet would never give him a single opportunity for saying even a couple of words on the subject. To be cheated of the chance of arguing was to Binoy the greatest possible punishment, for he knew that he could argue, and arrange his words skilfully, and that his power of justifying any particular side in a discussion was no uncommon gift. But whenever Lolita entered into conflict with him she never gave him an opportunity for argument, and to-day again the opportunity had not occurred.

Seeing a newspaper lying on the table in his impatience he snatched it up and suddenly saw that in one place it was marked in pencil. He read the passage and at once saw that he and Lolita were the objects of the discussion and of the comments that followed, and realised that Lolita would be always subjected to this kind of insult from the people of her community. It seemed to him therefore perfectly proper that a spirited girl like her should feel it contemptible on his part to spend his time in arguing fine points of social principle instead of trying to save her from such humiliation. He felt ashamed when he compared himself with this high-spirited girl and remembered her brave and complete indifference for society.

When Sucharita returned to Binoy, after having taken her own bath and given Satish his morning meal before sending him to school, she found him sitting moody and depressed, so she did not raise the subject of their previous discussion again.

Before he sat down to his meal Binoy omitted the usual ceremonial cleansing, and Harimohini expostulated: "Binoy since you don't observe any of our Hindu customs why don't you become a Brahmo?"

Binoy, feeling a little hurt, replied: "The very day I come to regard Hinduism as consisting of prohibitions with regard to touching, and prohibitions with regard to eating, and a lot of other meaningless rules and regulations, I shall become, if not a Brahmo, then a Christian, a Mussalman, or something of that sort. But I have not yet such a lack of faith in Hinduism."

When Binoy left Sucharita's house his mind was greatly disturbed, for it seemed as if he were receiving shocks from all sides, and as though he had reached a place that was void and without shelter!

Wondering why he had got into such an unnatural position, he walked slowly along with head bowed in thought, till he came to a square where he took a seat under a tree. Hitherto, whenever in his life any knotty question had arisen, he had taken it, whether great or small, to discuss with his friend, and a solution had always been found, but to-day that way was closed and he had to face it alone.

As the sun's rays began to penetrate to the shade where he was sitting he got up and went out into the road again, but he had not gone far when he suddenly heard Satish's voice calling: "Binoy Babu! Binoy Babu!" and a moment later his little friend had hold of his hand. It was Friday, and Satish was on his way home after his school had closed for the week-end.

"Come along Binoy Babu," pleaded Satish, "come home with me!"

"How can I?" asked Binoy.

"Why can't you?" persisted Satish.

"How will your people be able to bear me if I go so often?" explained Binoy.

Thinking such an argument entirely beneath his notice, Satish merely said: "No, come along!"

Satish was quite oblivious of the great calamity which had befallen Binoy in his relationship to their family, and Binoy's heart was profoundly moved at the thought of this boy's pure love for him. The completeness of the joy which he had found in the heaven of Paresh Babu's home was untouched only in this member of the family. On this day of catastrophes it was only in his mind that no cloud of doubt had arisen, and no blow from society had tried to destroy the bond. Putting his arm round the boy's neck Binoy said: "Come on, little brother, I will take you as far as the door of your house," and he felt as though in the embrace that he gave Satish, he got a touch of the sweetness which had surrounded the boy from his childhood in the love and affection of Sucharita and Lolita.

The uninterrupted flow of irrelevant chatter which Satish kept up constantly as he walked along sounded intensely sweet in Binoy's ears, and in this touch with a boy's sincerity of heart he was able to forget for a little the tangled puzzle of his own life.

To reach Sucharita's house they had to pass in front of Paresh Babu's, and Paresh Babu's sitting-room on the first floor could be seen from the street. As they passed in front of that room Binoy could not resist looking up once, and he saw Paresh Babu sitting at his table. It was impossible to see whether he was speaking or not, but Lolita was seated on a stool with her back to the road, close to Paresh Babu's chair, just like an obedient pupil.

The agitation that Lolita had felt as she left Sucharita's house had made her so unbearably restless that, finding no other means of checking her distress, she had gone quietly to Paresh Babu. There was reflected in him such a deep peace that often the impatient Lolita used to go and sit silently beside him in order to control her own restlessness. To-day Paresh Babu had asked: "What is it, Lolita?" to which she had replied: "Nothing, father. But this room of yours is so nice and cool."

Paresh Babu clearly understood that she had come to him to-day with a wounded heart, for in his own heart too there was a hidden pain. So he began gradually to introduce such subjects as would help to lighten the burden of the trivial joys and sorrows of the individual life.

At the sight of this confidential talk between father and daughter Binoy for a moment stood still, and to what Satish was saying he paid not the least attention. Satish was propounding a very abstruse problem of military tactics. He was inquiring whether it would not be possible to train a troop of tigers and by placing them in the front line of battle, between one's own army and the enemy, make victory certain. Up to this moment the flow of question and answer had been going on unobstructed, and on receiving this unexpected check he looked up at Binoy to see what was the matter. Following the direction of Binoy's glance he saw Lolita, and immediately called out: "Lolita Didi, Lolita Didi, see, I got hold of Binoy Babu on the way from school and have brought him home."

When Lolita jumped up from her chair, and Paresh Babu too turned to look into the street, Binoy became hot all over, feeling that he was responsible for all this to-do. However, he managed to say good-bye to Satish and to go into Paresh Babu's house.

When he got upstairs he found that Lolita was no longer there, and thinking that he must appear like a robber who has broken in upon their peace he took a seat with shy hesitation.

When the usual preliminaries of asking after each other's health, etc., were over, Binoy began at once: "Since I do not observe the rules and customs of Hindu society with much devotion, and in fact transgress them almost everyday, I have been thinking that it is my duty to take shelter in the Brahmo Samaj, and my wish is to be initiated by you."

This wish and determination had not taken clear shape in Binoy's mind even fifteen minutes before, and Paresh Babu was so surprised that he remained silent for a little. Then he said: "But have you considered the question carefully from every point view?"

"In this matter there is nothing much to be considered," answered Binoy. "It seems to me to be simply a question of right and wrong. It is a perfectly straightforward matter. With the teaching that I have had I cannot sincerely accept as religion a mere state of not transgressing certain rules and customs. It is for this reason that at every step inconsistencies appear, and so long as I remain connected with those who regard Hinduism with real devotion I shall merely be giving them shocks, and I have no doubt in my mind that this is very wrong of me. Without worrying myself at present about anything else I must be prepared to escape from this wrong, otherwise I shall not be able to preserve my self-respect."

Such a long explanation was quite unnecessary for Paresh Babu, but it was needed by Binoy himself to strengthen his determination. He felt his breast swell with pride as he thought of the battle between right and wrong in the midst of which he found himself, and in which he, taking the side of right, would have to be victorious. The honour of his manhood was at stake.

"Are your opinions at one with those of the Brahmo Samaj on matters of religious faith?" asked Paresh Babu.

"To tell you the truth," began Binoy, after a moment's silence, "there was a time when I thought that I had religious faith, and even used to have quarrels with many people on the subject, but now I realise that in matters of religious faith I am quite undeveloped. I have come to understand this much from knowing you. No real need of religion has occurred in my life, and because no real faith in it has grown in me I have up to now only followed the current religion of our society and upheld it by all sorts of skilful and hair-splitting arguments. I have never felt any need for thinking which religion is true; I have been merely going about trying to prove the truth of that religion which would bring me victory. The harder it became to prove, the more pride I took in proving it. I can't say even now whether I shall ever have a perfectly true and natural religious faith, but it is certain that if only I get into a favourable environment and meet with those who are an example to me, I shall make progress in that direction. At any rate I shall be freed from the humiliation of going about displaying, as though it was a flag of victory, the thing which does inner violence to my intelligence."

As he went on discussing his position with Paresh Babu, arguments favourable to his present state of mind began to take shape, and he began to speak with such enthusiasm that it appeared as if he had come to this firm decision after having weighed the pros and cons for many days.

Still Paresh Babu pressed him to take a little more time before deciding, which made Binoy think that Paresh Babu had some doubt as to his firmness of purpose. This only made him all the more obstinate, and he again and again declared that he was so sure of himself that there was no possibility of his being shaken from his determination. There was no mention made by either side of the proposal of marriage with Lolita.

At this point Bordashundari came in on the pretext of some housework, and when she had finished it she was about to leave the room without having shown any sign that she had seen Binoy there. Binoy thought that Paresh Babu would certainly call Bordashundari back to tell her this latest piece of news, but Paresh Babu did not say a word, in fact he did not consider that the time had arrived for speaking of it. He wanted to keep the matter a secret, but when Bordashundari showed so rudely her contempt for and anger against him, Binoy was not able to restrain himself. He followed her and bending down in obeisance at her feet, said: "I have come to you to-day to tell you that I want to be initiated into the

Brahmo Samaj. I know I am not worthy but my hope is that you will make me so."

Bordashundari heard him with astonishment and, turning back, slowly re-entered the room with a questioning look in Paresh Babu's direction.

"Binoy has requested me to initiate him," explained Paresh Babu.

On hearing this Bordashundari felt the pride of one who has made a conquest, but why was it that her joy was not unalloyed? She had an intense desire to teach Paresh Babu a lesson for once. She had again and again declared, with the assurance of a prophetess, that her husband would have to repent bitterly of his conduct, so when she saw how unmoved Paresh Babu was by the agitation which was going on all round him in their society, she felt an intense inward impatience, and now when all their difficulties seemed to be about to be nicely settled she could not feel pure unmixed delight. So she said with a solemn air: "If this proposal for initiation had only been made a few days earlier we should not have had to endure so much sorrow or humiliation."

"This is not a question of our troubles or humiliations," observed Paresh Babu. "Binoy desires to be initiated, that's all."

"Merely initiation?" questioned Bordashundari.

"God knows that I am at the root of all your sorrows or humiliations!" exclaimed Binoy.

"Look here, Binoy," said Paresh Babu, "do not undertake this business of initiation without fully comprehending it. I said to you before that you were not to take any step which would involve serious consequences because you are under the impression that we are in some social dilemma."

"That is true enough," chimed in Bordashundari, "but what I contend is that he has no right to sit still doing nothing after having involved us all in such a tangle."

"If instead of sitting still doing nothing," interposed Paresh Babu, "you simply become excited, then the tangle will only become more complicated. It's no use saying that it is one's duty to be doing something; often enough one's chief duty is not to do anything at all."

"Yes, of course," complained Bordashundari. "I'm a fool, and am not able to understand anything. But I want to know what is going to be decided about it—I've got plenty of work waiting for me to do."

"I would like to be initiated on Sunday, the day after tomorrow," said Binoy. "So if Paresh Babu—"

"No," interrupted Paresh Babu, "I can't undertake any initiation by which my family can hope for any benefit. You must apply to the Brahmo Samaj direct."

Binoy at once felt discouraged, for he had not reached the point at which he felt he wanted to apply for initiation in a formal kind of way to the authorities of the Brahmo Samaj—especially seeing that it was that very community which had coupled his name with that of Lolita. How could he have the face to compose a letter of application, and in what language could he write it? How would he be able to show his face after the letter had been published in the Brahmo papers? The letter would be read by Gora, and by Anandamoyi also! Besides that, it would not appear in its full context, and Hindu readers would see only an unexpected eagerness on Binoy's part to take initiation in the Brahmo Samaj, and this was not the whole truth. Binoy could not hide his shame unless the other facts were also made known.

On seeing that Binoy remained silent Bordashundari became alarmed, and said: "Oh, I forgot. Of course Binoy Babu does not know anyone besides ourselves in the Brahmo Samaj. But never mind, we can make all the necessary arrangements. I'll send for Panu Babu at once. There's not much time to lose. Sunday is so near."

As she finished speaking Sudhir passed the door on his way upstairs to the top floor, and Bordashundari called after him: "Sudhir, Binoy is going to be initiated into our Samaj on Sunday."

Sudhir was delighted, for in his heart he had always greatly admired Binoy, and the thought of getting him in the Brahmo Samaj filled him with joy. He had always considered it most unreasonable that a man who could write such excellent English as Binoy, and had such intelligence and education, should not be a member of the Brahmo Samaj. His heart swelled with pride at this proof that men of Binoy's stamp could not be happy outside his community, and he said: "But how can it be arranged by Sunday? You won't be able to make it sufficiently widely known." For Sudhir's desire was that this initiation of Binoy's should be proclaimed before all and sundry as a kind of example.

"No, no!" exclaimed Bordashundari, "it can easily be managed by Sunday. Go quickly, Sudhir, and call Panu Babu."

The unfortunate being, by whose example the excited Sudhir saw the invincible might of the Brahmo Samaj made manifest to all, was feeling very small! That which, at the time of argument and reasoning did not seem of great importance, made him feel very uncomfortable when it showed its face in the open.

At the suggestion of Panu Babu being summoned, Binoy got up to go, but Bordashundari did not want to let him off, and pressed him to stay, saying that Panu Babu would be there directly, and he need not wait long.

But Binoy said apologetically: "No, you must excuse me to-day."

He felt that if only he could get breathing space, away from the hedge that surrounded him, so as to get time to think things out more clearly, he would feel all right.

As he got up to go Paresh Babu also got up, and putting a hand on Binoy's shoulder, said: "Don't do anything hastily, Binoy—get some peace and quiet, and think things over well before deciding anything. Do not take a step which affects your whole life so seriously without fully understanding your own mind."

Bordashundari feeling inwardly quite exasperated with her husband, said: "Those who begin a task without thinking things out at the start, who sit still doing nothing till they have got themselves and others into a scrape, when they find that there is no way of escape then say: 'Sit down and think!' You may be able to settle down to thinking, but in the meantime our lives are in danger."

Sudhir accompanied Binoy when he went out of the house, for he was feeling a restlessness like that of someone who wishes to taste the dishes before sitting down to a fine feast. He was keen to take Binoy at once to his friends of the Brahmo community and, announcing the glad tidings, begin the festival of joy there and then, but at the sight of Sudhir's expansive enthusiasm Binoy became more and more depressed. When Sudhir proposed that the two of them should go together to Panu Babu's at once, Binoy, without paying the least attention to the suggestion, snatched his hand away from Sudhir's and fled.

After going some distance he saw Abinash with two or three members of his party tearing along somewhere at a tremendous speed, but they stopped on seeing Binoy, and Abinash exclaimed: "Good, here is Binoy Babu! Come. Binoy Babu, come along with us!"

"Where are you going?" asked Binoy.

"Why, we are going to Kashipore Garden to make things ready for Gourmohan Babu's penance ceremony."

"No," protested Binoy, "I haven't time to go just now."

"What do you mean?" cried Abinash. "Do you realise what a great event this is going to be? If it had been a light matter, why should Gourmohan Babu have made such a proposal at all? Nowadays it is necessary for the Hindus to proclaim their own strength, and this penance of Gourmohan Babu's is going to create great sensation amongst the people of our country! We are inviting all the celebrated pandits from all over the place, so that this will have its effect on the whole of Hindu society. People will realise that we are still living! They will know that Hinduism is not about to die!"

Managing somehow to escape from Abinash's wiles, Binoy went on his way.

FIFTY NINE

When Haran Babu arrived in response to Bordashundari's message, he looked very serious for a moment, and then said: "It is our duty to send for Lolita and discuss this matter with her."

On Lolita's coming, Haran Babu, with portentous solemnity, said: "Look here, Lolita, a time has come in your life of great responsibility. On one side is your religion, and on the other your inclination, and you will have to make your choice as to which of these you will follow!"

Having said this much he paused to see the effect on Lolita, for he felt that in face of such an example of a passion for righteousness all cowardice must tremble, and all insincerity be reduced to ashes—this glowing example of spiritual ardour of his was indeed a valuable asset to the Brahmo Samaj!

But Lolita did not answer a word, and as she remained silent Haran Babu went on: "Doubtless you have heard that Binoy Babu, in view of the position you are in, or for some other reason, is expressing his readiness to become a member of the Brahmo Samaj."

This was news to Lolita, and though she did not express any opinion on it, her eyes became bright, and she remained seated like an image in stone.

"Paresh Babu," continued Haran Babu, "is, of course, delighted at this obliging willingness of Binoy's, but it is for you to decide whether or not this is a matter for being pleased at. Therefore in the name of the Brahmo Samaj I request you to-day, putting aside this insane desire of yours and looking into your heart from the standpoint of religion only, to ask yourself this question: 'Is there any real cause for being happy about this?'"

As Lolita still remained silent, Haran Babu thought that he was making a great impression, so he went on with re-doubled enthusiasm: "Initiation! Is it necessary for me to say what a sacred moment in life the initiation ceremony is? And will you allow such a ceremony to be polluted! At the bidding of happiness, convenience, or personal attachment are we going to surrender our Samaj to the path of falsehood, and welcome insincerity as though we honoured it? Tell me, Lolita, are you going to permit yourself to be connected with this distressing incident in the history of the Brahmo Samaj all your life?"

Even at this question Lolita remained as she was, silent and motionless, the only change being that she tightened her grasp of the chair on which she was sitting. So Haran Babu went on again: "I have often observed how irresistible is the force of personal desire in weakening man's character, and I know too how one has to pardon man's weakness, but when that weakness affects not only one's own life but the lives of hundreds of others and shatters into fragments their only shelter, tell me, Lolita, whether you think that pardonable for a single moment? Has God given us the right to pardon such weakness?"

"No, no! Panu Babu!" cried Lolita, leaving her chair and standing in front of him, "you need not pardon us! We have all become accustomed to your attacks, and probably 'any forgiveness that you could offer would be absolutely unbearable to everyone!" and with these words she left the room!

Bordashundari was very much disturbed at what Haran Babu had been saying, for she by no means wanted to lose

Binoy, but all her importunity was in vain, so far as Haran Babu was concerned, and in the end she parted from him in anger. She was in a fix, for she had managed to get neither Paresh Babu nor Haran Babu on her side. No one could have foreseen her getting into such an inconceivable situation, and her opinion of Haran Babu underwent another change.

As for Binoy, so long as his idea of taking initiation had been hazy in his own mind, he had expressed his determination with great zeal, but when he saw that he would have to make formal application to the Brahmo Samaj, and that Haran Babu would be consulted on the matter, he shrank with horror from this open publicity. He could not think where he could go and with whom he could consult, finding it impossible even to go to see Anandamoyi about it. He did not feel inclined to go for a walk, so he went to his own lodgings and, going upstairs to his bedroom, threw himself on his bed.

Evening came, and when the servant entered with the lamp he was just on the point of sending it away when he heard Satish calling him from downstairs, "Binoy Babu! Binoy Babu!" On hearing Satish call him Binoy began to feel alive again, as though in the middle of a desert he had suddenly got a draught of water. At that moment Satish was the only person in the world who could console him, and all his lassitude disappeared at the sound of his voice. Calling out: "What, little brother, what is it?" he jumped from his bed and, without putting on his shoes, rushed downstairs, only to find waiting at the foot of the stairs leading into the little courtyard not only Satish but also Bordashundari. So he must again face that puzzle, and enter once more into that struggle!

Having taken them upstairs, Bordashundari ordered Satish to go and sit outside on the verandah, but Binoy, to relieve the misery of such a joyless banishment, gave him some picture books and took him into the next room, where there was a lamp.

When Bordashundari opened the attack by saying: "Binoy, as you do not know anybody in the Brahmo Samaj, you just write a letter for me to take to the minister of our church community and I will go round to-morrow morning and make all the necessary arrangements for your initiation on Sunday. You need not worry yourself a single moment longer," Binoy was so taken aback that he could not answer a word. But, nevertheless, he obediently wrote a letter and handed it to Bordashundari. He felt that no matter what happened he must find a way out from which there was no possibility of return and in which there could be no more question of hesitation.

Bordashundari also made a passing reference to Binoy's marriage with Lolita.

As soon as she had left him Binoy began to feel a certain disgust, so that even the memory of Lolita struck a harsh note in his mind. It seemed to him as if Bordashundari must have been encouraged by Lolita in this display of unseemly haste. Along with the waning of his own self-respect it was as though his respect for everyone else had abated.

Bordashundari, on the other hand, was thinking that on her return home she would have a piece of news to tell which would please Lolita, for she had discovered for certain that her daughter loved Binoy, and that way why there had been such a fuss in the Samaj about their marriage. For this she blamed everybody but herself. For several days she had practically not spoken to Lolita, but now that a way out had been found, largely by her own exertions, she was anxious to make it up with her wayward daughter by telling her the glorious news. Lolita's father had ruined everything, and even Lolita herself had not been able to guide Binoy aright. From Panu Babu too she had got no assistance. It had been for Bordashundari alone to cut the knot! Yes! Yes! One woman could manage what half-a-dozen men could not accomplish!

On reaching home Bordashundari heard that Lolita had gone to bed early, as she was not feeling well. She smiled to herself as she said: "I'll soon make her feel all right again!" and taking a lamp in her hand she went to the bedroom, where she found that Lolita had not yet gone to bed, but was reclining on her sofa, reading. Immediately Lolita sat upright, and asked: "Mother, where have you been?"

There was a sharpness in the question, for Lolita had heard that her mother had gone to Binoy's lodgings with Satish.

"I have been to see Binoy," answered Bordashundari.

"Why?" asked Lolita.

Why, indeed! said Bordashundari to herself somewhat angrily. Lolita can only think of me as her enemy! Ungrateful girl!

"That is why!" exclaimed Bordashundari, thrusting Binoy's letter out for Lolita to see. On reading the letter Lolita blushed scarlet, all the more when Bordashundari, in order to exaggerate her success, made out that she had not got the letter out of Binoy without considerable pressure! She could say with pride that, apart from herself no one would have had the ability to bring this matter to a successful issue!

Lolita, covering her face with her hands, lay down on the sofa, and her mother, thinking that she was shy of showing the intensity of her feelings openly, went out of the room.

Next morning when she went to get the letter, to take it to the Brahmo Samaj, she saw that someone had torn it into pieces!

SIXTY

Next evening, just as Sucharita was preparing to go to see
Paresh Babu, the servant came to announce that a
gentleman had called to see her. "What gentleman?" she
asked. "Is it Binoy Babu?" The servant replied that it was not
Binoy Babu, but a very tall fair gentleman. At this information
Sucharita started, and told the servant to show him upstairs.

Sucharita had not given a thought that day to what she
was wearing or how she was wearing it, and when she looked
in the mirror she was not at all satisfied with her appearance.
But there was no time to change, so giving a few hasty touches
to her hair, and adjusting her dress a little, she went into the
room. She had forgotten that on her table there were lying
copies of Gora's books, and there was Gora sitting right in
front of that table! The books were lying shamelessly before
his eyes, and she was unable either to remove them or to cover
them up.

"Auntie has been anxious to meet you for a long time,"
said Sucharita. "I will go and tell her you have come," and
she left the room, for she had not the courage of face Gora
alone.

After a few minutes Sucharita returned with Harimohini.

Harimohini had for some time past been hearing from
Binoy about Gora's life, and opinions, and his devoted faith,
and occasionally at midday she would request Sucharita to

read to her from his writings. Not that she was able to comprehend everything quite clearly, but she understood at least that Gora was a strict follower of the Scriptures and his writings were a protest against the loose principles of present-day society. At any rate they were a great convenience to her in encouraging her midday nap. She felt an admiration for Gora because nothing could be more wonderful and virtuous in her eyes than for an English-educated young man of modern times to take such a firm stand for orthodoxy. When she had first met Binoy in that Brahmo household she had been delighted with him, but gradually as she got to know him better, and especially when she had got a house of her own, the flaws in his conduct began to hurt her. Because she had relied too much on him she was beginning to reproach him unduly, and she was therefore looking forward to meeting Gora with the greater eagerness.

As soon as she set eyes on him she was astonished. Here was a Brahmin indeed! He was bright like the flame of some sacrificial fire! He resembled Mahadev in his lustrous radiance! She felt such a respect for him that when he stooped to make his *pronam* to her she shrank back in dismay.

"I have heard so much about you!" exclaimed Harimohini. "But when I see you I wonder how anyone could have the face to put you in gaol!"

"If people like you had been magistrates," laughed Gora, "then gaols would have been the haunts only of bats and rats!"

"No, my child," replied Harimohini, "there is no lack of thieves and cheats in this world. But was the Magistrate blind? One has only to look at your face to see that you are not a common person, that you are one of God's own people. Have you to put people in gaol simply because there is a gaol to be filled? Good gracious! What sort of justice is this?"

"The magistrates," explained Gora, "lest, by looking at men's faces, they should see the glory of God, do their work by keeping their eye on the Law books. Otherwise do you think they could have taken their food or got any sleep, while committing so many people to floggings, imprisonment, transportation, and even hanging?"

"When I have leisure," said Harimohini, "I get Radharani to read to me out of your writings, and I have been looking forward for a long time to the pleasure of hearing such words from your own lips. I am a poor foolish woman, and unfortunate into the bargain—I can neither understand nor give my mind to everything, but I have a firm belief that I shall be able to gain some wisdom from you!"

Gora, without contradicting her, modestly remained silent.

"You must take something to eat before you go," went on Harimohini. "It is a long time since I have been able to entertain a Brahimin boy like you. For to-day you must be satisfied with some sweetmeats, but another day I will invite you to a regular meal."

Sucharita being left alone, while Harimohini went out ot bring the light refreshments, became quite agitated.

"Did Binoy come to see you to-day?" asked Gora abruptly.

"Yes," replied Sucharita.

"I have not seen him since," said Gora, "but I know what he came about."

He paused, and Sucharita also, remained silent.

"You are trying," went on Gora, "to make Binoy marry according to your Brahmo rites! Do you think that fair?"

Being slightly goaded by this remark, all signs of shyness or hesitation on Sucharita's part vanished, and she looked straight at Gora as she replied: "Do you expect me to say that I do not think marriage according to our Brahmo rites is a good thing?"

"Be assured," answered Gora, "that from you I expect nothing of a trifling character. I look for much more from you than one can expect from ordinary sectarian people. I can say with the most absolute certainty that you do not belong to that class of people who work like coolies to increase the number of adherents to their own sect. I want you to understand yourself in your own way, and not to belittle yourself, misled by other people's opinions. You must realise in your own mind that you are not merely a member of any special party!"

Sucharita, summoning all her strength of mind to the argument, asked: "Do you not, then, belong to a particular party?"

"No," replied Gora, "I am a Hindu! A Hindu belongs to no party. The Hindus are a nation, and such a vast nation that their nationality cannot be limited within the scope of any single definition. Just as the ocean is not the same as its waves, so Hindus are not the same as sects."

"Then why," asked Sucharita, "if you have no party, is the party spirit so rife amongst Hindus?"

"Why," responded Gora, "when a man is struck does he defend himself? Because he has life. A stone can bear all sorts of blows quietly."

"If," inquired Sucharita, "Hindus count as a menace what I regard as the essence of religion, then what ought I to do? Tell me that!"

"Let me tell you," said Gora, "that when that which you consider to be a duty deals such a painful blow to that vast being known as the Hindu nation, then it is time for you to think seriously whether there is not some error or blindness in yourself, and whether you have really looked at the matter from every possible point of view. It is not right to resort to violence, taking for granted, through your own habits and indolence, that the beliefs of your society are the only true ones. When a rat gnaws a hole in the hull of a ship it considers only its own inclinations and convenience; it does not see that the advantage it gains by making a hole in such a huge shelter is very trifling compared with the immense loss it will cause to all. So you too ought to consider whether you are acting in the interests merely of your own sect or of the whole of mankind. Do you realise what the whole of mankind means? What a variety of needs it has, what different kinds of natures, what innumerable tendencies? All men do not stand at the same stage in the path—some are in front of the mountains, some on the shores of the sea, and some at the edge of the plains; though not one of them has the power to remain still, all have to keep moving. Do you want to impose the authority of your own sect upon everybody else? Do you want to shut your eyes and imagine that all men are alike and have been born into the world in order to become members of the sect known as the Brahmo Samaj? If that is your idea, then in what way do you differ from those robber nations who refuse to admit, because of their pride in physical force, that the differences between nations are in inestimable value to whole of mankind, and who imagine that the greatest blessing for humanity is that they should conquer all other nations of the world and bring them under their undisputed sway, thus reducing the whole earth to slavery?"

For a moment Sucharita forgot that Gora was arguing, her heart being profoundly moved by the marvellously solemn sound of his powerful voice. She did not feel that he was arguing, but the truths which he was expounding awoke a deep response in her mind.

"Your society," continued Gora, "did not create the millions of those who inhabit India. Is it for you to take upon yourself to dictate forcibly what path is best for these millions, what faith will satisfy their hunger, and by what actions they can become powerful? How can you wish to reduce to one and the same level an India of such vastness? When you find yourself being obstructed in the realisation of this impossible task you get angry with the country itself, and the greater the obstacles become the greater does your hatred and contempt become for those whom you wish to benefit! And yet you imagine that you worship the God who has made men different and wishes to keep them so. If you truly honour Him, then why can't you see clearly what His ordinances are, and why, in the pride of your own intellect and party, do you not acknowledge His intention?"

When Gora saw that Sucharita listened to him without attempting to make any answer his mind was filled with compassion, and when he began again after a slight pause his tone was more gentle: "Perhaps my words sound harsh to you, but don't revolt against me because you think I am a man of the opposite party. If I had thought of you merely as representing an opposing sect I would not have spoken a single word. But I am distressed when I see your natural liberality of mind confined within the narrow boundaries of a sect."

"No, no!" exclaimed Sucharita, blushing, "you must not be troubled about me. Go on talking and I will try to understand."

"I have not much more to say," said Gora. "Look at India with your clear intelligence, and love her with your sincerity of heart. But if you regard the people of India merely as non-Brahmos your vision will be distorted and you will feel a contempt for them,—you will only misunderstand them and will not see them in their completeness. God has created men differing from each other in ideas and in actions with a variety of beliefs and of customs, but fundamentally one in their humanity. There is something in all of them which is mine, which belongs to India as a whole, which, if only we can see it in its truth, will pierce through all littleness and incompleteness and reveal a vast and wonderful being through which the secret of the worship of centuries will be made clear. We shall see that the flame of sacrifice of past ages still burns through the ashes, and without doubt a day will come when, transcending the limits of time and place, that flame will kindle a fire throughout the world. Even to say in imagination that all the great deeds and words of India's manhood in past ages are false is to show dishonour to truth; it is nothing but atheism!"

Sucharita had been listening with her head bowed, but now she lifted her eyes and asked: "Then what do you tell me to do?"

"I have nothing more to say," answered Gora, "only this much I would add. You must understand that the Hindu religion takes in its lap, like a mother, people of different ideas and opinions; in other words, the Hindu religion looks upon man only as man, and does not count him as belonging to a particular party. It honours not only the wise but the foolish also, and it shows respect not merely to one form of wisdom but to wisdom in all its aspects. Christians do not want to acknowledge diversity; they say that on one side is the Christian religion and on the other eternal destruction, and between these two there is no middle path. And because we have studied under these Christians we have become ashamed of the variety there is in Hinduism. We fail to see that through this diversity Hinduism is coming to realise the oneness of all. Until we can free ourselves from this whirlpool of Christian teaching we shall not become fit for the glorious truths of our own Hindu religion!"

Sucharita not only heard what Gora was saying, his ideas seemed to become visible before her, and that distant future which Gora saw by the power of his contemplative vision revealed itself to her through his spoken words. Forgetting all her shyness, forgetting even herself, Sucharita sat looking up at Gora's face aglow with the radiance of his enthusiasm. She saw in that face a strength expressed by which all the great purposes in the world seemed to have been realised truly by esoteric power. Sucharita had heard many learned and intellectual people of her society discussing principles of truth, but Gora's words were not mere argument, they were a creation. They were so evident to the senses that they took possession at one and the same time of the body and of the mind. Sucharita to-day saw Indra with his thunderbolt; when the words struck her ears with their deep strong tones her heart trembled and keen flashes of lightning seemed to dance at every moment in her veins. She had not the power to think and see clearly where her opinions differed from those of Gora and where they were in harmony.

Satish came into the room at this moment, and as he always stood in awe of Gora, he kept as far away from him as possible, and going up to his sister said in a whisper: "Panu Babu has come." Sucharita started as though she had been struck, for she was in a frame of mind in which she would have given anything to be able to get rid of this unwelcome visitor. Thinking that Gora had not heard Satish's whispered remark she got up and hurried out of the room. She went straight downstairs, and addressing Haran Babu, said: "You must excuse me, but it will not be convenient for me to talk with you to-day."

"Why won't it be convenient?" queried Haran Babu.

"If you will call on my father to-morrow morning," said Sucharita, without answering his question, "you will be able to see me there."

"To-day I suppose you have visitors?" observed Haran Babu.

"I have no time to spare just now," said Sucharita, avoiding this question also. "I beg you to excuse me for to-day."

"But," persisted Haran Babu, "I heard the sound of Gourmohan Babu's voice from the street. He is here I suppose?"

Unable to avoid this direct inquiry, Sucharita said with a blush: "Yes, he is."

632 ❖ RABINDRANATH TAGORE OMNIBUS

"That's a good thing," exclaimed Haran Babu. "I want to have a word with him also. If you have any special work to do you can leave me to talk with Gourmohan Babu for a little." And without waiting for Sucharita's assent he went upstairs, followed by Sucharita, who, as she entered the room, said to Gora, without so much as a glance towards Haran Babu: "My aunt went to prepare some refreshments for you, I will just go and see her about it." With this remark she left the room hurriedly, while Haran Babu with a solemn face took possession of a chair.

"You seem to be looking rather ill," remarked Haran Babu.

"Yes," assented Gora. "I happen to have been undergoing recently some treatment for making me unwell."

"That is true," answered Haran Babu, softening his voice. "You must have suffered a good deal."

"Not much more than was hoped for," said Gora sarcastically.

"I have a matter to discuss with you in reference to Binoy Babu," said Haran Babu, changing the subject. "I expect you know that he is making preparations for being admitted into the Brahmo Samaj on Sunday?"

"No, I have not heard that," answered Gora.

"Do you approve of this step?" asked Haran Babu.

"Binoy does not ask for my approbation," replied Gora.

"Do you think," pursued Haran Babu, "that Binoy Babu's faith is sufficiently strong for him to be ready for initiation?"

"When he has expressed his willingness to be initiated," replied Gora, "then such a question is entirely superfluous."

"When we have a strong inclination towards something," observed Haran Babu, "then we do not give ourselves sufficient leisure for considering what we believe and what we do not believe. You know human nature."

"I don't engage in futile discussions on the subject of human nature," snapped Gora.

"Although," said Haran Babu, "my opinions and my society are not in accord with yours I entertain a great respect for you, and I know quite well that, whether your beliefs be true or false, no temptation will be able to make you waver in them. But—"

"Of course," interrupted Gora, "it would be a terrible loss to Binoy if he were deprived of that small amount of regard which you have managed to preserve for me! In this world the distinction between right and wrong is a necessary one, but if you want to determine the relative value of things by your own regard or lack of it, then do so by all means, but you must not expect everybody else to accept your verdict."

"Very well," said Haran Babu, "even if that question remains undecided no great harm will be done. But I want to ask you one question. Are you not going to make any objection to this attempt of Binoy's to marry into Paresh Babu's family?"

"Haran Babu!" exclaimed Gora, turning scarlet. "How can I discuss all these matters relating to Binoy with you? Since you are always talking about human nature, you ought at least to be able to understand that Binoy is my friend and not yours."

"I have raised this question," began Haran Babu, "because of its connection with the Brahmo Samaj, otherwise—"

"But I am nobody to the Brahmo Samaj," exclaimed Gora impatiently, "so of what value to me can this anxiety of yours be?"

Sucharita entered at this point in the discussion, and Haran Babu turned to her, and said: "Sucharita, I have a matter of great importance to talk to you about."

There was no special necessity for making this remark, but Haran Babu spoke deliberately just to show to Gora on what terms of special intimacy he was with Sucharita. She however, did not answer him, and Gora remained seated immovably in his chair, not showing the least sign of giving Haran Babu an opportunity for an uninterrupted talk.

"Sucharita," repeated Haran Babu, "come into the next room, as I have something to say to you."

Without taking any notice of his request Sucharita looked at Gora and said: "Is your mother well?"

"I have never known mother to be anything but well!" laughed Gora.

"Yes," assented Sucharita. "I have seen myself how easy she finds it to keep well."

Gora at once remembered how Sucharita had been to see Anandamoyi when he had been in gaol.

Haran Babu had meanwhile taken up a book which lay on the table, and after examining the title-page for the author's name was glancing at one or two passages.

Sucaharita looked uncomfortable and blushed, while Gora, knowing that it was one of his books, laughed slightly to himself.

"Gourmohan Babu," inquired Haran Babu, "this I suppose is some of your youthful writings?"

"I'm still youthful!" laughed Gora. "In the case of some species of animals youth soon passes, and with others it persists a long time."

Getting up from her chair Sucharita said: "Gourmohan Babu, your food must be ready by now! Will you come into the other room? Auntie will not come out before Panu Babu, so perhaps she is waiting for you."

This last remark was made by Sucharita as a special hit at Haran Babu. She had borne with so much that day that she could not refrain from returning at least one blow.

Gora got up, and the irrepressible Haran Babu observed: "Then I will wait for you here."

"Why wait here uselessly?" asked Sucharita. "It is late already."

But Haran Babu would not budge, so Sucharita and Gora went out of the room.

On seeing Gora in that house and noticing his behaviour towards Sucharita, Haran Babu's fighting spirit was aroused. Was it possible that Sucharita was going to slip out of the clutches of the Brahmo Samaj so easily? Was there no one who could rescue her? Somehow or other this would have to be stopped!

Taking a sheet of writing-paper Haran Babu wrote a letter to Sucharita. He was a man of certain fixed ideas, one of which was that whenever, in the name of truth, he administered a scolding to anyone his spirited words could never remain without some fruit. He never thought that words are not everything and that there is a reality known as the heart of man.

When, after a long talk with Harimohini, Gora went into Sucharita's room to fetch his stick it was already evening. A lighted lamp stood on Sucharita's desk. Haran Babu had gone, but lying on the desk, where it could not fail to be seen by anyone entering the room, was a letter addressed to Sucharita.

On catching sight of that letter Gora's heart became hard, for he had not a doubt who the letter was from. He knew that Haran Babu had a special claim on Sucharita, but he had not heard that his claims had met with any opposition. When that afternoon Satish had come in and announced to Sucharita the news of Haran Babu's arrival, and she had looked startled and had hurried downstairs, and when shortly afterwards she had returned in his company, Gora felt as if a harsh note had been struck. Then again when Sucharita had taken him out of the room to take refreshments and had left Haran Babu alone, although it had seemed to him rather rude behaviour, he had decided that such impoliteness was a sign of the intimacy of the relationship between the two. Now when he saw this letter lying on her table he received a great shock.

A letter is such a mysterious object. Because only the name is written outside, and all the vital matter is inside, a letter has a peculiar power of torturing people.

"I will call again to-morrow," announced Gora, looking towards Sucharita.

"Very well," she replied with averted eyes.

Just as he was on the point of taking leave Gora suddenly stopped and exclaimed: "Your place is in the solar system of India—you belong to my own country—it is impossible for you to be swept into the void by the tale of some wandering comet! When you are firmly established in your right place, then I will be able to relinquish you! People have made you believe that in that place your religion will forsake you—but I must tell you clearly that your truth and your religion is not merely the opinion or sayings of a few persons; it is united by countless threads with those all around you—you cannot root it up at will and plant it in a pot if you want to keep it bright and vigorous with life; if you want to raise it to full usefulness you will have to take your seat in the place which has been determined for you by the people of your country long before you were born. You must never say, 'I am nobody to them, and they are nobody to me.' If you speak so, then the truth of your religion and all your strength will vanish like a shadow. I can assure you that if your opinions draw you away from the place to which God has sent you, no matter where it may be, then your opinions will never be victorious. I will come again to-morrow."

As with these parting words he left the room the very air seemed to tremble for a long time after he had gone, and Sucharita remained sitting motionless like a statue.

SIXTY ONE

"Look here, mother," Binoy was saying to Anandamoyi, "to tell you the truth, every time I bow down before an idol I feel somehow ashamed. I have so far managed to conceal that feeling, in fact I have actually written several excellent articles in defence of idol worship. But I must tell you the truth, and I confess that when I make an obeisance to an idol my mind does not give its assent."

"Is your mind such a simple thing," exclaimed Anandamoyi, "you can never look at anything in its entirety, but must always regard things in their fine details? That is why you are so fastidious."

"That is true enough," assented Binoy. "Because I have such a keen intellect I am able to prove by hairsplitting arguments even what I do not believe in myself. All these religious principles that I have been defending so much all these days, I have been defending, not from the point of religion, but from the point of view of a party."

"That's what happens when there is no real attraction to religion," remarked Anandamoyi. "For then religion becomes merely a thing to take pride in, like wealth, or honour, or race."

"Yes," agreed Binoy. "We do not think of it as religion, but go about fighting for it because it is *our* religion. That's what I have been doing all this time, though I have not been able to deceive myself completely. Because I have feigned faith where my beliefs have not carried me I have all along felt ashamed of myself."

"Do you think I didn't understand that much?" exclaimed Anandamoyi. "You have always exaggerated more than ordinary people do, and from that it was easy to see that because there was a hollow space in your mind you had to use plenty of mortar to fill it up. So much would not have been so necessary if your faith had been simple."

"So I've come to ask you," went on Binoy, "whether it is good for me to pretend to have faith in something in which I do not believe?"

"Just listen!" exclaimed Anandamoyi. "Is it necessary to ask such a question?"

"Mother," said Binoy abruptly, "to-morrow I am going to be initiated into the Brahmo Samaj!"

"What do you say, Binoy?" exclaimed Anandamoyi in astonishment. "Surely that is not necessary!"

"I have just now been explaining to you its necessity, mother!" expostulated Binoy.

"With the faith that you have now, can't you stay on in our society?" asked Anandamoyi.

"If I did," answered Binoy, "I should be guilty of insincerity."

"Haven't you the courage to stay in your present community without being insincere?" inquired Anandamoyi. "The people of your community will persecute you no doubt, but can't you bear persecution?"

"Mother," began Binoy, "if I can't live according to the Hindu society, then—"

"If," interrupted Anandamoyi, "three hundred million people can live in the Hindu community, then why can't you do so?"

"But mother," expostulated Binoy, "if the members of the Hindu society say that I am not a Hindu, then can I make myself one by declaring violently that I am?"

"The people of my community call me a Christian," said Anandamoyi. "I never sit to eat with them in their social functions, but I don't see why I should have to accept their definition of me. I consider it wrong to try and escape from a position which I myself think to be the one I ought to be in."

Binoy was about to answer when Anandamoyi prevented him from speaking by continuing: "Binoy, I'm not going to allow you to argue about this, it is not a matter for argument! Do you think you can conceal anything from me? I can see that on the plea of arguing with me you are trying to deceive yourself forcibly. But do not try to throw dust in your eyes on a question of such serious importance!"

"But, mother," said Binoy with his face averted, "I have already sent a letter and given my word that I shall take initiation on Sunday."

"That can never be allowed," frowned Anandamoyi. "If you explain the situation to Paresh Babu he will never press you unduly."

"Paresh Babu showed no enthusiasm for this initiation," explained Binoy; "he is not going to take any part in the ceremony."

"Then you need not worry any further," exclaimed Anandamoyi, relieved.

"No, mother," cried Binoy, "there can be no turning back now that I have once given my word. That can never be."

"Have you told Gora?" asked Anandamoyi.

"I haven't seen Gora since I decided," answered Binoy.

"Why, isn't Gora at home now?" inquired Anandamoyi.

"No," replied Binoy. "I was told he had gone to Sucharita's house."

"Why, he was there yesterday!" exclaimed Anandamoyi in astonishment.

"He is there to-day also," observed Binoy.

As he spoke the sound of palanquin bearers came from the courtyard below, and Binoy, thinking that it was some female relative of Anandamoyi's who had arrived, went out.

It was, however, Lolita who had called and now made her *pronams* to Anandamoyi. Her visit was quite unexpected, and as Anandamoyi looked in astonishment at Lolita's face she understood that she had come because of the difficulty she was placed in through this affair of Binoy's initiation and all that it involved.

In order to introduce the question tactfully Anandamoyi began: "I am so pleased that you have called, little mother. Binoy was here only a moment since, and he was speaking of taking initiation into your community to-morrow."

"Why is he going to be initiated?" asked Lolita impatiently. "Has he any special necessity for doing so?"

"Is there then no necessity?" exclaimed Anandamoyi, amazed.

"None that I can think of!" answered Lolita.

Not being able to understand Lolita's meaning, Anandamoyi remained silent, with a questioning look in her direction.

"Suddenly to take his initiation in this manner will be humiliating for him," continued Lolita with eyes averted. "For what purpose is he going to accept this humiliation?"

"For what purpose? Does Lolita, then, not know? Is there nothing in this proposal to give Lolita happiness?" exclaimed Anandamoyi to herself, saying aloud: "To-morrow is the day settled, and as he has given his promise it is impossible to draw back now, that is what Binoy said."

With shining eyes Lolita turned to Anandamoyi, and said: "On all such matters there is no meaning in keeping one's promise—if it is necessary to change one's mind then one must do so."

"My dear," said Anandamoyi, "there's no need for you to feel shy before me, and I am going to speak quite openly to you. So far as I have been able to understand Binoy, no matter what his religious beliefs may be, I can see no need for him to leave his community, in fact he ought not to do so. He may say what he likes, but I can hardly believe that he does not realise that. But, my dear, you are not ignorant of what his thoughts are. He is certainly under the impression that without leaving his society he cannot be united to you. Do not feel shy, little mother, tell me frankly whether this is not true?"

"Mother," answered Lolita, lifting her eyes to Anandamoyi's, "before you I will not be reserved in the least. I assure you that I myself do accept all these ideas. I have come to the conclusion, after much thought, that it can never be necessary for a man to cut off all connection with his religion, his beliefs, or his society, no matter of what nature they may be, in order to be united with other men. If that were necessary then no friendship could exist between a Hindu and a Christian, and we ought to raise high walls round each sect and keep them each within its own fence."

"Ah!" exclaimed Anandamoyi, her face shining with delight, "I am so happy to hear you speak so. That is just what I say! When men differ in their virtues, natures, or beauty there is no obstacle in the way of their unity, so why should there be obstacles when it is a question of opinions or faith? Mother, you have given me new life! I was very anxious about Binoy. I know that he has given his whole heart to you, and if any of you were to receive a hurt he would be unable to bear it. So God knows how it has pained me to put any hindrances in his way. But how fortunate he is! Is it a small matter for him to get out of such a dilemma so easily? Let me ask you one question. Has this matter been discussed with Paresh Babu?"

"No, it hasn't" replied Lolita shyly, "but I am sure he will understand everything all right."

"If he were not able to understand," observed Anandamoyi, "then where did you get such strength of mind and intelligence? Let me call Binoy, for you ought to come to some conclusion about this face to face. And on this occasion let me tell you something. I have known Binoy from his childhood, and I can say with all the energy at my command that he is a boy who will be worthy of any troubles you may undergo for his sake. I have often thought that the one who would get Binoy for a husband would be fortunate. Once or twice proposals of marriage have been made but I could never be satisfied. To-day I see that his good fortune too is not small," and with these words Anandamoyi gave Lolita a kiss on her cheek, and then went to call Binoy. She then cleverly left the maidservant in the room with the two of them, and on the pretext of going to prepare some food for Lolita went to another part of the house.

To-day there was no time for shyness on the part either of Lolita or of Binoy. By the advent of this hard problem, which the lives of both of them had suddenly been called upon to solve, they were able to see their relationship to each other clearly and as something not to be trifled with. No mist of emotions cast a coloured screen between them. They took for granted, silently and humbly, without any discussion and without hesitation, the solemn fact that their two hearts were in harmony and the currents of their two lives were approaching each other like the Ganges and the Jumna to become one at some holy and sacred place. It was not society which called them, nor any particular opinion that united them; the bond between them was not an artificial one, and when they remembered this fact they felt that their harmony with one another had religion as its basis, a religion which was so deep and sincere that no trivial matter could dispute its claims, and no head of a panchayat could oppose it. Lolita, her face and eyes shining, commenced: "I could not bear the ignominy of feeling you accepted me by stooping to an act which would lower yourself in your own eyes. What I want is that you should remain where you are now without wavering."

"You also," assented Binoy, "will not have to stir from the place which you occupy now. If love is unable to acknowledge differences, then why are there differences anywhere in this world?"

They went on talking together for nearly twenty minutes, and the gist of what they decided was that they forgot they were Hindu or Brahmo, and only remembered that they were two human souls. This thought was like a steady and unflickering flame in their hearts.

SIXTY TWO

Paresh Babu was seated on the verandah in front of his
room, having finished his evening meditation. He was
quite still and the sun was about to set, when Binoy came to
him with Lolita and bent down to take the dust of his feet.

Paresh Babu was rather surprised at seeing the two of
them coming to see him together in this way, and as there
were no chairs nearby said: "Come, let us go inside my
room."

"No," replied Binoy, "don't get up," and he sat down on
the floor then and there, Lolita also taking a seat at a little
distance close to Paresh Babu's feet.

"We have come," explained Binoy, "to ask for your blessing
on us both. That will be our life's true initiation."

When Paresh Babu looked at him with questioning surprise
Binoy went on: "I will not take any vows to society which
bind me by word or rule. Your blessing is the only initiation
ceremony which can unite the lives of us two in truly humble
bonds. In devotion we place our hearts at your feet, and God
will bestow on us what is best for us through your hands."

"Then, Binoy, you are not going to become a Brahmo?"
asked Paresh Babu, after a few moments' silence.

"No!" replied Binoy.

"You want to remain in the Hindu community?" inquired
Paresh Babu.

"Yes!" answered Binoy.

Paresh Babu looked towards Lolita, and she, guessing what was in his mind, said: "Father, that which is my religion is my own and will always remain so. It may cause me inconvenience, and even bring me trouble, but I cannot believe that it can be in accordance with my religion that I should be separate from those who differ from me in their beliefs and customs."

Seeing that her father remained silent, she went on: "I used to imagine that the Brahmo Samaj was the only thing in the world—that everything outside it was mere shadow; that any separation from it was a separation from all that was true. But recently this idea has completely vanished."

Paresh Babu smiled rather sadly, and Lolita continued: "I cannot make you realise what a great change has taken place in me. I have seen many people in the Brahmo Samaj with whom I do not feel in the least at one and yet with whom my religious opinions are in agreement, and so I can see no meaning in saying that those who have taken shelter with me in a community called Brahmo are in a special way my own people, and all other people in the world must be kept at a distance!"

Patting his rebellious daughter gently on the back, Paresh Babu said: "When the mind is excited for any personal reason is it possible to judge anything truly? There is in mankind a continuity between past and future generations for the proper preservation of which society is necessary, and that necessity is not an artificial one. Have you not considered that it is your society upon which rests the burden of the distant future of all your coming generations?"

"There is the Hindu society," interposed Binoy.

"And if the Hindu society will not accept·responsibility for you, if it refuses?" inquired Paresh Babu.

"We shall have to take up the task of making it accept responsibility," answered Binoy, remembering Anandamoyi's words. "Hindu society has always given shelter to new sects, and it can be the society of all religious communities."

"That which in mere verbal argument appears as one thing," objected Paresh Babu. "becomes a very different matter when it comes to a question of action. Otherwise would anybody ever voluntarily forsake their old society? If you once begin to honour a society which wants to keep man's religious sense bound to one place by the fetters of external custom, then you will have to become for all your days mere wooden puppets."

"If," answered Binoy, "Hindu society remains in such a narrow condition then we must undertake the responsibility for rescuing it from that state. No one wants to reduce to ruins a fine building in order to get more light and air, when it would do just as well to enlarge its doors and windows!"

"Father!" chimed in Lolita, "I can't understand all these arguments. I personally have never determined to take the responsibility for the uplift of any society. But from all sides I am being pushed by such injustice that I can hardly breathe, and for no reason that I can see ought I to put up with this without protest. I don't clearly understand what I ought to do and what I ought not to do, but, father, I can't stand it."

"Wouldn't it be good to take a little more time?" asked Paresh Babu in a gentle tone. "Now your mind is upset."

"I have no objection to taking more time," answered Lolita, "but I know one thing for certain, and that is, untruth and injustice will simply go on increasing, and so I am dreadfully afraid least in desperation I should do something suddenly which would give you also pain. Don't think, father, that I have given no thought to this matter. I see clearly, after much consideration, that the teachings and impressions I have gained may bring me much suffering and shame outside the Brahmo Samaj, but I have no hesitation in my mind, rather I feel a kind of strength and joy. The only thing I am worried about, father, is lest anything that I may do should cause you pain," and saying this Lolita put her hands gently on Paresh Babu's feet.

"Mother," said Paresh Babu, laughing slightly, "if I relied only on my own intelligence, then I should have been sorry whenever anything was done contrary to my wishes or opinions. I can't say that the shock which has so suddenly come to you is altogether bad for you. I too once came out from my home in revolt, without a moment's thought as to whether it would be convenient or not. From these continual blows and counterblows from which society in these days is suffering it is easy to understand that His work of power is being accomplished. How can I know what He is bringing out as a whole from all this purificatory work of breaking? What to Him is the Brahmo Samaj? what is Hindu society?—He sees only Man," and for a moment he stopped speaking to retire into the still solitude of his own heart, closing his eyes in meditation.

"See here, Binoy" said Paresh Babu after a few moments' silence, "the social system of our country is intimately bound up with religious opinions— therefore with all our social observances religious practices have some connection. Surely you see that there is no possibility of your taking into the circle of your society those who are outside the circle of your religious opinions."

Lolita did not clearly follow this reasoning, because she had never seen the difference between their own society and other social systems. Her idea was that on the whole there was no great difference between the practices and customs of one society and those of another. Just as the distinction between themselves and Binoy was practically negligible, so also were the differences between different societies. In fact, she did not know that there was any special obstacle in the way of her being married according to Hindu rites.

"Are you referring to the fact that in our marriage ceremony we have to worship an idol?" asked Binoy.

"Yes," replied Paresh Babu, with a glance towards Lolita. "Will Lolita be able to assent to that?"

Binoy also looked towards her and saw from her face that her whole soul shrank from the idea.

Lolita had been carried by her feelings to a place which was altogether unfamiliar to her and full of pitfalls. Seeing this, Binoy's heart was touched with pity, and he felt that he would have to save her by taking to himself all the blows. It was as intolerable to see such indomitable enthusiasm for victory meeting the arrows of death as it was to see such a fine spirit return defeated. He would have not only to make her victorious but also to save her.

Lolita sat for a little with her head bowed, and then, lifting her gentle eyes to Binoy, she asked: "Do you really and truly believe in idols with all your heart?"

"No, I don't!" answered Binoy without a moment's hesitation. "An idol is not to me a god, it is merely a social symbol.

"Have you to acknowledge outwardly as a god what inwardly you regard only as a symbol?" inquired Lolita.

"I will not allow an idol at the wedding ceremony," said Binoy, looking towards Paresh Babu.

"Binoy," exclaimed Paresh Babu, getting up from his chair, "you have not thought out everything clearly. This is not a matter of your own opinion only nor of anyone else's. Marriage is not merely a personal affair, but is a social matter. Why do you forget that fact? Just think over the matter for a few days quietly, and don't settle like this all in a hurry."

Having said this Paresh Babu went out into the garden and began to walk up and down.

Lolita also was on the point of leaving the room, but she turned back and, addressing Binoy, said: "If our wish is not

a wrong one, I cannot understand why we should have to turn
back with heads bowed low in shame simply because it does
not entirely fall in with the injunctions of some society or
other. Do you mean to say that society has a place for conduct
that is false and no place for what is right?"

Binoy went slowly up to Lolita, and standing in front of
her, said: "I am not afraid of any society, and if the two of
us unite and take shelter in truth then where can you get a
society greater than that?"

At this moment Bordashundari came in like a storm, and,
standing before them both, exclaimed: "Binoy, I've heard that
you will not be initiated after all! Is that so?"

"I will take my initiation," answered Binoy, "from some
suitable guru, and not from any society."

"What then is the meaning of all this deceit and plotting?"
cried Bordashundari in a fury. "Tell me what you mean by
making all this fuss and deceiving me and the members of
our Samaj under the pretext of taking initiation? Haven't you
considered for a moment what ruin this means for Lolita?"

"It is not everyone in our Samaj who agrees to Binoy Babu
taking his initiation," interrupted Lolita. "Haven't you read
the papers? What is the need of taking such an initiation?"

"If he is not initiated, how can the marriage take place?"
asked Bordashundari.

"Why shouldn't it?" inquired Lolita.

"Will you marry according to Hindu rites?" asked
Bordashundari.

"That can be done," answered Binoy. "I will overcome
any obstacles there may be to it."

Boardashundari was speechless for a moment, and then
she said rudely: "Binoy, go! Go away from this house, and
never come back again!"

SIXTY THREE

Sucharita knew that Gora would certainly come that day, and from early morning she had been feeling agitated. With the joy she felt at the prospect of the visit there was mixed some fear, because the conflict which was taking place, at every step, between the habits and customs which had their roots in her very childhood, and the new life towards which Gora was drawing her, made her restless.

For instance on the previous day, when Gora had made his obeisance to the idol in her aunt's room, she had felt as if she had received a stab. She was unable to console herself by saying: "What does it matter if Gora does worship idols? What matters if that is his faith?"

Whenever she saw anything in Gora's conduct which came into conflict with the religious faith which was rooted in her own life she trembled with terror. Was God then going to give her no peace?

Harimohini to-day again took Gora into the room where her idol was, to show a good example to Sucharita so proud of her modern ideas, and to-day too Gora made an obeisance.

As soon as Sucharita had taken Gora downstairs again to the sitting-room she asked him: "Do you have faith in that idol?"

"Yes, of course I have!" answered Gora with a rather unnatural violence, while Sucharita, on hearing this reply, did not answer, but remained with head bent low.

Gora received a shock on seeing her humble and silent pain, and said hurriedly: "Look here, I will tell you the truth. Whether I have faith in idols or not I can't exactly say, but I respect the faith of my country. The worship which the whole country has evolved after so many centuries is something which I regard as worthy of devotion. I can never regard it, as the Christian missionaries do, with bitter looks."

Sucharita looked thoughtfully in Gora's face as he went on: "I know that it is very difficult for you to understand what I mean fully, because having been so long a member of a sect you have lost the power of seeing all these things clearly. When you see that idol in your aunt's room you see only a stone, but I see the tender heart of your aunt filled with devotion. Seeing that, how can I get angry or feel contempt? Do you imagine that divinity of the heart is a mere divinity of stone?"

"Is devotion in itself sufficient?" asked Sucharita. "Have you not to consider the object of the devotion?"

"In other words," exclaimed Gora, feeling rather excited, "you think that to worship a limited object as a god is an error. But have limits to be ascertained from the point of view of time and space? Remember this, that when you call to mind some text of Scripture you feel a great devotion in your heart, but, because that text is written on a page, are you going to decide its greatness by measuring the width of the page and counting the number of letters of which the text is composed? The unlimited character of the idea is a far greater thing than that of its extent in space! That small idol is to your aunt more truly unlimited than the endless sky decked with the sun, moon, and stars. You call that the unlimited which is unlimited in dimensions, so you have to close your eyes to picture it. I don't know whether this does you any good or not, but the heart's infinite can be seen even in such a small object as an idol with your eyes open. If it could not, then how could your aunt have held so fast to it when all her happiness in life had been destroyed? Could such a great void in her heart have been filled by a tiny stone like that if it had been mere play? The emptiness of the human heart could never be filled except by an unlimited feeling."

It was impossible for Sucharita to answer all these subtle arguments, and yet she felt quite unable to accept them as true. She merely suffered in silence without finding any remedy.

At the time of an argument Gora never felt the least pity for his opponents, he rather felt a malignant cruelty against them like that of a beast of prey. But to-day, on seeing her apparently accept defeat without a word, he felt distressed, and speaking more gently he went on: "I don't wish to say anything against your religious convictions. I only want to say that what you call abusively an idol is something that you cannot comprehend merely by seeing it with your eyes. Those who regard it with a tranquil mind, whose hearts find satisfaction in it, and whose natures find a refuge in it, they are the ones who know whether this idol is mortal or immortal, limited or limitless. I assure you that no worshipper in our country ever offers his devotion to what is limited— the joy of their worship is to lose the limits within the limited."

"But everyone is not a devotee," observed Sucharita.

"What does it matter to anyone what those who are not true devotees worship?" exclaimed Gora. "What do those in the Brahmo Samaj who are not true worshippers do? All their devotions are lost in fathomless emptiness. No, worse than that, more terrible than emptiness—their god is party spirit, their pride their priest! Have you never seen this bloodthirsty divinity being worshipped in your Samaj?"

"What you are saying about religion," inquired Sucharita, without answering Gora's question, "are you saying it from your own experience?"

"In other words," laughed Gora, "you want to know whether or not I have ever wanted God? No, I'm afraid my inclinations are not in that direction."

This was not said with the object of pleasing Sucharita, and yet she could not help heaving a sigh of relief. It was in some ways a comfort to her to know that on this subject Gora had not the right to speak with authority.

"I cannot claim to teach anyone about religion," continued Gora, "but I can never bear to see you laugh at the devotion of the people of my country. You are regarding the people of your country as fools and idolaters, but I want to call them all and say: 'No, you are not fools, you are not idolaters; you are wise, you are true worshippers.' By showing my reverence I want to awaken the soul of my country to the realisation that there is greatness in our religious principles and depth in our devotions. I want to arouse in them a pride in the wealth that they possess. I will not allow them to be humbled, nor will I permit them to become blind to the truth that is in them, or show contempt for themselves. This is my determination. And it is for this that I have come to you to-day. Ever since I first met you a new thought has been surging through my mind, a thought to which all these days I had been oblivious. I keep thinking that India can never be fully revealed only by looking at her men. Her manifestation will only be complete when she has revealed herself to our women. I have had an almost burning desire that I shall be able to see my country, standing by your side and looking at her with one united vision. For my India, as a man, I can only work and if necessary die, but who, except you, can light the lamp of welcome to her? If you stand aloof the service of India can never be beautiful."

Alas! Where was India? At what far distance was Sucharita? From where has this devotee of India come, this self-forgetful ascetic? Why had he pushed everyone aside to take his place at her side? Why had he left all and summoned her? Without any hesitation, and admitting no obstacles, he had said: "Without you, all will be in vain—it is to take you that I have come; if you remain in banishment the sacrifice will not be complete!" Sucharita's eyes filled with inexplicable tears, and as Gora looked at her face it seemed to him like a flower bedecked with careless dewdrops.

Although there were tears in her eyes she returned his gaze steadily and in entire self-forgetfulness, and before the fearless and unflinching look which she turned upon him, Gora's whole nature trembled as a marble palace trembles in an earthquake. Making a great effort at control, Gora pulled himself together and gazed out of the window. It was already evening, and above the narrow vista of the lane, where it joined the main road, the stars showed bright against a strip of open sky which was dark like a black stone. That strip of sky, and those few stars, how far did they carry Gora to-day from the accustomed world of his everyday life, and from the well-known round of his daily work! They had watched for ages the rise and fall of countless dynasties, the prayers and efforts of unnumbered centuries;— and yet, at the call of one human heart to another from the fathomless depths of life, those stars and that sky seemed to vibrate with some speechless hankering from the verge of the world! At this moment the stream of passers-by and all the noisy traffic of the busy Calcutta streets seemed to Gora unsubstantial as shadow pictures—none of the bustling sounds of the city reached his ears—he was looking into his own heart—there too all was still, and dark, and silent, like the sky, and there gazing from the eternal past of a never-ending future, were two tender eyes, filled with tears but steady and unflinching.

On suddenly hearing Harimohini's voice calling him to come and take some sweetmeats, Gora turned round, startled.

"No, not to-day," he said hurriedly. "You must excuse me to-day, for I must be going at once," and without waiting for

another word Gora went out with rapid steps. Harimohini
looked at Sucharita in astonishment, but she also left her,
leaving Harimohini shaking her head and exclaiming to herself,
"What's the matter now?"

Not long after this Paresh Babu called, and not finding
Sucharita in her room he went to Harimohini and asked her
where she was.

"How do I know?" asked Harimohini in a vexed tone.
"She was talking with Gourmohan Babu in the sitting-room
quite a long time; now I think she is walking up and down
on the roof."

"On the roof on such a cold night!" exclaimed Paresh
Babu in surprise.

"Let her enjoy the cold a little!" said Harimohini
impatiently. "The girls of these days are not harmed by the
cold."

As Harimohini was in a bad temper to-day she had not
called Sucharita to her meal, and Sucharita also was not
conscious of the passage of time.

On seeing Paresh Babu himself come out on to the roof
Sucharita was greatly distressed, and exclaimed: "Come in,
father, come downstairs. You will catch cold."

Sucharita got quite a shock when, on entering the lamp-
lit room, she saw how harassed Paresh Babu looked. He had
been all these days the father and guru of the fatherless child,
and now to-day she was being drawn away from him, severing
all the bonds which had united them since her childhood.
Sucharita felt as if she could never forgive herself. Paresh Babu
sat down wearily in a chair, and in order to hide the tears
which she found it difficult to control, Sucharita stood behind
him, passing her fingers lightly through his grey hair.

"Binoy is not willing to be initiated after all," remarked
Paresh Babu, and as Sucharita made no answer, he went on:
"I always had my doubts about this proposal for Binoy's

initiation, so I am not seriously disturbed at the turn things
have taken—but from what Lolita says I can see that she does
not feel there is any obstacle in the way of her marrying Binoy
even if he is not initiated."

"No!" exclaimed Sucharita almost violently. "No, father,
that must never be! Never, whatever happens!"

Sucharita did not usually display such unnecessary eagerness
when she spoke, so Paresh Babu was rather astonished at the
sudden outburst of impatience which was noticeable in her
tone. "What must never be?" he asked.

"Unless Binoy becomes a Brahmo, according to what rites
will the marriage be celebrated?" inquired Sucharita.

"According to Hindu rites," answered Paresh Babu.

"No, no, no!" exclaimed Sucharita, shaking her head
violently. "How can you suggest such a thing! You ought not
even to imagine such an idea. Lolita to be married, after
everything, with idol worship at the ceremony! I can never
consent to it!"

Was it because Gora had been attracting Sucharita's
mind that to-day she diplayed such unnatural impatience at
the idea of marriage in accordance with Hindu rites? The
real inner significance of this outburst was that she wanted
to hold on firmly to Paresh Babu, and say to him: "I will
never leave you. I am still a member of your Samaj, and still
hold your opinions; nothing will induce me to break away
from your teaching."

"Binoy has expressed his willingness to dispense with the
idol at the wedding ceremony," explained Paresh Babu, and
when Sucharita came from behind his chair and sat down in
front of him, he went on: "What do you say to that?"

"Then Lolita will have to go out of our community,"
observed Sucharita after a moment's silence.

"I have had to give much thought to this matter," said
Paresh Babu. "When any conflict occurs between an individual

and society, there are two things to be considered—first on whose side is the right, and secondly which side is the stronger. There is not the least doubt that of the two society is the stronger, so that the rebel against it will have to suffer. Lolita has again and again told me that she is not only ready to accept that suffering, but she regards it as a matter for rejoicing. If this is a fact, then, if I see nothing wrong in her action, how can I put obstacles in her way?"

"But, father, how can it take place?" asked Sucharita.

"I know," said Paresh Babu, "that it will land us all in a great difficulty, but when there is nothing wrong in Lolita marrying Binoy, when in fact she ought to do so, then I cannot think that it is my duty to respect an obstacle which society puts in the way. It can never be right that man should remain narrow and confined out of regard for society—rather society ought to become more liberal out of regard for the individual. Therefore I can never find fault with those who are ready to face the suffering their actions involve."

"Father," exclaimed Sucharita, "it is you who will have to suffer most in this matter."

"There is no need to worry about that," observed Paresh Babu.

"Father, have you given your consent?" asked Sucharita.

"No," replied Paresh Babu, "not yet. But I shall have to give it. In the path which Lolita is following who is there besides me who can give her his blessing, and who but God can be her helper?"

When Paresh Babu had gone Sucharita remained motionless. She knew how deeply he loved Lolita, and she had no difficulty in realising how anxious he must be feeling at letting that favourite daughter of his leave the accustomed path to enter on such a vast unknown. Yet, in spite of that, here he was at his age helping in this revolt, and showing so little sign of alarm! He never displayed his own strength in the least, and yet what great strength lay hidden, without any apparent effort, in the depth of his soul!

If it had been at any other time this insight into Paresh Babu's nature would not have struck her as strange, for she had known him from childhood, but to-day, as she had only just before been experiencing in her very soul the strokes of Gora, she could not avoid feeling the complete difference between these two types of people. How violent to Gora was his own will! And how ruthlessly he would push aside others and overwhelm them when he once applied that will with full force! Anyone who wanted to agree with Gora on any subject had to humble himself completely to Gora's will. To-day Sucharita had humbled herself and had even rejoiced in her humiliation, because she felt that by sacrificing herself she had gained greatly. Yet now, when her father went out of her lamp-lit room into the darkness, with head bowed in thought, she could not help comparing him with Gora in the pride of his youthful enthusiasm, and she felt that she wanted to dedicate her heart like an offering of flowers at his feet. For a long time she sat with her hands in her lap, still and silent like an image in a picture.

SIXTY FOUR

From early morning Gora's room was the scene of agitating discussions. First of all Mohim had come, puffing at his hookah, and had asked Gora: "Then, after all these days, Binoy has cut adrift from his chains, has he?"

Gora did not catch his meaning and looked inquiringly at him till he explained: "What's the use of keeping up this deception, tell me? Your friend's affairs are no longer a secret— they are being trumpeted abroad. Just read that!" and he handed to Gora a Bengali newspaper.

In it there appeared a very pungent article on the item of news which told of Binoy's intended initiation in the Brahmo Samaj that day. The writer used some very harsh language about the conduct of certain well-known members of the Brahmo Samaj, who were burdened with the responsibility of daughters, and who, while Gora was in gaol, had secretly tempted this weak-minded young man to leave his own ancient Hindu society for the sake of marriage into a Brahmo family.

When Gora observed: "I had not heard this news," Mohim at first did not believe him, and then began to express his astonishment at the depth of deceit displayed in Binoy's conduct. He exclaimed: "When, after having given his definite promise that he would marry Soshimukhi, he began to waver and shilly-shally, we ought to have realised that it was the beginning of his downfall."

Next came Abinash panting with excitement, and exclaiming: "Gourmohan Babu, what an affair this is! How could one have even dreamed it possible? That Binoy Babu should after all this—"

But Abinash was not able to complete his sentence. He felt such an intense pleasure in abusing Binoy that he was incapable of even pretending to be anxious on his account.

In less than no time all the important members of Gora's party came in turn, and when they were all gathered a heated discussion soon started on the subject of Binoy's conduct. The majority of them had only one comment to make, and it was, that this present affair was no matter for surprise, because they had all of them again and again noticed signs of weakness and hesitation in Binoy's character; in fact, they declared that Binoy had never surrendered himself wholeheartedly to their party. Many of them said that they had always felt how intolerable was the way in which he had tried, somehow or other, from the very beginning to put himself on an equality with Gourmohan. Where everyone else had kept himself at a proper distance out of respect, Binoy had forced himself on Gora, and made out that he was on terms of such intimacy that he appeared to be aloof from the rest of them, and equal in importance to Gora himself. Because Gora was fond of him they had all of them done their best to tolerate this extraordinary arrogance, and this was the deplorable sequel to that kind of unchecked vanity!

They said: "We may not be so well educated as Binoy Babu and we have not such great intelligence, but at least we have all along followed one principle, we don't say one thing and think another. For us it is impossible to do one thing to-day and quite the opposite to-morrow—you may call it foolishness on our part, or stupidity, or anything else you like!"

To all this Gora made no answer, but sat quite still without entering into the discussion at all.

When it was getting late and all his visitors had gone one by one, Gora saw that Binoy was going upstairs without coming into his room, so going out quickly he called, "Binoy!" and when Binoy turned back and entered the room, he said: "Binoy, I don't know whether or not I have done you any wrong, but it seems to me as if you were going to forsake me."

Binoy, having made up his mind beforehand that a quarrel with Gora was inevitable to-day, had hardened his heart, but when he saw how gloomy he was looking and felt the note of injured affection in his voice, in a moment the resolution with which he had been bracing himself vanished, and he said: "Brother Gora, you must not misunderstand me. Many changes come in our lives and we have to give up many things, but is that any reason why I should give up friendship?"

"Binoy," asked Gora after a moment's silence, "have you become a member of the Brahmo Samaj?"

"No, Gora, I have not, and I am not going to," answered Binoy. "But I don't want to lay much stress on that fact."

"What does that mean?" asked Gora.

"It means," answered Binoy, "that I no longer think that it is a matter of such tremendous importance whether I take initiation into the Brahmo Samaj or not."

"I want to ask you," said Gora, "what your idea was before and what it is now."

On hearing the tone of Gora's voice in this question Binoy girded himself for the conflict again, and said: "In the past, whenever I used to hear that anyone was becoming a Brahmo, I would feel very angry, and I devoutly hoped that some sort of punishment would follow. But nowadays I do not think like that. I feel that you can meet an opinion by another opinion, or one argument by another, but in matters in which the understanding is concerned it is barbarous to try and use anger as a punishment."

"Now when you see a Hindu become a Brahmo you will no longer feel angry," observed Gora, "but if you were to see a Brahmo doing penance to become a Hindu your whole body would burn with indignation, that's the only difference between your present position and your former one."

"You are saying that merely out of anger, not after due deliberation," observed Binoy.

"I tell you with the greatest respect for you," continued Gora, "that you ought to have done like this—if it had been my case I would have done so. If we had had something in our skins by which we could change our religious views as a chameleon changes its colour that would have been another matter—but I cannot make light of a thing that belongs to the heart. If no kind of opposition existed, and if you did not have to give toll in some form of punishment, then why, is such a serious matter as accepting or changing religious opinions, does a man arouse his whole intelligence? We must undergo some test as to whether we accept truth genuinely or not. Its consequences and penalties must be accepted. In the commerce of truth you cannot obtain the jewel and avoid the price."

The argument now went full speed ahead, and sparks began to fly as words clashed against words like arrows against arrows.

At last, when the war of words had gone on for a long time, Binoy stood up and said: "Gora, between your nature and mine there is a fundamental difference. Up to now that has been suppressed—whenever it wanted to raise its head I used to repress it, because I knew that where you saw any difference you did not know how to make a truce with it, that you always came running to attack it sword in hand. Therefore, in order to preserve my friendship with you I have all along been doing violence to my own nature. Now at last I have come to realise that no good has come of this and no good can come if it."

"Well then, now tell me openly what your intention is," said Gora.

"To-day I stand on my own feet!" exclaimed Binoy. "I can no longer admit the right of society to be pacified like a demon by daily human sacrifices. And whether I have to live or die, I am not going to wander, about with the noose of its injunctions fastened round my neck."

"Are you going to come out to slay the demon with a piece of straw like the Brahmin boy in the *Mahabharata?*" sneered Gora.

"Whether or not I shall succeed in slaying him with my straw I do not profess to know," answered Binoy, "but I at least refuse to admit his right to seize and chew me to pieces,—no, not even when he has begun chewing."

"It is becoming difficult to follow you now that you have begun to talk in allegories!" exclaimed Gora.

"It is not difficult for you to follow me," replied Binoy, "though it may be hard for you to accept what I say. You know as well as I do how meaningless are the bonds with which our society tries to fetter us in matters of eating, and touching and sitting, where man has a natural freedom based on religion. But you want to admit this high-handedness by being high-handed yourself. Let me tell you though that in this matter I will not submit to anyone's tryranny! I will admit the claims of society upon me only so long as society admits my claims upon it. If it refuses to regard me as a man, and wants to fashion me into a puppet of a machine I too will not worship it with my flowers and sandal paste—I will regard it as a machine of iron!"

"In other words, in short, you will become a Brahmo?" queried Gora.

"No!" replied Binoy.

"You will marιy Lolita?" inquired Gora.

"Yes," answered Binoy.

"A Hindu marriage?" asked Gora.

"Yes," replied Binoy.

"Has Paresh Babu given his consent?" inquired Gora.

"Here is his letter," said Binoy, handing Gora a letter which the latter read through twice carefully. At the end Paresh Babu had written:

"I do not intend to discuss whether this is good or bad for me personally; I do not even wish to raise the question as to whether it is likely to cause you both inconvenience or not. You both know what my faith and my opinions are, and what my community is, and it is not unknown to you what sort of teaching Lolita has received from her childhood and amidst what kind of social customs she has been brought up. You have chosen your path after due consideration of all these matters, and I have nothing to add. But do not imagine that I am surrendering the helm without any thought or because I am not able to come to any conclusion. I have considered the matter to the best of my ability, and this much I have realised, Binoy, because I have a deep regard for you personally, that there is no obstacle to your union from the standpoint of religion. Under such circumstances you are not bound to observe an obstacle which is raised only by society. I have only one thing to say to you in this connection— if you want to transcend the limitations of your societies then you must make yourselves greater than any society. Your love and your united lives must not only denote the beginning of some power of dissolution, but must show also a principle of creation and stability. It will not do merely for you to exhibit a sudden rashness, you must afterwards meet with daily heroism all the tasks of your united lives— for otherwise you will merely deteriorate. Society will no longer carry you along from outside on the level of ordinary life, and if you do not by your own strength become greater than ordinary people then you will simply fall behind them.

As for your future weal and woe I am full of apprehension, but I have no right to hinder you by these fears of mine, because those in this world who have the courage to try and solve in their own lives new problems of life are the ones who raise society to greatness! Those who merely live according to rule do not advance society, they only carry it along. Therefore I will not obstruct your path by my own anxiety and timidity. Follow what you feel to be right in the face of all obstacles, and may God help you. God never under any conditions binds His creation with fetters; He awakens it through constant changes to ever new life. Like messengers of that awakening of His you have set out along that difficult path, kindling your lives like torches. He who is the world's guide will show you the way. I can never admonish you to follow always along the path I have taken! One day, when I was your age, I too unloosened my boat from the ghat and floated it out to meet the storm, and I would listen to no one's warnings. Up to now I have never regretted it, and even if I had had cause to regret it, what of that? Man will make blunders, will be baffled, and will meet with sorrows, but he can never stand still; he will sacrifice his life for that which he believes to be his duty. It is thus that the sacred waters of the river of society are kept pure by being carried along in a never-ceasing current. This means that occasionally, for a short time, the banks of the river are broken and suffer loss, but to try and dam the current perpetually in fear of this would only be to invite stagnation and death. This I know for certain, and therefore I can surrender you both into the hands of that Power which is drawing you with irresistible force outside the rules of society and away from ease and comfort, and, making my obeisance to that Power with full devotion, I can pray that He may compensate you in your lives for all the slander and abuse you may suffer from and for the separation from your dear ones. It is He who has summoned you to take this difficult path, and He it is who will take you to your destination."

"Just as Paresh Babu has given his consent from his point of view," said Binoy, after Gora had read the letter and pondered over it in silence, "so you too, Gora must give your consent from your point of view."

"Paresh Babu can give his consent," observed Gora, "because he is in that current which is breaking the banks of the river. I cannot give mine because the current in which we are is that by which the bank has to be preserved from destruction. On this bank of ours it is impossible to say what vast relics of past centuries stand, but now let us carry on the work according to the laws of nature. You may abuse us or do anything you like because we build up our bank with stones, but on this ancient and holy place on which new silt has accumulated year after year it is not our intention to allow a lot of agriculturists to drive their ploughs through it. If that means loss to us then let it do so! That place is for our dwelling, not for ploughing. And when your agricultural department begins to slander us because of the hard stones we use we are not going to feel any heartfelt shame!"

"In other words, in short, you do not give your assent to this marriage of mine?" exclaimed Binoy.

"Certainly I will never do so!" answered Gora.

"And—" Binoy began, but Gora interrupted him with: "And I will have nothing more to do with you all."

"And if I had been one of your Mussulman friends?" asked Binoy.

"Then that would have been another matter," said Gora. "When one of its own branches is broken from a tree and falls, then the tree can never take it back again as before as part of itself—but it can give shelter to a creeper that climbs up it from outside, and even if the creeper is torn from the

tree in a storm there is no obstacle to its being gathered up
to the tree again. When you drift away there is no other path
for us than to separate ourselves entirely from you! It is for
that reason that society has such stringent rules and
prohibitions."

"That is why the reasons for separation ought not to have
been so slight, and the rules for separation so easy," replied
Binoy. "The bones of the arm are strong because, if they get
broken they take a long time to heal again, and so fractures
of the arm are not common. Will you not see how many
obstacles there are to working and coming and going easily
in a society in which a trifling blow causes a fracture which
can never be healed?"

"I don't have to worry about that," answered Gora. "Society
takes the burden of thinking so fully and completely on itself
that I am not even conscious that it is thinking. My hope is
that not only has it been considering this for thousands of
years, but that it is still preserving its integrity. Just as I have
never given a thought as to whether the earth is travelling
round the sun straight or crooked, whether it is making errors
or not, so far my lack of thought has not landed me in any
difficulty, so also is my attitude towards society."

"Brother Gora," laughed Binoy, "I have been saying all
that for a long time past—who could have suspected that to-
day again I would hear these words from your lips? I see that
I have to enjoy the penalty of having fabricated such long
speeches. But no good can come of arguing about it, for to-
day I have seen something at close quarters which I had not
realised so clearly before. I have understood to-day that the
course of human life is like that of a great river which, by
the force of its own swiftness, takes quite new and unforeseen
channels where before there was no current—such varied
currents and unpremeditated changes are part of God's purpose
for our lives. Life is not an artificial canal to be confined

within prescribed channels. When once this is clearly seen in our own lives then we shall not be able to be misled by any mere fabrications."

"When a moth is about to fall into the flame," observed Gora, "it uses just the same kind of argument as you are using—but to-day I am not going to waste time in trying to make you understand."

"That is a good thing," exclaimed Binoy, getting up from his chair, "then let me go, and see mother for a little."

When Binoy had gone Mohim came slowly into the room chewing as usual his betel, and asked: "So I suppose it's not to come off? Not convenient? For long enough I have been warning you to be careful—there have been signs of mischief for some time—but you would not listen to me. If only somehow at that time we had had the courage to force him to marry Soshimukhi then we should have had none of this worry. But who cares? In whom can I confide? That which you will not see for yourself you will never comprehend, even if I bore a hole in your skull. Is it a matter of little regret that a boy like Binoy should break up your party like this?"

"So there is no hope of getting Binoy back!" went on Mohim, seeing that Gora was silent. "However that may be, we have had worry enough through him in the matter of Soshimukhi's marriage. It will not do to delay any longer over this matter—you are aware of the nature of our society, if once it gets anyone into its clutches then it has no pity on him. So a bridegroom is—no, you need not be afraid, I'm not going to ask you to be a matchmaker. I've settled everything myself!"

"Who is the man?" inquired Gora.

"Your Abinash," answered Mohim.

"Has he agreed?" asked Gora.

"Abinash not agree indeed!" cried Mohim, "He's not like your Binoy. No, whatever you may say, it is easy to see that amongst all the members of your party Abinash is the one who has a real devotion for you! Why, when he heard the proposal that he should become a member of your family he fairly danced with joy. He said, 'What good fortune for me, what an honour!' When I raised the question of the amount of the dowry he put his hands over his ears, and exclaimed: 'You must excuse me, but do not speak to me about all that business!' I replied, 'Very well, I will discuss everything with your father,' and I went to him also. But I noticed a great difference between the father and the son. The former did not make the least attempt to stop his ears when the question of money was raised, rather as soon as he started to talk he began in such a strain that my hands became too paralysed to raise them to my ears. I saw too that in all such matters the boy showed the greatest respect for his father—altogether as if his father were the chief means of grace—I could see that it would be useless to employ him as a go-between. Without turning some Government securities into cash it will not be possible to bring this matter to a satisfactory conclusion. But, however that may be, you must say a little to encourage Abinash. One or two words from you—"

"Would not reduce the amount of the dowry by a single rupee," interrupted Gora.

"That I know," assented Mohim, "when respect for one's father brings with it some profit then it is hard to check it!"

"Is the matter definitely settled?" asked Gora.

"Yes," replied Mohim.

"Has the day been actually fixed?"

"Certainly it has," said Mohim. "The day of the full moon in *Magh*. That is not far off either. The boy's father says that it is no use having diamonds and jewels, but he wants very heavy ornaments. So I shall have to consult the goldsmith as to the best way to increase the weight of gold without increasing its cost."

"But what need was there to hurry things on at such a pace?" asked Gora. "Abinash is not likely to become a Brahmo soon, there's no fear of that."

"That is true," replied Mohim, "but haven't you noticed that father's health has been getting very bad lately. The more the doctors object the more does he merely increase the stringency of his rules. Nowadays that *sannyasi* with whom he has become intimate makes him bathe three times a day— and over and above that he has prescribed a form of yogic practice which is very nearly turning him inside out. It will be a great boon if Soshi's marriage can be celebrated while father is alive—I shan't have to worry much if I can accomplish the business before all the savings from my father's pension fall into the clutches of Oshkarananda Swami. I mentioned the subject to him yesterday, but I see that it won't be an easy matter. I am thinking that I shall have to drug this wretched *sannyasi* well for a few days and work the oracle through him. Be sure of one thing, that those of us who are family men and whose need of money is greatest, will not enjoy father's money! My difficulty is that another man's father is calling upon me without pity for cash, and my own father, the moment the question of money is raised, resorts to meditation and holding his breath. Am I to drown myself with this eleven-year-old girl tied round my neck?"

SIXTY FIVE

"Why didn't you take your food last night, Radharani?" inquired Harimohini.

"Why, what do you mean? I took my evening meal!" exclaimed Sucharita in astonishment.

"What did you eat? Here it is untouched!" said Harimohini, pointing to the previous night's meal with its covers still on.

Then Sucharita understood that she had forgotten all about her meal the previous evening.

"This is very bad!" pursued Harimohini in a harsh voice. "So far as I know Paresh Babu I am sure he will not like your going to such extremes; his very appearance gives peace to one. What do you think he would say if he were to know fully your present tendencies?"

There was no difficulty in Sucharita realising what Harimohini was hinting at, and for the first few moments her mind shrank within itself. She had never for an instant thought that the relationship between herself and Gora could be touched by the breath of scandal, as though it were nothing more than the most ordinary relationship between the sexes. So Harimohini's insinuation made her afraid. But the next moment she put aside her work, and sitting down with a determined air looked up at Harimohini. She decided, there and then, that she would not harbour in her mind the least feeling of shame with regard to Gora before anyone.

"You know, auntie, that last night Gourmohan Babu came here," she began. "The subject of my discussion with him took such a firm possession of my mind that I entirely forgot about my meal. If you had been there yesterday you would have heard a lot of interesting things."

But Gora's conversation was not exactly what Harimohini wanted to hear. Her desire was to listen to words of piety, but when Gora discoursed on matters of faith his words did not sound so sincere as to be palatable to her. It always seemed as if there were some adversary in front of him, and as if he were merely fighting against this opponent. Those who did not agree he simply wanted to force into acquiescence—but what had he to say to those who agreed with him? Harimohini was completely indifferent to the excitement Gora exhibited in argument. If the people of the Brahmo Samaj chose to follow their own opinions and did not mix with the Hindu community she was not in the least distressed at heart—so long as nothing occurred to separate her from those who were dear to her she was quite free from care. Therefore she did not get the least pleasure out of conversation with Gora, and when she further felt that he was getting an influence over Sucharita's mind his conversation became to her even more repulsive. In money matters Sucharita was entirely independent, and when it was a question of opinions, or faith, or conduct, she was quite free, so that from no point of view was Harimohini able to exercise any sort of control over her. And yet Harimohini, having no other support in her old age, was always much disturbed if anyone, except Paresh Babu, seemed to be getting any kind of influence over her. Harimohini's idea of Gora was that he was thoroughly insincere, and that his real object was to attract Sucharita to him on any sort of pretext. She even suspected that his primary object was to get hold of the property which Sucharita had in her own right. So, regarding Gora as her chief enemy, she braced herself to the task of thwarting him in every way she could.

There had been no mention of Gora coming again that day, and there was no particular reason why he should do so, but in his nature there was very little hesitation. When once he had set out to do a thing he never so much as gave a thought to the consequences, but went straight ahead like an arrow.

When Gora called early that morning Harimohini was at her devotions, and when Satish came to Sucharita, as she was busy arranging her books and papers, to tell her of Gora's arrival she was not greatly surprised. She had felt sure that he would come again.

"So Binoy has at last forsaken us," remarked Gora when he had taken a seat.

"Why?" asked Sucharita. "Why should he forsake us? He has not joined the Brahmo Samaj."

"If he had gone out into the Brahmo Samaj," answered Gora, "he would have been much closer to us than he is now. It is his holding so tightly to our Hindu society that hurts most. He would have done much better to have cleared out of our community altogether."

"Why do you regard society as of such excessive importance?" inquired Sucharita, feeling much pained. "Is it natural for you to place such implicit faith in society? Or is it rather that you force yourself to do so?"

"It is perfectly natural for me to force myself to do so under such circumstances as the present," said Gora. "When the earth under your feet begins to move then you have to apply greater force at every step! Now that opposition is coming from every side we naturally show some amount of exaggeration in our speech and conduct. That is nothing unnatural."

"Why do you think that the opposition you are meeting with from every side is wrong and unnecessary from start to finish?" asked Sucharita. "If society puts obstacles in the way of progress then it will have to receive some blows."

"Progress is like the waves in water," observed Gora. "By them the banks are broken—but I don't think it to be the chief duty of the banks to accept that breaking. Do not imagine that I never consider what is good or bad for society. Why, a sixteen-year-old boy of the present day can do that, it is so easy. But what is difficult is to see things in their completeness with the vision of faith."

"Is it only truth that we gain through faith?" asked Sucharita. "By faith we also sometimes misjudge things and get hold of what is false. Let me ask you one thing, can we have faith in idolatry? Do you believe in that as true?"

"I will try my best to tell you the truth about my attitude," answered Gora, after remaining silent for a moment. "At first I accepted all these things as true. I did not hastily oppose them because they happened to be contrary to European customs, and because there were a few very easy arguments which could be brought against them. In religious matters I have not myself realised anything very special, but I am not prepared to shut my eyes and repeat, like a lesson learnt by rote, that the worship of forms is the same as idolatry, or that the worship of images is the chief end of religious devotions. There is a place for imagination in Art, in Literature, and even in Science and History, and I will never admit that only in religion it has no place. The perfection of all man's powers is revealed in religion, and do you mean to say that the attempt made in our country to harmonise imagination with wisdom and devotion in idol worship does not reveal a truth to mankind greater than that of any other country?"

"In Greece and Rome also there was idol worship," argued Sucharita.

"In the idols of those countries," answered Gora, "there was not so much religious sense as a sense of beauty, whereas in our country imagination is very intimately interwoven with our philosophy and our faith. Our Krishna and Radha, and our Shiva and Durga, are not merely objects of historical worship, they are forms of the ancient philosophy of our race. Therefore the devotion of our Ramprashad, and our Chaitanyadev manifested itself by claiming the support of all these images. Where in the history of Greece or Rome do you see such an extreme devotion revealed?"

"Are you unwilling to admit that along with the changes of the ages some changes take place also in religion and society?" asked Sucharita.

"Why should I be unwilling?" exclaimed Gora. "But it won't do for those changes to be absolutely crazy ones—a child gradually grows up to be a man, but man does not suddenly become a cat or a dog. I want the changes in India to be along the path of India's development, for if you suddenly begin to follow the path of England's history then everything from first to last will be a useless failure. I am sacrificing my life to show you all that the power and greatness of our country have been preserved in our country itself. Can't you understand that?"

"Yes, I can understand that all right," answered Sucharita, "but all these ideas are so new to me that I had never given any thought to them before I heard them from you. Just as it takes some time before you get used to your surroundings in a new place so is it with me just now. I suppose it is because I am a woman that I haven't the power of realisation."

"Never!" exclaimed Gora. "I know many men with whom I have discussed these subjects for long enough, and they have no doubt at all that they have grasped the ideas perfectly, but I can assure you to your face that not a single one of them has been able to see what you have seen! When I first saw you I felt that you had an exceptionally keen insight, and that is why I have been coming to you so often and talking to you without any reserve. I have not felt the least hesitation in unfolding before you all my life's hopes."

"When you speak like that I feel very uneasy," expostulated Sucharita, "for I cannot comprehend what you hope from me, what I can give, what work I shall have to do, and how I shall be able to express the feelings that are crowding upon me with such rapidity. My one fear is that one day you will discover your mistake in having had such a belief in me."

"There can be no mistake there," shouted Gora in a voice of thunder. "I will show you what a tremendous power there is in you. You need not be in the least anxious—the burden of proving your worthiness has been taken on my shoulders— you have only to rely upon me!"

Sucharita made no reply to this, but that she was ready to rely upon him to the full was manifest even in her silence. Gora too remained silent, and for a long time there was not a sound in the room. In the lane outside the sound of the hawker's call could be heard and the jingling noise of the brass vessels he had for sale died gradually away as he passed from in front of the house.

Harimohini was on the way to the kitchen after having finished her morning devotions, and she had not the least idea that there was anyone in Sucharita's silent room, but when, on glancing in as she passed, she saw that Sucharita and Gora were seated together, without apparently exchanging a single word, she suddenly felt as though she had been struck by lightning, her anger was so intense. But, controlling herself as well as she could, she stood at the door and called: "Radharani!"

When Sucharita got up and came out to her she said sweetly: "To-day is the day for my lunar fast, and I am not feeling well. Please go to the kitchen and prepare the stove, while I sit with Gourmohan Babu a little."

When Sucharita saw what was her aunt's idea she went to the kitchen feeling rather uneasy in her mind, Gora meanwhile making his obeisance to Harimohini, who sat down without a word. After sitting with her lips pursed up for some minutes she at length broke the silence with: "You are not a Brahmo, are you?"

"No," replied Gora.

"Do you respect our Hindu society?" she asked.

"Of course I do," answered Gora.

"Then what do you mean by this kind of conduct?" snapped Harimohini.

Not being able to imagine what she was complaining of, Gora remained silent, looking towards her inquiringly.

"Radharani is grown up," pursued Harimohini, "and you are not a relation of hers, so what have you got to talk with her about so much? She is a woman, and has her housework to attend to, so what need has she of spending so much time gossiping? It will only distract her mind. You are an intelligent person—everybody is praising you—but whenever, in our country, was all this kind of thing permitted, and in what Scriptures do you find sanction for such conduct?"

This was a great shock to Gora, for it had never occurred to him that comment of this kind on his relationship with Sucharita could come from any quarter. He was silent for a little, and then explained: "She is a member of the Brahmo Samaj, and since I have seen her mixing with everyone freely like this I never thought anything of it."

"Well, even if she is a member of the Brahmo Samaj, you can never say that all this kind of thing is good," exclaimed Harimohini. "A vast number of people in these days have been awakened to consciousness by what you say, and how will they be able to respect you if they see you behaving like this? Last night you were talking with her till quite late, and you haven't finished your conversation with her yet, but must need come again this morning! From early this morning she has not been near either the store-room or the kitchen—and the little help she usually gives me on the eleventh day of the moon even that she has forgotten to give—what sort of teaching is this? There are girls in your own home—do you make them leave off all their household tasks and offer them this kind of instruction?—no, of course you don't, and if anyone else did so, would you think it a good thing?"

Gora had nothing to say in self-defence, he merely remarked: "Because of the teachings with which she has been brought up I never considered the matter from that point of view."

"Leaving aside all that teaching," cried Harimohini, "so long as she is living with me and so long as I am alive this kind of thing will not be tolerated. I have managed to get her a part of the way back. When she was in Paresh Babu's home there was even a rumour that she had become a Hindu through mixing with me. Then when we came to this house there were lengthy discussions with your Binoy which made everything topsy-turvy again. He apparently is going to marry into a Brahmo family! Well, let that be! I have managed to get rid of Binoy after a lot of trouble. And then there is a person called Haran Babu; whenever he used to call I would take Radharani and make her sit with me upstairs, so he got no chance of influencing her. In this way, after no end of trouble, I seem to be getting her back to reasonable opinions again nowadays. When she first came to this house she actually sat and took her meal with the whole of the rest of the family, but now I see that she has given up that nonsense, for she went and brought her own rice from the kitchen yesterday, and forbade the servant to bring her water. Now I beg of you, with folded hands, that you won't go and spoil her again. Everyone I had in the world has died and she is the only one I now have left to me—there is no one else whom I can call really my own. Do leave her alone! There are plenty of grown-up daughters in their house—see there is Labonya, and

Lilla, and they are both intelligent and educated. If you have anything to say, go and say it to them, no one will prevent you."

Gora sat absolutely dumbfounded, and, after a brief pause, Harimohini continued once more: "See here, she will have to be married, for she is more than old enough. What do you think, that she will remain for ever unmarried as she is now? Domestic work is a necessity for a woman."

Generally Gora never had any doubt on this question—his opinion was exactly the same, but he had never applied it to the case of Sucharita. His imagination had never pictured her as a wife, engaged in the task of housekeeping in the *zenana* of some family man. He had pictured her as continuing just as she was now.

"Have you thought at all about your niece's marriage?" asked Gora.

"One has to think about it, of course," answered Harimohini; "if I didn't think about it who would?"

"Will she be able to marry into the Hindu community?" inquired Gora.

"We shall have to try for that," said Harimohini. "If only there is no more trouble, and everything goes smoothly then I shall be able to manage it all right. In fact, I had come to a decision, but so long as she was in this state of mind I had not the courage to take any definite steps. Now that I have been noticing for the last two days that her mind is less stubborn I am hopeful again."

Gora felt that he ought not to ask any further questions on this subject, but he was unable to restrain himself, and he asked: "Have you thought of anyone yet as a bridegroom?"

"Yes, I have," replied Harmohini. "He is an excellent man—Kailash, my youngest brother-in-law. His wife died some time ago—and he has been waiting all this time for a suitable girl of grown-up age; otherwise do you think that such a boy would have remained unmarried? He would just suit Radharani."

The more keenly the thorn pricked him the more questions Gora asked about this Kailash.

It appeared that of all her brothers-in-law Kailash was the best educated. This had been due to his own efforts, but how far he had progressed in his education Harimohini was unable to say. In any case he was celebrated in his family for his learning. When the complaint against the village Postmaster had been sent to the General Post Office, Kailash had written it in such wonderful English that one of the heads of the Postal Department had come down to investigate the matter himself. All the inhabitants of his village had felt astonished at Kailash's ability. Yet, in spite of such learning, his devotion to matters of religion and the customs of his society had undergone no abatement.

When Kailash's whole history had been given Gora got up, made an obeisance to Harimohini, and left the room without a word, and going downstairs saw that Sucharita was engaged in cooking on the other side of the courtyard. When she heard the sound of Gora's footsteps she came and stood at the door, but when Gora went out, without looking to the right or the left, Sucharita heaved a deep sigh and went again to her work in the kitchen.

Just as he was leaving the lane for the main road Gora ran up against Haran Babu, who gave a slight laugh, and observed: "So early!"

Gora did not reply to this remark, but Haran Babu again asked: "You have just been to call there, I suppose? Is Sucharita at home?"

"Yes," said Gora, and walked away as fast as he could.

The moment Haran Babu entered the house he saw Sucharita through the door of the kitchen. She had no means of escape, and her aunt was nowhere near.

"I have only just this minute met Gourmohan Babu," observed Haran Babu. "I suppose he has been here till just now?"

Without making any answer to this remark Sucharita became suddenly very busy with her pots and pans—she behaved in fact as if she were so completely engaged that she had hardly time to breathe. But Haran Babu was not to be put off. Standing in the courtyard, outside the kitchen door, he began a conversation, in spite of the fact that Harimohini once or twice gave a warning cough from the stairs. Harimohini could easily have appeared before Haran Babu, but she knew for certain that, if she once allowed him to see her, neither she nor Sucharita would have any respite from the irrepressible enthusiasm of this persevering young man. So whenever she caught even the shadow of Haran Babu's presence she would draw her veil with a caution surpassing that of a newly married bride.

"Sucharita," said Haran Babu, "do you realise what you are doing? When will you eventually arrive? You have heard, I suppose, that Lolita is going to marry Binoy according to Hindu rites. You know who is responsible for this?"

Receiving no answer to this question, Haran Babu lowered his voice and said solemnly: "You are responsible!"

Haran Babu thought that Sucharita would be unable to bear the shock of such a dreadful charge, but seeing that she went on with her work without so much as looking up, he made his voice even more solemn, and shaking his finger at her, said: "Sucharita, I say again, you are repsonsible! Can you say, with your right hand on your heart, that for this you are not blameworthy before the whole Brahmo Samaj?"

Sucharita, for answer, put the frying-pan on the fire so that the oil began to splutter loudly.

Haran Babu continued: "It was you who brought Binoy Babu and Gourmohan Babu into your home, and encouraged them to such an extent that now they are more important in your eyes than all your most honoured friends in the Brahmo Samaj. Do you see what the result of this has been? And didn't I warn you to be careful from the very beginning? To-day what is the result? Now who can check Lolita? You think I suppose that the danger has ended with her! But that is not so! I have come to you to-day to warn you! Now it is your turn! Now you are doubtless repenting for the misfortune that has befallen Lolita, but the day is not far distant when you will not even have the grace to repent at your own downfall! But, Sucharita, there is still time to turn back! Just think for a moment, what great hopes once united us both—how brightly did duty shine before us, and how the whole future of the Brahmo Samaj spread out broadly before us—what resolutions we made together and how carefully we saved, every day, for the journey of life! Do you imagine that all that has been destroyed? Never! That field of our hopes is even now prepared. Only turn and look back once more! Come back again!"

At this moment the various kinds of vegetables which were frying in the boiling oil began to make a prodigious spluttering, and Sucharita began turning them over with the slicer in the approved manner; when Haran Babu remained silent, to see what the result of his summons to repentance was, Sucharita removed the frying-pan from the fire and putting it down, turned her face towards Haran Babu and said firmly: "I am a Hindu!"

"You are a Hindu!" exclaimed Haran Babu, completely taken aback.

"Yes, I am a Hindu!" Sucharita repeated, and she lifted the frying-pan on to the fire again and began to stir the vegetables vigorously.

"So Gourmohan Babu I suppose has been giving you initiation morning and evening, has he?" exclaimed Haran

Babu in a harsh voice, after recovering from the first effects of the shock.

"Yes," replied Sucharita without turning round, "I have been taking my initiation at his hands; he is my guru!"

Haran Babu had until now regarded himself as Sucharita's guru, and if he had heard that day that she loved Gora the news would not have been so bitter to him—but to hear from Sucharita's own lips that Gora had snatched away from him his rights as her guru struck him like a lash.

"However big a man your guru may be, do you imagine that the Hindu society will accept you?" sneered Haran Babu.

"I know nothing about that," answered Sucharita. "I do not understand your 'society,' but I know I am a Hindu!"

"Do you realise that the mere fact of your having remained so long unmarried is enough to outcaste you from the Hindu society?" asked Haran Babu.

"Do not trouble yourself uselessly over that question," answered Sucharita, "but I can tell you one thing, I am a Hindu!"

"You have abandoned all the religious teaching you have received from Paresh Babu at the feet of this new guru of yours, I suppose?" exclaimed Haran Babu.

"The Lord of my heart knows about my religion, and I do not propose to discuss it with anyone," said Sucharita. "But you can be certain of one thing, namely, that I am a Hindu!"

"Well let me tell you," exclaimed Haran Babu impatiently, "that no matter how big a Hindu you may think yourself you won't get any benefit from that. You haven't got another Binoy in your Gourmohan Babu, so you needn't hope that you will be able to get Gourmohan Babu even if you shout yourself hoarse by declaring yourself to be Hindu. It is an easy matter for him to assume the rôle of a guru and have you as his disciple, but don't even in your dreams think that he will take you into his home and set up housekeeping with you as his partner!"

Forgetting in a moment all her cooking Sucharita turned round like a flash of lightning and exclaimed: 'What is all this you are saying?"

"I say," replied Haran Babu, "that Gourmohan Babu will never think of marrying you!"

"Marry me?" exclaimed Sucharita, her eyes looking dangerously bright. "Did I not tell you that he is my guru?"

"That you did certainly," replied Haran Babu, "but we can understand also what you did not tell us!"

"Leave this house!" cried Sucharita. "You shall not insult me. Let me tell you now, once for all, that from to-day I will never come out in your presence again."

"Come out before me indeed!" sneered Haran Babu. "No you are a *zenana* lady! A proper Hindu housewife! 'Unseen even by the sun!' Now is Paresh Babu enjoying the full fruits of his sin! Let him enjoy in his old age the fruits of his own works, I say farewell to you all!"

Sucharita shut the kitchen door with a bang, and throwing herself on the floor tried to stifle the sound of her sobs, while Haran Babu went out of the house with his face dark with anger.

Harimohini had listened to every word of the conversation between the two, and what she had heard from Sucharita's own lips to-day was beyond her wildest hopes. Her heart swelled with joy and she exclaimed: "Why should it not be possible? What I have prayed for with such single-hearted devotion from my god, could that be all in vain?" And she went then and there to her prayer-room and, falling full length on the floor before her idol, promised that from that day she would increase the quantity of her offerings. Her worship, which for many days had been performed very peacefully under the influence of her sorrow, was to-day, in her realisation of a selfish hope, eager, hot and hungry.

SIXTY SIX

Gora had never spoken to anyone as he had been speaking to Sucharita. Up to now he had been bringing out before his hearers mere opinions, instructions, and speeches—to-day, before Sucharita, he was expressing his whole self. In the joy of this self-revelation there was not only a feeling of power, all his opinions and resolutions were filled with an emotional quality. His life was enveloped in beauty, and it seemed as though the gods were suddenly showering their nectar upon his religious devotions.

It was under the impulse of this joy that Gora had been visiting Sucharita for so many days consecutively without any thought of the consequences. But to-day, when he suddenly heard Harimohini's words, he remembered that once he had laughed mercilessly. He was startled at seeing himself landed in the same situation, through his own ignorance. Gora summoned all the senses at his command, just as a sleeping person who receives a sudden shock for which he is not prepared in an unknown place palpitates in dismay. Gora had over and over again preached that there are many powerful nations in this world which have been absolutely destroyed, and that India alone by reason of her restraint and the firmness with which she had kept to her old laws had been able to survive the adverse forces of the centuries. Nowhere would Gora admit the least laxity in these laws, and he would say that, though India had been plundered of all else, her soul was still lying hidden in the restraint of these inflexible regulations, and no oppressive rulers had the power to touch her body. So long as we are subject to some foreign nation we must observe strictly our own laws, and leave the question of their goodness or badness till later. A drowning man, clutching at a straw or any other object with which he can save his life, does not deliberate as to whether it is ugly or beautiful. Gora had over and over again declared himself thus. To-day also this was what he felt, and when Harimohini had abused him for his conduct he felt like a noble elephant pricked by the goad.

When Gora reached home he found Mohim seated on a bench outside the door without his shirt, smoking, as to-day was an office holiday. He followed Gora indoors, and called out: "Gora, listen to me, I want to have a talk with you."

"Do not be angry, brother," he continued when they were both seated in Gora's own room, "but let me first ask you whether you too have caught the same infection as Binoy? You seem to be going pretty frequently to that quarter, and getting very thick with them!"

"You needn't be afraid," said Gora, blushing.

"There is no saying, from the way I see things are going," observed Mohim. "You seem to think that it is something eatable which you can swallow without an effort and then come back home again! But that there is a hook in the bait you can see well enough from your friend's plight! No, don't run away! I haven't come to the point yet. I've heard that it is quite settled that Binoy is to marry into a Brahmo family, and I want to tell you beforehand that from now onwards we can't have anything more to do with him!"

"That goes without saying," assented Gora.

"But," continued Mohim, "if mother makes a fuss it will be a nuisance. We are family men and, as we are, we have to break our backs over the task of getting our girls and boys married. If in addition to that a branch of the Brahmo Samaj is established in our house then I shall have to go and live elsewhere."

"No, no, there will be no need for that!" assured Gora.

"Then proposal for Soshi's marriage is more or less settled," said Mohim. "But the future father-in-law will never be satisfied until he gets possession not only of the girl but of more than her weight in gold—for he is well aware that a human being is classed as 'Perishable Goods,' and gold lasts much longer. He has a keener eye for the sugar than for the pill! You lower him by calling him a father-in-law, he is so barefaced in his demands! It's going to cost me a pretty penny to be sure, but I've learnt a good lesson from him which will come in useful at the time of my own boy's marriage. I only wish I could be born again at this time, and with my father as go-between, could arrange for my own marriage—you may be sure I would see that I got the fullest benefit of being born a man. This is what is called manliness! To ruin completely a girl's father! Is that a small matter? Whatever you may say, brother, I can't go about with you singing victory to the Hindu society day and night; my voice all of a sudden becomes weak at the suggestion. My Tincowry's age is now only fourteen months—it took my spouse a long enough time to rectify the mistake of giving birth first of all to a daughter—but however that may be, Gora, you must do your best, with all your friends combined, to keep the Hindu society in a thriving state till my son is old enough to be married. After that the country can become Mohammedan, Christian, or anything else it likes, for all I care!"

"So I say," continued Mohim, on seeing Gora get up to go, "that it will never do to invite your Binoy to Soshi's marriage ceremony, for it would be foolish to give such an opening to more trouble. So you must begin from now to warn mother to be careful."

On entering Anandamoyi's room Gora found her seated at the table, with her spectacles on, engaged in making a list in an account book. She closed the book on seeing Gora and, taking off her spectacles, said: "Sit down."

"I want to consult you about something," observed Anandamoyi as soon as he was seated. "You have heard about Binoy's coming marriage of course."

"His uncle is angry about it," she continued, seeing that Gora was silent, "and none of his people will come to the wedding. And it is doubtful whether it can take place at Paresh Babu's so Binoy himself will have to make all the arrangements. So I was thinking that it would be most convenient if we could make use of that second storey of our house on the north, the lower storey is rented but the upper one is without a tenant just now."

"How would it be convenient?" inquired Gora.

"Who will look after the arrangements for his wedding if I don't?" explained Anandamoyi. "He will be in a great fix. But if the marriage were to take place in those rooms then I could easily manage everything from here without the least difficulty."

"That will be impossible, mother," said Gora, decisively.

"Why should it be impossible?" asked Anandamoyi. "I have obtained the permission of the master of the house."

"No, mother, the marriage can never be celebrated there," explostulated Gora, "I assure you. Do listen to me!"

"Why not?" asked Anandamoyi. "Binoy is not getting married according to their rites."

"That is all useless argument," objected Gora. "It is no use pleading like that with society. Let Binoy do what he likes, we can't give our approval to this marriage. There is no lack of houses in Calcutta. He has his own house."

Anandamoyi knew quite well that there were plenty of houses, but she could not bear to think of Binoy being deserted by all his friends and relations and having to marry like an unfortunate and friendless person managing somehow or other in a hired house. It was for this reason that she had settled in her mind to make use of that part of their house which was lying free, for Binoy's wedding. She would have been quite satisfied if only she could get the marriage celebrated in her own house without causing any opposition from society.

"If you are so averse to this idea," sighed Anandamoyi, "then we must hire a house somewhere else, I suppose. But that will mean a great strain on me. However, never mind that, if my idea is impracticable what's the use of thinking any more about it?"

"Mother, if you attend this marriage ceremony it will not be a good thing," objected Gora.

"Whatever are you saying, Gora?" exclaimed Anandamoyi. "If I don't attend our Binoy's wedding then who will, I should like to know?"

"No, it will never do mother," persisted Gora.

"Gora," answered Anandamoyi, "you may not agree with Binoy in your opinions, but is that any reason why you should become his enemy?"

"Mother," exclaimed Gora little excitedly, "it is wrong of you to say that. It's not a happy thing for me to feel that I can't rejoice on the occasion of Binoy's marriage. You know, if no one else does, how much I love him, but mother, this is not a question of love—friendship or enmity do not affect the matter in the least. Binoy is doing this with his eyes open to all its consequences. It is not we who are leaving him, but he who is forsaking us, so he is not receiving any greater blow than he could have been expecting."

"Gora," said Anandamoyi, "Binoy knows that you will have nothing whatever to do with this marriage of his, that is true enough. But he also knows that I can never desert him at so auspicious a moment of his life. I can tell you for certain that if Binoy knew that I would not give his bride my blessing then nothing would induce him to marry. Do you think that I don't know Binoy's mind?" and as she spoke she wiped a tear away.

The pain that Gora was feeling in his mind on Binoy's account troubled him greatly, till he remarked: "Mother, you must remember that you are a member of a society and that you are indebted to that society."

"Gora," exclaimed Anandamoyi, "haven't I been telling you again and again that I severed my connection with my society a long time ago? That is why society hates me so much and why I keep myself aloof from it."

"Mother," expostulated Gora, "that remark of yours hurts me more than everything else."

"My child," observed Anandamoyi, her tearful look seeming to take in the whole of Gora's body, "God knows that it is beyond my power to save you from that pain!"

"Very well," said Gora, getting up, "I will tell you what I must do. I will go to Binoy, and say to him that he must try to manage his marriage so as to avoid your becoming still more divorced from your society, for otherwise it will be very wrong and selfish of him."

"All right," laughed Anandamoyi, "you do whatever you can. Go and speak to him, and then I will see what happens."

When Gora had gone, Anandamoyi sat for a long time lost in thought, and then after some time had passed she got up slowly and went to her husband's quarters.

To-day it was the eleventh day of the moon, so Krishnadayal had made no preparations for his food. He had got hold of a new Bengali translation of a Hindu religious book, and was engaged in reading it, seated on a deerskin. On seeing Anandamoyi he became much disturbed, but she kept at a respectful distance from him, and seating herself in the doorway, remarked: "Look here, we are doing very wrong."

Krishnadayal considered himself quite outside the rights and wrongs of worldly affairs, so he inquired with an indifferent air: "What is wrong?"

"We ought not to deceive Gora another single day," explained Anandamoyi. "The situation is getting more and more complicated."

When Gora had raised the subject of his penance ceremony this question had occurred to Krishnadayal, but afterwards he had become so absorbed in the application of various methods of asceticism that he had found no further leisure to think about it.

"Soshimukhi's wedding is being talked of, and is likely to take place in the month of *Phalgun*," continued Anandamoyi. "Up to now, whenever there was to be any ceremony in our house, I used to take Gora off with me somewhere on some excuse or other, but there has never been a ceremony of very great importance until the present. But what shall we do with him on the occasion of Soshi's wedding? Tell me that. The evil increases everyday. I ask God's forgiveness twice everyday, and ask that He will let me bear any punishment that may be necessary. But I am all the time afraid that it will not be possible to hide it any longer, and that will mean a catastrophe for Gora. Now I want you to give me permission to speak out to him without reserve and let me bear what my fate has in store for me."

What is the meaning of this interruption to Krishnadayal's austerities which Indra has sent him? Lately his practice of asceticism had been very strict—he had been performing almost impossible feats with his breathing, and he had so reduced the quantity of his food that it would not be long before his stomach would be touching his backbone. And it was at such a time that such a calamity was befalling him!

"Are you mad?" exclaimed Krishnadayal. "If you make this known now I shall have to make some very difficult explanations—my pension will most certainly be stopped, and we may even have trouble with the police. What has been done has been done. Do what you can to put a check on things—and if you fail that will not be so terrible a crime."

Krishnadayal had decided that after his death they could do what they liked, but before it he wanted simply to be left to himself. Apart from that, if he did not pay any attention to what was happening to others without his knowledge, it would somehow come out all right.

Not being able to decide what ought to be done Anandamoyi looked very gloomy, and standing up for a little, said: "Don't you see how ill you are looking? Your body—"

"Body!" interrupted Krishnadayal with a slight laugh, and his voice was raised in impatience at such an exhibition of stupidity on the part of his wife. No satisfactory conclusion to this matter having been arrived at, Krishnadayal sat down again on his deerskin and plunged into his studies.

In the meantime Mohim was seated in the outer room with his *sannyasi*, engaged in an earnest discussion on the highest end of man and other deep principles of the religious life. Whether salvation was possible for a family man or not, was the question which he was propounding with such humble and anxious attention that it seemed that his whole life depended upon its answer. The *sannyasi* tried his best to console Mohim by saying that though salvation was not possible for a family man yet heaven was attainable, but Mohim was not to be comforted by such an assurance. It was salvation that he longed for. He had no use for a mere heaven! If only he could once get his daughter married off satisfactorily then he would devote himself to the service of the *sannyasi* and the attainment of salvation. There was no one who could divert him from this purpose! But to marry off his daughter was no easy matter. If only his guru would have pity on him!

SIXTY SEVEN

Remembering that there had been some amount of self-delusion in his relation with Sucharita, Gora determined to be more cautious. He felt that his laxity in following the accustomed path was due to the strong fascination which had made him forget his obligations to society.

When he had finished his morning worship Gora went into his room and found Paresh Babu waiting for him. On seeing him he felt a sudden thrill, for it was impossible for him not to feel that his relationship with Paresh Babu was of an especially intimate nature.

Gora having made his obeisance to him, Paresh Babu said: "You have of course heard of Binoy's coming marriage."

"Yes," assented Gora.

"He is not prepared to be married according to Brahmo rites," added Paresh Babu.

"In that case the marriage ought not to take place," observed Gora.

"We need not enter into an argument on that point," laughed Paresh Babu. "None of the members of our community will attend the wedding, and I have heard that none of Binoy's own relations will come. On my daughter's side there is only myself, and on Binoy's side I suppose there is no one but yourself, and that is why I have come to have a consultation with you."

"What is the use of consulting me about it?" exclaimed
Gora, shaking his head. "I will have nothing to do with the
affair."

"You will not?" said Paresh Babu, looking at him in
amazement.

For a moment Gora felt ashamed when he noticed Paresh
Babu's astonishment, but because he felt ashamed he exclaimed
with re-doubled firmness: "How is it possible for me to have
anything to do with it?"

"I know that you are his friend," observed Paresh Babu,
"and it is at such a time that the need of a friend is greatest,
is it not?"

"I am his friend that is true," answered Gora, "but that
is not the only tie I have in the world, nor the most important
either!"

"Gora," inquired Paresh Babu, "do you think that in
Binoy's conduct there has been anything wrong or irreligious
shown?"

"Religion has two aspects to it," answered Gora. "One
aspect is the eternal, the other the worldly. Where religion
is revealed through the laws of society you cannot disregard
it without bringing ruin on society."

"There are countless laws," said Paresh Babu, "but have
you to take it for granted that in every one of them religion
is revealed?"

Paresh Babu here touched Gora in such a spot that his
mind was stirred of itself, and from that stirring he reached
some definite conclusion. He in fact felt no further hesitation
in speaking quite freely of all that was in his heart. The main
purport of what he said was that, if we do not submit ourselves
completely to society through the restraining influence of
such laws, then we place obstacles in the way of the deepest
inner purpose for which society exists; for that purpose lies
concealed, and it is not within the power of everyone to see

it clearly. There we want to have some power, apart from that of our own judgment, by which we can show our respect for society.

Paresh Babu listened attentively to what Gora had to say up to the very end, and then when, feeling in his mind a little ashamed of his own boldness, he stopped, Paresh Babu said: "I agree in the main with what you have been saying. It is true enough that God has some special purpose to perform in every society, and that purpose is not completely evident to everybody. But it is man's task to try to see it clearly, and not to regard it as his chief aim in life to obey rules as though he were as unconscious as the branch of a tree."

"My point is this," explained Gora, "if we first of all obey society fully from every point of view then our consciousness of its real purpose will become clear! If we merely quarrel with it, we not only obstruct it but misunderstand it also."

"Truth cannot be tested except by opposition and obstacles," argued Paresh Babu, "the testing of truth has not been carried out once and for all by a group of learned men in some past age; truth has to be discovered anew through the blows and opposition it encounters from the people of every age. However that may be, I do not want to start a discussion on all these matters. I respect the freedom of the individual, for through the blows inflicted by the liberty of the individual we can know for certain what is everlasting truth, and what is transitory fancy. The welfare of society depends upon our knowing this or at least attempting to do so."

Having said this both Paresh Babu and Gora stood up, and Paresh Babu went on: "I had thought that out of respect for the Brahmo Samaj I would have to keep a little apart from this marriage ceremony, and that you, being Binoy's friend, would bring the whole matter to a satisfactory conclusion. In such circumstances a friend has an advantage over relations, for he does not have to bear the opposition of the community, but when you, too think it your duty to forsake Binoy, then I must assume the whole responsibility I shall have to manage the whole affair alone."

Gora did not know when he heard that word "alone" how truly alone Paresh Babu was. Bordashundari was against him, his own daughters were not pleased with him, and in fear of Harimohini's disapproval he had not even called Sucharita to consult her about this wedding. Then all the members of the Brahmo Samaj were at daggers drawn with him, and, as for Binoy's uncle, he had written two letters to Paresh Babu abusing him in most offensive terms as a kidnapper of youth, and an insincere and evil adviser.

As Paresh Babu was going out he was met at the door by Abinash and two or three other members of Gora's party. These young men, on seeing Paresh Babu, began to joke and laugh at him, but Gora turned on them indignantly and exclaimed: "If you have not the power to feel respect for a man who is worthy of honour, you might at least avoid such meanness as to jeer at him."

Gora found himself once more plunged into the affairs of his party in the old-accustomed channels. But how distasteful they were to him now! All seemed so flavourless, so insignificant. It was impossible to call this "work," it was so lifeless. Merely lecturing and writing like this and forming a party was not real work, rather it seemed to make the impossibility of work more widespread. Never before had Gora felt this so keenly. He was no longer attracted to all this; he wanted an absolutely true channel through which his life, trembling with his newly acquired power, could flow unobstructed.

In the meantime, the preparations for the ceremony of penance were going ahead, and in them at least Gora felt a certain amount of enthusiasm. This was to be a ceremony to cleanse him not only from the pollutions of his gaol life, but it was to make him pure again from every point of view, so that he could take as it were a new body for the field of his own work which he wanted to enter upon in his second birth. A dispensation for the penance had been obtained, the actual day had been fixed—preparations were being made for sending invitations to several well-known pandits from East and West, the wealthier members of Gora's party had collected money for the expenses, and all the members of the party were under the impression that at last a great work was going to be accomplished in their country. Abinash had had secret consultations with his own circle as to the possibility of getting the pandits, just when they were dispensing all the customary flowers, sandal-paste, grains of paddy, and sacred grass, to bestow the title of "The Light of the Hindu Religion" upon Gora. Several Sanskrit slokas were to be printed in letters of gold on a parchment which was to be signed by all the Brahmin pandits and would then be presented to Gora in a box of sandalwood. After that a fine edition of Max Müller's book on the *Rig Veda*, bound in the most expensive morocco cover, would be offered to him by the oldest and most honoured of the learned men present as a token of the blessings of India herself. In this way would be beautifully expressed, the appreciation they felt for Gora, who in the present fallen state of Hinduism had done so much to preserve the ancient forms of the Vedic religion.

In this manner, quite unknown to Gora, everyday amongst the members of his party discussions were taking place as to how best they could make the ceremony of that day most productive and pleasing to all concerned.

SIXTY EIGHT

Harimohini had received a letter from her brother-in-law, Kailash. He had written: "By the blessing of your gracious feet all are well here, and I hope you will remove all our anxiety about you by sending us good news of yourself." This he wrote in spite of the fact that from the moment Harimohini had left their house, they had not made the least effort to obtain any information as to her welfare. Having given the news of Khudi, Potol, Bhojohari, etc., Kailash wrote in conclusion: "I would like you to give me further particulars about the bride whom you have suggested for me in your last letter. You have said that she is about twelve or thirteen years of age, but exceptionally well developed for so young a girl, and looks quite grown-up. There is nothing to complain of about that, but I want you to make careful inquiries about the property which you mention, as to whether she has only a life-interest in it or whether it belongs to her without any qualifications. Then I can consult with my elder brothers, and I think they will raise no objection. I am glad to hear that she is firm in her devotion to the Hindu religion, but we must try our best to prevent it becoming known that she has lived so long in a Brahmo family, so do not mention this to anyone else. There is to be a bathing festival in the Ganges at the next lunar eclipse, and if I can manage it I shall come to Calcutta and shall be able to see the girl then."

So long Harimohini had been managing somehow to live in Calcutta, but as soon as a slight hope of being able to return to her father-in-law's house began to take shape in her mind she found it difficult to remain there patiently. Her banishment everyday became more unbearable to her, and if she could have had her way she would have spoken to Sucharita at once and tried to settle the day! But she had not the courage to be too hasty, for the more closely she came into contact with Sucharita the more clearly she realised that she was unable to understand her.

Harimohini, however, began to wait for her opportunity, and she started to keep a much stricter eye on Sucharita than before. She began even to lessen the time she had been accustomed to give to her devotions, as she did not want to let her companion out of her sight.

Sucharita on the other hand noticed that Gora had suddenly stopped coming, and though she felt sure that Harimohini had said something to him, she comforted herself by saying: "Well, even if he does not come—still he is my guru—my guru."

The influence of an absent guru is often much greater than that of one who is constantly present, for then the mind itself becomes filled from within when it feels the lack of the guru's presence. Where, if Gora had been with her in person, Sucharita would have argued with him, she now read his essays and accepted them without disputing them. If there was anything she could not understand she felt sure that if he had been there to explain she would have understood it!

But her hunger for the sight of his bright face and the sound of his thundering voice became so incessant that it seemed as if it were causing her very body to waste. From time to time she would think, with intense pain, how many people there were who could see Gora at any time of day or night without any difficulty, but who did not realise in the least the value of their privilege!

One afternoon Lolita came and, putting her arm round Sucharita's neck, said: "Well, sister Suchi!"

"What is it, sister Lolita?" asked Sucharita.

"Everything has been settled."

"What day is it to be?"

"Monday."

"Where?"

"I know nothing about all that, father knows that," replied Lolita with a shake of her head.

"Are you happy, sister?" inquired Sucharita, placing her arm round Lolita's waist.

"Why shouldn't I be happy?" exclaimed Lolita.

"Now that you have got everything you wanted," answered Sucharita, "and now that you will have no one else to quarrel with, I was afraid that your keenness would receive a check!"

"Why should there be a lack of people to quarrel with?" laughed Lolita. "Now it will not be necessary to search outside my own home!"

"So that's it, is it?" exclaimed Sucharita, playfully patting her on her cheek, "you are beginning to plan all that already are you? I will tell Binoy, there's still time! The poor fellow ought to be warned!"

"It's too late to warn your poor fellow now!" exclaimed Lolita. "There is no escape for him! The crisis which is mentioned in his horoscope is on him—now he will have to weep and beat his brow."

"But, really and truly, Lolita, I can't tell you how happy I am about it," said Sucharita, suddenly becoming serious. "I only pray that you may be worthy of a husband like Binoy."

"Fugh! Indeed! And is no one to become worthy of a wife like me?" exclaimed Lolita. "Just talk to him on that subject once and see what he has to say! Hear what his opinion is, and you will soon repent that you have so long failed to appreciate the affection of such an extraordinary and wonderful person—that you could have been so blind!"

"All right then, at last an expert has arrived on the scene," said Sucharita, "and there's no more cause for sorrow, for he has got what he wanted at the price he wanted to pay for it. So there will be no need for you to test the affection of inexperienced people like us!"

"No need indeed!" exclaimed Lolita. "There'll be plenty of need!" and she pinched Sucharita's cheek, slyly saying: "I want your affection always. It will never do if you cheat me by bestowing it elsewhere!"

"I will give it to no one else, no one else," said Sucharita assuringly, laying her cheek against Lolita's.

"To no one else?" asked Lolita. "Are you absolutely sure—to no one?"

Sucharita merely shook her head, whereupon Lolita sat at a little distance and said: "Look here, Suchi Didi, you know well enough, dear, that I should never have been able to bear it if you had given your affection to someone else. I have kept silent all this time, but to-day I will speak out. When Gourmohan Babu used to come to our house— no, Didi, you mustn't be shy—what I have to say I will say fully to-day, for though I never keep anything secret from you, so long I have somehow not been able to speak openly about this one thing, and I have often felt pained because of that. But, now that I am parting from you, I can't keep it to myself any longer. When Gourmohan Babu first began to come to our house I used to get very angry. Why was I angry? You used to think that I didn't understand anything, didn't you? I noticed that you never mentioned his name to me, and that only made me still more angry! It was unbearable to me to think that the time might come when you would love him more than me—no, Didi, you must let me finish—and I can't tell you what agony I endured for that reason. Now, too, you will not speak to me about him I know, but I am no longer angry about it. I can't tell you, dear, how happy I would be if you and—" but Sucharita suddenly interrupted her, by placing her hand over her mouth, and said:

"Lolita, I beg you, do not say such things! When I hear you speak like that, I feel like sinking into the ground!"

"Why not, sister, has he—" began Lolita, but Sucharita interrupted her once more in great distress. "No! No! No! You are talking as though you were mad! You ought not to speak of what one cannot even contemplate!"

"But, sister, this is affectation on your part," complained Lolita, being annoyed at her hesitation. "I've been watching very carefully, and I can assure you—"

But Sucharita would not let her finish. She snatched away her hands from Lolita's and went out of the room, with Lolita running after her, and saying: "Very well, I won't say any more about it."

"Never again!" begged Sucharita.

"I can't make such a serious promise as that," replied Lolita. "If my day comes then I will speak, otherwise not. That much I can promise."

For the past few days Harimohini had been keeping a constant eye upon Sucharita, following her about in such a way that it was impossible for her not to be aware of it, and this suspicion and vigilance became quite a burden to her. It made her feel impatient, and yet she could not say anything about it. To-day, when Lolita had gone, Sucharita sat down wearily at the table and, resting her head in her hands, began to weep, and when the servant brought in the lamp she sent it away again. Harimohini was at that time at her evening devotions, and when she saw Lolita going out of the house she came downstairs unexpectedly and, entering the room, called: "Radharani!"

Sucharita hastily wiped her eyes and stood up, as Harimohini attacked her with the question: "What's the matter?"

"I can't understand what all this foolishness is about!" exclaimed Harimohini in a hard voice, when she found that she got no answer to her query.

"Auntie," sobbed Sucharita, "why do you watch me and follow me about day and night?"

"Can't you understand why I do it?" asked Harimohini. "All this going without your food, and this weeping, what are they the signs of? I'm not a child, do you think I can't even understand that much?"

"Auntie," said Sucharita, "I assure you that you don't understand in the least. You are making such a dreadful blunder that at every moment I feel it growing more unbearable."

"Very well," replied Harimohini, "if I am making a blunder, then be good enough to explain everything to me fully."

"All right, I will explain," said Sucharita, making a great effort to control her feeling of shyness. "I have learnt something from my guru which is quite new to me, and to comprehend it properly needs great strength of mind—I am feeling the want of that—I find it difficult to be always quarrelling with myself. But Auntie, you have been taking a quite distorted view of our relationship, and you have driven him away, after insulting him. What you said to him was all a blunder, and what you are thinking about me is wholly false. In this you are doing wrong! It is beyond your power to lower a man like him, but what have I done that you should tyrannise over me like this?" As she spoke her voice became choked with sobs, and she had to leave the room.

Harimohini was taken aback, and said to herself: "Goodness me, whoever heard such talk?" Nevertheless she gave Sucharita a little time to recover before calling her to her evening meal.

"Look here, Radharani, I'm not a child," began Harimohini as soon as Sucharita was seated. "I have been brought up from childhood in what you call the Hindu religion, and have heard plenty of opinions about it. You know nothing of all this, and so Gourmohan is merely deceiving you by calling himself your guru. I have heard him talk every now and then, and there is nothing in keeping with traditional views in what he says— he invents some Scriptures of his own. It is easy enough for me to detect that, for haven't I a guru of my own? Let me advise you, Radharani, to have nothing to do with these things. When the time comes my guru will take you in hand, and will give you the right *mantrams*; there's no trickery about him. You need not be afraid, I will manage to get you into the Hindu community, no matter whether you have been in a Brahmo home, or not! Who will ever know about that? It is true your age is rather advanced— but there are plenty of girls who are over-developed for their age, and who is going to look up your birth certificate? Oh, when you have money everything can be managed! There will be no obstacles! Why, I have seen with my own eyes a low caste boy become high caste with the help of a little money! I will fix you up in such a good Brahmin family that no one will dare to say a word. Why, they are the leaders of the Hindu community. So you will not have to waste so many tears and entreaties on that guru of yours."

When Harimohini began this elaborate preamble Sucharita lost all appetite for her food, and she felt as if she could not swallow a morsel. But with a tremendous effort she managed quietly to eat something, because she knew that if she did not eat she would get such a lecture that she would be still more disgusted.

When Harimohini saw that she was getting no particular response she said to herself: "Oh, these people are beyond my comprehension! On the one hand she cries herself hoarse saying she is a Hindu, and then when she gets such an opportunity as this she won't listen. There will be no need to offer penance, and no explanations will be asked for; it will only be necessary to scatter a few rupees about and society will be easily managed, but if she fails to show enthusiasm even for this, how can she profess to be a Hindu?" Harimohini had not been long in discovering what a fraud Gora was, and she had come to the conclusion, when wondering what could be the cause of such colossal deceit, that Sucharita's good looks and her money were at the root of it all. The sooner she could rescue the girl, together with her Government securities, and transfer her to the safe fortress of her father-in-law's house the better for everyone concerned. But until her mind was a little more pliable it could not be managed, and so, in order to render it pliable, she began to talk day and night about her father-in-law's home. She gave all kinds of examples showing how unusual was their influence, and what almost impossible things they were able to accomplish in their community. She told her how many quite innocent people who had dared to oppose them had been persecuted by their society, and how many who had even eaten fowl cooked by Mohammedans had been able to continue along the difficult path of Hindu society with smiling faces, and to make it all the more plausible she described everything in detail with names and places.

Bordashundari had never concealed from Sucharita her wish that she should not come round to their house often, for she always took a sort of pride in what she called her frankness. Whenever she had occasion to use to anyone an unobstructed flow of severe abuse she never failed to refer to this virtue of hers. Therefore she expressed in language which was easy to understand that Sucharita need not expect any kind of decent treatment in her house, so Sucharita knew quite well that if she went often to their home Paresh Babu would have to suffer great disturbance to his peace and quiet. Therefore, unless there was some special need, she did not go, and Paresh Babu used to come round once or twice everyday to see her in her own home.

For some days, owing to pressure of work and various other anxieties, Paresh Babu had not been able to call, and everyday, in spite of a certain trouble and hesitation of mind, Sucharita had been hoping for him to come. She knew for certain that the deep relationship between them on which the welfare of them both depended could never at any time be broken, and yet there were one or two bonds, which were drawing her from outside, which gave her considerable pain and would not allow her to rest. On the other hand here was Harimohini, making her life everyday more unbearable. So, to-day, braving the displeasure of Bordashundari, Sucharita went to Paresh Babu's house. The high three-storyed building towards the west was casting a long shadow as the sun was setting, and in that shadow Paresh Babu was walking slowly up and down, alone with his head bent in thought.

"How are you, father?" asked Sucharita as she joined him in his walk.

Paresh Babu started on being thus suddenly interrupted in his meditations and, standing still for a moment, looked at Sucharita, and said: "I'm well, thank you, Radha!"

The two of them began to walk up and down together, and Paresh Babu remarked: "Lolita is to be married on Monday."

Sucharita had been thinking that she would ask him why he had not called her for consultation or help in the matter of this wedding, but she suddenly shrank from doing so, feeling that there was an obstacle somewhere on her own side. At any other time she would not have waited to be called.

But Paresh Babu himself introduced the very subject which she had been thinking about, by saying: "I was not able to ask your advice this time, Radha!"

"Why not, father?" asked Sucharita.

Without answering this question Paresh Babu remained looking inquiringly into her face, until Sucharita could no longer restrain herself, and said, with her face slightly averted: "You have been thinking that a change has taken place in my mind."

"Yes," assented Paresh Babu, "so I thought that I would not place you in an awkward position by making any request to you."

"Father," began Sucharita, "I have been intending to tell you everything, but I have not been able to see you lately. That's why I have come here to-day. I have not the power to explain everything to you quite clearly, and for that reason I am half-afraid lest you should not understand."

"I know that it is not easy to speak about these things simply," agreed Paresh Babu. "You have got something on your mind which is a question of emotions only, and although you feel it, it does not take tangible shape for you."

"Yes, it is exactly that!" exclaimed Sucharita, much relieved. "But how can I explain to you how strong that feeling is? It is exactly as if I had been re-born, and had attained a new consciousness. Never before have I seen myself from the same point of view as now. Up to now I never had any sort of relationship with either the Past or the Future of my country, but now I have got such a wonderful realisation in my heart of the greatness and truth of this relationship that I cannot forget it. Look here, father, I tell you the truth when I say that I am really a Hindu, though before this I could never have got myself to acknowledge it. Now I say, without any hesitation, and even with emphasis, that I am a Hindu! And I feel a great joy in the confession!"

"Have you looked at this question in all its aspects and with all its implications?" asked Paresh Babu.

"Have I in myself got the power of seeing it fully from every point of view?" answered Sucharita. "I can only say that

I have read widely on this subject and had many discussions on it. When I had not learnt to look at things in their true proportions, and was in the habit of exaggerating all the little details of Hinduism, then I felt a sort of hatred for Hinduism as a whole."

On hearing her speak like this Paresh Babu felt some astonishment. He understood clearly enough that Sucharita's mind was going through a transition of ideas, and because she had obtained something that was true she was feeling free from all doubt. It was not that she was being carried away by the current of some vague emotion which, in her infatuation, she was not able to comprehend.

"Father," continued Sucharita, "how can I say that I am an unimportant being separate from my caste and my country? Why can I not say, 'I am a Hindu'?"

"In other words," commented Paresh Babu, "you mean to ask me why I myself do not call myself a Hindu? If you come to think of it there is no very serious reason why I shouldn't, except that the Hindu Society itself refuses to acknowledge me as one. Another reason is that those whose religious opinions are in accordance with mine do not call themselves Hindus."

"I have explained to you," continued Paresh Babu, on seeing that Sucharita did not answer, "that none of these reasons are very serious ones, they are only external ones, and one can get along all right without admitting these obstacles. But there is a very deep inner reason, and it is that there is no way of obtaining entrance into the Hindu Society. At any rate there is no royal high road, though there may be some back-doors. That society is not one for all mankind—it is only for those whose destiny it is to be born Hindus."

"But all societies are like that," interposed Sucharita.

"No, there is no important society that is," replied Paresh Babu. "The portal of the Mussulman society stands open for all to enter—the Christian society also welcomes all. Even in the different branches of Christianity the same rule holds good. If I want to become English that is not absolutely impossible for me—if I live in England long enough and follow their customs, then I can be included in the English Society—it is not even necessary for me to become a Christian. It is easy enough to know how to enter a maze, but it is not so easy to know the way out. Now for a Hindu it is just the opposite. The way for entering their society is altogether closed, but there are thousands of ways out."

"But nevertheless, father," argued Sucharita, "the Hindus have suffered no loss all these centuries. The Hindu Society still lasts on."

"It takes time to realise when a society is suffering loss," answered Paresh Babu. "In olden times the back entrances to the Hindu Society were left open, and it used to be considered one of the glories of this country that one of non-Aryan nationality could become a Hindu. Even in the time of the Mohammedans the influence of Hindu rajas and zemindars could be felt everywhere, and for that reason there was no limit to the obstacles and punishments placed in the way of those who wanted to come out of the Hindu Society. Now that the English, by their laws, protect everyone there is not the same facility for forcibly closing the outlets of society by artificial means—that is why for some time past Hindus have been on the decrease in India and Mohammedans on the increase. If things go on like this, gradually the Mussulmans will predominate, and it will be wrong to call this country Hindustan."

"But, father," exclaimed Sucharita in distress, "isn't it the duty of all of us to prevent this happening? By forsaking the Hindus are we also to be the cause of still further loss? Now is just the time when we ought to hold with all the power at our command to our Hinduism."

"Merely by wishing it, can we keep anybody alive by holding tightly to them?" asked Paresh Babu, patting Sucharita affectionately on the back. "There is a natural law of protection, and he who forsakes that law of nature is naturally forsaken by all. The Hindu Society insults and abandons men, and for that reason nowadays it is becoming increasingly difficult to preserve our self-respect. In these days it is no longer possible to shelter ourselves behind a screen—the roads of the world are open in all directions, and people from all sides are invading our society—it is no longer possible, by raising walls, and building dams with codes of laws and scriptures, to cut ourselves off from all connection with everyone else. If the Hindu Society does not at once arouse all its accumulated forces, and gives free scope to this wasting disease, then this unobstructed connection with the outside world will deal it a deadly blow."

"I understand nothing about that," said Sucharita in a pained voice. "If this is true, that to-day all are forsaking it, then at such a time I at least will not forsake it. Because we are children of this unfortunate time we must all the more stand by our society in its distress."

"Mother," said Paresh Babu, "I will not say anything against the ideas that have awakened in your mind. Tranquillise yourself by worship, and try to judge everything by harmonising it with the truth that is in you, and the idea of the good that you feel—then gradually all will become clear to you. Do not lower Him, who is greater than all, before your country or before anyone, for that would be neither for your good nor for that of your country. With this thought in my mind I want to dedicate my whole spirit with undivided heart to Him— then I shall easily be able to be true in my relations with my country and with everyone."

At this point he was interrupted by a servant who handed him a letter.

"I have not got my spectacles," observed Paresh Babu, "and the light is getting dim, so will you read it to me please."

Sucharita took the letter and read it to him. The letter was from a Committee of the Brahmo Samaj, and was signed by many prominent members. It was to the effect that, seeing that Paresh Babu had consented to the marriage of one of his daughters according to non-Brahmo rites, and was actually himself preparing to take part in the wedding ceremony, the Brahmo Samaj felt itself unable to count him as a member of its governing body. If he had anything to say in self-defence then he should write a letter of explanation, which should be in the hands of the Committee before the coming Sunday, on which day a final settlement would be come to by a vote of the majority.

Paresh Babu took the letter and put it in his pocket, and Sucharita took his hand gently in hers and began walking up and down with him again. Gradually the evening darkness thickened, and in the adjoining lane a lamp was lighted.

"Father," said Sucharita softly, "it's time for your meditation. To-day I will join you at your devotions." And with these words she took him off to his solitary prayer-room, where the usual carpet was already spread, and a candle was burning. This evening Paresh Babu remained for a longer time than was his custom in meditation, and then after a brief spoken payer he rose to go. On leaving his room he saw Lolita and Binoy sitting silently outside the door. As soon as they saw him they stooped to his feet and made their *pronams* and he placed his hand on their heads in blessing, while to Sucharita he said: "Mother, to-morrow I will go to your house. Let me finish my work to-day?" and he went out of the room.

At that moment Sucharita was quietly weeping, and for some time she stood motionless in the darkness of the verandah like an image. Lolita and Binoy also remained silent for a long time.

When Sucharita was about to go Binoy came in front of her and said in a gentle voice: "Didi, won't you also give us your blessing?" And with these words he stooped and made his *pronam* to her.

What Sucharita replied was said in such a choking voice that only her God could hear.

Paresh Babu in the meanwhile had gone to his room to write his answer to the Brahmo Samaj Committee. In his letter he wrote: "Lolita's wedding will have to be managed by me, and if for this reason you give me up I will not regard it as wrong of you. In this matter I have only one prayer to offer to God, and it is that when I have been driven out of every society He will give me shelter at His own feet."

SIXTY NINE

Sucharita was very anxious to repeat to Gora all that she had been hearing from Paresh Babu. Did not Gora think that the India, towards which he had been directing her gaze and for which he had been trying to attract the intensest love of her heart, was already faced with destruction and threatened with loss? So long India had kept herself alive by some internal rules, so that Indians had not been compelled to exercise much care in the matter. But had not the time come to be watchful? Could we sit idly at home taking refuge in mere ancient rules as we had done heretofore?"

Sucharita thought to herself, "In this there is a work for me too to accomplish. What is that work? She felt that Gora ought, at such a time, to come to her and give her his commands, and show her the way. She was thinking that if only he had rescued her from all obstacles and contempt and set her in her rightful place, then the true value of her work would have far eclipsed all the trifling scandal and abuse of public opinion. Her mind became filled with pride in her own self, and she asked herself why Gora had not put her to the test, and called her to undertake some well-nigh impossible task—in the whole of his party was there a single man who could, like herself, sacrifice everything so easily? Did he not see the need for such eagerness and power for self-sacrifice? Was there not the least loss to the country in leaving her idle, surrounded and fenced in by public opinion? She put away from her the very thought of such lack of regard for her, and said to herself: "He can never mean to forsake me in such a manner! He will have to come back to me, he will have to search for me; he will have to get rid of the last trace of hesitation and shyness. No matter how great and powerful a man he may be, he has need of me, once he even said so with his own lips—how can he now forget this because of some mere idle talk?"

Satish now came running in and, standing beside her, said: "Didi!"

"What is it, little Mr. Chatterbox?" exclaimed Sucharita, putting her arm round his neck.

"On Monday, Lolita Didi is going to be married," answered Satish, "and for the next few days I am to go and stay at Binoy Babu's house. He has invited me."

"Have you spoken to Auntie about it?" inquired Sucharita.

"Yes, I have told Auntie," replied Satish, "and she was angry and said she did not know anything about all that, and that I must ask you, and what you thought best I could do! Didi, don't forbid me to go! My lessons will not suffer at all. I will read everyday, and Binoy Babu will help me."

"But you'll upset them all no end in a house where they are making such preparations," objected Sucharita.

"No, no, Didi," cried Satish, "I promise I won't upset them one little bit."

"Are you thinking of taking your dog, Khuda, with you?" asked Sucharita.

"Yes," answered Satish, "I must take him, for Binoy Babu told me specially to bring him. A separate invitation printed on red paper has been sent for him in his own name, and in it is written that he must bring his family to the wedding breakfast."

"Who are his family?" asked Sucharita.

"Why, of course, Binoy Babu says I am!" ejaculated Satish impatiently. "And, Didi, he told me to bring that organ too, so please do give it to me!—I promise not to break it."

"If only you would break it I would thank my stars!" exclaimed Sucharita. "Now at last I see why he has been calling you his friend so long! It was that he might get hold of that organ of yours, and so save the expense of having a band for his wedding! That's been his game, has it?"

"No, no, never!" cried Satish excitedly. "Binoy Babu says that he is going to make me his best man. What has the best man got to do, Didi?"

"Oh, he has to fast the whole day," explained Sucharita.

But Satish did not believe this for a moment. Then Sucharita, drawing him close up to her, asked: "Well, Mr. Chatterbox, what are you going to be when you grow up?"

Satish was ready with his answer, for having noticed what a model of exceptional learning and unobstructed power his teacher was, he had already made up his mind that he would be a schoolmaster when he grew up.

"There will be a lot of work to do," said Sucharita on being told of his ambition. "What do you say to us both joining and doing the work together? We shall have to work our hardest to make our country great! But do we need to make it great? What country is as great as ours? It is our own lives we shall have to make great! Do you know that? Do you understand?"

Satish was not a person to confess his inability to understand anything, so he said emphatically: "Yes!"

"Do you know how great our country is, and our race?" continued his sister. "How can I explain it to you? This is a wonderful country! How many thousands and thousands of years has God's purpose been working to make it surpass all other countries in the world? How many people from other lands have come to make this purpose complete? How many great men have taken birth in our land? How many great wars have had their scenes laid here? What great truths have found utterance here? What great austerities have been performed? From what a variety of standpoints has religion been studied? And how many solutions to the mystery of life have been found in this land? This is our India! You must know her as great, little brother, and never forget her or hold her in contempt! What I am telling you to-day you will have to comprehend one day—in fact I believe that you understand some of what I am saying even now. You will have to keep one thing in mind—that you have been born in a great country, and with all your soul you will have to work for her."

"And what will you do, Didi?" asked Satish, after a moment's silence.

"I too will take part in this work," answered Sucharita. "Will you help me?"

"Yes, I will!" said Satish, puffing out his chest with pride.

There was no one in the house to whom Sucharita could pour out what was pent up in her heart, so the whole force of its flood burst on the head of this little brother of hers. The language in which she spoke was hardly suitable for a boy of his age—but Sucharita was not deterred by that. She was so enthusiastic about the new knowledge she had gained that she felt she had only to explain fully what she herself had grasped, and old and young alike would be able to comprehend it, each according to his own ability—to keep anything back in the attempt to make it comprehensible to another's intelligence would be to distort the truth.

Satish's imagination was stirred, and he said: "When I am grown up, and when I have got a lot of money—"

"No! No! No!" exclaimed Sucharita. "Don't speak of money. Neither of us have any need of money, Mr. Chatterbox. The work we have to do will require our devotion, our lives."

At this moment Anandamoyi entered the room, and at sight of her the blood in Sucharita's veins began to dance. She made her obeisance to her, and Satish tried to follow suit, but he performed his act of greeting with poor grace, for making obeisances did not come quite naturally to him.

Anandamoyi drew Satish to her side and, kissing his head, turned to Sucharita, and said: "I've come to consult you about something, mother, for I see no one else to whom I can come. Binoy said that his wedding must take place at my house, but I objected to that, asking if he had become such a *nawab* that he could only be satisfied by the bride being married from his own home. But that could never be, so I have chosen a house not far from yours. I have just now come from there. Please speak to Paresh Babu and get his consent."

"Father will give his consent all right," assured Sucharita.

"After, that," pursued Anandamoyi, "you too must come there. The wedding is to be on Monday, and within these few days we have to make everything straight in the house. There is not much time! I could manage it all myself, but I know that Binoy would be greatly hurt if you didn't help. He could not bring himself to request you plainly—in fact he has not even mentioned your name to me—from that I can understand that on this point he feels some pain. It will never do for you to remain aloof—for that would hurt Lolita also."

"Mother, will you be able to attend this wedding?" exclaimed Sucharita in astonishment.

"Whatever do you mean?" asked Anandamoyi. "Why do you speak of 'attending' to me? Am I a mere outsider that you can use such a word? Why, this is Binoy's wedding! I must do everything for him on the occasion! But I have said to Binoy that in this marriage ceremony I am no connection of his, I am of the bride's party—he is coming to marry Lolita in my house!"

Anandamoyi's heart was filled with pity for Lolita, because, although she had her own mother, she had been cast out by her at this auspicious moment of her life. It was for this reason that she was trying so whole-heartedly to prevent the least sign on this occasion of a lack of regard or affection. Taking the place of her mother, she would dress Lolita with her own hands, would make all the arrangements for welcoming the bridegroom, and see that if two or three of the invited guests came they would receive a cordial reception. And she was determined to put the house into such a ship-shape condition that Lolita would feel at home in it as soon as she settled in.

"If you do this will you not get into trouble at all?" asked Sucharita.

"I may do, but what of that?" exclaimed Anandamoyi, remembering the fuss that Mohim had raised about it. "Even if there is a slight fuss, one has only to remain quiet for a little, and it will all be forgotten."

Sucharita knew that Gora would not attend the wedding, and she was eager to know whether he had made any attempt to prevent Anandamoyi also from taking any part in it. But she was not able to raise the question herself, and Anandamoyi never so much as mentioned Gora's name.

Harimohini had heard Anandamoyi arrive, but she took her time over her work before coming in to see her.

"Well, Didi, how are you?" she inquired. "I haven't seen you or heard news of you for a long time!"

"I've come to fetch your niece away," said Anandamoyi, without taking any notice of the complaint, and she explained what their intention was.

After sitting some time in silence, with a face full of displeasure, Harimohini at last said: "I can't take any part in this affair."

"No, sister, I don't ask you to go," said Anandamoyi. "You needn't be anxious about Sucharita, I will stay with her all along."

"Then let me speak out," exclaimed Harimohini. "Radharani is always saying that she is a Hindu, and as a matter of fact her tendency just now is in that direction. But if she wants to get into the Hindu community she will have to walk a bit cautiously. As it is, quite enough will be said about her, though I shall be able to manage somehow—but from now on she will have to be specially careful for a little. The first thing people will ask is why she is still unmarried at such an age—that question we shall be able, somehow or other, to avoid answering definitely—it is not that we cannot get her a good husband if we try, but if once she starts carrying on again in the old way, where can we check her, tell me? You belong to a Hindu family, so you understand well enough, so how can you have the face to talk like that? If you had had a daughter of your own, could you have sent her to take part in this wedding? Would you not have had to think about her own wedding also?"

Anandamoyi was so astonished that she could only gaze in amazement at Sucharita, who in her turn was blushing furiously.

"I don't want to force her to take part," observed Anandamoyi. "If she has any objection, then I—"

"Then I can make neither head nor tail of what your idea is," exclaimed Harimohini. "Your own son has been filling her with his Hindu notions, and now you come with these ideas of yours! Have you suddenly fallen from the sky?"

Where now was that Harimohini who, in Paresh Babu's house, had always been as timid as though she were a criminal, and who on noticing the least sign of approval on any one's part would hold on to him with all her might? To-day she stood like a tigress defending her own rights. She was all the time on tenterhooks, suspecting that all sorts of contrary forces were at work around her trying to snatch Sucharita away from her. She could not understand who was on her

side and who was against her—that was why she was so
uneasy in her mind to-day. Her heart was no longer finding
comfort in the god in whom she had taken shelter when she
had seen her whole world a void. Once she had been extremely
worldly, and when the strokes of inexorable misfortune had
made her detached from the world, she had never even in
thought contemplated the possibility of the least trace of
attachment for money, or houses, or relatives finding place
in her mind again. But now that her wound was slightly
healed the world again began to exercise its fatal fascination
for her, and with the accumulated hunger of many days all
the hopes and desires awoke in her as before. The speed of
returning again to that which she had renounced was so rapid
that she became even more restless than she had been when
she was actually in the world! On seeing the signs of this
change which had taken place within such a few days, in
Harimohini's face and eyes, in all her gestures and movements,
and in her words and behaviour, Anandamoyi was astonished
beyond measure, and her tender and affectionate heart was
filled with pained concern for Sucharita. If she had had the
least idea of the presence of this hidden danger she would
never have come to call Sucharita to the wedding, and now
the problem was how she could save her from the blow.

When Harimohini had made her veiled attack on Gora,
Sucharita got up without a word, and with bowed head left
the room.

"You needn't be afraid, sister," said Anandamoyi. "I did
not realise all this before, but I won't press her any more.
Don't you say anything to her either. She has been brought
up in one sort of way, and if you suddenly try to repress her
too much she will not be able to bear it."

"Do you think I do not understand that, at my age too?"
complained Harimohini. "Let her tell you to your face whether
I have ever given her any cause for trouble! She has done

whatever she liked, and I have never said a single word. I always say that if only God will let her live that is quite enough for me. Oh! my misfortune! I can hardly sleep for thinking of what may happen some day."

When Anandamoyi was leaving the house Sucharita came out of her room and made her *pronams* to her, and Anandamoyi put her hand affectionately on her head as she said: "I will come, my dear, and tell you all the news, so you need not get depressed. By God's grace the good work will be completed."

To this Sucharita made no answer.

Next morning, quite early, Anandamoyi took her maidservant, Lachmiya, to cleanse the house of the accumulated dust of many days, and just as she had absolutely flooded the floor with water Sucharita arrived on the scene. As soon as she saw her, Anandamoyi threw down her broom and clasped her to her breast, and then started in right earnest at the task of scrubbing, cleaning and washing everything in the house.

Paresh Babu had given to Sucharita sufficient money for covering the cost of all the necessary arrangements, and taking that as their treasury, they made a list and began to check all the items.

A little time afterwards Paresh Babu himself arrived with Lolita, whose home had become unendurable to her, for no one had the courage to speak a word to her, and their silence was like a blow at every turn. When, to crown everything, crowds of Bordashundari's friends began to call on her to express their sympathy, Paresh Babu thought it best to remove Lolita from the house altogether. At the time of parting Lolita went to take the dust of her mother's feet, and when she left the room Bordashundari remained seated with her face turned away, and there were tears in her eyes. Labonya and Lilla were in their heart of hearts quite excited about Lolita's marriage, and if they could have got the least excuse, on any pretext whatever, they would have gone running to attend the wedding. But when Lolita was bidding them farewell they remembered their stern duty to the Brahmo Samaj, and put on very solemn faces. At the door she caught a brief glimpse of Sudhir, but behind him was a group of elderly people, and so she was unable to have a word with him. On getting into the carriage she noticed something done up in paper in one corner of the seat, and on opening it she found a German silver vase on which was the inscription—"May God bless the happy pair," and tied to it was a card with the first letter of Sudhir's name. written on it. Lolita had made a firm determination not to let herself cry to-day, but, on getting this one and only token of affection from the friend of her childhood at the moment of leaving her father's home, she could not restrain her tears and they began to flow freely. Paresh Babu also wiped his eyes as he sat quietly in the corner.

"Come in, my dear, come in!" cried Anandamoyi, and she seized Lolita by both hands and took her into the room, as if she had been on the look-out for her.

"Lolita has left our house for good now," explained Paresh Babu when he had sent for Sucharita, and his voice trembled as he spoke.

"She will not lack for love and affection here, father," said Sucharita, taking his hand in hers.

When Paresh Babu was on the point of leaving again, Anandamoyi, drawing her head, came up to him and bowed to him, and Paresh Babu returned the bow as though slightly confused.

"Do not let yourself be in the least worried about Lolita," said Anandamoyi assuringly. "She will never suffer any sorrow at the hands of him to whom you are surrendering her. God has at last supplied what I have felt the want of so much. I have no daughter, and now I have got one. For a long time I have been hoping that in Binoy's bride I would find compensation for the lack of a daughter—and now God has at long last fulfilled my desire in such a wonderful way, and with such a girl, that I could never have even dreamed of such good fortune!"

This was the first time that Paresh Babu had received any consolation, or seen any shelter, from the very day that all this agitation about Lolita's marriage had commenced. Here was one place in the world where his heart found rest.

SEVENTY

S ince Gora's release from gaol so many visitors had been coming everyday to his house, that, with their discussions and adulation, he was so besieged that he could hardly breathe, and it became unbearable for him to remain at home. So he began to go about amongst the villages as he had done before.

He used to leave the house early in the morning after a slight meal, and would not return till late at night. Taking the train from Calcutta he would get out at some not far distant station, and wander about amongst the villages. There he would be the guest of potters, oil-vendors, and other low-caste men. These people could not understand why this huge, fair-skinned, Brahmin youth should visit them and inquire into their joys and sorrows, in fact they were often quite suspicious as to his motives. But Gora, thrusting aside all their doubts and hesitation, roamed about amongst them at will, and even when he sometimes heard them make unpleasant remarks he was not deterred.

The more he saw of their lives the more did one thought constantly occur to his mind. He saw that amongst these village people the social bondage was far greater than it was amongst the educated community. Night and day without ceasing every act of eating, drinking, social ceremony, and touching, in every home, was under the vigilant eyes of society. Every person had an absolutely simple faith in social custom—it never even occurred to them to question such matters. But this implicit faith in tradition and the bondage of society did not give them the least bit of strength for the tasks of their daily life. It is in fact doubtful whether in the whole world could be found a species of animal so impotent to judge what was for their own good, so helpless, and so cowardly. Apart from observing traditional customs their minds were completely unconscious of what was for their welfare, and even if it was explained to them they would not understand. They regarded prohibitions, by the threat of penalties and in the spirit of sectarianism, as greater than anything else in the world—it seemed as if their whole natures had become entangled from head to foot in a network of various penalties for transgressing against rules forbidding them to do this or that at every step—but this net was one woven by debt, and the bondage was one of creditors and of money-lenders, not the bondage of a king. In it there was no such unity as could make them stand firmly shoulder to shoulder in times of misfortune or prosperity. Gora could not help seeing that by this weapon of tradition and custom man was sucking the blood of man and was reducing him to poverty in a merciless fashion. How often did he see how, at the time of some social function, no one had the least pity for anyone else. The father of one poor fellow had been suffering for a long time from some disease, and nearly all the man's means had been expended on giving him medicines, special treatment and diet, and yet he had received not one particle of help from anyone—on the contrary the people of his village insisted that his father's chronic illness must be the penalty for some unknown sin he had committed and that he must therefore spend more money in a ceremony of penance. The unfortunate man's poverty and helplessness were known to everyone, but there was no pity for him. The same sort of thing happened in every kind of social function. Just as a police inquiry into a dacoity is a greater misfortune to a village than the dacoity itself, so the obsequies that have to be performed at the funeral of a parent are the cause of a more serious misfortune than the death itself of a father or mother. No one will accept the excuse of poverty or any other form of inability—no matter how it is accomplished society's heartless claim has to be satisfied to the very last farthing. On the occasion of a marriage the bridegroom's party adopt all sorts of tactics to make the burden of the girl's father as intolerable as possible, and show no trace of pity for the unfortunate man. Gora saw that society offers no help to a man at the time of his need, gives him no encouragement at the time of his misfortune, it merely afflicts him with penalties and humbles him to the dust.

In the educated community, in which he had been accustomed to move, Gora had forgotten this fact, because in that society a power to present a united front worked from outside for the common welfare. In that society many efforts towards unity could be observed, and the only thing to be feared was lest all their efforts after unity should be rendered fruitless through imitating others.

But Gora saw the image of his country's weakness, naked and unashamed, in the midst of the lethargy of village life where the blows from outside could not work so readily. He could see nowhere any trace of that religion which through service, love, compassion, self-respect and respect for humanity as a whole, gives power and life and happiness to all. The tradition which merely divided men into classes and separated class from class, driving to a distance even love itself, did not want to carry into effect the results of man's intelligent thinking, and only put obstacles at every step in the way of man's coming and going. In these villages the cruel and evil results of this blind bondage were so clearly seen by Gora in all kinds of ways (for he could see how, from a variety of standpoints, it attacked the work, wisdom, health, and religious principles of mankind), that it was no longer possible for him to delude himself by the web of delusion which his own mind had woven.

First of all Gora noticed that amongst the lower castes in the villages, owing to a scarcity in numbers amongst the females, or for some other reason, it was only possible to obtain a girl for marriage by offering a large dowry. Many men indeed remained unmarried all their lives, and many others did not marry till quite late in life. On the other hand there was a strict prohibition against widow remarriage. Owing to this, in many homes of the community, health was ruined, and the evil and inconvenience was felt by all alike. Everyone was forced to bear the burden of this ill fortune, and yet no one anywhere found means to remedy it. The Gora who in the educated community had not wanted traditional custom to be relaxed in any respect was the very man who gave to custom a direct blow here in the villages. He managed to win over the priests, but he could not get the people themselves to agree to his views. They simply became angry with him and exclaimed: "That's all very well, but you Brahmins should first adopt widow re-marriage, and then we will follow suit."

The chief cause of their anger was that they imagined Gora despised them because of their low caste, and that he had come to preach to them that it would be best for such people as they were to adopt a low standard of conduct.

During his wanderings through the village districts Gora had noticed one thing, namely, that amongst the Mohammedans there was something which enabled them to unite with one another. He had observed that when any misfortune or calamity occurred in a village the Mohammedans stood shoulder to shoulder in a way that the Hindus never did, and he often asked himself why there was such a great difference between communities which were such close neighbours. The answer that rose to his mind was one which he did not want to admit as the true one, for it pained him intensely to acknowledge that the Mussulmans were united by their religion, and not merely by custom and tradition. On the one hand, just as the bondage of custom did not render all their functions useless, so on the other the bond of religion made them very intimately one. Uniting together they had taken hold of something which was not merely negative but positive, by which they did not become merely debtors but owners of wealth—something at the summons of which man could in one moment easily sacrifice his very life, standing beside his comrades.

When, in his educated community, Gora had written, argued and lectured, it was in order to influence others, and it was natural for him to paint in rosy colours, through the power of his own imagination, the words which were intended to draw others into his own path. What was simple he had enveloped with subtle explanations, and in the moonlight of his own emotions he had given a fascinating picture of what was in reality a mere useless ruin. Because one party of people were opposed to his country, and regarded everything in the country as bad, Gora tried day and night, because of his intense love for his motherland, to cover everything behind the screen of his own brilliant feelings in order to save his country from the insult of such callous regard. Gora had learnt his lesson by heart. Not that he wanted to prove like a pleader that all was good, and that what from one point of view might be regarded as a fault from another might be regarded as a virtue—he believed all this with implicit faith. Even in the most impossible places he would stand erect and flaunt this faith of his with pride, holding it firmly in his hand like a flag of victory, in the face of the opposing party. His one motto was that first the people of one's country must be brought back to a true devotion to the motherland, and then other work could be undertaken.

But when he got out amongst the villages where he had no audience and where he had nothing to prove, where there was no need for awakening all the power of opposition at his command in order to lower in the dust all those who showed contempt and disrespect, he found it no longer possible to look at the truth through any kind of veil. The very intensity of his love for his country made his perception of truth all the keener.

SEVENTY ONE

With a shawl tied round his waist, wearing, a Tussore-silk coat, and carrying a canvas bag, Kailash presented himself to Harimohini and made his *pronams* to her. His age would be about thirty-five: he was short of stature, with a heavy face and tight skin. He had several days' growth on his chin, which looked like a stubble field.

Harimohini was overjoyed at seeing a member of her father-in-law's family after so long an interval, and exclaimed with delight: "Well, well, here is my Thakurpo! Sit down, sit down!" and she spread a mat for him to sit on, asking him whether he would like to have some water.

"No need, thank you," he replied, and observed: "You are looking very well."

"Well!" exclaimed Harimohini in annoyance, feeling that it was a kind of insult to say that she was in good health. "How can you say that?" and she proceeded to give a list of her various ailments, adding: "If only I could die I would be rid of this wretched body of mine!"

Kailash objected to this display of contempt for life, and although his brother was no more, as a proof that they all had the most heartfelt hope that Harimohini would live long, he said: "You mustn't talk like that. Why, if you were not alive I should not be in Calcutta now. I have at least got some sort of a shelter to my head in your home here."

After he had given all the news, from start to finish, of their relatives and neighbours in the village, Kailash suddenly looked about him, and asked: "So this is the house, I suppose?"

"Yes," replied Harimohini.

"It's a pucca¹ house I see," observed Kailash.

"Pucca indeed! I should think it is, every bit of it!" exclaimed Harimohini, trying to stimulate his enthusiasm.

He made careful note of the fact that the beams were of solid shal timber, that the doors and windows were not of mere mango wood. Whether the walls were of two or only one-and-a-half brick's thickness did not escape him either. He also inquired how many rooms there were both upstairs and downstairs, and on the whole he was quite satisfied with the results of his observations. It was difficult for him to make an estimate of the probable cost of building such a house, because he was not an expert in the matter of bricks and mortar and their price, but nevertheless, as he sat waggling his toes, he calculated to himself that it probably must have cost anything from fifteen to twenty thousand rupees. However, he did not say so openly, but observed: "What do you think, sister-in-law, it must have cost seven or eight thousand at least, don't you imagine?"

"What are you saying?" exclaimed Harimohini, expressing her surprise at his rustic ignorance. "Seven or eight thousand indeed! Why, it can't have cost a pice less than twenty thousand!"

Kailash began to examine everything within range of his vision with the utmost attention. He felt an intense satisfaction in the thought that, at a mere nod of his head, he might become sole lord of this well-built mansion with its beams of shal wood and its doors and windows of teak. He observed: "This is all right, but what about the girl?"

1 Pucca means solidly built.

"She has suddenly had an invitation to her aunt's house, and has gone there for three or four days," hurriedly replied Harimohini.

"Then how shall I be able to see her?" complained Kailash. "I have a lawsuit coming off in a day or so, and must leave again to-morrow.

"Let your lawsuit be for the present," said Harimohini; "you can't go away from here till this business is finished."

Kailash pondered for a moment and thought to himself: "Well, supposing I do drop the lawsuit they can only order a decree against me. And what of that? Let me take a good look round here first, and see what preparations for compensation are going on." Then suddenly his eyes caught sight of Harimohini's room where she did her puja, and he noticed some water had collected in one corner. In that room there was no drain or outlet, and in spite of that fact Harimohini everyday washed the floor with water, so that there was always a little collected in that corner of the room. Kailash was quite upset on seeing this, and exclaimed: "That's not right, sister-in-law!"

"Why, what's the matter?" asked Harimohini.

"Why, that water there! It will never do to let it accumulate like that," explained Kailash.

"But what can I do?" expostulated Harimohini.

"No, no, that will never do!" protested Kailash. "Why, the floor will get rotten! No, sister, let me tell you, in that room you must never throw any water."

Harimohini remained silent, until Kailash began to question her as to the personal appearance of Sucharita.

"You'll know soon enough when you see her,' said Harimohini. "I can say this much, that up to now there has been no such bride in your family."

"What do you say?" cried Kailash. "What about our second brother's—?"

"Pugh!" interrupted Harimohini. "Why, she can't bear any comparison with our Sucharita! Whatever you may say, your youngest brother's wife is much better-looking than your second brother's."

It should be explained that the second brother's wife was not a great favourite with Harimohini.

At these comparisons with the beauty of his second and youngest brothers' wives Kailash did not feel much enthusiasm, but he became lost in the contemplation of a creation of his own imagination, with almond-shaped eyes, a straight nose with arched eyebrows, and hair reaching down to her waist.

Harimohini saw that things were looking hopeful from her side. So much so, indeed, that even all the social flaws which existed on the girl's side were not likely to be counted as so serious after all.

SEVENTY TWO

Binoy knew that nowadays Gora went out very early in the morning, so on Monday, while it was still dark before dawn, he went to his house, going straight up to his bedroom on the top floor. On not finding him there, he inquired of a servant, who informed him that he was in his prayer-room at worship. Binoy was a little surprised on hearing this, and going there found him engaged in some puja. He wore a silk *dhutie*, and had on also a silk wrapper, but his immense body was for the most part bare, showing his fair skin. Binoy was still more astonished on seeing Gora actually doing his ceremonial puja.

On hearing the sound of footsteps Gora looked round, and on seeing Binoy, exclaimed in dismay: "Don't come into this room!"

"You needn't be afraid," assured Binoy. "I'm not coming in. But I have called to see you."

Gora then emerged, and after changing his clothes, took Binoy upstairs where they sat down, Binoy saying: "Brother Gora, do you know that to-day is Monday?"

"Of course it's Monday," laughed Gora, "the calendar is not likely to make a mistake, and as for you, you cannot make a blunder about what day .this is. At all events to-day is not Tuesday, that is sure."

"I know that you will probably not come," faltered Binoy, "but without at least speaking to you once to-day I could not take such a step. That is why I have come to you so early this morning."

Gora sat still without making any answer, and Binoy went on: "Then is it quite settled that you will not be able to attend my wedding?"

"No, Binoy, I shall not be able to go," replied Gora.

Binoy remained silent, and Gora, concealing the pain with which his heart was filled, said with a laugh: "And what does it matter, after all, if I do not go? You are victorious, for you are dragging mother there. I tried my hardest to prevent her from going, but I could not hold her back. So at last I have had to confess defeat at your hands even in my mother's case! Binoy, one by one all the countries of the map are being painted red. On my map there will soon be only myself left!"

"No, brother, don't blame me!" begged Binoy. "I told her again and again that she needn't come to my wedding, but she said: 'Look here, Binoy, those who will not go to your wedding will not go even if they are invited, and those who will go will go even if you forbid them to come, so you had much better keep quiet.' Well, Gora, you say you have had to admit defeat at my hands. But it is at the hands of your mother that you have had to admit defeat, not once only, but a thousand times! Where else could you find a mother like her?"

Although Gora had tried his best to dissuade Anandamoyi from attending Binoy's marriage ceremony he was not in his heart of hearts very much pained when, taking no account of his anger or distress, she refused to listen to him, in fact he really felt delighted. Feeling so certain that however great the gulf between Binoy and himself might become, Binoy could never be deprived of that part of his mother's immeasurable love which was showered upon him like nectar, Gora's heart was satisfied and at peace. From every other standpoint he might be separated ever so far from Binoy, but by this one bond of the imperishable love of a mother these two lifelong friends would be united by the closest and deepest ties for life.

"Then, brother, I will be going," said Binoy. "If it is quite impossible for you to come, then I shall not expect you, but do not harbour any displeasure in your mind against me. If only you could realise what a great purpose has been fulfilled in my life by this union, then you could never allow this marriage to cause a breach in our friendship. I can tell you that for certain." And as he spoke he got up to go.

"Binoy, sit down, do!" urged Gora. "The auspicious moment is not till to-night—what need of such hurry now?"

Binoy sat down again at once, his heart melted by this unexpected and affectionate request.

Then these two, after such a long interval, began to converse intimately as of old. Gora struck the same sweet note which was resounding to-day on Binoy's heartstrings, and Binoy began to talk without ceasing. How many very trifling events, which if he had written them down in plain black and white would have appeared futile and even ridiculous, were related by Binoy as though they had the oft-repeated sweetness of an epic poem set to music! The wonderful drama which was being staged in Binoy's heart was described by him with such skill of language that it became deeply touching and full of unsurpassable beauty. What was this unexampled experience in his life? This indescribable feeling with which his heart was filled,—did everyone experience it? Had everybody got the power of grasping hold of it? Binoy assured himself that in the ordinary relationship between man and woman in worldly society it was impossible that such a supremely lofty note could be heard, and again and again he told Gora that he must not compare it with the relationships of others. It was doubtful whether ever before quite what had happened to Binoy had occurred to anyone else! If such experiences had been universal, then the whole of human society would have become restless on every side with the surge of new life, just as, with the breath of spring, all the forests rejoice in their fresh leaves and blossoms. Then people would not have spent dull lives in sleeping and eating as they do now, and whatever had power or beauty in it would naturally have unfolded itself in a variety of shapes and colours. This was the golden wand, the touch of which no one could afford to neglect or remain insensitive to. By it even the most commonplace people became exceptional, and if once man tasted the strength of this rare experience he would acquire a knowledge of the truth of life.

"Gora," said Binoy ecstatically, "I can tell you for certain that the one means by which in a single moment man's whole nature can be awakened is this love—no matter what the reason is, there is no doubt that amongst us the manifestation of this love is weak, and therefore all of us are deprived of a complete realisation of ourselves—we don't know what is in us, we cannot reveal what is hidden within, and it is impossible for us to spend what is accumulated in our hearts—that is why there is such joylessness on every side, such want of cheerfulness! Therefore it is that, apart from one or two men like yourself, no one realises that there is so great a soul within each of us—the ordinary consciousness is quite blind to that fact."

The current of Binoy's enthusiasm was here interrupted by the sound of Mohim's loud yawning as he got up from his bed and went to wash his face and hands, so he rose and said farewell to Gora.

Gora heaved a deep sigh as he stood on the roof looking towards the rosy sky of approaching dawn. For a long time he walked up and down on the roof. To-day he did not go out on his usual visits to the villages.

That morning Gora felt in his own heart a longing and a void which he found it impossible to satisfy by any form of work. It was not only he himself, but the whole work of his life, that seemed to be stretching out its hands on high and saying—I want light, a bright and beautiful light. It was as if all the materials were ready, as if diamonds and jewels were not high-priced, and iron and nail were not difficult to get—only that tender and beautiful light of dawn, illumined by hope and consolation, where was that? To increase that which we already possess there is no need for any sort of exertion, but we await what should make it more manifest in radiance and loveliness.

When Binoy had said that when, at certain auspicious moments we find refuge in love between man and woman, an unspeakable and rare experience illumines our lives, Gora was not able to laugh it off as he had done before. He acknowledged to himself that this was no ordinary union of souls, it was a fulfilment of one's life, a relationship in which everything attained a greater value, which gave body to one's fancy, and filled the body with new life. It was not merely that it redoubled the powers of body and mind, it gave a new savour to life.

On this day, when Binoy was socially ostracising himself, his heart had awakened in Gora's heart a faultless harmony of music. Binoy himself had left him, but as the day wore on that music would not cease. Just as two rivers on their way to the ocean unite, so the current of Binoy's love, mingling with the love of Gora himself, resounded as wave fell upon wave. What Gora had been trying to hide from himself by any means he could devise, weakening it, obstructing it, and screening it from view, had now burst its banks and had revealed itself clearly and unmistakable. Gora no longer had the power to abuse it as improper or condemn it as contemptible.

The whole day was passed in such thoughts, and at last when the evening light was dissolving into dusk Gora took down a shawl and, throwing it over his shoulders, went out into the street, saying to himself: "I will claim what is mine. Otherwise I shall pass my life uselessly in this world."

There was not the least doubt in Gora's mind that in this whole world Sucharita was waiting for his summons, and he determined that that very evening he would make that summons final and complete.

As Gora passed through the crowded Calcutta streets it seemed as if he was untouched by anything or by anybody, for his mind was so intent on one object that it had passed beyond the limits of his body and was far away.

When he arrived in front of Sucharita's house, Gora suddenly regained consciousness. He had never before found the door of the house closed, but to-day it was not only closed, but when he gave it a push he found it was locked also. For a moment he stood in hesitation, then he began to knock two or three times loudly, until a servant came out, and seeing Gora in the dim light of evening, said without being asked: "The young lady is not at home."

"Where is she?" inquired Gora.

He was told that she had gone somewhere, two or three days back, to help in the preparations for Lolita's wedding.

For a moment Gora almost decided that he would go to attend the marriage ceremony, and as he was hesitating an unknown Babu came from inside the house and asked him: "What is it, sir? What do you want?"

"Nothing, thank you," replied Gora, after having looked him up and down from head to feet.

"Come in, won't you, and sit down a little, and have a smoke?" urged Kailash.

Kailash was finding life very dull for want of companionship, and if he could only get someone to come in to have a talk with him he would feel much relieved. During the daytime he managed to pass his time somehow by going, hookah in hand, to the end of the lane and watching the passers-by in the main thoroughfare, but when evening came and he had to retire to the house he nearly died of boredom. He had finished all the subjects which he had for discussion with Harimohini, for her topics of conversation were very limited in scope. So Kailash had placed a bed in the little room beside the front door, and taking his hookah he would now and then sit there discoursing with the servant, to pass the time.

"No, thank you, I can't stay now," answered Gora, and before Kailash's further request was out of his mouth he was on the other side of the lane.

Gora had a firm conviction in his mind that the majority of events in his life were not accidental, and that they were not merely the result of his own individual wishes. He believed that he had taken birth for the fulfilment of some special purpose of the Ruler of his country's destiny.

Therefore even the most trifling circumstances of his own life had for him a special significance, and to-day when in the very face of such a strong desire on his own part he found the door of Sucharita's house closed against him, and when he heard that Sucharita was not in the house, then he was firmly convinced that there was an inner meaning in this hindrance to his hopes. He who was directing his steps had make known to Gora His disapproval in this way. It was clear that in this life that door was closed, and Sucharita was not meant for him. For a man like Gora it would not do to be deluded by his own desires—he must be indifferent to joy or sorrow. He was a Brahmin of India, it was for him to worship the divine. Being on behalf of India, and his work was that of religious austerities. Desire and attachment were not for him, and Gora said to himself: "God has revealed to me plainly enough the form of attachment, and has shown me that it is not pure, and that in it there is no peace. Like wine it is red and pungent—it does not allow the mind to be tranquil, it makes one thing appear another—I am a *sannyasi,* in my realisation and worship it can have no place."

SEVENTY THREE

Sucharita, after having endured the tyranny of Harimohini for so long, felt a relief during these few days with Anandamoyi such as she had never experienced before. Anandamoyi drew her so naturally to herself that it was difficult for Sucharita to believe that she had ever been unknown to her or distant from her. She seemed somehow or other to understand everything that was in her mind, and even without speaking could make her feel quite at peace. Never before had Sucharita uttered the word "Mother" so whole-heartedly, and she used to invent all sorts of pretexts for calling out "Mother" even when there was not the least need for it. When, after all the arrangements for Lolita's wedding were completed, and she was lying tired out on her bed, she could think only one thought, and that was how could she now leave Anandamoyi, and she began to repeat to herself, "Mother! Mother! Mother!" and as she spoke her heart became so full that the tears began to flow, and the next moment she saw that Anandamoyi herself was standing beside her bed.

"Did you call for me?" asked Anandamoyi, stroking her head.

When Sucharita realised that she had called aloud, "Mother! Mother!" she was unable to answer the question, and, burying her face in Anandamoyi's lap, began to sob while

Anandamoyi, without speaking, tried to soothe her. That night Anandamoyi slept with her.

Anandamoyi did not like to leave as soon as Binoy's wedding was over, so she said: "These two are novices—how can I go before I get their domestic arrangements to run smoothly?"

"Then, mother, I will stay on with you for these few days," observed Sucharita.

"Yes, mother, let Suchi Didi stay on with us a few days," joined in Lolita eagerly.

Satish, on hearing of this proposal, came in dancing with joy, and, throwing his arms round Sucharita's neck, exclaimed: "Yes, Didi, I too will stay."

"But you have your lessons, Mr. Chatterbox," objected Sucharita.

"But Binoy Babu can teach me!" protested Satish.

"Binoy can't take on your tutoring now," observed Sucharita.

"Of course I can!" shouted Binoy from the next room. "How could I in one day become so preoccupied as to forget all that I have learnt through sitting up night after night at my studies?"

"Will your aunt give her consent?" asked Anandamoyi.

"I will send a letter to her," answered Sucharita.

"No, don't you write, I will write," suggested Anandamoyi.

Anandamoyi realised that if Sucharita herself expressed her wish to stay on Harimohini would feel hurt, but if she made the request then the anger would be directed against her and not against Sucharita.

In her letter Anandamoyi informed Harimohini that, in order to get the domestic arrangements straight in the new home, she would have to remain for a few days, and if she would consent to Sucharita staying on with her it would be a great help.

When Harimohini received this letter she felt not only angry but suspicious. She thought that now that she had put a stop to Gora's visits to her house, the mother was spreading a skilful net with which to snare Sucharita, and she saw clearly enough that this was a conspiracy between the son and his mother. She remembered now that she had taken a dislike to Anandamoyi from the first, when she had seen what her tendencies were.

If only she could get Sucharita safely married into the famous Roy family she would feel relieved of a great burden. How much longer could a man like Kailash, or anyone else for that matter, be kept waiting like this? The poor fellow was blackening the walls of the house with his smoking day and night without ceasing.

The morning after she had received the letter Harimohini took a servant and a palanquin and set out for Binoy's house arriving there to find Sucharita, Lolita and Anandamoyi making preparations for cooking in the room on the ground floor. From the upper storey the sound of Satish's shrill voice repeating English words, with their spelling and Bengali synonyms, startled the whole neighbourhood. When he was at home the sound of his voice was not so evident, but here, in order to give clear proof that his lessons were not being neglected, he paid particular attention to making his voice unnecessarily loud.

Anandamoyi welcomed Harimohini with great warmth, but without paying any attention to the politeness with which she was received Harimohini began without any preamble: "I have come to fetch Radharani."

"Very well, but sit down for a little, won't you?" invited Anandamoyi.

"No, thank you," answered Harimohini, "all my puja has to be performed yet, I haven't even finished my morning prayers—I must go back home at once."

Sucharita was employed in cutting up a pumpkin, and did not say a word until Harimohini, addressing her directly, said: "Don't you hear me? It's getting late."

Lolita and Anandamoyi remained silent, and Sucharita, putting aside her work, got up and said: "Come, auntie," and on her way towards the palanquin she took her aunt's hand and, drawing her into another room, said in a firm voice: "Since you have come to fetch me I will not turn you away in front of everybody,—I am going home with you, but I shall come back here to-day at noon."

"Just listen to her!" exclaimed Harimohini in vexation. "Then why don't you say that you will stay on here for good?"

"I can't stay on here for good!" answered Sucharita. "That is why I will not leave her so long as I have the opportunity of being with her."

This remark infuriated Harimohini, but as she did not feel it was an opportune moment for replying she said nothing.

"Well, mother, I'm just going home for an hour or two. I'll be coming back soon," said Sucharita smiling to Anandamoyi.

"Very well, my dear," replied Anandamoyi without asking any questions.

"I will be back at noon," whispered Sucharita to Lolita.

"Satish?" asked Sucharita, with an inquiring look, as she was standing in front of the palanquin.

"No, let Satish stay where he is," said Harimohini, feeling that Satish was a disturbing influence in the house and was better at a distance.

When they were both safely inside the palanquin Harimohini tried to introduce the subject of her discourse. She said: "Well, there's Lolita married off! That's a good thing. Paresh Babu need not worry any more about one of his daughters." And with these words as an introduction she dilated on the immense burden that an unmarried daughter was in a home, and showed what a cause of intolerable anxiety she was to her guardians.

"What can I say to you? I have no other cause for worry. Even when I am repeating the name of God this thought keeps coming to my mind. Really and truly, I tell you that I can't give my mind to the service of God as I used to. I say: Oh, God! you have taken everything else from me, why now are you fashioning this new noose to entangle me?"

It appeared then that this was a cause not only of worldly anxiety on the part of Harimohini, but it was an impediment in the path of her salvation. And yet on hearing of such a serious difficulty Sucharita remained silent! Harimohini was unable to understand exactly what Sucharita's idea was, but in accordance with the proverb that "silence gives consent," she interpreted her attitude as favourable to her own point of view, and thought that her victim's mind was yielding a little.

Harimohini now went on to hint how easily she had accomplished the very difficult task of opening the doors of Hindu society to a girl like Sucharita, and how she had managed so well that even when invited to the homes of big men such as Kulin Brahmins, Sucharita would be able to sit in one line with the rest of the guests at their feasts without anyone daring so much as to whisper an objection.

When the discourse had reached this point the palanquin arrived at the house. When they were about to go upstairs Sucharita noticed that in the little room by the front door the servant was rubbing oil on the body of some unknown gentleman, preparatory to his bath. This guest did not display the least shyness on seeing Sucharita—in fact he looked at her with intense, curiosity.

On going upstairs Harimohini explained that her brother in-law had come on a visit, and in view of what had gone before Sucharita guessed at once how the land lay. Harimohini tried to explain to her that in view of their having a visitor in the house it would be most impolite for her to leave again at midday, but Sucharita shook her head violently, and exclaimed: "No, auntie, I must go."

"Very well then," said Harimohini, "stay here to-day, and go to-morrow."

"When I have taken my bath I shall go and take my meal with father, and I will go to Lolita's from there," persisted Sucharita.

"But he has come to see you," blurted out Harimohini at last.

"What is the use of his seeing me?" inquired Sucharita blushing.

"Just listen to her!" exclaimed Harimohini. "In these days all this business cannot be managed without seeing! In my young days it was different. Why, your uncle never saw me until the first auspicious look in the marriage ceremony." And having given this broad hint she hastily went on to give further details of the preliminaries to her own wedding. She explained how, when the proposal for her own marriage was first brought up, two old and tried retainers from the famous Roy family came to her father's house, together with two servants in big turbans and with staffs in their hands, to see the girl. She described how excited her guardians were and what preparations were made in her home for the proper reception and feasting of these representatives from the Roy family. With a long sigh she ended up by saying: "In these days everything is different."

"You won't have to bother yourself much," urged Harimohini, "only see him for five minutes, that's all."

"No!" said Sucharita emphatically.

Harimohini was rather taken aback by the emphasis and decision which was expressed in this "No!" and said: "Very well, it will be all right even if you don't show yourself. There is no need for you to see each other—still Kailash is a modern young man, well educated—like you he has no respect for anything, and he said that he would see the bride with his own eyes. And as you appear in public before everybody I said there would be no difficulty in the way, and I would arrange for you to meet one day. But if you feel shy, then what does it matter if he doesn't see you?"

She then began to discourse on his wonderful education, how with one stroke of his pen he had got the village Postmaster into trouble, and how, whenever anybody in any of the neighbouring villages became involved in litigation, or had a petition to draw up, they would not move a single step without first consulting with Kailash. As for his character and nature it was almost unnecessary to speak. He had not wanted to marry again after his first wife's death, and in spite of the repeated request of his friends and relatives had preferred to obey the commands of his gurus. Harimohini had had to take no end of trouble to get him to hear of the present proposal. Do you think he wanted to listen? Such a high-class family too! And held in such great respect by society!

Sucharita however had not the least wish to be a cause of lowering that respect; she was not selfishly looking to her own glory. In fact, if it so happened that the Hindu community could find no place for her, she made it quite clear that she would not be in the least upset. This foolish girl was quite unable to realise that to have got Kailash's consent to this marriage after so much effort was a matter of no small honour for Sucharita—on the contrary she seemed to count it as an insult. Harimohini was perfectly disgusted at all this contrariness of modern times.

Then in her resentment she began to make all sorts of insinuations about Gora. She asked what position he had in society in spite of all his boasts about his being such a good Hindu. Who had any respect for him she would like to know?

And who had the influence to protect him from the penalties which his community would inflict upon him if, out of covetousness, he married some moneyed girl of the Brahmo Samaj? Why, all their money would have to be spent in bribing his friends to keep their mouths shut! And so on.

"Why are you talking like that, auntie?" expostulated Sucharita. "You know quite well that there is no foundation for what you are saying!"

"When one has reached my time of life," sneered Harimohini, "it is beyond anyone's power to mislead me. I keep my eyes and ears open. I see, hear, and understand everything and only keep silent from amazement."

She then expressed her firm conviction that Gora was plotting with his mother to marry Sucharita, and that the main object of this wedding was not a noble one. And she added that if she herself were not able to save Sucharita by the offer from the Roy family then in time Gora's conspiracy would be successful.

This was too much for even the forbearance of Sucharita, and she exclaimed: "Those of whom you are speaking are people whom I respect, and since it is impossible for you to comprehend in the least the nature of my relationship with them, there is only one course for me to follow—I must go away from here—when you are reasonable again and I can come and live with you alone, I will come back again."

"If you have no inclination for Gourmohan," urged Harimohini, "and if you are not going to marry him, then what fault have you to find with this husband? You are not going to remain unmarried?"

"Why not?" cried Sucharita. "I am not ever going to marry."

Harimohini opened her eyes wide in astonishment, and exclaimed: "And will you, till you are old, remain—?"

"Yes, till death!" said Sucharita.

SEVENTY FOUR

Sucharita's absence from home when he had been so anxious to see her caused Gora's mind to undergo a change. He felt that the reason why Sucharita had obtained such an influence over him was that he had been mixing too intimately with them all, and without himself being aware of it he had got entangled. In his pride he had overstepped the limits which had been prescribed, and by neglecting prohibitions had violated the customs of his country. It was not merely that if each one did not keep within the proper limits people did harm to themselves, whether knowingly or unknowingly, but they also lost their unmixed power of doing good to others. By association and intercourse with people many kinds of feelings become so strong that they obscure the power of our faith and our wisdom.

It was not only that by becoming intimate with the girls of a Brahmo family Gora had discovered this truth, for even where he had been mixing with ordinary people he was beginning to feel that he had lost himself in a whirlpool. For at every step a feeling of pity had been born in him which made him constantly think that such and such a thing was evil, and such a thing was wrong and ought to be got rid of. But had not this feeling of compassion merely distorted his power of judging between good and bad? The more inclined we are to regard things with pity the more completely do we

lose our power of seeing truth as a whole and unchanging—
we obscure what should be light by our compassion, as smoke
obscures the fire.

"Therefore," said Gora to himself, "it has always been
the rule in our country for those who have to bear the
burden of the welfare of all to remain aloof. The idea that
a king can protect his subjects by mixing intimately with
them is entirely without foundation. The kind of wisdom
that is needed by a raja in his relationship with his subjects
is defiled by association with them. It is for this reason that
the subjects surround their king of their own free will with
a halo of aloofness, for they realise that if their king
becomes their companion then the reason for his existence
disappears."

The Brahmin too should preserve this aloofness, this
detachment. The Brahmin who allows himself to get entangled
with the common people and sprawl in the mud of trade, who
in his greed for money ties round his neck the noose of the
Sudra and dies on the gallows, was so despised by Gora that
he hardly counted him as endowed with life—he regarded
such a man as inferior to the Sudras, for they at least were
true to their own caste, but such a one was dead to a sense
of his own Brahminhood, and was therefore impure. It was
because of such Brahmins that India was now passing through
a period of such defilement.

Gora was ready to-day to devote himself to the realisation
of the life-giving *mantram* of the Brahmins. He said to himself
that he must keep absolutely uncontaminated. "I do not stand
on the same level as others," he said. "For me friendship is
not necessary, and I do not belong to that common class of
people for whom the companionship of woman is a sweet to
be enjoyed, and for me too close a relationship with the vulgar
crowd is a thing to be completely shunned. Just as the earth
looks up to the sky in expectation of rain, so do they look

up to the Brahmins—if I come too close to them, who will
be able to give them life?"

Previous to this time Gora had never given his mind much
to worship of the gods, but now that he was so distressed he
was quite unable to control himself; his work seemed empty
to him, and his life to be half-drowned with tears, and so he
began to try what worship would do. He would sit motionless
in front of the idol and try to concentrate his mind entirely
on it, but he could not manage to arouse in himself the least
sign of real devotion. He could explain his god by his reason,
but without some sort of rhetorical figure for comparison he
could not grasp the idea. But rhetorical figures do not fill the
heart with devotion, and worship cannot be performed by
metaphysical exposition. Gora indeed found that it was when
he was launched on the current of argument with some one,
rather than when trying to perform puja in the temple, that
his mind was full of joy and moved with the spirit of devotion.
Still Gora did not give up—everyday he went through the
prescribed puja, and performed the rites regulated by Scripture.
He explained to his own mind that where the power of
uniting with all by one's feelings was absent, it was at least
left for one to unite through custom and rules. Whenever he
went into any village he would enter the village temple and,
sitting in meditation, would say to himself that that was his
proper place—on one side the god and on the other side the
worshipper, and between them, acting as a sort of bridge, the
Brahmin uniting them together. Gradually it dawned on Gora
that the feeling of devotion was not necessary for a Brahmin.
Devotion was a particular quality of the common people, and
the bridge which united the devotee with his faith was a
bridge of knowledge, and just as this united both together so
also it placed a limit between the two. If there were no gulf
of undiluted wisdom between the devotee and his deity then
everything would be distorted. Therefore the confusion caused

by devotion was not a thing to be enjoyed by Brahmins—it was for them to sit apart on the pinnacles of wisdom, and by their austerities preserve the mystery of the faith pure and undefiled for the enjoyment of the common crowds. Just as in the world there can be no rest for Brahmins, so in the worship of the gods there is for them no room for the enjoyment of devotion. This is the Brahmin's glory. In the world, restraint and obedience to rules was for Brahmins, and in their practice of religion, knowledge. Because his heart had obtained a victory over him, Gora had prescribed to his rebellious heart the punishment of banishment. But who would take the culprit into banishment? Where would the soldier be found to perform that duty?

SEVENTY FIVE

The preparations for Gora's penance ceremony were going on apace in the garden by the side of the Ganges. Abinash felt considerable regret that the place chosen for it was so far away from the centre of Calcutta that it would not attract much attention. He knew that Gora himself had no real need for making penance—the need was his country's, the people of which needed it for moral effect. So he felt it was necessary to hold the ceremony in the midst of a crowd.

But Gora would not consent, for the great sacrificial fire and the chanting of Vedic *mantrams* which he wanted, the middle of a crowded city such as Calcutta was unsuitable. For that a hermitage in the forest would have been more fitting. On the lonely bank of the Ganges, to the accompaniment of Vedic chants and lighted by the flames of the sacrificial fire, Gora would invoke ancient India, the teacher of the whole world, and bathing and purifying himself he would take his initiation from her into his new life. Gora cared nothing for "moral effect."

Finding no other way of satisfying this desire for publicity, Abinash took refuge in the Press, and, without telling Gora anything, he sent news of the coming ceremony to all the newspapers. Not only so—he wrote several long leading articles in which he made it known that so spirited and pure a Brahmin as Gora could not be contaminated by any sin, but he had taken upon his own shoulders all the faults of present-day fallen India and was going to perform penance on behalf of the whole country. He wrote: "Just as our country is suffering from the fetters of a foreign race as a result of its own wickedness, so Gourmohan Babu also has experienced in his own life the sorrow of prison shackles. So, as he was bearing in himself the sorrow of his country, and was prepared to practise penance himself for his country's evil conduct, so brother Bengalis, unhappy millions of India's children, you also should," etc. etc.

When Gora read all these effusions he was furiously angry, but Abinash was irrepressible. Even when Gora abused him he was unmoved—in fact he was rather pleased. He felt that his guru roamed in a higher realm of thought than others and did not understand all these worldly matters. It was the heavenly Narod who charmed Vishnu with the strains of his *vina* and made him create the holy Ganges, but to make it flow through the world of mortals was the task of the worldly King Bhagiratha—it was not a work for those who dwelt in heaven. These two tasks were absolutely distinct; so when Gora became furious at Abinash's outrages, Abinash merely smiled to himself, and his reverence for Gora grew still greater than before. He said to himself: "As our guru's face is like that of Shiva so in his thoughts he is just like Bholanath. He understands nothing, he has no commonsense, he gets angry at the least trifle, but it only takes a moment for him to become pacified."

As a result of Abinash's efforts this affair of Gora's penance ceremony began to cause a great sensation all around, and the number of people who came to Gora's house to see him or to be introduced to him was phenomenal. Everyday so many letters came for him from all over the country that he at last gave up reading them. In Gora's opinion all this public discussion of his penance destroyed the solemnity of the occasion—for it made it merely a kind of social function. This was a common fault of the times.

Krishnadayal never touched the newspapers nowadays, but the rumour of all these proceedings penetrated even into his retreat, and his attendant satellites dilated with great pride on their hopes that this worthy son of their revered friend would one day occupy a place equal to that of his holy father. He was already following in his footsteps, and they told the news of the approaching ceremony with great gusto, telling him with what éclat it was to be celebrated.

It is difficult to say how long ago it was since Krishnadayal had set foot in Gora's room. But to-day, putting aside his silk garments, he dressed in ordinary clothes and actually entered. But Gora was not to be seen there, and the servant informed him that he was in the household temple.

"Heavens! What need has he in the temple?" exclaimed Krishnadayal.

When he was informed that he was at worship he was still more alarmed, and went straight off to the door of the temple. There he saw that Gora was actually at his puja, and he called out to him from outside: "Gora!"

Gora stood up in surprise on seeing his father.

Krishnadayal had established in his own part of the house the worship of his own particular tutelary deity. The family were Vaishnabs, but he had become a *shakta,* and had not joined in the family worship for a long time. He now called to Gora: "Come, Gora, come out of there!"

"What does all this mean?" exclaimed Krishnadayal when Gora had come out. "What business have you in here?"

"There are Brahmins for doing puja," complained Krishnadayal when Gora made no answer. "They perform all the necessary ceremonies everyday—they carry on worship for the whole family, so what have you to do with all this?"

"There's nothing wrong in it, is there?" inquired Gora.

"Wrong indeed!" exclaimed Krishnadayal. "What do you mean? It is altogether wrong! What is the need for those who have not the right to do these things to meddle with them? It is a crime, I tell you! It is a crime not for you alone, but for the whole family!"

"If you look at things from the point of view of inner devotion, then there are very few people who have the right," replied Gora, "but do you mean to tell me that what our priest Ramhari has the right to do I have not?"

Krishnadayal suddenly found himself at a loss for an answer, and he remained silent for a little before replying: "Look here, to perform puja is the profession of Ramhari's caste. The gods do not regard that as a sin, in his profession, for if you once begin to find fault in that quarter then their occupation would be gone and the work of society would not be able to be carried on. But you have no excuse. What need have you to enter this room?"

It did not sound excessively unreasonable to hear a man like Krishnadayal saying that it was a fault for a strict Brahmin like Gora to enter the puja room, so Gora accepted this remark without protest. Then Krishnadayal went on: "And one other thing I have heard, Gora. Is it true that you have invited all the pandits to your penance ceremony?"

"Yes," confessed Gora.

"As long as I am alive I will never allow it!" exclaimed Krishnadayal excitedly.

"Why?" asked Gora, his whole mind up in arms.

"Why indeed!" cried Krishnadayal. "Did I not tell you the other day that you could not take part in a ceremony of penance?"

"Yes, you did tell me," assented Gora, "but you did not give me any reason."

"I don't see why I should give you any reason," answered Krishnadayal. "We are your elders and teachers, and must be respected, and it is a recognised law that without our permission you cannot take part in any religious ceremonies. You know, I suppose, about the ceremonies that have to be performed in memory of your ancestors?"

"Well, what is the hindrance for me there?" asked Gora in amazement.

"It is absolutely impossible for you!" exclaimed Krishnadayal in an angry voice. "I will not allow you to perform those ceremonies."

"Look here," expostulated Gora, feeling greatly hurt, "this is my own business. I am undertaking this penance for my own purification, so why are you uselessly arguing and showing so much anxiety about it?"

"See here, Gora," replied Krishnadayal, "don't go and make everything a matter for argument. This is not a subject that can be argued about. There are plenty of things that you have not yet the power to comprehend. Let me tell you once more—you are completely mistaken in thinking that you have obtained entrance into the Hindu religion. That is not in your power, for every drop of blood in your veins, your whole body from head to feet, is opposed to it. You cannot suddenly become a Hindu. The good work has to commence with every birth."

"I don't know anything about every birth," said Gora becoming flushed, "but cannot I claim the right which the blood of your lineage gives me?"

"Arguing again!" cried Krishnadayal. "Aren't you ashamed of contradicting me to my face? You call yourself a Hindu, but when are you going to get rid of that foreign temper of yours? You must listen to what I say, and put a stop to all this."

"If I don't perform penance," said Gora, after remaining silent for a little with head bowed, "then at Soshimukhi's wedding I shall not be able to sit with the rest of the guests."

"That will be all right!" exclaimed Krishnadayal eagerly. "What's the harm in that? We can arrange a separate seat for you."

"And I shall have to keep apart in our community as well," added Gora.

"That will be good," agreed Krishnadayal, and, on seeing Gora's astonishment at his eager approval, he added: "Just look at me, I never take my meals with anyone, even if I am invited. What connection have I got with my community? With your desire that your life should be as uncontaminated as possible it is better to follow the same path. As far as I can see that would be for your welfare."

At midday Krihnadayal sent for Abinash, and said to him: "Why are you all conspiring in leading Gora such a dance?"

"What do you mean?" asked Abinash. "It is rather your Gora who is leading us all! It is he who dances least!"

"But," expostulated Krishnadayal, "let me tell you that all this fuss about penance will never do. I can never allow it. You must put a stop to it at once."

Abinash thought what obstinacy this old man was showing. He knew of plenty of examples in history of the fathers of great men showing a complete lack of understanding of their sons, and he supposed Krishnadayal belonged to that class of fathers. If only, instead of spending his days and nights in the company of a lot of humbug *sannyasis*, Krishnadayal had learnt a few lessons from his own son he would have got far greater benefit!

But Abinash was a tactful person, and where he saw that argument would be fruitless, and that there was not much probability of "moral effect," he did not lose time in useless discussion. So he assented: "Very well, sir, if you do not approve then it can't take place. But all the arrangements have been made, and even the invitations have been sent off, and there is no time now to put it off—so let us do one thing, let Gora keep away, and we can perform the ceremony of penance, for there is no lack of sins in our country." And with this hope he pacified Krishnadayal.

Gora had never shown much respect for Krishnadayal's words, and to-day also his mind would not assent to obeying him. In that region of life which was greater than the life of society he did not consider himself bound to listen to the prohibitions of father and mother. Still, there was something this time which made him feel uncomfortable all day. A vague idea grew in his mind that there was some hidden truth at the back of what Krishnadayal had been saying. It was like some nightmare without shape which oppressed him, and which would not leave him. It seemed as if someone were trying to push him aside from every direction at once. His own loneliness to-day revealed itself, assuming huge proportions. In front of him was so vast a field of labour, and the work itself was so immense, but there was no one by his side.

SEVENTY SIX

It had been decided that as the ceremony was to take place next day Gora should go to the garden house that night, but just as he was getting ready to start Harimohini turned up unexpectedly. On seeing her Gora felt by no means pleased, and he said: "Oh, you have come—I have to go out immediately. Mother too is not here nowadays—if you want to see her, then—"

"No, thank you," answered Harimohini, "I have come to see you. You will have to sit down for a moment—I won't keep you long."

Gora sat down, and Harimohini immediately introduced the subject of Sucharita. She explained that she had got a great deal of benefit from the excellent teaching Gora had given her. So much so in fact that nowadays she would not take water touched by any and everybody, and she was well disposed towards everyone. "My goodness," she exclaimed, "you don't know what a worry she has been to me. If only you can guide her into the right path I shall be indebted to you for life. May god make you the ruler of a kingdom. May you get a girl of good family worthy of your noble descent, may your house prosper, and may you have good fortune, with wealth and children!"

She then went on to say that Sucharita was getting grown-up and it would not do to delay a single day longer than could be helped in getting her married. If she had been in a Hindu family she would by now have been the mother of a family of children. She felt sure that Gora would be of the same opinion as herself on the great impropriety of delaying her marriage any longer. Harimohini, after having borne for a long time the intolerable anxiety of trying to solve the problem of Sucharita's marriage, had at last, after great efforts and with many humble entreaties, got her brother-in-law Kailash to come to Calcutta. By the grace of God all the serious obstacles which had caused her so much fear and anxiety had been removed. Everything was settled. No dowry would be expected from the bride, and no objections would be raised on the score of her previous history—Harimohini had by her own skilful tactics managed all this—and now just at this moment, amazing to relate, Sucharita had become absolutely obstinate in her contrariness. What her idea was it was impossible for Harimohini to fathom—God alone knew whether someone had been influencing her, or whether she was attracted to somebody else.

"But," she continued, "I tell you plainly that the girl is not worthy of you! If she marries and settles in a village no one will know anything about her, and so things will somehow go smoothly. But you live in a city, and if you married her you would never be able to show your face in public again!"

"What are you talking about?" exclaimed Gora angrily. "Who ever told you that I wanted to marry her?"

"How can I say?" said Harimohini apologetically. "When I heard that it was mentioned in the newspaper I nearly died of shame!"

From this Gora understood that either Haran Babu, or some member of his party, had been writing about it in the Press, and he clenched his fist as he shouted: "It's a lie!"

"I know that," exclaimed Harimohini, startled by the thundering sound of Gora's voice. "Now I have a request to make to you which you must accede to. You must come round at once and see Radharani."

"Why?" inquired Gora.

"You must explain things to her," answered Harimohini. Gora's mind leapt at this proposal and he was ready to go immediately to Sucharita. His heart said: "Go and see her to-day for the last time! To-morrow is the day for your penance—after that you will be an ascetic. To-day there is only this brief part of the night left—you can see her only for a moment! There surely is no crime in that, and even if there is, to-morrow all will be consumed to ashes."

"Tell me what I have to explain to her?" asked Gora, after a short silence.

"Nothing more than this," answered Harimohini. "According to the Hindu ideals a grown-up girl like Sucharita ought to get married without delay, and that to get in the Hindu community such a good husband as Kailash is for a girl in her situation an unexpected piece of good fortune."

Gora's heart was pierced as with arrows, and when he remembered the man whom he had met at the door of Sucharita's house he felt as though he were being bitten by scorpions. It was unbearable for him to imagine for a single moment such a man gaining Sucharita as his wife. His mind revolted and he exclaimed to himself: "No, that can never be."

It was impossible for Sucharita to have such union with anyone else. Her deep still heart, filled to overflowing with the profundity of her thoughts and feelings, could never have revealed itself so fully before any other man, and never would it reveal itself at any future time. How wonderful it had been! How marvellous! What an indescribable presence had been made manifest in the innermost chamber of the abode of mystery! How often can man have such an experience, and how many men have seen such marvels? The man whose destiny had given him such a deep and true insight into Sucharita's character—who had felt her presence with his whole nature—had obtained Sucharita herself! How then could anyone else take possession of her?

"Is Radharani to remain unmarried like this all her days? Is such a fate possible for her?" exclaimed Harimohini.

That was true! To-morrow Gora was to perform his penance! After that he would have to be a completely pure Brahmin! Would then Sucharita all her days remain unmarried? In addition to that, had anyone the right to impose such a state on her for life? Was it possible for a woman to bear so heavy a burden?

Harimohini went on chattering, but Gora did not listen to what she was saying. He was pondering to himself: "My father has forbidden me so repeatedly to perform this ceremony of penance—has his prohibition no value? What I imagine my life to be meant for may be merely my imagination, and not in accordance with my nature. I shall be crippled for life if I try to carry an artificial burden, and by the perpetual weight of such a load I shall not be able to accomplish any task in life. I begin to see that my heart is entangled in desire! How can I shift this stone which weighs upon me? My father has somehow discovered that in my heart of hearts I am not a Brahmin, not an ascetic, and for that reason he has forbidden me so firmly."

Gora decided that he would go to Krishnadayal that very night, and would definitely ask him what he saw in him to make him say that the road of penance was closed to him. If only he could induce him to explain, he would be able to find a way of escape in that direction. Escape!

"Please wait a little, I'll be back again directly," said Gora to Harimohini, and he hurried to his father's quarters. He felt that there was something known to Krishnadayal by means of which he could get immediate liberation.

But the door of his father's retreat was closed, and even when he had knocked two or three times, it remained shut—no one responded to his knocks. From inside there came the scent of incense and sandalwood, for to-day Krihshnadayal, with one of his *sannyasis,* was deeply absorbed in some very intense method of yoga, and he was in the habit of closing all doors against outside intrusion on such occasions. That whole night no one would be allowed admittance on any pretext.

SEVENTY SEVEN

"No!" exclaimed Gora to himself, "my penance is not to-morrow! To-day it has begun. A greater fire is burning to-day than will be lighted to-morrow. At the commencement of my new life I have to offer up a great sacrifice, that is why God has awakened in my heart so strong a desire. Otherwise, why should such a strange thing have happened? There was no worldly probability of my becoming intimate with them, and a union of such contrary natures does not happen in this world in the ordinary course of events. Besides that, no one could even have dreamed that such an overpowering longing would awaken in the heart of a man so indifferent as myself. Up to now that which I have given to my country has been given too easily, and I have never been called upon to offer something which would be a real sacrifice to me! I could never understand before why people felt the least miserliness in giving up things for their country. But in such a great renunciation an ordinary gift will not do. Sorrow is needed for sacrifice, and my new birth can take place only if my very heart is pierced! To-morrow morning my ceremonial penance will be performed before the people of my community. And now, on the night before, the Lord of my life has come and knocked at the door of my heart. Unless in the depths of my soul an innermost penance is performed how can I accept purification to-morrow? When once I have offered up that gift which is the hardest of all to sacrifice, fully and completely, then I shall become truly poor and sanctified—then I shall be a Brahmin."

When Gora returned to Harimohini she said to him: "Please do come with me just this once! If you will come and say one word to her then all will be well."

"Why should I go?" protested Gora. "What relationship have I with her? None, none at all!"

"Why, she reveres you like a god, and respects you as her guru," replied Harimohini.

Gora's heart thrilled at these words, but he again protested:

"I don't see any need for me to go. There is no likelihood of my ever seeing her again."

"That is true," Harimohini smiled with pleasure, "It is not right to be seeing too much of a grown-up girl like that. But I can't let you off until my object is accomplished somehow. If I ever ask you to come again then you can refuse."

But Gora shook his head again and again. No more, never again! It was all over now. The offering to his God had been made, and he could not let the least spot sully its purity again. He would not go to see her.

When Harimohini realised that it would be impossible to move Gora she requested him: "Well, if it is absolutely impossible for you to go, then do one thing, please, write a letter to her."

Gora shook his head. That was impossible. He couldn't send a letter.

"Very well," said Harimohini, "write only just two lines for me! You are well versed in the Scriptures, I have come to obtain an injunction from you."

"An injunction for what?" asked Gora.

"Is it not the chief duty of a girl of proper age in a Hindu household to marry and take up domestic work?" explained Harimohini.

"Look here," said Gora after a moment's silence, "don't get me entangled in all this business. I'm not a pandit that I should give injunctions."

"Why don't you tell me plainly what it is you really wish in your innermost mind?" exclaimed Harimohini sharply. "In the beginning it was you who fashioned the noose—and now when the time comes for untying it you say: 'Don't entangle me!' What's the meaning of that? The real truth is you have no wish to make her mind clear."

At any other time Gora would have become hot with indignation at this remark, and would never have been able to bear even such a true accusation. But to-day his penance had begun, and he could not be angry. Further, he realised at the back of his mind that Harimohini had spoken the truth. He was cruel enough in cutting the strong ties which bound him to Sucharita, but he wanted to keep one fine thread on some excuse or other, a thread which could not be seen. He was not even yet prepared to sever his connection with Sucharita fully and finally.

But every vestige of miserliness must be removed, for it would never do for him to offer something with one hand while keeping back something with the other.

So he took out a piece of paper, and wrote with a firm bold hand:

"For women the path of life's true realisation is the welfare of all. The world may be full of joy or full of sorrow—the virtuous and chaste woman will accept it all and make it her chief religious duty to give form to her religion in her home."

"It would be a good thing if you could add a word or two in favour of our Kailash," suggested Harimohini on reading it.

"No, I don't know him," objected Gora. "I can't write anything about him."

Harimohini folded up this piece of writing with the utmost care and, tying it in the corner of her sari, set out for her home. Sucharita was still staying with Anandamoyi at Lolita's house, and Harimohini felt it would not be convenient to discuss the matter there lest Sucharita should hear Lolita and Anandamoyi saying things against the proposal and should hesitate. Fearing this, she sent a note to Sucharita, asking her to come round next day for the midday meal when she had a very important matter to discuss with her. She promised to let her return to Lolita's house the same afternoon.

Next morning Sucharita arrived with her mind made up to resist firmly, for she knew that her aunt was going to raise the question of her marriage again. She was determined to make an end of the whole business by giving a very firm and final answer to the proposal.

When she had finished her meal Harimohini began: "Yesterday evening I went round to see your guru."

Sucharita began to feel afraid. Had her aunt sent for her only to start insulting Gora again?

"Don't be afraid," said Harmohini reassuringly, "I didn't go round there to quarrel with him. I was all alone, and I thought to myself, why not go round there and listen to some of his excellent views. In the course of our conversation your name was mentioned, and I saw at once that his opinion agreed with mine. He does not regard it as good for girls to remain too long unmarried. In fact he says that according to the Scriptures it is actually unrighteous. It may be all right in European households but not in those of Hindus. I spoke quite openly about our Kailash, and I found that he took a very sensible view of the situation."

Sucharita felt ready to die of shame as Harimohini went on: "You respect him as your guru! So you must follow his advice!"

Sucharita remained silent, and Harimohini continued: "I said to him, 'Do please come and speak to her yourself, for she won't listen to what I say.' But he replied, "No, I must not see her again—it is forbidden by our Hindu society.' Then I said, 'Then what can be done?' And at last he wrote something with his own hand to give you. See, here it is!" and she slowly took out the piece of paper from the corner of her *sari,* and unfolding it spread it out before Sucharita for her to read.

As Sucharita read it, she felt as if she were suffocating, and sat stiff and motionless like a wooden doll.

There was nothing in what was written there which was either new or unreasonable. It was not that Sucharita differed from the opinions which were expressed. But that it should have been sent specially to her through Harimohini's hands seemed to suggest a meaning that gave her pain from various points of view. Why should this command come from Gora to-day specially? To be sure the day must come for Sucharita too when she would have to marry—but why was Gora in such a hurry on her account? Had Gora's work, so far as she was concerned, been absolutely finished? Was she a cause of injury to Gora in the discharge of his duties, or was she an obstacle in the path of his life's work? Had he nothing more to give to her, and had he nothing more to hope from her? She at any rate could not think so—she at least was still looking forward along the path. Sucharita tried her best to fight against the intolerable pain which she was feeling in her heart, but she could not get any consolation.

Harimohini gave Sucharita plenty of time to think matters over. She went and enjoyed her usual afternoon nap, and when she woke up and returned she found Sucharita sitting still and silent exactly as she had left her.

"Radhu," she said, "why are you so thoughtful, my dear? What is there in this matter to make you think so deeply? Has Gourmohan Babu written anything wrong?"

"No," replied Sucharita gently, "what he has written is quite true."

"Then, my child, what is the use of delaying matters?" exclaimed Harimohini, greatly encouraged.

"No, I don't want to delay things," answered Sucharita, "I will go and see father for a little."

"Look here, Radhu," objected Harimohini, "your father will never wish that you should marry into the Hindu community—but your guru, he—"

"Auntie," exclaimed Sucharita impatiently, "why will you talk again and again like that? I'm not going to speak to father about my marriage at all. I just want to see him, that's all!"

It was only in the close companionship of Paresh Babu that Sucharita could now find consolation.

On reaching his house she saw that he was packing some clothes in a trunk.

"Whatever does this mean?" asked Sucharita.

"Mother, I am going for a change to Simla," laughed Paresh Babu, "I am going by to-morrow morning's mail."

In this slight laugh of Paresh Babu's there lay concealed the history of a tremendous revolt which did not remain hidden from Sucharita. In his own home his wife, and outside it all his friends, did not give him a moment's peace, and if he could not get away somewhere to a distance for a time he would merely become the centre of a whirlpool. Sucharita received a great blow when she saw him packing his own trunk for a journey which was to begin next day. It was hard for her to think that there was no one of his own family who was there to help him in this task; so making Paresh Babu desist from his labours she first of all threw everything out of his trunk, and then, folding each garment with the greatest care, repacked all his things. His favourite books she packed carefully so that they should not get damaged by being shaken about, and as she was engaged at this work she gently asked Paresh Babu: "Father, are you going alone?"

"That won't be any difficulty for me, Radha!" assured Paresh Babu, detecting the pain which lay hidden in her question.

"No, father, I will accompany you," said Sucharita.

Paresh Babu looked in Sucharita's face, and she added: "Father, I promise not to be a nuisance."

"Why do you say that?" asked Paresh Babu. "When ever have you been a nuisance to me, little mother?"

"Unless I am near you, father, I can't get along at all," urged Sucharita. "There are many things which I do not yet understand, and unless you explain them to me I shall never reach the shore. Father, you tell me to rely upon my own intelligence—but I have not got that intelligence—I have no strength in my own mind. You must take me with you, father!"

Saying this she turned round and bent over the trunk, while from her eyes the tears began to fall.

SEVENTY EIGHT

When Gora had given the piece of writing into Harimohini's hand he felt as though he had sent a letter which meant the end of his relationship with Sucharita. But a deed or document is not finished with when it has merely been written. His heart would by no means give its consent, and although Gora had signed his name to it by the force of his own will-power his heart refused to witness it with its signature—it remained disobedient. So disobedient indeed that Gora all but decided to run round to Sucharita that very night! But just as he was about to start he heard the clock of the neighbouring church strike ten, and he suddenly realised that it was too late for anybody to be paying calls. After that he lay awake listening to the clock strike each hour, for he had not gone to the garden house that night after all. He had sent a message saying he would go in the morning.

Next morning he went to the riverside garden, but where was that strength and purity of mind with which he had resolved to enter upon the ceremony of penance?

Many of the pandits had already arrived, and others were expected. Gora gave them all a warm welcome, and they in their turn referred again and again, in the highest terms, to Gora's firm devotion to the eternal religion.

Gradually the garden became filled with confusion, and Gora went round superintending everything, but amidst all the uproar and the hurry of his work only one thought kept recurring to his mind, rising from the very depths of his heart. It was as though someone was saying to him, "You have done wrong! You have done wrong!" There was no time then for him to think clearly and discover whe   the wrong was—but he was quite unable to smother this deep feeling of his heart. In the midst of all these immense arrangements for the ceremony of penance some enemy, dwelling within the precincts of his own heart, was witnessing against him, saying. "The wrong still remains." This wrong was not a violation of rules and laws, it was not a blunder against the Shastras, or something opposed to religious practice,—it was a wrong which had been committed within his own nature. Therefore it was that Gora's whole soul revolted against all these preparations for the ceremony.

The time for beginning drew near. The place for the service had been made ready with a canopy and bamboo railings. But just when Gora was changing his clothes, after bathing in the Ganges, a disturbance was noticeable amongst the audience. A sort of uneasiness seemed to be spreading on all sides. At last Abinash, with a distraught face, came up to Gora, and said: "News has just come from your home, that Krishnadayal Babu is seriously ill. He has sent a carriage for you to return home immediately."

Gora hurried away at once, but when Abinash wanted to accompany him he said: "No, you must stay and look after the guests, it will not do for you to leave too."

When he entered Krishnadayal's room Gora saw that he was lying on his bed, and Anandamoyi was gently massaging his feet. He looked anxiously at both of them, until Krishnadayal made a sign for him to sit on a chair which had been placed ready for him.

"How is he now?" inquired Gora of his mother, when he was seated.

"He is slightly better," answered Anandamoyi. "The doctor *sahib* has been sent for."

Soshimukhi and a servant were also there, and Krishnadayal signed with his hand for them to go out. When he saw that there was no one else in the room he looked silently in Anandamoyi's face, and then, turning to Gora, said in a weak voice: "My time has come, and what I have kept concealed from you for so long I must tell you before I die. I cannot feel free otherwise."

Gora turned pale, and sat still and silent. For a long time no one said a word. Then Krishnadayal went on: "Gora, at that time I had no respect for our own society— that was why I made such a great blunder. And after it had once been committed there was no way back," and again he became silent. Gora, too, sat in silence without asking any question.

"I thought that it would never be necessary to let you know," continued Krishnadayal, "and that things could go on as they were doing always. But now I see that to be impossible, for after my death how could you take part in my funeral obsequies?"

It was evidently the thought of such a contingency that caused Krishnadayal to wince.

Gora became impatient to hear what was really the matter, and turning to Anandamoyi with an inquiring look, he said: "Tell me, mother, what does this mean? Have I not the right to join in the funeral rites?"

Anandamoyi had, up till this point, been sitting rigid, with her head bowed, but on hearing Gora's question she looked up and gazing steadily into Gora' eyes, said: "No, my child, you have not."

"Am I not then his son?" inquired Gora with a start of surprise.

"No," replied Anandamoyi.

With the explosive force of a volcanic eruption Gora brought out his next question: "Mother, are you not my real mother?"

Anandamoyi's heart was almost breaking as she answered in a dry tearless voice: "Gora, my child, you are the only son of mine. I am a childless woman, but you are more truly my son than a child born from my own body could have been."

"Then where did you get me?" inquired Gora looking towards Krishnadayal again.

"It was during the Mutiny," began Krishnadayal, "when we were at Etawa. Your mother, in fear of the Sepoys, took refuge one night in our house. Your father had been killed the previous day during the fighting. His name was—"

"There is no need to hear his name!" roared Gora. "I don't want to know the name."

Krishnadayal stopped in astonishment at Gora's excitement. He merely added: "He was an Irishman. That very night your mother died after giving birth to you. From that day you were brought up in our home."

In a single moment Gora's whole life seemed to him like some extraordinary dream. The foundations upon which, from childhood, all his life had been raised had suddenly crumbled into dust, and he was unable to understand who he was or where he stood. What he had called the past seemed to have no substance, and that bright future which he had looked forward to with such eagerness for so long had vanished completely. He felt as though he were like the dewdrop on the lotus leaf which comes into existence for a moment only. He had no mother, no father, no country, no nationality, no lineage, no God even. Only one thing was left to him, and that was a vast negation. What could he hold on to? What work could he undertake? From where could he begin life again? In what direction could he fix his gaze? And from whence could he gather, gradually day by day, materials for this new work of his? Gora was speechless in the midst of this strange void in which he had lost all sense of direction, and the look on his face made it impossible for another word to be spoken.

At this moment the English doctor arrived in the company of the Bengali physician. The doctor looked towards Gora with as much interest as he did at the patient, and wondered to himself who this extraordinary young man could be. For Gora still had on his forehead the sacred mark of the Ganges mud, and was still wearing the silk cloth which he had put on after his bath in the river. He had no shirt on, and his huge body showed through the scanty wrapper that was thrown over his shoulders.

At any time before this, on seeing an Englishman, Gora would have felt an instinctive antipathy, but to-day as the doctor was examining the patient he looked at him with peculiar eagerness. He was asking himself this question again and again: "Is this person then the one who is most closely related to me here?"

After having examined and questioned the patient, the doctor said: "Well, I don't see any very dangerous symptoms to speak of. There is nothing to be afraid of about the pulse, and there is nothing organically wrong anywhere. With care there is no reason at all why there should be a repetition of the symptoms."

When the doctor had gone Gora got up without a word, and was about to go, but Anandamoyi came running out from the next room where she had gone on the doctor's departure, and seizing Gora's hand, exclaimed: "Gora, my dear, you must not be angry with me, for that would break my heart."

"Why have you kept me in the dark for so long?" asked Gora. "There would have been no harm in your telling me."

"My child," began Anandamoyi, taking all the blame on her own shoulders, "I have committed this sin because I was afraid lest I should lose you. If in the end that happens, if to-day you leave me, I can blame no one but myself, Gora, but it would be the death of me, dearest!"

"Mother!" was all that Gora said in reply, but on hearing him utter that one word, all the pent-up tears which Anandamoyi had been holding back began to flow.

"Mother, now I must go to Paresh Babu's," said Gora.

"Very well, my dear, you go!" said Anandamoyi feeling a weight off her heart.

Krishnadayal, in the meantime, had become so greatly alarmed that, although there was no fear of his early death, he had told Gora his secret, and before Gora left the room he said: "Look here, Gora, I see no need for you to make this matter known to anyone. Only walk a little circumspectly, and go on more or less as you have been doing, and no one will be any the wiser."

Gora went out without making any reply to this suggestion, for on recollecting that he had no real relationship with Krishnadayal he felt a great relief.

Mohim had not been able to absent himself from his office without giving any intimation, so, when he had made all the necessary arrangements for the doctors and treatment of his father, he had gone to the office and obtained leave. He was on his way back home when he met Gora coming out of the house.

"Where are you off to?" asked Mohim.

"The news is good," said Gora. "The doctor has been and says there is no danger."

"What a mercy!" exclaimed Mohim, much relieved. "The day after to-morrow is the day on which Soshimukhi is to be married. So, Gora you must make things ready a little! And look here, you will have to warn Binoy beforehand, so that he may not turn up here on that day. Abinash is a very strict Hindu—he specially mentioned that no such people were to be invited to the wedding. And there is one other thing I want to say, brother. The head *sahib* from my office has been invited, so don't you go and drive him off with blows! You won't have to do much, just nod your head and say. 'Good evening, Sir.' There is nothing against that in your Scriptures. If you like you can get a special injunction from the pandits to make sure. You should understand, my boy, that they are the ruling class, there is nothing derogatory in your lowering your pride a little before them!"

Without making any reply to Mohim's remarks Gora went off.

SEVENTY NINE

Just as Sucharita was trying to conceal her tears by busying herself over the trunk, the servant arrived with the news that Gourmohan Babu had called. Quickly drying her eyes she put aside her work of packing just as Gora entered the room.

The Ganges mark was still on his forehead, and he was still wearing his silk cloth. He had not given a thought to his personal appearance, and had come dressed in a fashion such as no one would ordinarily think of paying a call in. Sucharita remembered the dress he had been wearing when he paid his first call at their house. She knew that on that day he had come in full war apparel, and she wondered whether this too was his fighting dress!

Gora, when he came in, knelt down before Paresh Babu and putting his head on the floor took the dust of his feet. Paresh Babu moved aside in distress, and lifting him up, exclaimed: "Come, come, my child, come and sit down!"

"Paresh Babu, I have now no more ties!" cried Gora.

"What ties?" inquired Paresh Babu in astonishment.

"I am not a Hindu!" explained Gora.

"Not a Hindu!" cried Paresh Babu.

"No, I am not a Hindu," continued Gora. "To-day I have been told that I was a foundling at the time of the Mutiny—my father was an Irishman! From one end of India to the other the doors of every temple are to-day closed against me—to-day in the whole country there is no seat for me at any Hindu feast."

Paresh Babu and Sucharita were both so dumbfounded that they were not able to make any remark.

"To-day I am free, Paresh Babu!" exclaimed Gora. "I need no longer fear being contaminated or becoming an outcaste— I shall not now have to look on the ground at every step to preserve my purity."

Sucharita gave one long look at Gora's glowing face, as he continued: "Paresh Babu, so long I have been trying to realise India with my whole life—I was finding obstacles at every turn—and day and night I have been trying always to make these obstacles objects of devotion. And in order to make that devotion firm in its foundations I have not been able to do any other work—that was my one and only task. For that reason every time I have come face to face with the real India I have turned back in fear—shaping an India with my unchanging and uncritical thought I have all this time been struggling against everything around me in my efforts to preserve my faith whole and entire in that impregnable fortress! To-day in a single moment that fortress of my own creation has vanished like a dream, and I, having got absolute freedom, suddenly find myself standing in the midst of a vast truth! All that is good or evil in India, all her joys and sorrows, all her wisdom and follies, have come in their fullness close to my heart. Now I have truly the right to serve her, for the real field of labour is spread out before me—it is not a creation of my own imagination—it is the actual field of welfare for the three hundred millions of India's children!"

This newly acquired experience of Gora's made him speak with such an intense enthusiasm that Paresh Babu, became quite agitated, and was unable to remain seated. He got up from his chair and stood as Gora went on:

"Can you follow what it is that I am trying to say? That which day and night I have been longing for but which I could not be, to-day at last I have become. To-day I am really an Indian! In me there is no longer any opposition between Hindu, Mussulman, and Christian. To-day every caste in India is my caste, the food of all is my food! Look here, I have wandered through many parts of Bengal, and have accepted hospitality in the lowest village homes—do not think that I have merely lectured before city audiences—but I have never been able to take my seat beside all equally—all these days I have been carrying about with me an unseen gulf of separation which I have never been able to cross over! Therefore in my mind there was a kind of void, which I tried by various devices to ignore. I tried to make that emptiness look more beautiful by decorating it with all kinds of artistic work. Because I loved India better than life itself I was quite unable to bear the least criticism of that part of it which I had got to know. Now that I have been delivered from those fruitless attempts at inventing such useless decorations I feel, Paresh Babu, that I am alive again!"

"When we obtain what is true," observed Paresh Babu, "then our soul gets satisfaction even in its incompleteness and imperfections—we do not even wish to dress it up in materials which are false."

"See here, Paresh Babu," said Gora, "last night I prayed to God that I might this morning enter into a new life! I asked that anything that had been false or impure, which had enveloped my life from childhood, might be completely destroyed and I might be born anew! God did not listen to my prayer in exactly the way which I had intended—He has startled me by the suddenness with which He has put into my hands His own Truth! I could never have even dreamed that He would wipe out all my impurity in so thorough a manner. To-day I have become so pure that I can never be afraid of contamination even in the house of the lowest of castes, Paresh Babu, this morning, with my heart absolutely bare I have prostrated myself wholly at the knees of my India—after so long I have at length fully experienced what is meant by the mother's lap!"

"Gora," said Paresh Babu, "call us too that we may share with you the birthright to rest in your mother's lap!"

"Do you know," asked Gora, "why, on getting my freedom to-day, the first thing I did was to come to you?"

"Why?" inquired Paresh Babu.

"It is you who have the *mantram* of that freedom," explained Gora, "and that is why to-day you find no place in any society. Make me your disciple! To-day give me the *mantram* of that Deity who belongs to all, Hindu, Mussulman, Christian, and Brahmo alike—the doors to whose temple are never closed to any person of any caste whatever—He who is not merely the God of the Hindus, but who is the God of India herself!"

A deep and tender expression of devotion lighted up Paresh Babu's face, and, lowering his eyes, he stood for some moments in silence.

Then Gora turned to Sucharita, who was sitting motionless on her chair.

"Sucharita," said Gora with a smile, "I am no longer your guru. I make known to you this prayer of mine—take my hand and lead me to this guru of yours?" and he held out his right hand towards her. Sucharita got up from her chair and put her hand in his, then Gora turned towards Paresh Babu, and the two together made their obeisance to him.

EPILOGUE

When Gora returned that evening to his home he found Anandamoyi sitting quietly on the verandah in front of his room.

He went up to her and, sitting down in front of her, laid his head at her feet, while Anandamoyi lifted his head and kissed him.

"Mother, you are my mother!" exclaimed Gora. "The mother whom I have been wandering about in search of was all the time sitting in my room at home. You have no caste, you make no distinctions, and have no hatred—you are only the image of our welfare! It is you who are India!"

"Mother!" went on Gora, after a moment's pause, "will you call Lachmiya and ask her to bring me a glass of water?"

MY BOYHOOD DAYS

I

The Calcutta where I was born was an altogether old-world place. Hackney carriages lumbered about the city raising clouds of dust, and the whips fell on the backs of skinny horses whose bones showed plainly below their hide. There were no trams then, no buses, no motors. Business was not the breathless rush that it is now, and the days went by in leisurely fashion. Clerks would take a good pull at the hookah before starting for office, and chew their betel as they went along. Some rode in palanquins, others joined in groups of four or five to hire a carriage in common, which was known as a "share-carriage". Wealthy men had monograms painted on their carriages, and a leather hood over the rear portion, like a half-drawn veil. The coachman sat on the box with his turban stylishly tilted to one side, and two grooms rode behind, girdles of yaks' tails round their waists, startling the pedestrians from their path with their shouts of "Hey-yo!"

Women used to go about in the stifling darkness of closed palanquins; they shrank from the idea of riding in carriages, and even to use an umbrella in sun or rain was considered unwomanly. Any woman who was so bold as to wear the new-fangled bodice, or shoes on her feet, was scornfully nicknamed "memsahib", that is to say, one who had cast off all sense of propriety or shame. If any woman unexpectedly encountered a stange man, one outside her family circle, her veil would promptly descend to the very tip of her nose, and she would at once turn her back on him. The palanquins in which women went out were shut as closely as their apartments in the house. An additional covering, a kind of thick tilt, completely enveloped the palanquin of a rich man's daughters and daighters-in-law, so that it looked like a moving tomb. By its side went the durwan carrying his brass-bound stick. His work was to sit in the entrance and watch the house, to tend his beard, safely to conduct the money to the bank and the women to their relatives houses, and on festival days to dip the lady of the house into the Ganges, closed palanquin and all. Hawkers who came to the door with their array of wares would grease Shivnandan's palm to gain admission, and the drivers of hired carriages were also a source of profit to him. Sometimes a man who was unwilling to fall in with this idea of going shares would create a great scene in front of the porch.

Our "jamadar" Sobha Ram, who was a wrestler, used to spend a good deal of time in practising his preaparatory feints and approaches, and in brandishing his heavy clubs. Sometimes he would sit and grind hemp for drink, and sometimes he would be quietly eating his raw radishes, tender leaves and all, when we boys would creep upon him and yell "Radhakrishna!" in his ear. The more he waved his arms and protested the more we delighted in teasing him. And perhaps— who knows?—his protests were merely a cunning device for hearing repeated the name of his favourite god.

There was no gas then in the city, and no electric light. When the kerosene lamp was introduced, its brilliance amazed us. In the evening the house-servant lit castor-oil lamps in every room. The one in our study-room had two wicks in a glass bowl.

By this dim light my master taught me from Peary Sarkar's First Book. First I would begin to yawn, and then, growing

more and more sleepy, rub my heavy eyes. At such times I
heard over and over again of the virtues of my master's other
pupil Satin, a paragon of a boy with a wonderful head for
study, who would rub snuff in his eyes to keep himself awake,
so earnest was he. But as for me—the less said about that the
better! Even the awful thought that I should probably remain
the only dunce in the family could not keep me awake. When
nine o'clock struck I was released, my eyes dazed and my
mind drugged with sleep.

There was a narrow passage, enclosed by latticed walls,
leading from the outer apartments to the interior of the
house. A dimly burning lantern swung from the ceiling. As
I went along this passage, my mind would be haunted by the
idea that something was creeping upon me from behind. Little
shivers ran up and down my back. In those days devils and
spirits lurked in the recesses of every man's mind, and the
air was full of ghost stories. One day it would be some servant
girl falling in a dead faint because she had heard the nasal
whine of Shañk-chunni. The female demon of that name was
the most bad-tempered devil of all, and was said to be very
greedy of fish. Another story was connected with the thick-
leaved *bādām* tree at the western corner of the house. A
mysterious Shape was said to stand with one foot in its
branches and the other on the third storey cornice of the
house. Plenty of people declared that they had seen it, and
there were not a few who believed them. A friend of my elder
brother's laughingly made light of the story, and the servants
looked upon him as lacking in all piety, and said that his neck
would surely be wrung one day and his pretensions exposed.
The very atmosphere was so enmeshed in ghostly terrors that
I could not put my feet into the darkness under the table
without them getting the creeps.

There were no water-pipes laid on in those days. In the
spring months of *Māgh* and *Fālgoon* when the Ganges water

was clear, our bearers would bring it up in brimming pots carried in a yoke across their shoulders. In the dark rooms of the ground floor stood rows of huge water jars filled with the whole year's supply of drinking water. All those musty, dingy, twilit rooms were the home of furtive "Things"—which of us did not know all about those "Things"? Great gaping mouths they had, eyes in their breasts, and ears like winnowing fans; and their feet turned backwards. Small wonder that my heart would pound in my breast and my knees tremble when I went into the inner garden, with the vision of those devilish shapes before me.

At high tide the water of the Ganges would flow along a masonry channel at the side of the road. Since my grandfather's time an allowance of this water had been discharged into our tank. When the sluices were opened the water rushed in, gurgling and foaming like a waterfall. I used to watch it fascinated, holding on by the railings of the south verandah. But the days of our tank were numbered, and finally there came a day when cartload after cartload of rubbish was tipped into it. When the tank no longer reflected the garden, the last lingering illusion of rural life left it. That *bādām* tree is still standing near the third storey cornice, but though his footholds remain, the ghostly shape that once bestrode them has disappeared for ever.

II

The palanquin belonged to the days of my grandmother. It was of ample proportions and lordly appearance. It was big enough to have needed eight bearers for each pole. But when the former wealth and glory of the family had faded like the glowing clouds of sunset, the palanquin bearers, with their gold bracelets, their thick ear-rings, and their sleeveless red tunics, had disappeared along with it. The body of the palanquin had been decorated with coloured line drawings, some of which were now defaced. Its surface was stained and discoloured, and the coir stuffing was coming out of the upholstery. It lay in a corner of the counting-house verandah as though it were a piece of common-place lumber. I was seven or eight years old at that time.

I was not yet, therefore, of an age to put my hand to any serious work in the world, and the old palanquin on its part had been dismissed from all useful service. Perhaps it was this fellow-feeling that so much attracted me towards it. It was to me an island in the midst of the ocean, and I on my holidays became Robinson Crusoe. There I sat within its closed doors, completely lost to view, delightfully safe from prying eyes.

Outside my retreat, our house was full of people, innumerable relatives and other folk. From all parts of the house I could hear the shouts of the various servants at their work. Pari the maid is returning from the bazaar through the front courtyard with her vegetables in a basket on her hip. Dukhon the bearer is carrying in Ganges water in a yoke across his shoulder. The weaver woman has gone into the inner apartments to trade the newest style of saries. Dinu the goldsmith, who receives a monthly wage, usually sits in the room next to the lane, blowing his bellows and carrying out the orders of the family; now he is coming to the counting house to present his bill to Kailash Mukherjee, who has a quill pen stuck over his ear. The carder sits in the courtyard cleaning the cotton mattress stuffing on his twanging bow. Mukundalal the durwan is rolling on the ground outside with the one-eyed wrestler, trying out a new wrestling fall. He slaps his thighs loudly, and repeats his "physical jerks" twenty or thirty times, dropping on all fours. There is a crowd of beggars sitting waiting for their regular dole.

The day wears on, the heat grows intense, the clock in the gate-house strikes the hour. But inside the palanquin the day does not acknowledge the authority of clocks. Our midday is that of former days, when the drum at the great door of the king's palace would be beaten for the breaking-up of the court, and the king would go to bathe in sandal-scented water. At midday on holidays those in charge of me have their meal and go to sleep. I sit on alone. My palanquin, outwardly at rest, travels on its imaginary journeys. My bearers, sprung from "airy nothing" at my bidding, eating the salt of my imagination, carry me wherever my fancy leads. We pass through far, strange lands, and I give each country a name from the books I have read. My imagination has cut a road through a deep forest. Tigers' eyes blaze from the thickets, my flesh creeps and tingles. With me is Biswanath the hunter; his gun speaks—Crack! Crack!—and there, all is still. Sometimes my palanquin becomes a peacock-boat, floating far out on the ocean till the shore is out of sight. The oars fall into the water with a gentle plash, the waves swing and swell around us. The sailors cry to us to beware, a storm is coming. By the tiller stands Abdul the sailor, with his pointed beard, shaven moustache and close-cropped head. I know him, he brings hilsa fish and turtle eggs from the Padma for my elder brother.

Abdul has a story for me. One day at the end of *Chaitra*[1] he had gone out in a dinghy to catch fish when suddenly there arose a great *Vaisākh* gale[2]. It was a tremendous typhoon and the boat sank lower and lower. Abdul seized the tow-rope in his teeth, and jumping into the water swam to the shore, where he pulled his dinghy up after him by the rope. But the story comes to an end far too quickly for my taste, and besides, the boat is not lost, everything is saved—that isn't what I call a story! Again and again I demand, "What next?" "Well," says Abdul at last, "after that there were great doings. What should I see next but a panther with enormous whiskers. During the storm he had climbed up a *pākur* tree on the village ghat on the other side of the river. In the violent wind the tree broke and fell into the Padma. Brother Panther came floating down on the current, rolled over and over in the water and reached and climbed the bank on my side. As soon as I saw him I made a noose in my tow-rope. The wild beast drew near, his big eyes glaring. He had grown very hungry with swimming, and when he saw me saliva dribbled from his red, lolling tongue. But though he had known many other men, inside and out, he did not know Abdul. I shouted to him, "Come on old boy", and as soon as he raised his forefeet for the attack I dropped my noose round his neck. The more he struggled to get free the tighter grew the noose, until his tongue began to loll out...." I am tremendously excited.

---

1. March-April.
2. Nor-wester, a very common phenomenon in Bengal in the beginning of the hot weather.

"He didn't die, did he Abdul?" I ask. "Die?" says Abdul, "He couldn't die for the life of him! Well, the river was in spate, and I had to get back to Bahadurganj. I yoked my young panther to the dinghy and made him tow me fully forty miles. Oh, he might roar and snarl, but I goaded him on with my oar, and he carried me a ten or fifteen hours' journey in an hour and a half! Now, my little fellow, don't ask me what happened next, for you won't get an answer."

"All right," say I, "so much for the panther; now for the crocodile?" Says Abdul, "I have often seen the tip of his nose above the water. And how wickedly he smiles as he lies basking in the sun, stretched at full length on the shelving sandbanks of the river. If I'd had a gun I should have made his acquaintance. But my license has expired....

"Still, I can tell you one good yarn. One day Kanchi the gypsy woman was sitting on the bank of the river trimming bamboo with a bill-hook, with her young goat tethered near by. All at once the crocodile appeared on the surface, seized the billy-goat by the leg and dragged it into the water. With one jump the gypsy woman landed astride on its back, and began sawing with her sickle at the throat of the "demon-lizard", over and over again. The beast let go of the goat and plunged into the water...."

"And then? And then?" comes my excited question. "Why," says Abdul, "the rest of the story went down to the bottom of the river with the crocodile. It will take some time to get it up again. Before I see you again I will send somebody to find out about it, and let you know." Abdul has never come again; perhaps he is still looking for news.

So much, then, for my travels in the palanquin. Outside the palanquin there were days when I assumed the role of teacher, and the railings of the verandah were my pupils. They were all afraid of me, and would cower before me in silence. Some of them were very naughty, and cared absolutely nothing for their books. I told them with dire threats that when they grew up they would be fit for nothing but casual labour. They bore the marks of my beatings from head to foot, yet they did not stop being naughty. For it would not have done for them to stop, it would have made an end of my game.

There was another game too, with my wooden lion. I heard stories of poojah sacrifices and decided that a lion sacrifice would be a magnificent thing. I rained blows on his back—with a frail little stick. There had to be a "mantra", of course, otherwise it would not have been a proper poojah:

"Liony, liony, off with your head,
    Liony, liony, now you are dead.
    Woofle the walnut goes clappety clap,
                Snip, snop, SNAP!"

I had borrowed almost every word in this from other sources; only the word walnut was my own. I was very fond of walnuts. From the words "clappety clap" you can see that my sacrificial knife was made of wood. And the word "snap" shows that it was not a strong one.

III

The clouds have had no rest since yesterday evening. The rain is pouring incessantly. The trees stand huddled together in a seemingly foolish manner; the birds are silent. I call to mind the evenings of my boyhood.

We used then to spend our evening in the servants' quarters. At that time English spellings and meanings did not yet lie like a nightmare on my shoulders. My third brother used to say that I ought first to get a good foundation of Bengali and only afterwards to go on to the English superstructure. Consequently, while other school-boys of my age were glibly reciting "I am up", "He is down", I had not even started on B, A, D, bad and M, A, D, mad.

In the speech of the nabobs the servants' quarters were then called "tosha-khana". Even though our house had fallen far below its former aristocratic state, these old high-sounding names, "tosha-khana", "daftar-khana", "baithak-khana", still clung to it.

On the southern side of this "tosha-khana", a castor oil lamp burned dimly on a glass stand in a big room; on the wall was a picture of Ganesh and a crude country painting of the goddess Kali, round which the wall lizards hunted their insect prey. There was no furniture in the room, merely a soiled mat spread on the floor.

You must understand that we lived like poor people, and were consequently saved the trouble of keeping a good stable.

Away in a corner outside, in a thatched shed under a tamarind tree, was a shabby carriage and an old horse. We wore the very simplest and plainest clothes, and it was a long time before we even began to wear socks. It was luxury beyond our wildest dreams when our tiffin rations went beyond Brajeswar's inventory and included a loaf of bread, and butter wrapped in a banana leaf. We adapted ourselves easily to the broken wrecks of our former glory.

Brajeswar was the name of the servant who presided over our mat seat. His hair and beard were grizzled, the skin of his face dry and tight-drawn; he was a man of serious disposition, harsh voice, and deliberately mouthed speech. His former master had been a prosperous and well-known man, yet necessity had degraded him from that service to the work of looking after neglected children like us. I have heard that he used to be a master in a village school. To the end of his life he kept this school-masterly language and prim manner. Instead of saying "The gentlemen are waiting", he would say "They await you", and his masters smiled when they heard him. He was as finicky about caste matters as he was conceited. When bathing he would go down into the tank and push back the oily surface water five or six times with his hands before taking a plunge. When he came out of the tank after his bath Brajeswar would edge his way through the garden in so gingerly a way that one would think he could only keep caste by avoiding all contact with this unclean world that God has made. He would talk very emphatically about what was right and what was wrong in manners and behaviour. And besides, he held his head a little on one side, which made his words all the more impressive.

But with all this there was one flaw in his character as *guru*. He cherished secretly a suppressed greed for food. It was not his method to place a proper portion of food on our plates before the meal. Instead, when we sat down to eat he would take one *luchi*[1] at a time, and dangling it at a little distance ask, "Do you want any more?" We knew by the tone of his voice what answer he desired, and I usually said that I didn't want any. After that he never gave us an opportunity to change our minds. The milk bowls also had an irresistible attraction for him—an attraction which I never felt at all. In his room was a small wired foodsafe with shelves in it. In it was a big brass bowl of milk, and *luchis* and vegetables on a wooden platter. Outside the wire-netting the cat prowled longingly to and fro sniffing the air.

From my childhood upwards these short commons suited me very well. Small rations cannot be said to have made me weak. I was, if anything, stronger, certainly not weaker, than boys who had unlimited food. My constitution was so abominably sound that even when the most urgent need arose for avoiding school, I could never make myself ill by fair means or foul. I would get wet through shoes, stockings and all, but I could not catch cold. I would lie on the open roof in the heavy autumn dew; my hair and clothes would be scaked, but I never had the slightest suspicion of a cough. And as for that sign of bad digestion known as stomachache, my stomach was a complete stranger to it, though my tongue made use of its name with mother in time of need. Mother would smile to herself and not feel the least anxiety; she would merely call the servant and tell him to go and tell my teacher that he should not teach me that evening. Our old-fashioned mothers used to think it no great harm if the boys occasionally took a holiday from study. If we had fallen into the hands of these present-day mothers, we should certainly have been sent to the teacher, and had our ears tweaked into the bargain. Perhaps with a knowing smile they would have dosed us with castor oil, and our pains would have been

---

1. Fried pancake known in Hindusthani as *puri*.

permanently cured. If by chance I got a slight temperature no one ever called it fever, but "heated blood". I had never set eyes on a thermometer in those days. Dr. Nilmadhav would come and place his hand on my body, and then prescribe as the first day's treatment castor oil and fasting. I was allowed very little water to drink, and what I had was hot, with a few sugar-coated cardamoms for flavouring. After this fast, the *mouralā fish* soup and soft-boiled rice which I got on the third day seemed a veritable food for the gods.

Serious fever I do not remember, and I never heard the name of malaria. I do not remember quinine—that castor oil was my most distasteful medicine. I never knew the slightest scratch of a surgeon's knife; and to this very day I do not know what measles and chicken-pox are. In short, my body remained obstinately healthy. If mothers want their children to be so healthy that they will be unable to escape from the school master, I recommended them to find a servant like Brajeswar. He would save not only food bills but doctor's bills also, especially in these days of mill flour and adulterated ghee and oil. You must remember that in those days chocolate was still unknown in the bazaar. There was a kind of rose lollipop to be had for a pice. I do not know whether modern boy's pockets are still made sticky by this sesamum-covered sugar-lump, with its faint scent of roses. It has certainly fled in shame from the houses of the respectable people of to-day. What has become of those cone-shaped packets of fried spices? And those cheap sesamum sweetmeats? Do they still linger on? If not, it is no good trying to bring them back.

Day after day, in the evenings, I listened to Brajeswar reciting the seven cantos of Krittibas' *Rāmayanā*. Kishori Chatterjee used to drop in sometimes while the reading was going on. He had by heart *Pānchāli*[2] versions of the whole

---

2. A kind of folk-version very popular in Bengal.

Rāmayanā, tune and all. He took possession at once of the seat of authority, and superseding Krittibas, would begin to recite his simple folk-stanzas in great style:

> "Lakshman O hear me
> Greatly I fear me
> Dangers are near me."

There was a smile on his lips, his bald head gleamed, the song poured from his throat in a torrent of sound, the rhymes jingled and rang verse after verse, like the music of pebbles in a brook. At the same time he would be using his hands and feet in acting out the thought. It was Kishori Chatterjee's greatest grief that Dadabhai, as he called me, could not join a troupe of strolling players and turn such a voice to account. If I did that, he said, I should certainly make my name.

By and by it would grow late and the assembly on the mat would break up. We would go into the house, to Mother's room, haunted and oppressed on our way by the terror of devils. Mother would be playing cards with her aunt, the inlaid parquet floor gleamed like ivory, a coverlet was spread on the big divan. We would make such a disturbance that Mother would soon throw down her hand and say, "If they are going to be such a nuisance, auntie, you'd better go and tell them stories." We would wash our feet with water from the pot on the verandah outside, and climb on to the bed, pulling "Didima" with us. Then it would begin—stories of the magical awakening of the princess and her rescue from the demon city. The princess might wake, but who could waken me? ... In the early part of the night the jackals would begin to howl, for in those days they still haunted the basements of some of the old houses of Calcutta with their nightly wail.

IV

When I was a little boy Calcutta city was not so wakeful at night as it is now. Nowadays, as soon as the day of sunlight is over, the day of electric light begins. There is not much work done in it, but there is no rest, for the fire continues, as it were, to smoulder in the charcoal after the blazing wood has burnt itself out. The oil mills are still, the steamer sirens are silent, the labourers have left the factories, the buffaloes which pull the carts of jute bales are stabled in the tin-roofed sheds. But the nerves of the city are throbbing still with the fever of thought which has burned all day in her brain. Buying and selling go on as by day in the shops that line the streets, though the fire is a little choked with ash. Motors continue to run in all directions, emitting all kinds of raucous grunts and groans, though they no longer run with the zest of the morning. But in those old times which we knew, when the day was over whatever business remained undone wrapped itself up in the black blanket of the night and went to sleep in the darkened ground-floor premises of the city. Outside the house the evening sky rose quiet and mysterious. It was so still that we could hear, even in our own street, the shouts of the grooms from the carriages of those people of fashion who were returning from taking the air in Eden Gardens by the side of the Ganges.

In the hot season of *Chaitra* and *Vaishākh* the hawkers
would go about the streets shouting "I-i-i-ce". In a big pot
full of lumps of ice and salt water were little tin containers
of what we called "kulpi" ice—nowadays ousted by the more
fashionable ices or "ice-cream". No one but myself knows
how my mind thrilled to that cry as I stood on the verandah
facing the street. Then there was another cry, "*Bela* flowers".
Nowadays for some reason one hears little of the gardeners
baskets of spring flowers—I do not know why. But in those
days the air was full of the scent of the thickly strung *bel*
flowers which the women and girls wore in their hairknots.
Before they went to bathe the women would sit outside their
rooms with a hand-mirror set up before them, and dress their
hair. The knot would be skilfully bound with the black hair-
braid into all sorts of different styles. They wore black-
bordered Chandernagore saries, skilfully crinkled before use
by pleating and twisting after the fashion of those days. The
barber's wife would come to scrub their feet with pumice and
paint them with red lac. She and her like were the
gossipmongers of the women's courts.

The crowds returning from office or from college did not
then, as they do now, rush to the football fields, clinging in
swarms to the foot-boards of the trams. Nor did they crowd
in front of cinema halls as they returned. There was some
active interest shown in drama, but alas! I was only a child
then.

Children of those times got no share in the pleasures of
the grown-ups, even from a distance. If we were bold enough
to go near, we should be told, "Off with you, go and play."
But if we boys made the amount of noise appropriate for
proper play, it would then be, "Be quiet, do." Not that the
grownups themselves conducted their pleasures and
conversation in silence, by any means; and now and again we
would stand on the fringe of their far-flung jubilations, as

though sprinkled by the spray of a waterfall. We would hang over the verandah on our side of the courtyard, staring across at the brilliantly lit reception-room on the other side. Big coaches would roll up to the portico one after another. Some of our elder brothers conducted the guests upstairs from the front door, sprinkling them with rose-water from the sprinkler, and giving each one a small buttonhole or nosegay of flowers. As the dramatic entertainment proceeded, we could hear the sobs of the "highcaste *kulin* heroine", but we could make out nothing of their meaning, and our longing to know grew intense. We discovered later that though the sobber was certainly highcaste, "she" was merely our own brother-in-law. But in those days grown-ups and children were kept apart as strictly as men and women with their separate apartments. The singing and dancing would go on in the blaze of the drawing-room chandeliers, the men would pull at the hookah, the women of the family would take their betel boxes and sit in the subdued light behind their screen, the visiting ladies would gather in these retired nooks, and there would be much whispering of intimate domestic gossip. But we children were in bed by this time, and lay listening as our maid-servants Piyari or Sankari told us stories—"In the moonlight, expanding like an opening flower..."

V

A little before our day it was the fashion among wealthy householders to run *jātrās* or troupes of actors. There was a great demand for boys with shrill voices to join these troupes. One of my uncles was patron of such an amateur company. He had a gift for writing plays, and was very enthusiastic about training the boys. All over Bengal professional companies were the rage, just as the amateur companies were in aristocratic circles. Troupes of players sprang up like mushrooms on all sides, under the leadership of some well-known actor or other. Not that either patron or manager was necessarily of high family or good education. Their fame rested on their own merits. *Jātrā* performances used to take place in our house from time to time. But we children had no part in them, and I managed to see only the preliminaries. The verandah would be full of members of the company, the air full of tobacco smoke. There were the boys, long-haired, with dark rings of weariness under their eyes, and, young as they were, with the faces of grown men. Their lips were stained black with constant betel chewing. Their costumes and other paraphernalia were in painted tin boxes. The entrance door was open, people swarmed like ants into the courtyard, which, filled to the brim with the seething, buzzing mass, spilled over into the lane and beyond into the Chitpore Road. Then nine o'clock would strike, and Shyam would swoop down on me like a hawk on a dove, grip my elbow with his rough, gnarled hand, and tell me that Mother was calling me to go to bed. I would hang my head in confusion at being thus publicly dragged away, but would bow to superior force and go to my bedroom. Outside all was tumult and shouting, outside flared the lighted chandeliers, but in my room there was not a sound and a brass lamp burned low on its stand. Even in sleep I was dimly conscious of the crash of the cymbals marking the rhythm of the dance.

The grown-ups usually forbade everything on principle, but on one occasion for some reason or other they decided to be indulgent, and the order went forth that the children also might come to the play. It was a drama about Nala and Damayanti. Before it began we were sent to bed till half-past eleven. We were assured again and again that when the time came we should be roused, but we knew the ways of the grown-ups, and we had no faith at all in these promises—*they* were adults, and *we* were children!

That night, however, I did drag my unwilling body to bed. For one thing, Mother promised that she herself would come and wake me. For another thing, I always had to pinch myself to keep myself awake after nine o'clock. When the time came I was awakened and brought outside, blinking and bewildered in the dazzling glare. Light streamed brightly from coloured chandeliers on the first and second storeys, and the white sheets spread in the courtyard made it seem much bigger than usual. On one side were seated the people of importance, senior members of the family, and their invited guests. The remaining space was filled with a motley crowed of all who cared to come. The performing company was led by a famous actor wearing a gold chain across his stomach, and old and young crowded together in the audience. The majority of the audience were what the respectable would call "riff-raff". The play itself had been written by men whose hands were trained only to the villager's reed pen, and who had never practised on the letters of an English copy book. Tunes, dances, and story had all sprung from the very heart of rural Bengal, and no pundit had polished their style.

We went and sat by our elder brothers in the audience, and they tied up small sums of money in kerchiefs and gave them to us. It was the custom to throw this money on to the stage at the points where applause was most deserved. By this means the actors gained some extra profit and the family a good reputation.

The night came to an end, but the play would not. I never knew whose arms gathered up my limp body, nor where they carried me. I was far too much ashamed to try to find out. I, a fellow who had been sitting like an equal among the grown-ups and doling out *baksheesh,* to be disgraced in this way before a whole courtyard full of people! When I woke up I was lying on the divan in my mother's room; it was very late, and already blazing hot. The sun had risen, but I had not risen!—Such a thing had never happened before.

Nowadays the city's pleasures flow on in an unbroken stream. There is always a cinema show somewhere, and whoever pleases may see it for a trifling sum. But in those days entertainments were few and far between, like water holes dug in the sandy bed of a dried up river, three or four miles apart. Like these too they lasted only a few hours, and the wayfarers hastily gathered round, drinking from their cupped hands to quench their thirst.

The old days were like a king's son who, from time to time on festive occasions, or according to his whim, distributes rich and royal gifts to all within his jurisdiction. Modern days are like a merchant's son, sitting at the cross-roads on some great highway with many kinds of cheap and tawdry goods spread glittering before him, and drawing his customers by highway and byway from every side.

VI

Brajeswar was the head-servant, and his second-in-command was called Shyam. He came from Jessore, and he was a real countryman, speaking in a dialect strange to Calcutta. He would say "tenārā" and "onārā" for "tārā" and "orā", "jāti" and "khāti" for "jete" and "khete". He used to call us affectionately "Domani". He had a dark skin, big eyes, long hair glistening with oil, and a strong, well-built body. He was really good at heart, and affectionate and kind to children. He used to tell us stories of dacoits. Dacoity stories filled men's houses then as universally as the fear of ghosts filled their minds. Even today dacoity is not uncommon; murder, assault and looting still take place, and the police still do not catch the right man. But nowadays this is only a news-item, it has none of the fascination of romance. In those days dacoities were woven into stories, and passed from mouth to mouth for long periods. In my childhood men were still to be met with who in their prime had been members of dacoit gangs. They were all past-masters in the science of the *lathi*, and were surrounded by disciples eager to learn the art of single-stick. Men salaamed at the very mention of their names. Dacoity then was usually not a mere matter of rash, headstrong bloodshed. As bodily strength and skill played their part, so did a generous, gallant mind. Moreover, gentlemen's houses often contained an exercise-ground for the practice of *lathi-*

fighting, and those who made a name on these grounds were acknowledged as masters even by dacoits, who gave them a wide berth. Many zemindars made a profession of dacoity. There was a story of a man of this class who had stationed his desperadoes at the mouth of a river. It was new moon, and poojah night, and when they returned, carrying a severed head to the temple in honour of Kali Kankali[1], the zemindar clapped his hands to his head and cried out, "What have you done? It's my son-in-law!"

We heard also about the exploits of the dacoits Raghu and Bishu. They used to give notice before they attacked, and there was nothing underhand in their dacoity. When their rallying-cry was heard in the distane, the blood of the villagers ran cold. But their code forbade them to lay hands on women. On one occasion, in fact, a woman even succeeded in "robbing the robbers", by appearing to them dressed as Kali, brandishing the goddess's heavy curved blade, and claiming their devout offerings.

One day there was a display of dacoits' wrestling feats in our house. They were all strong young fellows, big-made, dark-skinned, and long-haired. One man tied a cloth round a heavy grain-pounder, seized the cloth in his teeth, and then flung the pounder upwards and backwards over his shoulder. Another got a man to grasp him by his shaggy hair, and then whirled him round and round by a mere turn of his head. Using a long pole as support and lever, they leaped up to the second storey. Then one man stood with his hands clasped above his bent head, and others shot through the aperture like diving birds. They also showed how it was possible for them to manage a dacoity twenty or thirty miles away, and the same night be found sleeping peacefully in their beds like law-

---

1. The destructive aspect of the goddess Kali, pictured with a necklace of skulls.

abiding citizens. They had a pair of very long poles with a piece of wood lashed cross-wise in the middle of each as a foot-rest. These poles were called *rang-pā* (stilts). When walking with the tops of the poles held in the hands, and the feet on these footholds, one stride had the value of ten ordinary steps, and a man could run faster than a horse. I used to encourage boys at Santiniketan to practise stilt-walking—though without any idea of committing dacoity! My imagination mingled such pictures of dacoity feats with Shyam's stories with gruesome effect, so that I have often spent the evening with my arms huddled against my pounding heart!

Sunday was a holiday. On the previous evening the crickets were chirping in the thickets outside in the south garden, and the story was about Raghu the highwayman. My heart went pit-a-pit in the dim light and flickering shadows of the room. The next day in my holiday leisure I climbed into the palanquin. It began to move unbidden, its destination unknown, and my mind, enthralled still by the magic of the previous night's romance, knew a thrill of delicious fear. In the silent darkness my pulses attuned themselves to the rhythmic shouts of the bearers, and my body grew numb with terrified anticipation.

On the boundless expanse of plain the air quivers in the heat, in the distance glistens the Kali tank; the sand sparkles, the wide-spreading *pākur* tree leans from the bank of the river over the cracked, ruined *ghāt*. My romance-fed terrors are concentrated on that thick clump of reeds, and in the shade of the tree on that unknown plain. Nearer and nearer we approach, quicker and quicker beats my heart. Above the reeds can be seen the tips of one or two stout bamboo staves. The bearers will stop there to change shoulders. They will drink, and wind wet towels round their heads. And then?...

Then with a blood-curdling shout, the dacoits are upon us....

VII

From morning till night the mills of learning went on grinding. To wind up this creaking machinery was the work of *Shejadādā*[1], Hemendranath. He was a stern taskmaster, but it is useless now to try to hide the fact that the greater part of the cargo with which he sought to load our minds was tipped out of the boat and sent to the bottom. My learning at any rate was a profitless cargo. If one seeks to key an instrument to too high a pitch, the strings will snap beneath the strain.

Shejadādā made all arrangements for the education of his eldest daughter. When the time came he got her admitted into the Loreto Convent School, but even before that she had been given a foundation in Bengali. He also gave Protibha a thorough training in western music, which, however, did not cause her to lose her skill in Indian music. Among the gentlemen's families of that time she had no equal in Hindustani songs.

It is one merit of western music that its scales and exercises demand diligent practice, that it makes for a sensitive ear, and that the discipline of the piano allows of no slackness in the matter of rhythm.

Meanwhile she had learnt Indian music from her earliest years from our teacher Vishnu. In this school of music I also

---

1. Third elder brother.

had to be entered. No present-day musician, whether famous or obscure, would have consented to touch the kind of songs with which Vishnu initiated us. They were the very commonest kind of Bengali folk songs. Let me give you a few examples:

"A gypsy lass is come to town
    To paint tattoos, my sister.
The painting's nothing, so they tell,
Yet she on me has cast a spell,
And makes me weep and mocks me well,
    By her tattoos, my sister."

I remember also a few fragmentary lines, such as:

"The sun and moon have owned defeat,
    the firefly's lamp lights up the stage;
    the Moghul and the Pathan flag,
    the weaver reads the Persian page."

and:

"Your daugher-in-law is the plantain tree,
    Mother of Ganesh, let her be.
For if but one flower should blossom and grow
She will have so many children you won't
    know what to do."

Lines too come back to me in which one can catch a glimpse of old forgotten histories:

"There was a jungle of thorn and burr,
    Fit for the dogs alone;
    There did he cut for himself a throne..."
    The modern custom is first to practise scales—*sā-re-ga-ma*, etc., on the harmonium, and then to teach some simple Hindu songs. But the wise supervisor who was then in charge

of our studies understood that boyhood has its own childish needs, and that these simple Bengali words would come much more easily to Bengali children than Hindi speech. Besides this, the rhythm of this folk music defied all accompaniment by *tabla*. It danced itself into our very pulses. The experiment thus made showed that just as a child learns his first enjoyment of literature from his mother's nursery rhymes, he learns his first enjoyment of music also from the same source.

The harmonium, that bane of Indian music, was not then in vogue. I practised my songs with my *tamburā* resting on my shoulder, I did not subject myself to the slavery of the keyboard.

It was no one's fault but my own, that nothing could keep me for many days together in the beaten track of learning. I strayed at will, filling my wallet with whatever gleanings of knowledge I chanced upon. If I had been disposed to give my mind to my studies, the musicians of these days would have had no cause to slight my work. For I had plenty of opportunity. As long as my brother was in charge of my education, I repeated Brahmo songs with Vishnu in an absentminded fashion. When I felt so inclined I would sometimes hang about the doorway while *Shejadādā* was practising, and pick up the song that was going on. Once he was singing to the *Behāg* air, "O thou of slow and stately tread". Unobserved I listened and fixed the tune in my mind, and astounded my mother—an easy task—by singing it to her that evening. Our family friend Srikantha Babu was absorbed in music day and night. He would sit on the verandah, rubbing *chāmeli* oil on his body before his bath, his *hookāh* in his hand, and the fragrance of amber-scented tobacco rising into the air. He was always humming tunes, which attracted us boys around him. He never *taught* us songs, he simply sang them to us, and we picked them up almost without knowing it. When he could no longer restrain his enthusiasm, he would stand up and dance, accompanying himself on the *sitār*. His big expressive eyes shone with enjoyment, he burst into the song, *Mai chhōrō brajaki bāsari,* and would not rest content till I joined in too.

In matters of hospitality, people kept open house in those days. There was no need for a man to be intimately known before he was received. There was a bed to be had at any time, and a plate of rice at the regular meal times for any who chanced to come. One day, for example, one such stranger guest, who carried his *tamburā* wrapped in a quilt on his shoulder, opened his bundle, sat down, and stretched his legs at ease on one side of our reception room, and Kanai the *hookāh*-tender offered him the customary courtesy of the *hookāh*.

Pān, like tobacco, played a great part in the reception of guests. In those days the morning occupation of the women in the inner apartments consisted in preparing piles of *pān* for the use of those who visited the outer reception room. Deftly they placed the lime on the leaf, smeared catechu on it with a small stick, and putting in the appropriate amount of spice folded and secured it with a clove. This prepared *pān* was then piled into a brass container, and a moist piece of cloth, stained with catechu, acted as cover. Meanwhile, in the room under the staircase outside, the stir and bustle of preparing tobacco would be going on. In a big earthenware tub were balls of charcoal covered with ash, the pipes of the *hookāhs* hung down like snakes of *Nāgaloka,* with the scent of rosewater in their veins. This amber scent of tobacco was the first welcome extended by the household to those who climbed the steps to visit the house. Such was the invariable custom then prescribed for the fitting reception of guests. That overflowing bowl of *pān* has long since been discarded, and the caste of *hookāh*-tenders have thrown off their liveries and taken to the sweetmeat shops, where they knead up three-day-old *sandesh* and refashion it for sale.

That unknown musician stayed for a few days, just as he chose. No one asked him any questions. At dawn I used to drag him from his mosquito curtains and make him sing to me. (Those who have no fancy for regular study revel in study that is irregular). The morning melody of *Bansi hāmāri re* ... would rise on the air.

After this, when I was a little older, a very great musician called Jadu Bhatta came and stayed in the house. He made one big mistake in being determined to teach me music, and consequently no teaching took place. Nevertheless, I did casually pick up from him a certain amount of stolen knowledge. I was very fond of the song *Ruma jhuma barakhā āju bādara⁻ā* ... which was set to a *Kāfi* tune, and which remains to this day in my store of rainy season songs. But unfortunately just at this time another guest arrived without warning, who had a name as a tiger-killer. A Bengali tiger-killer was a real marvel in those days, and it followed that I remained captivated in his room for the greater part of the time. I realise clearly now what I never dreamed of then, that the tiger whose fell clutches he so thrillingly described could never have bitten him at all; perhaps he got the idea from the snarling jaws of the stuffed Museum tigers. But in those days I busied myself eagerly in the liberal provision of *pān* and tobacco for this hero, while the distant strains of *kānārā* music fell faintly on my indifferent ears.

So much for music. In other studies the foundation provided by *Shejadādā* was equally generously laid. It was the fault of my own nature that no great matter came of it. It was with people like me in view that Ramprosad Sen wrote, "O Mind, you do not understand the art of cultivation." With me, the work of cultivation never took place. But let me tell you of a few fields where the ploughing at least was done.

I got up while it was still dark and practised wrestling— on cold days I shivered and trembled with cold. In the city was a celebrated one-eyed wrestler, who gave me practice. On the north side of the outer room was an open space known as the "granary". The name clearly had survived from a time when the city had not yet completely crushed out all rural life, and a few open spaces still remained. When the life of the city was still young our granary had been filled with the whole year's store of grain, and the *ryots* who held their land on lease from us brought to it their appointed portion. It was here that the lean-to shed for wrestling was built against the compound wall. The ground had been prepared by digging and loosening the earth to a depth of about a cubit and pouring over it a maund of mustard oil. It was mere child's play for the wrestler to try a fall with me there, but I would manage to get well smeared with dust by the end of the lesson, when I put on my shirt and went indoors.

Mother did not like to see me come in every morning so covered with dust—she feared that the colour of her son's skin would be darkened and spoiled. As a result, she occupied herself on holidays in scrubbing me. (Fashionable housewives of today buy their toilet preparations in boxes from western shops; but then they used to make their unguent with their own hands. It contained almond paste, thickened cream, the rind of oranges and many other things which I forget. If only I had learnt and remembered the receipt, I might have set up a shop and sold it as "Begum Bilash" unguent, and made at least as much money as the *sandesh-wāllāhs*.) On Sunday mornings there was a great rubbing and scrubbing on the verandah, and I would begin to grow restless to get away. Incidentally a story used to go about among our school fellows that in our house babies were bathed in wine as soon as they were born, and that was the reason for our fair European complexions.

When I came in from the wrestling ground I saw a Medical College student waiting to teach me the lore of bones. A whole skeleton hung on the wall. It used to hang at night on the wall of our bedroom, and the bones swayed in the wind and rattled together. But the fear I might otherwise have felt had been overcome by constantly handling it, and by learning by heart the long, difficult names of the bones.

The clock in the porch struck seven. Master Nilkamal was a stickler for punctuality, there was no chance of a moment's variation. He had a thin, shrunken body, but his health was as good as his pupil's, and never once, unluckily for us, was he afflicted even by a headache. Taking my book and slate I sat down before the table, and he began to write figures on the blackboard in chalk. Everything was in Bengali, arithmetic, algebra and geometry. In literature I jumped at one bound from *Sitār Banabās*[2] to *Meghnādbadh Kābya*[3]. Along with this there was natural science. From time to time Sitanath Datta would come, and we acquired some superficial knowledge of science by experiments with familiar things. Once Heramba Tattvaratna, the Sanskrit scholar, came; and I began to learn the Mugdhabodh Sanskrit grammar by heart, though without understanding a word of it.

In this way, all through the morning, studies of all kinds were heaped upon me, but as the burden grew greater, my mind contrived to get rid of fragments of it; making a hole in the enveloping net, my parrot-learning slipped through its meshes and escaped—and the opinion that Master Nilkamal expressed of his pupil's intelligence was not of the kind to be made public.

In another part of the verandah is the old tailor, his thick-lensed spectacles on his nose, sitting bent over his sewing, and ever and anon, at the prescribed hours, going through the

---

2. "Sita in the Forest," by Iswarchandra Vidyasagar.
3. An Epic on the death of Meghnād (son of Rāvana in *Rām(E)yana*) by Michael Madhusudan Dutta.

ritual of his Namāz⁴. I watch him and think what a lucky fellow Niāmat is. Then, with my head in a whirl from doing sums, I shade my eyes with my slate, and looking down see in front of the entrance porch Chandrabhān the *durwan* combing his long beard with a wooden comb, dividing it in two and looping it round each ear. The assistant *durwan,* a slender boy, is sitting near by, a bracelet on his arm, and cutting tobacco. Over there the horse has already finished his morning allowance of gram, and the crows are hopping round pecking at the scattered grains. Our dog Johnny's sense of duty is aroused and he drives them away barking.

I had planted a custard-apple seed in the dust which continual sweeping had collected in one corner of the verandah. All agog with excitement, I watched for the sprouting of the new leaves. As soon as Master Nilkamal had gone, I had to run and examine it, and water it. In the end my hopes went unfulfilled—the same broom that had gathered the dust together dispersed it again to the four winds.

Now the sun climbs higher, and the slanting shadows cover only half the courtyard. The clock strikes nine. Govinda, short and dark, with a dirty yellow towel slung over his shoulder, takes me off to bathe me. Promptly at half past nine comes our monotonous, unvarying meal—the daily ration of rice, *dāl* and fish curry—it was not much to my taste.

The clock strikes ten. From the main street is heard the hawker's cry of "Green Mangoes"—what wistful dreams it awakens! From further and further away resounds the clanging of the receding brass-peddler, striking his wares till they ring again. The lady of the neighbouring house in the lane is drying her hair on the roof, and her two little girls are playing with shells. They have plenty of leisure, for in those days girls were

---

4. Muslim devotional exercises.

not obliged to go to school, and I used to think how fine it would have been to be born a girl. But as it is, the old horse draws me in the rickety carriage to my Andamans, in which from ten to four I am doomed to exile.

At half past four I return from school. The gymnastic master has come, and for about an hour I exercise my body on the parallel bars. He has no sooner gone than the drawing master arrives.

Gradually the rusty light of day fades away. The many blurred noises of the evening are heard as a dreamy hum resounding over the demon city of brick and mortar. In the study room an oil lamp is burning. Master Aghor has come and the English lesson begins. The black-covered reader is lying in wait for me on the table. The cover is loose; the pages are stained and a little torn; I have tried my hand at writing my name in English in it, in the wrong places, and all in capital letters. As I read I nod, then jerk myself awake again with a start, but miss far more than I read. When finally I tumble into bed I have at last a little time to call my own. And there I listen to endless stories of the king's son travelling over an endless, trackless plain.

VIII

When I see the roofs of modern houses, uninhabited by either men or ghosts, I realise vividly the change that has taken place between those times and these. I have already mentioned how the *brahma-daitya*[1] of the *bādām* tree has fled, unable to endure the modern atmosphere of excessive learning. On the cornice where rumour had it that he had rested his foot, the crows snatch and squabble over our discarded mango stones. And men too restrict themselves nowadays to the confined, boxed-in rooms of the lower storeys, and pass their time within four walls.

My mind goes back to the parapet-surrounded roof of the inner apartments. It is evening, and Mother has spread her mat and seated herself, with her friends gossiping round her. Their talk has no need of authentic information, it is only a means of passing the time. There was then no regular supply of valuable and varied ingredients to fill the day, which was not, as now, a closely woven mesh, but like a net of loose texture, full of holes. And therefore, stories and rumours, laughter and jokes, all in the lightest vein, filled both the social gatherings of the men and the women's assemblies. Among Mother's friends the first in importance was Braja

---

1. A class of formidable ghosts believed to be the spirits of departed Brahmins.

Acharji's sister, who was called "Acharjini". She was the daily purveyor of news to the company. Almost every day she picked up, (or made up!) and brought with her, every item of fantastic, ominous news in the country. By this means expenditure on all ceremonies calculated to avert impending calamity or the evil eye, was greatly increased.

Into this assembly I imported from time to time my recently acquired book-learning. I informed them that the sun is nine crores of miles distant from the earth. From the second part of my *ôju-Pāth* I recited a portion of Valmiki's *Rāmāyana* in the original complete with Sanskrit terminations. Mother was no judge of the accuracy of her son's pronunciation, but the range of his learning filled her with awe, and seemed to her far to outrun the nine-crore miles journey of light. Who would have thought that any except Naradmuni himself could recite all these *slōkas*?

This inner apartment roof was entirely the women's domain, and had a close conection with the store room. The sun's rays fell full upon it, so it was used for preparing lemons for pickle. The women used to sit there with brass vessels full of *kalāi* paste, and while their hair was drying they made pulse-balls with their deft, quick fingers. The maid-servants who had washed the soiled linen came here to spread it in the sun, for the *dhoby* had little work in those days. Green mangoes were cut in slices and dried into *āmsi*. The mango juice was poured layer after layer into black stone moulds of all sizes and all patterns[2]. A pickle of young jack-fruit stood there to season in sun-warmed mustard oil. Catechu, scented with the fragrant screw-pine, would be prepared with great care.

I had a special reason for remembering this item. When my school-master informed me that he had heard the fame

---

2. This preparation is called *āmsatta*.

of my family's screw-pine catechu, it was not difficult to understand his meaning. What he had heard of, he wished to become acquainted with. So to preserve the good name of my family, I occasionally climbed secretly to the roof containing the screw-pine catechu, and—what shall I say? "Appropriated" a piece or two sounds better than "stole". For even kings and emperors may make "appropriations" when need arises, or indeed even if it does not, but vulgar "stealing" is punished by prison or impaling.

In the pleasant sunlight of the cold weather it was the family tradition for the women to sit on the roof gossiping, driving off crows and passing the time of day. I was the only younger brother-in-law in the house, the guardian of my sister-in-law's "āmsatta", and her friend and ally in many other trival pursuits. I used to read to them from Bangādhipa Parājaya[3]. From time to time the duty of cutting up betel-nut would devolve on me. I could cut betel very finely. My sister-in-law would never admit that I had any other good quality, so much so that she even made me angry with God for giving me such a faulty appearance. But she found no difficulty in speaking in exaggerated fashion of my skill in cutting betel. Therefore the work of betel-cutting used to go on at a fine pace. But for a long time now, for want of anyone to encourage me, the hand that was so killed in fine betel-cutting has perforce busied itself in other fine work.

Around all this women's work spread on the roof there lingered the aroma of village life. These occupations belonged to the days when there was a pounding-room in the house, when confectionery balls were made, when the maid-servants sat in the evening rolling on their thighs the cotton wicks for the oil lamps, when invitations came from neighbours' houses to the ceremonies of the eighth day after birth. Modern

3. "The Defeat of the King of Bengal."

children do not hear fairy stories from their mothers' lips, they read them for themselves in printed books. Pickles and chutney are bought from the Newmarket by the bottleful, each bottle corked and sealed with wax.

Another relic of a bygone village life was the *chandimandap*, the outer verandah where the school was held. Not only the boys of the house, but those of the neighbourhood, also, made there their first attempt to search letters on palm-leaves. I suppose that I too must have traced out my first laborious letters on that verandah, but I have no clear memory of the child I then was, who seems as far removed as the farthest planet of the solar system, and I possess no telescope which can bring him into view.

The first thing I remember about reading after this is the terrible story of Ýanāmārka Muni's school, and of the *avatār* Narasiṃha tearing the bowels of Hiraṇyakaśipu; I think also that there was a lead-plate engraving of it in the same book— and I remember also reading a few *slōkas* of Chānakya.

My chief holiday resort was the unfenced roof of the outer apartments. From my earliest childhood till I was grown up, many varied days were spent on that roof in many moods and thoughts. When my father was at home his room was on the second floor. How often I watched him at a distance, from my hiding place at the head of the staircase. The sun had not yet risen, and he sat on the roof silent as an image of white stone, his hands folded in his lap. From time to time he would leave home for long periods in the mountains, and then the journey to the roof held for me the joy of a voyage through the seven seas. Sitting on the familiar first floor verandah I had daily watched through the railings the people going about the street. But to climb to that roof was to be raised beyond the swarming habitations of men. When I went on to the roof my mind strode proudly over prostrate Calcutta to where the last blue of the sky mingled with the last green of the earth; my eye fell on the roofs of countless houses, of all shapes and sizes, high and low, with the shaggy tops of trees between.

I would go up secretly to this roof, usually at midday. The midday hours have always held a fascination for me. They are like the night of the daytime, the time when the *Sannyāsi* spirit in every boy makes him long to quit his familiar surroundings. I put my hand through the shutter and drew the bolt of the door. Right opposite the door was a sofa, and I sat there in perfect bliss of solitude. The servants who acted as my warders had eaten their fill and become drowsy, and yawning and stretching had betaken themselves to sleep on their mats. The afternoon sunlight deepened into gold, and the kite rose screaming into the sky. The bangle-seller went crying his wares down the opposite lane. His sudden cry would penetrate to where the housewife lay with her loosened hair falling over her pillow, a maidservant would bring him in, and the old bangle-seller dexterously kneaded the tender fingers as he fitted on the glass bangles that took her fancy. The hushed pause of that old-world midday is now no more, and the hawkers of the silent time are heard no longer. The girl who in those days had married status, nowadays has still not attained it, she is learning her lessons in the second class. Perhaps the bangle-seller runs, pulling a rickshaw, down that very lane.

The roof was like what I imagined the deserts of my books to be, a sheer expanse of quivering haze. A hot wind ran panting across it, whirling up the dust, the blue of the sky paled above it. Moreover, in this roof desert there appeared an oasis. Nowadays the pipe water does not reach the upper floors, but then it ran even up to the second floor rooms. Like some young Livingstone of Bengal, alone and unaided, I secretly sought and found a new Niagara, the private bathroom. I would turn on the tap, and the water would run all over my body. I then took a sheet from the bed and dried myself, looking the picture of innocence.

Gradually the holiday drew towards its close, and four struck on the gateway clock. The face of the sky on Sunday evenings was always very ill-favoured. There fell across it the shadow of the coming Monday's gaping jaws, already swallowing it in dark eclipse. Below at last a search had been instituted for the boy who had given his guards the slip, for now it was tiffin time. This part of the day was a red-letter time for Brajeswar. He was in charge of buying the tiffin. In those days the shop-keepers did not make thirty or forty per cent profit on the price of *ghee,* and in odour and flavour the tiffin was still unpoisoned. When we were lucky enough to get them, we lost no time in eating up our *kochuri, singārā,* or even *ālur dom.* But when the time came round and Brajeswar, with his neck still further twisted, called to us, "Look *babu,* what I have brought you today", what was usually to be found in his cone of paper was merely a handful of fried groundnuts. It was not that I did not like this, but its attractiveness lay in its price. I never made the least objection, not even on the days when only sesamum *gojā* came out of the palm-leaf wrapper.

The light of day begins to grow murky. Once more with a gloomy spirit, I make the round of the roof. I gaze down at the scene below, where a procession of geese has climbed out of the tank. People have begun to come and go again on the steps of the *ghāt,* the shadow of the banyan tree lengthens across half the tank, the driver of a carriage and pair is yelling at the pedestrians in the street.

IX

In this way the days passed monotonously on. School grabbed the best part of the day, and only fragments of time in the morning and evening slipped through its clutching fingers. As soon as I entered the classroom, the benches and tables forced themselves rudely on my attention, elbowing and jostling their way into my mind. They were always the same—stiff, cramping, and dead. In the evening I went home, and the oil lamp in our study-room, like a stern signal, summoned me to the preparation of the next day's lessons. There is a kind of grass-hopper which takes the colour of the withered leaves among which it lurks unobserved. In like manner my spirit also shrank and faded among those faded, drab-coloured days.

Now and again there came to our courtyard a man with a dancing bear, or a snake charmer playing with his snakes. Now and again the visit of a juggler provided some little novelty. Today the drums of the juggler and snake-charmer no longer beat in our Chitpore Road. From afar they have salaamed to the cinema, and fled before it from the city. Games were few and of very ordinary kinds. We had marbles, we had what is called "bat-ball," a very poor distant relation of cricket, and there were also top-spinning and kite-flying. All the games of the city children were of this same lazy kind. Football, with all its running and jumping about on a big field, was still in its overseas home. And so I was fenced in by the deadly sameness of the days, as though by an imprisoning hedge of lifeless, withered twigs.

In the midst of this monotony there played one day the flutes of festivity. A new bride came to the house, slender gold bracelets on her delicate brown hands. In the twinkling of an eye the cramping fence was broken, and a new being came into view from the magic land beyond the bounds of the familiar. I circled around her at a safe distance, but I did not dare to go near. She was enthroned at the centre of affection, and I was only a neglected, insignificant child.

The house was then divided into two suites of rooms. The men lived in the outer, and the women in the inner apartments. The ways of the nabobs obtained there still. I remember how my elder sister was walking on the roof with the new bride at her side, and they were exchanging intimacies freely. As soon as I tried to go near, however, I brought reprimand on my head, for these quarters were outside the boundaries laid down for boys. I saw myself obliged to go back crest-fallen to my shabby retreat of former days.

The monsoon rain, rushing down suddenly from the distant mountains, undermines the ancient banks in a moment, and that is what happened now. The new mistress brought a new régime into the house. The quarters of the bride were in the room adjoining the roof of the inner suite. That roof was under her complete control. It was there that the leaf-plates were spread for the dolls' weddings. On such feast days, boy as I was, I became the guest of honour. My new sister-in-law could cook well, and enjoyed feeding people, and I was always ready to satisfy this craving for playing the hostess. As soon as I returned from school some delicacy made with her own hands stood ready for me. One day she gave me shrimp curry with yesterday's soaked rice, and a dash of chillies for flavouring, and I felt that I had nothing left to wish for. Sometimes when she went to stay with relatives and I did not see her slippers outside the door of her room, I would go in a temper and steal some valuable object from her room, and lay the foundation of a quarrel. When she returned and missed it, I had only to make such a remark as "Do you expect *me* to keep an eye on your room when you go away? Am I a watchman?" She would pretend to be angry and say, "You have no need to keep an eye on the room. Watch you own hands." Modern women will smile at the *naïveté* of their predecessors who knew how to entertain only their own brothers-in-law, and I daresay they are right. People today are much more grown-up in every way than they were then. Then we were all children alike, both young and old.

X

And so began a new chapter of my lonely Bedouin life on the roof, and human company and friendship entered it. Across the roof kingdom a new wind blew, and a new season began there. My brother Jyotidada played a large part in this change. At that time my father finally left our home at Jorasanko. Jyotidada settled himself into that outside second-floor room, and I claimed a little corner of it for my own.

No *purdah* was observed in my sister-in-law's apartments. That will strike no one as strange today, but it then sounded an unimaginable depth of novelty. A long time even before that, when I was a baby, my second brother had returned from England to enter the Civil Service. When he went to Bombay to take up his first post he astonished the neighbourhood by taking off his wife with him before their very eyes. And as if it was not enough to take her away to a distant province, instead of leaving her in the family home, he made no provision for proper privacy on the journey. That was a terrible breach of propriety. Even the relatives felt as if the sky had fallen on their heads.

A style of dress suitable for going out was still not in vogue among women. It was this sister-in-law who first introduced the manner of wearing the *sari* and blouse which is now customary. Little girls had not then begun to wear frocks or let their hair hang in plaits—at least not in our family. The little ones used to wear the tight Rajput pyjamas instead of the traditional *sari*. When the Bethune School was first opened my eldest sister was quite young. She was one of the pioneers who made the road to education easy for girls. She was very fair, uniquely so for this country. I have heard that once when she was going to school in her palanquin the police detained her, thinking her in her Rajput dress to be an English girl who had been kidnapped.

I said before that in those days there was no bridge of intimacy between adults and children. Into the tangle of these old customs Jyotidada brought a vigorously original mind. I was twelve years younger than he, and that I should come to his notice in spite of such a difference in age is in itself surprising. What was more surprising is that in my talks with him he never called me impudent or snubbed me. Thanks to this, I never lacked courage to think for myself. Today I live with children, I try all kind of subjects of conversation, but I find them dumb. They hesitate to ask questions. They seem to me to belong to those old times when the grown-ups talked and the children remained silent. The self-confidence that doubts and questions is the mark of the children of the new age; those of the former age are known by a meek and docile acceptance of what they are told.

A piano appeared in the terrace room. There came also modern varnished furniture from Bowbazar. My breast swelled with pride, as the cheap grandeur of modern times was displayed before eyes inured to poverty. At this time the fountain of my song was unloosed. Jyotidada's hands would stray about the piano as he composed and rattled off tunes in various new styles, and he would keep me by his side as he did so. It was my work to fix the tunes which he composed so rapidly by setting words to them then and there.

At the end of the day a mat and pillow were spread on the terrace. Nearby was a thick garland of *bel* flowers on a silver plate, in a wet handkerchief, a glass of iced water on a saucer, and some *chhānchi pān* in a bowl. My sister-in-law would bathe, dress her hair and come and sit with us. Jyotidada would come out with a silk *chaddar* thrown over his shoulders, and draw the bow across his violin, and I would sing in my clear treble voice. For providence had not yet taken away the gift of voice it had given me, and under the sunset sky my song rang out across the house-tops. The south wind came in great gusts from the distant sea, the sky filled with stars.

My sister-in-law turned the whole roof into a garden. She arranged rows of tall palms in barrels and beside and around them *chāmeli, gandharāj, rajanigandhā, karabi* and *dolan-champā*. She considered not at all the possible damage to the roof—we were all alike unpractical visionaries.

Akshay Chaudhuri used to come almost every day. He himself knew that he had no voice, other people knew it even better. In spite of that nothing could stop the flow of his song. His special favourite was the *Behāg* mode. He sang with his eyes shut, so he did not see the expression on the faces of his hearers. As soon as anything capable of making a noise came to hand, he took it and turned it into a drum, beating it in happy absorption, biting his lips with his teeth in his earnestness. Even a book with a stiff binding would do very well. He was by nature a dreamy kind of man, one could see no difference between his working days and his holidays.

The evening party broke up, but I was a boy of nocturnal habits. All went to lie down, I alone would wander about all night with the *Brahma-daitya*. The whole district was steeped in silence. On moonlight nights the shadows of the lines of palm-trees on the terrace lay in dream-patterns on the floor. Beyond the terrace the top of the *sishu* tree swayed and tossed in the breeze, and its leaves gleamed as they caught the light. But for some reason, what caught my eye more than anything was a squat room with a sloping roof built over the staircase of the sleeping house on the opposite side of the lane. It stood like a finger pointing for ever towards I knew not what.

It may have been one or two in the morning, when in the main street in front a wailing chant arose—*Bolō-Hari Hari-bōl.*[1]

---

1. Funeral chant of the Hindus.

XI

It was the fashion then in every house to keep caged birds. I hated this, and the worst thing of all to me was the call of a *koel* imprisoned in a cage in some house in the neighbourhood. *Bouthākrun*[1] had acquired a Chinese *shyama*. From under its covering of cloth its sweet whistling rose continuously, a fountain of song. Besides this there were other birds of all kinds, and their cages hung in the west verandah. Every morning a bird-seed and insect hawker provided the birds' food. Grass-hoppers came from his basket, and gram-flour for the grain-eating birds.

Jyotidada gave me proper answers in my difficulties, but as much could not be expected from the women. Once *Bouthākrun* took a fancy for keeping pet squirrels in cages. I said it wasn't right, and she told me not to set myself up to be her teacher. That could hardly be called a reasoned reply, and consequently, instead of wasting time in bickering, I privately set two of the little creatures free. After that too I had to listen to a certain amount of scolding, but I made no retort.

There was a permanent quarrel between us which was never made up, which was as follows.

---

1. Sister-in-law.

There was a smart fellow called Umesh. He used to go the rounds of the English tailoring shops and buy up for an old song all their scraps, remnants and strips of many coloured silk, and make up women's garments from them with the addition of a bit of net and cheap lace. He would open his paper parcel and spread them carefully out before the eyes of the women, extolling them as "the very latest fashion". The women could not resist the attraction of such a *mantra*, but I disliked it all intensely. Again and again, unable to contain myself, I made known my objections, but all the answer I got was "Don't be cheeky". I used to tell *Bouthākrun* that the old-fashioned black-bordered white saries, and the Dacca ones, were far better and more tasteful than these. I sometimes wonder, do modern brothers-in-law never open their mouths when they see their *Boudidis* robed in these modern georgette saries, with their faces painted like dolls? Even *Bouthākrun* decked out in Umesh's handiwork was not as bad as they are. Ladies then were at least not so guilty of forgery in dress or complexion.

I was however always beaten by *Bouthākrun* in argument, because she would never deign to give a logical answer; and I was beaten too in chess, in which she was an expert.

As I have referred to Jyotidada I ought to give a little more information about him, to make him better known. To do that I must go back to rather earlier days.

He had to go very often to Shelidah to see after the business of the zemindari. Once when he was travelling for this purpose he took me also with him. This was quite contrary to custom in those days, in fact it was what people would have called "altogether *too* much". He certainly considered that this travelling away from home was a kind of peripatetic schooling. He realised that my nature was attuned to ramblings in the open air, that in such surroundings it nourished itself spontaneously. A little later, when I was more mature, it was in Shelidah that my nature developed.

The old indigo factory was still standing, with the river Padma in the distance. The zemindari office was on the ground floor, and our living quarters on the upper floor. In front of them was a very large terrace. Beyond were tall casuarina trees, which had grown in stature with the growing prosperity of the indigo-trading sahebs. Today the blustering shouts of the sahebs are completely silent. Where is now the indigo factory's steward, that "messenger of death"? Where the troop of bailiffs, loins girded up and *lāthis* on shoulder? Where is the dining hall with its long tables, where the sahebs rode back from their business in the town and turned night into day? The feasting reached its height, the dancing couples whirled round the room, the blood coursed madly through the veins in the swelling intoxication of champagne—and the authorities never heard the appealing cries of the wretched *ryots,* whose weary journey took them only to the District Jail. All traces of those days have vanished, save one record alone—the two graves of two of the sahebs. The high casuarina trees bend and sway in the wind, and sometimes at midnight the grandsons and grand-daughters of the former *ryots* see the ghosts of the sahebs wandering in the deserted waste of garden.

Here I revelled in my solitude. I had a little corner room, and my days of ample leisure were spacious as the wide-spreading terrace. It was the leisure of a strange and unknown region, unfathomable as the dark waters of some ancient tank. The *bou-kathā-kao*[2] calls incessantly, my fancy unweariedly takes wing. Meantime my note-book is gradually filled with verses. They were like the blossoms of the mango-tree's first flowering in the month of *Māgh,* destined like them to wither forgotten.

---

2. Also called "makwa-pāko", an Indian species of cuckoo. Both names are imitations of the call.

In those days if a young boy, or still more a young girl, laboriously counted out the fourteen syllables and wrote two lines of verse, the wise critics of the country used to hail it as a unique and unparalleled achievement.

I saw in the papers and magazines the names of these girl-poets, and their verses also were published. Nowadays these carefully constructed metres and crude rhyming platitudes have vanished along with the names of their authors, and the names of countless modern girls have appeared in their stead.

Boys are less bold and far more self-conscious than girls. I do not remember any young boy-poet writing verse in those days, except myself. My sister's son, who was older than I, explained to me one day that if one poured words into a fourteen-syllable mould, they would condense into verse. I soon tried this magic formula for myself. The lotus of poetry blossomed in no time in this fourteen-syllabled form and even the bees found a foothold on it. The gulf between me and the poets was bridged, and from that time on I have struggled to overtake them.

I remember how, when I was in the lowest class of the *chhātra britti*[3] our superintendent Govinda Babu heard a rumour that I wrote poetry. He thereupon ordered me to write, thinking that it would redound to the credit of the Normal School. There was nothing for it but to write, to read my work before my class-mates, and to hear the verdict—"this verse is assuredly stolen goods". The cynics of that day did not know that when I increased in worldly wisdom I should grow shrewd in stealing, not words but thoughts. Yet it is these stolen goods which are valuable.

I remember once composing a poem in the *Payār* and *Tripadi* metres, in which I lamented that as one swims to pluck

___
3. This corresponds roughly to the modern transition from "primary" to "secondary" education.

the lotus it floats further and further away on the waves raised by one's own arms, and remains always out of reach. Akshay Babu took me round to the houses of his relatives and made me recite it to them. "The boy has certainly a gift for writing", they said.

Bouthākrun's attitude was just the opposite. She would never admit that I should ever make a success of writing. She would say mockingly that I should never be able to write like Bihari Chakravarti. I used to think despondently that even if I were placed in a far lower class than he, she would then be prevented from so disregarding her little poet-brother-in-law's disapprobation of women's fashions.

Jyotidada was very fond of riding. He actually took even *Bouthākrun* riding along Chitpore Road to the Eden Gardens. In Shelidah he gave me a pony, a beast that was no mean runner. He sent me to give the pony a run on the open *rath-talā* field.[4] I did as I was bidden, in continual imminent danger of a fall on that uneven ground. That I did not fall was solely because he was so determined that I should *not* do so .Shortly afterwards Jyotidada sent me out riding on the roads of Calcutta also. Not on the pony, but on a high-spirited thoroughbred. One day it galloped straight in through the porch, with me on its back, to the courtyard where it was accustomed to be fed. From that day on I had nothing more to do with it.

I have referred elsewhere to the fact that Jyotidada was a practised shot. He was always eager for a tiger-hunt. One day the *shikāri* Visvanath brought news that a tiger was living in the Shelidah jungle, and Jyotidada at once furbished up his gun and prepared for sport. Surprising to say, he took me with him. It never seemed to occur to him that there could be any danger.

---

4. The field reserved in a Bengali village for the celebration of the car-festival.

Visvanath was indeed an expert *shikāri*. He knew that there was nothing manly about hunting from a *māchān*. He would call the tiger out and shoot face to face, and he never missed his aim.

The jungle was dense, and in its lights and shadows the tiger refused to show himself. A rough kind of ladder was made by cutting footholds in a stout bamboo, and Jyotidada climbed up with his gun ready to hand. As for me, I was not even wearing slippers, I had not even that poor instrument with which to beat and humiliate the tiger. Visvanath signed to us to be on the alert, but for some time Jyotidada could not even see the tiger. After long straining of his bespectacled eyes he at last caught a glimpse of one of its markings in the thicket. He fired. By a lucky chance the shot pierced the animal's backbone, and it was unable to rise. It roared furiously, biting at all the sticks and twigs within reach, and lashing its tail. Thinking it over, I know that it is not in the nature of tigers to wait so long and patiently to be killed. I wonder if some one had had the forethought to mix a little opium with its feed on the previous night? Otherwise, why such sound sleep?

There was another occasion when a tiger came to the jungles of Shelidah. My brother and I set out on elephants to look for him. My elephant lurched majestically on, uprooting cane from the sugar-cane fields and munching as he went, so that it was like riding on an earthquake. The jungle lay ahead of us. He crushed the trees with his knees, pulled them up with his trunk and cast them to the ground. I had previously heard tales of terrible possibilities from Visvanath's brother Chamru, how sometimes the tiger leaps on to the elephant's back and clings there, digging in his claws. Then the elephant trumpeting with pain, rushes madly through the forest, and whoever is on his back is dashed against the trees till arms, legs and head are crushed out of all recognition. That day, as I sat my elephant, the image of myself thus being pounded to a jelly filled my imagination from first to last. For very shame I concealed my fear, and glanced from side to side in nonchalant fashion, as though to say, "Let me but catch a glimpse of the tiger, and then!..." The elephant entered the densest part of the jungle, and coming to a certain place, suddenly stood stock-still. The *māhout* made no attempt to urge it forward. He had clearly more respect for the tiger's powers as a *shikāri* than for my brother's. His great anxiety was undoubtedly that Jyotidada should so wound the tiger as to drive it to desperation. Suddenly the tiger leaped from the jungle, swift as the thunder-charged storm from the cloud. We are accustomed to the sight of a cat, dog, or jackal, but here were shoulders of terrific bulk and power, yet no sense of heaviness in that perfectly proportioned strength. It crossed the open fields at a canter in the full blaze of the midday sun. What loveliness, ease and speed of motion! The land was empty of crops; here indeed was a setting in which to feast one's eyes on the running tiger, this wide stretch of golden stubble drenched in the noonday sunlight.

There is one more story that may prove amusing. In Shelidah the gardener used to pluck flowers and arrange them in the vases. I took a fancy to write poetry with a pen dipped in the coloured essences of flowers. But the moisture that I could obtain by squeezing was not sufficient to wet the tip of my pen. I decided that it must be done by machinery. It would do, I thought, if I had a cup-shaped wooden sieve and a pestle revolving in it. It could be turned by an arrangement of ropes and pulleys. I made known my wants to Jyotidada. It may be that he smiled to himself, but he gave no outward sign. He issued instructions, and the carpenter brought wood. The machine was ready. I filled the wooden cup with flowers, but turn the ropes of the pestle as I would the flowers, merely turned to mud and not a drop of essence ran out. Jyotidada saw that the essence of flowers was incompatible with the grinding of machinery, yet he never laughed at me.

This was the only occasion in my life on which I tried my hand at engineering. It is said in the *sāstras* that there is a god who compasses the humiliation of those who ignore their own limitations. That god cast a mocking glance that day upon my engineering, and from that time I have not so much as laid hands on any kind of instrument, not even on a *sitār* or an *esrāj*.

I described in my *Reminiscences* how Jyotidada went bankrupt in his attempt to run a *swadeshi* steamer company on the rivers of Bengal in competition with the Flotilla Company. *Bouthākrun's* death had taken place before then. Jyotidada gave up his rooms on the third storey and finally built himself a house on a hill at Ranchi.

XII

A new chapter in the life of the third storey room now opened, as I took up my abode there. Up to that time it had been merely one of my gypsy haunts, like the palanquin and the granary, and I roamed from one to another. But when *Bouthākrun* came a garden appeared on the roof, and in the room a piano was established. Its flow of new tunes symbolised the changed tenor of my life.

Jyotidada used to arrange to have his coffee in the mornings in the shade of the staircase room on the eastern side of the terrace. At such times he would read to us the first draft of some new play of his. From time to time I also would be called upon to add a few lines with my unpractised hand. The sun's rays gradually invaded the shade, the crows cried hoarsely to each other as they sat on the roof keeping an eye upon the bread-crumbs. By ten o'clock the patch of shade had dwindled away and the terrace grew hot.

At midday Jyotidada used to go down to the office on the ground floor. *Bouthākrun* peeled and cut fruit and arranged it carefully on a silver plate, along with a few sweetmeats made with her own hands, and strewed a few rose petals over it. In a tumbler was coconut milk or fruit-juice or *tāl shāns* (fresh palmyra kernels), cooled in ice. Then she covered it with a silk kerchief embroidered with flowers, put it on a

Moradabad tray, and despatched it to the office at tiffin time, about one or two o'clock.

Just then *Bangadarśan*[1] was at the height of its fame, and *Suryamukhi* and *Kundanandini*[2] were familiar figures in every house. The whole country thought of nothing else but what had happened and what was gong to happen to the heroines.

When *Bangadarśan* came there was no midday nap for anyone in the neighbourhood. It was my good fortune not to have to snatch for it, for I had the gift of being an acceptable reader. *Bouthākrun* would rather listen to my reading aloud than read for herself. There were no electric fans then, but as I read I shared the benefits of *Bouthākrun's* hand fan.

---

1. A famous Bengali magazine edited by the well-known Bengali novelist, Bankim Chandra Chatterji.
2. Characters in Bankim Chandra's novel.

XIII

Now and again Jyotidada used to go for change of air to a garden house on the bank of the Ganges. The Ganges shores had then not yet lost caste at the defiling touch of English commerce. Both shores alike were still the undisturbed haunt of birds, and the mechanised dragons of industry did not darken the light of heaven with the black breath of their upreared snouts.

My earliest memory of our life by the Ganges is of a small two-storey house. The first rains had just fallen. Cloud shadows danced on the ripples of the stream, cloud shadows lay dark upon the jungles of the further shore. I had often composed songs of my own on such days, but that day I did not do so. The lines of Vidyapati came to my mind, *e bharā bādara māha bhādara śūnya mandira mōr.*[1] Moulding them to my own melody and stamping them with my own musical mood, I made them my own. The memory of that monsoon day, jewelled with that music on the Ganges shore, is still preserved in my treasury of rainy season songs. I see in memory the tree-tops struck ever and again by great gusts of wind, till their boughs and branches were tangled together in an ecstasy of play. The boats and dinghies raised their white sails and

---

1. Brimmed with rain is the month of Bhadra (August-September), empty my spirit's dwelling stands.

scudded before the gale, the waves leaped against the *ghāt* with sharp, slapping sounds. *Bouthākrun* came back and I sang my song to her. She listened in silence and said no word of praise. I must then have been sixteen or seventeen years old. We used to have arguments even then about various matters, but no longer in the old spirit of childish wrangling.

A little while after we removed to Moran's Garden. That was a regular palace. The rooms, of varying heights, had coloured glass in their windows, the floors were of marble, and steps led down from the long verandah to the very edge of the Ganges. Here a fit of wakefulness by night came upon me, and I used to pace to and fro, as I did later on the banks of the Sabarmati. That Garden is no longer in existence, the iron jaws of the Dundee Mills have crushed and swallowed it.

At the mention of Moran's Garden there comes back the memory of our occasional picnics under the *bakul* tree. The food owed its flavour not to spices but to the hands that prepared it. How I remember our sacred-thread ceremony, when we two boys were fed by *Bouthākrun* with the ceremonial rice and fresh ghee! For those three days we had our fill of tasty and savoury dishes.

It was a great annoyance to me that it was so difficult for me to fall ill. All the other boys in the house could manage it, and then they would enjoy *Bouthākrun's* personal care. Not only did they enjoy her care, but they took up all her time, and my own share of it was correspondingly diminished.

So came to an end that page of the history of the third storey, and with it *Bouthākrun* also passed away. After that the second floor became my own domain, but it was no longer as in the old days.

I have wandered in my story up to the very gateway of my young manhood. I must return to the territory of my boyhood once more.

Now I must give some account of my sixteenth year. At its very entrance stands *Bhārati*.[2] Nowadays the whole country seethes with the excitement of bringing out papers, and I can well understand the strength of that passion when I look back on my own madcap escapades. That a boy like me, with neither learning nor talents, should succeed in establishing himself in that *salon,* or at least in escaping reprimand there, shows what a youthful spirit was abroad everywhere. *Bangadarśan* was then the only magazine in the country controlled by a mature hand. As for ours, it was a medley of the mature and the crude. Baḍadada's contributions were as difficult to understand as they were to write; and side by side with them stood a story of mine, the raw verbosity of whose style I was too young to appraise, nor did others apparently possess the critical judgment to do so.

The time has come to say something of Baḍadada. Jyotidada held court in that third storey room, and Baḍadada in our south verandah. At one time he plunged into the deepest problems of metaphysics, far outside the range of our comprehension. There were few to listen to what he wrote and thought, and he would not lightly let any man go who showed himself willing to be audience. Nor would the man himself soon relinquish Baḍadada, but what he claimed from him was not alone the privilege of listening to metaphysics. One such man attached himself whose name I do not remember, but everyone called him "The Philosopher". My other brothers made great fun of him, not only about his love for mutton chops, but about his endless stream of varied and urgent necessities. Besides philosophy, Baḍadada then began to take

---

2. Monthly magazine founded by Jyotidada (Jyotirindranath Tagore) and first edited by the Poet's eldest brother Dwijendranath Tagore, referred to here as Baḍadada. It ran for about half a century.

great interest in the construction of mathematical problems. The verandah would be full of papers, covered with figures, flying about in the south wind. Baḍadada could not sing, but he used to play an English flute, not for the sake of the music, but in order to measure mathematically the notes of each scale. After that he occupied himself for a time in writing *Svapna-Prayāna*. To start with, he began to experiment in verse-making, weighing the sound-values of Sanskrit words in the scales of Bengali rhythm, and so creating new forms. Many of these attempts he retained, but many he threw away, and torn pages were scattered everywhere. After that he started to write his book of poems, but he rejected far more than he kept, for he was not easily satisfied with his work. We had not the sense to pick up and keep all these discarded lines. As he wrote he would read his work, and people would gather round him to listen. Our whole household was intoxicated with this wine of poetry. Sometimes in the midst of his reading he would burst into a great shout of laughter. His laughter was ample and generous as the skies, but woe betide the man who sat within reach when the fit took him; he received slaps on the back to shake his very soul. The south verandah was the living fountain of the life of Jorasanko, but the fountain dried up when Baḍadada went to live at the Santiniketan *asrama*. I remember, however, times spent in the garden opposite that south verandah, when with mind made listless by the touch of the autumn sun I composed and sang a new song: "Today in the autumn sun, in my dreams of dawn, a nameless yearning fills my soul." I remember also a song made in the quivering heat of one blazing noon: "In this listless abandon of spirit, I know not what games I kept on playing with my own self."

Another striking thing about Baḍadada was his swimming. He would swim backwards and forwards across our tank at least fifty times. When he lived at Panihati Garden he used to swim far out into the Ganges. With his example before us we also learned to swim as boys. We started to learn by ourselves. We would wet our pyjamas and then pull them up tight so as to fill them with air. In the water they swelled out round our waists like balloons, and we could not possibly sink. When I was older and stayed on the river-lands[3] of Shelidah, I once swam across the Padma. This was not as wonderful an achievement as it sounds. The Padma was full of alluvial islands which broke the force of its current, so that the feat was not worthy of any great respect. Still, it was certainly a story with which to impress others, and I have used it so many times. When I went as a boy to Dalhousie, my father never forbade me to wander about by myself. With an alpenstock in my hand I traversed the footpaths, climbing one hill after another. It was most amusing to scare myself with my own make-believe. Once while going steeply downhill I stepped on a heap of withered leaves at the foot of a tree. My foot slipped a little and I saved myself with my stick. But perhaps I might not have been able to stop myself! I wondered how long it would have taken to roll down the steep slope and fall into the waterfall far below. I described to Mother with picturesque inventiveness all that might have happened. Then, wandering in the deep pinewoods, I might suddenly have come upon a bear that also was certainly something worth talking about. As nothing ever really happened I stored up all these imaginary adventures in my mind. The story of my swimming across the Padma was much of a piece with this class of romances.

When I was seventeen I had to leave the editorial board of *Bhārati*, for it was then decided that I should go to England. Further it was considered that before sailing I should live with

---

3. Tracts of rich alluvial land often found as islands in the great rivers (Beng. *Char*).

Mejadādā[4] for a time to get some grounding in English manners. He was then a judge in Ahmedabad, and *Meja-Bouthākrun* and her children were in England, waiting for *Mejadādā* to get a furlough and join them.

I was torn up by the roots and transplanted from one soil to another, and had to get acclimatised to a new mental atmosphere. At first my shyness was a stumbling-block at every turn. I wondered how I should keep my self-respect among all these new acquaintances. It was not easy to habituate myself to strange surroundings, yet there was no means of escape from them; in such a situation a boy of my temperament was bound to find his path a rough one.

My fancy, free to wander, conjured up pictures of the history of Ahmedabad in the Moghul period. The judge's quarters were in Shahibag, the former palace grounds of the Muslim kings. During the daytime *Mejadādā* was away at his work, the vast house seemed one cavernous emptiness, and I wandered about all day like one possessed. In front was a wide terrace, which commanded a view of the Sabarmati river, whose knee-deep waters meandered along through the sands. I felt as though the stone-built tanks, scattered here and there along the terrace, held locked in their masonry wonderful secrets of the luxurious bathing-halls of the Begums.

We are Calcutta people, and history nowhere gives us any evidence of its past grandeur there. Our vision had been confined to the narrow boundaries of these stunted times. In Ahmedabad I felt for the first time that history had paused, and was standing with her face turned towards the aristocratic past. Her former days were buried in the earth like the treasure of the *yakshas*.[5] My mind received the first suggestion for the story of *Hungry Stones*.

---

4. Second brother, Satyendranath Tagore.
5. Demons who guard treasure.

How many hundred years have passed since those times! Then in the *nahabat-khānā*, the minstrel's gallery, an orchestra played day and night, choosing tunes appropriate to the eight periods of the day. The rhythmic beat of horses' hoofs echoed on the streets, and great parades were held of the mounted Turkish cavalry, the sun glittering on the points of their spears. In the court of the Pādshāh whispered conspiracies were ominously rife. Abyssinian eunuchs, with drawn swords, kept guard in the inner apartments. Rose-water fountains played in the *hamāms* of the Begums, the bangles tinkled on their arms. Today Shahibag stands silent, like a forgotten tale; all its colour has faded, and its varied sounds have died away; the splendours of the day are withered and the nights have lost their savour.

Only the bare skeleton of those old days remained, its head a naked skull whose crown was gone. It was like a mummy in a museum, but it would be too much to say that my mind was able fully to re-clothe those dry bones with flesh and blood and restore the original form. Both the first rough model, and the background against which it stood, were largely a creation of the fancy. Such patch-work is easy when little is known and the rest has been forgotten. After these eighty years even the picture of myself that comes before me does not correspond line for line with the reality, but is largely a product of the imagination.

After I had stayed there for some time *Mejadādā* decided that perhaps I should be less homesick if I could mix with women who could familiarise me with conditions abroad. It would also be an easy way to learn English. So for a while I lived with a Bombay family. One of the daughters of the house was a modern educated girl who had just returned with all the polish of a visit to England. My own attainments were only ordinary, and she could not have been blamed if she had ignored me. But she did not do so. Not having any store of

book-learning to offer her, I took the first opportunity to tell
her that I could write poetry. This was the only capital I had
with which to gain attention. When I told her of my poetical
gift, she did not receive it in any carping or dubious spirit,
but accepted it without question.. She asked the poet to give
her a special name, and I chose one for her which she thought
very beautiful. I wanted that name to be entwined with the
music of my verse, and I enshrined it in a poem which I made
for her. She listened as I sang it in the *Bhairavi* mode of early
dawn, and then said, "Poet, I think that even if I were on my
death-bed your songs would call me back to life." There is
an example of how well girls know how to show their
appreciation by some pleasant exaggeration. They simply do
it for the pleasure of pleasing. I remember that it was from
her that I first heard praise of my personal appearance,—
praise that was often very delicately given.

For example, she asked me once very particularly to
remember one thing: "You must never wear a beard. Don't
let anything hide the outline of your face." Everyone knows
that I have not followed that advice. But she herself did not
live to see my disobediene proclaimed upon my face.

In some years, birds strange to Calcutta used to come and
build in that banyan tree of ours. They would be off again
almost before I had learnt to recognize the dance of their
wings, but they brought with them a strangely lovely music
from their distant jungle homes. So, in the course of our life's
journey, some angel from a strange and unexpected quarter
may cross our path, speaking the language of our own soul,
and enlarging the boundaries of the heart's possessions. She
comes unbidden, and when at last we call for her she is no
longer there. But as she goes, she leaves on the drab web of
our lives a border of embroidered flowers, and for ever and
ever the night and day are for us enriched.

XIV

The Master-Workman, who made me, fashioned his first model from the native clay of Bengal. I have described this first model, which is what I call my boyhood, and in it there is little admixture of other elements. Most of its ingredients were gathered from within, though the atmosphere of the home and the home people counted for something too. Very often the work of moulding goes no further than this stage. Some people get hammered into shape in the book-learning factories, and these are considered in the market to be goods of a superior stamp.

It was my fortune to escape almost entirely the impress of these mills of learning. The masters and pundits who were charged with my education soon abandoned the thankless task. There was Jnanachandra Bhattacharya, the son of Anandachandra Vedāntabāgish, who was a B.A. He realised that this boy could never be driven along the beaten tract of learning. The teachers of those days, alas! were not so strongly convinced that boys should all be poured into the mould of degree-holding respectability. There was then no demand that rich and poor alike should all be confined within the fenced-off regions of college studies. Our family had no wealth then, but it had a reputation, so the old traditions held good, and they were indifferent to conventional academic success. From the lower classes of the Normal School we were transferred to De Cruz's Bengal Academy. It was the hope of my guardians that even if I got nothing else, I should get enough mastery of spoken English to save my face. In the Latin class I was deaf and dumb, and my exercise books of all kinds kept from beginning to end the unrelieved whiteness of a widow's cloth. Confronted by such unprecedented determination not to study, my class-teacher complained to Mr. De Cruz, who explained that we were not born for study, but for the purpose of paying our monthly fees. Jnana Babu was of a similar opinion, but found means of keeping me occupied nevertheless. He gave me the whole of *Kumārsambhava*[1] to learn by heart. He shut me in a room and gave me *Macbeth* to translate. Then Pundit Ramsarbaswa read *Sakuntalā* with me. By setting me free in this way from the fixed curriculum, they reaped some reward for their labours. These then were the materials that formed my boyish mind, together with what other Bengali books I picked up at random.

I landed in England, and foreign workmanship began to play a part in the fashioning of my life. The result is what is known in chemistry as a compound. How capricious is Fortune!—I went to England for a regular course of study, and a desultory start was made, but it came to nothing. *Meja-Bouthān* was there, and her children, and my own family circle absorbed nearly all my interest. I hung about around the school-room, a master taught me at the house, but I did not give my mind to it.

However, gradually the atmosphere of England made its impression on my mind, and what little I brought back from that country was from the people I came in contact with. Mr. Palit finally succeeded in getting me away from my own family. I went to live with a doctor's family, where they made me forget that I was in a foreign land. Mrs. Scott lavished

1. A work of Kalidasa.

on me a genuine affection, and cared for me like a mother. I had then been admitted to London University, and Henry Morley was teaching English literature. His teaching was no dry-as-dust exposition of dead books. Literature came to life in his mind and in the sound of his voice, it reached to our inner being where the soul seeks its nourishment, and nothing of its essential nature was lost. With his guidance, I found the study of the Clarendon Press books at home to be an easy matter and I took upon myself to be my own teacher. For no reason at all Mrs. Scott would sometimes fancy that I did not look well, and would become very worried about me. She did not know that the portals of sickness had been barred against me from childhood. I used to bathe every morning in ice-cold water—in fact, in the opinion of the doctors, it was almost a sacrilege that I should survive such flagrant disregard of the accepted rules!

I was able to study in the University for three months only, but I obtained almost all my understanding of English culture from personal contacts. The Artist who fashions us takes every opportunity to mingle new elements in his creation. Three months of close intimacy with English hearts sufficed for this development. Mrs. Scott made it my duty each evening till eleven o'clock to read aloud from poetic drama and history by turn. In this way I did a great deal of reading in a short space of time. It was not prescribed class study, and my understanding of human nature developed side by side with my knowledge of literature. I went to England but I did not become a barrister. I received no shock calculated to shatter the original framework of my life—rather East and West met in friendship in my own person. Thus it has been given me to realise in my own life the meaning of my name.[2]

---

2. The poet's name *Rabi* means the sun, which does not distinguish between East and West.

HUNGRY STONES

AND OTHER STORIES

Preface

The stories contained in this volume were translated by several hands. The version of 'The Victory' is the author's own work. The seven stories which follow it were translated by Mr. C.F. Andrews, with the author's help. Assistance has also been given by the Rev. E.J. Thompson, Panna Lal Basu, Prabhat Kumar Mukerji, and the Sister Nivedita.

The Hungry Stones

My kinsman and myself were returning to Calcutta from our Puja trip when we met the man in a train. From his dress and bearing we took him at first for an up-country Mahomedan, but we were puzzled as we heard him talk. He discoursed upon all subjects so confidently that you might think the Disposer of All Things consulted him at all times in all that He did. Hitherto we had been perfectly happy, as we did not know that secret and unheard-of forces were at work, that the Russians had advanced close to us, that the English had deep and secret policies, that confusion among the native chiefs had come to a head. But our newly acquired friend said with a sly smile: "There happen more things in heaven and earth, Horatio, than are reported in your newspapers." As we had never stirred out of our homes before, the demeanour of the man struck us dumb with wonder. Even on the most trivial topic he would quote science or comment on the Vedas or repeat quatrains from some Persian poet, and as we had no knowledge of science or the Vedas or Persian, our admiration for him increased, and my kinsman, a theosophist, was convinced that our fellow-passenger must have been supernaturally inspired by some strange magnetism or occult power or astral body. He listened with devotional rapture to even the tritest saying of our extraordinary companion, and secretly took notes of the conversation. I think that the man saw this and was pleased by it. When the train reached its junction, we stood in the waiting-room for our connection. It was 10 p.m., and since we heard that the train was likely to be quite late, because of something wrong in the lines, I spread my bed on the table and was about to lie down for a comfortable doze, when this extraordinary person began spinning the following yarn. Of course, I got no sleep that night.

"When, owing to a disagreement about some questions of administrative policy, I quit my post at Junagarh and entered the service of the Nizam of Hyderabad, they appointed me at once, as a strong young man, collector of cotton duties at Barich.

"Barich is a lovely place. The *Susta* chatters over stones and babbles on the pebbles, tripping through the woods like a skilful dancing girl. A flight of 150 steps rises from the river, above which, at the foot of the hills, stands a solitary marble palace. Nobody lives nearby; the village and the cotton market are far away.

"About 250 years ago, Emperor Mahmud Shah II built this lonely palace for his pleasure and luxury. In those days jets of rose-water spurted from its fountains, and on the cold marble floors of its spray-cooled rooms young Persian women sat, their hair dishevelled before bathing, and splashing their soft naked feet in the clear water of the reservoirs, would sing the *ghazals* of their vineyards, to the tune of a guitar.

"The fountains play no longer, the songs have ceased, white feet no longer step gracefully on the snowy marble. It is now the lonely home of men oppressed with solitude and deprived of the society of women. Karim Khan, my old office clerk, repeatedly warned me not to take up my abode there. 'Pass the day there if you like,' said he, 'but never stay the night.' I passed it off with a light laugh. The servants said that they would work till dark and then go away. I gave my assent.

The house had such a bad name that even thieves would not venture near it after dark.

"At first the solitude of the deserted palace weighed upon me like a nightmare. I would stay out, and work hard as long as possible, then return home at night, jaded and tired, go to bed and fall asleep.

"Before a week had passed, the place began to exert a weird fascination upon me. It is difficult to describe or to induce people to believe; but I felt as if the whole house was like a living organism slowly and imperceptibly digesting me by the action of some stupefying gastric juice.

"Perhaps the process had begun as soon as I set my foot in the house, but I distinctly remember the day on which I first was conscious of it.

"It was the beginning of summer, and the market being dull I had no work to do. A little before sunset I was sitting in an arm-chair near the water's edge below the steps. The *Susta* had shrunk and sunk low; a broad patch of sand on the other side glowed with the hues of evening; on this side the pebbles at the bottom of the clear shallow waters were glistening. There was not a breath of wind anywhere, and the still air was laden with an oppressive scent from the spicy shrubs growing on the hills close by.

"As the sun sank behind the hill-tops a long dark curtain fell upon the stage of day, and the intervening hills cut short the time in which light and shade mingle at sunset. I thought of going out for a ride, and was about to get up when I heard a footfall on the steps behind. I looked back, but there was no one.

"As I sat down again, thinking it to be an illusion, I heard many footfalls, as if a large number of persons were rushing down the steps. A strange thrill of delight, slightly tinged with fear, passed through my frame, and though there was not a figure before my eyes, I thought I saw a bevy of joyous maidens coming down the steps to bathe in the *Susta* in that summer evening. Not a sound was in the valley, in the river, or in the palace, to break the silence, but I distinctly heard the maidens' gay and mirthful laugh, like the gurgle of a spring gushing forth in a hundred cascades, as they ran past me, in quick playful pursuit of each other, towards the river, without noticing me at all. As they were invisible to me, so I was, as it were, invisible to them. The river was perfectly calm, but I felt that its still, shallow, and clear waters were stirred suddenly by the splash of many an arm jingling with bracelets, that the girls laughed and dashed and spattered water at one another, that the feet of the fair swimmers tossed the tiny waves up in showers of pearl.

I felt a thrill at my heart—I cannot say whether the excitement was due to fear or delight or curiosity. I had a strong desire to see them more clearly, but naught was visible before me. I thought I could catch all that they said if I only strained my ears; but however hard I strained them, I heard nothing but the chirping of the cicadas in the woods. It seemed as if a dark curtain of 250 years was hanging before me, and I would fain lift a corner of it tremblingly and peer through, though the assembly on the other side was completely enveloped in darkness.

"The oppressive closeness of the evening was broken by a sudden gust of wind, and the still surface of the *Susta* rippled and curled like the hair of a nymph, and from the woods, wrapt in the evening gloom, there came forth a simultaneous murmur, as though they were awakening from a black dream. Call it reality or dream, the momentary glimpse of that invisible mirage reflected from a far-off world, 250 years old, vanished in a flash. The mystic forms that brushed past me with their quick unbodied steps, and loud, voiceless laughter, and threw themselves into the river, did not go back wringing their dripping robes as they went. Like fragrance wafted away by the wind they were dispersed by a single breath of the spring.

"Then I was filled with a lively fear that it was the Muse that had taken advantage of my solitude and possessed me— the witch had evidently come to ruin a poor devil like myself making a living by collecting cotton duties. I decided to have a good dinner—it is the empty stomach that all sorts of incurable diseases find an easy prey. I sent for my cook and gave orders for a rich, sumptuous *moghlai* dinner, redolent of spices and *ghi.*

"Next morning the whole affair appeared a queer fantasy. With a light heart I put on a *sola* hat like the *sahebs,* and drove out to my work. I was to have written my quarterly report that day, and expected to return late; but before it was dark I was strangely drawn to my house—by what I could not say— I felt they were all waiting and that I should delay no longer. Leaving my report unfinished I rose, put on my *sola* hat, and startling the dark, shady, desolate path with the rattle of my carriage, I reached the vast silent palace standing on the gloomy skirts of the hills.

"On the first floor, the stairs led to a very spacious hall, its roof stretching wide over ornamental arches resting on three rows of massive pillars, and groaning day and night under the weight of its own intense solitude. The day had just closed, and the lamps had not yet been lighted. As I pushed the door open a great bustle seemed to follow within, as if a throng of people had broken up in confusion, and rushed out through the doors and windows and corridors and verandas and rooms, to make its hurried escape.

"As I saw no one I stood bewildered, my hair on end in a kind of ecstatic delight, and a faint scent of *attar* and unguents almost effaced by age lingered in my nostrils. Standing in the darkness of that vast desolate hall between the rows of those ancient pillars, I could hear the gurgle of fountains splashing on the marble floor, a strange tune on the guitar, the jingle of ornaments and the tinkle of anklets, the clang of bells tolling the hours, the distant note of *nahabat,* the din of the crystal pendants of chandeliers shaken by the breeze, the song of *bulbuls* from the cages in the corridors, the cackle of storks in the gardens, all creating round me a strange unearthly music.

"Then I came under such a spell that this intangible, inaccessible, unearthly vision appeared to be the only reality in the world—and all else a mere dream. That I, that is to say, Srijut So-and-so, the eldest son of So-and-so of blessed memory, should be drawing a monthly salary of Rs. 450 by the discharge of my duties as collector of cotton duties, and driving in my dog-cart to my office every day in a short coat and *sola* hat, appeared to me to be such an astonishingly ludicrous illusion that I burst into a horse-laugh, as I stood in the gloom of that vast silent hall.

"At that moment my servant entered with a lighted kerosene lamp in his hand. I do not know whether he thought me mad, but it came back to me at once that I was in very deed Srijut So-and-so, son of So-and-so of blessed memory, and that, while our poets, great and small, alone could say whether inside or outside the earth there was a region where unseen fountains perpetually played and fairy guitars, struck by invisible fingers, sent forth an eternal harmony, this at any rate was certain, that I collected duties at the cotton market at Barich, and earned thereby Rs. 450 per mensem as my salary. I laughed in great glee at my curious illusion, as I sat over the newspaper at my camp-table, lighted by the kerosene lamp.

"After I had finished my paper and eaten my *moghlai* dinner, I put out the lamps, and lay down on my bed in a small side-room. Through the open window a radiant star, high above the Avalli hills skirted by the darkness of their woods, was gazing intently from millions and millions of miles away in the sky at Mr. Collector lying on a humble camp-bedstead. I wondered and felt amused at the idea, and do not know when I fell asleep or how long I slept; but I suddenly awoke with a start, though I heard no sound and saw no intruder—only the steady bright star on the hilltop had set, and the dim light of the new moon was stealthily entering the room through the open window, as if ashamed of its intrusion.

I saw nobody, but felt as if some one was gently pushing me. As I awoke she said not a word, but beckoned me with her five fingers bedecked with rings to follow her cautiously. I got up noiselessly, and, though not a soul save myself was there in the countless apartments of that deserted palace with its slumbering sounds and waking echoes, I feared at every step lest any one should wake up. Most of the rooms of the palace were always kept closed, and I had never entered them.

"I followed breathless and with silent steps my invisible guide—I cannot now say where. What endless dark and narrow passages, what long corridors, what silent and solemn audience-chambers and close secret cells I crossed!

"Though I could not see my fair guide, her form was not invisible to my mind's eye,—an Arab girl, her arms, hard and smooth as marble, visible through her loose sleeves, a thin veil falling on her face from the fringe of her cap, and a curved dagger at her waist! Methought that one of the thousand and one Arabian Nights had been wafted to me from the world of romance, and that at the dead of night I was wending my way through the dark narrow alleys of slumbering Bagdad to a trysting-place fraught with peril.

"At last my fair guide stopped abruptly before a deep blue screen, and seemed to point to something below. There was nothing there, but a sudden dread froze the blood in my heart—methought I saw there on the floor at the foot of the screen a terrible negro eunuch dressed in rich brocade, sitting and dozing with outstretched legs, with a naked sword on his lap. My fair guide lightly tripped over his legs and held up a fringe of the screen. I could catch a glimpse of a part of the room spread with a Persian carpet—some one was sitting inside on a bed—I could not see her, but only caught a glimpse of two exquisite feet in gold-embroidered slippers, hanging out from loose saffron-coloured *paijamas* and placed idly on the orange-coloured velvet carpet. On one side there was a bluish crystal tray on which a few apples, pears, oranges, and bunches of grapes in plenty, two small cups, and a gold-tinted decanter were evidently awaiting the guest. A fragrant intoxicating vapour, issuing from a strange sort of incense that burned within, almost overpowered my senses.

"As with trembling heart I made an attempt to step across the outstretched legs of the eunuch, he woke up suddenly with a start, and the sword fell from his lap with a sharp clang on the marble floor.

"A terrific scream made me jump, and I saw I was sitting on that camp-bedstead of mine sweating heavily; and the crescent moon looked pale in the morning light like a weary sleepless patient at dawn; and our crazy Meher Ali was crying out, as is his daily custom, "Stand back! Stand back!!" while he went along the lonely road.

"Such was the abrupt close of one of my Arabian Nights; but there were yet a thousand nights left.

"Then followed a great discord between my days and nights. During the day I would go to my work worn and tired, cursing the bewitching night and her empty dreams, but as night came my daily life with its bonds and shackles of work would appear a petty, false, ludicrous vanity.

"After nightfall I was caught and overwhelmed in the snare of a strange intoxication. I would then be transformed into some unknown personage of a bygone age, playing my part in unwritten history; and my short English coat and tight breeches did not suit me in the least. With a red velvet cap on my head, loose *paijamas,* an embroidered vest, a long flowing silk gown, and coloured handkerchiefs scented with *attar,* I would complete my elaborate toilet, sit on a high-cushioned chair, and replace my cigarette with a many-coiled *narghileh* filled with rose-water, as if in eager expectation of a strange meeting with the beloved one.

"I have no power to describe the marvellous incidents that unfolded themselves as the gloom of the night deepened. I felt as if in the curious apartments of that vast edifice the fragments of a beautiful story, which I could follow for some distance, but of which I could never see the end, flew about in a sudden gust of the vernal breeze. And all the same I would wander from room to room in pursuit of them the whole night long.

"Amid the eddy of these dream-fragments, amid the smell of *henna* and the twanging of the guitar, amid the waves of air charged with fragrant spray, I would catch like a flash of lightning the momentary glimpse of a fair damsel. She it was who had saffron-coloured *paijamas,* white ruddy soft feet in gold-embroidered slippers with curved toes, a close-fitting bodice wrought with gold, a red cap, from which a golden frill fell on her snowy brow and cheeks.

"She had maddened me. In pursuit of her I wandered from room to room, from path to path among the bewildering maze of alleys in the enchanted dreamland of the nether world of sleep.

"Sometimes in the evening, while arraying myself carefully as a prince of the blood-royal before a large mirror, with a candle burning on either side, I would see a sudden reflection of the Persian beauty by the side of my own. A swift turn of her neck, a quick eager glance of intense passion and pain glowing in her large dark eyes, just a suspicion of speech on her dainty red lips, her figure, fair and slim, crowned with youth like a blossoming creeper, quickly uplifted in her graceful tilting gait, a dazzling flash of pain and craving and ecstasy, a smile and a glance and a blaze of jewels and silk, and she melted away. A wild gust of wind, laden with all the fragrance of hills and woods, would put out my light, and I would fling aside my dress and lie down on my bed, my eyes closed and my body thrilling with delight, and there around me in the breeze, amid all the perfume of the woods and hills, floated through the silent gloom many a caress and many a kiss and many a tender touch of hands, and gentle murmurs in my ears, and fragrant breaths on my brow; or a sweetly-perfumed kerchief was wafted again and again on my cheeks. Then slowly a mysterious serpent would twist her stupefying coils about me; and heaving a heavy sigh, I would lapse into insensibility, and then into a profound slumber.

"One evening I decided to go out on my horse—I do not know who implored me to stay—but I would listen to no entreaties that day. My English hat and coat were resting on a rack, and I was about to take them down when a sudden whirlwind, crested with the sands of the *Susta* and the dead leaves of the Avalli hills, caught them up, and whirled them round and round, while a loud peal of merry laughter rose higher and higher, striking all the chords of mirth till it died away in the land of sunset.

"I could not go out for my ride, and the next day I gave up my queer English coat and hat for good.

"That day again at dead of night I heard the stifled heart-breaking sobs of some one—as if below the bed, below the floor, below the stony foundation of that gigantic palace, from the depths of a dark damp grave, a voice piteously cried and implored me: "Oh, rescue me! Break through these doors of hard illusion, deathlike slumber and fruitless dreams, place me by your side on the saddle, press me to your heart, and,

riding through hills and woods and across the river, take me
to the warm radiance of your sunny rooms above!"

"Who am I? Oh, how can I rescue thee? What drowning
beauty, what incarnate passion shall I drag to the shore from
this wild eddy of dreams? O lovely ethereal apparition! Where
didst thou flourish and when? By what cool spring, under the
shade of what date-groves, wast thou born—in the lap of what
homeless wanderer in the desert? What Bedouin snatched
thee from thy mother's arms, an opening bud plucked from
a wild creeper, placed thee on a horse swift as lightning,
crossed the burning sands, and took thee to the slave-market
of what royal city? And there, what officer of the Badshah,
seeing the glory of thy bashful blossoming youth, paid for thee
in gold, placed thee in a golden palanquin, and offered thee
as a present for the seraglio of his master? And O, the history
of that place! The music of the *sareng*,[1] the jingle of anklets,
the occasional flash of daggers and the glowing wine of Shiraz
poison, and the piercing flashing glance! What infinite
grandeur, what endless servitude! The slave-girls to thy right
and left waved the *chamar*,[2] as diamonds flashed from their
bracelets; the Badshah, the king of kings, fell on his knees
at thy snowy feet in bejewelled shoes, and outside the terrible
Abyssinian eunuch, looking like a messenger of death, but
clothed like an angel, stood with a naked sword in his hand!
Then, O, thou flower of the desert, swept away by the blood-
stained dazzling ocean of grandeur, with its foam of jealousy,
its rocks and shoals of intrigue, on what shore of cruel death
wast thou cast, or in what other land more splendid and more
cruel?

"Suddenly at this moment that crazy Meher Ali screamed
out: "Stand back! Stand back!! All is false! All is false!!" I

---

1. A sort of violin.
2. Chamar: chowrie, yak-tail.

opened my eyes and saw that it was already light. My *chaprasi* came and handed me my letters, and the cook waited with a *salam* for my orders.

"I said: "No, I can stay here no longer." That very day I packed up, and moved to my office. Old Karim Khan smiled a little as he saw me. I felt nettled, but said nothing, and fell to my work.

"As evening approached I grew absent-minded; I felt as if I had an appointment to keep; and the work of examining the cotton accounts seemed wholly useless; even the *Nizamat*[3] of the Nizam did not appear to be of much worth. Whatever belonged to the present, whatever was moving and acting and working for bread seemed trivial, meaningless, and contemptible.

"I threw my pen down, closed my ledgers, got into my dog-cart, and drove away. I noticed that it stopped of itself at the gate of the marble palace just at the hour of twilight. With quick steps I climbed the stairs, and entered the room.

"A heavy silence was reigning within. The dark rooms were looking sullen as if they had taken offence. My heart was full of contrition, but there was no one to whom I could lay it bare, or of whom I could ask forgiveness. I wandered about the dark rooms with a vacant mind. I wished I had a guitar to which I could sing to the unknown; "O fire, the poor moth that made a vain effort to fly away has come back to thee! Forgive it but this once, burn its wings and consume it in thy flame!"

"Suddenly two tear-drops fell from overhead on my brow. Dark masses of clouds overcast the top of the Avalli hills that day. The gloomy woods and the sooty waters of the *Susta* were waiting in terrible suspense and in an ominous calm. Suddenly land, water, and sky shivered, and a wild tempest-blast rushed howling through the distant pathless woods,

---

3. Royalty.

showing its lightning-teeth like a raving maniac who had broken his chains. The desolate halls of the palace banged their doors, and moaned in the bitterness of anguish.

"The servants were all in the office, and there was no one to light the lamps. The night was cloudy and moonless. In the dense gloom within I could distinctly feel that a woman was lying on her face on the carpet below the bed—clasping and tearing her long dishevelled hair with desperate fingers. Blood was trickling down her fair brow, and she was now laughing a hard, harsh, mirthless laugh, now bursting into violent wringing sobs, now rending her bodice and striking at her bare bosom, as the wind roared in through the open window, and the rain poured in torrents and soaked her through and through.

"All night there was no cessation of the storm or of the passionate cry. I wandered from room to room in the dark, with unavailing sorrow. Whom could I console when no one was by? Whose was this intense agony of sorrow? Whence arose this inconsolable grief?

And the mad man cried out: "Stand back! Stand back!! All is false! All is false!!"

I saw that the day had dawned, and Meher Ali was going round and round the palace with his usual cry in that dreadful weather. Suddenly it came to me that perhaps he also had once lived in that house, and that, though he had gone mad, he came there every day, and went round and round, fascinated by the weird spell cast by the marble demon.

Despite the storm and rain I ran to him and asked: "Ho, Meher Ali, what is false?"

The man answered nothing, but pushing me aside went round and round with his frantic cry, like a bird flying fascinated about the jaws of a snake, and made a desperate effort to warn himself by repeating. "Stand back! Stand back!! All is false! All is false!!"

I ran like a mad man through the pelting rain to my office, and asked Karim Khan: "Tell me the meaning of all this!"

What I gathered from that old man was this: That at one time countless unrequited passions and unsatisfied longings and lurid flames of wild blazing pleasure raged within that palace, and that the curse of all the heart-aches and blasted hopes had made its every stone thirsty and hungry, eager to swallow up like a famished ogress any living man who might chance to approach. Not one of those who lived there for three consecutive nights could escape these cruel jaws, save Meher Ali, who had escaped at the cost of his reason.

I asked: "Is there no means whatever of my release?" The old man said: "There is only one means, and that is very difficult. I will tell you what it is, but first you must hear the history of a young Persian girl who once lived in that pleasure-dome. A stranger or a more bitterly heart-rending tragedy was never enacted on this earth."

Just at this moment the coolies announced that the train was coming. So soon? We hurriedly packed up our luggage, as the train steamed in. An English gentleman, apparently just aroused from slumber, was looking out of a first-class carriage endeavouring to read the name of the station. As soon as he caught sight of our fellow-passenger, he cried, "Hallo," and took him into his own compartment. As we got into a second-class carriage, we had no chance of finding out who the man was nor what was the end of his story.

I said: "The man evidently took us for fools and imposed upon us out of fun. The story is pure fabrication from start to finish." The discussion that followed ended in a lifelong rupture between my theosophist kinsman and myself.

The Victory

She was the Princess Ajita. And the court poet of King Nārāyan had never seen her. On the day he recited a new poem to the king he would raise his voice just to that pitch which could be heard by unseen hearers in the screened balcony high above the hall. He sent up his song towards the star-land out of his reach, where, circled with light, the planet who ruled his destiny shone unknown and out of ken.

He would espy some shadow moving behind the veil. A tinkling sound would come to his ear from afar, and would set him dreaming of the ankles whose tiny golden bells sang at each step. Ah, the rosy red tender feet that walked the dust of the earth like God's mercy on the fallen! The poet had placed them on the altar of his heart, where he wove his songs to the tune of those golden bells. Doubt never arose in his mind as to whose shadow it was that moved behind the screen, and whose anklets they were that sang to the time of his beating heart.

Manjari, the maid of the princess, passed by the poet's house on her way to the river, and she never missed a day to have a few words with him on the sly. When she found the road deserted, and the shadow of dusk on the land, she would boldly enter his room, and sit at the corner of his carpet. There was a suspicion of an added care in the choice of the colour of her veil, in the setting of the flower in her hair.

People smiled and whispered at this, and they were not to blame. For Shekhar the poet never took the trouble to hide the fact that these meetings were a pure joy to him.

The meaning of her name was the *spray of flowers*. One must confess that for an ordinary mortal it was sufficient in its sweetness. But Shekhar made his own addition to this name, and called her the Spray of Spring Flowers. And ordinary mortals shook their heads and said, Ah, me!

In the spring songs that the poet sang the praise of the spray of spring flowers was conspicuously reiterated; and the king winked and smiled at him when he heard it, and the poet smiled in answer.

The king would put him the question: "Is it the business of the bee merely to hum in the court of the spring?"

The poet would answer: "No, but also to sip the honey of the spray of spring flowers."

And they all laughed in the king's hall. And it was rumoured that the Princess Ajita also laughed at her maid's accepting the poet's name for her, and Manjari felt glad in her heart.

Thus truth and falsehood mingle in life—and to what God builds man adds his own decoration.

Only those were pure truths which were sung by the poet. The theme was Krishna, the lover god, and Rādhā, the beloved, the Eternal Man and the Eternal Woman, the sorrow that comes from the beginning of time, and the joy without end. The truth of these songs was tested in his inmost heart by everybody from the beggar to the king himself. The poet's songs were on the lips of all. At the merest glimmer of the moon and the faintest whisper of the summer breeze his songs would break forth in the land from windows and courtyards, from sailing-boats, from shadows of the wayside trees, in numberless voices.

Thus passed the days happily. The poet recited, the king listened, the hearers applauded, Manjari passed and repassed by the poet's room on her way to the river—the shadow flitted behind the screened balcony, and the tiny golden bells tinkled from afar.

Just then set forth from his home in the south a poet on his path of conquest. He came to King Nārāyan, in the kingdom of Amarapur. He stood before the throne, and uttered a verse in praise of the king. He had challenged all the court poets on his way, and his career of victory had been unbroken.

The king received him with honour, and said: "Poet, I offer you welcome."

Pundarik, the poet, proudly replied: "Sire, I ask for war."

Shekhar, the court poet of the king did not know how the battle of the muse was to be waged. He had no sleep at night. The mighty figure of the famous Pundarik, his sharp nose curved like a scimitar, and his proud head tilted on one side, haunted the poet's vision in the dark.

With a trembling heart Shekhar entered the arena in the morning. The theatre was filled with the crowd.

The poet greeted his rival with a smile and a bow. Pundarik returned it with a slight toss of his head, and turned his face towards his circle of adoring followers with a meaning smile.

Shekhar cast his glance towards the screened balcony high above, and saluted his lady in his mind, saying: "If I am the winner at the combat to-day, my lady, thy victorious name shall be glorified."

The trumpet sounded. The great crowd stood up, shouting victory to the king. The king, dressed in an ample robe of white, slowly came into the hall like a floating cloud of autumn, and sat on his throne.

Pundarik stood up, and the vast hall became still. With his head raised high and chest expanded, he began in his thundering voice to recite the praise of King Nārāyan. His words burst upon the walls of the hall like breakers of the sea, and seemed to rattle against the ribs of the listening crowd. The skill with which he gave varied meanings to the name Nārāyan, and wove each letter of it through the web of his verses in all manner of combinations, took away the breath of his amazed hearers.

For some minutes after he took his seat his voice continued to vibrate among the numberless pillars of the king's court and in thousands of speechless hearts. The learned professors who had come from distant lands raised their right hands, and cried, Bravo!

The king threw a glance on Shekhar's face, and Shekhar in answer raised for a moment his eyes full of pain towards his master, and then stood up like a stricken deer at bay. His face was pale, his bashfulness was almost that of a woman, his slight youthful figure, delicate in its outline, seemed like a tensely strung *vina* ready to break out in music at the least touch.

His head was bent, his voice was low, when he began. The first few verses were almost inaudible. Then he slowly raised his head, and his clear sweet voice rose into the sky like a quivering flame of fire. He began with the ancient legend of the kingly line lost in the haze of the past, and brought it down through its long course of heroism and matchless generosity to the present age. He fixed his gaze on the king's face, and all the vast and unexpressed love of the people for the royal house rose like incense in his song, and enwreathed the throne on all sides. These were his last words when, trembling, he took his seat: 'My master, I may be beaten in play of words, but not in my love for thee."

Tears filled the eyes of the hearers, and the stone walls shook with cries of victory.

Mocking this popular outburst of feeling, with an august shake of his head and a contemptuous sneer, Pundarik stood up, and flung this question to the assembly: "What is there superior to words?" In a moment the hall lapsed into silence again.

Then with a marvellous display of learning, he proved that the Word was in the beginning, that the Word was God. He piled up quotations from scriptures, and built a high altar for the Word to be seated above all that there is in heaven and in earth. He repeated that question in his mighty voice: "What is there superior to words?"

Proudly he looked around him. None dared to accept his challenge, and he slowly took his seat like a lion who had just made a full meal of its victim. The pandits shouted, Bravo! The king remained silent with wonder, and the poet Shekhar felt himself of no account by the side of this stupendous learning. The assembly broke up for that day.

Next day Shekhar began his song. It was of that day when the pipings of love's flute startled for the first time the hushed air of the Vrinda forest. The shepherd women did not know who was the player or whence came the music. Sometimes it seemed to come from the heart of the south wind, and sometimes from the straying clouds of the hill-tops. It came with a message of tryst from the land of the sunrise, and it floated from the verge of sunset with its sigh of sorrow. The stars seemed to be the stops of the instrument that flooded the dreams of the night with melody. The music seemed to burst all at once from all sides, from fields and groves, from the shady lanes and lonely roads, from the melting blue of the sky, from the shimmering green of the grass. They neither knew its meaning nor could they find words to give utterance to the desire of their hearts. Tears filled their eyes, and their life seemed to long for a death that would be its consummation.

Shekhar forgot his audience, forgot the trial of his strength with a rival. He stood alone amid his thoughts that rustled and quivered round him like leaves in a summer breeze, and sang the Song of the Flute. He had in his mind the vision of an image that had taken its shape from a shadow, and the echo of a faint tinkling sound of a distant footstep.

He took his seat. His hearers trembled with the sadness of an indefinable delight, immense and vague, and they forgot to applaud him. As this feeling died away Pundarik stood up before the throne and challenged his rival to define who was this Lover and who was the Beloved. He arrogantly looked around him, he smiled at his followers and then put the question again: "Who is Krishna, the lover, and who is Rādhā, the beloved?"

Then he began to analyse the roots of those names,—and various interpretations of their meanings. He brought before the bewildered audience all the intricacies of the different schools of metaphysics with consummate skill. Each letter of those names he divided from its fellow, and then pursued them with a relentless logic till they fell to the dust in confusion, to be caught up again and restored to a meaning never before imagined by the subtlest of wordmongers.

The pandits were in ecstasy; they applauded vociferously; and the crowd followed them, deluded into the certainty that they had witnessed, that day, the last shred of the curtains of Truth torn to pieces before their eyes by a prodigy of intellect. The performance of his tremendous feat so delighted them that they forgot to ask themselves if there was any truth behind it after all.

The king's mind was overwhelmed with wonder. The atmosphere was completely cleared of all illusion of music, and the vision of the world around seemed to be changed from its freshness of tender green to the solidity of a high road levelled and made hard with crushed stones.

To the people assembled their own poet appeared a mere boy in comparison with this giant, who walked with such ease, knocking down difficulties at each step in the world of words and thoughts. It became evident to them for the first time that the poems Shekhar wrote were absurdly simple, and it must be a mere accident that they did not write them themselves. They were neither new, nor difficult, nor instructive, nor necessary.

The king tried to goad his poet with keen glances, silently inciting him to make a final effort. But Shekhar took no notice, and remained fixed to his seat.

The king in anger came down from his throne—took off his pearl chain and put in on Pundarik's head. Everybody in the hall cheered. From the upper balcony came a slight sound of the movements of rustling robes and waist-chains hung with golden bells. Shekhar rose from his seat and left the hall.

It was a dark night of waning moon. The poet Shekhar took down his MSS. from his shelves and heaped them on the floor. Some of them contained his earliest writings, which he had almost forgotten. He turned over the pages, reading passages here and there. They all seemed to him poor and trivial—mere words and childish rhymes!

One by one he tore his books to fragments, and threw them into a vessel containing fire, and said: "To thee, to thee, O my beauty, my fire! Thou hast been burning in my heart all these futile years. If my life were a piece of gold it would come out of its trial brighter, but it is a trodden turf of grass, and nothing remains of it but this handful of ashes."

The night wore on. Shekhar opened wide his windows. He spread upon his bed the white flowers that he loved, the jasmines, tuberoses and chrysanthemums, and brought into his bedroom all the lamps he had in his house and lighted them. Then mixing with honey the juice of some poisonous root, he drank it and lay down on his bed.

Golden ankles tinkled in the passage outside the door, and a subtle perfume came into the room with the breeze.

The poet, with his eyes shut, said: "My lady, have you taken pity upon your servant at last and come to see him?"

The answer came in a sweet voice: "My poet, I have come."

Shekhar opened his eyes—and saw before his bed the figure of a woman.

His sight was dim and blurred. And it seemed to him that the image made of a shadow that he had ever kept throned in the secret shrine of his heart had come into the outer world in his last moment to gaze upon his face.

The woman said: "I am the princess Ajita."

The poet with a great effort sat up on his bed.

The princess whispered into his ear: "The king has not done you justice. It was you who won at the combat, my poet, and I have come to crown you with the crown of victory."

She took the garland of flowers from her own neck, and put it on his hair, and the poet fell down upon his bed stricken by death.

Once There Was A King

"Once upon a time there was a king."

When we were children there was no need to know who the king in the fairy story was. It didn't matter whether he was called Shiladitya or Shaliban, whether he lived at Kashi or Kanauj. The thing that made a seven-year-old boy's heart go thump, thump with delight was this one sovereign truth, this reality of all realities: "Once there was a king."

But the readers of this modern age are far more exact and exacting. When they hear such an opening to a story, they are at once critical and suspicious. They apply the searchlight of science to its legendary haze and ask: "Which king?"

The story-tellers have become more precise in their turn. They are no longer content with the old indefinite, "There was a king," but assume instead a look of profound learning, and begin: "Once there was a king named Ajatasatru."

The modern reader's curiosity, however, is not so easily satisfied. He blinks at the author through his scientific spectacles, and asks again: "Which Ajatasatru?"

"Every schoolboy knows," the author proceeds, "that there were three Ajatasatrus. The first was born in the twentieth century B.C., and died at the tender age of two years and eight months. I deeply regret that it is impossible to find, from any trustworthy source, a detailed account of his reign. The second Ajatasatru is better known to historians. If you refer to the new Encyclopedia of History..."

By this time the modern reader's suspicions are dissolved. He feels he may safely trust his author. He says to himself: "Now we shall have a story that is both improving and instructive."

Ah! how we all love to be deluded! We have a secret dread of being thought ignorant. And we end by being ignorant after all, only we have done it in a long and roundabout way.

There is an English proverb: "Ask me no questions, and I will tell you no lies." The boy of seven who is listening to a fairy story understands that perfectly well; he withholds his questions, while the story is being told. So the pure and beautiful falsehood of it all remains naked and innocent as a babe; transparent as truth itself; limpid as a fresh bubbling spring. But the ponderous and learned lie of our moderns has to keep its true character draped and veiled. And if there is discovered anywhere the least little peephole of deception, the reader turns away with a prudish disgust, and the author is discredited.

When we were young, we understood all sweet things; and we could detect the sweets of a fairy story by an unerring science of our own. We never cared for such useless things as knowledge. We only cared for truth. And our unsophisticated little hearts knew well where the Crystal Palace of Truth lay and how to reach it. But today we are expected to write pages of facts, while the truth is simply this:

"There was a king."

I remember vividly that evening in Calcutta when the fairy story began. The rain and the storm had been incessant. The whole of the city was flooded. The water was knee-deep in our lane. I had a straining hope, which was almost a certainty, that my tutor would be prevented from coming that evening. I sat on the stool in the far corner of the veranda looking down the lane, with a heart beating faster and faster. Every minute I kept my eye on the rain, and when it began to grow less I prayed with all my might: "Please, God, send some more rain till half-past seven is over." For I was quite ready to believe that there was no other need for rain except to protect one helpless boy one evening in one corner of Calcutta from the deadly clutches of his tutor.

If not in answer to my prayer, at any rate according to some grosser law of physical nature, the rain did not give up.

But, alas! nor did my teacher.

Exactly to the minute, in the bend of the lane, I saw his approaching umbrella. The great bubble of hope burst in my breast, and my heart collapsed. Truly, if there is a punishment to fit the crime after death, then my tutor will be born again as me, and I shall be born as my tutor.

As soon as I saw his umbrella I ran as hard as I could to my mother's room. My mother and my grandmother were sitting opposite one another playing cards by the light of a lamp. I ran into the room, and flung myself on the bed beside my mother, and said:

"Mother dear, the tutor has come, and I have such a bad headache; couldn't I have no lessons to-day?"

I hope no child of immature age will be allowed to read this story, and I sincerely trust it will not be used in text-books or primers for schools. For what I did was dreadfully bad, and I received no punishment whatever. On the contrary, my wickedness was crowned with success.

My mother said to me: "All right," and turning to the servant added: "Tell the tutor that he can go back home."

It was perfectly plain that she didn't think my illness very serious, as she went on with her game as before, and took no further notice. And I also, burying my head in the pillow, laughed to my heart's content. We perfectly understood one another, my mother and I.

But every one must know how hard it is for a boy of seven years old to keep up the illusion of illness for a long time.

After about a minute I got hold of Grandmother, and said: "Grannie, do tell me a story."

I had to ask this many times. Grannie and Mother went on playing cards, and took no notice. At last Mother said to me: "Child, don't bother. Wait till we've finished our game." But I persisted: "Grannie, do tell me a story." I told Mother she could finish her game to-morrow, but she must let Grannie tell me a story there and then.

At last Mother threw down the cards and said: "You had better do what he wants. I can't manage him." Perhaps she had it in her mind that she would have no tiresome tutor on the morrow, while I should be obliged to be back to those stupid lessons.

As soon as ever Mother had given way, I rushed at Grannie. I got hold of her hand, and, dancing with delight, dragged her inside my mosquito curtain on to the bed. I clutched hold of the bolster with both hands in my excitement, and jumped up and down with joy, and when I had got a little quieter, said: "Now, Grannie, let's have the story!"

Grannie went on: "And the king had a queen." That was good to begin with. He had only one.

It is usual for kings in fairy stories to be extravagant in queens. And whenever we hear that there are two queens, our hearts begin to sink. One is sure to be unhappy. But in Grannie's story that danger was past. He had only one queen.

We next hear that the king had not got any son. At the age of seven I didn't think there was any need to bother if a man had had no son. He might only have been in the way.

Nor are we greatly excited when we hear that the king has gone away into the forest to practise austerities in order to get a son. There was only one thing that would have made me go into the forest, and that was to get away from my tutor!

But the king left behind with his queen a small girl, who grew up into a beautiful princess.

Twelve years pass away, and the king goes on practising austerities, and never thinks all this while of his beautiful daughter. The princess has reached the full bloom of her youth. The age of marriage has passed, but the king does not return. And the queen pines away with grief and cries: "Is my golden daughter destined to die unmarried? Ah me! what a fate is mine."

Then the queen sent men to the king to entreat him earnestly to come back for a single night and take one meal in the palace. And the king consented.

The queen cooked with her own hand, and with the greatest care, sixty-four dishes, and made a seat for him of sandal-wood, and arranged the food in plates of gold and cups of silver. The princess stood behind with the peacock-tail fan in her hand. The king, after twelve years' absence, came into the house, and the princess waved the fan, lighting up all the room with her beauty. The king looked in his daughter's face, and forgot to take his food.

At last he asked his queen: "Pray, who is this girl whose beauty shines as the gold image of the goddess? Whose daughter is she?"

The queen beat her forehead, and cried. "Ah, how evil is my fate! Do you not know your own daughter?"

The king was struck with amazement. He said at last: "My tiny daughter has grown to be a woman."

"What else?" the queen said with a sigh. "Do you not know that twelve years have passed by?"

"But why did you not give her in marriage?" asked the king.

"You were away," the queen said, "And how could I find her a suitable husband?"

The king became vehement with excitement. "The first man I see to-morrow," he said, "when I come out of the palace shall marry her."

The princess went on waving her fan of peacock feathers, and the king finished his meal.

The next morning, as the king came out of his palace, he saw the son of a Brahman gathering sticks in the forest outside the palace gates. His age was about seven or eight.

The king said: "I will marry my daughter to him."

Who can interfere with a king's command? At once the boy was called, and the marriage garlands were exchanged between him and the princess.

At this point I came up close to my wise Grannie and asked her eagerly: "What then?"

In the bottom of my heart there was a devout wish to substitute myself for that fortunate wood-gatherer of seven years old. The night was resonant with the patter of rain. The earthen lamp by my bedside was burning low. My grandmother's voice droned on as she told the story. And all these things served to create in a corner of my credulous heart the belief that I had been gathering sticks in the dawn of some indefinite time in the kingdom of some unknown king, and in a moment garlands had been exchanged between me and the princess, beautiful as the Goddess of Grace. She had a gold band on her hair and gold earrings in her ears. She had a necklace and bracelets of gold, and a golden waist-chain round her waist, and a pair of golden anklets tinkled above her feet.

If my grandmother were an author how many explanations she would have to offer for this little story! First of all, every one would ask why the king remained twelve years in the forest? Secondly, why should the king's daughter remain unmarried all that while? This would be regarded as absurd.

Even if she could have got so far without a quarrel, still there would have been a great hue and cry about the marriage itself. First, it never happened. Secondly, how could there be a marriage between a princess of the Warrior Caste and a boy of the priestly Brahman Caste? Her readers would have imagined at once that the writer was preaching against our social customs in an underhand way. And they would write letters to the papers.

So I pray with all my heart that my grandmother may be born a grandmother again, and not through some cursed fate take birth as her luckless grandson.

So with a throb of joy and delight, I asked Grannie: "What then?"

Grannie went on: Then the princess took her little husband away in great distress, and built a large palace with seven wings, and began to cherish her husband with great care.

I jumped up and down in my bed and clutched at the bolster more tightly than ever and said: "What then?"

Grannie continued: The little boy went to school and learnt many lessons from his teachers, and as he grew up his class-fellows began to ask him: "Who is that beautiful lady who lives with you in the palace with the seven wings?"

The Brahman's son was eager to know who she was. He could only remember how one day he had been gathering sticks, and a great disturbance arose. But all that was so long ago that he had no clear recollection.

Four or five years passed in this way. His companions always asked him: "Who is that beautiful lady in the palace with the seven wings?" And the Brahman's son would come back from school and sadly tell the princess: "My school companions always ask me who is that beautiful lady in the palace with the seven wings, and I can give them no reply. Tell me, oh, tell me who you are!"

The princess said: "Let it pass to-day. I will tell you some other day." And every day the Brahman's son would ask: "Who are you?" and the princess would reply: "Let it pass to-day. I will tell you some other day." In this manner four or five more years passed away.

At last the Brahman's son became very impatient, and said: "If you do not tell me to-day who you are, O beautiful lady, I will leave this palace with the seven wings." Then the princess said: "I will certainly tell you to-morrow."

Next day the Brahman's son, as soon as he came home from school, said: "Now, tell me who you are." The princess said: "To-night I will tell you after supper, when you are in bed."

The Brahman's son said: "Very well"; and he began to count the hours in expectation of the night. And the princess, on her side, spread white flowers over the golden bed, and lighted a gold lamp with fragrant oil, and adorned her hair, and dressed herself in a beautiful robe of blue, and began to count the hours in expectation of the night.

That evening when her husband, the Brahman's son, had finished his meal, too excited almost to eat, and had gone to the golden bed in the bedchamber strewn with flowers, he said to himself: "To-night I shall surely know who this beautiful lady is, in the palace with the seven wings."

The princess took for her the food that was left over by her husband, and slowly entered the bedchamber. She had to answer that night the question, who was the beautiful lady who lived in the palace with the seven wings. And as she went up to the bed to tell him she found a serpent had crept out of the flowers and had bitten the Brahman's son. Her boy-husband was lying on the bed of flowers, with face pale in death.

My heart suddenly ceased to throb, and I asked with choking voice: "What then?"

Grannie said: "Then..."

But what is the use of going on any further with the story? It would only lead on to what was more and more impossible. The boy of seven did not know that, if there were some "What then?" after death, no grandmother of a grandmother could tell us all about it.

But the child's faith never admits defeat, and it would snatch at the mantle of death itself to turn him back. It would be outrageous for him to think that such a story of one teacherless evening could so suddenly come to a stop. Therefore the grandmother had to call back her story from the ever-shut chamber of the great End, but she does it so simply: it is merely by floating the dead body on a banana stem on the river, and having some incantations read by a magician. But in that rainy night and in the dim light of a lamp death loses all its horror in the mind of the boy, and seems nothing more than a deep slumber of a single night. When the story ends the tired eyelids are weighed down with sleep. Thus it is that we send the little body of the child floating on the back of sleep over the still water of time, and then in the morning read a few verses of incantation to restore him to the world of life and light.

The Home-Coming

Phatik Chakravorti was ringleader among the boys of the village. A new mischief got into his head. There was a heavy log lying on the mudflat of the river waiting to be shaped into a mast for a boat. He decided that they should all work together to shift the log by main force from its place and roll it away. The owner of the log would be angry and surprised, and they would all enjoy the fun. Every one seconded the proposal, and it was carried unanimously.

But just as the fun was about to begin, Mākhan, Phatik's younger brother, sauntered up, and sat down on the log in front of them all without a word. The boys were puzzled for a moment. He was pushed, rather timidly, by one of the boys and told to get up: but he remained quite unconcerned. He appeared like a young philosopher meditating on the futility of games. Phatik was furious. "Mākhan," he cried, "if you don't get down this minute, I'll thrash you!"

Mākhan only moved to a more comfortable position.

Now, if Phatik was to keep his regal dignity before the public, it was clear he ought to carry out his threat. But his courage failed him at the crisis. His fertile brain, however, rapidly seized upon a new manoeuvre which would discomfit his brother and afford his followers an added amusement. He gave the word of command to roll the log and Mākhan over together. Mākhan heard the order, and made it a point of honour to stick on. But he overlooked the fact, like those who attempt earthly fame in other matters, that there was peril in it.

The boys began to heave at the log with all their might, calling out, "One, two, three, go." At the word 'go' the log went; and with it went Mākhan's philosophy, glory and all.

All the other boys shouted themselves hoarse with delight. But Phatik was a little frightened. He knew what was coming. And, sure enough, Mākhan rose from Mother Earth blind as Fate and screaming like the Furies. He rushed at Phatik and scratched his face and beat him and kicked him, and then went crying home. The first act of the drama was over.

Phatik wiped his face, and sat down on the edge of a sunken barge on the river bank, and began to chew a piece of grass. A boat came up to the landing, and a middle-aged man, with grey hair and dark moustache, stepped on shore. He saw the boy sitting there doing nothing, and asked him where the Chakravortis lived. Phatik went on chewing the grass, and said: "Over there," but it was quite impossible to tell where he pointed. The stranger asked him again. He swung his legs to and fro on the side of the barge, and said: "Go and find out," and continued to chew the grass as before.

But now a servant came down from the house, and told Phatik his mother wanted him. Phatik refused to move. But the servant was the master on this occasion. He took Phatik up roughly, and carried him, kicking and struggling in impotent rage.

When Phatik came into the house, his mother saw him. She called out angrily: "So you have been hitting Mākhan again?"

Phatik answered indignantly: "No, I haven't; who told you that?"

His mother shouted: "Don't tell lies! You have."

Phatik said suddenly: "I tell you, I haven't. You ask Mākhan!" But Mākhan thought it best to stick to his previous statement. He said: "Yes, mother. Phatik did hit me."

Phatik's patience was already exhausted. He could not bear this injustice. He rushed at Mākhan and hammered him with blows: "Take that," he cried, "and that, and that, for telling lies."

His mother took Mākhan's side in a moment, and pulled Phatik away, beating him with her hands. When Phatik pushed her aside, she shouted out: "What! you little villain! would you hit your own mother?"

It was just at this critical juncture that the grey-haired stranger arrived. He asked what was the matter. Phatik looked sheepish and ashamed.

But when his mother stepped back and looked at the stranger, her anger was changed to surprise. For she recognised her brother, and cried: "Why, Dada! Where have you come from?"

As she said these words, she bowed to the ground and touched his feet. Her brother had gone away soon after she had married, and he had started business in Bombay. His sister had lost her husband while he was in Bombay. Bishamber had now come back to Calcutta, and had at once made enquiries about his sister. He had then hastened to see her as soon as he found out where she was.

The next few days were full of rejoicing. The brother asked after the education of the two boys. He was told by his sister that Phatik was a perpetual nuisance. He was lazy, disobedient, and wild. But Mākhan was as good as gold, as quiet as a lamb, and very found of reading. Bishamber kindly offered to take Phatik off his sister's hands, and educate him with his own children in Calcutta. The widowed mother readily agreed. When his uncle asked Phatik if he would like to go to Calcutta with him, his joy knew no bounds, and he said: "Oh, yes, uncle!" in a way that made it quite clear that he meant it.

It was an immense relief to the mother to get rid of Phatik. She had a prejudice against the boy, and no love was lost between the two brothers. She was in daily fear that he would either drown Mākhan some day in the river, or break his head in a fight, or run him into some danger or other. At the same time she was somewhat distressed to see Phatik's extreme eagerness to get away.

Phatik, as soon as all was settled, kept asking his uncle every minute when they were to start. He was on pins and needles all day long with excitement, and lay awake most of the night. He bequeathed to Mākhan, in perpetuity, his fishing-rod, his big kite, and his marbles. Indeed, at this time of departure his generosity towards Mākhan was unbounded.

When they reached Calcutta, Phatik made the acquaintance of his aunt for the first time. She was by no means pleased with this unnecessary addition to her family. She found her own three boys quite enough to manage without taking any one else. And to bring a village lad of fourteen into their midst was terribly upsetting. Bishamber should really have thought twice before committing such an indiscretion.

In this world of human affairs there is no worse nuisance than a boy at the age of fourteen. He is neither ornamental nor useful. It is impossible to shower affection on him as on a little boy; and he is always getting in the way. If he talks with a childish lisp he is called a baby, and if he answers in a grown-up way he is called impertinent. In fact any talk at all from him is resented. Then he is at the unattractive, growing age. He grows out of his clothes with indecent haste; his voice grows hoarse and breaks and quavers; his face grows suddenly angular and unsightly. It is easy to excuse the shortcomings of early childhood, but it is hard to tolerate even unavoidable lapses in a boy of fourteen. The lad himself becomes painfully self-conscious. When he talks with elderly people he is either unduly forward, or else so unduly shy that he appears ashamed of his very existence.

Yet it is at this very age when in his heart of hearts a young lad most craves for recognition and love; and he becomes the devoted slave of any one who shows him consideration. But none dare openly love him, for that would be regarded as undue indulgence, and therefore bad for the boy. So, what with scolding and chiding, he becomes very much like a stray dog that has lost his master.

For a boy of fourteen his own home is the only Paradise. To live in a strange house with strange people is little short of torture, while the height of bliss is to receive the kind looks of women, and never to be slighted by them.

It was anguish to Phatik to be unwelcome guest in his aunt's house, despised by this elderly woman, and slighted on every occasion. If she ever asked him to do anything for her, he would be so overjoyed that he would overdo it; and then she would tell him not to be so stupid, but to get on with his lessons.

The cramped atmosphere of neglect in his aunt's house oppressed Phatik so much that he felt that he could hardly breathe. He wanted to go out into the open country and fill his lungs and breathe freely. But there was no open country to go to. Surrounded on all sides by Calcutta houses and walls, he would dream night after night of his village home, and long to be back there. He remembered the glorious meadow where he used to fly his kite all day long; the broad river-banks where he would wander about the livelong day singing and shouting for joy; the narrow brook where he could go and dive and swim at any time he liked. He thought of his band of boy companions over whom he was despot; and, above all, the memory of that tyrant mother of his, who had such a prejudice against him, occupied him day and night. A kind of physical love like that of animals; a longing to be in the presence of the one who is loved; an inexpressible wistfulness during absence; a silent cry of the inmost heart for the mother, like the lowing of a calf in the twilight;— this love, which was almost an animal instinct, agitated the shy, nervous, lean, uncouth and ugly boy. No one could understand it, but it preyed upon his mind continually.

There was no more backward boy in the whole school than Phatik. He gaped and remained silent when the teacher asked him a question, and like an overladen ass patiently suffered all the blows that came down on his back. When other boys were out at play, he stood wistfully by the window and gazed at the roofs of the distant houses. And if by chance he espied children playing on the open terrace of any roof, his heart would ache with longing.

One day he summoned up all his courage, and asked his uncle: "Uncle, when can I go home?"

His uncle answered: "Wait till the holidays come."

But the holidays would not come till November, and there was a long time still to wait.

One day Phatik lost his lesson-book. Even with the help of books he had found it very difficult indeed to prepare his lesson. Now it was impossible. Day after day the teacher would cane him unmercifully. His condition became so abjectly miserable that even his cousins were ashamed to own him. They began to jeer and insult him more than the other boys. He went to his aunt at last, and told her that he had lost his book.

His aunt pursed her lips in contempt, and said: "You great clumsy, country lout. How can I afford, with all my family, to buy you new books five times a month?"

That night, on his way back from school, Phatik had a bad headache with a fit of shivering. He felt he was going to have an attack of malarial fever. His one great fear was that he would be a nuisance to his aunt.

The next morning Phatik was nowhere to be seen. All searches in the neighbourhood proved futile. The rain had been pouring in torrents all night, and those who went out in search of the boy got drenched through to the skin. At last Bishamber asked help from the police.

At the end of the day a police van stopped at the door before the house. It was still raining and the streets were all flooded. Two constables brought out Phatik in their arms and placed him before Bishamber. He was wet through from head to foot, muddy all over, his face and eyes flushed red with fever, and his limbs all trembling. Bishamber carried him in his arms, and took him into the inner apartments. When his wife saw him, she exclaimed: "What a heap of trouble this boy has given us. Hadn't you better send him home?"

Phatik heard her words, and sobbed out loud: "Uncle, I was just going home; but they dragged me back again."

The fever rose very high, and all that night the boy was delirious. Bishamber brought in a doctor. Phatik opened his eyes flushed with fever, and looked up to the ceiling, and said vacantly: "Uncle, have the holiday come yet? May I go home?"

Bishamber wiped the tears from his own eyes, and took Phatik's lean and burning hands in his own, and sat by him through the night. The boy began again to mutter. At last his voice became excited: "Mother," he cried, "don't beat me like that! Mother! I am telling the truth!"

The next day Phatik became conscious for a short time. He turned his eyes about the room, as if expecting some one to come. At last, with an air of disappointment, his head sank back on the pillow. He turned his face to the wall with a deep sigh.

Bishamber knew his thoughts, and, bending down his head, whispered: "Phatik, I have sent for your mother."

The day went by. The doctor said in a troubled voice that the boy's condition was very critical.

Phatik began to cry out: "By the mark!—three fathoms. By the mark—four fathoms. By the mark—." He had heard the sailor on the river-steamer calling out the mark on the plumb-line. Now he was himself plumbing an unfathomable sea.

Later in the day Phatik's mother burst into the room like a whirlwind, and began to toss from side to side and moan and cry in a loud voice.

Bishamber tried to calm her agitation, but she flung herself on the bed, and cried: "Phatik, my darling, my darling."

Phatik stopped his restless movements for a moment. His hands ceased beating up and down. He said: "Eh?"

The mother cried again: "Phatik, my darling, my darling."

Phatik very slowly turned his head and, without seeing anybody, said: "Mother, the holidays have come."

My Lord, The Baby

I

Raicharan was twelve years old when he came as a servant to his master's house. He belonged to the same caste as his master, and was given his master's little son to nurse. As time went on the boy left Raicharan's arms to go to school. From school he went on to college, and after college he entered the judicial service. Always, until he married, Raicharan was his sole attendant.

But, when a mistress came into the house, Raicharan found two masters instead of one. All his former influence passed to the new mistress. This was compensated for by a fresh arrival. Anukul had a son born to him, and Raicharan by his unsparing attentions soon got a complete hold over the child. He used to toss him up in his arms, call to him in absurd baby language, put his face close to the baby's and draw it away again with a grin.

Presently the child was able to crawl and cross the doorway. When Raicharan went to catch him, he would scream with mischievous laughter and make for safety. Raicharan was amazed at the profound skill and exact judgment the baby showed when pursued. He would say to his mistress with a look of awe and mystery: "Your son will be a judge some day."

New wonders came in their turn. When the baby began to toddle, that was to Raicharan an epoch in human history. When he called his father Ba-ba and his mother Ma-ma and Raicharan Chan-na, then Raicharan's ecstasy knew no bounds. He went out to tell the news to all the world.

After a while Raicharan was asked to show his ingenuity in other ways. He had, for instance, to play the part of a horse, holding the reins between his teeth and prancing with his feet. He had also to wrestle with his little charge, and if he could not, by a wrestler's trick, fall on his back defeated at the end, a great outcry was certain.

About this time Anukul was transferred to a district on the banks of the Padma. On his way through Calcutta he bought his son a little go-cart. He bought him also a yellow satin waist-coat, a gold-laced cap, and some gold bracelets and anklets. Raicharan was wont to take these out, and put them on his little charge with ceremonial pride, whenever they went for a walk.

Then came the rainy season, and day after day the rain poured down in torrents. The hungry river, like an enormous serpent, swallowed down terraces, villages, cornfields, and covered with its flood the tall grasses and wild casuarinas on the sandbanks. From time to time there was a deep thud as the river-banks crumbled. The unceasing roar of the main current could be heard from far away. Masses of foam, carried swiftly past, proved to the eye the swiftness of the stream.

One afternoon the rain cleared. It was cloudy, but cool and bright. Raicharan's little despot did not want to stay in on such a fine afternoon. His lordship climbed into the go-cart. Raicharan, between the shafts, dragged him slowly along till he reached the rice-fields on the banks of the river. There was no one in the fields, and no boat on the stream. Across the water, on the farther side, the clouds were rifted in the west. The silent ceremonial of the setting sun was revealed in all its glowing splendour. In the midst of that stillness the child, all of a sudden, pointed with his finger in front of him and cried: "Chan-na! Pitty fow."

Close by on a mud-flat stood a large *Kadamba* tree in full flower. My lord, the baby, looked at it with greedy eyes, and Raicharan knew his meaning. Only a short time before he had made, out of these very flower balls, a small go-cart; and the child had been so entirely happy dragging it about with a string, that for the whole day Raicharan was not made to put on the reins at all. He was promoted from a horse into a groom.

But Raicharan had no wish that evening to go splashing knee-deep through the mud to reach the flowers. So he quickly pointed his finger in the opposite direction, calling out: "Oh, look, baby, look! Look at the bird." And with all sorts of curious noises he pushed the go-cart rapidly away from the tree.

But a child, destined to be a judge, cannot be put off so easily. And besides, there was at the time nothing to attract his eyes. And you cannot keep up for ever the pretence of an imaginary bird.

The little Master's mind was made up, and Raicharan was at his wits' end. "Very well, baby," he said at last, "you sit still in the cart, and I'll go and get you the pretty flower. Only mind you don't go near the water."

As he said this, he made his legs bare to the knee, and waded through the oozing mud towards the tree.

The moment Raicharan had gone, his little Master went off at racing speed to the forbidden water. The baby saw the river rushing by, splashing and gurgling as it went. It seemed as though the disobedient wavelets themselves were running away from some greater Raicharan with the laughter of a thousand children. At the sight of their mischief, the heart of the human child grew excited and restless. He got down stealthily from the go-cart and toddled off towards the river. On his way he picked up a small stick, and leant over the bank of the stream pretending to fish. The mischievous fairies of the river with their mysterious voices seemed inviting him into their play-house.

Raicharan had plucked a handful of flowers from the tree, and was carrying them back in the end of his cloth, with his face wreathed in smiles. But when he reached the go-cart there was no one there. He looked on all sides and there was no one there. He looked back at the cart and there was no one there.

In that first terrible moment his blood froze within him. Before his eyes the whole universe swam round like a dark mist. From the depth of his broken heart he gave one piercing cry: "Master, Master, little Master."

But no voice answered "Chan-na." No child laughed mischievously back: no scream of baby delight welcomed his return. Only the river ran on, with its splashing, gurgling noise as before,—as though it knew nothing at all, and had no time to attend to such a tiny human event as the death of a child.

As the evening passed by Raicharan's mistress became very anxious. She sent men out on all sides to search. They went with lanterns in their hands, and reached at last the banks of the Padma. There they found Raicharan rushing up and down the fields, like a stormy wind, shouting the cry of despair: "Master, Master, little Master!"

When they got Raicharan home at last, he fell prostrate at this mistress's feet. They shook him, and questioned him, and asked him repeatedly where he had left the child; but all he could say was that he knew nothing.

Though every one held the opinion that the Padma had swallowed the child, there was a lurking doubt left in the mind. For a band of gipsies had been noticed outside the village that afternoon, and some suspicion rested on them. The mother went so far in her wild grief as to think it possible that Raicharan himself had stolen the child. She called him aside with piteous entreaty and said: "Raicharan, give me back my baby. Oh! give me back my child. Take from me any money you ask, but give me back my child!"

Raicharan only beat his forehead in reply. His mistress ordered him out of the house.

Anukul tried to reason his wife out of this wholly unjust suspicion: "Why on earth," he said, "should he commit such a crime as that?"

The mother only replied: "The baby had gold ornaments on his body. Who knows?"

It was impossible to reason with her after that.

II

Raicharan went back to his own village. Up to this time he had had no son, and there was no hope that any child would now be born to him. But it came about before the end of a year that his wife gave birth to a son and died.

An overwhelming resentment at first grew up in Raicharan's heart at the sight of this new baby. At the back of his mind was resentful suspicion that it had come as a usurper in place of the little Master. He also thought it would be a grave offence to be happy with a son of this own after what had happened to his master's little child. Indeed, if it had not been for a widowed sister, who mothered the new baby, it would not have lived long.

But a change gradually came over Raicharan's mind. A wonderful thing happened. This new baby in turn began to crawl about, and cross the doorway with mischief in its face. It also showed an amusing cleverness in making its escape to safety. Its voice, its sounds of laughter and tears, its gestures, were those of the little Master. On some days, when Raicharan listened to its crying, his heart suddenly began thumping wildly against his ribs, and it seemed to him that his former little Master was crying somewhere in the unknown land of death because he had lost his Chan-na.

Phailna (for that was the name Raicharan's sister gave to the new baby) soon began to talk. It learnt to say Ba-ba and Ma-ma with a baby accent. When Raicharan heard those familiar sounds the mystery suddenly became clear. The little Master could not cast off the spell of his Chan-na, and therefore he had been reborn in his own house.

The arguments in favour of this were, to Raicharan, altogether beyond dispute:

(i) The new baby was born soon after his little Master's death.

(ii) His wife could never have accumulated such merit as to give birth to a son in middle age.

(iii) The new baby walked with a toddle and called out Ba-ba and Ma-ma. There was no sign lacking which marked out the future judge.

Then suddenly Raicharan remembered that terrible accusation of the mother. "Ah," he said to himself with amazement, "the mother's heart was right. She knew I had stolen her child." When once he had come to this conclusion, he was filled with remorse for his past neglect. He now gave himself over, body and soul, to the new baby, and became its devoted attendant. He began to bring it up, as if it were the son of a rich man. He bought a go-cart, a yellow satin waistcoat, and a gold-embroidered cap. He melted down the ornaments of his dead wife, and made gold bangles and anklets. He refused to let the little child play with any one of the neighbourhood, and became himself its sole companion day and night. As the baby grew up to boyhood, he was so

petted and spoilt and clad in such finery that the village
children would call him "Your Lordship," and jeer at him;
and older people regarded Raicharan as unaccountably crazy
about the child.

At last the time came for the boy to go to school. Raicharan
sold his small piece of land, and went to Calcutta. There he
got employment with great difficulty as a servant, and sent
Phailna to school. He spared no pains to give him the best
education, the best clothes, the best food. Meanwhile he lived
himself on a mere handful of rice, and would say in secret:
"Ah! my little Master, my dear little Master, you loved me
so much that you came back to my house. You shall never
suffer from any neglect of mine."

Twelve years passed away in this manner. The boy was
able to read and write well. He was bright and healthy and
good-looking. He paid a great deal of attention to his personal
appearance, and was specially careful in parting his hair. He
was inclined to extravagance and finery, and spent money
freely. He could never quite look on Raicharan as a father,
because, though fatherly in affection, he had the manner of
a servant. A further fault was this, that Raicharan kept secret
from every one that himself was the father of the child.

The students of the hostel, where Phailna was a boarder,
were greatly amused by Raicharan's country manners, and I
have to co...ess that behind his father's back Phailna joined
in their fun. But, in the bottom of their hearts, all the students
loved the innocent and tender-hearted old man, and Phailna
was very fond of him also. But, as I have said before, he loved
him with a kind of condescension.

Raicharan grew older and older, and his employer was
continually finding fault with him for his incompetent work.
He had been starving himself for the boy's sake. So he had
grown physically weak, and no longer up to his work. He
would forget things, and his mind became dull and stupid.

But his employer expected a full servant's work out of him, and would not brook excuses. The money that Raicharan had brought with him from the sale of his land was exhausted. The boy was continually grumbling about his clothes, and asking for more money.

III

Raicharan made up his mind. He gave up the situation where he was working as a servant, and left some money with Phailna and said: "I have some business to do at home in my village, and shall be back soon."

He went off at once to Baraset where Anukul was magistrate. Anukul's wife was still broken down with grief. She had had no other child.

One day Anukul was resting after a long and weary day in court. His wife was buying, at an exorbitant price, a herb from a mendicant quack, which was said to ensure the birth of a child. A voice of greeting was heard in the courtyard. Anukul went out to see who was there. It was Raicharan. Anukul's heart was softened when he saw his old servant. He asked him many questions, and offered to take him back into service.

Raicharan smiled faintly, and said in reply: "I want to make obeisance to my mistress."

Anukul went with Raicharan into the house, where the mistress did not receive him as warmly as his old master. Raicharan took no notice of this, but folded his hands, and said: "It was not the Padma that stole your baby. It was I."

Anukul exclaimed: "Great God! Eh! What! Where is he?"

Raicharan replied: "He is with me. I will bring him the day after to-morrow."

It was Sunday. There was no magistrate's court sitting. Both husband and wife were looking expectantly along the road, waiting from early morning for Raicharan's appearance. At ten o'clock he came, leading Phailna by the hand.

Anukul's wife, without a question, took the boy into her lap, and was wild with excitement, sometimes laughing, sometimes weeping, touching him, kissing his hair and his forehead, and gazing into his face with hungry, eager eyes. The boy was very good-looking and dressed like a gentleman's son. The heart of Anukul brimmed over with a sudden rush of affection.

Nevertheless the magistrate in him asked: "Have you any proofs?"

Raicharan said: "How could there be any proof of such a deed? God alone knows that I stole your boy, and no one else in the world."

When Anukul saw how eagerly his wife was clinging to the boy, he realised the futility of asking for proofs. It would be wiser to believe. And then—where could an old man like Raicharan get such a boy from? And why should his faithful servant deceive him for nothing?

"But," he added severely, "Raicharan, you must not stay here."

"Where shall I go, Master?" said Raicharan, in a choking voice, folding his hands; "I am old. Who will take in an old man as a servant?"

The mistress said: "Let him stay. My child will be pleased. I forgive him."

But Anukul's magisterial conscience would not allow him. "No," he said, "he cannot be forgiven for what he has done."

Raicharan bowed to the ground, and clasped Anukul's feet. "Master," he cried, "let me stay. It was not I who did it. It was GOD."

Anukul's conscience was worse stricken than ever, when Raicharan tried to put the blame on God's shoulders.

"No," he said, "I could not allow it. I cannot trust you any more. You have done an act of treachery."

Raicharan rose to his feet and said: "It was not I who did it."

"Who was it then?" asked Anukul.

Raicharan replied: "It was my fate."

But no educated man could take this for an excuse. Anukul remained obdurate.

When Phailna saw that he was the wealthy magistrate's son, and not Raicharan's, he was angry at first, thinking that he had been cheated all this time of his birthright. But seeing Raicharan in distress, he generously said to his father: "Father, forgive him. Even if you don't let him live with us, let him have a small monthly pension."

After hearing this, Raicharan did not utter another word. He looked for the last time on the face of his son; he made obeisance to his old master and mistress. Then he went out, and was mingled with the numberless people of the world.

At the end of the month Anukul sent him some money to his village. But the money came back. There was no one there of the name of Raicharan.

The Kingdom of Cards

Once upon a time there was a lonely island in a distant sea where lived the Kings and Queens, the Aces and the Knaves, in the Kingdom of Cards. The Tens and Nines, with the Twos and Threes, and all the other members, had long ago settled there also. But these were not twice-born people, like the famous Court Cards.

The Ace, the King, and the Knave were the three highest castes. The fourth caste was made up of a mixture of the lower Cards. The Twos and Threes were lowest of all. These inferior Cards were never allowed to sit in the same row with the great Court Cards.

Wonderful indeed were the regulations and rules of that island kingdom. The particular rank of each individual had been settled from time immemorial. Every one had his own appointed work, and never did anything else. An unseen hand appeared to be directing them wherever they went,—according to the Rules.

No one in the Kingdom of Cards had any occasion to think: no one had any need to come to any decision: no one was ever required to debate any new subject. The citizens all moved along in a listless groove without speech. When they fell, they made no noise. They lay down on their backs, and gazed upward at the sky with each prim feature firmly fixed for ever.

There was a remarkable stillness in the Kingdom of cards. Satisfaction and contentment were complete in all their rounded wholeness. There was never any uproar or violence. There was never any excitement or enthusiasm.

The great ocean, crooning its lullaby with one unceasing melody, lapped the island to sleep with a thousand soft touches of its wave's white hands. The vast sky, like the outspread azure wings of the brooding mother-bird, nestled the island round with its downy plume. For on the distant horizon a deep blue line betokened another shore. But no sound of quarrel or strife could reach the Island of Cards, to break its calm repose.

II

In that far-off foreign land across the sea, there lived a young Prince whose mother was a sorrowing queen. This queen had fallen from favour, and was living with her only son on the seashore. The Prince passed his childhood alone and forlorn, sitting by his forlorn mother, weaving the net of his big desires. He longed to go in search of the Flying Horse, the jewel in the Cobra's hood, the Rose of Heaven, the Magic Roads, or to find where the Princess Beauty was sleeping in the Ogre's castle over the thirteen rivers and across the seven seas.

From the Son of the Merchant at school the young Prince learnt the stories of foreign kingdoms. From the Son of the Kotwal he learnt the adventures of the Two Genii of the Lamp. And when the rain came beating down, and the clouds covered the sky, he would sit on the threshold facing the sea, and say to his sorrowing mother: "Tell me, mother, a story of some very far-off land."

And his mother would tell him an endless tale she had heard in her childhood of a wonderful country beyond the sea where dwelt the Princess Beauty. And the heart of the young Prince would become sick with longing, as he sat on the threshold, looking out on the ocean, listening to his mother's wonderful story, while the rain outside came beating down and the grey clouds covered the sky.

One day the Son of the Merchant came to the Prince, and said boldly: "Comrade, my studies are over. I am now setting out on my travels to seek my fortunes on the sea. I have come to bid you good-bye."

The Prince said: "I will go with you."

And the Son of Kotwal said also: "Comrades, trusty and true, you will not leave me behind. I also will be your companion."

Then the young Prince said to his sorrowing mother: "Mother, I am now setting out on my travels to seek my fortune. When I come back once more, I shall surely have found some way to remove all your sorrow."

So the Three Companions set out on their travels together. In the harbour were anchored the twelve ships of the merchant, and the Three Companions got on board. The south wind was blowing, and the twelve ships sailed away, as fast as the desires which rose in the Prince's breast.

At the Conch Shell Island they filled one ship with conchs. At the Sandal Wood Island they filled a second ship with sandal-wood, and at the Coral Island they filled a third ship with coral.

Four years passed away, and they filled four more ships, one with ivory, one with musk, one with cloves, and one with nutmegs.

But when these ships were all loaded a terrible tempest arose. The ships were all of them sunk, with their cloves and nutmeg, and musk and ivory, and coral and sandal-wood and conchs. But the ship with the Three Companions struck on an island reef, hurled them safe ashore, and itself broke in pieces.

This was the famous Island of Cards, where lived the Ace and King and Queen and Knave, with the Nines and Tens and all the other members—according to the Rules.

III

Up till now there had been nothing to disturb that island stillness. No new thing had ever happened. No discussion had ever been held.

And then, of a sudden, the Three Companions appeared, thrown up by the sea,—and the Great Debate began. There were three main points of dispute.

First, to what caste should these unclassed strangers belong? Should they rank with the Court Cards? Or were they merely lower-caste people, to be ranked with the Nines and Tens? No precedent could be quoted to decide this weighty question.

Secondly, what was their clan? Had they the fairer hue and bright complexion of the Hearts, or was theirs the darker complexion of the Clubs? Over this question there were interminable disputes. The whole marriage system of the island, with its intricate regulations, would depend on its nice adjustment.

Thirdly, what food should they take? With whom should they live and sleep? And should their heads be placed south-west, north-west, or only north-east? In all the Kingdom of Cards a series of problems so vital and critical had never been debated before.

But the Three Companions grew desperately hungry. They had to get food in some way or other. So while this debate went on, with its interminable silence and pauses, and while the Aces called their own meeting, and formed themselves into a Committee, to find some obsolete dealing with the question, the Three Companions themselves were eating all they could find, and drinking out of every vessel, and breaking all regulations.

Even the Twos and Threes were shocked at this outrageous behaviour. The Threes said: "Brother Twos, these people are openly shameless!" And the Twos said: "Brother Threes, they are evidently of lower caste than ourselves!"

After their meal was over, the Three Companions went for a stroll in the city.

When they saw the ponderous people moving in their dismal processions with prim and solemn faces, then the Prince turned to the Son of the Merchant and the Son of the Kotwal, and threw back his head, and gave one stupendous laugh.

Down Royal Street and across Ace Square and along the Knave Embankment the quiver of this strange, unheard-of laughter, the laughter that, amazed at itself, expired in the vast vacuum of silence.

The Son of the Kotwal and the Son of the Merchant were chilled through to the bone by the ghost-like stillness around them. they turned to the Prince, and said: "Comrade, let us away. Let us not stop for a moment in this awful land of ghosts."

But the Prince said: "Comrades, these people resemble men, so I am going to find out, by shaking them upside down and outside in, whether they have a single drop of warm living blood left in their veins."

IV

The days passed one by one, and the placid existence of the Island went on almost without a ripple. The Three Companions obeyed no rules nor regulations. They never did anything correctly either in sitting or standing or turning themselves round or lying on their back. On the contrary, wherever they saw these things going on precisely and exactly according to the Rules, they gave way to inordinate laughter. They remained unimpressed altogether by the eternal gravity of those eternal regulations.

One day the great Court Cards came to the Son of the Kotwal and the Son of the Merchant and the Prince.

"Why," they asked slowly, "are you not moving according to the Rules?"

The Three Companions answered: "Because that is our *Ichcha* (wish)."

The great Court Cards with hollow, cavernous voices, as if slowly awakening from an age-long dream, said together: "*Ich-cha!* And pray who is *Ich-cha*?"

They could not understand who *Ichcha* was then, but the whole island was to understand it by-and-by.

The first glimmer of light passed the threshold of their minds when they found out, through watching the actions of the Prince, that they might move in a straight line in an opposite direction from the one in which they had always gone before. Then they made another startling discovery, that there was another side to the Cards which they had never yet noticed with attention. This was the beginning of the change.

Now that the change had begun, the Three Companions were able to initiate them more and more deeply into the mysteries of *Ichcha*. The Cards gradually became aware that life was not bound by regulations. They began to feel a secret satisfaction in the kingly power of choosing for themselves.

But with this first impact of *Ichcha* the whole pack of cards began to totter slowly, and then tumble down to the ground. The scene was like that of some huge python awaking from a long sleep, as it slowly unfolds its numberless coils with a quiver that runs through its whole frame.

V

Hitherto the Queens of Spades and Clubs and Diamonds and Hearts had remained behind curtains with eyes that gazed vacantly into space, or else remained fixed upon the ground.

And now, all of a sudden, on an afternoon in spring the Queen of Hearts from the balcony raised her dark eyebrows for a moment, and cast a single glance upon the Prince from the corner of her eye.

"Great God," cried the Prince, "I thought they were all painted images. But I am wrong. They are women after all."

Then the young Prince called to his side his two Companions, and said in a meditative voice: "My comrades! There is a charm about these ladies that I never noticed before. When I saw that glance of the Queen's dark, luminous eyes, brightening with new emotion, it seemed to me like the first faint streak of dawn in a newly created world."

The two Companions smiled a knowing smile, and said: "Is that really so, Prince?"

And the poor Queen of Hearts from that day went from bad to worse. She began to forget all rules in a truly scandalous manner. If, for instance, her place in the row was beside the Knave, she suddenly found herself quite accidentally standing beside the Prince instead. At this, the Knave, with motionless face and solemn voice, would say: "Queen, you have made a mistake."

And the poor Queen of Hearts' red cheeks would get redder than ever. But the Prince would come gallantly to her rescue and say: "No! There is no mistake. From to-day I am going to be Knave!"

Now it came to pass that, while every one was trying to correct the improprieties of the guilty Queen of Hearts, they began to make mistakes themselves. The Aces found themselves elbowed out by the Kings. The Kings got muddled up with the Knaves. The Nines and Tens assumed airs as though they belonged to the Great Court Cards. The Twos and Threes were found secretly taking the places specially reserved for the Fours and Fives. Confusion had never been so confounded before.

Many spring seasons had come and gone in that Island of Cards. The Kokil, the bird of Spring, had sung its song year after year. But it had never stirred the blood as it stirred it now. In days gone by the sea had sung its tireless melody. But, then, it had proclaimed only the inflexible monotony of the Rule. And suddenly its waves were telling, through all their flashing light and luminous shade and myriad voices, the deepest yearnings of the heart of love!

VI

Where are vanished now their prim, round, regular, complacent features? Here is a face full of love-sick longing. Here is a heart beating wild with regrets. Here is a mind racked sore with doubts. Music and sighing, and smiles and tears, are filling the air. Life is throbbing; hearts are breaking; passions are kindling.

Every one is now thinking of his own appearance, and comparing himself with others. The Ace of Clubs is musing to himself that the King of Spades may be just passably good-looking. "But," says he, "when I walk down the street you have only to see how people's eyes turn towards me." The King of Spades is saying: "Why on earth is that Ace of Clubs always straining his neck and strutting about like a peacock? He imagines all the Queens are dying of love for him, while the real fact is——" Here he pauses, and examines his face in the glass.

But the Queens were the worst of all. They began to spend all their time in dressing themselves up to the Nines. And the Nines would become their hopeless and abject slaves. But their cutting remarks about one another were more shocking still.

So the young men would sit listless on the leaves under the trees, lolling with outstretched limbs in the forest shade. And the young maidens, dressed in pale-blue robes, would come walking accidentally to the same shade of the same forest by the same trees, and turn their eyes as though they saw no one there, and look as though they came out to see nothing at all. And then one young man more forward than the rest in a fit of madness would dare to go near to a maiden in blue. But, as he drew near, speech would forsake him. He would stand there tongue-tied and foolish, and the favourable moment would pass.

The Kokil birds were singing in the boughs overhead. The mischievous South wind was blowing; it disarrayed the hair, it whispered in the ear, and stirred the music in the blood. The leaves of the trees were murmuring with rustling delight. And the ceaseless sound of the ocean made all the mute longings of the heart of man and maid surge backwards and forwards on the full springtide of love.

The Three Companions had brought into the dried-up channels of the Kingdom of Cards the full flood-tide of a new life.

VII

And, though the tide was full, there was a pause as though the rising waters would not break into foam but remain suspended for ever. There were no outspoken words, only a cautious going forward one step and receding two. All seemed busy heaping up their unfulfilled desires, like castles in the air, or fortresses of sand. They were pale and speechless, their eyes were burning, their lips trembling with unspoken secrets.

The Prince saw what was wrong. He summoned every one on the Island and said: "Bring hither the flutes and the cymbals, the pipes and drums. Let all be played together, and raise loud shouts of rejoicing. For the Queen of Hearts this very night is going to choose her Mate!"

So the Tens and Nines began to blow on their flutes and pipes; the Eights and Sevens played on their sackbuts and viols; and even the Twos and Threes began to beat madly on their drums.

When this tumultuous gust of music came, it swept away at one blast all these sighings and mopings. And then what a torrent of laughter and words poured forth! There were daring proposals and mocking refusals, and gossip and chatter, and jests and merriment. It was like the swaying and shaking, and rustling and soughing, in a summer gale, of a million leaves and branches in the depth of the primeval forest.

But the Queen of Hearts, in a rose-red robe, sat silent in the shadow of her secret bower, and listened to the great uproarious sound of music and mirth that came floating towards her. She shut her eyes, and dreamt her dream of love. And when she opened them she found the Prince seated on the ground before her gazing up at her face. And she covered her eyes with both hands, and shrank back quivering with an inward tumult of joy.

And the Prince passed the whole day alone, walking by the side of the surging sea. He carried in his mind that startled look, that shrinking gesture of the Queen, and his heart beat high with hope.

That night the serried, gaily-dressed ranks of young men and maidens waited with smiling faces at the Palace Gates. The Palace Hall was lighted with fairy lamps and festooned with the flowers of spring. Slowly the Queen of Hearts entered, and the whole assembly rose to greet her. With a jasmine garland in her hand, she stood before the Prince with downcast eyes. In her lowly bashfulness she could hardly raise the garland to the neck of the mate she had chosen. But the Prince bowed his head, and the garland slipped to its place. The assembly of youths and maidens had waited her choice with eager, expectant hush. And when the choice was made, the whole vast concourse rocked and swayed with a tumult of wild delight. And the sound of their shouts was heard in every part of the Island, and by ships far out at sea. Never had such a shout been raised in the Kingdom of Cards before.

And they carried the Prince and his Bride, and seated them on the throne, and crowned them then and there in the Ancient Island of Cards.

And the sorrowing Mother Queen, on the far-off island shore on the other side of the sea, came sailing to her son's new kingdom in a ship adorned with gold.

And the citizens are no longer regulated according to the Rules, but are good or bad, or both, according to their *Ichcha*.

The Devotee

I

At a time when my unpopularity with a part of my readers had reached the nadir of its glory, and my name had become the central orb of the journals, to be attended through space with a perpetual rotation of revilement, I felt the necessity to retire to some quiet place and endeavour to forget my own existence.

I have a house in the country some miles away from Calcutta, where I can remain unknown and unmolested. The villagers there have not, as yet, come to any conclusion about me. They know I am no mere holiday-maker or pleasure-seeker; for I never outrage the silence of the village nights with the riotous noises of the city. Nor do they regard me as an ascetic, because the little acquaintance they have of me carries the savour of comfort about it. I am not, to them a traveller; for, though I am a vagabond by nature, my wandering through the village fields is aimless. They are hardly even quite certain whether I am married or single; for they have never seen me with my children. So, not being able to classify me in any animal or vegetable kingdom that they know, they have long since given me up and left me stolidly alone.

But quite lately I have come to know that there is one person in the village who is deeply interested in me. Our acquaintance began on a sultry afternoon in July. There had been rain all the morning, and the air was still wet and heavy with mist, like eyelids when weeping is over.

I sat lazily watching a dappled cow grazing on the high bank of the river. The afternoon sun was playing on her glossy hide. The simple beauty of this dress of light made me wonder idly at man's deliberate waste of money in setting up tailors' shops to deprive his own skin of its natural clothing.

While I was thus watching and lazily musing, a woman of middle age came and prostrated herself before me, touching the ground with her forehead. She carried in her robe some bunches of flowers, one of which she offered to me with folded hands. She said to me, as she offered it: "This is an offering to my God."

She went away. I was so taken aback as she uttered these words, that I could hardly catch a glimpse of her before she was gone. The whole incident was entirely simple, but it left a deep impression on my mind; and as I turned back once more to look at the cattle in the field, the zest of life in the cow, who was munching the lush grass with deep breaths, while she whisked off the flies, appeared to me fraught with mystery. My readers may laugh at my foolishness, but my heart was full of adoration. I offered my worship to the pure joy of living, which is God's own life. Then, plucking a tender shoot from the mango tree, I fed the cow with it from my own hand, and as I did this I had the satisfaction of having pleased my God.

The next year when I returned to the village it was February. The cold season still lingered on. The morning sun came into my room, and I was grateful for its warmth. I was writing, when the servant came to tell me that a devotee, of the Vishnu cult, wanted to see me. I told him, in an absent way, to bring her upstairs, and went on with my writing. The Devotee came in, and bowed to me, touching my feet. I found that she was the same woman whom I had met, for a brief moment, a year ago.

I was able now to examine her more closely. She was past that age when one asks the question whether a woman is beautiful or not. Her stature was above the ordinary height, and she was strongly built; but her body was slightly bent owing to her constant attitude of veneration. Her manner had nothing shrinking about it. The most remarkable of her features were her two eyes. They seemed to have a penetrating power which could make distance near.

With those two large eyes of hers, she seemed to push me as she entered.

"What is this?" she asked. "Why have you brought me here before your throne, my God? I used to see you among the trees; and that was much better. That was the true place to meet you."

She must have seen me walking in the garden without my seeing her. For the last few days, however, I had suffered from a cold, and had been prevented from going out. It had, perforce, to stay indoors and pay my homage to the evening sky from my terrace. After a silent pause the Devotee said to me: "O my God, give me some words of good."

I was quite unprepared for this abrupt request, and answered her on the spur of the moment: "Good words I neither give nor receive. I simply open my eyes and keep silence, and then I can at once both hear and see, even when no sound is uttered. Now, while I am looking at you, it is as good as listening to your voice."

The Devotee became quite excited as I spoke, and exclaimed: "God speaks to me, not only with His mouth, but with His whole body."

I said to her: "When I am silent I can listen with my whole body. I have come away from Calcutta here to listen to that sound."

The Devotee said: "Yes, I know that, and therefore I have come here to sit by you."

Before taking her leave, she again bowed to me, and touched my feet. I could see that she was distressed, because my feet were covered. She wished them to be bare.

Early next morning I came out, and sat on my terrace on the roof. Beyond the line of trees southward I could see the open country, chill and desolated. I could watch the sun rising over the sugar-cane in the East, beyond the clump of trees at the side of the village. Out of the deep shadow òf those dark trees the village road suddenly appeared. It stretched forward, winding its way to some distant villages on the horizon, till it was lost in the grey of the mist.

That morning it was difficult to say whether the sun had risen or not. A white fog was still clinging to the tops of the trees. I saw the Devotee walking through the blurred dawn, like a mist-wraith of the morning twilight. She was singing her chant to God, and sounding her cymbals.

The thick haze lifted at last; and the sun, like the kindly grandsire of the village, took his seat amid all the work that was going on in home and field.

When I had just settled down at my writing-table, to appease the hungry appetite of my editor in Calcutta, there came a sound of footsteps on the stair, and the Devotee, humming a tune to herself, entered, and bowed before me. I lifted my head from my papers.

She said to me: "My God, yesterday I took as sacred food what was left over from your meal."

I was startled, and asked her how she could do that.

"Oh," she said, "I waited at your door in the evening, while you were at dinner, and took some food from your plate when it was carried out."

This was a surprise to me, for every one in the village knew that I had been to Europe, and had eaten with Europeans.

I was a vegetarian, no doubt, but the sanctity of my cook would not bear investigation, and the orthodox regarded my food as polluted.

The Devotee, noticing my sign of surprise, said: "My God, why should I come to you at all, if I could not take your food?"

I asked her what her own caste people would say. She told me she had already spread the news far and wide all over the village. The caste people had shaken their heads, but agreed that she must go her own way.

I found out that the Devotee came from a good family in the country, and that her mother was well-to-do, and desired to keep her daughter. But she preferred to be a mendicant. I asked her how she made her living. She told me that her followers had given her a piece of land, and that she begged her food from door to door. She said to me: "The food which I get by begging is divine."

After I had thought over what she said, I understood her meaning. When we get our food precariously as alms, we remember God the giver. But when we receive our food regularly at home, as a matter of course, we are apt to regard it as ours by right.

I had a great desire to ask her about her husband. But as she never mentioned him even indirectly, I did not question her.

I found out very soon that the Devotee had no respect at all for that part of the village where the people of the higher castes lived.

"They never give," she said, "a single farthing to God's service; and yet they have the largest share of God's glebe. But the poor worship and starve."

I asked her why she did not go and live among these godless people, and help them towards a better life. "That," I said with some unction, "would be the highest form of divine worship."

I have heard sermons of this kind from time to time, and I am rather fond of copying them myself for the public benefit, when the chance comes.

But the Devotee was not at all impressed. She raised her big round eyes, and looked straight into mine, and said:

"You mean to say that because God is with the sinners, therefore when you do them any service you do it to God? Is that so?"

"Yes," I replied, "that is my meaning."

"Of course," she answered almost impatiently, "of course, God is with them: otherwise, how could they go on living at all? But what is that to me? My God is not there. My God cannot be worshipped among them; because I do not find Him there. I seek Him where I can find Him."

As she spoke, she made obeisance to me. What she meant to say was really this. A mere doctrine of God's omnipresence does not help us. That God is all-pervading,—this truth may be a mere intangible abstraction, and therefore unreal to ourselves. Where I can see Him, there is His reality in my soul.

I need not explain that all the while she showered her devotion on me she did it to me not as an individual. I was simply a vehicle of her divine worship. It was not for me either to receive it or to refuse it: for it was not mine, but God's.

When the Devotee came again, she found me once engaged with my books and papers.

"What have you been doing," she said, with evident vexation, "that my God should make you undertake such drudgery? Whenever I come, I find you reading and writing."

"God keeps his useless people busy," I answered; "otherwise they would be bound to get into mischief. They have to do all the least necessary things in life. It keeps them out of trouble."

The Devotee told me that she could not bear the encumbrances, with which, day by day, I was surrounded. If she wanted to see me, she was not allowed by the servants to come straight upstairs. If she wanted to touch my feet in worship, there were my socks always in the way. And when she wanted to have a simple talk with me, she found my mind lost in a wilderness of letters.

This time, before she left me, she folded her hands, and said: "My God! I felt your feet in my breast this morning. Oh, how cool! And they were bare, not covered. I held them upon my head for a long time in worship. That filled my very being. Then, after that, pray what was the use of my coming to you yourself? Why did I come? My Lord, tell me truly,— wasn't it a mere infatuation?"

There were some flowers in my vase on the table. While she was there, the gardener brought some new flowers to put in their place. The Devotee saw him changing them.

"Is that all?" she exclaimed. "Have you done with the flowers? Then give them to me."

She held the flowers tenderly in the cup of her hands, and began to gaze at them with bent head. After a few moments' silence she raised her head again, and said to me: "You never look at these flowers; therefore they become stale to you. If you would only look into them, then your reading and writing would go to the winds."

She tied the flowers together in the end of her robe, and placed them, in an attitude of worship, on the top of her head, saying reverently. "Let me carry my God with me."

While she did this, I felt that flowers in our rooms do not receive their due need of loving care at our hands. When we stick them in vases, they are more like a row of naughty schoolboys standing on a form to be punished.

The Devotee came again the same evening, and sat by my feet on the terrace of the roof.

"I gave away those flowers," she said, "as I went from house to house this morning, singing God's name. Beni, the head man of our village, laughed at me for my devotion, and said: 'Why do you waste all this devotion on Him? Don't you know He is reviled up and down the countryside?' Is that true, my God? Is it true that they are hard upon you?"

For a moment I shrank into myself. It was a shock to find that the stains of printers' ink could reach so far.

The Devotee went on: "Beni imagined that he could blow out the flame of my devotion at one breath! But this is no mere tiny flame: it is a burning fire. Why do they abuse you, my God?"

I said: "Because I deserved it. I suppose in my greed I was loitering about to steal people's hearts in secret."

The Devotee said: "Now you see for yourself how little their hearts are worth. They are full of poison, and this will cure you of your greed."

"When a man," I answered, "has greed in his heart, he is always on the verge of being beaten. The greed itself supplies his enemies with poison."

"Our merciful God," she replied, "beats us with His own hand, and drives away all the poison. He who endures God's beating to the end is saved."

II

That evening the Devotee told me the story of her life. The stars of evening rose and set behind the trees, as she went on to the end of her tale.

"My husband is very simple. Some people think that he is a simpleton; but I know that those who understand simply, understand truly. In business and household management he was able to hold his own. Because his needs were small, and his wants few, he could manage carefully on what we had. He would never meddle in other matters, nor try to understand them.

"Both my husband's parents died before we had been married long, and we were left alone. But my husband always needed some one to be over him. I am ashamed to confess that he had a sort of reverence for me, and looked upon me as his superior. But I am sure that he could understand things better than I, though I had greater powers of talking.

"Of all the people in the world he held his Guru Thakur (spiritual master) in the highest veneration. Indeed it was not veneration merely but love; and such love as his is rare.

"Guru Thakur was younger than my husband. Oh! how beautiful he was.

"My husband had played games with him when he was a boy; and from that time forward he had dedicated his heart and soul to this friend of his early days. Thakur knew how simple my husband was, and used to tease him mercilessly.

"He and his comrades would play jokes upon him for their own amusement; but he would bear them all with long suffering.

"When I married into this family, Guru Thakur was studying at Benares. My husband used to pay all his expenses. I was eighteen years old when he returned home to our village.

"At the age of fifteen I had my child. I was so young I did not know how to take care of him. I was fond of gossip, and liked to be with my village friends for hours together. I used to get quite cross with my boy when I was compelled to stay at home and nurse him. Alas! my child-God came into my life, but His playthings were not ready for Him. He came to the mother's heart, but the mother's heart lagged behind. He left me in anger; and ever since I have been searching for Him up and own the world.

"The boy was the joy of his father's life. My careless neglect used to pain my husband. But his was a mute soul. He has never been able to give expression to his pain.

"The wonderful thing was this, that in spite of my neglect the child used to love me more than any one else. He seemed to have the dread that I would one day go away and leave him. So even when I was with him, he would watch me with a restless look in his eyes. He had me very little to himself, and therefore his desire to be me with was always painfully eager. When I went each day to the river, he used to fret and stretch out his little arms to be taken with me. But the bathing *ghat* was my place for meeting my friends, and I did not care to burden myself with the child.

"It was an early morning in August. Fold after fold of grey clouds had wrapped the midday round with a wet clinging robe. I asked the maid to take care of the boy, while I went down to the river. The child cried after me as I went away.

"There was no one there at the bathing *ghat* when I arrived. As a swimmer, I was the best among all the village women. The river was quite full with the rains. I swam out into the middle of the stream some distance from the shore.

"Then I heard a cry from the bank, 'Mother!' I turned my head and saw my boy coming down the steps, calling me as he came. I shouted to him to stop, but he went on, laughing and calling. My feet and hands became cramped with fear. I shut my eyes, afraid to see. When I opened them, there, at the slippery stairs, my boy's ripple of laughter had disappeared for ever.

"I got back to the shore. I raised him from the water. I took him in my arms, my boy, my darling, who had begged so often in vain for me to take him. I took him now, but he no more looked in my eyes and called 'Mother.'

"My child-God had come. I had ever neglected Him. I had ever made Him cry. And now all that neglect began to beat against my own heart, blow upon blow, blow upon blow. When my boy was with me, I had left him alone. I had refused to take him with me. And now, when he is dead, his memory clings to me and never leaves me.

"God alone knows all that my husband suffered. If he had only punished me for my sin, it would have been better for us both. But he knew only how to endure in silence, not how to speak.

"When I was almost mad with grief, Guru Thakur came back. In earlier days, the relation between him and my husband had been that of boyish friendship. Now, my husband's reverence for his sanctity and learning was unbounded. He could hardly speak in his presence, his awe of him was so great.

"My husband asked his Guru to try to give me some consolation. Guru Thakur began to read and explain to me the scriptures. But I do not think they had much effect on my mind. All their value for me lay in the voice that uttered them. God makes the draught of divine life deepest in the heart for man to drink, through the human voice. He has no better vessel in His hand than that; and He Himself drinks His divine draught out of the same vessel.

"My husband's love and veneration for his Guru filled our house, as incense fills a temple shrine. I showed that veneration, and had peace. I saw my God in the form of that Guru. He used to come to take his meal at our house every morning. The first thought that would come to my mind on waking from sleep was that of his food as a sacred gift from God. When I prepared the things for his meal, my fingers would sing for joy.

"When my husband saw my devotion to his Guru, his respect for me greatly increased. He noticed his Guru's eager desire to explain the scriptures to me. He used to think that he could never expect to earn any regard from his Guru himself, on account of his stupidity; but his wife had made up for it.

"Thus another five years went by happily, and my whole life would have passed like that; but beneath the surface some stealing was going on somewhere in secret. I could not detect it; but it was detected by the God of my heart. Then came a day when, in a moment, our whole life was turned upside down.

"It was a morning in midsummer. I was returning home from bathing, my clothes all wet, down a shady lane. At the bend of the road, under the mango tree, I met my Guru Thakur. He had his towel on his shoulder and was repeating some Sanskrit verses as he was going to take his bath. With my wet clothes clinging all about me I was ashamed to meet him. I tried to pass by quickly, and avoid being seen. He called me by my name.

"I stopped, lowering my eyes, shrinking into myself. He fixed his gaze upon me, and said: 'How beautiful is your body!'

"All the universe of birds seemed to break into song in the branches overhead. All the bushes in the lane seemed ablaze with flowers. It was as though the earth and sky and everything had become a riot of intoxicating joy.

"I cannot tell how I got home. I only remember that I rushed into the room where we worship God. But the room seemed empty. Only before my eyes those same gold spangles of light were dancing which had quivered in front of me in that shady lane on my way back from the river.

"Guru Thakur came to take his food that day, and asked my husband where I had gone. He searched for me, but could not find me anywhere.

"Ah! I have not the same earth now any longer. The same sunlight is not mine. I called on my God in my dismay, and He kept His face turned away for me.

"The day passed, I know not how. That night I had to meet my husband. But the night is dark and silent. It is the time when my husband's mind comes out shining, like stars at twilight. I had heard him speak things in the dark, and I had been surprised to find how deeply he understood.

"Sometimes I am late in the evening in going to rest on account of household work. My husband waits for me, seated on the floor, without going to bed. Our talk at such times had often begun with something about our Guru.

"That night, when it was past midnight, I came to my room, and found my husband sleeping on the floor. Without disturbing him I lay down on the ground at his feet, my head towards him. Once he stretched his feet, while sleeping, and struck me on the breast. That was his last bequest.

"Next morning, when my husband woke up from his sleep, I was already sitting by him. Outside the widow, over the thick foliage of the jack-fruit tree, appeared the first pale red of the dawn at the fringe of the night. It was so early that the crows had not yet begun to call.

"I bowed, and touched my husband's feet with my forehead. He sat up, starting as if waking from a dream, and looked at my face in amazement. I said:

"'I have made up my mind. I must leave the world. I cannot belong to you any longer. I must leave your home.'

"Perhaps my husband thought that he was still dreaming. He said not a word.

"'Ah! do hear me!' I pleaded with infinite pain. 'Do hear me and understand! You must marry another wife. I must take my leave.'

"My husband said: 'What is all this wild, mad talk? Who advises you to leave the world?'

"I said: 'My Guru Thakur.'

"My husband looked bewildered. 'Guru Thakur!' he cried. 'When did he give you this advice?'

"'In the morning,' I answered, 'yesterday, when I met him on my way back from the river.'

"His voice trembled a little. He turned, and looked in my face, and asked me: 'Why did he give you such a behest?'

"'I do not know,' I answered. 'Ask him! He will tell you himself, if he can.'

"My husband said: 'It is possible to leave the world, even when continuing to live in it. You need not leave my home. I will speak to my Guru about it.'

" 'Your Guru,' I said, 'may accept your petition; but my heart will never give its consent. I must leave your home. From henceforth, the world is no more to me.'

"My husband remained silent, and we sat there on the floor in the dark. When it was light, he said to me: 'Let us both come to him.'

"I folded my hands and said: 'I shall never meet him again.'

"He looked into my face. I lowered my eyes. He said no more. I knew that, somehow, he had seen into my mind, and understood what was there. In this world of mine, there were only two who loved me best—my boy and my husband. That love was my god, and therefore it could brook no falsehood. One of these two left me, and I left the other. Now I must have truth, and truth alone."

She touched the ground at my feet, rose and bowed to me, and departed.

Vision

I

When I was a very young wife, I gave birth to a dead child, and came near to death myself. I recovered strength very slowly, and my eyesight became weaker and weaker.

My husband at this time was studying medicine. He was not altogether sorry to have a chance of testing his medical knowledge on me. So he began to treat my eyes himself.

My elder brother was reading for his law examination. One day he came to see me, and was alarmed at my condition.

"What are you doing?" he said to my husband. "You are ruining Kumo's eyes. You ought to consult a good doctor at once."

My husband said irritably: "Why! what can a good doctor do more than I am doing? The case is quite a simple one, and the remedies are all well known."

Dada answered with scorn: "I suppose you think there is no difference between you and a Professor in your own Medical College."

My husband replied angrily: "If you ever get married, and there is a dispute about your wife's property, you won't take my advice about Law. Why, then, do you now come advising me about Medicine?"

While they were quarrelling, I was saying to myself that it was always the poor grass that suffered most when two kings went to war. Here was dispute going on between these two, and I had to bear the brunt of it.

It also seemed to me very unfair that, when my family had given me in marriage, they should interfere afterwards. After all, my pleasure and pain are my husband's concern, not theirs.

From that day forward, merely over this trifling matter of my eyes, the bond between my husband and Dada was strained.

To my surprise one afternoon, while my husband was away, Dada brought a doctor in to see me. He examined my eyes very carefully, and looked grave. He said that further neglect would be dangerous. He wrote out a prescription, and Dada sent for the medicine at once. When the strange doctor had gone, I implored my Dada not to interfere. I was sure that only evil would come from the stealthy visits of a doctor.

I was surprised at myself for plucking up courage to speak to my brother like that. I had always hitherto been afraid of him. I am sure also that Dada was surprised at my boldness. He kept silence for a while, and then said to me: "Very well, Kumo. I won't call in the doctor any more. But when the medicine comes you must take it."

Dada then went away. The medicine came from the chemist. I took it—bottles, powders, prescriptions and all—and threw it down the well!

My husband had been irritated by Dada's interference, and he began to treat my eyes with greater diligence than ever. He tried all sorts of remedies. I bandaged my eyes as he told me, I wore his coloured glasses, I put in his drops, I took all his powders. I even drank the cod-liver oil he gave me, though my gorge rose against it.

Each time he came back from the hospital, he would ask me anxiously how I felt; and I would answer: "Oh! much better." Indeed I became an expert in self-delusion. When I found that the water in my eyes was still increasing, I would console myself with the thought that it was a good thing to get rid of so much bad fluid; and, when the flow of water in my eyes decreased, I was elated at my husband's skill.

But after a while the agony became unbearable. My eyesight faded away, and I had continual headaches day and night. I saw how much alarmed my husband was getting. I gathered from his manner that he was casting about for a pretext to call in a doctor. So I hinted that it might be as well to call one in.

That he was greatly relieved, I could see. He called in an English doctor that very day. I do not know what talk they had together, but I gathered that the Sahib had spoken very sharply to my husband.

He remained silent for some time after the doctor had gone. I took his hands in mine, and said: "What an ill-mannered brute that was! Why didn't you call in an Indian doctor? That would have been much better. Do you think that man knows better than you do about my eyes?"

My husband was very silent for a moment, and then said with a broken voice: "Kumo, your eyes must be operated on."

I pretended to be vexed with him for concealing the fact from me so long.

"Here you have known this all the time," said I, "and yet you have said nothing about it! Do you think I am such a baby as to be afraid of an operation?"

At that he regained his good spirits. "There are very few men," said he, "who are heroic enough to look forward to an operation without shrinking."

I laughed at him: "Yes, that is so. Men are heroic only before their wives!"

He looked at me gravely, and said: "You are perfectly right. We men are dreadfully vain."

I laughed away his seriousness: "Are you sure you can beat us women even in vanity?"

When Dada came, I took him aside: "Dada, that treatment your doctor recommended would have done me a world of good; only unfortunately I mistook the mixture for the lotion. And since the day I made the mistake, my eyes have grown steadily worse; and now an operation is needed."

Dada said to me: "You were under your husband's treatment, and that is why I gave up coming to visit you."

"No," I answered. "In reality, I was secretly treating myself in accordance with your doctor's directions."

Oh! what lies we women have to tell! When we are mothers, we tell lies to pacify our children; and when we are wives, we tell lies to pacify the fathers of our children. We are never free from this necessity.

My deception had the effect of bringing about a better feeling between my husband and Dada. Dada blamed himself for asking me to keep a secret from my husband: and my husband regretted that he had not taken my brother's advice at the first.

At last, with the consent of both, an English doctor came and operated on my left eye. That eye, however, was too weak to bear the strain; and the last flickering glimmer of light went out. Then the other eye gradually lost itself in darkness.

One day my husband came to my bedside. "I cannot brazen it out before you any longer," said he; "Kumo, it is I who have ruined your eyes."

I felt that his voice was choking with tears, and so I took up his right hand in both of mine and said: "Why! you did exactly what was right. You have dealt only with that which was your very own. Just imagine, if some strange doctor had come and taken away my eyesight. What consolation should I have had then? But now I can feel that all has happened for the best; and my great comfort is to know that it is at your hands I have lost my eyes. When Ramchandra found one lotus too few with which to worship God, he offered both his eyes in place of the lotus. And I have dedicated my eyes to my God. From now, whenever you see something that is a joy to you, then you must describe it to me; and I will feed upon your words as a sacred gift left over from your vision."

I do not mean, of course, that I said all this there and then, for it is impossible to speak these things on the spur of the moment. But I used to think over words like these for days and days together. And when I was very depressed, or if at any time the light of my devotion became dim, and I pitied my evil fate, then I made my mind utter these sentences, one by one, as a child repeats a story that is told. And so I could breathe once more the serener air of peace and love.

At the very time of our talk together, I said enough to show my husband what was in my heart.

"Kumo," he said to me, "the mischief I have done by my folly can never be made good. But I can do one thing. I can ever remain by your side, and try to make up for your want of vision as much as is in my power."

"No," said I. "That will never do. I shall not ask you to turn your house into an hospital for the blind. There is only one thing to be done—you must marry again."

As I tried to explain to him that this was necessary, my voice broke a little. I coughed, and tried to hide my emotion, but he burst out saying:

"Kumo, I know I am a fool, and a braggart, and all that, But I am not a villain! If ever I marry again, I swear to you— I swear to you the most solemn oath by my family god, Gopinath—may that most hated of all sins, the sin of parricide, fall on my head!"

Ah! I should never, never have allowed him to swear that dreadful oath. But tears were choking my voice, and I could not say a word for insufferable joy. I hid my blind face in my pillows, and sobbed, and sobbed again. At last, when the first flood of my tears was over, I drew his head down to my breast.

"Ah!" said I, "why did you take such a terrible oath? Do you think I asked you to marry again for your own sordid pleasure? No! I was thinking of myself, for she could perform those services which were mine to give you when I had my sight."

"Services!" said he, "services! Those can be done by servants. Do you think I am mad enough to bring a slave into my house, and bid her share the throne with this my Goddess?"

As he said the word "Goddess," he held up my face in his hands, and placed a kiss between my brows. At that moment the third eye of divine wisdom was opened, where he kissed me, and verily I had a consecration.

I said in my own mind: "It is well. I am no longer able to serve him in the lower world of household cares. But I shall rise to a higher region. I shall bring down blessings from above. No more lies! No more deceptions for me! All the littlenesses and hypocrisies of my former life shall be banished for ever!"

That day, the whole day through, I felt a conflict going on within me. The joy of the thought, that after this solemn oath it was impossible for my husband to marry again, fixed its roots deep in my heart, and I could not tear them out. But the new Goddess, who had taken her new throne in me, said: "The time might come when it would be good for your husband to break his oath and marry again." But the woman, who was within me, said: "That may be; but all the same an oath is an oath, and there is no way out." The Goddess, who was within me, answered: "That is no reason why you should exult over it." But the woman, who was within me, replied: "What you say is quite true, no doubt; all the same he has taken his oath." And the same story went on again and again.

At last the Goddess frowned in silence, and the darkness of a horrible fear came down upon me.

My repentant husband would not let the servants do my work; he must do it all himself. At first it gave me unbounded delight to be dependent on him thus for every little thing. It was a means of keeping him by my side, and my desire to have him with me had become intense since my blindness. That share of his presence, which my eyes had lost, my other senses craved. When he was absent from my side, I would feel as if I were hanging in mid-air, and had lost my hold of all things tangible.

Formerly, when my husband came back late from the hospital, I used to open my window and gaze at the road. That road was the link which connected his world with mine. Now when I had lost that link through my blindness, all my body would go out to seek him. The bridge that united us had given way, and there was now this unsurpassable chasm. When he left my side the gulf seemed to yawn wide open. I could only wait for the time when he should cross back again from his own shore to mine.

But such intense longing and such utter dependence can never be good. A wife is a burden enough to a man, in all conscience, and to add to it the burden of this blindness was to make his life unbearable. I vowed that I would suffer alone, and never wrap my husband round in the folds of my all-pervading darkness.

Within an incredibly short space of time I managed to train myself to do all my household duties by the help of touch and sound and smell. In fact I soon found that I could get on with greater skill than before. For sight often distracts rather than helps us. And so it came to pass that, when these roving eyes of mine could do their work no longer, all the other senses took up their several duties with quietude and completeness.

When I had gained experience by constant practice, I would not let my husband do any more household duties for me. He complained bitterly at first that I was depriving him of his penance.

This did not convince me. Whatever he might say, I could feel that he had a real sense of relief when these household duties were over. To serve daily a wife who is blind can never make up the life of a man.

II

My husband at last had finished his medical course. He went away from Calcutta to a small town to practise as a doctor. There in the country I felt with joy, through all my blindness, that I was restored to the arms of my mother. I had left my village birthplace for Calcutta when I was eight years old. Since then ten years had passed away, and in the great city the memory of my village home had grown dim. As long as I had eyesight, Calcutta with its busy life screened from view the memory of my early days. But when I lost my eyesight I knew for the first time that Calcutta allured only the eyes: it could not fill the mind. And now, in my blindness, the scenes of my childhood shone out once more, like stars that appear one by one in the evening sky at the end of the day.

It was the beginning of November when we left Calcutta for Harsingpur. The place was new to me, but the scents and sounds of the countryside pressed round and embraced me. The morning breeze coming fresh from the newly ploughed land, the sweet and tender smell of the flowering mustard, the shepherd-boy's flute sounding in the distance, even the creaking noise of the bullock-cart, as it groaned over the broken village road, filled my world with delight. The memory of my past life, with all its ineffable fragrance and sound, became a living present to me, and my blind eyes could not tell me I was wrong. I went back, and lived over again my childhood. Only one thing was absent: my mother was not with me.

I could see my home with the large peepul trees growing along the edge of the village pool. I could picture in my mind's eye my old grandmother seated on the ground with her thin wisps of hair untied, warming her back in the sun as she made the little round lentil balls to be dried and used for cooking. But somehow I could not recall the songs she used to croon to herself in her weak and quavering voice. In the evening, whenever I heard the lowing of cattle, I could almost watch the figure of my mother going round the sheds with lighted lamp in her hand. The smell of the wet fodder and the pungent smoke of the straw fire would enter into my very heart. And in the distance I seemed to hear the clanging of the temple bell wafted up by the breeze from the river bank.

Calcutta, with all its turmoil and gossip, curdles the heart. There, all the beautiful duties of life lose their freshness and innocence. I remember one day, when a friend of mine came in, and said to me: "Kumo, why don't you feel angry? If I had been treated like you by my husband, I would never look upon his face again."

She tried to make me indignant, because he had been so long calling in a doctor.

"My blindness," said I, "was itself a sufficient evil. Why should I make it worse by allowing hatred to grow up against my husband?"

My friend shook her head in great contempt, when she heard such old-fashioned talk from the lips of a mere chit of a girl. She went away in disdain. But whatever might be my answer at the time, such words as these left their poison; and the venom was never wholly got out of the soul, when once they had been uttered.

So you see Calcutta, with its never-ending gossip, does harden the heart. But when I came back to the country all my earlier hopes and faiths, all that I held true in life during childhood, became fresh and bright once more. God came to me, and filled my heart and my world. I bowed to Him, and said:

"It is well that Thou has taken away my eyes. Thou art with me."

Ah! But I said more than was right. It was a presumption to say: "Thou art with me." All we can say is this: "I must be true to Thee." Even when nothing is left for us, still we have to go on living.

III

We passed a few happy months together. My husband gained some reputation in his profession as a doctor. And money came with it.

But there is a mischief in money. I cannot point to any one event; but, because the blind have keener perceptions than other people, I could discern the change which came over my husband along with the increase of wealth.

He had a keen sense of justice when he was younger, and had often told me of his great desire to help the poor when once he obtained a practice of his own. He had a noble contempt for those in his profession who would not feel the pulse of a poor patient before collecting his fee. But now I noticed a difference. He had become strangely hard. Once when a poor woman came, and begged him, out of charity, to save the life of her only child, he bluntly refused. And when I implored him myself to help her, he did his work perfunctorily.

While we were less rich my husband disliked sharp practice in money matters. He was scrupulously honourable in such things. But since he had got a large account at the bank he was often closeted for hours with some scamp of a landlord's agent, for purposes which clearly boded no good.

Where has he drifted? What has become of this husband of mine,—the husband I knew before I was blind; the husband who kissed me that day between my brows, and enshrined me on the throne of a Goddess? Those whom a sudden gust of passion brings down to the dust can rise up again with a new strong impulse of goodness. But those who, day by day, become dried up in the very fibre of their moral being; those who by some outer parasitic growth choke the inner life by slow degrees,—such men reach one day a deadness which knows no healing.

The separation caused by blindness is the merest physical trifle. But, ah! it suffocates me to find that he is no longer with me, where he stood with me in that hour when we both knew that I was blind. That is a separation indeed!

I, with my love fresh and my faith unbroken, have kept to the shelter of my heart's inner shrine. But my husband has left the cool shade of those things that are ageless and unfading. He is fast disappearing into the barren, waterless waste in his mad thirst for gold.

Sometimes the suspicion comes to me that things are not so bad as they seem: that perhaps I exaggerate because I am blind. It may be that, if my eyesight were unimpaired, I should have accepted the world as I found it. This, at any rate, was the light in which my husband looked at all my moods and fancies.

One day an old Musalman came to the house. He asked my husband to visit his little grand-daughter. I could hear the old man say: "Babu, I am a poor man; but come with me, and Allah will do you good." My husband answered coldly: "What Allah will do won't help matters; I want to know what you can do for me."

When I heard it, I wondered in my mind why God had not made me deaf as well as blind. The old man heaved a deep sigh, and departed. I sent my maid to fetch him to my room. I met him at the door of the inner apartment, and put some money into his hand.

"Please take this from me," said I, "for your little grand-daughter, and get a trustworthy doctor to look after her. And—pray for my husband."

But the whole of that day I could take no food at all. In the afternoon, when my husband got up from sleep, he asked me: "Why do you look so pale?"

I was about to say, as I used to do in the past: "Oh! It's nothing"; but those days of deception were over, and I spoke to him plainly.

"I have been hesitating," I said, "for days together to tell you something. It has been hard to think out what exactly it was I wanted to say. Even now I may not be able to explain what I had in my mind. But I am sure you know what has happened. Our lives have drifted apart."

My husband laughed in a forced manner, and said: "Change is the law of nature."

I said to him: "I know that. But there are some things that are eternal."

Then he became serious.

"There are many women," said he, "who have a real cause for sorrow. There are some whose husbands do not earn money. There are others whose husbands do not love them. But you are making yourself wretched about nothing at all."

Then it became clear to me that my very blindness had conferred on me the power of seeing a world which is beyond all change. Yes! It is true. I am not like other women. And my husband will never understand me.

IV

Our two lives went on with their dull routine for some time. Then there was a break in the monotony. And aunt of my husband came to pay us a visit.

The first thing she blurted out after our first greeting was this: "Well, Kumo, it's a great pity you have become blind; but why do you impose your own affliction on your husband? You must get him to marry another wife."

There was an awkward pause. If my husband had only said something in jest, or laughed in her face, all would have been over. But he stammered and hesitated, and said at last in a nervous, stupid way: "Do you really think so? Really, Aunt, you shouldn't talk like that."

His aunt appealed to me. "Was I wrong, Kumo?"

I laughed a hollow laugh.

"Had not you better," said I, "consult some one more competent to decide? The pickpocket never asks permission from the man whose pocket he is going to pick."

"You are quite right," she replied blandly. "Abinash, my dear, let us have our little conference in private. What do you say to that?"

After a few days my husband asked her, in my presence, if she knew of any girl of a decent family who could come and help me in my household work. He knew quite well that I needed no help. I kept silence.

"Oh! there are heaps of them," replied his aunt. "My cousin has a daughter who is just of the marriageable age, and as nice a girl as you could wish. Her people would be only too glad to secure you as a husband."

Again there came from him that forced, hesitating laugh, and he said: "But I never mentioned marriage."

"How could you expect," asked his aunt, "a girl of decent family to come and live in your house without marriage?"

He had to admit that this was reasonable, and remained nervously silent.

I stood alone within the closed doors of my blindness after he had gone, called upon my God and prayed: "O God, save my husband."

When I was coming out of the household shrine from my morning worship a few days later, his aunt took hold of both my hands warmly.

"Kumo, here is the girl," said she, "we were speaking about the other day. Her name is Hemangini. She will be delighted to meet you. Hemo, come here and be introduced to your sister."

My husband entered the room at the same moment. He feigned surprise when he saw the strange girl, and was about to retire. But his aunt said: "Abinash, my dear, what are you running away for? There is no need to do that. Here is my cousin's daughter, Hemangini, come to see you. Hemo, make your bow to him."

As if taken quite by surprise, he began to ply his aunt with questions about the when and why and how of the new arrival.

I saw the hollowness of the whole thing, and took Hemangini by the hand and led her to my own room. I gently stroked her face and arms and hair, and found that she was about fifteen years old, and very beautiful.

As I felt here face, she suddenly burst out laughing and said: "Why! what are you doing? Are you hypnotising me?"

That sweet ringing laughter of hers swept away in a moment all the dark clouds that stood between us. I threw my right arm about her neck.

"Dear one," said I, "I am trying to see you." And again I stroked her soft face with my left hand.

"Trying to see me?" she said, with a new burst of laughter. "Am I like a vegetable marrow, grown in your garden, that you want to feel me all round to see how soft I am?"

I suddenly bethought me that she did not know I had lost my sight.

"Sister, I am blind," said I.

She was silent. I could feel her big young eyes, full of curiosity, peering into my face. I knew they were full of pity.

Then she grew thoughtful and puzzled, and said, after a short pause:

"Oh! I see now. That was the reason your husband invited his aunt to come and stay here."

"No!" I replied, "you are quite mistaken. He did not ask her to come. She came of her own accord."

Hemangini went off into a peal of laughter. "That's just like my aunt," said she. "Oh! wasn't it nice of her to come without any invitation? But now she's come, you won't get her to move for some time, I can assure you!"

Then she paused, and looked puzzled.

"But why did father send me?" she asked. "Can you tell me that?"

The aunt had come into the room while we were talking. Hemangini said to her: "When are you thinking of going back, Aunt?"

The aunt looked very much upset.

"What a question to ask!" said she, "I've never seen such a restless body as you. We've only just come, and you ask when we're going back!"

"It is all very well for you," Hemangini said, "for this house belongs to your near relations. But what about me? I tell you plainly I can't stop here." And then she held my hand and said: "What do you think, dear?"

I drew her to my heart, but said nothing. The aunt was in a great difficulty. She felt the situation was getting beyond her control; so she proposed that she and her niece should go out together to bathe.

"No! we two will go together," said Hemangini, clinging to me. The aunt gave in, fearing opposition if she tried to drag her away.

Going down to the river Hemangini asked me: "Why don't you have children?"

I was startled by her question, and answered: "How can I tell? My God has not given me any. That is the reason."

"No! That's not the reason," said Hemangini quickly. "You must have committed some sin. Look at my aunt. She is childless. It must be because her heart has some wickedness. But what wickedness is in your heart?"

The words hurt me. I have no solution to offer for the problem of evil. I sighed deeply, and said in the silence of my soul: "My God! Thou knowest the reason."

"Gracious goodness," cried Hemangini, "what are you sighing for? No one ever takes me seriously."

And her laughter pealed across the river.

V

I found out after this that there were constant interruptions in my husband's professional duties. He refused all calls from a distance, and would hurry away from his patients, even when they were close at hand.

Formerly it was only during the mid-day meals and at night-time that he could come into the inner apartment. But now, with unnecessary anxiety for his aunt's comfort, he began to visit her at all hours of the day. I knew at once that he had come to her room, when I heard her shouting for Hemangini to bring in a glass of water. At first the girl would do what she was told; but later on she refused altogether.

Then the aunt would call, in an endearing voice: "Hemo! Hemo! Hemangini." But the girl would cling to me with an impulse of pity. A sense of dread and sadness would keep her silent. Sometimes she would shrink towards me like a hunted thing, who scarcely knew what was coming.

About this time my brother came down from Calcutta to visit me. I knew how keen his powers of observation were, and what a hard judge he was. I feared my husband would be put on his defence, and have to stand his trial before him. So I endeavoured to hide the true situation behind a mask of noisy cheerfulness. But I am afraid I overdid the part: it was unnatural for me.

My husband began to fidget openly, and asked how long my brother was going to stay. At last his impatience became little short of insulting, and my brother had no help for it but to leave. Before going he placed his hand on my head, and kept it there for some time. I noticed that his hand shook, and a tear fell from his eyes, as he silently gave me his blessing.

I well remember that it was an evening in April, and a market-day. People who had come into the town were going back home from market. There was the feeling of an impending storm in the air; the smell of the wet earth and the moisture in the wind were all-pervading. I never keep a lighted lamp in my bedroom, when I am alone, lest my clothes should catch fire, or some accident happen. I sat on the floor in my dark room, and called upon the God of my blind world.

"O my Lord," I cried, "Thy face is hidden. I cannot see. I am blind. I hold tight this broken rudder of a heart till my hands bleed. The waves have become too strong for me. How long with thou try me, my God, how long?"

I kept my head prone upon the bedstead and began to sob. As I did so, I felt the bedstead move a little. The next moment Hemangini was by my side. She clung to my neck, and wiped my tears away silently. I do not know why she had been waiting that evening in the inner room, or why she had been lying alone there in the dusk. She asked me no question. She said no word. She simply placed her cool hand on my forehead, and kissed me, and departed.

The next morning Hemangini said to her aunt in my presence: "If you want to stay on, you can. But I don't. I'm going away home with our family servant."

The aunt said there was no need for her to go alone, for she was going away also. Then smilingly and mincingly she brought out, from a plush case, a ring set with pearls.

"Look, Hemo," said she, "what a beautiful ring my Abinash brought for you."

Hemangini snatched the ring from her hand.

"Look, Aunt," she answered quickly, "just see how splendidly I aim." And she flung the ring into the tank outside the window.

The aunt, overwhelmed with alarm, vexation, and surprise, bristled like a hedgehog. She turned to me, and held me by the hand.

"Kumo," she repeated again and again, "don't say a word about this childish freak to Abinash. He would be fearfully vexed."

I assured her that she need not fear. Not a word would reach him about it from my lips.

The next day before starting for home Hemangini embraced me, and said: "Dearest, keep me in mind; do not forget me."

I stroked her face over and over with my fingers, and said: "Sister, the blind have long memories."

I drew her head towards me, and kissed her hair and her forehead. My world suddenly became grey. All the beauty and laughter and tender youth, which had nestled so close to me, vanished when Hemangini departed. I went groping about with arms outstretched, seeking to find out what was left in my deserted world.

My husband came in later. He affected a great relief now that they were gone, but it was exaggerated and empty. He pretended that his aunt's visit had kept him away from work.

Hitherto there had been only the one barrier of blindness between me and my husband. Now another barrier was added,—this deliberate silence about Hemangini. He feigned utter indifference, but I knew he was having letters about her.

It was early in May. My maid entered my room one morning, and asked me: "What is all this preparation going on at the landing on the river? Where is Master going?"

I knew there was something impending, but I said to the maid: "I can't say."

The maid did not dare to ask me any more questions. She sighed, and went away.

Late that night my husband came to me.

"I have to visit a patient in the country," said he. "I shall have to start very early to-morrow morning, and I may have to be away for two or three days."

I got up from my bed. I stood before him, and cried aloud: "Why are you telling me lies?"

My husband stammered out: "What—what lies have I told you?"

I said: "You are going to get married."

He remained silent. For some moments there was no sound in the room. Then I broke the silence:

"Answer me," I cried. "Say, yes."

I shouted out with a loud voice: "No! I shall never allow you. I shall save you from this great disaster, this dreadful sin. If I fail in this, then why am I your wife, and why did I ever worship my God?"

The room remained still as a stone. I dropped on the floor, and clung to my husband's knees.

"What have I done?" I asked. "Where have I been lacking? Tell me truly. Why do you want another wife?"

My husband said slowly: "I will tell you the truth. I am afraid of you. Your blindness has enclosed you in its fortress, and I have now no entrance. To me you are no longer a woman. You are awful as my God. I cannot live my everyday life with you. I want a woman—just an ordinary woman— whom I can be free to chide and coax and pet and scold."

Oh, tear open my heart and see! What am I else but that,—just an ordinary woman? I am the same girl that I was when I was newly wed,—a girl with all her need to believe, to confide, to worship.

I do not recollect exactly the words that I uttered. I only remember that I said: "If I be a true wife, then, may God be my witness, you shall never do this wicked deed, you shall never break your oath. Before you commit such sacrilege, either I shall become a widow or Hemangini shall die."

Then I fell down on the floor in a swoon. When I came to myself, it was still dark. The birds were silent. My husband had gone.

All that day I sat at my worship in the sanctuary at the household shrine. In the evening a fierce storm, with thunder and lightning and rain, swept down upon the house and shook it. As I crouched before the shrine, I did not ask my God to save my husband from the storm, though he must have been at that time in peril on the river. I prayed that whatever might happen to me, my husband might be saved from this great sin.

Night passed. The whole of the next day I kept my seat at worship. When it was evening there was the noise of shaking and beating at the door. When the door was broken open, they found me lying unconscious on the ground, and carried me to my room.

When I came to myself at last, I heard some one whispering in my ear: "Sister."

I found that I was lying in my room with my head on Hemangini's lap. When my head moved, I heard her dress rustle. It was the sound of bridal silk.

O my God, God! My prayer has gone unheeded! My husband has fallen!

Hemangini bent her head low, and said in a sweet whisper: "Sister, dearest, I have come to ask your blessing on our marriage."

At first my whole body stiffened like the trunk of a tree that has been struck by lightning. Then I sat up, and said, painfully, forcing myself to speak the words: "Why should I not bless you? You have done no wrong."

Hemangini laughed her merry laugh.

"Wrong!" said she. "When you married it was right; and when I marry, you call it wrong!"

I tried to smile in answer to her laughter. I said in my mind: "My prayer is not the final thing in this world. His will is all. Let the blows descend upon my head; but may they leave my faith and hope in God untouched."

Hemangini bowed to me, and touched my feet. "May you be happy," said I, blessing her, "and enjoy unbroken prosperity."

Hemangini was still unsatisfied.

"Dearest sister," she said, "a blessing for me is not enough. You must make our happiness complete. You must, with those saintly hands of yours, accept into your home my husband also. Let me bring him to you."

I said: "Yes, bring him to me."

A few moments later I heard a familiar footstep, and the question: "Kumo, how are you?"

I started up, and bowed to the ground, and cried: "Dada!"

Hemangini burst out laughing.

"You still call him elder brother?" she asked. "What nonsense! Call him younger brother now, and pull his ears and tease him, for he has married me, your younger sister."

Then I understood. My husband had been saved from that great sin. He had not fallen.

I knew my Dada had determined never to marry. And, since my mother had died, there was no sacred wish of hers to implore him to wedlock. But I, his sister, by my sore need had brought it to pass. He had married for my sake.

Tears of joy gushed from my eyes, and poured down my cheeks. I tried, but I could not stop them. Dada slowly passed his fingers through my hair. Hemangini clung to me, and went on laughing.

I was lying awake in my bed for the best part of the night, waiting with straining anxiety for my husband's return. I could not imagine how he would bear the shock of shame and disappointment.

When it was long past the hour of midnight, slowly my door opened. I sat up on my bed, and listened. They were the footsteps of my husband. My heart began to beat wildly. He came up to my bed, held my hand in his.

"Your Dada," said he, "has saved me from destruction. I was being dragged down and down by a moment's madness. An infatuation had seized me, from which I seemed unable to escape. God alone knows what a load I was carrying on that day when I entered the boat. The storm came down on the river, and covered the sky. In the midst of all my fears I had a secret wish in my heart to be drowned, and so disentangle my life from the knot in which I had tied it. I reached Mathurganj. There I heard the news which set me free. Your brother had married Hemangini. I cannot tell you with what joy and shame I heard it. I hastened on board the boat again. In that moment of self-revelation I knew that I could have no happiness except with you. You are a Goddess."

I laughed and cried at the same time, and said: "No, no, no! I am not going to be a Goddess any longer. I am simply your own little wife. I am just an ordinary woman."

"Dearest," he replied, "I have also something I want to say to you. Never again put me to shame by calling me your God."

On the next day the little town became joyous with the sound of conch shells. But nobody made any reference to that night of madness when all was so nearly lost.

The Babus of Nayanjore

I

Once upon a time the Babus of Nayanjore were famous landholders. They were noted for their princely extravagance. They would tear off the rough border of their Dacca muslin, because it rubbed against their skin. They could spend many thousands of rupees over the wedding of a kitten. On a certain grand occasion it is alleged that in order to turn night into day they lighted numberless lamps and showered silver threads from the sky to imitate sunlight. Those were the days before the flood. The flood came. The line of succession among these old-world Babus, with their lordly habits, could not continue for long. Like a lamp with too many wicks burning, the oil flared away quickly, and the light went out.

Kailas Babu, our neighbour, is the last relic of this extinct magnificence. Before he grew up, his family had very nearly reached its lowest ebb. When his father died, there was one dazzling outburst of funeral extravagance, and then insolvency. The property was sold to liquidate the debt. What little ready money was left over was altogether insufficient to keep up the past ancestral splendours.

Kailas Babu left Nayanjore and came to Calcutta. His son did not remain long in this world of faded glory. He died, leaving behind him an only daughter.

In Calcutta we are Kailas Babu's neighbours. Curiously enough our own family history is just the opposite to his. My father got his money by his own exertions, and prided himself on never spending a penny more than was needed. His clothes were those of a working man, and his hands also. He never had any inclination to earn the title of Babu by extravagant display, and I myself, his only son, owe him gratitude for that. He gave me the very best education, and I was able to make my way in the world. I am not ashamed of the fact that I am a self-made man. Crisp bank-notes in my safe are dearer to me than a long pedigree in an empty family chest.

I believe, this was why I disliked seeing Kailas Babu drawing his heavy cheques on the public credit from the bankrupt bank of his ancient Babu reputation. I used to fancy that he looked down on me, because my father had earned money with his own hands.

I ought to have noticed that no one showed any vexation towards Kailas Babu except myself. Indeed it would have been difficult to find an old man who did less harm than he. He was always ready with his kindly little acts of courtesy in times of sorrow and joy. He would join in all the ceremonies and religious observances of his neighbours. His familiar smile would greet young and old alike. His politeness in asking details about domestic affairs was untiring. The friends who met him in the street were perforce ready to be button-holed, while a long string of questions of this kind followed one another from his lips:

"My dear friend, I am delighted to see you. Are you quite well? How is Shashi? and Dada—is he all right? Do you know, I've only just heard that Madhu's son has got fever. How is he? Have you heard? And Hari Charan Babu—I have not seen him for a long time—I hope he is not ill. What's the matter with Rakkhal? And, er—er, how are the ladies of your family?"

Kailas Babu was spotlessly neat in his dress on all occasions, though his supply of clothes was sorely limited. Every day he used to air his shirts and vests and coats and trousers carefully, and put them out in the sun, along with his bed-quilt, his pillow-case, and the small carpet on which he always sat. After airing them he would shake them, and brush them, and put them on the rock. His little bits of furniture made his small room decent, and hinted that there was more in reserve if needed. Very often, for want of a servant, he would shut up his house for a while. Then he would iron out his shirts and linen with his own hands, and do other little menial tasks. After this he would open his door and receive his friends again.

Though Kailas Babu, as I have said, had lost all his landed property, he had still some family heirlooms left. There was a silver cruet for sprinkling scented water, a filigree box for otto-of-roses, a small gold salver, a costly ancient shawl, and the old-fashioned ceremonial dress and ancestral turban. These he had rescued with the greatest difficulty from the money-lenders' clutches. On every suitable occasion he would bring them out in state, and thus try to save the world-famed dignity of the Babus of Nayanjore. At heart the most modest of men, in his daily speech he regarded it as a sacred duty, owed to his rank, to give free play to his family pride. His friends would encourage this trait in his character with kindly good-humour, and it gave them great amusement.

The neighbourhood soon learnt to call him their Thakur Dada.[1] They would flock to his house, and sit with him for hours together. To prevent his incurring any expense, one or other of his friends would bring him tobacco, and say: "Thakur Dada, this morning some tobacco was sent to me from Gaya. Do take it, and see how you like it."

---

1. Grandfather.

Thakur Dada would take it, and say it was excellent. He would then go on to tell of a certain exquisite tobacco which they once smoked in the old days at Nayanjore at the cost of a guinea an ounce.

"I wonder," he used to say, "I wonder if any one would like to try it now. I have some left, and can get it at once."

Every one knew that, if they asked for it, then somehow or other the key of the cupboard would be missing; or else Ganesh, his old family servant, had put it away somewhere.

"You never can be sure," he would add, "where things go to when servants are about. No, this Ganesh of mine,— I can't tell you what a fool he is, but I haven't the heart to dismiss him."

Ganesh, for the credit of the family, was quite ready to bear all the blame without a word.

One of the company usually said at this point: "Never mind, Thakur Dada. Please don't trouble to look for it. This tobacco we're smoking will do quite well. The other would be too strong."

Then Thakur Dada would be relieved, and settle down again, and the talk would go on.

When his guests got up to go away, Thakur Dada would accompany them to the door, and say to them on the door-step: "Oh, by the way, when are you all coming to dine with me?"

One or other of us would answer: "Not just yet, Thakur Dada, not just yet. We'll fix a day later."

"Quite right," he would answer. "Quite right. We had much better wait till the rains come. It's too hot now. And a grand rich dinner such as I should want to give you would upset us in weather like this."

But when the rains did come, every one was very careful not to remind him of his promise. If the subject was brought up, some friend would suggest gently that it was very inconvenient to get about when the rains were so severe, that it would be much better to wait till they were over. And so the game went on.

His poor lodging was much too small for his position, and we used to condole with him about it. His friends would assure him they quite understood his difficulties: it was next to impossible to get a decent house in Calcutta. Indeed, they had all been looking out for years for a house to suit him, but, I need hardly add, no friend had been foolish enough to find one. Thakur Dada used to say, after a long sigh of resignation: "Well, well, I suppose I shall have to put up with this house after all." Then he would add with a genial smile: "But, you know, I could never bear to be away from my friends. I must be near you. That really compensates for everything."

Somehow I felt all this very deeply indeed. I suppose the real reason was, that when a man is young stupidity appears to him the worst of crimes. Kailas Babu was not really stupid. In ordinary business matters every one was ready to consult him. But with regard to Nayanjore his utterances were certainly void of common sense. Because, out of amused affection for him, no one contradicted his impossible statements, he refused to keep them in bounds. When people recounted in his hearing the glorious history of Nayanjore with absurd exaggerations he would accept all they said with the utmost gravity, and never doubted, even in his dreams, that any one could disbelieve it.

II

When I sit down and try to analyse the thoughts and feelings that I had towards Kailas Babu, I see that there was a still deeper reason for my dislike. I will now explain.

Though I am the son of a rich man, and might have wasted time at college, my industry was such that I took my M.A. degree in Calcutta University when quite young. My moral character was flawless. In addition, my outward appearance was so handsome, that if I were to call myself beautiful, it might be thought a mark of self-estimation, but could not be considered an untruth.

There could be no question that among the young men of Bengal I was regarded by parents generally as a very eligible match. I was myself quite clear on the point, and had determined to obtain my full value in the marriage market. When I pictured my choice, I had before my mind's eye a wealthy father's only daughter, extremely beautiful and highly educated. Proposals came pouring into me from far and near; large sums in cash were offered. I weighed these offers with rigid impartiality, in the delicate scales of my own estimation. But there was no one fit to be my partner. I became convinced, with the poet Bhabavuti, that

In this world's endless time and boundless space
One may be born at last to match my sovereign
grace.

But in this puny modern age, and this contracted space of modern Bengal, it was doubtful if the peerless creature existed as yet.

Meanwhile my praises were sung in many tunes, and in different metres, by designing parents.

Whether I was pleased with their daughters or not, this worship which they offered was never unpleasing. I used to regard it as my proper due, because I was so good. We are told that when the gods withhold their boons from mortals they still expect their worshippers to pay them fervent honour, and are angry if it is withheld. I had that divine expectance strongly developed in myself.

I have already mentioned that Thakur Dada had an only grand-daughter. I had seen her many times, but had never mistaken her for beautiful. No thought had ever entered my mind that she would be a possible partner for myself. All the same, it seemed quite certain to me that some day or other Kailas Babu would offer her, with all due worship, as an oblation at my shrine. Indeed—this was the secret of my dislike—I was thoroughly annoyed that he had not done it already.

I heard he had told his friends that the Babus of Nayanjore never craved a boon. Even if the girl remained unmarried, he would not break the family tradition. It was this arrogance of his that made me angry. My indignation smouldered for some time. But I remained perfectly silent, and bore it with the utmost patience, because I was so good.

As lightning accompanies thunder, so in my character a flash of humour was mingled with the mutterings of my wrath. It was, of course, impossible for me to punish the old man merely to give vent to my rage; and for a long time I did nothing at all. But suddenly one day such an amusing plan came into my head, that I could not resist the temptation of carrying it into effect.

I have already said that many of Kailas Babu's friends used to flatter the old man's vanity to the full. One, who was a retired Government servant, had told him that whenever he saw the Chota Lord Sahib he always asked for the latest news about the Babus of Nayanjore, and the Chota Lord had been heard to say that in all Bengal the only really respectable families were those of the Maharaja of Burdwan and the Babus of Nayanjore. When this monstrous falsehood was told to Kailas Babu he was extremely gratified, and often repeated the story. And wherever after that he met this Government servant in company he would ask, along with other questions:

"Oh! er—by the way, how is the Chota Lord Sahib? Quite well, did you say? Ah, yes, I am so delighted to hear it! And the dear Mem Sahib, is she quite well too? Ah, yes! And the little children—are they quite well also? Ah, yes! that's very good news! Be sure and give them my compliments when you see them."

Kailas Babu would constantly express his intention of going some day and paying a visit to the Sahib. But it may be taken for granted that many Chota Lords and Burra Lords also would come and go, and much water would pass down the Hoogly, before the family coach of Nayanjore would be furnished up to pay a visit to Government House.

One day I took Kailas Babu aside, and told him in a whisper: "Thakur Dada, I was at the Levee yesterday, and the Chota Lord happened to mention the Babus of Nayanjore. I told him that Kailas Babu had come to town. Do you know, he was terribly hurt because you hadn't called. He told me he was going to put etiquette on one side, and pay you a private visit himself this very afternoon."

Anybody else could have seen through this plot of mine in a moment. And, if it had been directed against another person, Kailas Babu would have understood the joke. But after all he had heard from his friend the Government servant, and after all his own exaggerations, a visit from the Lieutenant-Governor seemed the most natural thing in the wold. He became highly nervous and excited at my news. Each detail of the coming visit exercised him greatly—most of all his own ignorance of English. How on earth was that difficulty to be met? I told him there was no difficulty at all: it was aristocratic not to know English: and, besides, the Lieutenant-Governor always brought an interpreter with him, and he had expressly mentioned that this visit was to be private.

About midday, when most of our neighbours are at work, and the rest are asleep, a carriage and pair stopped before the lodging of Kailas Babu. Two flunkeys in livery came up the stairs, and announced in a loud voice, "The Chota Lord Sahib has arrived." Kailas Babu was ready, waiting for him, in his old-fashioned ceremonial robes and ancestral turban, and Ganesh was by his side, dressed in his master's best suit of clothes for the occasion. When the Chota Lord Sahib was announced, Kailas Babu ran panting and puffing and trembling to the door, and led in a friend of mine, in disguise, with repeated salaams, bowing low at each step, and walking backward as best he could. He had his old family shawl spread over a hard wooden chair, and he asked the Lord Sahib to be seated. He then made a high-flown speech in Urdu, the ancient Court language of the Sahibs, and presented on the golden salver a string of gold *mohurs,* the last relics of his broken fortune. The old family servant Ganesh, with an expression of awe bordering on terror, stood behind with the scent-sprinkler, drenching the Lord Sahib, touching him gingerly from time to time with the otto-of-roses from the filigree box.

Kailas Babu repeatedly expressed his regret at not being able to receive his Honour Bahadur with all the ancestral magnificence of his own family estate at Nayanjore. There he could have welcomed him properly with due ceremony. But in Calcutta he was a mere stranger and sojourner—in fact a fish out of water.

My friend, with his tall silk hat on, very gravely nodded. I need hardly say that according to English custom the hat ought to have been removed inside the room. But my friend did not dare to take it off for fear of detection; and Kailas Babu and his old servant Ganesh were sublimely unconscious of the breach of etiquette.

After a ten minutes' interview, which consisted chiefly of nodding the head, my friend rose to his feet to depart. The two flunkeys in livery, as had been planned beforehand, carried off in state the string of gold *mohurs,* the gold salver, the old ancestral shawl, the silver scent-sprinkler, and the otto-of-roses filigree box; they placed them ceremoniously in the carriage. Kailas Babu regarded this as the usual habit of Chota Lord Sahibs.

I was watching all the while from the next room. My sides were aching with suppressed laughter. When I could hold myself in no longer, I rushed into a further room, suddenly to discover, in a corner, a young girl sobbing as if her heart would break. When she saw my uproarious laughter she stood upright in passion, flashing the lightning of her big dark eyes in mine, and said with a tear-choked voice: "Tell me! What harm has my grandfather done to you? Why have you come to deceive him? Why have you come here? Why—"

She could say no more. She covered her face with her hands, and broke into sobs.

My laughter vanished in a moment. It had never occurred to me that there was anything but a supremely funny joke in this act of mine, and here I discovered that I had given the cruellest pain to this tenderest little heart. All the ugliness of my cruelty rose up to condemn me. I slunk out of the room in silence, like a kicked dog.

Hitherto I had only looked upon Kusum, the grand-daughter of Kailas Babu, as a somewhat worthless commodity in the marriage market, waiting in vain to attract a husband. But now I found, with a shock of surprise, that in the corner of that room a human heart was beating.

The whole night through I had very little sleep. My mind was in a tumult. On the next day, very early in the morning, I took all those stolen goods back to Kailas Babu's lodgings, wishing to hand them over in secret to the servant Ganesh. I waited outside the door, and, not finding any one, went upstairs to Kailas Babu's room. I heard from the passage Kusum asking her grandfather in the most winning voice: "Dada, dearest, to tell me all that the Chota Lord Sahib said to you yesterday. Don't leave out a single word. I am dying to hear it all over again."

And Dada needed no encouragement. His face beamed over with pride as he related all manner of praises which the

Lord Sahib had been good enough to utter concerning the ancient families of Nayanjore. The girl was seated before him, looking up into his face, and listening with rapt attention. She was determined, out of love for the old man, to play her part to the full.

My heart was deeply touched, and tears came to my eyes. I stood there in silence in the passage, while Thakur Dada finished all his embellishments of the Chota Lord Sahib's wonderful visit. When he left the room at last, I took the stolen goods and laid them at the feet of the girl and came away without a word.

Later in the day I called again to see Kailas Babu himself. According to our ugly modern custom, I had been in the habit of making no greeting at all to this old man when I came into the room. But on this day I made a low bow, and touched his feet. I am convinced the old man thought that the coming of the Choat Lord Sahib to his house was the cause of my new politeness. He was highly gratified by it, and an air of benign severity shone from his eyes. His friends had flocked in, and he had already begun to tell again at full length the story of the Lieutenant-Governor's visit with still further adornments of a most fantastic kind. The interview was already becoming an epic, both in quality and in length.

When the other visitors had taken their leave, I made my proposal to the old man in a humble manner. I told him that, "though I could never for a moment hope to be worth of marriage connection with such an illustrious family, yet... etc. etc."

When I made clear my proposal of marriage, the old man embraced me, and broke out in a tumult of joy: "I am a poor man, and could never have expected such great good fortune."

That was the first and last time in his life that Kailas Babu confessed to being poor. It was also the first and last time in his life that he forgot, if only for a single moment, the ancestral dignity that belongs to the Babus of Nayanjore.

Living or Dead?

I

The widow in the house of Saradasankar, the Ranihat zemindar, had no kinsmen of her father's family. One after another all had died. Nor had she in her husband's family any one she could call her own, neither husband nor son. The child of her brother-in-law Saradasankar was her darling. For a long time after his birth, his mother had been very ill, and the widow, his aunt Kadambini, had fostered him. If a woman fosters another's child, her love for him is all the stronger because she has no claim upon him—no claim of kinship, that is, but simply the claim of love. Love cannot prove its claim by any document which society accepts, and does not wish to prove it; it merely worships with double passion its life's uncertain treasure. Thus all the widow's thwarted love went out towards this little child. One night in *Sraban* Kadambini died suddenly. For some reason her heart stopped beating. Everywhere else the world held on its course; only in this gentle little breast, suffering with love, the watch of time stood still for ever.

Lest they should be harassed by the police, four of the zemindar's Brahmin servants took away the body, without ceremony, to be burned. The burning-ground of Ranihat was very far from the village. There was a hut beside a tank, a huge banian near it, and nothing more. Formerly a river, now completely dried up, ran through the ground, and a part of the watercourse had been dug out to make a tank for the performance of funeral rites. The people considered the tank as part of the river and reverenced it as such.

Taking the body into the hut, the four men sat down to wait for the wood. The time seemed so long that two of the four grew restless, and went to see why it did not come. Nitai and Gurucharan being gone, Bidhu and Banamali remained to watch over the body.

It was a dark night of *Sraban*. Heavy clouds hung in starless sky. The two men sat silent in the dark room. Their matches and lamp were useless. The matches were damp, and would not light for all their efforts, and the lantern went out. After a long silence, one said: "Brother, it would be good if we had a bowl of tobacco. In our hurry we brought none."

The other answered: "I can ran and bring all we want."

Understanding why Banamali wanted to go,[1] Bidhu said: "I daresay! Meanwhile, I suppose I am to sit here alone!"

Conversation ceased again. Five minutes seemed like an hour. In their minds they cursed the two who had gone to fetch the wood, and they began to suspect that they sat gossiping in some pleasant nook. There was no sound anywhere, except the incessant noise of frogs and crickets from the tank. Then suddenly they fancied that the bed shook slightly, as if the dead body had turned on its side. Bidhu and Banamali trembled, and began muttering: "Ram, Ram." A deep sigh was heard in the room. In a moment the watchers leapt out of the hut, and raced for the village.

After running about three miles, they met their colleagues coming back with a lantern. As a matter of fact, they *had* gone

---

1. From fear of ghosts, the burning-ground being considered haunted..

to smoke, and knew nothing about the wood. But they declared that a tree had been cut down, and that, when it was split up, it would be brought along at once. Then Bidhu and Banamali told them what had happened in the hut. Nitai and Gurucharan scoffed at the story, and abused Bidhu and Banamali angrily for leaving their duty.

Without delay all four returned to the hut. As they entered, they saw at once that the body was gone; nothing but an empty bed remained. They stared at one another. Could a jackal have taken it? But there was no scrap of clothing anywhere. Going outside, they saw that on the mud that had collected at the door of the hut there were a woman's tiny footprints, newly made. Saradasankar was no fool, and they could hardly persuade him to believe in this ghost story. So after much discussion the four decided that it would be best to say that the body had been burnt.

Towards dawn, when the men with the wood arrived they were told that, owing to their delay, the work had been done without them; there had been some wood in the hut after all. No one was likely to question this, since a dead body is not such a valuable property that any one would steal it.

II

Every one knows that, even when there is no sign, life is often secretly present, and may begin again in an apparently dead body. Kadambini was not dead; only the machine of her life had for some reason suddenly stopped.

When consciousness returned, she saw dense darkness on all sides. It occurred to her that she was not lying in her usual place. She called out "Sister," but no answer came from the darkness. As she sat up, terror-stricken, she remembered her death-bed, the sudden pain at her breast, the beginning of a choking sensation. Her elder sister-in-law was warming some milk for the child, when Kadambini became faint, and fell on the bed, saying with a choking voice: "Sister, bring the child here. I am worried." After that everything was black, as when an inkpot is upset over an exercise-book. Kadambini's memory and consciousness, all the letters of the world's book, in a moment became formless. The widow could not remember whether the child, in the sweet voice of love, called her "Auntie," as if for the last time, or not; she could not remember whether, as she left the world she knew for death's endless unknown journey, she had received a parting gift of affection, love's passage-money for the silent land. At first, I fancy, she thought the lonely dark place was the House of Yama, where there is nothing to see, nothing to hear, nothing to do, only an eternal watch. But when a cold damp wind drove through the open door, and she heard the croaking of frogs, she remembered vividly and in a moment all the rains of her short life, and could feel her kinship with the earth. Then came a flash of lightning, and she saw the tank, the banian, the great plain, the far-off trees. She remembered how at full moon she had sometimes come to bathe in this tank, and how dreadful death had seemed when she saw a corpse on the burning-ground.

Her first thought was to return home. But then she reflected: "I am dead. How can I return home? That would bring disaster on them. I have left the kingdom of the living; I am my own ghost!" If this were not so, she reasoned, how could she have got out of Sardasankar's well-guarded zenana, and come to this distant burning-ground at midnight? Also, if her funeral rites had not been finished, where had the men gone who should burn her? Recalling her death-moment in Saradasankar's brightly-lit house, she now found herself alone in a distant, deserted, dark burning-ground. Surely she was no member of earthly society! Surely she was a creature of horror, of ill-omen, her own ghost!

At this thought, all the bonds were snapped which bound her to the world. She felt that she had marvellous strength, endless freedom. She could do what she liked, go where she pleased. Mad with the inspiration of this new idea, she rushed from the hut like a gust of wind, and stood upon the burning-ground. All trace of shame or fear had left her.

But as she walked on and on, her feet grew tired, her body weak. The plain stretched on endlessly; here and there were paddy-fields; sometimes she found herself standing knee-deep in water.

At the first glimmer of dawn she heard one or two birds cry from the bamboo-clumps by the distant houses. Then terror seized her. She could not tell in what new relation she stood to the earth and to living folk. So long as she had been on the plain, on the burning-ground, covered by the dark night of *Sraban,* so long she had been fearless, a denizen of her own kingdom. By daylight the homes of men filled her with fear. Men and ghosts dread each other, for their tribes inhabit different banks of the river of death.

III

Her clothes were clotted in the mud; strange thoughts and walking by night had given her the aspect of a madwoman; truly, her apparition was such that folk might have been afraid of her, and children might have stoned her or run away. Luckily, the first to catch sight of her was a traveller. He came up, and said: "Mother, you look a respectable woman. Wherever are you going, alone and in this guise?"

Kadambini, unable to collect her thoughts, stared at him in silence. She could not think that she was still in touch with the world, that she looked like a respectable woman, that a traveller was asking her questions.

Again the man said: "Come, mother, I will see you home. Tell me where you live."

Kadambini thought. To return to her father-in-law's house would be absurd, and she had no father's house. Then she remembered the friend of her childhood. She had not seen Jogmaya since the days of her youth, but from time to time they had exchanged letters. Occasionally there had been quarrels between them, as was only right, since Kadambini wished to make it clear that her love for Jogmaya was unbounded, while her friend complained that Kadambini did not return a love equal to her own. They were both sure that, if they once met, they would be inseparable.

Kadambini said to the traveller: "I will go to Sripati's house at Nisindapur."

As he was going to Calcutta, Nisindapur, though not near, was on his way. So he took Kadambini to Sripati's house, and the friends met again. At first they did not recognise one another, but gradually each recognised the features of the other's childhood.

"What luck!" said Jogmaya. "I never dreamt that I should see you again. But how have you come here, sister? Your father-in-law's folk surely didn't let you go!"

Kadambini remained silent, and at last said: "Sister, do not ask about my father-in-law. Give me a corner, and treat me as a servant: I will do your work."

"What?" cried Jogmaya. "Keep you like a servant! Why, you are my closest friend, you are my——" and so on and so on.

Just then Sripati came in. Kadambini stared at him for some time, and then went out very slowly. She kept her head uncovered, and showed not the slightest modesty or respect. Jogmaya, fearing that Sripati would be prejudiced against her friend, began an elaborate explanation. But Sripati, who readily agreed to anything Jogmaya said, cut short her story, and left his wife uneasy in her mind.

Kadambini had come, but she was not at one with her friend: death was between them. She could feel no intimacy for others so long as her existence perplexed her and consciousness remained. Kadambini would look at Jogmaya, and brood. She would think: "She has her husband and her work, she lives in a world far away from mine. She shares affection and duty with the people of the world; I am an empty shadow. She is among the living; I am in eternity."

Jogmaya also was uneasy, but could not explain why. Women do not love mystery, because, though uncertainty may be transmuted into poetry, into heroism, into scholarship, it cannot be turned to account in household work. So, when a woman cannot understand a thing, she either destroys and forgets it, or she shapes it anew for her own use; if she fails to deal with it in one of these ways, she loses her temper with it. The greater Kadambini's abstraction became, the more impatient was Jogmaya with her, wondering what trouble weighed upon her mind.

Then a new danger arose. Kadambini was afraid of herself; yet she could not flee from herself. Those who fear ghosts fear those who are behind them; wherever they cannot see there is fear. But Kadambini's chief terror lay in herself, for she dreaded nothing external. At the dead of night, when alone in her room, she screamed; in the evening, when she saw her shadow in the lamp-light, her whole body shook. Watching her fearfulness, the rest of the house fell into a sort of terror. The servants and Jogmaya herself began to see ghosts.

One midnight, Kadambini came out from her bedroom weeping, and wailed at Jogmaya's door: "Sister, sister, let me lie at your feet! Do not put me by myself!"

Jogmaya's anger was no less than her fear. She would have liked to drive Kadambini from the house that very second. The good-natured Sripati, after much effort, succeeded in quieting their guest, and put her in the next room.

Next day Sripati was unexpectedly summoned to his wife's apartments. She began to upbraid him: "You, do you call yourself a man? A woman runs away from her father-in-law, and enters your house; a month passes, and you haven't hinted that she should go away, nor have I heard the slightest protest from you. I should take it as a favour if you would explain yourself. You men are all alike."

Most men have such an unreasoning fondness for their wives that they willingly allow themselves to be put in the wrong. Although Sripati was prepared to touch Jogmaya's body, and swear that his kind feeling towards the helpless but beautiful Kadambini was no whit greater than it should be, he could not prove it by his behaviour. He thought that her father-in-law's people must have treated this forlorn widow abominably, if she could bear it no longer, and was driven to take refuge with him. As she had neither father nor mother, how could he desert her? So saying, he let the matter drop, for he had no mind to distress Kadambini by asking her unpleasant questions.

His wife, then, tried other means of attack upon her sluggish lord, until at last he saw that for the sake of peace he must send word to Kadambini's father-in-law. The result of a letter, he thought, might not be satisfactory; so he resolved to go to Ranihat, and act on what he learnt.

So Sripati went, and Jogmaya on her part said to Kadambini: "Friend, it hardly seems proper for you to stop here any longer. What will people say?"

Kadambini stared solemnly at Jogmaya, and said: "What have I to do with people?"

Jogmaya was astounded. Then she said sharply: "If *you* have nothing to do with people, *we* have. How can we explain the detention of a woman belonging to another house?"

Kadambini said: "Where is my father-in-law's house?"

"Confound it!" thought Jogmaya. "What will the wretched woman say next?"

Very slowly Kadambini said: "What have I to do with you? Am I of the earth? You laugh, weep, love; each grips and holds his own; I merely look. You are human, I a shadow. I cannot understand why God has kept me in this world of yours."

So strange were her look and speech that Jogmaya understood something of her drift, though not all. Unable either to dismiss her, or to ask her any more questions, she went away, oppressed with thought.

IV

It was nearly ten o'clock at night when Sripati returned from Ranihat. The earth was drowned in torrents of rain. It seemed that the downpour would never stop, that the night would never end.

Jogmaya asked: "Well?"

"I've lots to say, presently."

So saying, Sripati changed his clothes, and sat down to supper; then he lay down for a smoke. His mind was perplexed.

His wife stifled her curiosity for a long time; then she came to his couch and demanded: "What did you hear?"

"That you have certainly made a mistake."

Jogmaya was nettled. Women never make mistakes, or, if they do, a sensible man never mentions them; it is better to take them on his own shoulders. Jogmaya snapped: "May I be permitted to hear how?"

Sripati replied: "The woman you have taken into your house is not your Kadambini."

Hearing this, she was greatly annoyed, especially since it was her husband who said it. "What! I don't know my own friend? I must come to you to recognise her! You are clever, indeed!"

Sripati explained that there was no need to quarrel about his cleverness. He could prove what he said. There was no doubt that Jogmaya's Kadambini was dead.

Jogmaya replied: "Listen! You've certainly made some huge mistake. You've been to the wrong house, or are confused as to what you have heard. Who told you to go yourself? Write a letter, and everything will be cleared up."

Sripati was hurt by his wife's lack of faith in his executive ability; he produced all sorts of proof, without result. Midnight found them still asserting and contradicting. Although they were both agreed now that Kadambini should be got out of the house, although Sripati believed that their guest had deceived his wife all the time by a pretended acquaintance, and Jogmaya that she was a prostitute, yet in the present discussion neither would acknowledge defeat. By degrees their voices became so loud that they forgot that Kadambini was sleeping in the next room.

The one said: "We're in a nice fix! I tell you, I heard it with my own ears!" And the other answered angrily: "What do I care about that? I can see with my own eyes, surely?"

At length Jogmaya said: "Very well. Tell me when Kadambini died." She thought that if she could find a discrepancy between the day of death and the date of some letter from Kadambini, she could prove that Sripati erred.

He told her the date of Kadambini's death, and they both saw that it fell on the very day before she came to their house. Jogmaya's heart trembled, and even Sripati was not unmoved.

Just then the door flew open; a damp wind swept in and blew the lamp out. The darkness rushed after it, and filled the whole house. Kadambini stood in the room. It was nearly one o'clock, and the rain was pelting outside.

Kadambini spoke: "Friend, I am your Kadambini, but I am no longer living. I am dead."

Jogmaya screamed with terror; Sripati could not speak.

"But, save in being dead, I have done you no wrong. If I have no place among the living, I have none among the dead. Oh! whither shall I go?" Crying as if to wake the sleeping Creator in the dense night of rain, she asked again: "Oh! whither shall I go?"

So saying, Kadambini left her friend fainting in the dark house, and went out into the world, seeking her own place.

V

It is hard to say how Kadambini reached Ranihat. At first she showed herself to no one, but spent the whole day in a ruined temple, starving. When the untimely afternoon of the rains was pitch-black, and people huddled into their houses for fear of the impending storm, then Kadambini came forth. Her heart trembled as she reached her father-in-law's house; and when, drawing a thick veil over her face, she entered, none of the doorkeepers objected, since they took her for a servant. And the rain was pouring down, and the wind howled.

The mistress, Saradasankar's wife, was playing cards with her widowed sister. A servant was in the kitchen, the sick child was sleeping in the bedroom. Kadambini, escaping every one's notice, entered this room. I do not know why she had come to her father-in-law's house; she herself did not know; she felt only that she wanted to see her child again. She had no thought where to go next, or what to do.

In the lighted room she saw the child sleeping his fists clenched, his body wasted with fever. At sight of him, her heart became parched and thirsty. If only she could press that tortured body to her breast! Immediately the thought followed: "I do not exist. Who would see it? His mother loves company, loves gossip and cards. All the time that she left me in charge, she was herself free from anxiety, nor was she troubled about him in the least. Who will look after him now as I did?"

The child turned on his side, and cried, half asleep: "Auntie, give me water." Her darling had not yet forgotten his auntie! In a fever of excitement, she poured out some water, and, taking him to her breast, she gave it him.

As long as he was asleep, the child felt no strangeness in taking water from the accustomed hand. But when Kadambini satisfied her long-starved longing, and kissed him and began rocking him asleep again, he awoke and embraced her. "Did you die, Auntie?" he asked.

"Yes, darling,"

"And you have come back? Do not die again."

Before she could answer disaster overtook her. One of the maidservants coming in with a cup of sago dropped it, and fell down. At the crash the mistress left her cards, and entered the room. She stood like a pillar of wood, unable to flee or speak. Seeing all this, the child, too, became terrified, and burst out weeping: "Go away, Auntie," he said, "go away!"

Now at last Kadambini understood that she had not died. The old room, the old things, the same child, the same love, all returned to their living state, without change or difference between her and them. In her friend's house she had felt that her childhood's companion was dead. In her child's room she knew that the boy's "Auntie" was not dead at all. In anguished tones she said: "Sister, why do you dread me? See, I am as you knew me."

Her sister-in-law could endure no longer, and fell into a faint. Saradasankar himself entered the zenana. With folded hands, he said piteously: "Is this right? Satis is my only son. Why do you show yourself to him? Are we not your own kin? Since you went, he has wasted away daily; his fever has been incessant; day and night he cries: 'Auntie, Auntie.' You have left the world; break these bonds of *maya*.[2] We will perform all funeral honours."

Kadambini could bear no more. She said: "Oh, I am not dead, I am not dead. Oh, *how* can I persuade you that I am not dead? I am living, living!" She lifted a brass pot from the ground and dashed it against her forehead. The blood ran

---

2. Illusory affection binding a soul to the world.

from her brow. "Look!" she cried, "I am *living*!" Saradasankar stood like an image; the child screamed with fear, the two fainting women lay still.

The Kadambini, shouting "I am not dead, I am not dead," went down the steps to the zenana well, and plunged in. From the upper story Saradasankar heard the splash.

All night the rain poured; it poured next day at dawn, was pouring still at noon. By dying, Kadambini had given proof that she was not dead.

"We Crown Thee King"

When Nabendu Sekhar was wedded to Arunlekha, the God of marriage smiled from behind the sacrificial fire. Alas! what is sport for the gods is not always a joke to us poor mortals.

Purnendu Sekhar, the father of Nabendu, was a man well known amongst the English officials of the Government. In the voyage of life he had arrived at the desert shores of Rai Bahadurship by diligently plying his oars of *salaams*. He held in reserve enough for further advancement; but at the age of fifty-five, his tender gaze still fixed on the misty peak of Raja-hood, he suddenly found himself transported to a region where earthly honours and decorations are naught, and his *salaam-*wearied neck found everlasting repose on the funeral pyre.

According to modern science, force is not destroyed, but is merely converted to another form, and applied to another point. So Purnendu's *salaam*-force, constant handmaid of the fickle Goddess of Fortune, descended from the shoulder of the father to that of his worthy son; and the youthful head of Nabendu Sekhar began to move up and down, at the doors of high-placed Englishmen, like a pumpkin swayed by the wind.

The traditions of the family into which he had married were entirely different. Its eldest son, Pramathanath, had won for himself the love of his kinsfolk and the regard of all who knew him. His kinsmen and his neighbours looked up to him as their ideal in all things.

Pramathanath was a Bachelor of Arts, and in addition was gifted with common sense. But he held no high official position; he had no handsome salary; nor did he exert any influence with his pen. There was no one in power to lend him a helping hand, because he desired to keep away from Englishmen, as much as they desired to keep away from him. So it happened that he shone only within the sphere of his family and his friends, and excited no admiration beyond it.

Yet this Pramathanath had once sojourned in England for some three years. The kindly treatment he received during his stay there overpowered him so much that he forgot the sorrow and the humiliation of his own country, and came back dressed in European clothes. This rather grieved his brothers and his sisters at first, but after a few days they began to think that European clothes suited nobody better, and gradually they came to share his pride and dignity.

On his return from England, Pramathanath resolved that he would show the world how to associate with Anglo-Indians on terms of equality. Those of our countrymen who think that no such association is possible, unless we bend our knees to them, showed their utter lack of self-respect, and were also unjust to the English—so thought Pramathanath.

He brought with him letters of introduction from many distinguished Englishmen at home, and these gave him some recognition in Anglo-Indian society. He and his wife occasionally enjoyed English hospitality at tea, dinner, sports and other entertainments. Such good luck intoxicated him, and began to produce a tingling sensation in every vein of his body.

About this time, at the opening of a new railway line, many of the town, proud recipients of official favour, were invited by the Lieutenant-Governor to take the first trip.

Pramathanath was among them. On the return journey, a European Sergeant of the Police expelled some Indian gentlemen from a railway-carriage with great insolence. Pramathanath, dressed in his European clothes, was there. He, too, was getting out, when the Sergeant said: "You needn't move, sir. Keep your seat, please."

At first Pramathanath felt flattered at the special respect thus shown to him. When, however, the train went on, the dull rays of the setting sun, at the west of the fields, now ploughed up and stripped of green, seemed in his eyes to spread a glow of shame over the whole country. Sitting near the window of his lonely compartment, he seemed to catch a glimpse of the downcast eyes of his Motherland, hidden behind the trees. As Pramathanath sat there, lost in reverie, burning tears flowed down his cheeks, and his heart bursted with indignation.

He now remembered the story of a donkey who was drawing the chariot of an idol along the street. The wayfarers bowed down to the idol, and touched the dusty ground with their foreheads. The foolish donkey imagined that all this reverence was being shown to him. "The only difference," said Pramathanath to himself, "between the donkey and myself is this: I understand to-day that the respect I receive is not given to me but to the burden on my back."

Arriving home, Pramathanath called together all the children of the household, and lighting a big bonfire, threw all his European clothes into it one by one. The children danced round and round it, and the higher the flames shot up, the greater was their merriment. After that, Pramathanath gave up his sip of a tea and bits of toast in Anglo-Indian houses, and once again sat inaccessible within the castle of his house, while his insulted friends went about from the door of one Englishman to that of another, bending their turbaned heads as before.

By an irony of fate, poor Nabendu Sekhar married the second daughter of this house. His sisters-in-law were well educated and handsome. Nabendu considered he had made a lucky bargain. But he lost no time in trying to impress on the family that it was a rare bargain on their side also. As if by mistake, he would often hand to his sisters-in-law sundry letters that his late father had received from Europeans. And when the cherry lips of those young ladies smiled sarcastically, and the point of a shining dagger peeped out of its sheath of red velvet, the unfortunate man saw his folly, and regretted it.

Labanyalekha, the eldest sister, surpassed the rest in beauty and cleverness. Finding an auspicious day, she put on the mantel-shelf of Nabendu's bedroom two pairs of English boots, daubed with vermilion, and arranged flowers, sandal-paste, incense and a couple of burning candles before them in true ceremonial fashion. When Nabendu came in, the two sisters-in-law stood on either side of him, and said with mock solemnity: "Bow down to your gods, and may you prosper through their blessings."

The third sister Kiranlekha, spent many days in embroidering with red silk one hundred common English names such as Jones, Smith, Brown, Thomson, etc., on a *chadar*. When it was ready, she presented this *namavali*[1] to Nabendu Sekhar with great ceremony.

The fourth, Sasankalekha, of tender age and therefore of no account, said: "I will make you a string of beads, brother, with which to tell the names of your gods—the sahibs." Her sisters reproved her, saying: "Run away, you saucy girl."

Feelings of shame and irritation assailed by turns the mind

---

1. A namavali is a sheet of cloth printed all over with the names of Hindu gods and goddesses and worn by pious Hindus when engaged in devotional exercises.

of Nabendu Sekhar. Still he could not forgo the company of his sisters-in-law, especially as the eldest one was beautiful. Her honey was no less than her gall, and Nabendu's mind tasted at once the sweetness of the one and the bitterness of the other. The butterfly, with its bruised wings, buzzes round the flowers in blind fury, unable to depart.

The society of his sisters-in-law so much infatuated him that at last Nabendu began to disavow his craving for European favours. When he went to *salaam* the Burra Sahib, he used to pretend that he was going to listen to a speech by Mr. Surendranath Banerjea. When he went to the railway station to pay respects to the Chota Sahib, returning from Darjeeling, he would tell his sisters-in-law that he expected his youngest uncle.

It was a sore trial to the unhappy man placed between the cross-fires of his Sahib and his sisters-in-law. The sisters-in-law, however, secretly vowed that they would not rest till the Sahibs had been put to rout.

About this time it was rumoured that Nabendu's name would be included in the forthcoming list of Birthday honours, and that he would mount the first step of the ladder to Paradise by becoming a Rai Bahadur. The poor fellow had not the courage to break the joyful news to his sisters-in-law. One evening, however, when the autumn moon was flooding the earth with its mischievous beams, Nabendu's heart was so full that he could not contain himself any longer, and he told his wife. The next day, Mrs. Nabendu betook herself to her eldest sister's house in a palanquin, and in a voice choked with tears bewailed her lot.

"He isn't going to grow a tail," said Labanya, "by becoming a Rai Bahadur, is he? Why should you feel so very humiliated?"

"Oh no, sister dear," replied Arunlekha, "I am prepared to be anything—but not a Rai Bahadur*ni*." The fact was that in her circle of acquaintances there was one Bhutnath Babu, who was a Rai Bahadur, and that explained her intense aversion to that title.

Labanya said to her sister in soothing tones: "Don't be upset about it, dear; I will see what I can do to prevent it."

Babu Nilratan, the husband of Labanya, was a pleader at Buxar. When the autumn was over, Nabendu received an invitation from Labanya to pay them a visit, and he started for Buxar greatly pleased.

The early winter of the western province endowed Labanyalekha with new health and beauty, and brought a glowing colour to her pale cheeks. She looked like the flower-laden *kasa* reeds on a clear autumn day, growing by the lonely bank of a rivulet. To Nabendu's enchanted eyes she appeared like a *malati* plant in full blossom, showering dew-drops brilliant with the morning light.

Nabendu had never felt better in his life. The exhilaration of his own health and the genial company of his pretty sister-in-law made him think himself light enough to tread on air. The Ganges in front of the garden seemed to him to be flowing ceaselessly to regions unknown, as though it gave shape to his own wild fantasies.

As he returned in the early morning from his walk on the bank of the river, the mellow rays of the winter sun gave his whole frame that pleasing sensation of warmth which lovers feel in each other's arms. Coming home, he would now and then find his sister-in-law amusing herself by cooking some dishes. He would offer his help, and display his want of skill and ignorance at every step. But Nabendu did not appear to be at all anxious to improve himself by practice and attention. On the contrary he thoroughly enjoyed the rebukes he received from his sister-in-law. He was at great pains to prove every day that he was inefficient and helpless as a new-born babe in mixing spices, handling the saucepan, and regulating the heat so as to prevent things getting burnt—and he was duly rewarded with pitiful smiles and scoldings.

In the middle of the day he ate a great deal of the good food set before him, incited by his keen appetite and the coaxing of his sister-in-law. Later on, he would sit down to a game of cards—at which he betrayed the same lack of ability. He would cheat, pry into his adversary's hand, quarrel—but never did he win a single rubber, and worse still, he would not acknowledge defeat. This brought him abuse every day, and still he remained incorrigible.

There was, however, one matter in which his reform was complete. For the time, at least, he had forgotten that to win the smiles of Sahibs was the final goal of life. He was beginning to understand how happy and worthy we might feel by winning the affection and esteem of those near and dear to us.

Besides, Nabendu was now moving in a new atmosphere. Labanya's husband, Babu Nilratan, a leader of the Bar, was reproached by many because he refused to pay his respects to European officials. To all such reproaches Nilratan would reply: "No, thank you,—if they are not polite enough to return my call, then the politeness I offer them is a loss that can never be made up for. The sands of the desert may be very white and shiny, but I would much rather sow my seeds in black soil, where I can expect a return."

And Nabendu began to adopt similar ideas, all regardless of the future. His chance of Rai Bahadurship throve on the soil carefully prepared by his late father and also by himself in days gone by, nor was any fresh watering required. Had he not at great expense had laid out a splendid race-course in a town, which was a fashionable resort of Europeans?

When the time of Congress drew near, Nilratan received a request from headquarters to collect subscriptions. Nabendu, free from anxiety, was merrily engaged in a game of cards with his sister-in-law, when Nilratan Babu came upon him with a subscription book in his hand, and said: "Your signature, please."

From old habit Nabendu looked horrified. Labanya, assuming an air of great concern and anxiety, said: "Never do that. It would ruin your race-course beyond repair."

Nabendu blurted out: "Do you suppose I pass sleepless nights through fear of that?"

"We won't publish your name in the papers," said Nilratan reassuringly.

Labanya, looking grave and anxious, said: "Still, it wouldn't be safe. Things spread so, from mouth to mouth—"

Nabendu replied with vehemence: "My name wouldn't suffer by appearing in the newspapers." So saying, he snatched the subscription list from Nilratan's hand, and signed away a thousand rupees. Secretly he hoped that the papers would not publish the news.

Labanya struck her forehead with her palm and gasped out: "What—have you—done?"

"Nothing wrong," said Nabendu boastfully.

"But—but—," drawled Lahanya, "the Guard-sahib of Sealdah Station, the shop-assistant at Whiteaway's, the syce-sahib of Hart Bros.—these gentlemen might be angry with you, and decline to come to your Poojah dinner to drink your champagne, you know. Just think, they mightn't pat you on the back when you meet them again!"

"It wouldn't break my heart," Nabendu snapped out.

A few days passed. One morning Nabendu was sipping his tea, and glancing at a newspaper. Suddenly a letter signed "X" caught his eye. The writer thanked him profusely for his donation, and declared that the increase of strength the Congress had acquired by having such a man as he within its fold, was inestimable.

Alas, father Purnendu Sekhar! Was it to increase the strength of the Congress that you brought this wretch into the world?

But the cloud of misfortune had its silver lining. That he was not a mere cypher was clear from the fact that the Anglo-Indian community on the one side and the Congress on the other were each waiting patiently, eager to hook him, and land him on their own side. So Nabendu, beaming with pleasure, took the paper to his-sister-in-law, and showed her the letter. Looking as though she knew nothing about it, Labanya exclaimed in surprise: "Oh, what a pity! Everything has come out! Who bore you such ill-will? Oh, how cruel of him, how wicked of him!"

Nabendu laughed out, saying: "Now—now—don't call him names, Labanya. I forgive him with all my heart, and bless him too."

A couple of days after this, an anti-Congress Anglo-Indian paper reached Nabendu through the post. There was a letter in it, signed "One who knows," and contradicting the above report. "Those who have the pleasure of Babu Nabendu Sekhar's personal acquaintance," the writer went on, "cannot for a moment believe this absurd libel to be true. From him to turn a Congresswalla is as impossible as it is for the leopard to change his spots. He is a man of genuine worth, and neither a disappointed candidate for Government employ nor a briefless barrister. He is not one of those who, after a brief sojourn in England, return aping our dress and manners, audaciously try to thrust themselves on Anglo-Indian society, and finally go back in dejection. So there is absolutely no reason why Babu Nabendu Sekhar," etc., etc.

Ah, father Purnendu Sekhar! What a reputation you had made with the Europeans before you died!

This letter also was paraded before his sister-in-law, for did it not assert that he was no mean, contemptible scallywag, but a man of real worth?

Labanya exclaimed again in feigned surprise: "Which of your friends wrote it now? Oh, come—is it the Ticket

Collector, or the hide merchant, or is it the drum-major of the Fort?"

"You ought to send in a contradiction, I think," said Nilratan.

"Is it necessary?" said Nabendu loftily. "Must I contradict every little thing they choose to say against me?"

Labanya filled the room with a deluge of laughter. Nabendu felt a little disconcerted at this, and said: "Why? What's the matter?" She went on laughing, unable to check herself, and her youthful slender form waved to and fro. This torrent of merriment had the effect of overthrowing Nabendu completely, and he said in pitiable accents: "Do you imagine that I am afraid to contradict it?"

"Oh dear, no," said Labanya; "I was thinking that you haven't yet ceased trying to save that race-course of yours, so full of promise. While there is life, there is hope, you know."

"That's what I am afraid of, you think, do you? Very well, you shall see," said Nabendu desperately, and forthwith sat down to write his contradiction. When he had finished, Labanya and Nilratan read it through, and said: "It isn't strong enough. We must give it them pretty hot, mustn't we?" And they kindly undertook to revise the composition. Thus it ran: "When one connected to us by ties of blood turns our enemy he becomes far more dangerous than any outsider. To the Government of India, the haughty Anglo-Indians are worse enemies than the Russians or the frontier Pathans themselves—they are the impenetrable barrier, for ever hindering the growth of any bond of friendship between the Government and people of the country. It is the Congress which has opened up the royal road to a better understanding between the rulers and the ruled, and the Anglo-Indian papers have planted themselves like thorns across the whole breadth of that road," etc., etc.

Nabendu had inward fear as to the mischief this letter might do, but at the same time he felt elated at the excellence of its composition, which he fondly imagined to be his own. It was duly published, and for some days comments, replies, and rejoinders went on in various newspapers, and the air was full of trumpet-notes, proclaiming the fact that Nabendu had joined the Congress, and the amount of his subscription.

Nabendu, now grown desperate, talked as though he was a patriot of the fiercest type. Labanya laughed inwardly, and said to herself: "Well—well—you have to pass through the ordeal of fire yet."

One morning when Nabendu, before his bath, had finished rubbing oil over his chest, and was trying various devices to reach the inaccessible portions of his back, the bearer brought in a card inscribed with the name of the District Magistrate himself! Good heavens!—What would he do? He could not possibly go, and receive the Magistrate Sahib, thus oil-besmeared. He shook and twitched like a *koi*-fish, ready dressed for the frying pan. He finished his bath in a great hurry, tugged on his clothes somehow, and ran breathlessly to the outer apartments. The bearer said that the Sahib had just left after waiting for a long time. How much of the blame for concocting this drama of invented incidents may be set down to Labanya, and how much to the bearer, is a nice problem for ethical mathematics to solve.

Nabendu's heart was convulsed with pain within his breast, like the tail of a lizard just cut off. He moped like an owl all day long.

Labanya banished all traces of inward merriment from her face, and kept on inquiring in anxious tones: "What has happened to you? You are not ill, I hope?"

Nabendu made great efforts to smile and find a humorous reply. "How can there be," he managed to say, "any illness within your jurisdiction, since you yourself are the Goddess of Health?"

But the smile soon flickered out. His thoughts were: "I subscribed to the Congress fund to begin with, published a nasty letter in a newspaper, and on the top of that, when the Magistrate Sahib himself did me the honour to call on me, I kept him *waiting*. I wonder what he is thinking of me."

Alas, father Purnendu Sekhar, by an irony of fate I am made to appear what I am not.

The next morning, Nabendu decked himself in his best clothes, wore his watch and chain, and put a big turban on his head.

"Where are you off to?" inquired his sister-in-law.

"Urgent business," Nabendu replied. Labanya kept quiet.

Arriving at the Magistrate's gate, he took out his card-case.

"You cannot see him now," said the orderly peon icily.

Nabendu took out a couple of rupees from his pocket. The peon at once *salaamed* him and said: "There are five of us, sir." Immediately Nabendu pulled out a ten-rupee note, and handed it to him.

He was sent for by the Magistrate, who was writing in his dressing-gown and room slippers. Nabendu *salaamed* him. The Magistrate pointed to a chair with his finger, and without raising his eyes from the paper before him said: "What can I do for you, Babu?"

Fingering his watch-chain nervously, Nabendu said in shaky tones: "Yesterday you were good enough to call at my place, sir—"

The Sahib knitted his brows, and, lifting just one eye from his paper, said: "I called at you place! Babu, what nonsense are you talking?"

"Beg your pardon, sir," faltered out Nabendu. "There has been a mistake—some confusion," and wet with perspiration, he tumbled out of the room somehow. And that night, as he lay tossing on his bed, a distant dream-like voice came into his ear with a recurring persistency: "Babu, you are a howling idiot."

On his way home, Nabendu came to the conclusion that the Magistrate denied having called, simply because he was highly offended.

So he explained to Labanya that he had been out purchasing rose-water. No sooner had he uttered the words than half-a-dozen chuprassis wearing the Collectorate badge made their appearance, and after *salaaming* Nabendu, stood there grinning.

"Have they come to arrest you because you subscribed to the Congress fund?" whispered Labanya with a smile.

The six peons displayed a dozen rows of teeth and said: "*Bakshish*—Babu-sahib."

From a side room Nilratan came out, and said in an irritated manner: "*Bakshish?* What for?"

The peons, grinning as before, answered: "The Babu-Sahib went to see the Magistrate—so we have come for *bakshish.*"

"I didn't know," laughed out Labanya, "that the Magistrate was selling rose-water nowadays. Coolness wasn't the special feature of his trade before."

Nabendu, in trying to reconcile the story of his purchase with his visit to the Magistrate, uttered some incoherent words which nobody could make sense of.

Nilratan spoke to the peons: "There has been no occasion for *bakshish;* you shan't have it."

Nabendu said, feeling very small: "Oh, they are poor men—what's the harm of giving them something?" And he took out a currency note. Nilratan snatched it away from Nabendu's hand, remarking: "There are poorer men in the world—I will give it to them for you."

Nabendu felt greatly distressed that he was not able to appease these ghostly retainers of the angry Siva. When the peons were leaving, with thunder in their eyes, he looked at them languishingly, as much as to say: "You know everything, gentlemen; it is not my fault."

The Congress was to be held at Calcutta this year. Nilratan went down thither with his wife to attend the sittings. Nabendu accompanied them.

As soon as they arrived at Calcutta, the Congress party surrounded Nabendu, and their delight and enthusiasm knew no bounds. They cheered him, honoured him, and extolled him up to the skies. Everybody said that, unless leading men like Nabendu devoted themselves to the Cause, there was no hope for the country. Nabendu was disposed to agree with them, and emerged out of the chaos of mistake and confusion as a leader of the country. When he entered the Congress Pavilion on the first day, everybody stood up and shouted "Hip, hip, hurrah!" in a loud outlandish voice, hearing which our Motherland reddened with shame to the root of her ears.

In due time the Queen's birthday came, and Nabendu's name was not found in the list of Rai Bahadurs.

He received an invitation from Labanya for that evening. When he arrived there, Labanya with great pomp and ceremony presented him with a robe of honour, and with her own hand put a mark of red sandal paste on the middle of his forehead. Each of the other sisters threw round his neck a garland of flowers woven by herself. Decked in a pink *Sari* and dazzling jewels, his wife Arunlekha was waiting in a side room, her face lit up with smiles and blushes. Her sisters rushed to her, and, placing another garland in her hand, insisted that she also should come and do her part in the ceremony, but she would not listen to it; and that principal garland, cherishing a desire for Nabendu's neck, waited patiently for the still secrecy of midnight.

The sisters said to Nabendu: "To-day we crown thee King. Such honour will not be done to anybody else in Hindoostan."

Whether Nabendu derived any consolation from this, he alone can tell; but we greatly doubt it. We believe in fact, that he will become a Rai Bahadur before he has done, and the *Englishman* and the *Pioneer* will write heart-rending articles lamenting his demise at the proper time. So, in the meanwhile, Three Cheers for Babu Purnendu Sekhar! Hip, hip, hurrah—Hip, hip, hurrah—Hip, hip, hurrah!

The Renunciation

I

It was a night of full moon early in the month of *Phalgun*. The youthful spring was everywhere sending forth its breeze laden with the fragrance of mango-blossoms. The melodious notes of an untiring *papiya*,[1] concealed within the thick foliage of an old *lichi* tree by the side of a tank, penetrated a sleepless bedroom of the Mukerji family. There Hemanta now restlessly twisted a lock of his wife's hair round his finger, now beat her *churi* against her wristlet until it tinkled, now pulled at the chaplet of flowers about her head, and left it hanging at her face. His mood was that of an evening breeze which played about a favourite flowering shrub, gently shaking her now this side, now that, in the hope of rousing her to animation.

But Kusum sat motionless, looking out of the open widow, with eyes immersed in the moonlit depth of never-ending space beyond. Her husband's caresses were lost on her.

At last Hemanta clasped both the hands of his wife, and shaking them gently, said: "Kusum, where are you? A patient search through a big telescope would reveal you only as a

---

1. One of the sweetest songsters in Bengal. Anglo-Indian writers have nicknamed it the "brain-fever bird," which is a sheer libel.

small speck—you seem to have receded so far away. O, do come closer to me, dear. See how beautiful the night is."

Kusum turned her eyes from the void of space towards her husband, and said slowly: "I know a *mantra*[2] which could in one moment shatter this spring night and the moon into pieces."

"If you do," laughed Hemanta, "pray don't utter it. If any *mantra* of yours could bring three or four Saturdays during the week, and prolong the nights till 5 P.M. the next day, say it by all means."

Saying this, he tried to draw his wife a little closer to him. Kusum, freeing herself from the embrace, said: "Do you know, to-night I feel a longing to tell you what I promised to reveal only on my death-bed. To-night I feel that I could endure whatever punishment you might inflict on me."

Hemanta was on the point of making a jest about punishments by reciting a verse from Jayadeva, when the sound of an angry pair of slippers was heard approaching rapidly. They were the familiar footsteps of his father, Harihar Mukerji, and Hemanta, not knowing what it meant, was in a flutter of excitement.

Standing outside the door Harihar roared out: "Hemanta, turn your wife out of the house immediately."

Hemanta looked at this wife, and detected no trace of surprise in her features. She merely buried her face within the palms of her hands, and, with all the strength and intensity of her soul, wished that she could then and there melt into nothingness. It was the same *papiya* whose song floated into the room with the south breeze, and no one heard it. Endless are the beauties of the earth—but alas, how easily everything is twisted out of shape.

---

2. A set of magic words.

II

Returning from without, Hemanta asked his wife: "Is it true?"

"It is," replied Kusum.

"Why didn't you tell me long ago?"

"I did try many a time, and I always failed. I am a wretched woman."

"Then tell me everything now."

Kusum gravely told her story in a firm unshaken voice. She waded barefooted through fire, as it were, with slow unflinching steps, and nobody knew how much she was scorched. Having heard her to the end, Hemanta rose and walked out.

Kusum thought that her husband had gone, never to return to her again. It did not strike her as strange. She took it as naturally as any other incident of everyday life—so dry and apathetic had her mind become during the last few moments. Only the world and love seemed to her as a void and make-believe from beginning to end. Even the memory of the protestations of love, which her husband had made to her in days past, brought to her lips a dry, hard, joyless smile, like a sharp cruel knife which had cut through her heart. She was thinking, perhaps, that the love which seemed to fill so much of one's life, which brought in its train such fondness and depth of feeling, which made even the briefest separation so exquisitely painful and a moment's union so intensely sweet, which seemed boundless in its extent and eternal in its duration, the cessation of which could not be imagined even in births to come—that this was that love! So feeble was its support! No sooner does the priesthood touch it than your "eternal" love crumbles into a handful of dust! Only a short while ago Hemanta had whispered to her: "What a beautiful night!" The same night was not yet at an end, the same *papiya* was still warbling, the same south breeze still blew into the

room, making the bed-curtain shiver; the same moonlight lay
on the bed next the open window, sleeping like a beautiful
heroine exhausted with gaiety. All this was unreal! Love was
more falsely dissembling than she her-self!

III

The next morning Hemanta, fagged after a sleepless night,
and looking like one distracted, called at the house of Peari
Sankar Ghosal. "What news, my son?" Peari Sankar greeted
him.

Hemanta, flaring up like a big fire, said in a trembling
voice: "You have defiled our caste. You have brought
destruction upon us. And you will have to pay for it." He
could say no more; he felt choked.

"And *you* have preserved my caste, prevented my ostracism
from the community, and patted me on the back affectionately!"
said Peari Sankar with a slight sarcastic smile.

Hemanta wished that his Brahman-fury could reduce Peari
Sankar to ashes in a moment, but his rage burnt only himself.
Peari Sankar sat before him unscathed, and in the best of
health.

"Did I ever do you any harm?" demanded Hemanta in
a broken voice.

"Let me ask you one question," said Peari Sankar. "My
daughter—my only child—what harm had she done your
father? You were very young then, and probably never heard.
Listen, then. No, don't you excite yourself. There is much
humour in what I am going to relate.

"You were quite small when my son-in-law Nabakanta ran
away to England after stealing my daughter's jewels. You
might truly remember the commotion in the village when he
returned as a barrister five years later. Or, perhaps, you were
unaware of it, as you were at school in Calcutta at the time.
Your father, arrogating to himself the headship of the

community, declared that if I sent my daughter to her husband's home, I must renounce her for good, and never again allow her to cross my threshold. I fell at your father's feet, and implored him, saying: 'Brother, save me this once. I will make the boy swallow cow-dung, and go through the *prasyaschittam* ceremony. Do take him back into caste.' But your father remained obdurate. For my part, I could not disown my only child, and, bidding good-bye to my village and my kinsmen, I betook myself to Calcutta. There, too, my troubles followed me. When I had made every arrangement for my nephew's marriage, your father stirred up the girl's people, and they broke the match off. Then I took a solemn vow that, if there was a drop of Brahmin blood flowing in my veins, I would avenge myself. You understand the business to some extent now, don't you? But wait a little longer. You well enjoy it, when I tell you the whole story; it is interesting.

"When you were attending college, one Bipradas Chatterji used to live next door to your lodgings. The poor fellow is dead now. In his house lived a child-widow called Kusum, the destitute orphan of a Kayestha gentleman. The girl was very pretty, and the old Brahmin desired to shield her from the hungry gaze of college students. But for a young girl to throw dust in the eyes of her old guardian was not at all a difficult task. She often went to the top of the roof, to hang her washing out to dry, and, I believe, you found your own roof best suited for your studies. Whether you two spoke to each other, when on your respective roofs, I cannot tell, but the girl's behaviour excited suspicion in the old man's mind. She made frequent mistakes in her household duties, and, like Parbati,[3] engaged in her devotions began gradually to renounce food and sleep. Some evenings she would burst into tears in the presence of the old gentleman, without any apparent reason.

---

3. The wife of Shiva the Destroyer.

"At last he discovered that you two saw each other from the roofs pretty frequently, and that you even went the length of absenting yourself from college to sit on the roof at midday with a book in your hand, so fond had you grown suddenly of solitary study. Bipradas came to me for advice, and told me everything. 'Uncle,' said I to him, 'for a long while you have cherished a desire to go on a pilgrimage to Benares. You had better do it now, and leave the girl in my charge. I will take care of her.'

"So he went. I lodged the girl in the house of Sripati Chatterji, passing him of as her father. What happened next is known to you. I feel a great relief to-day, having told you everything from the beginning. It sounds like a romance, doesn't it? I think of turning it into a book, and getting it printed. But I am not a writing-man myself. They say my nephew has some aptitude that way—I will get him to write it for me. But the best thing would be, if you would collaborate with him, because the conclusion of the story is not known to me so well."

Without paying much attention to the concluding remarks of Peari Sankar, Hemanta asked: "Did not Kusum object to this marriage?"

"Well," said Peari Sankar, "it is very difficult to guess. You know, my boy, how women's minds are constituted. When they say 'no,' they mean 'yes.' During the first few days after her removal to the new home, she went almost crazy at not seeing you. You, too, seemed to have discovered her new address somehow, as you used to lose your way after starting for college, and loiter about in front of Sripati's house. Your eyes did not appear to be exactly in search of the Presidency College, as they were directed towards the barred windows of a private house, through which nothing but insects and the hearts of moon-struck young men could obtain access. I felt very sorry for you both. I could see that your studies were being seriously interrupted, and that the plight of the girl was pitiable also.

"One day I called Kusum to me, and said: 'Listen to me, my daughter. I am an old man, and you need feel no delicacy in my presence. I know whom you desire at heart. The young man's condition is hopeless too. I wish I could bring about your union.' At this Kusum suddenly melted into tears, and ran away. On several evenings after that, I visited Sripati's house, and, calling Kusum to me, discussed with her matters relating to you, and so I succeeded in gradually overcoming her shyness. At last, when I said that I would try to bring about a marriage, she asked me: 'How can it be?' 'Never mind,' I said, 'I would pass you off as a Brahmin maiden.' After a good deal of argument, she begged me to find out whether you would approve of it. 'What nonsense!' replied I; 'the boy is well-nigh mad as it were—what's the use of disclosing all these complications to him? Let the ceremony be over smoothly and then—all's well that ends well. Especially, as there is not the slightest risk of its ever leaking out, why go out of the way to make a fellow miserable for life?'

"I do not know whether the plan had Kusum's assent or not. At times she wept, and at other times she remained silent. If I said, 'Let us drop it then,' she would become very restless. When things were in this state, I sent Sripati to you with the proposal of marriage; you consented without a moment's hesitation. Everything was settled.

"Shortly before the day fixed, Kusum became so obstinate that I had the greatest difficult in bringing her round again. 'Do let it drop, uncle,' she said to me constantly. 'What do you mean, you silly child,' I rebuked her; 'how can we back out now, when everything has been settled?'

" 'Spread a rumour that I am dead,' she implored. 'Send me away somewhere.'

" 'What would happen to the young man then?' said I. 'He is now in the seventh heaven of delight, expecting that his long-cherished desire would be fulfilled to-morrow; and to-day you want me to send him the news of your death? The result would be that to-morrow I should have to bear news of his death to you, and the same evening your death would be reported to me. Do you imagine, child, that I am capable of committing a girl-murder and a Brahmin-murder at my age?'

"Eventually the happy marriage was celebrated at the auspicious moment, and I felt relieved of a burdensome duty which I owed to myself. What happened afterwards you know best."

"Couldn't you stop after having done us an irreparable injury?" burst out Hemanta after a short silence. "Why have you told the secret now?"

With the utmost composure, Peari Sankar replied: "when I saw that all arrangements had been made for the wedding of your sister, I said to myself: 'Well, I have fouled the caste of one Brahmin, but that was only from a sense of duty. Here, another Brahmin's caste is imperilled, and this time it is my plain duty to prevent it.' So I wrote to them saying that I was in a position to prove that you had taken the daughter of a *sudra* to wife."

Controlling himself with a gigantic effort, Hemanta said: "What will become of this girl whom I shall abandon now? Would you give her food and shelter?"

"I have done what was mine to do," replied Peari Sankar calmly. "It is no part of my duty to look after the discarded wives of other people. Anybody there? Get a glass of cocoanut milk for Hemanta Babu with ice in it. And some *pan* too."

Hemanta rose, and took his departure without waiting for this luxurious hospitality.

IV

It was the fifth night of the waning of the moon—and the night was dark. No birds were singing. The *lichi* tree by the tank looked like a smudge of ink on a background a shade less deep. The south wind was blindly roaming about in the darkness like a sleep-walker. The stars in the sky with vigilant unblinking eyes were trying to penetrate the darkness, in their effort to fathom some profound mystery.

No light shone in the bedroom. Hemanta was sitting on the side of the bed next the open window, gazing at the darkness in front of him. Kusum lay on the floor, clasping her husband's feet with both her arms, and her face resting on them. Time stood like an ocean hushed into stillness. On the background of eternal night, Fate seemed to have painted this one single picture for all time—annihilation on every side, the judge in the centre of it, and the guilty one at his feet.

The sound of slippers was heard again. Approaching the door, Harihar Mukerji said: "You have had enough time,—I can't allow you more. Turn the girl out of the house."

Kusum, as she heard this, embraced her husband's feet with all the ardour of a lifetime, covered them with kisses, and touching her forehead to them reverentially, withdrew herself.

Hemanta rose, and walking to the door, said: "Father, I won't forsake my wife."

"What!" roared out Harihar, "would you lose your caste, sir?"

"I don't care for caste," was Hemanta's calm reply.

"Then you too I renounce."

The Cabuliwallah

My five years' old daughter Mini cannot live without chattering. I really believe that in all her life she has not wasted a minute in silence. Her mother is often vexed at this, and would stop her prattle, but I would not. To see Mini quiet is unnatural, and I cannot bear it long. And so my own talk with her is always lively.

One morning, for instance, when I was in the midst of the seventeenth chapter of my new novel, my little Mini stole into the room, and putting her hand into mine, said: "Father! Ramdayal the door-keeper calls a crow a krow! He doesn't know anything, does he?"

Before I could explain to her the differences of language in this world, she was embarked on the full tide of another subject. "What do you think, Father? Bhola says there is an elephant in the clouds, blowing water out of his trunk, and that is why it rains!"

And then, darting off anew, while I sat still making ready some reply to this last saying: "Father! what relation is Mother to you?"

"My dear little sister in the law!" I murmured involuntarily to myself, but with a grave vase contrived to answer: "Go and play with Bhola, Mini! I am busy!"

The window of my room overlooks the road. The child had seated herself at my feet near my table, and was playing softly, drumming on her knees. I was hard at work on my seventeenth chapter, where Protap Singh, the hero, had just caught Kanchanlata, the heroine, in his arms, and was about to escape with her by the third-story window of the castle, when all of a sudden Mini left her play, and ran to the window, crying: "A Cabuliwallah! a Cabuliwallah!" Sure enough in the street below was a Cabuliwallah, passing slowly along. He wore the loose soiled clothing of his people, with a tall turban; there was a bag on his back, and he carried boxes of grapes in his hand.

I cannot tell what were my daughter's feelings at the sight of this man, but she began to call him loudly. "Ah!" I thought, "he will come in, and my seventeenth chapter will never be finished!" At which exact moment the Cabuliwallah turned, and looked up at the child. When she saw this, overcome by terror, she fled to her mother's protection, and disappeared. She had a blind belief that inside the bag, which the big man carried, there were perhaps two or three other children like herself. The pedlar meanwhile entered my doorway, and greeted me with a smiling face.

So precarious was the position of my hero and my heroine, that my first impulse was to stop and buy something, since the man had been called. I made some small purchases, and a conversation began about Abdurrahman, the Russians, the English, and the Frontier Policy.

As he was about to leave, he asked: "And where is the little girl, sir?"

And I, thinking that Mini must get rid of her false fear, had her brought out.

She stood by my chair, and looked at the Cabuliwallah and his bag. He offered her nuts and raisins, but she would not be tempted, and only clung the closer to me, with all her doubts increased.

This was their first meeting.

One morning, however, not many days later, as I was leaving the house, I was startled to find Mini, seated on a bench near the door, laughing and talking, with the great Cabuliwallah at her feet. In all her life, it appeared, my small daughter had never found so patient a listener, save her father. And already the corner of her little *sari* was stuffed with almonds and raisins, the gift of her visitor. "Why did you give her those?" I said, and taking out an eight-anna bit, I handed it to him. The man accepted the money without demur, and slipped it into his pocket.

Alas, on my return an hour later, I found the unfortunate coin had made twice its own worth of trouble! For the Cabuliwallah had given it to Mini, and her mother catching sight of the bright round object, had pounced on the child with: "Where did you get that eight-anna bit?"

"The Cabuliwallah gave it me," said Mini cheerfully.

"The Cabuliwallah gave it you!" cried her mother much shocked. "O Mini! how could you take it from him?"

I, entering at the moment, saved her from impending disaster, and proceeded to make my own inquiries.

It was not the first or second time, I found, that the two had met. The Cabuliwallah had overcome the child's first terror by a judicious bribery of nuts and almonds, and the two were now great friends.

They had many quaint jokes, which afforded them much amusement. Seated in front of him, looking down on his gigantic frame in all her tiny dignity, Mini would ripple her face with laughter, and begin: "O Cabuliwallah! Cabuliwallah! what have you got in your bag?"

And he would reply, in the nasal accents of the mountaineer: "An elephant!" Not much cause for merriment, perhaps; but how they both enjoyed the witticism! And for me, this child's talk with a grown-up man had always in it something strangely fascinating.

Then the Cabuliwallah, not to be behindhand, would take his turn: "Well, little one, and when are you going to the father-in-law's house?"

Now most small Bengali maidens have heard long ago about the father-in-law's house; but we, being a little new-fangled, had kept these things from our child, and Mini at this question must have been a trifle bewildered. But she would not show it, and with ready tact replied: "Are you going there?"

Amongst men of the Cabuliwallah's class, however, it is well known that the words *father-in-law's house* have a double meaning. It is a euphemism for *jail*, the place where we are well cared for, at no expense to ourselves. In this sense would the sturdy pedlar take my daughter's question. "Ah," he would say, shaking his fist at an invisible policeman, "I will thrash my father-in-law!" Hearing this, and picturing the poor discomfited relative, Mini would go off into peals of laughter, in which her formidable friend would join.

These were autumn mornings, the very time of year when kings of old went forth to conquest; and I, never stirring from my little corner in Calcutta, would let my mind wander over the whole world. At the very name of another country, my heart would go out to it, and at the sight of a foreigner in the streets, I would fall to weaving a network of dreams,— the mountains, the glens, and the forests of his distant home, with his cottage in its setting, and the free and independent life of far-away wilds. Perhaps the scenes of travel conjure themselves up before me, and pass and repass in my imagination all the more vividly, because I lead such a vegetable existence that a call to travel would fall upon me like a thunderbolt. In the presence of this Cabuliwallah I was immediately transported to the foot of arid mountain peaks, with narrow little defiles twisting in and out amongst their towering heights. I could see the string of camels bearing the merchandise, and the company of turbanned merchants carrying some of their queer old firearms, and some of their spears, journeying downward towards the plains. I could see—But at some such point Mini's mother would intervene, imploring me to "beware of that man."

Mini's mother is unfortunately a very timid lady. Whenever she hears a noise in the street, or sees people coming towards the house, she always jumps to the conclusion that they are either thieves, or drunkards, or snakes, or tigers, or malaria, or cockroaches, or caterpillars, or an English sailor. Even after all these years of experience, she is not able to overcome her terror. So she was full of doubts about the Cabuliwallah, and used to beg me to keep a watchful eye on him.

I tried to laugh her fear gently away, but then she would turn round on me seriously, and ask me solemn questions.

Were children never kidnapped?

Was it, then, not true that there was slavery in Cabul?

Was it so very absurd that this big man should be able to carry off a tiny child?

I urged that, though not impossible, it was highly improbable. But this was not enough, and her dread persisted. As it was indefinite, however, it did not seem right to forbid the man the house, and the intimacy went on unchecked.

Once a year in the middle of January Rahmun, the Cabuliwallah, was in the habit of returning to his country, and as the time approached he would be very busy, going from house to house collecting his debts. This year, however, he could always find time to come and see Mini. It would have seemed to an outsider that there was some conspiracy between the two, for when he could not come in the morning, he would appear in the evening.

Even to me it was a little startling now and then, in the corner of a dark room, suddenly to surprise this tall, loose-garmented, much bebagged man; but when Mini would run in smiling, with her "O Cabuliwallah! Cabuliwallah!" and the two friends, so far apart in age, would subside into their old laughter and their old jokes, I felt reassured.

One morning, a few days before he had made up his mind to go, I was correcting my proof sheets in my study. It was chilly weather. Through the window the rays of the sun touched my feet, and the slight warmth was very welcome. It was almost eight o'clock, and the early pedestrians were returning home with their heads covered. All at once I heard an uproar in the street, and, looking out, saw Rahmun being led away bound between two policemen, and behind them a crowd of curious boys. There were blood-stains on the clothes of the Cabuliwallah, and one of the policemen carried a knife. Hurrying out, I stopped them, and inquired what it all meant. Partly from one, partly from another, I gathered that a certain neighbour had owed the pedlar something for a Rampuri shawl, but had falsely denied having bought it, and that in the course of the quarrel Rahmun had struck him. Now in the heat of his excitement, the prisoner began calling his enemy all sorts of names, when suddenly in a verandah of my house appeared my little Mini, with her usual exclamation: "O Cabuliwallah! Cabuliwallah!" Rahmun's face lighted up as he turned to her. He had no bag under his arm to-day, so she could not discuss the elephant with him. She at once therefore proceeded to the next question: "Are you going to the father-in-law's house?" Rahmun laughed and said: "Just where I am going, little one!" Then seeing that the reply did not amuse the child, he held up his fettered hands. "Ah," he said, "I would have thrashed that old father-in-law, but my hands are bound!"

On a charge of murderous assault, Rahmun was sentenced to some years' imprisonment.

Time passed away, and he was not remembered. The accustomed work in the accustomed place was ours, and the thought of the once free mountaineer spending his years in prison seldom or never occurred to us. Even my light-hearted Mini, I am ashamed to say, forgot her old friend. New companions filled her life. As she grew older, she spent more of her time with girls. So much time indeed did she spend with them that she came no more, as she used to do, to her father's room. I was scarcely on speaking terms with her.

Years had passed away. It was once more autumn and we had made arrangement for our Mini's marriage. It was to take place during the Puja Holidays. With Durga returning to Kailas, the light of our home also was to depart to her husband's house, and leave her father's in the shadow.

The morning was bright. After the rains, there was a sense of ablution in the air, and the sun-rays looked like pure gold. So bright were they that they gave a beautiful radiance even to the sordid brick walls of our Calcutta lanes. Since early dawn to-day the wedding-pipes had been sounding, and at each beat my own heart throbbed. The wail of the tune, Bhairavi, seemed to intensify my pain at the approaching separation. My Mini was to be married to-night.

From early morning noise and bustle had pervaded the house. In the courtyard the canopy had to be slung on its bamboo poles; the chandeliers with their tinkling sound must be hung in each room and verandah. There was no end of hurry and excitement. I was sitting in my study, looking through the accounts, when some one entered, saluting respectfully, and stood before me. It was Rahmun the Cabuliwallah. At first I did not recognise him. He had no bag, nor the long hair, nor the same vigour that he used to have. But he smiled, and I knew him again.

"When did you come, Rahmun?" I asked him.

"Last evening," he said, "I was released from jail."

The words struck harsh upon my ears. I had never before talked with one who had wounded his fellow, and my heart shrank within itself when I realised this, for I felt that the day would have been better-omened had he not turned up.

"There are ceremonies going on," I said, "and I am busy. Could you perhaps come another day?"

At once he turned to go; but as he reached the door he hesitated, and said: "May I not see the little one, sir, for a moment?" It was his belief that Mini was still the same. He had pictured her running to him as she used, calling "O Cabuliwallah! Cabuliwallah!" He had imagined too that they would laugh and talk together, just as of old. In fact, in memory of former days he had brought, carefully wrapped up in paper, a few almonds and raisins and grapes, obtained somehow from a countryman, for his own little fund was dispersed.

I said again: "There is a ceremony in the house, and you will not be able to see any one to-day."

The man's face fell. He looked wistfully at me for a moment, said "Good morning," and went out.

I felt a little sorry, and would have called him back, but I found he was returning of his own accord. He came close up to me holding out his offerings, and said: "I brought these few things, sir, for the little one. Will you give them to her?"

I took them and was going to pay him, but he caught my hand and said: "You are very kind, sir! Keep me in your recollection. Do not offer me money!—You have a little girl: I too have one like her in my own home. I think of her, and bring fruits to your child—not to make a profit for myself."

Saying this, he put his hand inside his big loose robe, and brought out a small and dirty piece of paper. With great care he unfolded this, and smoothed it out with both hands on my table. It bore the impression of a little hand. Not a photograph. Not a drawing. The impression of an ink-smeared hand laid flat on the paper. This touch of his own little daughter had been always on his heart, as he had come year after year to Calcutta to sell his wares in the streets.

Tears came to my eyes. I forgot that he was a poor Cabuli fruit-seller, while I was—But no, what was I more than he? He also was a father.

That impression of the hand of his little *Pārbati* in her distant mountain home reminded me of my own little Mini.

I sent for Mini immediately from the inner apartment. Many difficulties were raised, but I would not listen. Clad in the red silk of her wedding-day, with the sandal paste on her forehead, and adorned as a young bride, Mini came, and stood bashfully before me.

The Cabuliwallah looked a little staggered at the apparition. He could not revive their old friendship. At last he smiled and said: "Little one, are you going to your father-in-law's house?"

But Mini now understood the meaning of the word "father-in-law," and she could not reply to him as of old. She flushed up at the question, and stood before him with her bride-like face turned down.

I remembered the day when the Cabuliwallah and my Mini had first met, and I felt sad. When she had gone, Rahmun heaved a deep sigh, and sat down on the floor. The idea had suddenly come to him that his daughter too must have grown in this long time, and that he would have to make friends with her anew. Assuredly he would not find her as he used to know her. And besides, what might not have happened to her in these eight years?

The marriage-pipes sounded, and the mild autumn sun streamed round us. But Rahmun sat in the little Calcutta lane, and saw before him the barren mountains of Afghanistan.

I took out a bank-note and gave it to him, saying: "Go back to your own daughter, Rahmun, in your own country, and may the happiness of your meeting bring good fortune to my child!"

Having made this present, I had to curtail some of the festivities. I could not have the electric lights I had intended, nor the military band, and the ladies of the house were despondent at it. But to me the wedding-feast was all the brighter for the thought that in a distant land a long-lost father met again with his only child.